True Freeze

Allanto

Shingyong
Mountains

Danziyi

Celestial
Palace

Sea of
Flowers

Xusan

Blue
Sea

Sand Snake

The Original Temple
of the Tiandi

THE ART OF PROPHECY

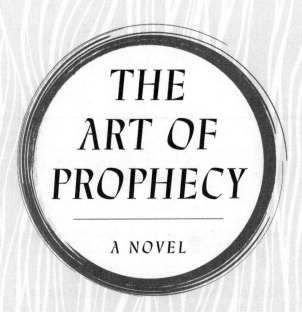

THE ART OF PROPHECY

A NOVEL

THE WAR ARTS SAGA: BOOK ONE

WESLEY CHU

NEW YORK

Published in the United States by Del Rey, an imprint of Random House, a division of Penguin Random House LLC, New York.

DEL REY and the CIRCLE colophon
are registered trademarks of Penguin Random House LLC.

Hardback ISBN 978-0-593-23763-2
International edition ISBN 978-0-593-50104-7
Ebook ISBN 978-0-593-23764-9

Endpaper map: Sunga Park

Printed in Canada on acid-free paper

randomhousebooks.com

2 4 6 8 9 7 5 3 1

First Edition

Book design by Jo Anne Metsch

To Hunter & River

ACT I

CHAPTER ONE

BROKEN TOYS

The line of broken soldiers stretched out of the training pit and around the arena, spilling out onto the streets. They came in all types and sizes: men, women, tall, short, fat, emaciated, and with varying numbers of limbs. A few were fully armored, others only in loincloths. All looked like they had stared death in the face and wished not to have survived it.

Ling Taishi leaned over the balcony overlooking the pit. Most of the soldiers—volunteer fodder—kept their eyes low and their shoulders slumped, working hard to avoid attention and hide their defects, inside and out. Taishi could tell what ailed them with just a glance, not that she cared. She had run out of pity years ago. The more pressing thought on her mind as she scanned their ranks was how this rabble could possibly put up a fight against anyone.

An official with his beard trimmed and oiled to a point approached her, his gold-laced crimson robe flapping against his knees. The broccoli shape of his tall black hat placed him as the high lord of the palace. "It is time, emissary. Please allow me to escort you to your seat. I have arranged refreshments. Peaches from my own estates, harvested just a season ago and spirited here for your pleasure."

Taishi struggled to recall his name. "Thank you, Palacelord Faaru."

The palacelord led her across the balcony toward an elevated dais, rambling on about his stupid fruit the entire time. "They are so succulent you will believe it is nectar from heaven. My orchards are renowned among all of the Enlightened States."

Taishi's face drooped further with each passing description. If the man was as good with training boys as he was with selling fruit, the world could rest easy. Fortunately, it was a short walk to her seat. She sat down on a bed of cushions reserved for high-ranking officials and guests of the court. Taishi technically held no rank and belonged to no court. She had been sent here as an emissary by one of her former students, who also happened to be both her landlord *and* her actual lord. Saan, the Duke of Shulan, wanted her to appraise how the Prophesied Hero of the Tiandi's education was coming along. She had wanted to refuse the assignment, but the terms he offered were too good to pass up: tax exemption for life and not going to jail for refusing her duke. Taishi was not a big fan of taxes or imprisonment.

As soon as she settled in, the rest of the crowds on the balcony took their places in the tier below her platform. The arena was surprisingly packed for a simple training session. Taishi wondered how many in the audience were actually paid spectators. As Faaru had promised, a servant appeared with a platter of peaches piled in a pyramid, and placed it on the small table next to her. Taishi was tempted to grab one from the bottom, or better yet wave it off, but being old and irritable was no excuse for poor manners. She plucked the top one and absently bit into it as the guards below cleared the training pit. She stopped and stared at the golden juice sticking to her fingers. *By the Queen's rotted ovaries, the man wasn't lying. These are damn good peaches.*

The palacelord appeared out of nowhere and hovered nearby as she gnawed on the peach, his eyes staring intently. He was sneaky for such a large man. Taishi fought the urge to spit the peach out and sour her face, but there was no sense in wasting quality fruit. She had to give the man his due and so offered him a slight tilt of his head. The palacelord beamed.

The training session was about to begin. Somewhere above, drums rumbled as the lazy and scattered applause from the crowd betrayed their true enthusiasm for the event. Taishi failed to mask her growing irritation. She checked the water clock at the time table. It was nearly noon. Half the day was already wasted.

The first group of toy soldiers paraded into the pit and milled about, uncertain and disorganized. They were ten volunteers in a random assortment of weapons and armor, no two looking like they belonged in the same unit. Taishi pitied this pathetic bunch, these loyal soldiers of the States who hadn't died in the war, but hadn't necessarily survived it either. Now they were left to eke out a living the only way they could: becoming training toys to a boy playing war. There was the pikeman with the distant stare. The swordswoman with the shaking hands. The young man missing the rest of his arm below the elbow cowering behind her . . . Taishi shifted her own mangled arm hanging useless by her side. Well, one should never underestimate a cripple.

The training overseer stood and clapped his hands. "You all have the honor of aiding in the training of the undefeated Champion of the Five Under Heaven, the terror of the Katuia Hordes, and the savior of the Zhuun people. Fight bravely, but remember your place. The penalty for injuring him is death. The penalty for drawing his blood is death. The penalty for refusing to engage is death." The overseer continued, rambling off another ten or fifteen rules. By the time he was done, Taishi wasn't sure how any fighting was possible. "Any questions?" he intoned.

The small group looked dejected, and as baffled as she was. One woman wearing half the banded armor of a light cavalry unit raised her spear. "What if he's about to kill us?"

"Then die honorably. Try not to if you want to get paid."

"Wait," another asked. "He can attack us, but we can't attack him?" This had to be his first day.

The training overseer sounded hassled. "Of course you are allowed to fight back. Just don't injure him."

Faaru leaned in. "Are you enjoying the delicacies, emissary?" Her muffled slurp was answer enough. She helped herself to a second peach and slipped a third into her pocket. He gestured toward the pile of peaches. "If you wish for more, emissary, you need only ask."

The palacelord was being awfully pushy about his silly fruit. Then she noticed the decorations on the plate. A long string of gold liang looping through the peaches at the base. The coins, ducal-stamped from the Gyian mint, formed a glimmering yellow snake linked together through each liang's square hole. That much money was more than enough to pay off most emissaries. Far too generous, in fact, which made Taishi only more suspicious. She looked back at Faaru, and his smile widened until the corners of his mouth nearly touched his long earlobes.

There was a reason Saan had sent her instead of the usual court buffoon. Taishi ignored the bribe and turned her attention back to the pit. "Get on with this. I have other things to do with my day." *Like soaking my feet in a hot bucket.*

He stiffened and gestured to the overseer. "As you wish, emissary."

The overseer began to speak again, his voice carrying across the arena. "Behold, Wen Jian, the Prophesied Hero of Legend, the savior of the Zhuun people, the one foretold by the Tiandi Prophets, under the sign of a thousand stars, to fulfill his destiny and lead the mighty armies of the Enlightened States to victory over the terrible, evil, savage hordes of the Katuia Clans, break the immortality of their Eternal Khan, and bring everlasting peace to the Children of Zhuun. Bear witness . . ."

Taishi rolled her eyes. So much stupid pomp. She mouthed silently and carried her whisper on the wind to the man's ear. "Skip the rest."

The overseer's voice cracked. He glanced around and then cleared his throat. "Let the round begin."

There were still a few seconds of excessive drumbeating and fanfare before the gates below the balcony finally opened. Five imposing figures in heavy armor cut long shadows into the sand. They wore elaborate helmets shaped like animal heads, which she thought was a nice touch, and moved with the swagger of opera villains. They looked like the guardians of the gate to some mystic zoo. Taishi was entertained.

Meanwhile, the sacrificial lambs on the other side of the arena looked as if they were about to soil themselves. Following the five horned warriors appeared a much more diminutive figure, but to much greater applause. About damn time. Taishi crossed her arms and leaned forward. She had met many legendary masters in her day, but this was the first time she was going to see a legend.

Her initial impression of the Hero of Prophecy was lukewarm. The hero everyone was fawning over was a scrawny teenager wearing only black breeches cut off just below the knee. His skinny chest was defined but flat, his arms were taut but stick-thin, and his skin was pale as ox milk. His black headband made his dark hair stick out like a bird's nest, but his round boyish face was clean and manicured.

"Put a shirt on before you blind someone," she muttered.

Her first thought was that it was strange for the hero to be so lightly armored compared with his bodyguards, but of course a teacher couldn't check a student's form and technique under several layers of armor.

The boy flourished his sword above his head, and then moved his hands apart to reveal that it was in fact two identical blades. He twirled the two swords around his body and loosed a reasonable attempt at a war cry, his voice cracking at the tail end.

Taishi raised an eyebrow. "This should be interesting."

Double straight swords: a bold choice, a weapon that was very difficult to master. It was Taishi's personal opinion that double straight swords were the wrong weapons in every fight, no exceptions. She leaned forward and studied the stillness within him: His eyes were up and steady, his footwork relaxed, his form and balance proper, his guard held correctly. So far so good. Like a prize horse, he looked the part. But as her own father and master had taught her a lifetime ago, *You can tell a war artist's true ability in three moves. Everything else is just a rooster's strut.*

His pitiful challengers advanced, the boy moved, and the action unfolded more or less as expected. Jian and his overdressed bodyguards fanned out. The toy soldiers made halfhearted attempts at combat, while the demon-helmed guards basically postured picturesquely in the background. The boy did actually do all the work, if it could be called that.

Taishi hated to admit it, but at first she was grudgingly impressed. He looked good. His movements were crisp, his balance and ability to change directions impressive, and his reflexes sublime. Her eyes sparkled as the boy effortlessly transitioned between techniques. Most important, she could tell by the snap and fluidity of his attacks that his jing, his energy, was strong. Taishi couldn't recall the last time she had witnessed such martial beauty in one so young.

"He might actually be as good as his legend," she marveled.

And yet, he should have been dead five times over.

"Should have gotten stabbed there," she counted under her breath. "And there. Dead there, there again. There goes his left arm." The longer the melee continued, the more problems she found. It wasn't so much the boy's abilities or technique that were at fault, it was the way he put everything together. In isolation, each movement was timed and executed flawlessly. Once she examined the fight in its entirety, however, something looked off. It was in the flow of the battle, the almost rhythmic pacing of the action, the stuttering exchanges, and the awkward angles.

"He's overthinking, and no one else is actually trying," she muttered. The boy didn't bother with his defense, because no one posed anything remotely resembling a threat.

As the round continued, the smile that had crept onto her face faded, replaced with a forced neutrality that she kept up for as long as she could, but inevitably melted into a scowl as if she smelled something rancid. Once she realized what was happening, she couldn't help but notice it in every movement, every exchange. If the boy made a mistake, his opponent would actually hesitate to compensate for it. It wasn't real. His opponents were making sure the boy looked good. This whole thing wasn't choreographed, but maybe it should have been; then maybe Jian's many flaws wouldn't stand out so easily.

Jian squared up with his last remaining challenger. The man feinted, then swung his horse-cutter in a long overhead swing. Taishi could have taken a nap in the time it took the blade to reach its target. The boy blocked it competently and countered. Block, parry, dodge. The two moved as if underwater until Jian finally jabbed his opponent in the thigh.

All of the fodder had been vanquished, left writhing on the sand. The poor cripple missing a hand almost lost his other one, having suffered a deep gash down the length of his arm that would require stitches. The rest of the sad rabble picked themselves up and dragged themselves to the other side of the training grounds.

The crowd all rose to their feet when the last soldier fell, clapping as if that Champion of the Five Under Heaven had just single-handedly beaten back the Katuia Hordes, bare-chested, with only his hands. Taishi stayed in her seat. The peaches had been more impressive than what she had just seen.

The overseer banged on his gong. "There will be a fifteen-minute intermission between rounds," he declared, again to scattered applause. "Bring out the refreshments." A small army of attendants came jogging out onto the pits, carrying tables and chairs and food and drink.

Taishi frowned. "Fifteen minutes? Refreshments?"

"The young hero needs to recuperate between rounds, emissary," Faaru explained. "It gives the masters the opportunity to dispense their wisdom."

Taishi's gaze drifted to a group of eight extravagantly dressed men hurrying down the stairs into the pit and clustering around the boy, jockeying with one another to whisper in his ear. All wore colorful pageant sashes over one shoulder. A *beauty pageant for old ugly self-important men*, Taishi thought. She nudged Faaru. "Who are those peacocks?"

"Those are the young hero's teachers," exclaimed Faaru, his chest puffing out. "As you can see, we've recruited the finest masters from across the Enlightened States. The one speaking is Master Sun. Next to him is Master Hili, then Master Pai, Master Ningzhu, Master Luda . . ."

Taishi stopped listening after that. Of course. That explained the color-coding. It was the latest rage among war arts schools. It gave the students some stupid sense of tangible accomplishment to cling to. These lofty titles, ranks, silly sashes, fancy names were all nothing more than marketing ploys for those who lived outside the lunar court, the secretive underground community of war artists residing on the fringes of order and society.

She reminded herself that the masters charged with training the Prophesied Hero were political appointees and had little to do with any actual ability or skill. She turned her nose. "The corruption of the States extends even to our salvation."

Still, eight war arts masters, one student. *How does that even work? A student with more than one master only makes for an indecisive student. In the heat of battle, which master's voice would ring loudest?* Taishi flicked her hand toward those masters and drew their voices back to her.

"Use the front sweep next time against a shield."

"Jump downward, thrust when their guard is low."

"Feint first. That's why you have two blades."

"Double thrust. Always be on the attack."

That answered her question: It didn't. It was a dizzying amount of information, some contradictory. The poor boy must be so confused.

One of the peacocks noticed Taishi staring and broke off from the group. He approached the dais and offered her a generous bow and a wide smile, exposing two rows of yellow teeth. "Such an honor to meet you again, Master Ling. Truly one of the grand legendary masters. I once had the privilege of witnessing your feats at the Shulan Moon Festival Tournament. You were spectacular, truly invincible that day. I'm sure you still would be"—he glanced at the mangled arm hanging useless by her side—"if it weren't for your unfortunate injury."

Still can beat you senseless with only one arm, you puffed-up fungal wart. She offered him a withering glance. "Who are you again? Apologies. Along with my useless arm, I also suffer from face blindness."

"Sinsin. Master Le Sinsin. As you can likely tell from the hero's movements, he leans heavily on my family style. If I—"

"That tells me all I need to know." Taishi put a hand up to Sinsin's face before he could say another word. She turned to Faaru. "Start the next round."

"But the intermission—"

"Now!"

The palacelord blanched and then bowed. He signaled to the over-seer, who had also taken a seat to take advantage of the refreshments. The man quickly replaced his pear-shaped hat and gave the order to clear the floor. The audience grumbled as they returned to their seats.

"Uncle Faaru, what is the meaning of this? Why is this break so short? Who is that woman?" a high-pitched voice said across the pit. Jian was staring straight at her. He had just sat down and was having his forehead dabbed with a wet cloth.

"Uncle"? The ends of Taishi's lips curled.

"It's no one you need to be concerned about, savior of the Zhuun," replied Faaru, waving with both arms, swishing his giant sleeves about.

"We can't start the next round yet. We haven't finished our refresh-ments. My unit needs to rest."

Bonus points for being considerate, offset by the fact the boy thought those five clowns fighting alongside him actually needed rest after three minutes of posing. His people looked uncertain. Three stood up and reached for their helmets while the remaining two stayed seated and continued to slurp their drinks.

The new group of sad fodders that had just been led into the pit for the slaughter looked equally puzzled. These poor cracked eggs were even more pathetic than the last: an old man and two women equipped with matching broadswords and shields. They were probably from the same regiment. They were joined by two others, a sickly man with ema-ciated arms wearing wooden armor and wielding an oversized ax, and another man wearing only a tight loincloth held together by a few des-perate threads and holding a mancatcher over his shoulder. The re-maining four looked like peasants carrying farming tools.

The two sides faced each other once more. Taishi wrapped her hands around the railing and squeezed until her knuckles turned white. This was a waste of time. She was tempted to just leave. She had just started to rise out of her seat when a wicked little spark tickled her. She decided instead to stay and prove a point. Taishi really did love making fools of fools.

As the overseer began his long-winded introduction, Taishi carried her whisper to the graybeard leading the fodders. "Seize the advantage while they are unprepared. Move first."

He hesitated. "But we're supposed—"

"Now, soldier. Split that gap on the right flank. You have a straight shot at your target. Seize your moment."

Her whispers spoke to his desires. Soldiers, no matter how beaten down, never lost their taste for victory. Taishi just had to reawaken that part of them. A glint appeared in his eyes as he clenched his jaw and raised his shield to his body. Someone down in the pit was finally taking the fight seriously.

The graybeard, used to following orders, did as he was told and charged, much to the confusion of his squad. He ran between two of Jian's heavily encumbered bodyguards, who were thrown off by the grizzled veteran's sudden, aggressive tactic. They just stood there, ex-changing I-thought-*you*-were-supposed-to-get-him looks. Their confusion was brief, because the women behind the graybeard, also pushed by Taishi's whispers, crashed into them a moment later. The audience next to Taishi sat up in their seats. For the first time possibly ever, a real fight was brewing below.

Jian looked like a startled rabbit as the soldier bore down on him, shield up and blade forward. He sidestepped the charge clumsily and made a looping swing with his sword that bounced off the edge of his opponent's well-placed shield. The graybeard gave Jian little quarter as he pressed forward, poking at the many holes in the boy's defense. If it weren't for the old man's old reflexes and the young man's young reflexes, the fight might have ended right there.

Faaru hissed at the overseer. "What is the meaning of this? End the round. End the round!"

"No," Taishi barked. "Ring that gong and I'll put your head through it." The overseer froze in mid-swing and then threw his hands up as if trying to surrender.

The ends of her lips curved upward as she gleefully scattered more encouragement and orders. "Are you meat for the butcher or are you fighting soldiers of the Enlightened States? Use your numbers. They've abandoned the center. The Ram-Head is overextended. You two farm boys, Hoe and Shovel, get on either side of him. Mancatcher, come around behind and take Bull from the back. Sword and Boards, get around Lion's flank. You two with the spears, pull back. No, your other back, you idiots."

Bull and Lion were quickly brought down while the other animals were busy retreating to the boy's rescue. By the time they had cut down the graybeard, the odds had turned. Ram got speared in the back while Rooster got bashed in the back of the head. That left the hero and Bear, who found themselves outnumbered.

On the balcony, Faaru stomped his way to the overseer, grabbed the mallet from his hand, shoved the man aside. He was about to signal the end of the round when Taishi flicked her hand, snapped the gong off its hinges, and sent it rolling on its side down the stairs. "Finish the round. I want to see a winner."

"But—"

Taishi looked him square in the eye. He shut up, but not before whispering something in the overseer's ear. Taishi pulled the sound over to her.

"Call in the second group. Hurry."

Four more animal heads ran into the pit, some still strapping on their armor. The fifth hopped in a moment later, trying to lace his sandal. The fodders would not have noticed these reinforcements had Taishi not sent them a warning. They regrouped to face the new threat, but now they were sandwiched and facing off six to seven, the advantage to the animal heads.

Jian looked tentative, lost. This was probably the first time he had had to deal with uncertainty in the pit. It took him a moment to collect himself. He charged one of the farmers sword-first, piercing his gut. Then Jian waved to rally the rest of his unit.

That earned him Taishi's approval. The audience in the stands broke out into a chant, encouraging the young hero, applauding when he stabbed one of the spearmen who, because of a bad leg, was not able to retreat quickly enough.

Taishi gritted her teeth as the animals closed in on her outnumbered and overmatched renegades. Her eyes darted around the grounds. Her options were limited up here. She had only so much to work with. She should probably let it go. Her ragtag squad would likely lose now, but her point had been made. The rest of this exercise was irrelevant. Winning or losing in practice was just about pride.

Taishi let herself sink back down into the pillows and fingered another peach. She was about to take another bite out of it when she hesitated. Her pride wouldn't allow her to lose, not even during practice. She chucked the peach into the pit, bouncing it off the helm of Snake. Then Taishi shot out of her seat, finding a soft, whimsical air current to carry her across the arena. The currents here were tame, lazy, forcing her to jump across three more before her toes touched down on the helmet of Elephant, bounded off the shoulder of what she thought looked like a fox, and landed in the sand between her troops and this tacky menagerie.

Snake pulled up short, mouth wide, the ax in his hand quivering.

A wry smile grew on her face. "You're allowed to try to hit me."

Snake accepted her challenge and made a good effort as the tip of his blade nearly gashed her robe when he streaked past her. With three quick strikes of the tips of her fingers, Taishi sent him flying off to the side. Fox came next, followed closely by Wolf, or possibly Badly-Designed-Monkey? Fox was blinded by a puff of air before Taishi slapped the consciousness out of him. Wolf-Monkey swung a heavy mace at full force, a killing blow. She diverted its trajectory with the tips of her fingers. He followed up with a series of snapping kicks, which she danced around like a leaf swirling in the breeze.

Taishi countered with her own soft kick to the flesh of his neck, a blow that would have crushed the man's throat if she had wished it.

Faaru ran down the stairs to the pit, his generous robes fluttering as he flapped his arms. "This has gone far enough. Stop this at once!"

Taishi sent her whispers to the squad around her. "This is your chance. Seize your glory."

These were true soldiers who had lived through real war, survived death, and sacrificed everything to end up disposable practice targets. They obeyed. They had nothing left to lose, and a trapped enemy was the deadliest. They surged past her, surrounding and hacking at the boy's remaining animals.

Taishi stood in their midst, intervening with only a few more whispers. Within seconds, it was over. The Prophesied Hero was surrendering to a farmer and a naked man. The loincloth had not survived the fight.

The arena fell silent, save for the labored panting of the participants as they picked themselves up off the sand. Jian stood in the middle of it all, stunned. His various masters seemed no less so.

The ego was a fragile thing; Taishi knew well enough.

Taishi helped the axman who was struggling to stand. She gave him a pat on the rear as encouragement and wiped her dirtied hands on his shoulders before launching herself back to the balcony. Two delicate steps off the railing and floor and she was back in her seat, reaching for a peach.

Taishi turned to Faaru. "My office, now."

The palacelord looked equal parts terrified and confused. "But you don't have an office . . ." He froze, and then dropped to his knees, his head bowed low.

She did now.

CHAPTER TWO

THE HERO OF PROPHECY

Wen Jian, the Hero of Prophecy, Champion of the Five Under Heaven, savior of the Zhuun People, terror of the Katuia Hordes, was having a tough day. He had just lost the first match of his life, broken his favorite practice sword against a wall in a fit of anger, received two splinters, and had now missed dinner because of a summons from Uncle Faaru.

Jian left the tower he called his home, ritualistically slapping the stone placard with the inscription TOWER OF ETERNAL HEROISM, and crossed over to the now-deserted Heavenly Grounds. He ignored the crowd of long shadows and soft stampede of footsteps that trailed behind him as he made his way to the Heart of the Tiandi Throne at the center.

The King, blazing gold, was just about to set for the day while the Queen neared her zenith as she followed her husband across the sky. Their twin children, the Prince and Princess, were just beginning their ascent, climbing from the southern horizon. The night this time of the year was particularly bright with all three moons shining fiercely, adding hints of blue, green, and purple respectively to the landscape.

Jian's mind raced furiously, mostly in circles, as he hurried to answer Uncle Faaru's summons. A hundred worries plagued him as he relived the humiliating events of the morning. What had happened? How had he lost? He had done everything right. Had the masters canceled this evening's training to discuss his failure? He hoped so. Someone had to take responsibility for this unacceptable development. He was the Prophesied Hero. No one was allowed to do this to him.

He could come to only one logical conclusion: The peasant woman—the one Jian had originally taken for a servant who had forgotten her uniform—must have cheated. Why was *she* important enough for all the masters to fret over? She had thrown him off guard when she had leaped off the balcony and attacked him unprovoked. He hadn't been ready. It wasn't fair. She shouldn't have been allowed to do that.

Jian fought his anxiety and shoved his hands deep into his pockets. Heroes did not bite their nails. Heroes did not cry. It was times like this Jian was grateful that he was alone with his thoughts. He would have been dreadfully ashamed if his masters or Uncle Faaru saw him in such a state.

He was the greatest prodigy in all the Enlightened States. Everyone told him so. Constantly! It was his destiny to become a great warrior, to lead the Zhuun to victory over the vicious, evil Khanate Hordes and to bring peace to the world. That's why he had been born into this world and lived here in the Celestial Palace. It was why all the best masters had been gathered to train him. It was why, throughout his entire life, he had been undefeated in the training pit. Because all of these were true, so the only explanation was that the old woman had cheated in order to make him look bad. But why?

Jian was both relieved and enraged. Too many people depended on him for him to fail. Cheating for the sake of shaming him was unacceptable. He brooded, his fingers curling into fists and threatening to punch holes in his pockets. A muffled growl escaped his lips as he stomped the tiles toward the Heart of the Tiandi Throne.

He stepped to the base of the Thousand Steps to Wisdom—it was technically only 814 steps—and sprinted up. A small parade of footsteps and heavy breathing followed as he bounded up three steps at a time.

He reached the top slightly winded and sucked in two long breaths. Jian hadn't meant to sprint all the way up, but his body tended to run alongside his mind when he fretted. It wouldn't do to make his appearance looking out of sorts. He held out his hand. "Handkerchief."

No one appeared. A second ticked by. Jian didn't bother masking his annoyance as he shook his free hand. A few moments later, the heavy breathing caught up to him. The towel attendant, a grizzled old man, stuttered a profuse apology and bowed low before dabbing Jian's forehead with a silken wipe. It didn't help much. Not in this weather.

Jian held out another hand. "Drink."

The cupbearer appeared, holding a tray of chilled peach juice. The boy was equally out of breath and had spilled some of it on his sleeve. Jian let it go. He went through so many cup boys he couldn't keep them straight. He looked again and corrected himself: cup *girl*.

"I need to take another bath," he muttered.

"Yes, savior of the Zhuun," another voice piped up from behind him. "It'll be ready by the time you return from the throne room." A pair of footsteps faded down the stairs.

Jian walked up to the grand entryway into the Heart of the Tiandi Throne. Two members of his retinue had hurried ahead to the large double doors and were waiting to open them and present him. He acknowledged Horashi and Riga with a curt nod as he stopped and straightened his wrinkled robe as best he could. Unlike the rest of his retinue, Jian's personal bodyguards were not replaceable or disposable.

The two honor guards, one a grizzled veteran nearing the end of his tenure while the other was still entering his prime, were both in dress armor with silver-plated sabers hanging off their waists. Both were decorated war artists who had pledged their lives to serve and defend against all threats to his person.

Instead of giving the signal, Jian took in several deep breaths as he gathered his thoughts and mustered his confidence. His fingers whitened as they curled tightly around the intricate black wooden lacquered patterns on the door frame.

"Are you ready, savior?" asked Horashi, the older one with a patchwork of sparse, unruly short hair, and the scars to mark his long and distinguished career. "Is something on your mind?"

A sigh escaped Jian's lips. "I'm just angry."

Riga, the younger one with an unmarked face and full mane of black hair pulled into a ponytail, held on to the other handle. "Angry about losing the sparring match?" Riga was new, a recent replacement for a previous bodyguard who had died during a Katuia assassination attempt nine months ago. He was polite enough, but Jian chafed at the fact the man rarely showed proper deference.

"I didn't lose. It wasn't a fair fight."

His bodyguard shrugged. "Battles aren't always fair. I once cut in line at the brothel for the most popular girl. Seven people jumped me."

"Seven on one doesn't seem fair at all," agreed Jian.

Riga shrugged and patted his belt. "The only thing that wasn't fair was I still had my sword."

Horashi crinkled his forehead. "Your five heavily armed guards against those broken soldiers they picked up off the street wasn't a fair fight?" Deep lines etched his bald head. "Fair to whom?"

The older bodyguard was the only person in the palace that could speak to Jian so directly. Horashi had been at Jian's side for as long as Jian could remember. Throughout the years, a carousel of attendants and bodyguards had come and gone, but he had been the one constant. Horashi had been a young man when he had first come into Jian's service. No one would accuse him of that now.

"Who cares about fair?" argued Riga. "The only people who are concerned about fairness are stupid or dead."

"In war, perhaps," said Horashi. "In the arena, rules and honor must be observed."

"Enough," said Jian, absentmindedly. The two didn't see eye to eye on much, and always made their differences loudly known. It gave him headaches. Horashi and Riga obeyed immediately. Jian crossed his arms. "That old woman cheated. That loss shouldn't count. I remain undefeated. I'll present my case to the masters and have today's results annulled."

"It's only a practice . . ." A sigh escaped Horashi's lips. "As you say, savior."

"I'm ready now. Open the door." Jian tugged at his sleeves. "It's time we remind everyone why they're here."

Before the doors opened, Horashi bent down and adjusted his collar. The older man wet his thumb and wiped Jian's cheek and brow. When Jian shied away, Horashi broke into a grin and tousled his hair. "Now you look the part of the hero. Remember, confidence through humility."

The doors swung open and struck the arrival gong. His two body-guards walked in first, then Jian, and then his attendants. He was about to call for the Voice of the Throne Room to announce him when he paused. There was no Voice present. In fact, there was no formal audience here. The throne room was empty except for a small group of people at the base of the throne at the far end, all with their backs turned to him.

Their commotion filled the space. Everyone was speaking angrily, their words muddling as they echoed across the expansive room. Their bickering sounded like a night bazaar. Undeterred by this lack of reception, Jian stormed into the Hall of the Edified Thoughts with Horashi and Riga flanking him. It wasn't until he had almost reached the group that someone finally noticed him.

The peasant woman who had interrupted his training was standing at the center of the commotion. She stepped out from the group and leveled a finger over Jian's shoulder. "Who by the Queen's skirt are they?"

A surge of indignation coursed through Jian. That wasn't the sort of greeting he was used to. "How dare you . . . You address . . ." The words died in his throat under her gaze.

"No, not you." She pointed past his shoulder. "Them."

Jian followed her finger, confused. He raised his chin, defiantly. "They're my attendants. They see to my needs and comfor—"

"Get out. You are all dismissed."

Jian would not back down so easily. "I need them!"

"Out now!"

The poor attendants milled back and forth, trying to decide which order to follow, each trying to shrink behind another. Finally, to Jian's chagrin, they took the side of the thunderous peasant woman. The cup-bearer, in tears, approached Jian and bowed, offering her cup. Then she fled the room. The rest of his retinue followed suit, until only Horashi and Riga remained. His two stalwart bodyguards crossed their arms defiantly.

The woman whipped her attention back toward Faaru. "That proves my point exactly!"

Faaru broke away from the group and placed himself between Jian and the woman. "Great savior of the Zhuun, if I may introduce Master Ling Taishi, of the Windwhispering School of the Zhang lineage. Family style—"

"That will be enough, Faaru," she replied, not taking her eyes off Jian.

"Today was an outrage, Uncle." Jian was comforted by Faaru standing close by. "My training is important, and cannot be disrupted by any peasant who . . ."

His voice trailed off. For the first time, Jian noticed the heaviness in the air. This was not a happy room. Wang wore his fighting face. Sinsin looked more offended than usual, and Sun was sniffing loudly as if trying to hold back tears. The only person who did not look outraged or devastated was this Ling Taishi person. Who was she, and who had ever heard of a master who didn't announce their family line? That was the first thing all his masters made him memorize when he began his tutelage under them. Was she not proud of her lineage?

Jian tried to meet her gaze, but his eyes slipped away the moment they met hers, and he found himself counting his toes. "Master Ling," he managed to mumble. He tried to face her again, but those eyes . . . His fled to the safety of the floor the second time he tried, then retreated to the group of friendly faces. "What is going on, masters?"

Ningzhu folded his arms. "Master Ling believes we have been deficient in your training."

"She feels some of us who have dedicated our lives to you aren't necessary," added Sun.

"She implies that we are poor and ineffective masters," said Hili.

"She even went as far as to accuse me of being a fraud," added Jang.

"Now, now," said Faaru. "I'm sure the emissary wasn't being literal."

Taishi sneered. "Oh no, I was. The lot of you frauds and sycophants are a pathetic disgrace to your titles and stations."

The masters erupted at the insult. Only Faaru, who looked decidedly uncomfortable and nervous, and Taishi remained silent. She looked bored. The old woman pulled a peach from her pocket and bit into it.

"Now, now," said Faaru, waving his arms out trying to calm the room. "Let us remain civil!"

"She told me to my face I had bought my title," said Sinsin.

"Well, when you foreclosed on Chin's school and then just took his place . . ." Wang interjected.

"How dare you! It was a legal and legitimate transfer of ownership."

The two men lunged at each other and had to be restrained. All of his masters were shaking their fists, loudly making their cases for why their particular discipline was necessary in the war against the Katuia Hordes.

"What if Jian had to fight mounted cavalry? My family's style specializes in spear. The hordes' cavalry number greater than the stars."

"What if he faces archers? I teach my student to catch arrows midflight."

Jian caught himself nodding to every single one. All of his masters were important and filled a specific role in his training. He would not be nearly as accomplished without each of them.

"Don't you see, emissary," Faaru exclaimed. "This is exactly why I have gathered such a diverse group of masters from all corners of the land. This is so our young Prophesied Hero is prepared for all eventualities."

Taishi threw her peach pit over her shoulder and wiped her hands on her peasant robes. She held up a hand as if expecting that to quiet the masters. When no one obeyed, she barked a command that rumbled like thunder through the room. "Silence!"

The sheer force of this woman's presence made the hair on the back of Jian's neck stand as her word lingered in the air. She fixed him with a steely look. To his credit, this time he kept his face leveled, although his entire body clenched. She spoke again, in a crisp, commanding voice. "Show me a fist, boy."

How dare she? No one called him a boy. Didn't she know who he was? He swallowed the words. Instead, he did as he was told and raised an open hand, then curled his fingers into his palm. This was obviously a trick question. Jian spoke confidently. "There are several types of fists based on family style." He made a fist and bent his wrist. "There's the rolling fist favored by the Wang style." Out of the corner of his eye, he caught Wang nodding approvingly for being named first. Jian curled his knuckles next in a slant. "This is the Jang cutting punch." He extended the knuckle of his forefinger. "Hili ape fist." Knuckles up. "Pai knife punch." Flat palm. "Sinsin family super chop punch."

Wang snorted. "That's not even a fist."

The two masters went at it again.

Jian's cheeks burned. This sort of quarreling happened often, but usually behind closed doors. Both men were like uncles to him. He pushed on and curled his fingers into claws. "The Luda eagle claw—"

Taishi held up a hand. "That's enough. Show me your guard."

Jian obliged. This time, he started with Master Ningzhu's since he hadn't gotten the chance to demonstrate the Ning straight-arm punch technique. He crossed his wrists. "This is the Ning family holy cross. This is the single Jang side guard. This is the Sun hacking block—"

Taishi reached out and slapped Jian. The blow wasn't fast or particularly hard. Jian saw her hand moving toward his face slowly and was momentarily confused. He had plenty of time to block, duck, or counter it. At the very least steel himself for the hit. Instead, Jian just watched as her palm connected with his cheek. His head snapped to the side and he tumbled to the ground. Fortunately, the rug was thick.

A collective gasp filled the room.

"All these blocking techniques for what?" Taishi shook her head. "It took the unity of all the believers of the Tiandi Prophecy to find this boy. Every child in fifteen generations brought forth to the Tiandi monks for testing. Hundreds of the loyal traveling hundreds of miles for nearly a hundred years. Emperor Xuanshing, may his greatness everlast, made it his life's mission to find the Hero of Prophecy. When he passed, the five states of Zhuun honored him by burying their conflict and offered his home to train and raise the savior. Each state tithed a tenth of their soldiers and resources as tribute to defend the prophecy." Then Taishi pointed at Jian. "And this is what you've done with him?"

"Hey!" The protest involuntarily shot out of Jian's lips. He could take only so much. He burned inside.

Taishi did not appear to hear his outburst. "Instead of preparing him, teaching him the ways of the masters or war arts, each of you has tried to put your own imprint on him, to possess him and call him your own. Instead of serving the people, you sought glory, not only at the expense of the boy, but at the expense of all Zhuun."

The looks on his masters' faces were mixed. Some were angry, some ashamed. All looked uncomfortable. Jian was having trouble standing still. No one had ever spoken about him like this. No one would dare! It angered him even more to hear her disparage his masters. They weren't perfect, yes, but they were *his*.

The masters weren't the only ones facing Taishi's wrath. She turned on Faaru next. "And you, Peachlord, where are the boy's other instructors?"

Faaru stuttered. "W-What?"

"You brought him eight supposed war arts masters, but where are his other teachers? Who is teaching him strategy, tactics, and diplomacy? Who is teaching him calligraphy? Can he even read? Can that soft melon of his do even basic dog-piss math?"

Palacelord Faaru's face broke out in fat beads of sweat, and he looked unsteady on his feet. "His masters provide all the instruction he needs. I assure you he will be ready when the time comes."

"I can *too* read . . ." Jian sputtered. The words died in his throat when Taishi turned toward him. Her attention was terrible. ". . . Well, sort of," he finished in a much smaller voice.

"He can too read, sort of," she mimicked. "I was informed before I was dragged all the way across the Jagged Peak Mountains that I was going to witness legendary greatness. That this Hero of Prophecy, Champion of the Five Under Heaven, was a once-in-a-lifetime sight.

So far, all I've seen is a bunch of wounded throwaway soldiers and eight fools teaching an arrogant and spoiled boy to fight like a fool."

Jian finally found his voice. "You cannot talk to me like this!"

She ignored him. "Palacelord Faaru, I have decided. I am taking over the boy's training. From this point on, he will become my responsibility. I just hope it's not too late."

Sinsin raised an arm as if a schoolboy asking a question. "What about us?"

She snapped, "You're all dismissed. I want every one of you gone from the palace before the next King's dawn."

The fire burning inside Jian finally exploded. If his masters were too honorable and respectful to defend themselves, then he, their disciple, would stand for them. Rage inflamed his courage. "It is *you* who will leave at once, woman. You are only an emissary sent by the Duke of Shulan. You think you can tell us what to do because you cheated in the pit. Well, there is no cheating in real life." Taishi looked as if she were sucking on a sour plum. For some reason, Jian had expected a different reaction. He continued. "I am the Prophesied Hero of Zhuun. My masters stay. I command it. They have made me the warrior I am. I am ready to fight the hordes' Khan now if needed. I bet I can easily beat him even now."

Taishi studied him intently as he puffed his chest. This time, he did not wilt under her intense gaze. What was the worst she could do? Strike him dead? Slap him again? He dared her to try. To the Zhuun, he was practically a god.

"Oh, are you, boy?" To his great discomfort, Taishi smiled. "What do you know about this Khan?"

Jian raised his chin. "He is a beast: half man, half horse. He is strong as a mountain but dumb as the boulders. He rules over the savage hordes through fear and plunder. I will put him down like any rabid animal."

This time Taishi did break into a chuckle. For some reason, the happier she looked, the more frightening she appeared. "Is that what these fools who have never sniffed a battlefield tell you about him? Well, I've stood on the opposite side of the field against the Khan. My blade has kissed his. He is a savage, but not in the way you think." She almost sounded enchanted. "Taller than any man has a right to be. Hair that flows on the currents of the Grass Sea, a voice that rumbles the earth. He is a force of nature on the battlefield. Feet like a dancer, hands like a painter, and the mouth of a poet." She paused. "Somewhat. His prose could use a little refinement."

"What?" Jian became confused. "Whose side are you supposed to be on?"

She shrugged. "You'll see if you are ever unfortunate enough to stand in his way. You had better hope it is still many years from now, boy, because the Eternal Khan is an artist with death, a god of war, the right hand of violence. He kills creatively, slaughtering by the dozens, by the hundreds, for sport." She stepped closer. Her breath smelled like peaches, with hints of opium and rot.

"In battle, the Khan is a whirlwind, equal parts savagery, skill, and masterful tactics. He has the strength of a giant and the speed of a serpent. He rides an elephant into battle and decimates entire squads with one charge. In the Battle of Northern Pengnin, he and just fifty of his riders outmaneuvered and decimated six hundred soldiers, killing two master generals. Then they razed a town of three thousand. *Including the children.*"

Just when Jian had found the courage to stand up to Taishi, something about her voice pierced his mind and broke his will. Her words, infused with the power of her jing, evoked terrible images. A giant silhouette stepped out from within the tall lilting blades of a grass forest and stalked toward him with lightning and thunder announcing his approach. The dark figure had long fangs and sharp claws and possibly four arms, one wielding a spear as tall as a house. The tip of that phantom spear touched his chest, slicing through his skin like rice paper. Jian tried to scream, but only a pained gasp escaped his lips.

The spear went in deeper, cutting bone and sinew, and then plunged through his back. Terror seized his chest. His stomach clenched. He tried to pull away again, but a vise-like grip held him.

The room swayed, and he focused to see Taishi's weathered face close to his, her rough, scarred hand wrapped around his wrists like a claw. "After he flays and kills you, he'll tear your arms from your body to pick his teeth. He'll use your severed head as a goblet, and wear your skin as a cloak. That is the Eternal Khan that you are fated to fight. And you say you're ready to face him on the field?"

When Jian opened his mouth, no words came. Phantom pain and stark terror seized his breath. Then, Wen Jian, the Prophesied Hero of the Zhuun, Champion of the Five Under Heaven, savior of the Zhuun people, destined to lead the Enlightened States over the savage Khanate Hordes of Katuia, threw up peach juice all over Ling Taishi's feet, and fainted.

CHAPTER THREE

POETRY IN MOTION

Jalua stared at the tall blade of grass swaying in the breeze. He shoved it aside, only to have it rebound and shove him back. A hiss erupted from his throat as he hacked at the giant weed with his ax until the stem lay bent in a dozen places. Then, slowly, the accursed weed stood itself back up, with only a few tooth marks from his ax betraying the violence Jalua had inflicted on it. He gave up and ducked his head under the tall blade of grass bowing over the narrow, winding path. The stupid grass had won again, as it had the other hundred times his squad had crossed this field.

Jalua hated the Grass Sea. It was an endless plain of indestructible plants, each as tall as a tree. The grasses here were impossible to kill: difficult to cut, tough to flatten, and resilient even against fire. And it wasn't for want for trying: In the early days of the war, the Enlightened States had uprooted and burned the grasses and even salted the earth. But the overgrown green blades, the true lords of these wild and resilient lands, always came back.

Unfortunately, the Grass Sea was also home to the Katuia Hordes. These savages would swarm out from the Grass Sea and raid the

Zhuun's rich farmlands, then scurry back into the tall weeds before the Enlightened States' armies could pursue. Now it was up to Jalua's patrol, and hundreds of others like it, to give the army advance warning of horde incursions.

Jalua craned his neck back and scanned the few bits of blue that broke past the green spears. He finally found a sliver of the King just to his left. They were still heading in the right direction. It was easy to get twisted around in this jungle. More important, they were almost at the halfway mark, which meant it was time for the patrol to begin working their way back to friendly territory.

The Grass Sea made Jalua feel like a tiny bug, and that was unnerving. From the day he had slipped out of his mam's womb, Jalua had been a big boy, with a big mouth, a big appetite, and a big voice. He was always a head taller than the other children—and a head wider and several heads meaner. When he was still crawling, he would eat the dog's food after finishing his own. When the dog snapped at him, he bit it. When he was a boy, he would take the other children's lunches. When they complained, he would bite them as well. When Jalua was a grown man and past his biting phase, he stole food from the local shops. He had then tried to beat up the town's entire magistrate watch, but he hadn't been quite big enough for that.

Instead of losing his hands—the penalty for theft—Jalua joined the army, which ended up being the best decision he had ever made. The army loved big, strong men with big, loud mouths. His sergeant had looked him up and down like a slab of meat and promoted him to corporal on the spot. Being big was a great talent, he had declared. Size couldn't be taught. It could only be nurtured, so the army fed him plenty. From that point, Jalua had quickly risen in the ranks. Being a leader was easy. He just had to yell and push people around, things he had done well all his life. Within a season of bellowing and threatening, Jalua was promoted to unit commander. And he still got to eat as much as he liked.

The Grass Sea was the only place that ever made him feel small, like one of the insects that crawled through the weeds of his family's garden, right before he'd bring his meaty foot down upon it for a satisfying squish. And if he were a bug, that meant there was a stomping boot in his future.

Just as his imagination was about to get the better of him, some plants to the east rustled. He held up a fist. The rest of his squad stopped along the winding path and retreated behind cover among the stalks. One of his men yelped as he fell into an innocent-looking puddle that turned out to be neck-deep. The sea was sneaky like that.

"What is it, Captain?" asked Manji, the newest recruit in the unit. Jalua liked to keep the fresh meat close to him at all times and send them out on the most dangerous assignments. It helped him cut down on replacing his veterans and remembering names.

Jalua slid his ax out of its holster and pointed toward the source of the noise. "Something in the weeds. Check it out."

"Why me?"

Jalua shook his ax threateningly. "Because I'm a lot worse than what's in there."

Manji, his face already a mess of blue and purple from having once been on the receiving end of Jalua's wrath, gulped and rose from his hiding place. He managed a step forward before Jalua smacked him on the side of the head. "Your spear, fool. Lose another and I'll attach it to your asshole."

The boy, barely sixteen, scampered back to pick it up and then began to pick his way toward the noise. He squeezed between several clusters of grass, looked back once apprehensively, and was then swallowed up by the tangled foliage.

Jalua signaled for the rest of the squad to stay behind cover. The wind had picked up overhead, causing the grasses to rustle as the blades brushed against one another. Somewhere just in the darkness beyond, cicadas and birds joined the chorus. A pack of coyotes laughed, probably celebrating a kill. Some of the men became restless as vertigo took hold of them, which was common. Everything in here was always moving in one direction or another. The only way to stay sane was if you moved with the land.

Jalua flinched when a spider the size of his hand lowered itself to a large leaf and crawled directly in front of him. It chittered softly as it sized him up. "Hey there, you ugly little thing," he cooed, raising his free hand next to it. The spider stared at him for a few seconds, as if considering his offer, and then its eight furry legs moved one by one onto his fingers before coming to a rest on the back of his hand.

He raised his arm so the spider was eye level. "Thought you'd get the jump on me, eh? Wanted a bite of juicy Jalua, eh?" Then he smashed the flat of his ax onto the spider. He grinned as fragments of legs and guts and green goo dripped down his forearm. "Nasty bug. I hate this place," he muttered. "Where in the ten depths of hell did that lazy Manji go? I swear, if I have to send someone after him, I'm going to cleave him in two."

His answer came a moment later in the form of a high-pitched shriek from the darkness. Manji burst out of the thickets, his spindly legs pedaling as hard as they could in the soft mud. He looked shaken, his face white and his eyes bulging like the twin moons. His hands were up in the air as if he were looking for someone to whom to surrender.

The boy was just about to speed past when Jalua stretched out a beefy arm and clotheslined him. Manji hit the ground back-first with a wheeze. Jalua scowled at the boy writhing at his feet, clutching his neck. "What happened to your spear, soldier? What did I say I'd do to you if you lose it again?"

Manji's mouth opened and closed, managing only a squeak. He rolled his eyes upward and pointed back the way he had come. Jalua squinted at the narrow path leading into the darkness.

At first, the sea was still save for the breeze. Then he heard it: twigs snapping and plants crunching, soon followed by labored breathing and . . . singing? The grass was suddenly violently parted as a very large and very naked man burst into the clearing.

Jalua's jaws dropped in consternation and jealousy. Mostly jealousy. It was easily the biggest man he had ever seen in his life. "Piss on me! That is a big boy."

The man, if he could be called that, charged the patrol. Jalua managed to save himself by diving to the side into a shallow pond. His entire body was submerged and all he could see in the muddy water were the green tentacles of man-eating kelp and schools of ugly gray eels with sharp, pointy teeth. That was when Jalua remembered he couldn't swim. He sucked in a gulp of rancid water and began to choke, flailing and kicking his legs. He managed to get his head up above water for a moment before sinking back down.

The moment Jalua's feet touched the pond floor, he pushed back up to the surface. His head broke through a second time. Then he stood up and realized the water was only chest-deep. Jalua vomited up rancid water and wiped his brow, scowling at the dozens of small black leeches sucking on his arms. His axes were gone. Jalua was never going to live this down. He looked over at the battle that had unfolded while he had gone for a dip. Maybe he wouldn't need to. The giant naked man was making mincemeat of his patrol.

Jalua was once again stunned by this specimen of a man. *That really is a big boy!* Even worse, with his thick eyebrows, long sideburns, and overly long topknot, he was obviously a Kati savage. In fact, this brute looked like he had jumped straight out of one of those stories Zhuun mothers told their children to frighten them into eating their congee.

Big Boy rampaged with reckless abandon through rows of soldiers armed with spears and shields, winning the contest of wills as they scattered against the onslaught. He clipped one soldier, knocking him to the ground, then stopped. He paused in the middle of the clearing, leaning off to one side and staggering before careening forward again, knocking down two more.

All the while Big Boy was screaming in his strange tongue. No, not screaming, but singing or shouting some battle chant in a low baritone. While Jalua stood there, mesmerized, Big Boy grabbed Manji by the collar, lifted him off the ground with one arm, and then threw him all the way across the clearing, right over Jalua's head and into the pond.

That snapped Jalua out of his stupor. Big Boy here may be a beast of a man, but he was still only a man. A pack of hyenas could pull down a lion given the right motivation, and Jalua had thirty such dogs in his unit. He waded his way back onto land and began barking orders. "Form up. Spears out. Close in like lovers, you tick-loving, stick-humping dogs. The next man who shows me his ass is going to get it split open! Someone put some gods-pig-sticking arrows in that oversized piece of pork!"

It took a few more loud curses and several more threats before he managed to rouse his men to order. They formed up quickly enough, more out of self-preservation than discipline. Within seconds, they had the rabid naked man encircled, their spears threatening him from every side. Jalua's best archer, Wanko, rose from behind the row of shields and shot an arrow. Big Boy snatched it out of the air mid-flight. The archer gasped and shot another, only to have that swatted aside like an annoying gnat. The giant man glared at the archer and went straight for him.

Jalua's stomach churned. Not only were they facing a giant, he appeared to be highly skilled in the war arts. Size and skill. How unfair. That unpredictable movement, the unsteady weaving to dodge attacks, could it be the famed Drunken style? That was supposed to be a myth!

The line of spearmen who were supposed to protect Wanko broke and scattered. The poor archer found himself standing alone as the giant man barreled toward him. To his credit, and stupidity, Wanko stood his ground and fumbled for another arrow, managing to draw and loose it at the very last moment.

Big Boy staggered, tumbled several steps to the side, and then collapsed facedown, skidding a few feet along the soft ground before coming to a rest at Wanko's feet.

There was a stunned silence, and then Jalua let out a triumphant cry as he pushed past his men. "You got him! Way to stand tall, Wanko. See? I told you all those times I screamed in your face during drills would help."

Wanko looked confused. "I didn't hit him. He just kind of lurched forward. The shot went over his head." He pointed at an arrow in the distance sticking out of the soft earth.

Jalua's breath caught in his throat. It *was* the fabled Drunken Fist! He stared at the body lying facedown in several inches of water. What an amazing display of skill. He grabbed the nearest body and shoved him forward. "Singhy, check out the big boy and tell me if he's still alive."

Singhy looked as if he was about to refuse, then thought better of it. The soldier slowly advanced on the body, his spear trembling in his grasp.

"Is he dead?" someone asked.

That would have been too easy. Singhy had almost reached the body when Big Boy shuddered and rolled onto his side, pulling his knees to his chest in a fetal position. Singhy jumped back, then gingerly poked Big Boy's leg with the tip. He looked back at Jalua. "Sir, he's sleeping. I think he's drunk."

"Drunk like Drunken-style drunk?"

"No, more like my ba after an all-night binge at the room salon."

As soon as he turned his back to Big Boy, the big man popped to his feet. Before anyone could shout a warning, a meaty hand smacked Singhy on the side of the head, knocking the consciousness out of him before he even hit the ground. Singhy landed limply in another shallow puddle and probably would have drowned if one of the other soldiers hadn't fetched him out.

Then Big Boy scrunched his face, hung his head, and threw up. Jalua was at a complete loss. Was this man a legendary war artist or just an idiot Kati who had drunk too much, stripped off all his clothes, and wandered out naked into the Grass Sea? Jalua decided that it didn't matter: The savage had attacked his men and that was all he really needed to know. He signaled to his remaining soldiers. "Just kill him. We'll sort this out later."

His men, already rattled, shouted half-throated battle cries as they converged. Just as they were about to skewer Big Boy, he must have found his second wind. The first over-eager sap who reached him was brutally disarmed when Big Boy grabbed his shield and violently yanked it away. Unfortunately for the soldier, the shield was lashed to his forearm, and the disarmament included his elbow on down.

The next three soldiers came at him from opposite sides. Somehow, even at close range, all three missed their intended target. No weapons, no matter how close, could find their mark. Blades seem to turn aside from his skin. Spear thrusts glanced away. Big Boy retaliated by taking all three out at once, launching himself into the air to kick two in the faces before landing on the third, smashing his head into the soft mud. It was a spectacular display of strength and skill.

Jalua snatched the nearest pike and joined the fray. He aimed for the crack on Big Boy's ass and charged, only to somehow streak right past him. He stopped and turned just in time to take a foot to the gut. He gasped and watched helplessly as the giant Kati wound up and back-handed him across the face. Jalua found himself half blind with a mouthful of mud and wet grass a moment later. The side of his face hurt so bad he thought his eyeball had popped out. His men continued to scream behind him.

Jalua nearly stayed down to play dead this time, but then decided he could never live down that shame. He pushed himself back to his feet, grabbing the shoulder of his nearest soldier for support. Big Boy had taken out three more spearmen while still singing loudly and off-key. By now, at least half of the unit was down.

Jalua turned to the man he was leaning on. "Cairon, you speak Kati. What's this madman saying?"

Cairon listened intently. "He's not making any sense. He's saying something about being the lord of the weeds and bog. The east is dark. The sky green. And, um, broken feathers in the wind?" The soldier's brow furrowed. "Actually I think it's poetry."

"Poetry?"

Jalua looked on as the giant plucked a bow out of an archer's hands and wrapped it around the man's neck. There was something familiar about this guy. There were descriptions, rumors, reports, whispered by drunk soldiers about an enemy this size with this savagery and mastery.

Then every nerve in Jalua's body tingled and his muscles clenched. "Of course. It can't be anyone else. It's the bloody bear-humping Khan, but why is he naked? And drunk for that matter?" This realization should have made him even more terrified, but it made him only greedier. "This is too good to be true. Imagine what will happen if we're the ones to kill him."

"But," stammered Cairon. "He's the Eternal Khan. He's literally immortal. It says so in his title."

"Maybe it's because no one has tried hard enough," snapped Jalua. "Listen, boys," he bellowed loudly. "This egg-hatcher is the Khan of all the Katuia Hordes. Slaughter this naked hairless savage and your names will be etched among the stars until the last of days. This is the day you become legends."

Jalua's men cheered and attacked the Khan with renewed vigor, which resulted in only more of them getting put down more quickly. It didn't matter. The idea of being rich proved to be a far greater motivation than any threat Jalua could have lobbed at them.

"Form up again! Like professional soldiers, you motherless, neutered pufferflies!" Jalua barked, grabbing another spear. While his men were keeping the Khan busy, he circled, biding his time as his men slowly closed in on the Khan instead of blindly charging at him. "Entrench and hold him. Collapse in, now!"

The spearmen converged on the Khan from three sides. Most of the spears missed their mark, but that was fine. The Khan knocked a few more men over, but the rest of the patrol attacked him again. Still Jalua waited. All his men had to do was hold the Khan in place. The opening came a moment later. Jalua seized it. He gripped the spear close to his body and hurtled it forward with all his might, ramming the tip into the royal big boy's back.

The Khan shuddered and roared as the spear went through his body. A look of puzzlement stretched on his face as he glanced down at the bloody spear tip protruding through his chest. The moment seemed to stretch as realization dawned on his drunken face. The Khan staggered left and right, and then fell to his knees.

His death knell was surprisingly muted, not so much an extended histrionic outburst as a short, burpy gasp. The last thing the Eternal Khan of the savage Katuia Hordes did before the life left his eyes was to release his bowels, spraying an impressive amount of shit between his legs before keeling over on top of it. Near-black blood oozed from the spear wound as his breathing stopped.

A long silence followed. None of the men moved. Even the Grass Sea appeared to have calmed, as if paying its last respects to the Eternal Khan, the legendary demi-god who could not be killed, the man from whom blades would turn aside out of respect and arrows missed out of fear. Whom Jalua had just killed.

Jalua couldn't believe what had just happened. He stared at his hands still gripping the spear shaft. He struggled for words but found none. Finally, he began to do what he did best. Jalua began to yell, his voice carrying across the Grass Sea so loudly it sent a flock of starlings up into the air. "I did it! Me! I'm going to be famous. I'm going to be jewels-on-my-balls rich! I'm going to marry a princess."

He began jumping up and down in the air. His joy was infectious. Soon the survivors of his unit joined in. Even nature seemed to celebrate the victory: Everything around them suddenly came alive. Insects chirped, small rodents skittered along the ground, and hundreds of birds took flight from their nests, nearly blotting out the sky. Even a herd of antelopes bounded past their celebration.

It was too late by the time they actually heard the rumbling. Manji must have heard it first. While everyone was celebrating around him, Manji pushed his way to Jalua and furiously patted his shoulder, his voice drowned by the cheers. He jovially returned the gesture, smacking Manji across the side of the head, knocking him over.

Manji quickly picked himself back up. There was fear in his eyes. "Captain, listen!"

It took a minute before Jalua realized that the boy was frightened and a whole other minute before he managed to quiet the rest of his squad with waves of his arm. Then they all heard it too, a familiar high-pitched shriek followed by a deep, rhythmic sputter.

"Bixi!" Jalua yelled.

It was too late.

The walls of tall grass surrounding them crumpled as a squat turtle-shaped monster made of metal burst into the clearing. Four archers leaned out of an armored nest situated on top of the Katuia wargear, raining arrows down at the Zhuun soldiers. Fat, squat spikes protruding from the machine's wheels whirled and chewed up everything in its path as it rolled over the wet and uneven terrain. The bixi plowed into the cluster of soldiers, running over two and impaling four before the rest could scatter, and then it screamed its namesake war cry as a plume of steam shot into the air.

The tip of one of the spikes grazed Jalua, slicing through his armor as if it were wool. He rolled to his feet and fumbled for a weapon. Any weapon. He seemed to keep losing them today. He was about to try to rally his men again when ten more bixis in a tight formation appeared.

Jalua's breath caught. It was a full-blown attack. He wanted to sound the retreat, but it wasn't necessary. He was alone in the clearing. His soldiers had already fled. Blasted cowardly mutts. Jalua knew better than to try to run at this point. Either the bixis were going to get them or the archers riding on top would. Or some monster residing within the Grass Sea if he just ran blind. His only choice now was how to die.

What awful luck. Something had finally swung his way and now he wouldn't even get a chance to enjoy it. Of course these damn Kati would have been searching for their naked Eternal Khan. Not so damn eternal, was he? Killed by this guy right here! Still, Jalua would have liked to have gotten a little rich and a whole lot of famous before he died. He cursed and decided to make his stand.

Perhaps it was his last bit of pride that made Jalua remember his duty. He fumbled in his pack and pulled out a signal. He had no time to plant it in the ground so he cracked the fuse and held the stick in his hand. Pointing it upward, Jalua screamed his last cry of big-man defiance. The signal lit a moment later, shooting a burst of light into the sky before exploding into spherical burst of yellow and red.

"Now you're going to get it, you Kati assholes! When the army comes, you tell them Zin Jal—" Jalua raised his fist and roared just as one of the bixis crushed him beneath its giant, spiked wheels, like a boot on a bug.

CHAPTER FOUR

LESSONS

An uneasy sensation tickled the back of Jian's brain the moment he opened his eyes. The water clock sitting in a small alcove on the opposite wall had run dry, and the King was already far along into his morning climb across the sky. A quick glance about the room told him that his training garb hadn't been laid out. Nor were his attendants waiting to dress him. There was no scroll keeper with whom to review the morning's lessons.

Most important, where was breakfast?

He reached over to the side of the bed and pulled the long green silk cord hanging from the ceiling. A soft gong rang overhead and echoed through bell ducts behind the ceiling. Jian waited until the sound drifted away and settled into a low hum. No one appeared at the servants' door. Frowning, he sat up and pulled the orange, yellow, and red cords. Three more tones sounded in harmony, all with the same result. One of his favorite things to do as a child was to pull all twelve ropes for the full harmonization, which his attendants had not much appreciated. Within seconds, his entire room would be filled with people seeing to his needs. He would send them away and do it all over again.

But today, the symphony of gongs summoned none of his staff. When no one responded, especially to the red cord, which was supposed to be pulled only if his well-being was at risk, Jian reached for the knife hidden behind a latch in his headboard and rolled off the bed. If Riga and Horashi weren't close by, then something was definitely wrong. Was it an attack? Had the Kati sent assassins to massacre his servants in the night? He waited and listened. The reverberation faded to stillness, and the Tower of Eternal Heroism was quiet, silent in a way it had never been before.

Jian kept his head down as he scampered to the window overlooking the rest of the Celestial Palace. The morning attendants had obviously not come: The drapes would have been opened, the morning bath drawn, and the aroma of the first course would be filling the room. Jian swept the drapes aside and looked out. His heart hammered in his chest. Everyone had disappeared. No guards in sight, no servants moving about, not even the many horses or dogs. It was as if every living soul had suddenly departed.

Something was *very* wrong. Jian dove under the window and somersaulted from cover to cover until he crossed to the other side of the room. He paused behind his heavy desk and then slid behind his sparring dummy. Still no sounds other than his quick, short breaths, for which he was ashamed.

"To show breath is to show weakness," Hili had recited during his many long training sessions.

Jian crept out from behind the dummy and hurried into his weapons closet. He had been only six years old when the Katuia had sent their first assassin. An old woman hired on to the cleaning staff had tried to poison his undergarments. There had been many more attempts since, ranging from creepy invisible Kati who melded into the walls to deadly warriors who cut their way through half the garrison. Horashi had killed three assassins by himself over the years. Riga currently had a job because his predecessor had jumped in front of an arrow meant for Jian.

Regardless, these new assassins would find him more difficult prey. The weapons closet was a long narrow room. It was his favorite place in the tower, and housed every imaginable weapon, neatly organized on hooks and shelves from floor to ceiling: melee weapons, from bastard swords to long, broad axes decked out with intricate carvings on both blade and hilt, on racks; baskets of munitions—arrows, caltrops, throwing daggers—to the side; and on the opposite wall, an array of armors, here a heavy dueling full-plate suit, there a set of banded wood greaves for cavalry work and black cloth wraps for clandestine operations.

But if Jian was to be fighting off a small army of Katuia assassins, he must look the part of an epic hero of legend. His lips curled into a smile at the sight of gold and green glinting in the back corner.

When Jian emerged moments later, he had transformed into a glittering, shining tank. He admired himself at the mirror before stepping out of the armory. He was a beaming image of a glorious hero of legend, wearing green plate armor with an illustration of a Pixiu, a ferocious cat creature with long sharp fangs and brightly feathered wings, whose presence heralded the arrival of a powerful force. The gauntlets and greaves of this set of armor were shaped like sharpened furry paws, which Jian quite fancied.

On his person was strapped a veritable trove of incredibly valuable armaments, so that he appeared not unlike a porcupine of shining, glimmering death. On his left hip sat a golden straight sword, next to two glittering daggers. Across his back, a tear-away bandolier held his bone-carved staff, a diamond-etched spear, and an onyx-gem-wrapped bow with matching quiver. On his right hip hung a glass-etched chain whip. Jian had pondered bringing the horse-cutter as well, but the large sword with the extended handle was so heavy he nearly fell over as soon as he pulled it off the wall. He decided against bringing it and left it lying in the middle of the floor. What he was equipped with now should be more than enough against the savage enemy.

Jian left the armory feeling invincible and ready for battle, if it were not for the fact the helmet hugged his ears too tightly and its weight pulled his head backward. Sure, the onyx-wrapped bow pinched his hand on the draw, and the golden sword was not exactly the most balanced blade. But surely his martial skills, long practiced in the halls of the tower, would overcome any disadvantage from his gear.

He had everything he needed to take on an army of horde assassins while letting his foes know they were vanquished by the Champion of the Five Under Heaven. Sinsin would be proud. "Looking the part is as important as playing the part," his master always said.

Ready to take on the world, Jian drew the saber in one hand and gripped the knife in the other as he crept across the room, doing his best to minimize the clanging noises made with every step. He stopped at the door and pushed it open a sliver. The hallway, like everywhere else in the palace, was empty. Neither of the two guards were there, but strangely, their bodies were not even lying around. No blood, no broken furniture. No signs of struggle whatsoever.

He reversed the grip on his knife and hugged the wall as he made his way down the winding staircase that wrapped around the outer wall of his tower. The main foyer was, perhaps unsurprisingly, abandoned too. Jian took no chances, leaping from cover to cover, rolling over a chair, and sliding behind a table. The sword and bow strapped to his back got tangled with his legs and his quiver kept tipping over and leaving a trail of arrows on the floor.

It took Jian twenty minutes to reach the front entrance of his tower. As soon as he stepped out onto the street, he jumped the railing and re-treated into the alley, hiding in the small depression of a door reserved for servants. He took stock of his environment and continued on, scurrying from shadow to shadow.

In some ways, even with all the noise he was making, it was too quiet. Jian never realized how used he was to the pitter-patter sounds his retinue made until they were no longer there. He was now truly alone, and the silence felt alien and eerie. His skin crawled, and he fought a suffocating surge of panic. What would his masters do?

Master Pai's lessons rang in his head: "When under attack, it is the hero's responsibility to find and kill the enemy."

At the time, Jian had thought it was very sound advice. He gritted his teeth and steeled his resolve as he painstakingly crept to the edge of the

Heavenly Grounds. The Heart of the Tiandi Throne was the symbol of the prophecy and the old seat of the former Zhuun empire. If the enemy had come, they would be there.

He scanned the wide-open expanse of the Heavenly Grounds. Still no activity save for the occasional leaf dancing with the breeze. He would have to sprint across the grounds and up the Thousand Steps without cover to reach the throne room. Taking a deep breath, Jian burst from the shadow of the building out into the open, his feet churning as fast as he could move. He half expected to hear arrows whistling around him. The Katuia, if it was indeed those savages, were famed archers and would certainly be on the lookout. Fortunately, his masters had always praised his unnatural speed.

It was about the time he reached the steps that the weight from all his gear started slowing him down. Jian had fought in full armor before, but running with it was a new experience. The weight of the weapons didn't help. He began shedding gear. First the staff a quarter of the way up the stairs, then the spear a hundred steps later. He lost the helm at around six hundred steps, and then the chain whip. By the time he reached the top, he was so exhausted, he fell to the ground and rolled onto his back, his arms and legs splayed out. If the Katuia were going to shoot him now, then fine.

After he caught his breath, Jian sat up and pulled the bow off his shoulder. The quiver had overturned halfway up the run. Still panting, he held out his hand. "Drink." Then he remembered. "Oh."

Jian stood up and scanned the rest of the palace. He should have seen someone, anyone, by now. There were no archer snipers, no assassins lurking in the shadows, nothing. Maybe this place actually was abandoned. Instead of going around through the servants' door as he had originally planned, Jian just walked up to the front entrance. He was too tired to sneak around anymore. He pushed through the double doors and made it two steps when he saw the first living soul. In some ways he wished it had been an assassin.

Taishi, that hateful old woman, was sitting on the throne up on the dais, leaning on one arm casually while peering at him from behind a teacup. Jian gripped his saber and marched up to her. "It's a capital offense to sit on the throne. Not even *I* am allowed. It's a symbol that the States have no emperor. You can be hanged for this."

She eyed him disdainfully. "It took you long enough to find your way here," she remarked. "I was informed that you rose with the King."

"My attendants did not wake me. They have all gone missing," he replied. "What are you doing here? I ordered you gone from the palace."

"Drinking tea. Waiting for you." Taishi took a long, exaggerated sip. "I dismissed your attendants. In fact I've barred anyone from entering the palace until further notice."

Jian blanched. "What about my masters? This morning is Master Wang's session."

"Especially those useless fools." A small smirk betrayed the old woman. She was enjoying this. "Wang and a few others with any self-respect left the city this morning."

"Well, call him back. I need him. I need all of my masters."

"You need nothing of the sort. The only things fools can teach are foolish things." She took another sip of her tea. "They were tasked to raise a leader of the Zhuun. Instead, they've given us a monkey to put on a show."

It was a slap in the face. To say that his masters were a joke meant that Jian was the punch line. "You can't talk to me like this," he hollered. "I'm the Prophesied Hero of the—"

"That's another thing I'm changing," she cut him off. "No one is calling you a hero or champion anymore. No more special little swaddled star. You are nothing until you have accomplished something. Until then, you are only a spoiled boy playing at hero, walking around parroting the idiocy of lesser men."

"Bring everyone back, all the attendants and my masters immediately," he screamed. "That's an order."

She ticked off another finger. "No more giving orders until you've earned that right too. Authority is earned, not given. A strong leader is forged, not born. There will be no more groveling servants and scraping sycophants. No corrupt masters and lords fawning over you to seek advantage. You are a soldier and a student. And from this point on, *my* student. I am taking over your training. You are now my ward and responsibility. It is past time you begin walking the true path of a war arts master to reach your full potential. Now, come here." She held out her opened palm with her half-empty cup resting on it. "Your first lesson is humility. Pour me more tea, boy. Dash of honey."

Jian tried very hard at that moment to kill Taishi with his glare. "Pour it yourself, you hateful, crippled hag." He swatted at the cup.

Taishi flexed her palm and bounced the porcelain teacup straight up into the air as his hand passed underneath. The cup rose up to his eye level and then fell, leaving a stream of tea following it back down. Not a drop was spilled. Jian tried again, but succeeded only in grabbing a handful of her sleeve. He yanked hard, causing the cup to slip from her palm. The top of her foot tapped it as it fell, and the cup bounced back up again. It landed on the top of her foot, and she then sent it leaping upward again, landing perfectly and completely unspilled back onto her palm. She held it out. "Refill. My. Tea."

Jian turned his back to her. "I don't need to put up with this." He recognized a power struggle when he saw one. His masters waged continuous ones against one another. As the most important person in all of Zhuun, this was beneath him. The Enlightened States needed him more than he needed them. Jian stomped away, the sound of his heavy boots echoing around the cavernous ceiling of the throne room. "I'm going to instruct Palacelord Faaru to have you shot next time you step foot into the Celestial Palace." He managed to make it five steps before he felt a light tap on the crown of his head, and then Taishi landed in front of him, the teacup still in her hand.

"The front gates are locked, and the walls are too tall to climb. I'll offer one chance to escape me, however. If you can smash this cup, then I will unlock the gates, and you will never see me again. Otherwise, serve me tea and begin your training."

"I hate you!"

Taishi shrugged.

This time Jian didn't hold back, aiming a killing blow as he went at her with renewed fury. His heel missed rearranging her nose by inches. He followed up with the Ningzhu family switch kick, Sun family double thrust. The almighty Jang lunge. Taishi gave an exaggerated yawn as she avoided his blows, her arms and legs swaying away from his attacks like a feather blown about by the wind. He might as well have been batting air. Jian quickly wore down; missed strikes were often more draining than ones that found their marks. Then to his shock, she slapped him. Again. Hard this time.

Her open palm came flying toward his left cheek and past it, swiveling his head to the side and rattling his skull. A giant bell rang in his head as his knees gave out and he spun in a complete circle and crashed to the ground.

"Stop slapping me!" Jian probably should have taken a moment to collect himself, but in his fury he bounded to his feet right away. He did not see her palm until it connected with his right cheek. As he stumbled, she slapped his ear, breaking his equilibrium, and then slapped him once again in the solar plexus, causing the air to rush out of his lungs. A moment later, he was on the floor again, this time facedown.

Jian was a little slower to get up. A whimper escaped him. His head was still ringing and the world swaying when he wobbled onto his hands and knees. He came at her again: Sinsin sucker punch followed by the Wang sweep, and then the—no, he changed his mind and switched to the Hili hammer fist. It was all for naught.

"You move with the grace of a two-headed donkey when you don't run a set routine." Taishi calmly shifted out of range. His attacks were only just missing her. Jian extended farther, thinking the next blow would be the one to find its mark. He tried harder and harder until he found himself precariously off balance.

"You are also easily taunted into making mistakes." She stuck her foot out and his legs disappeared from under him as the world flipped upside down. His head bounced off the gold and purple tiles once, twice, three times. A high-pitched whine escaped his lips.

Jian gnashed his teeth and picked himself up once more. He took a step forward and got slapped on the nose. He took two more swift shots to the forehead and neck before he finally penetrated the diminutive woman's guard. Then, he wasn't sure how she did it, but Taishi bumped him with her tiny hips and he went flying. None of his masters had ever hit him so hard before. Jian landed roughly sprawled on the marble floor. He forced himself to his knees.

"A good warrior knows when to submit," she droned.

"A good warrior keeps his mouth shut." Jian grabbed the half-empty pot of tea that had spilled onto the floor. He flung the contents at her.

"First thing we've agreed on," she conceded as she parted the spray of liquid with a brush of her hand.

Their next exchange went as well as the last. Still, that did not cure Jian's stubbornness. Five more times he picked himself up and went at her. Five more times she slapped him to the ground. Each subsequent time he rose more slowly than before.

After six more attempts, Jian lay on the floor, his body stinging and numb, but it was his ego that hurt most. Losing for the first time in his life yesterday could have been a fluke. Twice now in so many days shattered his will. He was supposed to be this invincible warrior, the savior of the Zhuun, the greatest hero since the dawn of the Enlightened States. Yet here he was, being easily manhandled and insulted by a miserable old woman who told him that he was not only a disappointment, but also a fraud.

Whatever little self-control he had left failed him then. Jian began to cry, shoulder-shaking sobs that racked his entire body. Nothing made sense anymore. The thought of being an absolute failure smacked him over and over. He had let everyone down. Jian brought his knees to his chest and turned away from Taishi, his face burning with shame.

"Heroes betray no emotion," Wang had lectured the first time he had cried as a little boy.

"The true warrior steels his nerves," Ningzhu had added.

"Heroes do not cry. Babies cry. Which are you?" Sinsin had practically yelled into his face.

The other masters had only stared at him in quiet disappointment and disdain every time his emotions got the better of him. Jian had learned to sniff quickly and wipe the tears away. Now it was too much to keep in. Jian didn't know how long he stayed on the ground, bawling like a child.

A hand touched his shoulder. "You fought well, boy. Better than I gave your masters credit for." Taishi knelt beside him. Jian tried to brush her away and cover his face. She touched his hand softly and lowered it. "There's no shame in tears. Nor in defeat. Both can be great sources of strength."

He sniffed and sat up to face her. "It doesn't make me weak?"

A small smile, the first he had seen on her face, appeared. "There is nothing weak about being in tune with your emotions. There is great strength once you learn to harness it. I *want* you to care so deeply it brings tears to your eyes."

Jian sat up and wiped at the wetness and snot running down his face. His body still ached, but he knew it would not last long. He was surprised by the old woman's gentleness. Perhaps it was the light, but at that moment the old, hateful woman didn't look hateful at all. There was almost a kind maternal aura to her, a warmth he had not noticed before. He sniffed. "Does that mean you'll return my attendants?"

Taishi made a sound somewhere between a snort and a laugh. She stood up. "Don't be stupid. Now go clean yourself up and get some breakfast."

"But I don't know how to cook."

"I guess you'll starve then."

CHAPTER FIVE

BY FIRE

Taishi's relationship with her new student was not off to an auspicious start. She had told herself that the first day would be hardest, that it would get better as time wore on. She had most definitely been wrong. She thought she had gotten through to him when he had cried, but he had still refused to serve her tea. The next day, Jian tested the gates. The day after, he explored the cellars. The one after that, he probed the Celestial Palace's walls for vulnerabilities. The boy was a stubborn one, and while she approved of a little grit in her students, this one was a mound of stupidity.

A person is their truest self when alone. These were the revered monk Goramh's last words before he disappeared into the Diyu Mountains, never to be seen again. Either he really enjoyed his truest self or he had starved on that desolate rock. In either case, Taishi took his wisdom to heart.

She carefully observed the boy from afar, staying mostly out of sight as Jian pouted through his days. He was shockingly unexciting and unimaginative for someone around whom a prophecy and religion were built, and upon whom an entire people's salvation depended.

On the third day, he tried to break the teacup again, which left him in a sour mess. He spent the rest of the morning trying to make food, which in itself would have been an entertaining spectacle if it were not for the fact that he set fire to the kitchen.

Taishi almost intervened then, but she decided to see how he resolved the little crisis. She learned quite a bit. The boy panicked easily, but also regained his senses quickly once his nerves settled. His planning was methodical and his decisions logical, both fine traits. She could work with that. Unfortunately, it took him too long to figure things out. By the time he moved into action, the kitchen's roof had already collapsed. Fortunately, the palace had three more kitchens for him to set on fire.

Seeing the wreckage of his little accident had left a small smile on her lips. In many ways, he reminded her of another boy who had trained under her. Sanso had been equally destructive and stubborn, but also resilient and full of drive. Now, *that* boy had grit.

Jian spent his mornings searching for a way to escape the palace and the afternoons mournfully looking over the palace walls at Hengyu, the small town that was built expressly to support the Celestial Palace. Then he would hole up in one of the studies to read those silly scrolls his former masters had written. Then he would try to break her teacup again. Every time Jian challenged her, he came prepared for the fight with a new plan based on what he had learned from their last bout, and then tried something new to beat her. She appreciated the effort at strategizing and rewarded his diligence with fists instead of opened palms as a sign of respect.

On the sixth morning, Jian finally got smart and came at her with weapons. Unfortunately for him, he chose double straight swords again. Stupid boy. On the seventh, a spear. The eighth, a rope dart. That last one was a disaster. She left him tied up in his own rope, and was mildly alarmed to find him still tied up on the ninth morning.

That night, after another long day of watching Jian mope around the palace, Taishi grabbed a gourd of plum wine and retreated to her residence at the top of the Eyes of the Earth Tower on the eastern edge of the palace. The view of the Kunlai Mountain from the tower reminded her of home, which would be her first destination the moment she finished this assignment. If she was honest with herself, her life might end before this assignment did, however. It had been a long time since Taishi had taught, and she was quickly reminded how much she despised the role. Now all the awfulness of working with a student came rushing back: the angst, the whininess, the blank looks, the stubborn insolence.

Jian had his moments, flashes of brilliance that made her breath catch. It was these glimmers of his potential in between long stretches of annoyance that reminded Taishi of a time when she used to love teaching a certain boy who could have been special. Who *had been* special. Sanso. Her own child. The fog blanketing her past momentarily lifted, awakening long-forgotten feelings of pride and accomplishment that came with nurturing greatness.

But those memories also brought forth old wounds: pain, anguish, and regret. Taishi would quickly bury those still-raw emotions before they dragged her to a dark pit. There was a reason she had eschewed teaching for so long and refused to take on another student.

But somehow, in a fit of righteous outrage and patriotic indignation and admittedly a fair amount of snobbery, she had bullied her way into this role again, and now she wasn't sure what to do. Even worse, she was teaching a student who was even more unruly, rebellious, and resistant to learning than her son had ever been. Somewhere out there, Sanso was having a hearty laugh at his mam's expense.

"It's for the good of the Enlightened States," she muttered as she brought the mostly empty gourd up to her lips. If only her words would manage to convince herself.

Now she was stuck in a self-imposed prison teaching this brat. Whether he fulfilled the prophecy six weeks or sixty years from now, making sure the Prophesied Hero of the Zhuun lived up to his destiny was now her responsibility. She would need at least a decade to give him even a slim chance of surviving an encounter with the Khan.

Who was she kidding? Even ten years wouldn't be enough. The Khan would pulverize the boy into fine turnip paste. Taishi looked down

at her useless arm; she would know. The man was an impressive creature, in body and mind. Especially in body. The memory brought a smile
to her face: the dark hurricane eyes and an earthquake-rumbling voice
to match. If only he had stopped trying to sound smart. Taishi and the
Khan had maintained a pleasant and professional relationship over the
years, one born out of mutual respect from both their exalted reputations within the lunar court. Every time their paths crossed, the two
would sit down for tea, swap stories, and debate technique and martial
styles, sometimes for hours on end. Only after their bodies were refreshed and their minds fed would they then return to the sordid business of trying to kill each other. Both, obviously, had yet to succeed,
although Taishi had to admit he had come far closer than she. The Eternal Khan's moniker was well earned.

Taishi retreated unsteadily to her wooden canopy bed and plopped
into the cushions, her mind cloudy with wine and exhaustion. A yawn
escaped her lips as the room blinked away. The wine gourd slipped from
her fingers and landed on its plump end, spinning around a few turns
before finally coming to rest on its side, the dregs spilling over the side of
the bed and staining the expensive rug.

Watching the tiny red waterfall made Taishi homesick. The last winter season of the year's cycle always brought floods to the Cloud Pillars.
It generally made starting fires an exercise in misery and crossing rope
bridges a daily life-or-death excursion, but it was also when nature came
alive. The flowers that clung to the precipitous peaks would blossom as
they cascaded down the sheer faces of the soaring cliffs while thousands
of small, gushing, bouncing waterfalls tumbled off the sheer edges with
abandon. The Cloud Pillars was the most beautiful place in the world in
the last season, regardless of how miserable of a place it was to live. That
was why Taishi had chosen to live there; and why she had very few
neighbors. That was a feature, not a detractor. She missed it dreadfully,
and it made her question every day what could have made her leave.

Taishi retreated from the spill and moved deeper into the enclosure
of the canopy bed. The servants would come in and clean it up in the
middle of the night. As much as she wanted Jian to believe the two of
them were completely alone within the walls of the Celestial Palace, it

wasn't a realistic proposition. This palace was palatial. Even with only the two of them occupying it, it needed constant maintenance and care. And it wasn't like *she* was going to keep this place tidy. What tickled Taishi to no end was that Jian was completely oblivious to the fact that for nearly two weeks, without any other souls here save her, his room and the facilities remained immaculately clean. The boy had lived such a life of luxury and privilege that the very thought that furniture got dusty and things got misplaced went completely over his head.

"At least he is learning that food doesn't magically appear," Taishi chuckled as she drifted off to sleep.

It felt like no sooner had her eyes closed than they flew back open to darkness. She was suffocating. There was no shine from the moons, no shadows in the corners, no silhouettes lurking just outside her bed. There was simply blackness. Her breath was labored as something pressed down on her face, covering her mouth and nose. Taishi tried to flail her good arm, but found it trapped in place. A strange, tremendous pressure weighed on her chest. Her body began to seize.

More curious than frightened, she soothed her mind and willed it to wrestle control of her body away from her panicked nerves. A veil of calm drifted over her, and she was in control again. Taishi managed to shift her head side to side, and felt the smooth but now-wet silk rub along her skin.

Of course.

Taishi waited until her body was completely loose, almost as if she had returned to slumber, or was dead. She counted one, two, three beats, and then she threw all her force upward, sending her entire body shooting toward the ceiling, tearing through the canopy above the bed and then flipping a complete somersault in the air before landing on one foot on the corner bedpost.

A surprised and pained cry followed her sudden eruption. Taishi looked down at Jian tumbling on the floor, sliding all the way to the far wall. He huddled behind the attempted murder weapon, a red cushion vectored with glittery sequins.

"Really, a pillow?" she thundered.

Fueled partially by wine and partially by being so violently woken, Taishi's rage was a lightning storm on an otherwise calm, black night. This cheeky child had just tried to smother her in her sleep. Unforgivable! There were a few unspoken rules in the lunar court. Trying to assassinate your master ranked somewhere near the top of the list. Rudely interrupting her sleep was probably not far behind.

Taishi cut across the room like a hawk diving toward a field mouse. Jian only had time to look panicked and throw his arms up as she grabbed his shirt and yanked him roughly to his feet. She had tolerated his disrespect so far, more than any self-respecting master should have. "Next time you want to suffocate someone, leverage your body. This technique is called the Fool Carrying the Water Jug." She grabbed his head and trapped it close to her torso, then used her forearm to torque it sideways. Then she squeezed, immediately cutting off his circulation. Jian began to beat at her furiously and ineffectively. "Now you can't breathe and are completely helpless." She shifted her weight to one leg. "This is the Cheating Scale. See how your pain feels ten times worse?" She dropped to one knee. His frantic flailing went limp, like a puppet with its strings cut. Only his labored breathing gave any indication that she wasn't holding a corpse. "Lastly, the Python's Embrace. There is nothing you can do at this point. All I have to do is count to ten, and then I'm free to pick your pockets for loose change."

The lines on Jian's face receded, fury and indignance replaced by something like placid acceptance. He looked almost at peace. It took Taishi up to the count of six before sanity reclaimed her mind. She let go, and Jian crumpled to the ground. For a moment, she worried that it was she who had gone too far, and muttered a prayer that the boy took more than a six-count to kill. Fortunately, his fingers twitched a moment later, his chest spasmed, and then Jian fell into a fit of body-shaking coughs. It was very difficult for Taishi to mask her relief.

Her poor temperament had gotten the best of her again. "A heap of trouble" was an understatement for what would have befallen her if she had accidentally, or not so accidentally, killed the savior of the Tiandi Prophecy in a fit of drunken rage. There probably was no coming back from that, not for her or for the Zhuun people. Like it or not, she needed the brat. They all did.

She knelt next to him and patted his back as if she were trying to burp a newborn. When he finally appeared to have calmed from his fits of sobs and coughs, Taishi tried gentleness and encouragement, at least as much as she could muster. "That was a foolish thing to do. Still, I give you credit for thinking outside the box."

Jian slapped her hand aside and rolled to his feet, his hands balled into fists and his face red and wet. "I hate you! You're the worst thing that ever happened to me." Then he fled the room. Her bedside manner could use a little fine-tuning.

Taishi watched him go and shook her head. "No, boy, the worst thing that will happen to you is if you don't start listening to me." She rose to her feet and wiped her hands. "Well, this has been a disaster." She debated whether she should go after him. His emotions were raw but would only fester if she let them linger. She looked over at her shattered canopy bed and then back at the water clock. With a sigh, she walked over to the bed and pulled out the blanket, shook out the dust and debris, and went back to sleep on the sofa.

Taishi didn't see Jian the next day. She searched all the usual spots, the new kitchen, the training room, all the possible exits. He was nowhere to be found. She didn't think much of it. The boy had had a traumatic night and was probably holed up somewhere licking his wounds and clutching one of his very gaudy decorative weapons. She decided to give him time before they resumed their work. She was probably the last person he wanted to see.

To her utter dismay, her sleep was interrupted the next night as well. This time, however, Taishi had gone to bed sober and her heightened senses woke her the moment someone crept into her quarters. As soon as the figure neared, she lashed out with the Swallow Dances, her family heirloom. The plain straight sword with its unusual metallic blue tint had been passed down from father to son for centuries, the story of its origins much warped by a hundred retellings. As far as Taishi knew, she was the first woman to ever own this legendary weapon. And as far as she was concerned, she was also the most skilled.

The Swallow Dances sang and shimmered in the still air as it lashed out and kissed skin. She turned the edge downward and pressed, forcing the intruder to their knees. "How dare you try this again . . ."

Faaru burst into tears, his hands laced together as he begged for mercy. "Forgive me, Master Ling, for disturbing you. Please don't kill me."

Her blade disappeared as if it were never there. "What is it, Peachlord?"

"It's the savior, master. He's trying to escape the Celestial Palace."

Taishi stifled a yawn. "He's been trying to do that since the first day, and stop calling him that."

"Yes, master. But he's trying to climb down the south wall. He's stuck now and is in danger of plummeting to his death. Master Sinsin tried but is unable to reach him."

"What?" Taishi leaped out of bed, leaving the palacelord blubbering on his knees. She jumped out the window and glided down the roof, her feet touching lightly on the tip of the upturned eave before landing on the spine of a nearby roof. She sped to the other end of the building before bounding off again, landing on top of the adjacent chimney and then off a flagpole. She continued moving from building to building until she reached the parapet on the southeastern corner of the outer wall.

It took her old eyes several squints in the darkness before she sighted the small figure dangling halfway down. At the base of the wall was a cluster of soldiers, with Sinsin standing just below the boy as if positioning himself to catch him if he fell. What by the enlightened imprint of Goramh's ass was that fraud still doing here?

Taishi focused on the boy. Whatever credit she had given Jian for thinking outside the box last night was immediately wiped away by his trying to rappel down a hundred-foot wall with fifty feet of rope. Even more stupid was that it had taken him climbing all the way to the end of the rope before he realized he was in trouble.

Cursing, Taishi leaped over the side of the wall, skidding down until her foot caught resistance, then angling in a slant toward Jian, her right shoulder leaning against the wall for stability. She cursed the Khan's name as she pedaled small steps while struggling against the swirling winds beneath her feet.

Jian saw her approach from afar. His expression was mixed, as if he wasn't sure if he should be grateful she was coming to his rescue or not.

A crosswind slammed into Taishi as she neared the boy, causing her to miss a step. She fell off the current she was gliding on and pitched downward headfirst, her face smashing into the stone wall, sending her careening off. She recovered by pushing off on another thread of another breeze, but it left the right side of her face scraped raw and her vision blurry. She blinked and wiped the blood away as she caught the rope with her good hand.

Taishi took a breath. A younger Taishi wouldn't have given this jump a second thought. Unfortunately that was a lifetime and many battles ago. This was definitely much harder than it needed to be, not to mention a little embarrassing. It was a good thing this was the dead of night without a large audience.

Apparently, Jian didn't think so. "That was incredible."

Taishi grunted. "Your former masters are obviously lacking." She loosened her grip and slid down the rope. She stuck her foot out. "Can you grab on?"

He stared at her dangling foot and hesitated only briefly before letting go of the rope with one hand. He batted at her a few times before finally catching her foot. Jian teetered, one hand on the rope and one hand wrapped around her ankle. She could feel his nails digging into her flesh. It didn't show on his face, but he was terrified. More important, though, he stayed focused.

It took a few more seconds before Jian finally let go of the rope and wrapped both hands around her. Taishi immediately felt the strain from his full weight. Her grip slipped a few inches.

"Lock your muscles," she yelled over the howl of the wind. "Tighten your jing if you know how. Then hold on." She kicked, pulling his entire body weight up. He flew upward a few feet just past her shoulder level. The two of them looked as if they were going to miss their connection, and then he managed to wrap his arms around her shoulder.

Taishi lost a few more inches along the rope. "I'm going to get us up now. Can you hang on tight?" Jian answered with several sharp nods as he buried his face in her neck and tried to squeeze the life out of her.

Taishi cursed every step as she began the long trek back up the rope with only one arm while a teenager wrapped his arms and legs around her body. She would walk up a few steps, release her grip on the rope, and regrip it again higher up. Each grasp sent shock waves of aches through her entire body.

She didn't know how long it took her to get to the top, only that she nearly didn't make it when they were only a few feet away. That would have been certain death, and an embarrassing one at that. She was still pretty certain there was an audience standing beneath them to spread the word about how the great Master Ling Taishi and the Prophesied Hero of the Zhuun died by falling off the wall that was supposed to protect him.

The second Taishi climbed over the top and tumbled onto the ground, she shucked Jian off and rolled onto her back, gasping. Jian, on his hands and knees, tried to stand, and then he fell back next to her in a similar state. His chest heaved; his shirt was drenched with sweat.

"What are you tired for?" she muttered. "I did all the work."

She wasn't sure how long the two lay there, just that by the time she stirred again, the King was rising on the horizon. It was a good thing Faaru had assigned watchers to the palace, or she would have been too late. She looked over to the side and saw the exhausted boy still lying there with his eyes closed. She reached out and whacked him lightly across the face.

"That's two stupid things you've done today."

Jian's eyes flared open and he groaned. He looked resigned, miserable. Finally he spoke. "How did you fly like that across the walls?"

"It wasn't flying," she grunted. "Flying's impossible unless you have wings."

"None of my other masters can do that. Master Wang can run up a wall of a house onto the roof. That's about it. Horashi and Riga can do some stuff, but nothing like this."

"Wang is the only one of your teachers worthy of being called a master then, and barely that. If I recall, the Wang family style trains their toes and fingers to be strong enough to grip walls. That's a different technique. Some train for powerful legs. Others learn to lighten their bodies. Windwhispers learn to harness the currents." She shook her head. "With all your training, boy, you should have been able to channel your jing by now."

"They've never even spoken of it. Sinsin calls it silly parlor tricks." Jian sat up. "They've all emphasized that I had to train for every weapon and fighting style in order to be prepared for anything."

Taishi shook her head. "The master of everything is a master of nothing. The truth is, it doesn't matter which style you learn as long as it is a true path. Regardless of technique or family style, all the war arts lead to the same end."

A long silence passed. No one spoke except the breeze whistling its morning tune.

Jian broke the silence first. "Thank you for saving my life."

A truce.

Taishi was slightly ashamed that it was the boy who offered it first. She sat up. "I have been harsh on you, Wen Jian. We've had a rough beginning to our relationship. Perhaps we can take this opportunity to start over."

A sly look appeared on Jian's face. "You mean I don't have to be grateful that you saved my life, and you'll forget that I tried to kill you?"

Cheeky little piss monkey.

Taishi chuckled. "Only if you learn respect and obey your master."

"You can teach me how to fly?"

"Better than that, I'll give you a chance to live up to your legend. Maybe even survive your destiny, boy."

"Will you stop calling me 'boy'?"

Taishi was loath to agree to anything. Students did not bargain with their masters. In this case, however, she made an exception. "I'll think about it, Wen Jian." She immediately regretted her decision.

The boy sensed an opening. He crossed his arms. "I'll consider letting you observe and assist in my training. I won't kowtow to you."

Taishi rolled her eyes. "I'll have none of that around me anyway. Kowtowing is for lords and insecure fools. However, you'll do what I say."

"Fine," he conceded. "But you're not my master until I accept you."

Sharp words nearly leaped off Taishi's tongue, then she reconsidered. "That's fair." A relationship between a master and student was deeply personal, and had to be accepted by both sides. Taishi stood up. "Very well. Now pick yourself up off the floor and get to the training room. We have much work to do. I'll be waiting for you there." She turned to leave and stopped at the top of the stairs. "Also before you go to the training grounds, brew me a fresh pot of tea."

Jian flashed her his pinkie finger and wiggled it. It was an insult usually requiring a duel to satisfy. So much for a fresh start.

"Ungrateful little whelp," muttered Taishi. A smile perked on her face as she walked down the stairs.

It was *a* start.

CHAPTER SIX

THE RETURN

It was early into the night and Salminde the Viperstrike, hailing from the Katuia clan and capital city of Nezra, had just settled into her sleep sack after a long day of travel, and within moments was already flirting with Zharia, the spirit storyteller of dreams. Though her mind was at rest, Sali, as she was known to those with whom she shared a hearth, had never felt as awake as she did at that moment with her barely conscious mind soaking in the sounds and sensations of the Grass Sea.

This land was always alive, but never more so than under the shine of the moons. Her heart sang along with the cadence of the rustling jungle, celebrating the abundant life that could be found everywhere through-out the Grass Sea: in the air, in the plants, and beneath her feet. Sali in-haled the scent of soil, vegetation, and rot, feeling a warmth bubble deep within her being even as the cool, wet air chilled her skin.

After two long years—a full six cycles—raiding Gyian lands far to the north near the white devils' country, it was good to be finally home. It never failed to surprise Sali to rediscover how much she missed the rhythmic living earth rolling once more beneath her feet, as if a part of her had been cut off. The cold, soulless earth of the Zhuun lands had a way of dulling the senses. It had taken her nearly six weeks, but she was now finally entering the heart of the Grass Sea, and her long-dormant connection to this land was reawakening once more.

Sali's wandering mind hummed as it continued to drink in her surroundings A nearby monkey howled somewhere from the direction of her feet. It was followed by a similar, slightly deeper howl, from the monkey's rival. A violent rustling followed, and then a flock of starlings took flight. Beneath her on the jungle floor, her mare snored in long labored breaths. The soft creature, Zhuun-bred and unused to the humidity of the Grass Sea, especially during autumn of the third cycle, had been wheezing ever since they first stepped from firm ground to the constantly rolling earth shifting beneath her hooves.

The lullaby of the Grass Sea had nearly rocked her to sleep when she first heard it: the sound of voices and hoofbeats clopping on the ground. Sali became more alert to her surroundings for moments at a time, her senses searching, listening. A warrior's mind never drifted far from consciousness. She pried one eye open, and then the other, but made no movement to leave the cocoon of her warm, safe campsite, nestled in the sheath of a blade of grass swaying in the breeze some twenty feet off the ground. Traffic was not uncommon along this route, although it was a strange time of the day for traveling through these dangerous and constantly shifting lands. One misstep could plummet someone into a bottomless pool that had opened up one day and disappeared the next.

Sali glanced upward, seeing the sky in full bloom. Two bright moons hung close together just beyond the jungle canopy while the southern horizon glowed purple, heralding the impending arrival of the third. To her side, hanging off the sliver of grass, was a small kiln serving as her hearth. It had extinguished hours ago but still emanated warmth.

The approaching strangers were getting closer, louder. There were four or five souls by their noises, riding on four mounts and with at least one woman among them. Their voices were quiet but conversational. A man and woman were disagreeing about a honking sound they had heard some way back. The man believed it a dire hippo. The woman, a fire peacock in heat. Both were likely mistaken since either creature would have slaughtered the lot before they ever got close enough to hear its crooning. If Sali had to guess, she'd surmise it was a death worm, which, contrary to its name, was completely harmless.

The conversation abruptly died as they passed underneath her encampment, and the world quieted again, save for that quarreling pair of monkeys going at it for another round. A choir of cicadas, which had gone on intermission earlier, returned with another song. Their symphony was now joined by the rattle of a giant snake slithering across a low branch.

A contented but also slightly sad sigh escaped her lips. While it was good to be home again and surrounded by these familiar trappings of the Grass Sea, Sali wished she could have returned under different circumstances.

She closed her eyes and allowed her mind to drift toward slumber. Sali was just about to take another walk with Zharia when her eyes flared open. Something was amiss, felt amiss, sounded amiss. She wasn't sure what exactly, however.

Sali listened intently. The sounds of the Grass Sea were still there: the starlings, the quarreling monkeys, and the slithering snake.

That was when it hit her.

Sali sat up abruptly and craned her head over the side of the sheath. She stared at the ground. Her jaw dropped. Outrage burned in her and ruined the otherwise peaceful zen state she had been enjoying. "My horse . . . How dare they!"

Sali shot to her feet and scanned the winding path. It was near pitch-black, save for the intermittent lances of moonbeams piercing through the canopy, illuminating the ground with hues of blue, green, and cyan. She massaged her eyelids with her thumb and forefinger, concentrating her jing into her gaze. The world turned a green hue, helping the darkness clear.

There, near the far bend, several outlines were moving. Sali leaped to a nearby branch, nearly getting tangled up with the snake. The branch dipped under her weight and then sprang her forward. She landed on a blade of grass and hopped to another, carefully leaping her way toward the thieves across the jungle canopy.

Blade jumping was a popular and exhilarating pastime for Katuia children, one in which Sali had once excelled. It was also usually forbidden by the clan elders because serious injuries if not death were all too common. Not only did blade jumpers risk falling, they sometimes fell victim to four-winged scaled kunpeng whale-birds, giant horned Gudiao eagles, or many other such predators that hunted the skies above, often hoping to find a child-sized morsel. No one enforced this rule, however, since almost every Katuia had played this game at some point in their youth.

After several leaps along the canopy, Sali landed softly beside her roan, who now was standing alone. The mare greeted Sali with a nuzzle, completely unperturbed that she had just been stolen, and continued chewing a mouthful of hay. The sect marking was hanging in plain sight on the horse's neck, which should have been a strong enough warning for anyone with ill intentions.

Sali spun slowly, eyeing the edge of the clearing. "What are you doing here by yourself, horse?" The two had been together since Sali had relieved a Zhuun officer wearing a panda head atop his helm of her, and they had developed a friendly working relationship. Sali grabbed the reins and was about to lead the mare back to camp when something tickled the back of her neck. She smelled an ambush. She was being watched. It wasn't some innate ability or jing, just her instincts honed from years of battle.

Her fingers drifted down to her waist where her weapon, a whip known as a tongue, was coiled at rest. She gripped the familiar curved mahogany handle, feeling the static of its vibration as its thousands of tiny diamond-shaped metallic links came alive.

Five camouflaged figures rose from the nothing around her. The only thing that betrayed their presence was the shimmering of the air around them as they emerged. The more these shimmers moved, the more the air around them smeared as if a child were finger-painting on a canvas. Then, as if wiped clean of colors, the shimmers dulled into darkened silhouettes until they finally revealed five armed individuals. By this type of camouflage technique and the way they held their low stances, these appeared to be members of the Ikuan sect from the city of Ankar.

What were they doing here? More important, why where they trying to rob her?

Undaunted, Sali directed her ire at them, stating the obvious. "You disgraceful wretches stole my horse! How dare you stoop to such craven acts."

"Does it matter?" said one to her left. "A horse rides the same regardless of who rode her last."

"Since when do People of the Sea steal from our own hearths? We raid the Zhuun, not each other," she spat. "And to steal a horse is a low crime unworthy of the Ikuan sect." In Katuia culture, to steal a horse amounted to worse than murder. It meant abandoning someone to make their own way through the Grass Sea.

"The hearth is extinguished," said one to her left.

"The Sacred Braid is cut," added another.

"Give up your weapons and food, bitch," barked the one directly in front rather eloquently. She added hastily, "And your horse. Give up your horse too, and you might live."

Sali pulled her cloak aside to reveal her bone-scale armor, its dull fossilized pieces identifying her as a viperstrike. That sent an anxious titter through the five. Two of her attackers hesitated. Two more began backing away. Only now had they realized their grave error.

The rude one, who appeared to be leading this outfit, did not appear deterred by Sali. She drew a jagged double-sided machete that widened into an ax-like fan. Definitely Ikuan. "The Khan's dead, and so is Ankar, and so is the rest of Katuia," the leader spat. "So unless you want to join them, bitch, you better shut your—"

Sali's hands blurred as she snapped her tongue from her hip, cracking the air and slicing open the speaker's hand, sending her machete spinning gracefully over the side of the pod. The woman was fortunate her fingers were not sailing alongside her sword.

The closest Ikuan looked too spooked to make a move. Hmm. Maybe they really *hadn't* noticed the sect marking on the horse. Not that it mattered anymore. This crime could not go unpunished.

Sali retracted the tongue just as one of the thieves tried to take her head off with a spiked weighted club. She sent a jolt through the tongue, stiffening its spine until it became a long spear a head taller than she. The hardened tongue clashed with the club and guided it harmlessly aside, sinking it into the soft ground. She spared a killing thrust with the point of the spear, and instead whipped him across the chin with the butt.

The second Ikuan made it two steps toward her before a sharp thrust with the tips of her fingers to his throat sent him writhing to the ground. She whirled to face the third, who tried to slice her back open with his machete. He was joined by the foulmouthed woman coming from her opposite side. Sali faced off both and parried them handily, wielding her tongue as a staff. She danced between the two, avoiding them easily. Every time they struck at her, she bit back even harder. The two Ikuans found themselves on the defensive as her tongue twirled and flexed in the air around her.

The combat abilities between their two sects were at the far opposite ends. Ikuans, while excellent scouts and spies, and serviceable assassins, were not exactly known for their melee prowess. It didn't make them any less brave, but they were still relatively ineffective against someone like Sali.

The man made the first mistake, lunging a hair too hard and losing his balance. Sali rapped him on the side of the head with one end of the spear while tripping the woman with the other end. They collided together in a tangled heap, barely avoiding skewering each other. Sali casually knocked the man across the temple as she stepped out of the way.

That left two more: the foulmouthed woman who was picking herself out of the muck, and a younger man who had not made a move the entire fight. Of course, the group's neophyte. This must have been a sect unit before they had forsaken their honor and abandoned their duties. The poor boy likely had little choice in the matter.

"Salvage what little dignity you have left and surrender." Not bothering to glance at the neophyte, Sali thrust the spear in his direction, the point stopping just close enough to miss his nose. At this point, she was showing off, but also trying to make a point. The boy tripped over himself backpedaling and fell, and then the ground around him gave way.

He must have landed on a particularly soft patch. There was a rush of water and the hole became a new pond.

The boy's head dipped below the murky water for several seconds, long enough for the freshly made pool's surface to calm. And then he broke it violently again, flailing his arms and screaming before resubmerging.

Both Sali and the remaining Ikuan stared.

"Can he swim?" Sali asked.

The look on the woman's face signaled that she had no clue.

"We should probably save the lad, yeah?"

The foulmouthed woman met her suggestion with suspicion, but then nodded and took a step toward the pond. Sali beat her to it. Just as the neophyte's arms broke the water's surface again, her tongue snapped out and lashed around his wrist. She immediately began to lose her footing as she curled the tongue around her forearm to get a better grip. The boy was big and waterlogged, and the ground around her feet was soft and slippery. Sali also realized she had turned her back to the woman and was now defenseless.

Sali looked over at the woman, who was just standing there nursing her cut hand. "Some help?"

The woman hesitated for a split second, then probably decided that his life was worth more than trying to take on Sali again. She scampered over to Sali, and together they pulled the neophyte back up from the pond. Once the boy was safe, Sali made a show of curling her tongue and hooking it on its holster. She scanned the rest of the Ikuans, who were still in the process of picking themselves up off the ground.

Sali continued admonishing them. "You say the Sacred Braid is broken, but you're the ones breaking it. You say the hearth is extinguished, but you're the ones putting it out. What do you have to say in your defense before I pass judgment?"

"Who do you think you are to judge us?" their leader hissed. At least she wasn't calling Sali a bitch anymore.

"You saved me just so you can kill me?" the neophyte hacked in between breaths.

One of the others approached her and squinted. "I've never seen anyone flick a tongue so smoothly. Who are you?"

"My name is Salminde."

The older man's eyes widened. "You're not just a viperstrike, you're a Will of the Khan!"

"I am one of Nezra's Eldest," Sali conceded. "And yes, I am a Part of the Whole."

"You're on your Return." Another spoke with reverence. He fell to his knees.

"Yes, the Return," she replied, grimly.

A strangled cry gurgled from the foulmouthed woman, and then she charged Sali. That was not the response Sali expected. Her tongue nearly snapped again, but then the woman threw herself at her feet. "A hundred forgivenesses, Salminde," she sobbed. "We did not know it was you." The rest soon followed her lead.

"Forgive us," the others begged. "We didn't know it was your horse."

"It shouldn't matter if it was mine or not," she scoffed. "But I understand how you could have missed the sect mark."

"So you won't kill us?" asked the neophyte.

Sali shook her head. "That's not for me to decide. You shame your sect and Ankar with this lawlessness. If you cut the Sacred Braid, you must face punishment."

That earned her a fresh bout of tears and pleas. "We had no choice. The hearths are cold now. We're starving."

"The Sacred Braid has unraveled."

"Ankar is no more. No other city will take our people in."

Sali fixated on that last bit, turning to the man mumbling it. It appeared he was suffering from a broken jaw. "What do you mean by that? What happened to Ankar?"

The Ikuans exchanged baffled looks. The neophyte hesitantly raised his arm. "You mean you don't know?"

"Of course I know about the Khan. We all grieve for him," she said curtly. "What else happened?"

The woman pointed off to the side. "See for yourself."

Sali followed her finger off to the side, past the tree line. At first, she saw nothing, but then as her gaze rose she noticed something large and dark jutting up toward the sky. It couldn't be natural. The edges were too smooth and the corners too straight. Besides, nothing that large could sit on the surface of the Grass Sea for long. She decided to take a closer look.

"You lot. Stay right there," she ordered. "I order it as a Will of the Khan."

"Yes." They bowed, collectively staying there, alternating between heart-saluting—throwing their fists over their hearts—and bowing profusely. At least not all tradition and civility had fallen to the wayside.

Sali pushed her way into the thickets, being careful with each step. One wrong move and she could end up like the neophyte, plummeting into the bottomless abyss beneath the Grass Sea's layer of land. That was why it was so dangerous to travel at night.

It didn't take long to pick her way to a crushed field. By the looks the damage was no more than a month or two old. Many of the giant blades of grass were still flattened, slowly springing back up to standing. That meant something large, a city most likely, was responsible for this damage. Sali tilted her head the same angle as she studied the large structure jutting unnaturally toward the sky. Though the surface was covered with a thick layer of vegetation, there was no mistaking what she saw at one side: wheels and tracks.

This was the mangled wreckage of a city pod, one of dozens of large mobile structures that linked together to form their moving capital cities. This particular pod appeared to be one of the outer edges. What resembled a docking crane and watchtower still stood atop its platform. One end of the pod was completely submerged while the other end tipped up into the air; half of its wheels were missing and the track that rolled around them was broken and dangling like large jungle vines.

Sali knelt and checked the earth around the pod. Most of the evidence had washed away, but some of the deeper wounds still offered memories of what had transpired. She rubbed the grass blades bent unnaturally between her fingers and felt the length of the stems. Month-old scabs and faint stress marks ran all the way to the base of the plants. Fresh water had pooled around the bruises where the pod punctured the ground. Her mother used to say that rain was nature's way of healing the wounds inflicted by people. Some wounds, however, were too deep to wash away.

Sali stood and followed the path of destruction. With the angle of the breaks and the crisscrossing lines, whatever had caused this had come from the west, and it had come quickly, cutting a wide swath without concern for the sacred sea beneath her feet. Sali backtracked around the pod and found another set of tracks. This time it was a pair of perfectly straight puddles, one shallow and green, the other filled with a black ooze, like half-day-old blood. Sled tracks and dried grease. By the width of the impressions in the earth, not just any tracks, but heavy carryalls. This entire field was the wake of an entire city in full retreat.

Sali walked up to the pod and examined it, looking for telltale signs of its origin and its death. Was this pod part of Ankar? What had caused its destruction? Why was a city pod so close to the Zhuun border this time of year? Katuia capital cities did not travel during the last cycle of the year when the Son and all three moons littered the sky. Nothing made sense.

There was an old Katuia saying: "Wage war at dawn. Hunt during the day. Drink in the evenings." It was sound advice, and referred not only to the times of the day, but also to the three cycles of seasons in the year. The first cycle was the most temperate, with the coolest summers and warmest winters, so it was usually the most pleasant for raids and battles. The second yielded the best harvest and was generally when the cities traveled to follow herd migrations.

The third cycle had the harshest of all seasons: stormy springs, searing summers, howling autumns, and frigid winters. This cycle was when the clans stayed close to the hearth. It was when their people reconnected with families and allies to prepare for the raids of the following year. Fortunately this cycle was also the shortest, lasting only two months. Soon, a new year would arise, bringing back the first cycle of mild weather with only the sun and moon in the sky. They would then be joined by the green moon in the second cycle, and the purple in the third.

Katuia astronomers had always theorized that the number of moons contributed to the increasingly harsh weather. Sali could not understand how a moon could do such a strange thing, but she paid no attention to those people who spent their lives looking up at the stars. The seasons and cycles were the way they had always been. No other knowledge was necessary save for how their people lived in balance with the world around them.

Finding a nearby sprawl of grass, Sali squeezed between two blades near its crown and began to crawl toward its tip. The slightly sticky feel of the grass under her fingers brought her back to simpler times. Sali and her best friend, Jiamin, had always been climbing and jumping along these patches, sometimes all the way up to the canopies, each daring the other to see who could climb higher, who could get closer to the tip. They had spent much of their childhood in the Grass Sea canopies, either blade jumping or, even more risky, playing along the tops of the Grass Sea ceiling, seeing who could make the most dangerous climbs, runs, and jumps along the jungle canopy. Mali, her little bud of a sister, was often close behind, always trying to prove she could keep up. She never could, of course, at least not with Sali. No one could except for Jiamin, but he rarely bothered to tempt the same fates.

They were all so free and light back then, long before Sali had shaved the sides of her head and declared her intention as a warrior. Long before she had donned the scale armor and learned how to snap death with her tongue. Long before she had become a viperstrike and engaged in a never-ending war and seen the deaths of her friends and clan mates.

Sali continued to climb until she reached the highest arc of the blade. Just as her weight caused the tip to dip and bounce back, she reached up and pulled herself to the next blade, navigating it until she could reach the next, each one bringing her closer to the pod. She eventually ran out of grass to climb.

She stood up carefully. Balancing precariously on the increasingly narrow piece of grass, she continued to inch forward, pushing down slightly, feeling the blade's bounce react to her weight. With each bob, the grass pushed back harder. Finally, Sali timed the last bounce and sprang toward the pod.

Her feet slipped on the mud-coated surface, threatening to send her sliding into a newly formed lake on the other side. Every step she took sent her skidding three more. The platform undulated unsteadily as she grabbed a hold of a beam post. It was indeed an end-pod, one stationed at the edge of a city. It had four structures: a watchtower, a crane, a guardhouse, and a small garage to house bixis, the squirrel gliders, and other assorted vehicles.

The first thing that came to mind was relief. This platform wasn't part of Nezra; she knew every pod in her home city up close. Each city was born from a different clan and was built from a different part of the Grass Sea. Nezra hailed from the far northeastern edge. Her skin was painted green, like young ivy, and her flesh was bamboo, koa, and macassar. This pod was painted yellow with twisted iron bones and sun-bleached teak flesh. The iron of these bones was hammered, which meant its city likely came from the southeast, likely Ankar as those Ikuans had indicated.

How had this pod ended up here, and were there others?

Sali focused on the watchtower creaking at the edge of the pod. She drew her tongue and, with a snap of her wrist, extended its tip to the nest on top of the uppermost platform. As it retracted, the tongue pulled her with it, up and onto the watch nest. She landed lightly and perched on the thin railing.

Sali looked out from this perch and her breath caught in her throat. From here to the horizon, as far as she could see on either side, now under the full glow of the three moons, the fractured corpses of the cities of Katuia littered the sea. Pods, too many to count, lay broken, burned, splintered, and crushed, each a small wreckage in an ocean of green. Some belched black smoke; others seemed to have already burned to a charred iron frame. Others still had almost succumbed to the flora of the sea itself.

There must have been a great battle here. These were the corpses of more than one city—two, possibly three. The buildings still standing looked dilapidated, some with roofs caved in, some missing walls. Just past where she stood was the ruin of another pod from Ankar, and then another farther along. The city left a trail of pods that ended halfway to the horizon. At the end was a large cluster of pods arrayed in a rough circle. Ankar's final resting place.

Sali didn't know how long she stared at the shattered remnants of her civilization, but she couldn't look away. She counted the pods, trying to determine which other cities had fallen and whose people were lost. How many of her friends and comrades were dead? Swallowed up by the depths of the Grass Sea? She thought of Mali and Jiamin again, and muttered a prayer of thanks that her proud grandfather, once the clan chief of Nezra, did not have to bear witness to the fall of a Katuia city. She held on to a glimmer of hope: None of these pods looked like Nezra. It was a small blessing, and a selfish one, but Sali could not lie to her own heart.

Sali eventually spied a city far to the southeast. It was barely a speck, but unmistakable. A large spot of black in the sea of green. Chaqra, the Black City and final resting place of the Khan, still stood a few days' ride away. That was where she could find the answers and put to rest this compulsion driving her.

Sali leaped down off the pod the way she came, bouncing off a nearby blade and then clinging to the stem of a weed as she slid down to the ground. She hurried back to the gyre where she had left her honorbound prisoners and was unsurprised but mildly disappointed to find them gone. Sali suppressed her irritation. Their cities were broken, and her people now flouted their honor. It was almost too much to bear. At least they left her horse this time.

She was tempted to hunt these criminals down, but the Pull of the Khan had no more patience. Upon seeing the Black City of Chaqra, the Pull had flared up with renewed urgency.

It was time for Salminde the Viperstrike, the Will of the Khan, to return home to fulfill her solemn and final duty, and merge her part of the Eternal Khan's soul back with the Whole.

It was time for Sali to die.

CHAPTER SEVEN

MASTER AND STUDENT

The Crane Swoops Over the Lake.

Wave Hands Like Rolling Storm.

The Hungry Monk Grinds the Grain.

"Slow down," Taishi barked from her stool. "There's no ribbon for finishing first."

"I can do this in my sleep," he replied without missing a breath as he slipped into Green Snake Slithers in the Tall Weeds.

Taishi grunted as she sipped tea. He probably could. Just as the first time she witnessed him in action, she was enamored of the boy's potential. Though she was having him run through fundamental movements, Jian was executing them with speed and precision. His form was powerful, decisive, and effortless. He changed directions and linked techniques smoothly, like water babbling down a stony brook. The boy's body and mind were in sync, his balance exceptional, and the jing that flowed inside him had more potential than any she had ever seen.

Still, a pretty sparkle couldn't mask all the cracks. Any warm body could learn to run forms. His true abilities lagged far behind his training and capabilities. It was a crime that he couldn't control his jing by now.

The ability to manifest jing was the true indicator of a war artist's mastery. That was what allowed one to appear unnaturally strong or fast, to control the elements, to seemingly fly. It was a difficult hurdle to externally manifest jing, one often celebrated by both student and master. That was the true difference between just any war artist and those with real ability.

Fifteen was young to manifest jing, but not unheard of for the truly talented, especially with proper training. Taishi herself had first shown glimpses of her ability at thirteen, Sanso at twelve. Jian was paying the price for a gaggle of idiots getting to him first. It was an embarrassment. So much time and potential wasted. Or perhaps Jian simply didn't have the talent to make that leap. Taishi couldn't be sure. He was certainly diligent enough.

Taishi wasn't sure how to address this problem. The boy was too skilled to simply wipe clean and start over, but he also had too many holes in his training to evolve further. He was at a dead end. It was like trying to fix a house infested with termites. It would be better just to burn the house down and rebuild. Except the boy wasn't a house to just demolish. Taishi scratched her chin as she puzzled over this conundrum.

While Taishi watched Jian practice, a memory of Sanso running through the exact same form filled her mind. The two both had that intense focus that made their faces furrow as if they were scowling. It was technically a tell—a war artist's face should remain neutral in battle—but Taishi had always found the raisin-brow endearing.

Both boys had the same hurriedness in their movements as well, as if finishing first meant they were winning. When Jian exhaled and shouted during his form, she could almost hear Sanso's voice. The two were so similar in so many ways, equally great and equally impatient, and both wanted to do more than they were able or ready to do. And just like with Sanso, watching Jian move made her fall in love with the *art* of war all over again.

"Stop, stop," she drawled. "Your form bores me. You only know one speed. It's like you're hurrying so you can go piss. Your movements need space to pause and breathe, but the jing within you is spinning in place. It should be coursing through your body, reaching the tips of your fingers and toes. You're better off just standing still."

"I can't listen and focus at the same time," he retorted. "My masters always gave feedback after I finished the form."

"Ah, so listening and moving is too difficult for you?" she mocked. "What about thinking and breathing? Imagine how distracted you would be if you had a Katuia sickle buried in your back."

That was another problem. Unlearning his bad habits simply required time and repetition. That she could correct. But the boy's focus broke far too easily. Everything threw him off. Taishi once saw a buzzing fly break his form. A servant walking across his line of sight caused him to drop his horse-cutter.

Finally, Taishi had seen enough. She rose from her seat and flipped the hourglass on the table. "You've been in such a hurry to move fast. Now I want to see you move still. Horse stance until the water drains."

A scowl flashed across his face, and then slowly drained away, reluctantly. For now, he was honoring their arrangement. Jian dragged his feet to a spot in front of her, spread his stance wide, and then crouched down with his fists chambered at his sides. Once he had accepted Taishi's guidance, even if she wasn't his master, they had settled into an adequate working relationship. He still bristled at her every command, but he did as he was told. It didn't matter to Taishi how much the boy—Jian, she corrected herself—liked her commands, as long as he followed them. At the very least this week wasn't ending in quite the same disaster as the last.

Taishi leaned back in her chair. "I want to go over the teachings of Zhangan and Marci."

Jian was disciplined enough to keep his head locked forward and his eyes staring ahead, unfocused, commonly referred to as the thousand-mile-stare. "Actually, I have a suggestion regarding my training."

Taishi tapped the side of the hourglass. It was an hour of slow-moving drips. She'd been hoping for a quieter life after she was discharged from the war, but this wasn't what she had in mind. "Go on."

"I was just thinking. You and I are practically strangers. Some of my masters have trained with me since I was young. They know me well. Perhaps it would be wise to bring one back."

Taishi's face melted a little at the thought, but she continued to humor the boy. Yes, the boy. "Do you have someone in mind?"

"Master Sinsin hasn't left yet. Maybe you can bring him on in an advisory role."

That man was a fungus that would not go away. There was only one way to kill fungus. "And you think this will help."

Jian broke form by nodding vigorously.

"This is your idea? Not Sinsin's?"

There was a slight hesitation. "Of course not."

That was another deep failing she would have to remedy. The last thing the Zhuun needed was for their Prophesied Hero to be a laughably offensive liar.

"*Your* idea has merit," said Taishi, standing up. "I assume you know exactly where Sinsin is right now. Please have him meet me at the northwestern tower. We can discuss a possible arrangement for his services."

Jian nodded enthusiastically and scurried away, thankful to skip the hour-long stance. Add "gullible" to the list of traits she was going to have to beat out of him. Taishi splashed the remainder of her tea onto the ground and strolled to her meeting with Master Sinsin.

Fifteen minutes later, she had him dangling over the side of the wall.

"Please, please," Sinsin screamed. His toes clawed at the stones for dear life.

"What did I tell you the day you were dismissed?" she pressed.

"To leave the palace at once . . . but the responsibility of raising the Hero of Prophecy is so heavy. Surely you could use some support, someone with inside knowledge. I can be of great assistance to you. Perhaps—"

"Did I ask for help?" she hissed. "What were my exact words?"

Sinsin scrunched his face. "You said . . . your exact words were 'get your fungus-rotted empty vessel out of here.'"

"So why is this empty vessel still here speaking to me?"

"I've trained with Jian for over six years. I know everything about him. I know his weaknesses and strengths. I know how to motivate—"

Taishi let go of his sleeve and Sinsin began to tip over the side. He experienced a moment of free fall before she grabbed the front of his shirt again. She wouldn't admit it, but she had almost muffed that grab. Sinsin was still screaming for several seconds after she had a hold on him. Unfortunately, the strong winds had sent the bottom of his robes almost horizontal and Taishi got a front-row view of his pants staining as he blubbered for his life.

Taishi turned away in disgust. That was when she saw it. At first, she thought it a mirage, but several blinks and squints did not make the vision disappear. There, snaking up Qilin Road from the distant horizon, like a golden serpent with scales glittering in the sheen of the King, Queen, and Prince. It required several squints for her aged eyes to notice the fluttering green banner.

"What is Waylin doing here?" she muttered. From the size of the procession, the Duke of Xing seemed to be on his way here in person. A second glimmer out of the corner of her eye caught Taishi's attention. Her gaze followed the light and she saw another procession approaching the palace from Shojo Road. This one was much closer, and the yellow banners of the Caobiu State could not be mistaken. At the head of the procession riding in her legendary peacock chariot was Duchess Sunri herself.

Taishi's mouth fell open and her breath caught. What in the name of the Goramh's marble scrotum was going on? If two of the five dukes of Zhuun were here, something significant was about to happen. It could mean anything. They could be here to settle a dispute, work out a trade agreement, or even declare war on each other.

A chill passed through her. Or worse. They were going to have a wedding.

The Prophesied Hero needed a few more years to mature and train before he could lead the Zhuun to victory over the Eternal Khan and the Katuia. These fracturing dukes had to hold it together just a little longer. A marriage between the two states would skewer the delicate peace they kept, and plunge the Zhuun into civil war. Taishi would bet her good arm that the wedding ritual would end with bloodshed, assuming the other dukes allowed it to get that far. Any hope of defeating the Katuia would disappear in a wisp of smoke.

Taishi actually almost did let Sinsin plummet to his death this second time. Only his frantic cry reminded her that he was still dangling over the side of the wall. Taishi heaved him back onto the pathway and stomped away.

"Thank you for sparing my life, master," he blubbered. "Does that mean you'll let me—"

"If every step you take from this point on isn't carrying you closer to the front gates, then I'll make sure you never take another step again."

Taishi left Sinsin to clean up his own mess and hurried down to the Heavenly Grounds. The center of the palace was a hive of chaos and panic. The staff certainly knew what was coming; they had just neglected to mention it to her. Hosting one of the five dukes was a major event, usually requiring several days of preparation. Two was exponentially more difficult, with the host having to juggle not only the demands and comforts of two dukes, but the peace between their finicky retinues. Luckily, it was still an easy half day's journey for those slow processions to hike up Wunshan Mountain to reach the Celestial Palace.

Taishi found Faaru crossing the grounds, barking instructions to attendants like a general planning a battle. The bald man's robes had only a few buttons clinging together to keep him respectable. His mushroom hat was missing, the few wisps of hair on his knotty head were frazzled, and the collar around his neck was drenched with sweat. He was speaking so quickly his words slurred together as if he were drunk. Spittle continuously sprayed out of his mouth, and he was huffing heavily as if someone had just loosed a pack of dogs on him.

"Take out the winter's stores. The next season's as well. Just take them all out. Bring up all the caskets. I don't care if some haven't aged. Send three wagons to Hengyu to procure more. Give them a marker for credit. Head out to all the farms. We'll take whatever livestock they can spare. Yes, put that on marker too. Draft any servants from the local merchants you can find. Tell them we'll put that on marker as—" He roared when one of his attendants asked a question that displeased him. "I don't care if they don't want a marker. Rob them then!"

Taishi fell in line as he passed her, taking the opportunity to find out what was going on as he paused from his chatter to wheeze for breath. "Palacelord, do you know why Waylin and Sunri are coming? You might want to ready the Celestial Guard in case this situation deteriorates."

"It's not just them," he snapped reflexively, then he realized whom he was addressing. He continued in a more respectful tone. "Pardon my hastiness, master, but it's for all five dukes. Dongshi arrived last night. Saan and Yanso are arriving later this evening."

Taishi was stunned. She could count on one hand the number of times all five heads of the Enlightened States were in one place. The first was at the emperor's funeral. The second was when the Hero of Prophecy was discovered. That meant the only reason they could be meeting now was . . .

"Where's Jian?"

Sheer worry appeared to have given Faaru a spine. "How am I supposed to know?" he snapped. "You should be taking care of your own ward. Now if you'll excuse me, I have a thousand tasks to complete."

Taishi let that jibe slide. A thought slammed into her head and she froze. The palacelord was right. She *did* have to take care of her own ward. She hurried away from this chaos of activity as she prepared her own list of things that she had to do with Jian before this event.

Thirty minutes later, Taishi barged into the Tower of Eternal Heroism. As she bounded up the stairs, she reminded herself for the twentieth time to take a chisel to that stupid placard displaying the tower's name. In fact, she planned to eventually ban all references to "hero" in the Celestial Palace.

She kicked open Jian's bedroom and found him sticking his body half out the window facing the Heavenly Grounds. He rocked back inside and beamed from ear to ear as he jumped excitedly. "Can you believe this? All five dukes are here, to see me! Have you ever seen so many soldiers?" He looked over her shoulder. "Who are they?"

Taishi pointed to her left and right. "That's the Mistress of Etiquette.

He's the Court Facemaker. The bald one is a tailor I pulled off the streets." She clapped her hands. "Get to it."

The Mistress of Etiquette immediately began asking Jian how much instruction he had in courtly manners, which of course ended up being none. From how to properly bow to the dukes to recognizing the ranks and functions of the court via the hats to properly holding chopsticks, Jian was in many ways more uncultured than commoners. They at least knew how to address their lords.

Taishi had been so busy she kept forgetting to tell Faaru to put out a call for educators. The boy needed to know more than eight ways to throw a punch. She needed to hire teachers: philosophers, mathematicians, politicians . . . and probably someone to teach him how to dress himself. He would need to be versed in diplomacy, cultures, logistics, art, and etiquette. Half of a leader's job was to not be an idiot. The other half was to not act like an ignorant peasant. If Jian were to succeed in killing the Khan and bringing peace to the Enlightened States, he would need allies. His most important battles would be waged at the negotiating table.

While the Mistress of Etiquette worked on Jian's posture, the facemaker got busy matching Jian's skin tone. "This just won't do," the older gentleman huffed, his hands whipping several different colors together like an artist. "The savior's face is weathered like a farmer. His hands cracked like a bricklayer. I'll need days to soften his complexion and make him presentable."

"You have three hours." Taishi turned to the tailor. "Go through the boy's wardrobe. Choose his finest robe and then stitch the colors of the five states around his wrists and collar. No matter what, keep the green away from the white, and the blue away from the yellow. The red must never be in between two other colors."

The tailor looked confused. "But . . ."

"Just do it," snapped Taishi. "Also, as the Hero of Prophecy, he must wear a silver waistband with matching trim. Do not use commoner gray or I swear I will hang you off this tower with that very cloth. All of us need to be presentable at the dukes' pleasure."

The poor man's eyes widened and then he swallowed, bowing. "Yes, master."

All of us. That meant her as well. Taishi closed her eyes. She grabbed the tailor by the collar before he could slip away. "I'll need clothing to match the boy's."

The poor man's face turned white. "An entire robe? In a day?"

"In a few hours." She walked up to Jian and raised his chin with her finger. A fleeting image of Sanso flashed through her head. "Listen closely, Jian, the five dukes coming together is not an event to celebrate. Anything can happen. A civil war may break out. One of them may decide to kidnap you to hold as leverage over the others, possibly marry you off to one of their daughters. Sunri might decide to just marry you herself. For all we know, they may call you forth to fulfill your destiny today." Before he could reply, she poked his nose with her finger. "You're *not* ready. Don't even think about it. No matter what, you are not to leave the tower without me by your side. Do you understand?"

"I—"

"Don't talk. Just nod."

He nodded.

"Good." Taishi sat down in a chair and crossed her arms, and watched over the Mistress of Etiquette, the facemaker, and the tailor as they worked.

Within a few short hours, the three managed to pull off a minor miracle. Jian was bathed, was groomed, and had the mop on top of his head cut and styled into a semblance of presentability for court. His skin was oiled like a pig's, and his face powdered white. To even Taishi's approval, the tailor turned out a perfectly adequate set of matching robes for the two.

The Mistress of Etiquette did what she could with the time she had. "He won't make a fool of himself as long as he doesn't dine with them," she proclaimed stiffly.

Everything was passable, barely. That was good enough. All that was left was to wait for the eventual summons. She ordered the Mistress of Etiquette to bring her some tea and settled in for the duration.

Taishi had not expected to wait long, at the very latest until after the evening meal. She was surprised to still be waiting well after the Queen began her nightly ascent. Surely at least one of the five rulers would have asked to meet with the Hero of the Tiandi Prophecy. Taishi began to worry. Something was wrong.

She herself finally turned in when the Twins reached their midnight peak.

Jian had fallen asleep after exhausting himself first with anticipation, then boredom. Taishi retired for the night to the guest room. "I'm too old to stay up this late," she grumbled as she scrubbed off the facemaker's gunk. "And too old to wear this crap. No amount of powder is going to erase the last forty years."

No sooner had she wiped the last of the powder off her face and slipped into bed than there was a knock on the door. "Master Ling Taishi, you are being summoned."

"Piss, are you serious? At this hour?" Taishi bolted out of bed and swung the door open, her nightshirt threatening to reveal more than anyone needed to see.

The Court Voice awaiting her at the other side did not flinch. If he noticed her impropriety, he did not show it. "All Zhuun wait at the pleasure of their divine dukes."

"Of course they do. I'll wake the hero."

The Voice shook his head. "Only your presence is requested, master."

Taishi hesitated, and then nodded. "Give me a minute. Let me dress and put my face on."

"The five are not to be kept waiting. Only modesty is required."

The five? All five rulers of the Enlightened States wanted to meet with her. By herself. In the middle of the night. Taishi's stomach churned as she bit back her worry.

She hastily threw on the robe the tailor had sewn for her and followed the Court Voice down the stairs to an intricately and richly adorned rickshaw. Behind it were half a dozen men on horseback. Official summons indeed. Taishi climbed inside. The Voice climbed onto the back, and the rickshaw rumbled forward. Her unease grew as the Tower of Eternal Heroism disappeared from view. Taishi did not like leaving Jian alone, but it couldn't be helped. Summonses by the dukes were not to be trifled with.

The Tiandi Throne was the obvious stop. It was the only place in the Celestial Palace fit for the dukes of the Enlightened States. What Taishi wasn't prepared for, however, were the thousands of soldiers standing at attention in neat columns and rows on the Heavenly Grounds, all wearing their respective state colors. Banners and flags flapped in the wind. Lanterns hanging off spears swayed in a brilliant array, tiny lights against the dark night. There was a gap between two of the groups of soldiers just wide enough for the rickshaw to turn and cut through toward the throne room. Taishi also noted that while their banners and tunics were ceremonial, their armor and weapons were not.

"Don't they ever sleep?" she said to no one in particular as the cart's wooden wheels ground against the stone. She was also interested to note that the soldiers were facing the throne, not away. These men standing watch all night were not looking for an outside threat; they were guarding against one another.

The rickshaw pulled to the bottom of the stairs, and a stool was quickly placed next to it. The Voice exited first and offered Taishi a hand. She ignored him as she stepped out, looked up at the Thousand Steps to Heaven, and sighed. "Let's get on with this."

To her delight, a palanquin of servants appeared a moment later to ferry her up the stairs. By the time Taishi had reached the top, she was beginning to reconsider all her disdain for court life. She wondered if Saan's offer to make her Court Warmaster was still good.

The large doors opened with the sound of a gong, and the Voice announced Taishi's arrival. She was momentarily disoriented when she walked in. The cavernous throne room felt strangely desolate. It was dark inside save for the dais, where the throne resided. The throne itself was empty, but five cushioned seats were lined up in front of it.

That empty seat was the price of peace.

Nestled on the cushions were the rear ends of the five who one day hoped to change that.

It took Taishi a few moments to realize that the room was actually brimming with people. Not just people, but the personal guards of the dukes, the infamous Mute Men, also known as the Quiet Death. Bodyguards trained from childhood to protect nobility, the Mute Men were elite warriors who had their tongues cut off and were never taught to read. Fanatic devotion. They rarely left the dukes' sides, standing like silent statues until action was required. Taishi had witnessed these black-clad nightmares fight many times, and considered their reputations well earned. It was said that the mere sight of approaching Mute Men's winged cloaks fluttering in the wind could cause entire militias to surrender or cities to throw open their gates.

The rest of the assembly hall, the side corridors, and the balconies above were all filled with the silhouettes of the advisers, diplomats, and scholars. They were shrouded in darkness until their wisdom or input was required. Only the area around the throne was brightly lit, to the point of being almost blinding.

Taishi had been so busy taking in the environment like a commoner that she hadn't realized the dukes were already holding an audience. A small group of men were standing on their knees before the five, talking over one another. Their animated and garbled buzzing echoed through the room. It wasn't until she distinctly heard her name spoken that Taishi realized who they were. Faaru and all eight of Jian's former masters. Here. Giving testimony about her, and about him.

So much for leaving town. *I swear I will hunt them all down and hang them by their fat toes.*

"And then," Hili continued. "Right during the most critical time in the hero's training, she bans us from the palace. We pleaded for her to see wisdom, but Master Ling was adamant in her selfish and cruel ways."

Sunri, the Duchess of Caobiu, the Desert Lioness, former emperor's concubine who had risen to become the general of all of the emperor's armies, and likely still the most eligible woman in Zhuun, gave that gaggle of useless men the exact look they deserved. Her jet-black hair was intricately embroidered and twisted up, and held together by a golden phoenix crown, which Taishi thought was honestly a bit presumptuous. The duchess loosed a long, derisive sigh and drummed her long fingernails against the side of her famously sharp chin. "And how prepared is our hero? His training is incomplete? He is not ready yet?"

"Oh we're very close," said Pai. "Or at least we were. I daresay we don't know how much damage Ling has done to the hero. She must be recalled, and we must be reinstated. For the good of the Enlightened States!"

Waylin, the former emperor's brother-in-law's cousin (of some description or another) who had somehow weaseled and killed his way up, looked over at Sunri and then back at the masters. Waylin was the least imposing of the dukes, but had the support of most of the nobility. "Why would the emissary who was sent to check the hero's progress take matters into her own hands?"

Jang huffed, sucking in a labored breath. He was a large bald man with a thick beard and an even thicker waistline. "I believe Master Ling's ambition is to usurp the hero's training and take credit for his successes once he fulfills his destiny."

Several of his peers nodded. "It's a disgrace," someone barked.

"Despicable." More chatter as each man tried to sound more indignant than the next.

That continued for a few moments longer before Dongshi, the cunning Duke of Lawkan, the former emperor's whisperlord and leader of the brutal secret police, the Ten Hounds, belched. He looked amused as he turned toward the end. "Well, Saan, what do you have to say for yourself? She's your emissary. You're the one who gave her the Ducal Mandate. Why would she undermine the masters?"

Saan of Shulan, the second and only surviving son of the late emperor, looked nothing like his lazy, bald father. Tall, with a mane of carefully coifed hair and always with a layer of dark eyeliner, he was known as the Painted Tiger. A fierce and famed war artist, Saan and his allies at the court had been on the western front putting down the Straw Hat Rebellion when the old emperor died. By the time word of his father's death reached him, the empire had already fragmented. He opted not to plunge his people into civil war, a decision that likely saved them from obliteration by the Katuia Hordes.

Taishi was fond of Saan, but was secretly glad the emperor's stupid-looking nub hat and gaudy golden chain did not rest on that man's head and shoulders. Anyone else playing the Way of the Courts would not have allowed themselves to be sent away to the distant front so easily. Saan was an honorable and brave warrior who strictly followed Goramh's Tenets of Nobility, but, to put it bluntly, Saan had a head as soft as an overripe melon baking in the sun. He could fight his way through a hundred men but couldn't count to twenty-one without help.

Fortunately for him, Saan's simplemindedness sometimes resulted in profundity, which was how Taishi ended up here at the Celestial Palace in the first place. Now he pointed toward her, smiled, and said, "Why don't you ask her yourself?"

Before she realized what was happening, two servants carrying lanterns appeared next to her, illuminating her for all the throne room to see.

Dongshi squinted. "Well, Master Ling? Is what these masters say true? Are you trying to steal the Hero of Prophecy all for yourself?"

Taishi became the focus of a hundred pairs of glimmering eyes reflecting the lights of the lanterns back at her. She may have been one of the great masters of the war arts, but she was still that shy little girl when it came to crowds. She gulped and coughed and found her fingers itchy and sweaty. She was trying to come up with something flowery and diplomatic to save face, but came up short. The seconds ticked by.

Finally, Taishi decided to go with a neutral answer. "I believe the noble and wise dukes can judge for themselves once they see the Champion of the Five Under Heaven in action."

Saan spoke. "But you, Master Ling, have actually fought the Eternal Khan before. How would our hero have fared against him?"

Squashed like a shit-eating shit beetle. Taishi tried to go with something gentler, but diplomacy was truly escaping her right now. She heard herself saying, "As of right now, Wen Jian can't fight his way out of an old women's knitting circle. The Khan would chew through that boy like a snack and then use his bones to pick his teeth."

Saan cut off the outraged masters' fresh round of yapping. "So the boy isn't ready. That is why Master Ling took the steps she thought necessary. He is no threat to anyone." The way he spoke those last words caught Taishi's attention. What did he mean by that?

Yanso of Gyian spoke next. "Let me understand this properly." He began ticking off his fingers. "As part of our truce, each state agreed to tithe ten percent of our resources and military powers to maintain and protect the Celestial Palace for the Hero of Prophecy, to prepare him to defeat the Katuia Hordes. The boy lives like an emperor in the emperor's former home with a very well-equipped and very expensive standing army protecting him. After fifteen years, all we have to show for our considerable cost is a useless boy who may or may not defeat my ten-year-old daughter in a duel?" He began to laugh, his voice echoing loudly across the room.

Yanso was easily the smartest, the richest, and widely acknowledged to be the most powerful of the five dukes. The former purselord just happened to have had control of the gold repository and factories that minted all the liang when the emperor died. That vast wealth guaranteed him power and control of Gyian State. Aside from this, Yanso's daughter was quite the prodigy.

She bowed. "Yanliu sets a high bar, my lord."

Saan pressed. "But as of right now, he isn't ready."

Taishi bowed deeply. "Far from it, my lord."

He turned to the other dukes. "If this is indeed the case, the cost has already been sunk. We should just follow the simplest solution and send everyone home."

Home? Taishi couldn't believe what she was hearing. "What about the Tiandi Prophecy?" she asked. "Wen Jian is not beneath saving. He has great potential. We still have time—"

Saan cut her off. "That's enough, Master Ling."

The other dukes exchanged glances. Sunri spoke next. "Two weeks ago, one of our patrols in the Grass Sea was attacked by a giant, naked, drunk man. The patrol fought valiantly, but the giant killed everyone in the unit down to the last, except for one lone survivor, footman Ho Manji, who claimed to have killed this giant."

"There are many giants among the hordes. Hell, the riders of Keenyan are all two heads taller tha—"

"A thought we shared, Master Ling," interrupted Sunri. "But it has been verified: The Eternal Khan of the Katuia is dead."

Taishi was stunned. "The God of the Grass? The Immortal Horseman? The man who cannot be killed . . . has fallen?"

"A spear through the back," replied Sunri matter-of-factly. "Ho Manji's story is likely riddled with lies, but it does not matter. Our great enemy is no more."

"Shortly after he died," added Yanso, "that unit's position was overrun by the entire horde army. All their mounted cavalry, their metal dragons and bixis, and four of their twelve cities. It was an ill-planned attack, no doubt ordered in haste to save their Khan."

Taishi was still in shock. "What of the battle?"

A smile grew on Yanso's face. "Total victory. The Army of the Enlightened routed the hordes, scattered their riders, and razed several of their cities."

"We five are on our way to the signing of the armistice," said Waylin. "We just stopped by the Celestial Palace to meet so we can agree on the terms for their unconditional surrender."

"This is joyous news," said Taishi, still not believing it. "When the people—"

"Word of this will not reach the masses until the armistice is signed, and we know what to do about the Tiandi Prophecy and the supposed Champion of the Five Under Heaven," Sunri interrupted. "That is a ducal decree on pain of death. We must determine how to deal with the Tiandi faithful."

"Can you believe this superstitious peasant shit?" spat Waylin. "Winning the war isn't good enough for them. They insist on winning the war *their* way. Damn fanatics."

"The question," said Dongshi slowly, "is what do we do with this hero now that he is no longer necessary."

"As Master Ling said," said Saan. "He is weak and is no threat to anyone."

"Of course you would say that," retorted Sunri. "Wen Jian is from your region. He would make a useful pawn."

"May I remind you," added Waylin, "that an entire religion practically sprang from the earth around him. Even with the prophecy broken, he will carry influence wherever he goes."

Saan shook his head. "Who cares about those fools? Once it is revealed that the prophecy is no longer necessary, they will wither away all on their own. His followers will move on to other legends. Perhaps even some prophecies divined by our own soothsayers."

Dongshi slapped his drink down. "Someone will find a way to manipulate him to their own advantage. I won't allow it. He belongs to all five of us, or to none."

Sunri agreed. "That boy remains a threat as long as he lives."

"We cannot simply kill the boy," said Saan. "That will only make a martyr out of him."

"That's true," Dongshi conceded. "It's harder to kill martyrs after they're dead."

Yanso was quiet as the others went back and forth. When he finally spoke, it was with a solution. "None of us can have him, and after what we've heard, I suspect none of us want him. The hero cannot be killed, but it appears he is a hassle to all of us alive unless he dies of natural causes. I propose we send him off to a distant monastery. Declare that he intends to live a life of meditation. Let him fade into obscurity. Eventually, the religion will fade away, and all this tithing we did will have been a very expensive lesson for us all."

Saan frowned. "What is the difference between housing him here and in some faraway monastery?"

Yanso barked a crude laugh. "So we don't have to pay for this heavens-forsaken palace and army anymore. We have all paid too much. The Tiandi Prophecy has been a costly gold brick around all our necks for years. Send the boy away with a bribe and let the monks deal with feeding and clothing him."

Saan still looked uncertain, but the decision was four to one. Jian's fate was sealed. The dukes would ship him away to a monastery the location of which only they would know. Chances were, no one would ever hear from him again until some report came out in half a century about him dying from old age or disease. It wasn't a good solution for the boy, but it was acceptable to the dukes, and that was all that mattered. Something didn't sit right with Taishi, however.

Sunri looked to Faaru. "See that the boy is ready to travel immediately, Palacelord. Begin winding down all operations in the Celestial Palace. Leave only a skeleton staff to maintain the facilities and grounds."

"As you wish, my lords." Faaru bowed profusely.

"Now for the important matter at hand. The armistice," said Sunri. "A once-in-a-generation opportunity. How do we get fat off these savages so they can't start another war?"

The other dukes laughed.

Just like that, Jian was forgotten. The Prophecy of the Tiandi was dead, ending without even a whimper.

Everyone else bowed and began to file out of the throne room. As Taishi turned to depart, Waylin called after her. "Master Ling, stay. You had a long, glorious career fighting the hordes. You've spent many years living in the Grass Sea. Your insight on them will be most welcome."

There was nothing Taishi wanted to do less right now than help the dukes squeeze out every last drop of blood the Katuia had left. But she had no choice. "I would be honored." She bowed deeply and took her place next to the group of scholars waiting in the darkened balcony. Taishi suffered in silence for the next hour, with only her grinding teeth betraying her nerves. Though she remained perfectly still, her mind raced in every direction, and nearly all her thoughts ended in a dark place.

CHAPTER EIGHT

FALL OF THE PROPHECY

S oft hands shook Jian awake. His eyes flared open, and he found himself staring at eyes that were slightly too close together in a pudgy face with sparse facial hair. For a moment, he thought he was dreaming. He blinked. No, the face was still there. Master Sinsin's face was a breath away from his. Next to him was Master Jang. Hili and Ningzhu were at the foot of the bed. Luda and Sun stood on the left side of the bed. His masters had returned. They were all staring at him with bright eyes and wide smiles.

"What are you all doing here?" Jian sat up and yawned, then he counted again. "Where are Master Wang and Master Pai?"

Luda shook his head. "Those two have decided to move on to other positions."

Jian was sorely disappointed by that news. Wang and Pai were by far his favorite masters. They were the ones who had treated him most like a son. He swung his feet over the side of the bed and stretched. "What happened? I thought I was supposed to see the dukes last night."

Fading purple light shone through the window, slowly giving way to a strong orange hue. The Princess was hiding from her father. Dawn approached.

"Yes, Great Hero," said Ningzhu. "That's why we are here. The dukes have seen the wisdom in our training and restored us to our rightful position as your guides. They give us the honor of bringing you to their presence."

"It's about time. How dare they make me wait so long!" As far as he was concerned, the Hero of Prophecy was at the very least on equal footing with the dukes. Jian jumped out of bed and hurried to the mannequin still wearing the robe the tailor had made him. He quickly dressed and adjusted the belt around his waist, just like the tailor had shown him. "Summon the facemaker."

"That won't be necessary," said Ningzhu. "The lords have asked to meet with you in an informal setting. They simply wish to get acquainted with the savior of our people."

That was even better. Jian had already forgotten most of what the Mistress of Etiquette had tried to drill into his head the previous night. He left the room with his masters close behind. Riga and Horashi flanked him; the rest trailed after him down the curved stairs. It was just like old times again. It felt good.

He stopped at the base and looked back the way they came. "What happened to Master Ling?"

"Taishi has been released from service," said Sinsin with a smirk. "The dukes saw through her greed, that she was trying to usurp your destiny, and in their wisdom returned you to our care. She is an evil woman, and you would be wise to unlearn her teachings."

Jian should have been glad, but his feelings were mixed. He relished stability and routine, and was happy to have his masters back. But from his short time with Taishi, he knew none of them could teach him to fly or glide down walls or punch through stone. He had often dreamed of punching holes in the walls and escaping beyond the palace. The least she could have done was say goodbye. The old woman was mean, but he had sensed that they were starting to understand each other.

Two columns of rickshaws flanked by a full dozen cavalry honor guards, the Mute Men no less, awaited him outside his tower. Jian beamed with pride as he climbed inside the lead carriage. He waved at the bowing attendants as his procession passed and raised a fist in salute at the soldiers wearing different-colored uniforms. Some saluted back, while others looked at him curiously. Jian wished he was wearing his gem-encrusted golden armor.

They turned onto the open Heavenly Grounds where Jian gasped with delight at the rows upon rows of soldiers arrayed at attention in perfect symmetry. He waved to them as well. None waved back. He shook with anticipation as they approached the turn toward the Heart of the Tiandi Throne and was bewildered when the rickshaw continued past it, moving along the edge of the grounds.

"Why are we turning away from the Tiandi Throne?" he asked.

"Duchess Sunri herself thought a picnic in the grove would be more appropriate for breakfast," explained Sinsin. "Like I said earlier, the dukes wish to meet you in a less formal, more intimate setting. In many ways, as the holy son of the Zhuun, all five consider you family." Sinsin's smile felt hollow.

His nursemaids had raised him on tales of the dukes. Sunri, the fiercest and most beautiful woman in all the land, could challenge the Queen for her throne in heaven. Saan the Painted Tiger: Where he walked, death walked alongside him. Shrewd Dongshi, the self-proclaimed lord of knowledge, who knew your mind better than you did yourself. Yanso, the lord whose veins flowed with gold and wisdom. And Waylin, the emperor's brother or cousin of some sort, the villain in just about every story.

They entered the northern garden and proceeded to a small grove with clusters of willow trees and a pond in the shape of a crescent moon fed by waters from a whistling waterfall. The only way to enter the grove was over a small red wooden bridge that arched high over the pond. It was scenic and quiet, save for a small group of frogs singing alongside the willows shifting in the breeze. A flock of redheaded herons took to the air as they passed.

The rickshaws circled and dropped off their passengers, and then the masters led Jian to a quiet cottage. It had been a long time since he had explored this part of the palace. It was usually boring here, and the groundskeepers were strict and had no respect for his position. There were also a lot of bees, of which he was secretly deathly afraid.

Riga and Horashi had gone ahead of them and were already waiting at the door. They bowed as he approached, far more formally than usual, which was a nice touch. Being considered an equal to a duke could do that to bodyguards, even ones who had known you since you were a child.

Horashi opened the door and everyone filed into what appeared to be a storeroom. It was empty except for racks of gardening tools on the walls and barrels of fertilizer stacked on one side. A rough wooden table with a bench sat on the opposite end.

Jian's forehead furrowed. This was not what he expected for a picnic with the dukes. "Master Sinsin, what's the meaning of this? Where is everyone?"

Sinsin knelt down to Jian's level and patted him on the cheek. Then, without saying a word, he left the room. One by one, his masters approached, muttering limp goodbyes and wishing him luck on his next journey. Jang, the last master to leave the room, could barely look him in the eye. His face was wet, and the words he mumbled were nearly imperceptible. "Walk toward heaven, Jian."

Jang stopped and spoke with Horashi in a soft voice. It wasn't soft enough. "Remember the dukes' orders. No signs of violence. It has to look natural. There *will* be a revolt otherwise. We will be waiting in the grove."

Horashi nodded. Riga pulled out a silk rope.

That was when the realization of what was about to happen hit Jian. It was a sudden, viscous, nauseating sensation not unlike a punch in the stomach. His mind reeled. Panic gripped his chest. He stared at Horashi, the wrinkled familiar face of the man who had watched over him since he was a small. The constant, reassuring presence that was rarely out of sight and almost never out of earshot. It was as if his own heart had turned on him. The assurance and pride in Jian's voice were gone, and he sounded like the frightened child he was. His eyes watered. "Why?"

"I'm sorry, Jian," said Horashi. "Fortune changes with a flip of the coin."

"What did I do wrong? I'm sorry. Whatever it is, I didn't mean it."

Horashi bit his lips. His eyes glistened. "It's nothing you did, son. You were born to bad circumstances." He tousled Jian's hair one last time, which made Jian feel even worse.

"But the prophecy needs me," he pleaded. "I'm the savior of our people."

Horashi's shoulders slumped. "The Khan is dead. Felled in battle. The war is over. The Enlightened States have won. Now the dukes are just cleaning up. You're too dangerous alive. They fear your influence. They think one of the others will use you as a pawn."

Jian didn't hear anything much else except that the Khan was dead. "That's impossible," he whispered. "*I'm* supposed to kill him."

A heavy sigh escaped the older man. "It seems the prophecy was . . . mistaken."

Those words hit almost as heavily as Horashi's betrayal. Jian stumbled. It was a good thing his knees stubbornly refused to give way. He continued to stare at his friend's face, reality still sinking in. "My whole life is a lie."

The room swayed as he blinked back tears. Nothing made sense. Jian didn't flinch when Horashi gently wrapped the silk rope around his neck. Horashi's usual cool broke and he looked away, choking up.

Riga, leaning against the wall next to the door, yawned. "Get on with it. Kill him already. I for one am glad this assignment is over. If I had to play butler to this spoiled brat for one more day, I swear I would slit his throat myself."

Horashi put his hand on his hilt. "Shut up, you bull drinker! I swear I'll gut you from neck to balls if you say another word."

Riga eyed Horashi, a sneer growing on his face. His hand lowered to his saber. "I'd like to see you try. Disobeying the dukes' order is treason. I'll have every justification to dice you up."

Blades hissed out of their scabbards. The two men squared off, circling in the cramped space. Jian, still standing in the middle with the silk rope dangling around his neck, didn't move. He didn't know what was going on. He stayed frozen, his mind confused, his body numb. He was about to tell them, out of habit, to stop arguing, then realized what would happen if he did.

The two men were screaming and waving their blades at each other when Riga held up a hand and looked up at the ceiling. "Did you hear that?"

"Hear what?" spat Horashi.

Jian listened. A thunking was coming from above them. Wooden beams creaked, and then the ceiling collapsed, raining debris and dust into the room. A body dropped down, landing lightly between the two bodyguards.

Taishi looked curiously at the two men with their blades drawn. "Am I interrupting something?" She kicked Horashi in the chest, sending him flying across the room and slamming into the far wall.

Riga's saber nearly took her head off, but she ducked and spun. Taishi made no attempt to counter as she danced away. The bodyguard pressed his attack, trying to find an opening. He jabbed high and then slashed low, each strike inches from finding its mark.

Taishi didn't seem concerned as her arm fluttered at the air in a seemingly random way. The saber never touched her, and as the attack continued, Riga became more desperate. Then he executed his specialty, throwing the saber spinning horizontally in the air at Taishi's neck. She ducked, and it passed overhead. Jian stared as the saber shot past her and then came spinning back. He wanted to yell a warning, but no sound escaped his lips.

His help wasn't needed, however.

As the spinning blade returned, Taishi slapped it, changing the balance and sending it twirling between her two fingers. She pointed it at Riga. The blade blurred as it struck him in the chest, passing straight through his body and sinking halfway into the stone wall.

Riga staggered, his hands clutching the red bloom on his chest. He stared at Taishi, eyes wide. "That was really spectacular." Then he pitched forward and fell onto his face.

Taishi was already moving to the other target. She beckoned at the saber and it wiggled free from the wall, flying into her grasp. She leveled it at the still-unconscious Horashi's chest.

That was when Jian finally found his voice. "No!" He rushed in between Taishi and Horashi, his arms spread out. "Stop."

Taishi shot him a crooked frown. "Wasn't he trying to kill you?"

"Yes, sort of. But he hesitated."

"Not good enough." She slapped Jian on the side of his head with the flat of the blade. "Out of the way."

Jian held his ground. "Spare him. Please."

Taishi was about to slap him again when she threw her arm up. "Fine, I'll spare that one. If your lack of war art ability doesn't get you killed, your softness surely will."

"Did the dukes really order my death?" he asked.

"The official command was to exile you to some far-off mountain monastery, but that was fairly clearly just a ploy." She mused. "I knew something felt wrong with their decree. The dukes do not allow loose ends. That also explained why Saan was so angry. Unfortunately, Jian, you became a liability the moment the Khan died." She began patting the bodies. "Those shortsighted fools. You're lucky I'm far more prudent and much less cruel."

"What are you doing?" asked Jian.

"Looking for liang. I didn't exactly have time to pack before I saved you. We're going to need some money if we're to escape the palace."

There was a heavy knock on the door, followed by a muffled voice. "Is everything all right in there? We heard noises."

"My masters," whispered Jian.

"*Former* masters. Pai and Wang were the only ones with the dignity not to participate in this charade," she hissed. "Am I allowed to kill them or do those treacherous sycophants get to live as well?"

"Can you do something in between killing and letting them live?"

"Like, maim them?"

"No! Just knock them out or something."

A guttural sound came out of Taishi's mouth reminiscent of a snarl. "Fine. Stay here until I'm done." She opened the door mid-knock and threw a punch, snapping Hili's head back and sending his body flying out of sight. Taishi slammed the door shut behind her.

The men outside began to scream.

Jian stood there, wondering how long he had to wait inside the hut. Wondering if he should go out and help. Help who, though? He couldn't bear the thought of betraying his masters, even if they had turned on him. But what if six masters were too much for even Taishi to take on? Perhaps Jian had better go out and help her after all.

He rolled up his sleeves and psyched himself up for a fight. The shock of the betrayal, learning that the prophecy was a lie, that he was not the champion of his people, just a nobody, was starting to wear off. In its place was a growing, burning rage. He had spent his entire life trapped in the Celestial Palace, all for nothing. He never knew his parents because of this prophecy, all for nothing. He had done nothing but train in war arts for nothing. And now he had learned that he wasn't even very good at any of this. They had wasted his life, and now they all wanted to kill him!

Jian was not going to tolerate this anymore. It was time he took his destiny into his own hands. He stomped to the door and flinched when a body flew through the window, spraying glass shards and wood fragments all over the room. Master Ningzhu, body broken and twisted, raised a bloodied and battered face toward Jian. He tried to speak and managed a moan before he slumped over.

Before Jian could ask him if he was all right, another crack shook the building. Jian ducked again as a black leather shoe somehow broke through the thick wooden door. He crept up and examined the shoe, only to realize that the leg was still attached. Hesitantly, Jian swung the door open, and saw Master Sinsin swing with it, hanging upside down by one leg.

Jian's mouth opened as he watched the end of the carnage. Three of the masters were still fighting. Masters Hili and Sun were on opposite sides of Taishi, attacking her at the same time, but somehow getting the worst of the exchanges. Master Luda was on the far side of the clearing struggling to stand. His muddy robe and a long brown streak running along the grass behind him told the story of how he had gotten there.

Jian stared, mouth agape, as Taishi pummeled the two men. He had always thought his former masters the best; they were certainly skilled. But now he realized he never knew what true war art skill was until he saw Taishi. She dodged and stepped just out of range of both their attacks almost casually, and when she attacked, it was as if thunder flowed through her body.

Even with just one arm, she blocked all of Sun's prickling punches, and then her palm shot out, whipping him in the face, sending him flipping backward in a complete somersault. Just as quickly, she turned to meet Hili's slower, more powerful looping hammer swings. Jian used to watch in awe and clap when some of Hili's swings would crack tree trunks. Small tree trunks. Yet somehow Taishi managed to block Hili's attacks and remain standing, although the impact sent a ring of dust expanding from where she stood.

Hili must have wondered how she did that as well. His eyes widened. "How—"

Then she kicked both his knees in rapid succession, and he howled, falling face-first. As she stood over him, Taishi grimaced and clutched her chest. Hili's attack must have hurt her. The show of weakness lasted a few seconds as she recovered from the pain.

By now Luda had made it back from the far end of the clearing. He snarled, waved his arms over his head in the Luda family claw, and charged Taishi from behind. This time, Jian didn't hesitate. He rushed out and intercepted Luda before he could reach her. He raised his guard and dared Luda to cut him down. His former master's eyes widened for a moment, and then he actually tried to do it. Jian blocked the first claw swipe and managed to duck the second, but that was as far as he got.

They were no longer training, and his former masters were no longer holding back. Luda's movements were much faster and more powerful than Jian was used to. He did not hold a candle to Taishi, but he was still a master. The clawed hand gripped Jian's forearm and raked downward, easily cutting through the cloth of his robe and slicing his flesh open. Jian tried to twist away, but Luda's grip was like pincers. He tried to retaliate with a punch that fell woefully short, and then Luda had his other clawed hand wrapped around his neck.

Luda roared. "How dare you turn on your master?"

"You tried to kill me," Jian choked through gritted teeth. "You're not my master anymore." He lashed out wildly. Both of them were surprised when Jian's punch found its mark, striking Luda in the eye and turning his head. The man blinked and snarled.

"You impudent dog." Luda's curled fingers widened and he drew his arm back.

Jian had seen the Luda family death move only during practice. He didn't believe it actually existed or worked. Half the styles claimed to have death moves. It was of course hard to prove any of their effectiveness. Jian, his neck still in Luda's grip, flailed his arms. Luda's claw struck Jian in the chest over his heart, his fingers digging deep into the flesh. The shock reverberated through Jian's body. He looked down. That was when he realized.

His heart had stopped beating.

Jian tried to cry out; no breath came. He tried to move his arms; they were heavy like iron, and then he couldn't feel them at all. His legs were rooted to the ground. He began to tip over. The look on Luda's face was rage mixed with incredulity, as if he were surprised the move had actually worked. The world began to darken.

Taishi appeared out of nowhere. Her hand sliced horizontally across Luda's face. A stream of blood burst out, and he screamed, clutching what had been his good eye. Taishi struck him once more in the chest with her palm, adding another mud skid to the previously manicured meadow.

She turned to Jian and touched the marks on his chest. Her eyes widened with deep concern. Her hand was a blur as she struck him several times with two fingers: on the base of his neck, over his heart, then once more on his solar plexus. She turned him around, and a sudden hard blow pitched Jian forward. Black blood spewed from his lips. His veins felt as if they were on fire, and then he could breathe again.

"I . . ." He couldn't form words.

Taishi held him up by his shoulders. "What did I tell you about staying inside, boy?"

"I wanted to help," he mumbled, although he wasn't sure the sounds were making it past his lips.

Taishi half carried, half dragged him back to the clearing. She stopped when the squad of Quiet Death pulled up at the other side of the bridge. She yanked them both into the brush.

"Can . . ." He breathed heavily. "Can you beat them?"

"I'm not in the mood to fight a dozen fully armored Mute Men on horseback, no." She paused. "I mean I probably could, but I'm not going to try." She glanced up at the waterfall and dragged him back toward it. She whistled. "Peachlord, are you there?"

Faaru crept out of the bushes a second later. "Is Jian safe?"

Seeing Faaru there hit Jian almost as hard as Horashi betraying him. "Uncle Faaru is in on it too? He wants me dead as well?"

"No, stupid boy. He's the one who warned me about this and guided me here. Faaru, is there a way out?"

Faaru pointed at the waterfall. "The water flows through an underground stream coming down from the mountains. If you're strong, you can swim upstream to escape."

Taishi glanced at Jian. Doubt flashed on her face. "A cripple and a boy . . ." She shook her head. "We'll have to risk it."

"You'd best hurry then," said Faaru, urging them on.

Taishi nodded. "Thank you, Faaru. I had judged you wrong. You are a good man."

"Just get the boy to safety, Master Ling."

The palacelord looked down at Jian. He bowed. "It's been an honor, Wen Jian, Hero of the Tiandi Prophecy, Champion of the Five Under Heaven . . . my boy." The way he said it was completely different from the way Taishi did.

Jian caught himself swallowing back tears, and then he slumped forward into Faaru's embrace. "I'm going to miss you," he sobbed.

Faaru, body shaking as well, stroked the back of his head. "Lead a long and happy life, son."

"None of us will do that if we stick around much longer," said Taishi.

Taishi looped Jian's arm over her shoulder and carried him, bounding up to a rock, then a branch, and then up to the cliff halfway up the waterfall. Jian looked down. The last thing he saw was Uncle Faaru waving his arms at three of the Mute Men as they approached. And then one of them cut him down.

The spray from the waterfall masked his tears as Taishi continued to work her way up to the top of the cliff, a fistful of his shirt in her hand. Jian's head lolled as she jostled him up to the top of the waterfall, then up to the entrance of the underground stream.

"It's getting cold," he whispered between chattering teeth.

She laid him down and pressed her ear to his chest. "I'm not going to lose you now, boy, especially with all the trouble I'm in. This is going to hurt." Taishi stabbed two more pressure points along his neck, and once on both temples.

Everything went black.

Whether he was out for seconds or hours, he did not know. The next moment, Jian blinked his eyes open and found himself staring up at both the Prince and Princess playing in the night sky. He was drenched. Taishi, hovering over his body, was as well.

Jian sat up, opened his mouth, and promptly vomited up half of the Razor River. He struggled to breathe as his body spasmed several more times. For some reason, his body couldn't push out whatever water was still trapped inside him, and he was drowning. Taishi appeared and rolled him onto his side. She slapped his back several times, and he spewed out what felt like the other half of the river.

Finally, he fell onto his back. It took a moment for his eyes to focus on Taishi again. "Something's wrong. Everything feels numb."

She struck him several more times on his pressure points.

The next time Jian spat, the liquid was black.

"What is happening to me?"

"That bastard Luda poisoned your blood. I've temporarily relieved the effects, but it won't last long. I can't cure this."

"What does that mean?" Jian asked.

Taishi, for the first time, looked worn and defeated. She shook her head, resigned. "I'm sorry, boy, but you're dying."

CHAPTER NINE

THE SOUL OF THE KHAN

Sali pressed on for four more days. She dozed on horseback by day, letting her savvy roan pick her way over the uneven paths, and stopped only a few hours at night to let the mare rest. Nights were also a dangerous time to travel. The Grass Sea's thick canopies obstructed the shine of the Celestial Family, leaving the jungle floor in near blackness. And so Sali did her best to stay alert all night, intently watching the ground.

Even by day, shadows and pitfalls awaited their every step. Her mare nearly broke her leg several times, and on one occasion they both nearly drowned when Sali walked her directly off a ledge where both were swept away by an underwater current.

Sali didn't need to climb past the grass canopy to track the stars: The Khan's Pull was the only compass she needed. The closer she got to his soul's resting place, the stronger the draw. This compulsion crawled all over her skin. Over the last few hours, she began to find it difficult to breathe, her breaths turning shallow and forced. She had to grit her teeth to keep them from rattling. The need to Return was so overwhelming, it was all she could do to stay upright and move forward one step at a time.

The tops of the jagged black spires of Chaqra became visible past the canopy in the early evening of the third day, just before dusk reduced the twisted structures to gnarled silhouettes. The land was shrouded in darkness, with neither the moons nor the sun showing their faces. Sali and the mare were ambling forward solely on instinct, ignoring the protests from her sore backside and legs.

By dawn of the fourth day, it was all she could manage to stay upright in the saddle. That would have been the ultimate humiliation, to die in a fall hours away from her destination, not to mention the hassle it would cause the shamans to lose another piece of the Khan's soul. Sali and the poor mare continued ambling mindlessly in the direction that the throbbing in her chest demanded. In the back of her head, she imagined she heard the faint, familiar welcoming whistles and hisses, the roaring clang of furnaces, followed by morning chants. Sali was so exhausted and delirious, her mind so numb, that nothing registered. The noise just sounded like echoes of memories in her head.

That was what made it so easy to get captured.

One moment she was slumped on the mare's back, the next a dozen black-clad warriors wielding swords and tall shields with numbered tattoos on their faces—the number of their kills—had her surrounded. "Identify yourself," someone ordered.

Sali recognized their black garb. Towerspears, or vigilant spears as they were often named. These were the spirit shamans' personal army, handpicked from among all the clans and often chosen more for their fanaticism than their skill in defending their holiest city. Contrary to their name, the towerspears also never used spears—or resided in towers, now that she thought about it.

Sali gave them a dull stare. "About time you found me. I'm almost on top of you."

"It's a viperstrike!"

Technically she was *the* Viperstrike, of the first among seventeen viperstrikes from her sect, but that was a moot point.

The squadlead who recognized her heart-saluted, putting his fist over his chest. "You honor us with your Return, Will of the Khan." The other towerspears fell to their knees.

Sali remembered what her position meant to these warriors, especially in Chaqra. She did her best to sit up and not look so much like the wreck she felt like. "The Return to the Rebirth," she recited. "Lead on."

The squadlead gestured to his squad, and they spread out in formation around her, an honor guard of sorts. The warriors of Katuia did not believe in such things. Guards were required only for those who could not protect themselves. To assign guards to someone meant they were either weak or so important that custom had to be disregarded for the greater good. In this case, it seemed, Sali was both.

Her escort led her through several clusters of sickly-looking grass, as after a drought. That should have been impossible considering the season they had just weathered. Then Sali realized why it looked unwell. The flora around here had been trampled multiple times by track vehicles, abused by prolonged exposures to exhaust from the cities, and subjected to continuing proximity to humans.

"When did we turn into land-chained?" she muttered.

Sali got her answer a moment later. Her escort led her through several more blooms of grass before finally taking her to what she could describe only as a large refugee camp. Sali could only gape. Sprawling before her eyes was a field of cut and trampled blades, flattened lands of uprooted plants, and fires, dozens of them, dotting the landscape. The people here were living in makeshift tents and hovels, crowded together in disorder and squalor. Many huddled near firepits. Others sat aimlessly on the ground, despondent, their eyes haunted, their strength sapped. A group of children, many barefoot and shirtless, were playing in a stream, the waters polluted with floating debris. The sea underneath their feet had to be groaning from the weight and misery.

She was furious. "These fires are touching the ground. This is sacrilege."

The lead shook his head. He too looked uncomfortable. "The shamans have made exceptions to ease the people's plight."

Sali closed her eyes. She could rattle off half a dozen heretical actions in front of her eyes with just a glance. Things had to be really bad if the shamans allowed this. It was still not acceptable, regardless of circumstances.

It didn't take long for her to attract curious eyes, and then for word of her arrival to spread. Soon enough, people were flocking to catch a glimpse of her. The Wills of the Khan, twelve in number, were parts of his soul, and considered an extension of his being. Upon his death, it was every Will of the Khan's duty to Return and join him at his final resting place in the Sanctuary of the Eternal Moor. Only after they all reunited, after he was made whole again, would he be at full strength to reincarnate to his next life and continue to lead their people to salvation.

The towerspears began clearing the way, but it wasn't necessary. The seemingly endless throng parted before her. Most, if not all, placed their fists over their hearts as she passed. Sali returned the courtesy, keeping her eyes fixed forward, avoiding looking at the pitiful masses entirely. It was inappropriate for someone of her position to stare at commoners.

Eventually, after the excruciating passage through the refugee camp, an end-pod of Chaqra came into view. The space beneath it was even more crowded than the field. Most there appeared to be waiting for something. She didn't know what until a ship ramp tilted out and lowered to ground level. The once orderly refugees began to jostle one another, pushing their way onto the ramp.

The squad leading Sali began to push back, using their shields and clubs to make space. At first the crowd appeared to overwhelm the towerspears, but slowly they got beaten back. She clicked her tongue irritably. Try as she might, it was difficult to ignore their wailing and begging to be let in.

Her escort ended at the base of the ramp. Sali needed help getting off the mare. Her knees buckled when they touched the ground, but between the mare and the squadlead, she managed not to fall on her face. He also tried to help with her gear, but she would have none of that. It was bad enough getting an escort. If someone was carrying her things for her as well, she would never have been able to face the warriors she commanded, let alone her fellow viperstrikes. Jiamin would never have let her live it down.

Sali slung her gear over her shoulder and gave the roan a gentle pat before handing her off to the lead. "She's a strong horse, but skittish in space. Worthy to breed for the fields, but not for war."

The squadlead nodded, taking the reins. "I'll see that she is honored with good work before she feeds the people."

The Katuia, with few exceptions, did not give character to their animals or objects. The mare was simply called what she was, as would be a stallion, or a dog. It was the same with their objects. A tool, be it a horse or hammer or sword, should be allowed to fulfill its purpose without the taint of human qualities.

Sali scratched the back of the horse's ear one last time. She had enjoyed the mare's company, the gentle and patient creature far more accommodating than the usually temperamental and strong-willed warhorses to which Sali was accustomed. "May your fruitful labors continue, mare." She turned toward the pod, and then stopped. "One more thing, squadlead. No more fires on the ground. Figure out another way. Difficult times are no excuse for desecration."

She walked stiffly up the ramp, all too aware of the hundreds of eyes and outstretched hands clamoring to be allowed to join her in the city. Once again she showed them respect by placing her fist to her chest and looking straight ahead.

A man who looked more beard than person was waiting for her at the top. Sali broke into a smile and cupped one side of his face with her palm while he did the same to her. Their foreheads touched. "Jhamsa."

"Chaqra honors your Return, Will of the Khan."

"Stop it."

A wry grin appeared on his face, and the formality in his voice dropped. "Sali, my dear child. I have missed you. I had feared something had happened to you on your journey home."

"The last cycle of the year isn't clear and easy days, Spirit Shaman," she replied drily. "Our Khan chose the worst time to die."

"Indeed. I honor you for holding to your sacred vows, Sali."

Not like she had had much of a choice.

He gestured for her to follow him to the end of the pod and across a rope bridge. "Come, you must be exhausted. You should rest before the ritual."

"How many have arrived?" she asked.

"Besides the four who passed before the Eternal Khan, three perished during the rescue of the Eternal Khan's body. They have not been recovered, and may never be. Soul Seekers are trying to find their bodies to recover his fragments, but the devastation on the battlegrounds is vast. Two arrived a few weeks ago and have already rejoined the Whole. The only ones left in the world, other than you, are Molari and Poli."

"Take me to him," she ordered.

Jhamsa hesitated. "You've had a long journey. Allow Chaqra the honor of opening our hearth. The ceremony can wait a few days."

Sali shook her head. "My head is rattling so hard I fear my teeth may fall out. I do not need an audience to honor my death. What I wish for is to sleep in peace tonight."

Sadness briefly flashed across the shaman's face. He looked as if he was about to refuse her, and then nodded. "Your loyalty to duty honors and shames me, Will of the Khan."

Jhamsa led her across the end-pod, which, like the one from Ankar, had a garage and a guardhouse on one side. On the other was a row of large tower crossbows. Sali had always thought it a pity. Chaqra was by far the most heavily armed of the Twelve, but because of its significance, it had never seen battle, at least not in her lifetime. Of course, before the time of the Sacred Braid and the war with the Zhuun, the cities had clashed with one another, until the city with the most weapons mounted on its pods became Katuia's head of government.

They continued to the next pod, which housed several smithies—black, armor, weapon, steam—as well as a tinker shop. From there, the bridge forked toward three different pods. Like all Katuia cities, every pod was carried across the Grass Sea on tracks powered by steam engines set in the lower levels. They were all interconnected like a giant spiderweb, and the residents of the city could cross from one section to another; if necessary, each pod could disengage from its neighbors and reconnect where needed.

Welcome memories rushed into Sali's thoughts as they strolled through the Black City. Nezra's clan chief, Faalan, had been Sali's uncle, and her family hailed from a long line of viperstrikes, so Sali had often come to the capital when she was a little girl. She remembered long days running across these same bridges with Jiamin, Mali, and the children of other chiefs. She could still hear their uncontrolled laughter as they caused trouble overturning carts and pestering towerspears while chasing one another throughout the webbed city. Poor Mali had always been falling behind. Sali admitted to often being an inconsiderate sister. Jiamin, on the other hand, always gentle, never failed to pick Mali up and carry her on his back.

Those had been much happier times, when constant war seemed a world away. Most of Sali's childhood friends, like her, had shaved the sides of their heads and taken on their clan style, which probably meant that most of them were now dead. Sali could almost feel the ghosts of her past running and giggling across these bridges as she made this lonely walk.

The next pods housed warehouses, garrisons, and administrative and engineering buildings that kept the city running and the people cared for. What Sali did not see here were many that housed people. Most people of a city did not live on the city, but moved alongside it.

"What happened to the Khan?" she asked as they began to cross the next rope bridge.

The look on the shaman's face told her everything before he opened his mouth. "You know how the Khan gets in his melancholic moods, the burden of being the Eternal One, the slow attrition of our war. In the past few months, he began to disappear for days. We allowed it because . . . he had always been sensitive . . . He needed privacy and time to collect his thoughts. We gave him space."

"That doesn't explain how the Katuia, in the span of a cycle, lost four cities. This is a disaster."

"We lost seven cities."

"Seven!" Sali stumbled and had to grab on to the roped railing to stay upright. "How is that possible?"

Jhamsa's body deflated as his gaze fell to the ground. "The Khan was gone longer than usual and had wandered too close to the Zhuun borders. One of our scouting parties was watching his whereabouts, but kept their distance. Then a Zhuun patrol stumbled on him . . ."

This time, Sali did stop in her tracks. "There is no chance a Zhuun patrol could defeat the Khan in battle."

Jhamsa's voice fell to a hush, even though they were alone. "He had been on the drink for several days. By the time the Zhuun found him, he could barely stand, so I'm told."

Sali closed her eyes and gnashed her teeth. She tasted blood on her tongue. "So it only took a group of Zhuun grunts to kill the Eternal Khan who cannot die."

The shaman nodded. "We launched an attack in an effort to save him. The advance scouts destroyed the patrol but were chased down by the enemy's counterattack. More of our forces caught up to the group stealing the Khan's body, but then they themselves were annihilated by the Zhuun's main force. We had no choice then but to launch cities."

"We have never been able to match the Zhuun in numbers," spat Sali. "Why did we not just retreat into the sea when we were faced with defeat?" Then she realized. "The body. The immortal lineage of the Khan."

Jhamsa nodded. "We could not retreat."

The Katuia believed that after the death of every Khan, his soul reincarnated into another of the people. It was their holy duty to seek out the vessel of the new Khan and bring him to the Sanctuary of the Eternal Moor to complete his rebirth. Only then could he ascend, take his natural form, and lead the Katuia people once more. The shamans claimed that the only way the Khan's soul could ever die was if his body was not brought back to the temple. In a thousand years, the line of the Khan had remained unbroken. Sali was eternally thankful that it would not be her generation that broke it, although their people had paid a dear price.

The last section of pods were the council buildings and temples. They were nearing the heart of Chaqra, which meant every step was bringing Sali closer to death. These were her last moments. She should have been at peace. Her duty to Katuia had been fulfilled, and her place among her ancestors on the Wheel of Life assured. Her next life would return her as a more perfect and complete being.

Still, Sali was not at peace. She could not be. As much as she tried to ignore the pressing question on her mind, she could not hide from it any longer. She had to know. "Jhamsa, I did not see pods from Nezra on my journey here. Do you know its fate?" Sali's voice was quiet.

The spirit shaman hesitated. "Sali, it is heresy."

It was taboo to ask, and forbidden for the spirit shaman to answer. Tradition required Wills of the Khan shed their past on the day of their Return so that the soul was clean and unburdened for the next reincarnation. To hold on to their previous lives could weigh down the Khan's soul during its reincarnation.

"Please, heart-father, I must know. If I am to depart this world today, I need to know of my family."

Jhamsa looked as if he was about to refuse her. But the determination on her face, the desperation in her eyes could not be dismissed. He turned away, his face twisted in anguish. He replied in a hushed voice. "Sali, I would have preferred to spare you the suffering, but an old man cannot refuse his heart-daughter's last wish." His voice broke as he continued. "During the battle, Nezra sacrificed itself by moving to the front to shield our people while they searched for the Khan's body. Your city took the heaviest losses. Nezra was crippled and unable to escape. The city is no more. I am sorry."

It took several moments for Sali to process that idea. Her home was gone. The Glittering Emerald Beacon would never roll again. The bamboo flesh of the buildings, the curved arches, the many stairways that led to the skies. If all her people were gone, was she the last to remember her city? And once Sali returned to the Whole, would Nezra fade from the stories as well?

She squeezed her eyes shut and tried to hold on to those memories, knowing they would probably disappear once her soul returned to the Whole. Perhaps if she thought hard enough, the next Khan would keep those memories as well.

"Are all my people dead?" she asked.

"From what we could tell," said Jhamsa slowly, "those on Nezra who survived the battle either died in defense of their city or were captured." He hesitated. "I have the honor of informing you that your family fought with valor to the last in defense of their hearth."

That felt strangely hollow. It was rare for a city to join a battle, but when it did, the entire populace fought. They did not send only the warriors to fight. Everyone worked in the defense of their home, the elderly and children included. Everyone had their role.

She nodded. "Thank you, Spirit Shaman. I can now Return in peace."

That was a lie. Not that it mattered. At this stage, mere steps away from joining the Whole, nothing mattered. Everything hurt. Badly. Sali wanted to fall to her knees and weep. She wanted to draw her tongue and charge alone toward Zhuun lands and extract as much blood and vengeance as she could before the land-chained struck her down. She wanted to do anything—everything—else except to walk into the Sanctuary of the Eternal Moor and lie down to die. But she couldn't, and it wouldn't make a difference anyway. Dying and Returning her soul to the Whole, however, was necessary to strengthen the Khan as he continued his eternal journey into his next life in this world.

Sali sighed, and swallowed her grief. "I am ready."

Jhamsa looked as if he was finished, then added, "Sali, my dear, it may be of little solace to you, but Mali survived. She was captured by Zhuun soldiers when they overran the city."

Hearing that was a punch to the gut. Sali should have been happy that her sister was alive. Strangely, she was not. At least with death she knew that Mali was at peace, and they could possibly see each other again in their next incarnation. Now Sali was escaping this life to the next, and Mali was left alone enslaved by the enemy, imprisoned in an alien land.

The two continued in silence over the last bridge. The impossibly tall black spires of the Sanctuary of the Eternal Moor loomed high in the sky before her. It was now the tomb of the thirty-seventh Khan of the Katuia, and every other Khan before him.

Sali had come here only once before, and to this day seeing it instilled an icy fear and awe within her. Cut from onyx, spark stones, and vantam gems, the temple was the symbol of the Khan's rebirth. It was where his body was always laid to rest, and where his reincarnated vessel was confirmed and sanctified. It was the tallest structure in Chaqra, all of Katuia in fact. The Sanctuary of the Eternal Moor stood alone and had the effect of absorbing all light around it, making the temple appear displaced from another dimension.

Jhamsa paused at the base of the temple and craned his head upward. A contented exhale escaped his lips. "Every time I stand in this beautiful place, I am instilled with reverence for our ancestors. Oh, how they were able to accomplish such grandeur."

If Sali were to be honest, it was a hideous structure, with a squat base and twisted branches that snaked in all directions, like a diseased tree or a crushed sea urchin. Sali kept her opinions to herself. "It's magnificent."

They reached the entrance to the Sanctuary of the Eternal Moor, two thick mahogany doors encrusted with vantam gems and lined with spark stones. Staring at it felt oppressive. Being so close made Sali feel small.

Jhamsa turned to Sali. "Are you sure you won't change your mind? Once you pass through these doors, the ritual begins, and you cannot turn back. Why don't you stay for a few days? Allow an old man some final memories with his heart-daughter."

"My duty is now a burden I cannot resist." Sali shook her head with a heavy, long breath. "Besides, there is nothing left for me here in this world."

The spirit shaman nodded. "I understand." He clutched her shoulders and pulled her into a hard embrace. "Your sacrifice will never be forgotten. Your Return to the Whole will bless our people and reincarnate our Khan stronger than ever."

"Goodbye, heart-father. I am glad yours is the last face I see before the end."

He smiled. "My dear Sali. This is not the end, but a transition. The next time we meet, a Soul Seeker will be introducing you to me anew."

Soul Seekers. Adventurers who explored the Grass Sea to seek out the next vessel for the Eternal Khan's soul. As a little girl, Sali had often dreamed of declaring herself a Soul Seeker. Although considered lowly in rank, they were the source of many stories that fed the imaginations of Katuia children. Never in her life had she thought she would instead become a part of the Khan's soul. Fate was strange that way.

Sali embraced Jhamsa one last time and stared at the doors to the tomb. Once she entered, her time on this world would end. As one of the Wills of the Khan, she was destined to join the other eleven of the Blood to return to his soul, so in his next life they may continue living, as it had been for nearly a thousand years.

Sali took one last breath of the Grass Sea and walked through the doors. Inside was an altar decorated with incense and gold plates of dried fruits and meats, vases of peat wine and rich molted skins of giant serpents.

On the other side of the altar lay, or stood in this case, the Eternal Khan, the man who could not die, quite dead now, arranged on a slanted slab in the middle of the room. Behind him were twelve more slabs. Four contained mummies, Wills who had passed before he had. Three were marked. They were souls of the Wills whose bodies were never recovered and were doomed to spend an eternity searching for their way back to the Whole. Two other slabs were freshly occupied by the bodies of Shianka and Trishan.

The last three slabs were reserved for Molari, Poli, and of course Sali. She decided to take the empty one in the middle. She liked the idea of being surrounded by friends. Several shamans emerged but kept their distance, waiting patiently to serve and bathe her before she drank the nectar.

She closed her eyes, thought of her clan and of Nezra, the glimmering glass windows and the green steam pipes. The way the aft pods always ran slower than the rest of the city. Its famous celebrations. Mostly, she thought of her family: her parents, her dozens of cousins and uncles and aunts. All dead defending their hearth. As they would have wanted.

She thought inevitably of Mali, her little sprout of a sister, who had never been fit for battle, but whose mind had been destined for far greater things. Mali, now in the clutches of the evil Zhuun. That hurt her deeper than she cared to admit.

"Are you ready, Will of the Khan?" asked a shaman.

Sali took a deep breath and stared ahead. "Leave me. I need a moment."

The four—the oldest among them could not have been older than twenty, Mali's age—looked confused at first, but Sali's sharp glance sent them scurrying and bowing as they shuffled out of the room. The doors closed with an echo that shook the tomb.

Now that she was alone, Sali let the mask of the Will of the Khan fall. She no longer needed to be the calm forceful representative of the Khan, no longer his serene unyielding voice. She closed her eyes, inhaled deeply, feeling the cool air flow, joined by the faint odors of dust and formaldehyde. This was her final resting place.

She stayed rooted to the floor, unsure what she should feel. Was it honor, piety, pride? Was she content with her accomplishments in this life? All Sali felt anymore was the hole in her heart. She felt . . . incomplete. It certainly wasn't the fear of death. To her people, dying was as normal as waking to a new day. No, something else was pulling her back. Her life did not feel satisfied. It felt unfinished, but she didn't know why.

What she really had to do right now, though, was get something off her chest.

Sali walked up to the Eternal Khan of the Katuia's body, and put one opened palm to her forehead, then one to her chest. Her peace and love toward him from her heart and mind. "Hello, Jiamin." Then she slapped him across the face. "You. Blind. Ball-less. Selfish. Asshole. How *could* you? Ohhh, but you did. You couldn't help yourself. You were always so fragile in your might. Now here you are. I should be surprised. But we both knew, didn't we, Jiamin? Deep within ourselves, I had hoped so much for more from you, but you proved me correct."

She choked up with fresh grief as she stared at the Khan, the god of her people who could not be killed. At the leader of all Katuia, their people's symbol of strength, salvation, and glory. At the tired man carrying the unwanted responsibility of his people on his shoulders. At the scared boy burdened with the heaviest weight. At her best friend.

Weeks of pent-up emotions overwhelmed her. Or years, if she was honest, and that was all that was left to her now, wasn't it? Sali was hurt, she grieved, she wept. She was just so angry. She wanted to sweep the stupid contents of the altar onto the floor. She wanted to beat Jiamin senseless for having the audacity to die on her. Sali had all these things she wanted to scream at him. Now was her chance.

Sali stared and leveled a finger at Jiamin. "You didn't have to be the Khan. You could have said no. You *should* have said no."

That was a lie. No one had ever refused the honor, not in nearly a thousand years. It wasn't a choice; it was fate. The Khan was chosen by a higher power before even being born.

But Sali remembered everything. She had been there. Jiamin had badly wanted to refuse the honor. It was a mistake, he had pleaded to her. He couldn't have been whom the seekers sought when they arrived at his home and verified his ascendancy against the signs of the stars. He wasn't strong enough. He didn't *want* it, which was unheard of. Every boy and girl in Katuia dreamed of becoming the Khan. Everyone but Jiamin. At the time, as an ignorant child, she had thought the very fact that he did not seek to become the Khan was what made him worthy of it. Now she knew the truth. He was being honest, and no one had believed him. *She* hadn't believed him.

Sali had been at his side the entire time, and had been the second to become Jiamin's Will, after his brother. Now he was gone, as were their people, as she would soon be. Because he hadn't said no. Now she would join him even as their cities lay broken, their people scattered, enslaved. She would abandon them as he had abandoned them, because though no one would dare speak it, Sali knew that was the truth. She knew Jiamin better than anyone.

In her heart, she knew his death hadn't been a mistake. Jiamin had struggled with his place as the Khan his entire life. The physical transformation that changed all who became Khan had twisted his mind and scarred his soul. The weight of living up to the title, the heavy weight of leadership, and the crushing responsibility, had overwhelmed and broken his gentle soul, so Jiamin found a way out, not considering the consequences of his actions. The destruction of their cities. The enslavement of their people. The extinction of their way of life.

All because he hadn't said no.

Sali closed her eyes again. She thought of Nezra, of her people, of her broken family tree, and then of Mali. Possibly the last of her line, the seed that would likely never sprout a sapling. Mali. Her sister was still alive. Out there in Zhuun lands. Sali's heart thundered in her chest as the seconds ticked by. Then her eyes blinked open. It all became so clear.

Sali embraced and kissed her oldest and dearest friend on the lips. "I know what I must do now. You didn't say no, but I can. I need to make this right. I'm sorry I can't join you, Jiamin. Not yet. You'll understand."

Sali turned and walked away from her final resting place. She pushed the doors open with a slam, startling Jhamsa and the shamans waiting on the other side.

The elder spirit shaman gaped. "Salminde, what are you doing? You cannot come out once you go inside. You must stay and fulfill your duty as a Will of—"

"I'm not finished yet," Sali replied, not looking back as she walked away from the temple. "I am declaring myself a Soul Seeker. I'm going to find the next Khan."

CHAPTER TEN

THE ESCAPE

Throughout her long, distinguished life, Taishi had learned, experienced, and accomplished much. She was the head of a rare and deadly war art and one of the foremost masters of her generation. She could glide across the air, crack stone with a single blow, and carry a whisper hundreds of feet away. She could kill most enemies with one arm—not that she had much of a choice. Her ability to cow her enemies with her skill and her cutting tongue was legendary. There were few things in this world that Taishi could not do.

One of them, it seemed, was starting a fire.

The sky was filled with storm clouds, and Taishi was in a sour mood. She didn't give a bitch's udder where the Queen and her damn children were in the sky. She had just spent most of the evening hidden in the shadow of a ledge surrounded by thorny pear trees that weren't bearing fruit, trying to bang two rocks together with only one hand. Two hours and not one spark.

Taishi hadn't been this frustrated since the time she spent a month stalking a Tiandi-monk-turned-serial-killer only to find out after she caught him that she had been following the wrong fat, bald man the entire time. Or the first time she'd met the Khan, and instead of fighting to the death, they had turned their duel into a staring contest, with both standing still for four hours. Wait, no, that encounter had been tense and exhilarating. That young, chiseled body. The diamond-black lagoons of his eyes . . .

Taishi pulled her mind back to the putrid, miserable, wet present and hurled the rocks away in disgust. If only she had learned a war art skill that could flare the oil in a person's body or cause the air to combust. One of her ex-lovers, the plump and fun-loving Chakan, had had that skill. The people west of Shulan duchy had developed a war art that was as exotic as the tattoos on their faces. He could ignite his entire arm and summon flickers of fire to orbit around his body. It was not a particularly powerful or useful ability, but it made for a great party trick. Except one night when he was drunk and showing off, he had burned down a high-ranking Lawkan official's summer home. Chakan had of course fled the Enlightened States, along with most of Taishi's possessions from the room they shared. That was the last time anyone had heard from him. As far as she was concerned, he was better off staying missing. The fourteen-year-old warrant for his arrest was still active, though that was the least of his concerns.

Taishi looked up as the puffy clouds overhead rumbled. The temperature had dropped precipitously since the King had settled in for the night. A few raindrops pattered the grass around her hiding place, a precursor of what was to come. Without a fire or a civilized place to sleep, she and Jian were bound for another miserable night.

She admitted she hadn't thought this plan through very well, if at all. To begin with, Faaru's warning had come almost too late. Taishi had barely made it to the grove in time, mainly because she had to stop to ask for directions on the way. She was very fortunate to have barged in on Jian's bodyguards when she had. Otherwise, she probably would . . . still be living in luxury at the Celestial Palace or accompanying Duke Saan, also probably in luxury, or back at the Cloud Pillars. Taishi clenched her teeth and stared soberly at the bed of twigs she had gathered. Now that she put it that way . . .

But Taishi *had* rescued Jian, and that was as far as she had thought ahead. She didn't have an escape plan ready: no provisions, no mounts, no place in mind to go, nothing whatsoever. For the past four days, she and Jian had fled northwest, in the general direction of the Cloud Pillars, but home was several hundred miles away, so it definitely was not a feasible destination. She just didn't know where else to go. Taishi was mildly surprised that they had eluded capture this long.

Her gaze settled on Jian's face. He looked so peaceful, almost innocent, as he slept under a blanket of damp moss—not the oblivious, spoiled, entitled brat that she found him when he was awake. She closed her eyes. That was unfair. It wasn't the boy's fault. He had been fed a diet of praise and lies his entire life.

Still, why had she risked her life and reputation to save him? The little ingrate had whined the entire time they'd been on the lam. So what if protecting a helpless boy from murderers was righteous. This wasn't a moral world. People died all the time. What was one more? Why did she have to let herself get dragged down with him?

She had tried to reason through it for much of their journey. Her head kept telling her that the boy was still important, regardless of whether the prophecy was actually finished. If the Khan truly was dead, then there was nothing left to do or say. But what if there was more to the prophecy, or if they had been interpreting it wrong all this time? Then it would be foolish to discard Jian. The dukes were being shortsighted, more focused on the expenses and the risk of having a legend walk freely. A living legend with a religion built around him would make a powerful enemy or an asset to a rival duke. None of them, with the exception of possibly Saan, had truly believed in the Tiandi Prophecy to begin with. They'd followed along only to please the old emperor and to appease the masses, especially the religious fanatics.

That wasn't why Taishi had saved him, however. What did she care about the dumb ramblings of old religious men who smoked too much opium? It didn't matter to her if it ever came true, or if it failed for that matter. Taishi could count the number of years she had left on her hands. Well, count them twice on her good hand. She had no surviving family or loved ones to cherish or protect. If she died tomorrow, a few other war artists might raise a cup, but that would be about it. That was all her legacy amounted to.

So why was she here, a damn fugitive in the cold, protecting a boy she honestly didn't even care for that much?

She hated to admit it, but the real reason—the only reason Taishi had killed those fraud masters and incurred the wrath of all five dukes of the Enlightened States—was Sanso. There was so much of Jian that reminded Taishi of her boy. Jian looked nothing like Sanso, but they shared so many similarities, even if many of them set her teeth on edge. Both were arrogant, entitled, and often sniveling, but both were also earnest, honest, and occasionally thoughtful. They also thought far too highly of their own abilities.

"You're the one getting soft, Taishi," she grumbled. "He's not Sanso, and nothing you do will ever make it right, so stop wasting your time."

The right thing to do, the smart thing, was to hand him over to the dukes and beg for mercy. Perhaps even plead her case to spare Jian. Surely the dukes would see the wisdom of keeping him alive for a while, just until everyone was sure the prophecy was truly dead. Most of the dukes would probably kill her for disobedience to set an example, but Saan might support her case. In the Enlightened States, the support of one duke was all anyone needed. It wasn't too late to fix things.

Jian shifted in his sleep. Taishi reached out to brush away a strand of errant hair tickling his nose. Jian's eyes fluttered open, and he stared at her outstretched hand. "What are you doing? You're not going to eat me, are you?"

"What? Shut up," she snapped. "Why would you say that?"

He scooted to a seating position. "You look hungry."

She *was* famished. "I don't eat spoiled eggs, but yes, I'm hungry. Come on, it's going to rain soon. We passed by a farm settlement a little way back. I want a roof over our heads tonight."

"What about the Mute Men?"

"What about them? Get moving, boy."

Jian reluctantly removed the cocoon of moss wrapped around him. He groaned and stretched his arms. His legs shook like those of a newborn calf taking its first steps when he stood. He took a deep breath and fell into a hack of coughing. Traces of black blood flew from his lips. His teeth chattered as he wrapped his hands around his body. "It's so cold here."

Taishi touched his forehead. It burned. His face was pale, and he was sweating. The boy was getting steadily worse. Dark-blue veins ran up his neck, across his chest, and down his arms and legs. The black blood would have killed him by now if it weren't for Taishi slowing its flow with the application of pressure and cloth tourniquets. It wasn't enough. The boy needed to see a real healer—one she hoped to find in that settlement.

As they backtracked, she kept an eye on Jian between watching the sky as the rain clouds grew darker and puffier and scanning the nearby trees and fields. He wasn't wrong: They did have to worry about the Mute Men. The dukes had sent a team of the Quiet Death to retrieve them, and she doubted they cared about what state she and Jian were brought back in.

She'd discovered the plot the first night when, while trying to buy a horse at a hunting lodge, she had overhead a few men talking about the Mute Men staying in one of the guest rooms above. They had quickly fled. On the third day—after she had hidden Jian in an abandoned earthen home and gone foraging for food—she discovered a pair of the Mute Men crossing the river. She'd barely gotten back to Jian in time to escape. It would be only a matter of time before they were found.

The rain began to come down just as the settlement came into sight. It was a small farming community with only six streets, surrounded by terraced rice fields. Taishi eyed the rows of squat houses with suspicion. Outside of the commanderies and large cities, most of the villages and settlements were similar to this one here. Small settlements were particularly dangerous: There were no strangers in those communities, so news of any visitors spread like syphilis in an army camp. The Mute Men would definitely have canvassed anyplace where people gathered and would have notified the local magistrates. The peasants would never dare tempt the wrath of the personal guards of the dukes of the Enlightened States.

Taishi preferred to stay as far from here as possible. She looked over at her ward as the wind picked up: Jian shivered uncontrollably and sucked in several quick, shallow breaths, his eyes glazed and his footsteps uneven. The sky had opened up, and rain was coming down in heavy sheets by the time they crossed the last rice field. She had to help keep him upright as they reached the first set of buildings. The rain was actually a blessing in disguise, giving her cover as she slowly hobbled her way out in the open. At the very least the boy needed a roof over his head, or he might not survive the night.

They found shelter under a long awning on one side of an unused pigpen. Jian groaned as she threw his arm around her shoulder and dragged him to a relatively dry corner that held several dirty bales of hay. She touched his forehead again. She had avoided people as best she could, but now she had no choice. There had to be someone at the settlement who could help him: a veterinarian or midwife or herbalist. She'd even settle for one of those idiot blood drainers if they knew anything about medicine.

"Stop being a baby," she muttered, laying him down.

Jian's eyes were closed, and his head lolled to one side.

"I'm going to find help," she said, unconvinced that was possible. "I'll be back as soon as I can."

No response came; Jian had already faded into unconsciousness. Taishi checked her surroundings and inched away onto the deserted street. In small communities, the inn served as the heart of the settlement. It was where travelers stayed and locals gathered for drinks and gossip. If she was going to find help, it would be there. At the very least she could get them something to eat.

She walked up and down the streets until she found a door with a faded sign that looked like the Zhingzi word for "food." She gritted her teeth and opened the door to find the crowded common room of an inn. Eight round tables and a bench on the far side were filled with farmers and some merchants chatting loudly, making the small room sound much larger than it actually was. The air was fragrant, the scent of garlic, ginger, oil, and cooked meats wafting from the kitchen, inevitably joined by the smell of cow shit and the sweat of a group of unwashed men packed tightly together.

Every set of eyes turned toward the door and stayed fixed on her for several seconds. Taishi did her best to look innocent and innocuous, like a little old lady, as she hunched a little lower and hobbled casually to the nearest unoccupied seat, which incidentally was on the far end of the room. When it became apparent where she was heading, the four farmers already sitting there quickly cleared away. So much for country hospitality.

Well, Taishi didn't want company anyway. She made herself comfortable and signaled to the plump man who looked like the owner. "Boss, over here." Out of the corner of her eye, she noticed that most were still staring. The jolly-looking plump man she'd signaled approached and threw down several brisk but awkward bows. "What can I do for you, madam?"

"Four plates of hot buns. Anything with meat. Banana leaf rice." She paused. "Toss in some sweet buns too, if you have any."

He fixed her with a narrow stare. "Do you have money?"

Taishi jingled out the strings of copper she had lifted from Jian's bodyguards. The innkeeper grudgingly signaled to an equally plump woman, who began weaving her way through the crowd.

The first basket that came to the table held sweet barbecue buns. The smell made Taishi's toes curl. She immediately stuffed one into her mouth. Next came egg yolk buns, then pork belly, lotus, yam, and then lastly red bean buns. Taishi stuffed them into her mouth nearly as fast as they were presented to her, saving one or two in each basket for Jian.

While she was stuffing her face, Taishi gestured to the innkeeper to lean in. It took a few tries before she could formulate the words with the food in her mouth. "Good boss. My grandson took ill on the journey here. You know, the rain, the cold, the bugs. Is there a healer in your fine community? I can pay." She jingled the strings again.

His eyes widened briefly, and then he bowed while shaking his head. "My deepest sorrows, madam, there are no healers in our humble settlement. The closest one would be in Jiayi, about six hours by wagon to the east. Please excuse me." The innkeeper retreated to deal with the other patrons. He spoke with a few of the younger field hands, and they stood up and left, relieving some of the crowdedness and foul smell.

Jiayi. One of Sunri's commanderies. That name sounded familiar, but Taishi wasn't sure from when or where. She hadn't even known they had wandered so close to Caobiu lands. Caobiu State was the smallest of the five, with only four commanderies, but it had by far the largest military. The military was, in fact, Caobiu's primary industry. Sunri loved counting soldiers, marching them to their deaths, and then drafting more. She really needed a better hobby. Every aspect of her state—military, cultural, societal—revolved around building a bigger and deadlier army. Taishi could be sure every heavily fortified commandery had their descriptions plastered over every guardhouse. Not exactly a welcoming situation for two fugitives.

Taishi beckoned for the innkeeper again. "Well, boss, if there isn't a healer here, would you by chance know anyone who can arrange transportation? He's very sickly."

The innkeeper shook his head too quickly. "I'm sorry, madam. The weather, you see."

This man's words were as fishy as his breath . . . Sharp words leaped to Taishi's tongue. She was about to give this egg-hatcher a lashing when she realized what was going on. She rolled her eyes and slapped the table. "You already fetched them, didn't you."

The innkeeper looked slightly abashed. "The Quiet Death came around searching for an older woman or a boy about fifteen. He gave the mayor a flare with orders to signal them the moment we see or hear anything." He shook his head. "We're just farmers, peaceful folks. We don't want any trouble, especially with the duchess. You understand."

She did. Sunri was well known for having long mastered the fine art of tyrannical despotism. Taishi tried to negotiate. "Can you at least hold off for a bit before shooting the flare?"

A loud sound followed by several smaller ones that were definitely not rain popped just outside the inn. A sharp, yellowish light illuminated the window. Taishi sighed. So much for that.

"Fine. How about you at least tell them we ran into the eastern woods?"

The look he gave her told her otherwise. "Sorry, madam. They'll cut our tongues out if they find out we lied."

"Thanks a lot." Taishi shot to her feet and consolidated the remaining buns into one basket.

"Excuse me, madam, the banana leaf rice will be out in a moment. Your total will be . . ." The innkeeper began to count.

She shot him a look of death and shouldered past him, daring anyone to stop her. No one did. As she headed for the door, the plump woman walked out of the kitchen with a plate of banana leaf rice. Taishi stopped and swiped that as well.

She burst out of the door and sprinted toward Jian's pigpen, hugging the buildings as she neared. Even with the rain, she could smell the sulfur from the flare. With luck, she could grab Jian and be far away before the Mute Men answered it.

Taishi had almost reached him when she saw a group of black-cloaked riders gallop into the settlement. She leaped and rode the wind onto an adjacent roof and flattened herself against the tiles, watching as the group circled and then split apart. Eleven Mute Men by her count. Technically four women among that bunch. Sexist bastards.

The mute *people* split up, some moving toward the other end of the settlement while four headed toward the inn. Two were left on the road adjacent to the pigpen where Jian was hiding. Taishi stayed still, watching for an opening.

None came.

The seconds ticked by. Taishi bided her time. In battle, only fools hurried, and they either learned or died learning. This was too many Mute Men, even for her, although truthfully, she didn't know how skilled Mute Men were in battle. She wasn't willing to test their abilities with Jian's life at stake.

Or perhaps this was a divine sign for her to leave while she still had her head on her body. Taishi had tried her best to protect the boy, but she didn't owe him anything. She had paid her dues to the Zhuun, lost the use of an arm for her efforts. Maybe the dukes were right all along. Maybe by killing the boy, they were taking a political pawn off the table and keeping peace throughout the Enlightened States. Maybe it was the dukes who were prudent and Taishi who was being unwise.

This could be her last chance to extract herself from this terrible situation. Throw herself at the mercy of the dukes. Maybe flee home and never show her face again. As long as they had the boy, what did anyone care about her? They would probably care enough to hang her if they caught her, but certainly not enough to hunt her down. After all, she hadn't done anything seriously wrong so far. In the dukes' eyes, killing the bodyguards and masters was only a minor infraction. It wasn't as if she had killed any of their Mute Men. There was no coming back from that. To strike a mute man was to strike a duke, and that could never be forgiven. The Mute Men were unrelenting. They would hunt her until her dying breath.

Taishi was tempted to take the easy way out. Just because you were one of the greatest war arts masters of your generation didn't mean you weren't full of self-doubt. She nearly caved in to her fears and was about to stand on the roof to surrender when Jian's sleeping face filled her mind, then began to blur—perhaps from her tears or the rain falling from the sky obstructing her vision—and was soon replaced by the face of another.

The two boys were similar in so many ways. Taishi had loved Sanso intensely and accepted his many flaws, because he was her boy and he was perfect. He was young, talented, and brash. He'd needed guidance and protection, not only from the world but from himself. Taishi, in her own blindness and pride, had failed her son in all the ways a mother could have failed. Now all she had were memories and regret, and no chance to undo all the mistakes she had made.

Until now. Taishi clenched her teeth. Here she was on the cusp of failing another boy who needed her guidance, a boy who was bad-tempered but who she knew in her heart had a good soul worth saving. She'd almost surrendered him just now—because she was too weak. She was not going to fail this boy. Not this time. Not with her ancestors judging her with their judging eyes.

She waited until both mute people—one was a woman—were look-ing away, and then she sent a cry on the wind and carried it well away from where she hid. She couldn't get it far—the heavy rain and winds hampered its movement—but it did the trick. Both mute people turned when they heard a woman's cry just at the edge of the near rice field.

Taishi stood and flew across the street on the torrential wind, in her haste nearly losing control and careening into a wooden wall adjacent to the pigpen. That would be a fantastic and humiliating way to die. She could imagine the snickers throughout the lunar court.

She managed to correct course and veer away from the wall, slip just under the awning, and crash into a stack of bales, sending an explosion of hay into the air. She spun to the ground and peered through the de-stroyed bales to see if the mute people had noticed her. Fortunately, the heavy rain had masked any noise from her botched landing. The mute people were still poking around the rice field, searching for the source of the voice she had sent dancing in the wind.

Taishi crept over to Jian, who hadn't moved. Fearing that she was going to find a corpse, she was relieved to feel breath, albeit faint, when she put a finger under his nose. She put a hand over his mouth and nudged him gently. "Jian, boy, wake up. We need to go. The Mute Men are here."

It took a few tries before he roused. Jian glanced at her with unfo-cused eyes, and then a smile broke out on his face. "Hey, Taishi, just the person I wanted to talk to. I . . . I have to tell you something." His words were slurred.

"Not now," she hissed. "We need to go. The Mute Men are here."

"I have to tell you something," he insisted. "It . . . it will only take a moment. It's important."

A growl climbed up her throat. They didn't have time for this. The boy was clearly delirious. "Fine, what is it? Quickly, please."

He pulled his mouth close to her ear. "I just . . . I just wanted you to know that I'm really sorry I tried to murder you."

That stopped Taishi in her tracks. It was the nicest thing Jian had said to her. It actually touched her heart, a little. She slapped him lightly on the face a few times. "That's nice. Now get up."

"I don't feel good."

"I don't care. We have to get out of here."

They crept the opposite direction from the two mute people, over the wooden gates and down the adjoining side street. Visibility was poor with the rain so heavy. Taishi waited several beats before dragging Jian across the road. They continued weaving from cover to cover toward the north end of the settlement before finally huddling between a shack and a giant rain-collector pot that was already overflowing.

The road leading out to the hills looked unguarded, but the fields in front were flat for several hundred yards. Taishi was tempted to make a break for it and hope for the best, but caution made her stay. Her patience was rewarded a few moments later when two more Mute Men rode past to the end of the street. There was little chance she or Jian could get away across any of the fields before they were seen and run down. They were trapped. It was only a matter of time before the Mute Men discovered them.

Unless she killed the Mute Men now—if she could. Taishi wasn't even sure. The Mute Men—mute people—had a secretive society. Most of their feats were shrouded in legends and rumors. Few knew how they fought because few survived the fights. Taishi admitted to being curious, almost eager, to test them, to see if these strange creatures were as good as their reputation. In any case, she might not have the choice to avoid confrontation.

Fight two now or possibly fight all eleven later, which was certain death. Taishi made her decision. With luck, they could steal the horses and ride away, then spend the rest of their lives looking over their shoulders—and that was the best-case scenario. *Maybe if—* A clicking sound distracted Taishi from her thoughts.

She nudged Jian in the ribs. "Be quiet. I can hear your teeth rattling from here."

"I can't stop it. I'm so cold and wet."

Taishi dug out a bun and stuffed it into his mouth. "Don't eat it all at once."

But of course he did. She didn't blame him, and gave him two more. "Try to make these last the next five minutes. Now follow me. We're going to creep along that ditch on the side of the road. I'm going to kill those two Mute Men, and then we take their horses and ride as fast as we can. Got it?"

She didn't wait for him to acknowledge as she crept forward, then sprinted across the muddy road and slid down into the ditch. The freezing water at the bottom reached her knees. She found her own teeth chattering soon enough as numbness crept up her legs. That was a problem.

Taishi looked back just in time to see Jian slide down and slip head-first into the water. He sputtered up a moment later. She put her finger to her lips and led him across the ditch. The slope was steep, so unless the Mute Men leaned over the side to look down, she and Jian should be able to move directly below them.

Once situated, she waited for the right moment. One quick distraction, and then—

Something tugged at her sleeve. She turned to face Jian. "What is it?"

"Can I help?"

"No, stay here."

"But—"

She put her hand over his mouth and peeked over the lip of the ditch. The two Mute Men had turned away toward someone approaching from the settlement. A moment later, she heard the sounds of hoofbeats and wooden wheels grinding. She hesitated, then climbed up to risk a better look as the Mute Men converged on a merchant dragging a wagon. This was unexpected. Why would anyone travel in this weather?

Now was the time to strike, but Taishi hesitated. Even if she caught them by surprise, she didn't like these odds. Chances were, if the fight lasted for more than a few seconds, the others would come. She waited as the Mute Men searched the wagon and then let the merchant proceed.

A new plan formed in her head. She waved for Jian to climb up the slope to join her. As the merchant's wagon neared their location, she sent a blast of air back toward the water collector she'd seen earlier, smashing the large pot with a loud crack and sending gushing water onto the ground.

As the Mute Men turned to investigate, Taishi pushed Jian out of the ditch. "Go!"

The two scampered up onto the road and raced to the wagon. The merchant had only a second to open his mouth before she dove behind him and jabbed a knife into the base of his spine. "Keep going. No one gets hurt."

The merchant had to be an experienced robbery victim. He stayed relaxed and continued on as if there was nothing the matter. The muddy stretch of road led them slowly around the bend and up a rolling hill. Taishi didn't relax the blade until the settlement was well out of sight.

She slipped the blade back in its sheath. "Thank you for not panicking, good man."

The merchant swiveled his head back. "I assumed you two weren't going to rob me. You're a little too old to be a bandit, yeah?"

Taishi really wanted to draw her knife on him again. She let it slide. "We mean you no harm. My grandson and—"

He held up a hand. "No, no, I don't want to know your name or anything about you. Let's just keep this relationship professional. I assume you two are the ones the Mute Men are after, so the less I know the better."

"Uh. What Mute Men?"

The merchant barked a laugh. "It makes no difference to me." He shrugged and turned back toward the road. "That's why I decided to leave that settlement at night during pouring rain. The Quiet Death make my skin crawl. Anyplace that has a bunch of those creepy things lurking about is not a place I want to be." He paused. "So now that I helped you escape, is there anything else you need, or can you get off my wagon?"

"We need a ride."

He sighed. "Where to?"

Taishi really had no idea. As usual, she hadn't thought ahead. She blurted out the first thing that came to mind. "Jiayi."

The merchant made a face. "That's the opposite direction. I don't suppose you'd settle for anywhere else. There's nothing there except the military complex and war arts schools. The market there is oversaturated, and the army always pays less than half market value. I still have twelve bags of rice and five crates of bitter melons to unload. Look, I'm heading to Chenshi. It's two days' ride but I'll drive you all the way there."

"The boy won't last." That was when a long-forgotten memory about Jiayi resurfaced. Every time Taishi heard about that commandery, it reminded her of something. Not something, someone. The old memory bubbled to the surface: Guando or Guanno, something like that. It was a long time ago and she hadn't really been into him, but it was a lead. She shook her head. "No, we need to go to Jiayi."

"Can I refuse?"

"I can still stab you in the back."

"Madam, this is a very poor show of gratitude."

She shrugged. "The boy is sick." Taishi decided to try another tactic. "If you take us there, you'll be handsomely rewarded."

The farmer gave her a distrusting stare. "Is that true?"

She shrugged again. "Maybe. Wouldn't it be nice if it were?"

The merchant sighed. "Very well."

A large crunch sounded behind them. Both turned to see Jian wading through a bag of pears. He looked up, wide-eyed, an entire pear stuck in his mouth.

"Hey," shouted the merchant. "What happened to not robbing me?"

It took most of the night for the wagon to reach Jiayi. Taishi buried Jian and herself under several sacks of rice between a few baskets of cabbage and three crates of bitter melons. Jian's condition continued to worsen with the chill and wet. He was running a fever, and his lips had turned a shade of purple. His breathing was labored. Taishi pressed his body close to hers for warmth as the wagon jostled them with every rock and hole on the muddy road. Even though she was exhausted, she feared falling asleep, wondering if she would wake next to a corpse.

Taishi checked Jian's pulse. "Just a little longer, boy. Don't you dare give up now."

This tight little space in the back of a wagon reminded Taishi all too much of another journey she had taken a lifetime ago, vastly different but also hauntingly similar: not a merchant's wagon, but a funeral wagon. Sanso, cold to the touch like Jian, had lain peacefully on the wooden table, looking almost asleep. Taishi had lain beside her boy all the way to the burial site. That too had been an uncomfortable, bumpy ride.

Taishi dozed off much sooner than she intended. The merchant probably could have killed them or had them arrested at any time. She woke to sharp voices nearby, guards obviously, and was pleasantly surprised to find that she was still free. For now.

The merchant was speaking rapidly with what sounded like two or three guards. Were they at a checkpoint? Had they arrived at Jiayi? Had he driven them straight to a Caobiu garrison to collect his reward? *Was* there even a reward for her and Jian's capture? Truthfully, she would feel awfully offended if there wasn't. She squirmed. Their wagon was not quite full. It certainly would not hold up to any degree of scrutiny if the guards came poking about.

The seconds ticked by. Taishi half expected the merchant to betray her. She had hijacked his wagon. To her mild surprise, one of the guards said, "Welcome to Jiayi. Stay out of trouble." They began to move again.

A little while later, the sack of rice that covered them was removed. The merchant's scraggly face appeared. "You're here. Can you get out of my wagon now?"

Taishi was tempted to make him take her to find who she was looking for, but even her shamelessness had its limits. She scrambled out of the wagon and slung Jian across her back. "Thank you, good man. I'm sorry to have forced you."

He waved his hands. "It's all right. I understand why. I have two young sons myself. Your boy looks like he's on his deathbed. I hope he makes it." He looked around, resigned. "I don't suppose that reward you offered actually exists."

"I'm afraid not," she replied. "If you leave me your name and address..."

The merchant quickly waved his hands. "No offense, madam, but the Mute Men are after you. I would rather not have my name anywhere on your person."

"Understood." Taishi offered him a deep bow. "You are a good man."

He nodded. "I guess that will have to be my reward."

And that was the end of that. Taishi began her search for her acquaintance-she-wasn't-that-into from long ago. It didn't take long for her to find him. There were dozens of war arts schools in Jiayi, and they all advertised. It took Taishi just a quick scan before the memory returned. The man's name was actually Guanshi, and he owned a small but reputable war arts school at the eastern edge of the Rose Ridge District several gates over. Taishi cursed every step of the way as she carried the sleeping Jian on her back through the narrow and dirty streets.

Like many military cities, Jiayi looked more like a fortress, which was typical of commanderies, which were administration hubs for the surrounding region. Jiayi was divided into districts, each sectioned off by tall walls for defense. All of the buildings were packed tightly together, split by wide main streets and a maze of narrow alleyways. The King had not risen yet, but there was enough predawn light to guide her through the mostly empty streets, even with the paint on the street signs mostly peeled off. The only other people out seemed to be errand boys fetching water or picking up supplies.

Taishi crossed a bridge spanning an open sewer, then passed an alley littered with bodies slumped against the walls. The smell of the commandery reminded her why she hated urban areas in general. The worst of everything—actual shit being the least of the worst—was always dumped onto the streets.

The King was just peeking over the horizon when Taishi and Jian reached a walled-off school with a large sign in red letters emblazoned over large double doors: LONGXIAN NORTHERN FIST SCHOOL OF WAR. Underneath it, in smaller letters: EMPLOYMENT GUARANTEED AFTER GRADUATION. COME FOR A FREE TRIAL CLASS.

"Free trial class, my bony backside," she muttered. "How pathetic."

Taishi laid Jian down at the shadow of the doorway, and then she tried to jump over the outer wall of the school. It took her two tries to clear it, the first failing pitifully as her sore muscles refused to respond properly. Even on the second attempt, her foot slipped on the tiles of the narrow roof on top of the wall. Her knees cracked several clay tiles and knocked them loose as she began to fall. She managed to claw onto the spine of the roof. When she rolled off to land inside the wall, she nearly smashed her head on a planter.

This was not Taishi's finest hour.

Groaning, she pushed herself to her feet and removed the wooden bar locking the front gate, then pulled Jian inside. "You stay here," she said between deep breaths. "I'll go wake . . ." The master's name escaped her again. "Whatever his name is." It had been so brief and so long ago, you could hardly fault her.

Taishi stood up, turned to the inner courtyard, and barely ducked a looping piece of wood swinging for her head. She retreated as a young man wielding a three-sectional staff followed up his attack with several more flurries, each narrowly missing their mark.

The three-sectional staff was an uncommon weapon. Made from three pieces of wood linked together at the ends, it was very difficult to master. In Taishi's opinion, if there was one weapon more worthless than double straight swords, it was the three-sectional. To her surprise, this young man was very skilled with it. Plus, Taishi was exhausted, which made their melee somewhat competitive. Not really.

Their exchange continued for several more seconds. Three-sectionals were tricky weapons to fight, with unpredictable attacks that could come from many angles. Her assailant's arms also seemed to blur as he moved, making it even more difficult for Taishi to track. Either it was the young man's jing at work or her eyes were going bad. Oh yes, this was one of Guan-Something-Man's Longxian traits. Taishi found an opening a moment later when he tried to trap her crippled arm in a lock with his weapon.

The young man frowned when he didn't get his desired result. Taishi took the opportunity to grab one of the sticks and bop him on the head, just enough to hurt. The young man stumbled back, rubbing his forehead.

He glowered and reset his stance. "You made a big mistake, thief."

Taishi's sharp retort died in her throat. She hated herself for doing this, but to save time and possibly Jian's life, she decided to borrow a line from that merchant. "Boy, I am way too old to be a thief. Now go wake Guanning."

The young man looked confused.

"Guanpi, Gongshi." She gave up. "Your master. Go wake your damn master. Get moving."

He got moving.

CHAPTER ELEVEN

A FRESH START

Jian remembered Master Luda death-punching him in the chest, his veins feeling like they were scalding in hot oil. Everything was hazy after that. To be honest, part of him felt he owed his former master an apology: No one ever believed any war artist who claimed to know some form of death punch. Out of all his masters, only Luda had boasted that knowledge, and the rest had teased him relentlessly about it. Being on the receiving end of a death touch was a pretty awful way to confirm its existence.

He had faded in and out of consciousness for most of their escape from the Celestial Palace. He did recall being tired and cold, and distinctly remembered Taishi prodding him with her fingers regularly. She had explained in one of his rare moments of lucidity that she was using pressure points to slow the flow of bad blood and to prevent his jing from getting poisoned. Whatever that meant.

The rest of his memory of their flight from the palace was a collection of flashes, waking dreams that may or may not have actually happened: being pulled underwater, unable to breathe, for several minutes. Feeling his skin burn as if on fire while lying in moss during a thunderstorm. Asking Taishi if he was going to die, and being told that only stupid people die. He wasn't sure if she'd just been trying to make him feel better, but it hadn't helped.

Lastly, he remembered apologizing to Taishi for trying to kill her, and then falling into a ditch. One of those had definitely happened; he wasn't sure which. He drew a complete blank after that, the world alternating between freezing and burning, as if he had died and neither afterworld wanted him so they kept tossing him back and forth.

After what felt like an eternity of that hot and cold, Jian's eyes suddenly opened with a start as ice coursed through his body. He tried to move, but found his wrists restrained. He tried to sit up, but strong hands held him down. He opened his mouth to scream. Someone stuck a cloth into his mouth. He screamed anyway.

Jian struggled for a while before his eyes finally adjusted to the dim light. An old woman—another old woman who was not Taishi—hovered close by. She was palming his jaw and staring straight into his eyes. Then she turned to a young woman on the other side of Jian. "Keep his head straight before he blinds himself."

What, blind who? Him? Jian began to thrash even more, until the woman raised her palm and smacked him on the nose as if he were a bad dog. "Stop it." Jian's eyes watered; he did as he was told.

The woman wore what looked like a white nightgown. No, a black-collared white robe that fell all the way to the floor. Sitting on top of her head like a crown was a plain black cap that pulled her forehead back. The woman on the other side was also dressed in white, wearing what looked like a matching white cook's apron. Her headdress was just a plain white wrap holding together a plume of black curly hair that exploded outward in all directions from the top of her head.

Jian focused his attention back on the older woman, who had suddenly produced several needles, each as long as his finger. She began running them one by one under an open flame. His eyes bulged. Was she going to poke those things into him? He tried to scream through the cloth in his mouth, to little effect, and then he began to gag.

"Be careful," snapped the woman. "What did I tell you about pushing the rag in too deep? He's going to choke."

"Sorry, master."

The woman looked irritated. "Never mind. We'll do this the easy way."

She plucked one of the needles between her fingers and stabbed Jian right between the eyes. She stuck several more in him in rapid succession, sticking him on the crown of the forehead, his temples, his eyebrow, and several points under his jaw and on his nose. Her hands moved so fast he barely managed to utter a cry of protest. A few seconds later, his face went numb and his cheeks sagged. His jaw locked up and he lost all sensation in his face.

"Now," said the woman, studying his eyes from different angles. "This isn't going to feel good." *Wait, what?* Worse than he already felt?

Jian tried to tell her not to do whatever she was going to do, but the sound seemed trapped in his chest. He was completely helpless.

The woman held a very large needle in each hand. She held them close to his face, then stabbed him in the eyes. "Not feeling good" was an understatement. Jian's head exploded as if he had just been smashed by ten of Luda's death touches. It was an *interesting* experience, suffering so much pain with his body unable to express it. So Jian screamed internally for what felt like hours before he finally passed out from exhaustion.

He wasn't sure how long he was out, but when he woke again, everything was completely dark. He still couldn't move and he still couldn't scream, but at least his hearing still functioned perfectly.

"Will he survive, master acupuncturist?" That was definitely Taishi's voice.

The needle woman replied. "Perhaps. We will know more by morning. The poison had already seeped into his liver and kidneys. Fortunately, his jing is strong—unnaturally strong, in fact. Who is he to you? How did you come by him?"

"Just a boy I found and took pity on."

The acupuncturist did not sound convinced. "We'll know more about the boy's health within the next day or so. Either he'll be sitting up begging for food or you'll be paying for a funeral ceremony. I'll leave my apprentice here to watch over him."

A man's voice joined the conversation. "Thank you, Doctor Kui. I apologize again for the way Xinde woke you in the middle of the night. I assure you it won't happen again, and I will pay for a new window."

"Your senior was quite emphatic, Master Guanshi. It was understandable. That boy's life was measured in hours when I reached him. But I am charging you for this session. This was difficult work, and far outside our retainer agreement."

"I see." Guanshi did not sound pleased. "Master Nai, can you pay the acupuncturist?"

"No," Taishi replied curtly.

A brief silence passed.

"Fine," muttered Guanshi. "Speak with Zhaosun before you leave."

"You are a paragon of virtue and generosity, noble master," replied Master Kui. "Now pay attention, apprentice. Monitor the patient's temperature. If any part of his body turns purple, relieve the pressure. Six needles to the kidneys. If he gets cold, three to the heart and then to his major meridians to open his pathways. If there are any more symptoms of the black blood, or if his skin gets hot, send for me immediately. Don't try to cure it on your own, understand?"

"Yes, master," a high-pitched voice replied. "I will look after him like I would my own mother."

The master acupuncturist snorted. There was more shuffling and goodbyes, then fading footsteps. Jian thought he was alone again, but then a hushed conversation began.

The man asked. "So who is he really, Taishi? Is he yours?"

"Don't be absurd. Like I said. Just a boy I took pity on. We were attacked while on the road."

"No common brigand knows a death touch. Which style?"

"It doesn't matter, Guanshi. Are we agreed?"

"You ask for much, and offer little in return."

"I guess I haven't changed much over the years, then. Thank you, Guanshi. I see you've done well for yourself. This school looks prosperous."

"Business has been good. But look at you, a legendary master under the lunar court."

"Legendary and poor. I'd much rather just be rich."

"Perhaps. It's . . . it's good to see you again, Taishi."

"Shut up, Guanshi."

Their voices trailed off, and then Jian was truly alone again. The sounds around him were the only indication that time was passing: muffled voices and wood creaking, birds singing outside the window, and crickets chirping at night.

He dreamed again, but this time his mind took him somewhere else. There was a stranger with a scar across his lip. A bald woman with almond-colored skin and large eyes and a scream that never ended. He remembered being happy, then being alone. Then he blinked and the world faded. The next thing he saw was Horashi, his earliest memory and his earliest friend. His faithful and trusted guardian who tried to kill him.

Jian blinked one last time and found himself on the streets, begging for coin. The image from the water in a wooden bowl by his feet betrayed a face aged with wear, deep lines reflecting a difficult life. A useless one.

He continued to slip in and out of different levels of consciousness. Sometimes he dreamed that he was awake, other times he dreamed that he was dreaming. When awake, he would listen and then sleep, wake and sleep again. After either the fifth or sixth time he fell asleep in darkness, he finally opened his eyes to light.

His vision was blurry. He saw nothing but blots of brown, green, and white. Something blue and very bright began to fill the space, poking into his head like tiny knives. He opened his mouth and flinched when dryness cut into his throat. Jian struggled to get his bearings. Slowly, his eyes focused.

He was in a plain room. Wooden sliding doors. A wall with a row of windows along the ceiling. To his right was a small table. On the table was a plain water pitcher. Jian focused immediately on that. His throat throbbed. The girl in the white robe was sitting there, dozing, with her head resting on her arms. Her apprentice cap was resting on its side next to her, revealing cascading curls of black hair splayed across the table.

"Water." The words barely escaped his lips. "Water."

The girl didn't budge.

He would have to fetch it himself. Jian tried to sit up and was surprised to find that his wrists were no longer bound. He inched his way up into a sitting position and reached for the pitcher. His fingers had nearly managed to curl around the handle when he tipped over and fell off the bed.

This time his groan was definitely audible. At least he could feel his face again. "Hey," he managed to say, his voice hoarse. "Help. Girl, water."

The girl's eyes fluttered open and she raised her head. The apprentice acupuncturist appeared roughly Jian's age, with delicate features and pale skin. She yawned and glanced at the empty bed, and then her gaze lowered to Jian sprawling on the floor. "The name's not 'Girl.' It's Meehae." She closed her eyes again.

Jian tried to grab on to the table and pull himself up, but his arms and legs weren't cooperating. He gave up. "Water. I need water, Meehae."

Her eyes remained closed. "Do I look like a servant, boy?"

"You're not a very good doctor. You're supposed to take care of me."

"You're alive, aren't you?"

It took Jian several seconds before figuring out the magic phrase. "Please, Meehae, can you get me some water?"

Her eyes opened again, and her entire face brightened. "Sure." She reached over and handed him the pitcher.

Jian gulped it greedily, water pouring down his neck and chest. He nearly forgot to breathe while he was drinking and slumped onto the side of the bed after he emptied the pitcher, his chest heaving. "I needed that. Help me up."

Meehae looked down at him, her eyebrows furrowed. "And you were doing so well."

"Please."

She grabbed him by the arm and helped him back to the bed. He was about to collapse back down on the pillow when she held him tightly by the shoulder. "Gently. You still have forty-six needles all over your face and body."

"What?"

"How do you think you're still alive? Master Kui drained the poison from your body and purified your jing." She felt his forehead and adjusted some of the needles. "You're still feverish. Let me fix that."

"Didn't your master tell you to get her if my skin is hot?"

Meehae nodded, and stuck him anyway. Jian yelped and flinched with every poke, but whatever she was doing worked. The chill quickly subsided and he felt better. His vision eventually cleared as she adjusted the needles on his face. The apprentice acupuncturist was diminutive, with a young face and typical Zhuun features: a fair complexion, a slightly disheveled nest of curly black hair under her apprentice cap, and a small nose and bright wide eyes accentuated by a pair of wired spectacles. A smattering of freckles dotted her cheeks, and her eyebrows furrowed every time she squinted, which was quite often.

She was still fussing with him when another figure appeared at the doorway. "So he lives. Three days to come back to the land of the living. You lose, Meehae."

"The third doesn't count until the King is on his descent. You're the one who owes *me* lunch," Meehae shot back good-naturedly, sticking her tongue out. It may have been the light, but her face had turned a shade darker. She sounded flustered, her words picking up speed.

"I don't recall the exact parameters of our arrangement, so I will trust your fine memory." The young man grinned. "Besides, it is always a good idea to be kind and generous to the person who patches you up."

Meehae gestured to Jian. "Something you can teach this egg here."

"I'm sure he will soon enough, if what I hear is true." The young man looked out the door. "Hey, Gwaiya, tell Master Nai that he's awake."

"Yes, senior," a girl replied.

"You guys made a bet on my death?" Jian felt a little offended by this. *And who is Master Nai?*

The young man who walked into the room was tall and broad-shouldered and had an air of confidence. His face was long and narrow, with a distinctly square jawline and strong eyes that seemed to demand all the attention in the room. Jian wasn't sure if he should be annoyed or intimidated by someone so good-looking, but all he felt was a strange subconscious urge to be the young man's friend.

The young man squatted down until he was eye level with Jian and bowed, touching a fist to his opened palm. "We're glad you pulled through, friend. My name is Xinde. I am the first senior of the Longxian War Art Academy. You must be hungry."

"I'm fine," he mumbled. He really wasn't. He was starving and still thirsty, but something about Xinde's perfect teeth, bright smile, and friendly demeanor made Jian deeply insecure.

Xinde looked puzzled. "I still don't understand why anyone would death-touch you. That is very high-level."

For some reason, that rubbed Jian the wrong way. Why, was he not worth the effort to kill? "I'll have you know you're addressing the Hero—"

"Hiro," said Taishi, storming into the room. The look she shot him was enough. He shut up while she pretended to dote over him. "I was worried your fever would never break. You're looking better already. You had your auntie Nai worried sick. I expect you to be walking soon." In case he didn't get the hint, she pinched him hard on the arm. A whisper on the wind spoke into his ear. "Don't let them know who you are. I was going to say your name is Lu Hanhuo, but Lu Hiro will do. Now shut up and play along."

"Much better," said Jian slowly. "Thank you, Master . . ."

"Nai, dummy," the whisper hissed again.

". . . Nai," Jian finished.

"Apprentice Meehae, would you be so kind as to fetch your master?" asked Taishi. "And Senior Xinde, could you please ask your master to join us as well?"

The apprentice acupuncturist bowed. "Yes, Master Nai. Make sure he doesn't disturb the needles on his face."

The moment they were alone, Taishi grabbed Jian's shoulders. "Listen to me carefully, boy. I can't protect you anymore. From this point on, no one can know who you are. Being invisible, a nobody, will be the only thing that can save your life."

"You're not staying with me?" For some reason, that broke Jian's heart.

Taishi shook her head. "I can't, Jian. The Quiet Death will not give up. I need to lead the Mute Men away. You need to stay hidden here, where it's safe."

"But you said you were going to be my master."

Taishi looked away. For a moment, honest pain flashed on her face. "I know. I'm sorry. It's no longer possible. Guanshi can teach you war arts. He is a good man."

"But I want *you* to teach me."

"It's probably for the best. I'm a terrible master anyway."

"No! That is simply not true."

For the first time that he could remember, emotion racked Taishi's face. She wrapped her hand around his head and pulled him in close. "Don't be stupid, boy. You are your own person now. No prophecy to control you, no walls to lock you in. You have a second chance now. Be free, Jian."

Tears welled in Jian's eyes. He began to sob. "I'm sorry I wasn't good enough."

"That's not it. It was never your fault, boy." Taishi appeared to change her mind. Even during an emotional exchange she had to be bluntly honest. "I mean, well, you need work, son, but that's beside the point. But look, you can now carve out your own life. Create your own destiny."

"But I want to stay with you," he pleaded. "Please don't leave me. Everyone else in my life has. You're the only person I have left."

A set of footsteps grew louder just outside the room.

Taishi whispered to him furiously. "I'll check up on you often. I promise. Now listen carefully. No matter what, no one must know who you are. As far as anyone is concerned, you are a runaway farm boy who lived on the streets. You do not know any war art, so you must not under any circumstances show any skill. You are a complete novice. Do you understand? Your life depends on it."

A tall man near Taishi's age arrived in the room. He was obviously the master of this school, with a plump, soft face and extremely thick eyebrows. His white hair, pulled back and tied in a neat bun on top of his head, matched his white robe.

The master nodded at Taishi and then sat down next to Jian. "Hello, boy."

Why did everyone keep calling him boy?

"I am Master Guanshi Kanyu. I am known by most as just Guanshi," the man continued. "Master . . . Nai has informed me that you wish to study at the Longxian War Arts Academy. She says you cannot pay but will be willing to earn your keep as an indentured servant. Your chores will be to work in the kitchen during meals, launder the clothes every night, and maintain the grounds. You will obey the masters, seniors, and servants, and do all that is asked of you, anything that the school requires. It will be a hard life, but a worthwhile investment for your future. In ten years' time, you will be released from your indenture. Do you agree to the terms?"

Jian wasn't sure what indenture was, but he didn't like the sound of this one bit. He was about to object when something flicked him hard in the ear. He flinched, but there was nothing there. Taishi was standing on the opposite side of the room, looking off into space.

"Yes, Master Guanshi," Jian replied hesitantly, "I do."

"Very well then. What's your name?"

Jian, head still groggy and confused, struggled through his many names. "Lu, Lu Ji . . . Lu Hiro, master."

"Initiate Lu Hiro, come forth and bow to your master."

Jian recoiled at the order. He bowed to no one. His gaze flitted to Taishi again, who now stared at him expectantly. Wen Jian bowed to no one, but Lu Hiro was a nobody, a street rat, a runaway farm boy who kowtowed to everyone. Jian bit down on his lips and clenched his teeth as he dropped to his knees. He stared at his new master for several moments before throwing his head down to the floor. "Master Guanshi."

ACT II

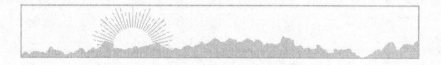

CHAPTER TWELVE

INTERMISSION

An elderly couple appeared at the doorway to the prayer hall, their silhouettes casting long shadows. Lee Mori squinted as they contributed to the offering vase. The pair looked familiar, regulars wearing the same Tenth Day Prayer best that they had worn for decades. He should have known their names, but with things the way they had been recently, he had too much else on his mind.

He ransacked his memory right up to the moment they puttered up to him, bowing deeply. "Holy day, Templeabbot."

Mori pressed his palms together and went with his default. "Welcome faithful Children of the Tiandi."

After a few yawn-inducing pleasantries about the weather and the crops and something about new and old life and being one with heaven, the pair continued to the large Celestial Mosaic of the Tiandi—heaven, earth, and hell—at the end of the hall, where they picked their colored incense sticks from the three rows of vases arranged on the left wall. The man chose gray, the woman copper and green. He was sick. She was praying for luck and a plentiful harvest. The two knelt before the mosaic to pray in low tones, occasionally bowing and shaking the incense.

Mori gestured to the nearby initiate. "Bring cushions for those devout."

The initiate, leaning against a column gazing off into nothing, stared blankly for several beats before replying. "Yes, Templeabbot." When he finally got moving, it was languidly and almost as slowly as the elderly couple. A disapproving rumble grew inside Mori's throat. Six months ago, he would have taken a switch to the boy's backside for such insolence. The world had been a vastly different place six months ago.

The couple were only on their second prayer, and Mori had been a Tiandi monk long enough to accurately judge how much time most devout needed in front of the mosaic. These two were going to take a while, so he took the opportunity to step out from the shade and into the warmth of the King's light.

The winter months brought strong gusts from the mountains down to the plateaus. It didn't help that the oversized roof caught many of the air currents and funneled them into the building, creating a wind tunnel through the prayer hall. The draft chilled the bones and wreaked havoc on the hundreds of candles that needed to stay burning during the entire Tenth Day Prayer. The initiates waged a constant, losing battle to keep them all lit. The architect of this prayer hall must have either never considered the necessities of the Tenth Day Prayer ceremonies or been a sadist.

Mori strolled to the entrance of the hall and exchanged nods with Solum, the Hansoo brother guarding the entrance, or more specifically the offering vase. "How fare we today?"

Solum glanced down into the vase's belly and replied with a grunt.

Mori offered a wry smile. "We may have to cut back on rations."

The massive war monk raised one of his hands, as big as another man's head, and curled it into a fist.

"For the initiates, of course," Mori added quickly. He patted the war monk's shoulder, jingling the dozen iron rings wrapped around his forearm, and continued outside. Spring of the second cycle had finally arrived, and with it rain showers, receding snows, and new life. The greenery on the temple grounds was already shifting with the weather. The trees lining the perimeter of the monastery had just entered their bloom. The stiff breezes from the mountains shook the branches, launching flurries of cherry petals into the air, showering the temple grounds with pink and white confetti. A family of geese was frolicking in the pond and a pair of cranes, lovers, glided elegantly in the air on their expansive wings.

Beautiful days like this were rare, and could not have been painted more perfectly by the divine. Mori admired the sparsely peopled temple grounds as a long, deep sigh escaped his lips. "Everything has gone to shit."

The Tenth Day Prayer used to be an all-day affair, sometimes lasting well into the night. Six months ago, the left half of the temple grounds would have been packed with devout commoners, forming a line that would snake up and down and then out the front gates. The right side would hold a slightly smaller but equally busy line of businessmen, merchants, the educated and skilled. These well-to-dos could afford the line's minimum donation requirements and enjoyed a faster trip to the prayer hall. The nearest line, set behind the row of cherry trees, was reserved for nobility, those who not only had the means to afford speed, but also held positions and ranks of influence.

Now there was no need for lines at all. These days the temple was lucky if Tenth Day Prayer lasted past noon. Mori glanced at the water clock hanging off the pole in the center of the grounds. In today's case, it had barely lasted two hours past opening gong. If this drastic drop in the numbers of the devout—and more important in their donations—could happen here in the Temple of the Tiandi in Vauzan, the capital of Shulan, the most pious duchy, then it was surely happening everywhere else in the Enlightened States.

Mori was musing about the death of his religion when he was interrupted by the sound of giggling children. He looked down the stairs at a large family with the five children babbling excitedly as they made a game of chasing one another up and down the steps. He grimaced. It was all he could do not to look even more downtrodden. Their parents, minor nobility by the looks of their attire and by the fact they could afford to keep this many children alive and fed, laughed along as a hapless nurse tried to corral the gaggle.

The children rushed straight past Mori to Solum. The Hansoo were always the most popular attraction with children. How could the plain regular monks, or even the templeabbot, compete with these giant, muscular war monks with their iron rings jingling on those tree-trunk arms? This was the reason why the Hansoo were positioned so prominently during public ceremonies next to the offering vase. Where children gathered, their parents, preferably with coin, soon followed.

Mori watched as the parents caught up with their brood. The annoyed mother flippantly gestured to the nurse to gather her flock like a shepherd, while the father made a modest donation. Mori sniffed at the coin pincher, his lips pursed and eyes lowering after the nobleman as he hastened back to his family. They passed him without so much as a bow. Mori didn't mind being ignored by the nobility. The wealthy demonstrated their devotion to the Tiandi with their large donations, while the poor showed theirs with piety.

As the abbot of the temple, the latter was what Mori cared about. A small voice in his head chastised him for such blasphemy, but that didn't make it any less true, especially in these . . . interesting . . . times. What had once been a celebrated, almost required, event, the Tenth Day Prayer was now an afterthought for all save the most pious. He did what he could to keep the business of the Tiandi religion in order. As the templeabbot, he was responsible for three dozen monks, twice that number of initiates, and two Hansoo brothers. Over the past few months, there had been a record number of desertions. It was up to him to be the rock that the waves of uncertainty broke upon in these trying times.

After spending most of the day shepherding the few devout, Mori retired to the temple heart sanctum. Calling his residence a sanctum was a bit ambitious, but it was tradition for templeabbots to reside at the centers of their temples. The heart sanctum was little more than a sitting room, a prayer room, and a bedroom-office. The heart sanctum in the Vauzan temple was spacious for a monk, but modest by secular standards.

He paused at his drinks cabinet and examined his collection of floral and fruit-flavored waters. These were one of the few indulgences he allowed himself in his otherwise austere life. He plucked and sniffed the lemon-water and salak decanters before deciding against both. None spoke to him this evening; this was just one of those days when his mind demanded a stiffer drink. Again with these errant thoughts. Blasphemy seeped into his mind more frequently of late.

No sooner had he sat down at his desk than Tuhan, the pillow-retrieving initiate who was being notably more disciplined, knocked on the door and entered. The young man was moving quickly as he gently placed the offering vase on Mori's desk. He palmed his hands together and bowed fervently. Mori had taken the time earlier to give the boy a stern talking-to and made him stand on his knees facing the corner, as punishment.

"Is there any other way I can serve the Tiandi, Templeabbot?" the initiate asked, standing taller than before.

Mori hid his smile by focusing on the papers at his desk. "The prayer hall?"

"Mopped and polished. The candles have been put away and the incense vases refilled."

"The grounds?"

"Swept and cleaned." The initiate added, "Brothers Nan and Gramo were kind enough to assist me."

Not giving credit to his friends would have earned him another switching. Mori pulled the vase closer. "You are finished for the night, but you are assigned kitchen duties at dawn—" He sniffed and glanced up, his eyes narrowing. His anger roiled. "Have you broken with the Tiandi, initiate?" It wasn't a question. Mori's look dared him to lie.

"I . . ." Tuhan's face whitened. "I . . . Brother Nan returned from his errand with some plum wine. I—"

Mori silenced him with his narrowed eyes. To behave insolently because of these circumstances was one thing; to break the Vow of Abstinence was a level worse. His hand reflexively reached for the spare switch he kept behind his desk.

Tuhan dropped to his knees as tears streamed down his face. "Forgive me, Templeabbot. Things have just been so difficult these past few months, ever since the prophecy was proven to be a lie. I feel so lost. I don't know what to believe anymore." The young man dissolved into a fit of long sniffs and body-racking sobs.

Mori gripped the switch tightly. He knew exactly how Tuhan felt. If an abbot who had pledged his life's work to the Tiandi could feel this doubt, what chance did an initiate have? He put the switch down. "I understand your struggle. These are difficult times for the Tiandi. We must hold on to our faith and trust in the divine's plans."

"But . . . but the broken prophecy . . ."

"You think too much about the outcome of the prophecy, my child, when you should be focusing on its path," said Mori gently. "The Prophecy of the Tiandi is a tool. The divine used it as a beacon to unite our people. The prophecy guided us to victory against our enemies. If the purpose of the Tiandi is to raise the Zhuun and bring them together, then it has already succeeded beyond measure."

"You mean, it doesn't matter that the Eternal Khan was not killed by the Champion of the Five Under Heaven?"

Mori nodded. "The prophecy's original purpose has been fulfilled. The Enlightened States are victorious and stand as the center and envy of the world. What the prophecy offers us now is another opportunity to lift ourselves closer to the Tiandi. Enlightenment is forged through failure."

"Victory is earned through defeat," Tuhan recited. The initiate's face slowly changed from puzzlement to incredulity to awe. "So the Tiandi intentionally broke the prophecy. The failure of the prophecy is not a failure at all, but a test for the devout?"

Something like that.

At this point, Mori wasn't sure what to believe anymore, but a good monk had to empathize with the people's fears and anxieties while a good abbot had to manipulate them, and Mori was one of the best. He placed a comforting hand on the initiate's shoulder. "The Tiandi has offered you the opportunity to turn your weakness into strength. I want you to go to Brothers Nan and Gramo. Show them the strength of the devout. Retrieve their sinful spirits and bring them to me."

"I will, Templeabbot, I will. Thank you, thank you." Tuhan bowed profusely. "I will rise from this! I will not fail you again!"

The initiate ran off. He returned a short while later with his drinking companions in tow. The three were carrying seven gourds of plum wine and two drinking urns. Mori had to suffer through the three throwing themselves at his feet, begging forgiveness and pledging to walk in the path of the Celestial Family something-something. He had to cover the growing smirk on his face. He may have been a senior and the temple-abbot of one of the grandest temples in the Enlightened States, but that didn't make him a saint. Not that what they were saying wasn't important. It was just awfully repetitive and tiresome. In Mori's estimation, religion could use a little less piety.

Mori waited patiently for the initiates to finish expunging their sins and sent them away. Once again alone in his sanctum, he collapsed into his chair and stared at the trove of alcohol scattered on his desk. He was about to set it out for disposal when he hesitated. His eye flitted to his shelf of scented water and then back to his desk. Once the idea had wormed its way into his head, it became impossible to expunge. He stared at the gourds for several minutes until his resolve fully crumbled.

"Just one drink. The Tiandi is forgiving," he muttered, uncorking a gourd. The contents smelled like they could kill a horse and grease the cart it was pulling at the same time. He poured just a little into one of the urns. His first drink in decades sent shivers down his body. The subsequent sips became easier to manage. Soon it was as if no time had passed at all.

A figure in dark robes stepped out from inside his closet. "Is that all for you, or is there enough to share?"

The shock of an intruder standing in his heart sanctum didn't faze Mori whatsoever. This wasn't the first time he had been marked by an assassin. The politics of the Tiandi brotherhood were surprisingly cutthroat. Mori lobbed the urn at the intruder and then dove for the two-handed war club leaning in the corner. It had been years since he had touched the hefty weapon, and it felt heavier than he remembered, nearly throwing out his back as he hoisted it.

"This is hallowed ground, friend," he said. "I urge you to consider your soul and—"

The cloaked figure, who hadn't moved, limply waved her hand, almost dismissively. The war club twisted in his grasp and socked him on the forehead, knocking him down.

Dazed and now fazed, Mori scrambled to his feet and pawed the walls for support as he cried for help. "Intruder in the sanctum! Brother Solum, to me. Help, help!"

A voice whispered in both his ears. "If you value the life of your Hansoo, you might want to keep your mouth shut, my autumn orchid."

Several brief long-forgotten memories fluttered into Mori's consciousness. Memories from another life. There was only one person in the world who called him orchid—pretty, high-maintenance, and easily crumbling—and who could talk into his head this way. He gaped. "Taishi, by the Tiandi, is that you?"

A still-familiar face emerged from the darkness. "Hello, Mori. The years have made us strangers again. You're looking bald."

The blood rushed into his face, and his heart went double time. Taishi wore her trademark smile. It was how he always envisioned her whenever she crossed his mind. To this day, she had never managed to make it look friendly. Age had touched her like it had him, but it had not marred her beauty. She was still breathtaking.

Alongside the rush of locked-away memories, however, came also a good deal of panic. The two had not parted on good terms, and Taishi's temper, at least back then, had been legendary.

There was also the calamitous news of her embroilment in the corruption of the Prophesied Hero of the Tiandi, and her responsibility for the boy going missing. Mori hadn't wanted to believe the rumors, but upon further introspection, he realized that kidnapping the hero was the exact sort of stunt Taishi would pull. Wrought by indecision, he stared at her wide-eyed. In some ways, he would have preferred facing an assassin.

Taishi broke the ice first. "I'm not here to kill you, Mori."

Well, at least that. The tension visibly left his body.

"Although I have good reason to."

He tensed right back up. He considered calling for Solum again, just in case, but the Hansoo brother would be no match for the legendary Ling Taishi. He tried a different tactic. "I'm glad you're not here to kill me, but we're still not getting back together."

That earned him an actual smile, which quickly blinked away. Her face looked as if she were chewing on something unpleasant. "I need your help."

Mori was intrigued. Those words were difficult for the Taishi he had known. He gestured at the chair across from his desk. "Make yourself comfortable."

She accepted his invitation, snatching one of the gourds and sniffing it. She wrinkled her nose, but poured herself a drink. She glanced up and hovered the gourd over the other urn.

Mori joined her at the desk. "Might as well. For old times'—"

The front door to the heart sanctum blew off its hinges and flew across the sitting room, splintering against the far wall. Solum charged inside with a thunderous roar, leaving a Hansoo-shaped opening in the doorway. The war monk, chest heaving and rings around his forearms jingling, looked around the room furiously before settling upon the two sitting calmly at the desk, the creases of rage on his face replaced by confusion. He looked at Taishi, then at Mori, then at the gourds of alcohol. His eyes widened and his gaze returned to Mori, because of course that was what shocked him.

"Templeabbot?" He spoke in a low, quivering voice, far too gentle for someone who cut such an imposing figure.

Mori did his best to stay calm. "Apologies, good Brother Solum. An old friend surprised me with an unexpected visit. My friend, uh . . ."

". . . Nai," said Taishi smoothly, offering Solum a bright smile. "Nai Roha."

"My good friend Mistress Nai startled me, that's all."

"Your friend, who you mistook for an assassin, visits you in your sanctum during the Queen's reign well after the temple doors close for the evening?" Solum frowned, gradually coming to a scandalous conclusion.

"Since you put it that way," muttered Mori under his breath. He said aloud, "Everything is fine, my diligent brother. I didn't mean to cause an alarm. You may go."

Staring suspiciously, Solum looked as if he was going to object before finally putting his palms together and bowing. "Your word, Temple-abbot." He turned to Taishi. "Have a good evening, mistress." His tone dripped disapproval.

Mori was tempted to ask Solum to stay close, but there was no way to do so tactfully without raising suspicions. He watched with slight worry as the Hansoo brother bowed again and reluctantly took his leave. Fortunately, there was no longer a door to close behind him in case he needed to shout for help again.

Once they were alone again, Mori turned his attention back to Taishi. "Before I help you, I have to ask. Is it true?"

Taishi snorted. "Which rumor? Did I kill the Hero of Prophecy and toss his body into the Grass Sea? Have I purposely lied to the dukes and led Jian astray to line my own pockets? Did I corrupt and seduce the boy hero, and turn him against his own people? Did I go on a murdering rampage in the Celestial Palace and kill all the masters? Take your pick."

A long, awkward silence hung in the air.

"Well, did you?" Mori asked, finally.

"No!" Taishi scoffed, and then quickly amended her emphatic declaration. "All right, except for that last part. I may have slain a few of his worthless masters during our escape." Her brow furrowed. "But not all of them!"

"So you did break the prophecy?"

"Don't be a fool. That asinine, bungling Khan got himself gutted all on his own, naked with his bits flailing about."

Taishi spent the next hour recounting her version of what had happened at the Celestial Palace six months earlier. How the hero's masters had been taking advantage of their positions and training Jian poorly. How the dukes had decided to kill the boy off after the Khan's death in order to keep him away from the others. And how they had used her as a scapegoat to cover up Jian's disappearance.

After she finished, Mori sat there, his mind processing everything. "Then you *are* responsible for everything, including the Champion of the Five Under Heaven's disappearance."

"I saved his life," she snapped. "Those dukes were petty and shortsighted. All they could see was a pawn to take off the board in their game for the golden mantle."

"But if the prophecy is broken, then what use is he anymore?"

"Fate may still have need of him. We can't be sure. There is no returning from death. We have to keep him safe until then. That's why I need your help."

Mori pondered her words. He did not doubt her tale. Taishi was probably guilty of all the crimes she was accused of committing, but in his heart he knew that the woman he had loved had had good reasons. Then again, the woman sitting across from him now was not the woman he had known. He didn't know what to believe. "How can I be of assistance to the legendary outlaw Ling Taishi?"

One end of Taishi's lips curled upward. She kept looking at him as she forwent the urn and swigged directly from the gourd that she had appropriated. She smacked her lips as if trying to rid herself of a bad taste and then wiped her mouth with her sleeve. "Mori, I'm going to get to the bottom of why things went so sideways with the prophecy. I need to understand why it broke so spectacularly, and if there's a way to fix it."

Mori stared at her as if a third eye had suddenly opened up on her forehead. "What's to fix? The Eternal Khan is dead and the Enlightened States are victorious. What more can you ask for?"

Taishi leaned forward, jabbing him with her finger. "I've been all over the Enlightened States, Mori. I've seen the aftermath of the Khan's death. The dukes have turned their eyes from Katuia and inward toward one another. The armies are bored and desperate for relevance—a volatile mixture—and the people are abandoning the Tiandi in droves. Is this how things were supposed to happen? Does this feel like the era of peace, prosperity, and enlightenment promised by the divine after the prophecy is fulfilled, or is everything just broken now? At the very least I need confirmation that the Tiandi has no more use for Wen Jian."

Taishi's summary wasn't wrong, but it also demonstrated her lack of faith. He took the gourd from her hand. "What makes you think I have answers to any of your questions, Taishi? If I actually knew the path ahead, I would be singing of it to the masses, preaching it at the five courts, and bringing it to the flock in every corner of the Enlightened States, instead of sitting here wasting my time with insolent initiates and criminal ex-lovers."

Taishi's jaw tightened. "You're the templeabbot of the largest temple in all the Enlightened States. Don't you want answers?"

"I don't need answers when I have faith." He took her gourd and poured generously into his urn. "Have you ever considered that this has been the plan of the Tiandi all along? To use the prophecy to bring the people together all those hundreds of years ago when we most needed it? And now that the people are united—"

Taishi knocked the urn out of his hand as he brought it up to his lips. "I know you well enough to know when you're talking out of your prettier end. I'm not one of your overboiled twits you can heap that drivel upon."

Time had not dulled her edge one bit. Mori picked up the urn staining his rug. He fixed her with the look he gave initiates who needed a talking-to. "If you are seeking my counsel, here it is. Forget about it. The divine works in its own ways. If the prophecy is broken, then it is as the Tiandi wills it. Let the River of Fate carve its own course. It's for the greater good."

"Really?" Taishi's voice was sharp. "Tell me, Mori. How has your pretty temple fared since news broke that the Khan died and the savior of the Zhuun disappeared? Have they flocked in droves to hear your wisdom and seek the blessings of the Tiandi?"

"The devout are having a difficult time with this transition," Mori conceded, failing to muffle a sigh.

Taishi leaned in with her piercing brown eyes. "The potato-brained Eternal Khan, the immortal ruler of the savage Katuia Hordes, the scourge of the Zhuun *and eater of babies*, met his untimely end at the hands of a lowly soldier wielding a sharpened broomstick! How does that happen? How do you kill a god-king? An entire religion, centuries of faith, hundreds of temples, thousands of devout, all dedicated to a prophecy that is gone"—she jabbed her forefinger upward—"with a poke up his ass. His death not only broke the Katuia people, it broke the Tiandi religion. Who wants to believe in a religion whose core belief has been proven false, let alone donate to it?"

Mori couldn't argue with that logic. He had often claimed that actually discovering the Champion of the Five Under Heaven was the worst thing that could have happened to their religion. He had so far been proven correct. He opened his palms up toward the sky. "What shall pass, will pass. Our fates are in the hands of the heavens. Like all trials, it will pass. Faith is cyclical. People turn to religion during hard times, and away when they are prosperous. The Enlightened States may be at peace for the first time in centuries, and the economy may be booming, but fortunes are like the tides: They will advance and recede. The crops will inevitably fail, nature will unleash her tempest, and men will wage their wars once more."

She snorted. "The economy is prosperous off the forced labor of the Katuia people."

"Indentured servitude is a fair price for peace and reparations."

Taishi growled and spat. "Indentured servitude. Listen to yourself. What pitiful excuses everyone makes to justify this atrocity."

"Unfortunately, the noble and wise dukes did not seek the Tiandi monks' counsel when they negotiated the armistice," replied Mori drily. "From what I understand, the terms were merciful. One of their capital cities working for one of ours every cycle. It isn't too much to ask."

"Merciful!" Taishi spat. "I was passing through Gyian when their city of Jomei arrived at Allanto at the beginning of the year. Yanso had insisted his duchy be served first. They moved along Kyubi Road single file on tracks stretching to the horizon. Men, women, and children lined up like cattle, disarmed, and then herded into pens. Pens, Mori. For the next three months, they were forced to work the fields: digging, planting, harvesting; slaving from dawn to nightfall under the watchful eyes of soldiers who cracked them with whips and beat them with sticks. I saw fields of men digging the earth with their bare hands because the soldiers were too fearful to provide tools. The women forced to work the mills for days without rest. Even the little ones"—her eyes brimmed—"had to do the jobs of cart horses, dragging supplies. They were afforded barely any food, even less rest, and paid with coppers to their debt.

"The Katuia are a proud people, a warrior society, and the Zhuun, supposedly civilized, humiliated and treated them like animals, just because we won, and because we are an angry and vengeful people." Taishi blinked and leveled her fury at Mori. "Forced cheap labor is the source of our economic boom. Where was Tiandi's guidance on that?"

Mori shifted uncomfortably. "I didn't realize." He had heard stories, gossip, but had chosen to discard it all as rumors. Slavery was forbidden by the Tiandi, and had been outlawed soon after the religion had come to prominence, but indentured servitude had quickly risen to take its place. In Taishi's view, the distinction between the two was paper-thin.

Taishi shook with emotion. "The hordes killed my brothers, and I spent the better part of a decade waging war against them, desperately hoping to find peace. But now . . . I just can't stand what is happening to those poor souls." She inhaled deeply and expunged her anger with her breath.

Mori knew little of Taishi's life other than the gossip and songs that grew from her exploits. She had completely cut herself off from him after he pledged himself fully to the Tiandi, refusing his every attempt to maintain any sort of relationship, to his deep disappointment and hurt. He had thought their bond stronger and more resilient. Still, he had been proud of all her accomplishments, and was a little wistful he had not had the chance to share those experiences with her. He could have, if he had made other choices in life. He *was* proud of her now, regardless. Mori hurried to dispel the fog of the past threatening to settle over him.

Taishi continued to rant, her fingers stabbing every which way. "But that's not why I'm here. I want to find out how the Prophecy of the Tiandi could have gone so wrong. I need to speak with someone who knows, or better yet, with the source. Can you at least direct me to the original Temple of the Tiandi?"

Mori was stumped and, to be honest, stumped that he was stumped. It was peculiar that in all the years he had studied the Tiandi, followed by all his decades as a monk, he had never wondered exactly where the

originating Temple of the Tiandi was located. It had never even occurred to him to visit. All he knew was that it was somewhere to the
south, outside of Zhuun borders, considered a difficult and treacherous
journey. That was why the Tiandi monks of previous generations had
had the wisdom to build temples all over the Enlightened States. People were much more likely to donate to the divine if they could do so
close by.

He struggled mightily to offer an answer fitting a templeabbot. Finally, he went with, "I can't help you."

Taishi's jaw clenched and her eyes narrowed. "You mean you won't
tell me?"

"I mean I have no idea where the original temple is located. It's—"
He pointed to the south. "—somewhere in that direction."

"How is this possible? It's the centerpiece of your damn religion!"

Mori's mind raced. Taishi wasn't wrong; he *should* know, but information like this was considered ancient, almost irrelevant, history. Most
of his training as a monk centered on studying scriptures, maintaining
temple grounds, and the necessary skill of eliciting donations from the
masses. Abbots-in-training had to learn how to deal with the nobility
and handle finances. Where an old temple was located simply wasn't
relevant. Only the fanatics cared enough to wallow in ancient history.

Mori was tempted to turn her away. Her foolish quest would lead
only to pain and doubt. Better to be shielded with ignorance than to suffer the truth. In a way, shielding with ignorance was what all Tiandi
monks were doing now.

Perhaps this was the test. Maybe the Tiandi was finally giving him
the opportunity to be the holy man he had always dreamed of being. He
had tried to believe that achieving the rank of abbot was a sign of his
faith, but he knew better. Becoming templeabbot had nothing to do
with his piety and everything to do with the fact that he was organized,
was competent, and could do math. Mori stared at the gourd in his hand
and, feeling loathsome, set it aside. He craned his head behind him and
studied the painting of the Celestial Mosaic hanging on the wall. Seeing
it filled him with warmth and inspiration. Maybe this was his chance to
truly serve the divine.

"I'll look into this."

Taishi must have somehow seen the change in him. "Thank you. I know it will take some time, but I can wait."

"I will send word if my research uncovers something. How can I reach you?"

She studied him suspiciously for a few moments before leaning in and speaking in a low voice. "I'm hiding in my family's crypt in a burial mountain about a day's ride east."

Mori nodded. "I know of it. There're three within a two-day journey surrounding Vauzan, and only one toward the east."

"If you find something, send a letter to a death shepherd named Foo. Address it to Nai."

"I will do my best."

"Thank you. I should leave now before your initiates think something is up."

"That's probably best."

Taishi stood. She opened her mouth, and then changed her mind. For a moment, the hard-nosed legendary warrior's visage softened, bringing back more memories of their gentler moments. "It was good to see you again, Mori. I'm glad to see you've achieved everything you wished for."

For some reason, her words stung. He glanced up at the ceiling and then around the room. "Perhaps the problem is people wish for the wrong things. And I miss your company as well." Mori had more to say, but that was as much impropriety as he would allow himself.

Taishi hesitated as she turned to leave. "Do you remember that picnic? Our first spring together?"

He knew exactly what she was thinking of. His cheeks burned to this day. "In the orange Ginko forest. That's a memory I prefer you forget. Some awful poetry was spoken that day."

"The meter needed work," she agreed. "But those images lingered. Your earlier terrible stuff was always my favorite. I just want you to know that." Taishi turned to leave.

"Wait," he called after her. "How did you get into the monastery?" The woman he knew wasn't exactly stealthy.

Taishi glanced over her shoulder. "It wasn't hard. I bribed one of your young monks with a couple gourds of wine. He let me right in." She flashed him one last trademark smile and was gone.

Mori sat alone in the dark long after she was gone, and then glowered at the wine gourds scattered about his desk. Tomorrow was going to be a rough day for the initiates.

CHAPTER THIRTEEN

FINAL RESTING PLACE

Taishi lay on her deathbed, her off-key hum resonating against the walls. A wisp of smoke from the candle made her eyes itch as she traced the path of a long crack across the curved ceiling. Large patches of black soot stained the stone, giving the impression of storm clouds floating across a gray, dreary sky. She doubted that any of it had been scrubbed or maintained. What exactly was she tithing to the death shepherds for?

Taishi had been on the run ever since Jiayi, returning to the Cloud Pillars to find Mute Men canvasing the sparsely populated mountain ranges and valleys. Her picture was plastered in every commandery, every village, every outpost, every drinking bar, and the price on her head was on the mind of every bounty hunter, soldier, ruffian, and other idiot looking to make a name for themselves. It was coming up on a year of being on the run, and though Taishi had finally found a small respite in the sanctuary of her family's crypt, its welcome had long worn away.

She had been holed up here for months, cold, weary, and bored. Mostly bored. Taishi wasn't even sure what she was waiting for anymore. What had begun as waiting for the manhunt to die down had turned to waiting for Mori to pass along information and now had turned into general malaise. Waiting for news from the outside world. Waiting to die. Taishi had always assumed her end would come on the battlefield, a quick, violent death, preferably glorious and for a noble cause in the midst of chaos and cacophony. Instead, she was dying slowly, quietly, alone, and with what felt like no cause at all. What a waste.

Taishi sighed and rested her head back on the cold stone slab, her empty stomach rumbling. She had run out of food two days ago, and had been too indifferent to do anything about it. At least it was comfortable here, as chilly crypts half buried in the sides of mountains went. And she was going to die with family around. Taishi craned her neck to the side and stared at the two empty slabs to her right. Nothing in her heart stirred at the sight. Her brothers had perished fighting in the war before she was born, their bodies never recovered from the Grass Sea. They were just two names in her family tree, though in a way she owed them everything.

"Thanks for dying, boys. You made my miserable life possible."

The only reason Taishi's parents had decided to try for another child was so her father could have a son to carry on the Zhang windwhispering line. She glanced up at the two embalmed bodies resting on slabs on the elevated platform behind her. Munnam had been bitterly disappointed when the newest addition to the Ling family hadn't had a penis, and had spent Taishi's childhood reminding her of her "inadequacies." Munnam had been a distant and stern father, and a crueler master, but to his credit, he had trained her as well as either of his sons.

"Still passed your test, Ba." Even after all these years, Taishi couldn't hide the bitterness in her thoughts.

Taishi's hatred for her father burned brighter than all the stars in the heavens, so much so she hadn't hesitated when he had finally offered her the chance to attempt the final test. She had been ready, eager even, knowing full well the consequences of success. The final test a windwhispering student overcame to elevate their status to master was to absorb their own master's sound, which merged the war artist's essence with their jing, amplifying their abilities by multitudes. *Absorption* was a gentle way to say "killing." A more accurate description was the student ripped the jing out of their master, instantly killing him. If the student failed, then the whiplash of their master's jing from the failed attempt would surge back and claim the student's life instead. It was why this particular windwhispering branch was always only single-lineage. This final technique was what elevated the Zhang lineage to its legendary status as opposed to those hundreds of other styles under the lunar court. It was also why Taishi, after Sanso, refused to ever take on another student.

Taishi was never sure if her own father was happy that she had passed. Munnam hadn't reacted when she successfully wrested the teacup from his hands. His face remained passive even when she demonstrated perfect control and seized the air surrounding them. He hardly looked surprised when she was able to wrestle his currents out of his grasp. It was only at that final moment when Taishi had succeeded in absorbing his sound, shattering his principal meridians and drawing in his jing, shattering most of the bones in his body, that her father had looked at her in a way that almost resembled pride.

A bastard to the end.

"True power requires true sacrifice," Munnam had told her over and over.

Taishi didn't really know what he'd meant until the moment she stood over his shattered body. The flash of memory made her breath catch. That final display of affection—or approval or whatever it had been—had broken Taishi. She had stood over him as the new Zhang grandmaster windwhisper, wearing the mantle of the eighteenth in an unbroken line, and wept like the child she had been. To this day, she hadn't forgiven him, although she wasn't exactly sure for what.

Taishi looked past her feet at the platform below, where a single slab held the last embalmed body. Her eyes squeezed shut as she fought down the surge of grief cutting into her heart. She would have been happy, ecstatic, to offer Sanso the same opportunity her father had given her.

It was sickening how much better she felt being close to him. That was one argument for just giving up and dying here and now. If Taishi had died like her brothers in some distant land, then her body would have been lost. Who knew if her spirit could ever find its way home. At least now in this crypt, it was guaranteed she could spend the rest of eternity with her son.

A scraping sound, like stones grinding together, echoed against the walls and interrupted her reflection. Taishi, annoyed, mulled whether she should investigate the disturbance. She was tempted to let the intruder discover her on the deathbed, but then her stomach growled again. She checked herself to see if she was covered. She wasn't, and quickly buttoned up her robe.

The intruder, a young man wearing the faded robe of a death shepherd, appeared a moment later, breathing laboriously as he dragged a heavily laden burlap sack along the ground. A primal instinct overtook Taishi, and she practically flew from the stone slab toward him. The death shepherd had only a panicked moment to drop the sack when she pounced on it, rummaging through its contents until she produced a loaf of bread. She tore into it like a starving animal catching its first morsel in weeks.

The young death shepherd bowed profusely. "My deepest apologies, Master Ling. The trade caravan was late due to the weather, and my elder forbade hiking up the mountain under inclement conditions."

"Mhmm, mmmhm." Taishi tried to tell the young shepherd it was all right, but she was having trouble prioritizing breathing over swallowing food, let alone forming a coherent sentence. She settled for reaching out and giving him a pat on the head.

Several minutes passed before she took a respite from gorging herself. Taishi tore a piece of smoked jerky in two and chewed on it, a contented sigh escaping her lips. She tossed him two strings of copper liang. "Anything to drink, Foo?"

The strings disappeared into his pocket as if by sleight of hand. Foo swung a second pack off his shoulder and held it out. Nine skins of water and two gourds of wine. Taishi would have much preferred the ratio reversed, but this would have to do. She tossed the young man another string.

"There's one more thing." Foo pulled out a rolled-up parchment with a broken yellow seal.

Taishi raised an eyebrow. It had been a long three months. She had all but given up on hearing from Mori. "Did you read it?"

"Apologies, Master Ling. The messenger did not know who to deliver it to, so it was passed around my brothers and sisters until it finally came to me."

Likely story. The letter was not addressed to anyone, nor was it signed, but Taishi immediately recognized Mori's impeccable calligraphy. He used to compose rather beautiful letters to her back when they were in love, long before she had made a name for herself as a war artist. His beautiful handwriting brought a rush of memories. Lee Mori had been the kindest, most patient, and most educated man to woo her, which honestly was not a high bar. These traits were not common among war artists. He was different from the sort of people she typically associated with.

That same kindness, patience, and intelligence often made him insufferable, but how she had loved him. That flame still had a small ember, if she was being honest. He was the only man who had ever left her, who had broken her heart. The two had met while he was attending Sunsheng, studying to become a monk. Taishi was young, brash, and passionate. Without vocalizing it, she thought their love was so strong, so deep, so necessary for them both, that Mori surely would choose to be with her. Such hubris, such stupidity. In the end, her dreams of the two of them—the mighty war artist and the philosopher-poet-bard-cook—wandering the Enlightened States together, quelling evil, earning fat contracts and fame, were crushed to dust when the noodle-limbed love-of-her-life actually donned that ugly fish-tail initiate's hat and became a Tiandi monk.

Three hours after Taishi had rushed out of the ceremony, sobbing and heartbroken, she had thrown up for the first time. She had done so again the next morning, and then learned shortly after that Sanso was on his way. By then, Taishi couldn't have very well shared the news with Mori, but she had tried, begging him to reconsider. Mori was too good a man and would have done the right thing had she told him everything, but she wanted him to *choose* to stay with her. That was one of the problems with having choices. The two had fought and pleaded and argued all night, and in the end Taishi had lost her temper, and Mori had nearly lost his life. Taishi had never regretted not telling Mori. In the end, Sanso had been *her* son and *her* disciple. She hadn't needed the Tiandi or Mori to muddle that, and she certainly didn't need to open up old wounds with him now.

She swallowed that last bitter thought and focused on the letter. Like all his other correspondence, it was longer than it needed to be. Mori had a way with words, but he also liked to use far too many of them to say far too little. Reading was admittedly not one of Taishi's strengths. It took her several passes over some of his wordier passages before she finally figured out where she needed to go. Mori even offered a contact, a man named Wu Chown, assuming he still lived there. Included was a small wooden disk with the marks of the abbot of the Vauzan temple carved on one side. Mori's instructions were to present it to the temple-abbot at the original Temple of the Tiandi.

He was kind enough to wish her luck, and asked that she not break into his temple again.

"I had to make sure you weren't going to run," she muttered.

Taishi rubbed the seal between her fingers. She was tempted to ignore the letter. Searching for the temple and finding out what had happened to the broken prophecy was the furthest thing from her mind. Spending nearly three months in her family's crypt had changed her perspective. She flipped the letter to the blank back page, digging for any other clues or messages from the man she had once loved. She was slightly disappointed but unsurprised that he had kept their communication strictly to business. Mori had always worn his school uniform perfectly when they were together.

That was when she noticed that Foo was still standing there, fidgeting awkwardly with the frayed ends of his faded robes. The poor boy was still waiting for his coin. Death shepherds were a sect of the Tiandi, but its lowest branch. This was the sect where all the initiates who could not test into any other sect were placed. They were the caretakers of the deceased and lived lonely, quiet lives on the many burial mountains that dotted the Enlightened States.

Their divine purpose was to prepare the earthly vessels for their journey to the afterlife, guiding souls to heaven or to hell. In reality, they spent their lives cleaning, embalming, and painting the dead. Supposedly, the souls of the deceased took on the appearance of the body they left behind, so it was big business to pretty up the corpses. The death shepherds' other duties revolved around pulling weeds, dusting crypts, maintaining the mountain passes, and chasing off grave robbers.

Though they had one of the most important jobs, death shepherds were paid very poorly, which explained Initiate Foo moonlighting as a pack mule smuggling supplies up the mountain for her. She tossed him a silver coin for the delivery. "Get some roast duck next time. I'm tired of gnawing on dried meat."

The young man hesitated. "A hundred sorrows, but that will not be possible."

She made a face. "How about salted fish then?"

The death shepherd looked frightened, the quivering extending to his voice. "You don't understand, Master Ling. My deepest apologies, but this arrangement cannot continue."

She shot him a withering look. "I can't pay you more if that's what you're asking."

The death shepherd shook his head. "It's not that. Your family's crypt is near the top of the mountain. The journey up here and then back to the funeral temple takes an entire day, and you're asking me to make it every five days. The other shepherds are starting to question my absences."

"Can't you just walk faster?"

He pointed at the sack at her feet. "It's a long, difficult hike up the mountain."

"What if you bring twice the supplies each time so you make fewer trips?"

"It's a really long, really difficult hike up the mountain," he repeated.

Taishi grimaced. The boy had a point. There was no winning. "All right, I lied. I can pay a little more." She really couldn't, but the young shepherd was currently her only link to the outside world.

The death shepherd bowed his head, miserable. "It's not about the money, truly."

If Foo was unable or unwilling to continue smuggling her supplies, Taishi's time here had come to an end. She eyed the stone slab reserved for her deathbed. One way or another.

"Maybe you could move to another crypt," Foo was suggesting. "One closer to the base of the mountain. I can always send warning if—"

Taishi threw up a hand, silencing him. There it was: faint voices, the echoes of brief conversations. Light metal clanging, heavy breathing, footsteps. Several, four or five pairs.

"You were followed." Taishi blew out the nearest candle and flicked her finger toward the one at the opposite end of the room, extinguishing it as well.

Foo looked stricken. "I'm so terribly sorry, master. I swear, I did not mean to—"

Taishi silenced him with a look and inched down the corridor. She flattened against the cold wall and closed her eyes. They were getting closer.

"It's so dark and chilly in here."

"Watch your step. Shutter that lantern. You'll give us away."

"This place smells like death."

Taishi arched an eyebrow.

"I hate being around dead people. It makes my blood freeze."

"You really should find another line of work then."

And rolled her eyes.

Taishi relaxed. This was a group of buffoons: grave robbers or bounty hunters or scavengers or whatever. They certainly wouldn't pose much of a problem. In all her years, after hundreds of fights and dozens of battles, she had never met an opponent who was stupid and still dangerous. This basket of eggs would prove little trouble. Maybe *they* had coin *she* could rob.

One of them must have finally realized that their voices carried deep into the crypt. "Quiet, fools," a woman barked. "You'll alert him of our presence."

Taishi perked up. "Him"? What were they after here? Certainly not the death shepherd's sad sack of supplies. She leaned against the wall and waited eagerly.

The first two appeared a moment later, a short hefty man with a soft, spongy midsection, followed closely by a tall, lanky bald one with a sharp nose. She couldn't tell in the darkness, but they looked young and ragtag, wearing light to no armor. Bounty hunters, perhaps? Long clubs dangled at their waists. Why weren't they drawn? Did they not expect danger? No, that wasn't it; they intended to take their target unharmed.

Taishi waited until the second pair passed, this time a young man and woman in similar garb, then pounced. She streaked out of her hiding spot and clapped the man's ear. His eardrum ruptured, he staggered as if drunk and crumpled to the ground. If she had been a little quicker, Taishi might have remained undetected before any of the eggs were any wiser, but she was admittedly out of practice and the chill atop the burial mountain had made her joints stiff.

The woman caught sight of Taishi before she could disappear back into the shadows. She cried out and fumbled for her club, another clue to their inexperience. Taishi flicked the woman's thumb with a shot of air, sending the club flipping out of her grasp.

"Who is that?" a new voice practically screamed. "Wait, that's not the boy. By the Tiandi, that's the evil master!"

Someone smacked her across the back with a club. Taishi barely noticed it. She whirled around and kicked her assailant, sending him flying onto a tomb and tumbling off the other side. Panic ensued among the other bounty hunters, and they ended in a tangle of limbs and dropped weapons in the middle of the floor. Two of the bounty hunters had tried to charge her, but Taishi barely had to step aside for the rotund one to run right by. She stuck out her leg and sent him flying headfirst into the wall. The tall one didn't even make it to her. He had drawn his club and was charging at her when the top of his head clipped a low-hanging piece of stalactite, flipping him onto his back.

Taishi stared at this comedy of ineptitude, actually at a loss for words. These eggs were almost too stupid to live. The wise thing to do was not to leave any loose ends. If she let them live, they would absolutely sell her out. Others would inevitably come for her.

A light illuminated the room as Foo, holding a candle, rushed to the middle of the fracas. He gawked. "Ningi, what are you doing here?"

The girl raised her head from the floor. She looked abashed.

Taishi glared at Foo sharply. "You know this rabble?"

"They're my brethren from the funeral temple."

Taishi's face hardened. She wasn't a tolerant person, and betrayal was the one thing she could never forgive. She clenched her fists and advanced on Foo.

"No!" Ningi wailed and threw herself across the floor to land between Taishi and Foo. The others followed suit, prostrating themselves around her, blubbering and kowtowing for forgiveness. Taishi grimaced. There were few things worse than a pathetic enemy. Her warrior instincts still warned her to just kill them and be done with them, but a little voice in her head urged mercy. These so-called bounty hunters may have been too stupid to live, but they were also too stupid to kill.

"Damn that stupid boy," she muttered. The softness inside her was spreading. Taishi pointed at the girl. "What's going on? How did you find me? Speak."

"Brother Foo's been stealing food up the mountain for weeks," the girl managed to say between long, labored sniffs.

"You said you bought the food," Taishi spat at Foo.

He looked embarrassed. "Sometimes I, maybe, borrowed from our temple stores. No one noticed."

"Oh, everyone noticed," the girl continued. "I followed him up here one day and realized it was the evil master Ling Taishi's family crypt. That's when we realized Foo might be hiding the Prophesied Hero of the Tiandi and came to see for ourselves. We didn't mean any harm."

Taishi gritted her teeth. "Watch who you're calling evil." She pointed at the clubs. "So you all thought you would come up here and capture the hero then? Maybe hand him to the dukes for a fat reward, right?"

"He's an escaped criminal. We're just doing our duty to the Enlightened States." The girl hesitated, looking abashed. "The bounties for the Prophesied Hero just increased."

Taishi swept her finger across the group. "You sad bunch of eggs are too pathetic to be bounty hunters. Stick to tending to the dead." She furrowed her brow. "Just how large is the hero's bounty now?"

"Ten strings of gold liang."

Taishi couldn't help but gape. No wonder these children wanted to jump in the game. "And how much did they increase mine to?"

The girl looked confused. "It stayed the same."

Taishi's face darkened. Those cheapskate dukes had put Jian's bounty at over five times hers. Ridiculous! She was one of the grandmasters of the war arts, a heroine of the Zhuun. Practically a national treasure. He was just a spoiled boy accidentally thrown into a mistaken and now-broken prophecy. What an outrage!

An irritated growl climbed up her throat. This was what it all came down to. How had the prophecy gotten things so wrong? The birth of the prophecy had been a seminal moment to the Zhuun. The people had been weary from centuries of war. They had rallied around the Prophecy of the Tiandi. It had given them hope, stiffened their spines in the face of utter collapse. It had given them purpose, a signal that the terrible times would pass. That was the difference between a tunnel and the abyss. That lone glimmer of light on the other end. Now, after centuries of faith, the prophecy was revealed to be nothing more than a hoax.

No matter how many times she tried, Taishi couldn't let it go. The journey to this moment was just as important as the unexpected outcome. Even though events had resolved favorably for the Zhuun, it left a taste of ash in her mouth. Generations had placed their faith in the prophecy. They had fought and struggled and sacrificed their lives and dreams to see it fulfilled. An entire religion had been born. It couldn't just end like this, could it? Taishi had to find out. The people needed— she needed—closure. At the very least they had to confirm that the Eternal Khan was truly dead and that Jian was free from his destiny.

Her gaze drifted to Sanso's tomb at the far end of the crypt, her face softening. It wasn't time, not yet. Taking a deep breath, she rounded on the pretend bounty hunters. "Do you know who I am?" It was more a statement—or a threat—than a question.

The tall one, now shining a large bump on his forehead, exchanged looks with the girl. He volunteered, "You're the evil, I mean, the great war arts master, Ling—"

The girl cut him off, shaking her head vigorously. "There's no one here. We followed our brother Foo to see if he needed help cleaning this esteemed family's crypt."

"Smart girl," muttered Taishi. "Now, I suggest the rest of you be as smart as your friend. You don't ever want to see me again." She turned to Foo. "Our arrangement is finished. I won't need your services anymore. Clean up the crypt so it looks as if I were never here."

"Where are you going—" Her glare cut him off. The stupid, slow learners finally caught on and bowed. "Yes, Master Ling."

"And scrub the damn ceiling this time," Taishi snapped as she turned her back to them to pack.

CHAPTER FOURTEEN

THE TASTE OF FREEDOM

Jian woke to his new neighbors quarreling at an obscene hour of the morning. The scattered rays of the King had not yet pierced the veil of night, the city outside still slept like a drunk in an alley, and it was so cold Jian's breath steamed in the air. The young couple, a pair of bush warblers, had moved in a few months ago and had built a nest on the corner rafter. He hadn't minded at first, appreciating the company, until one morning when their occasional warbling was joined by the frantic and insistent squeaks of four hatchlings. The young family's chatter filled his room every morning, but Jian didn't have the heart to evict them. At least now he was never late for morning chores.

He yawned and uncurled his body, his arms and legs escaping the warmth of his jute blanket, his toes extending past the foot of the bed. That wouldn't have happened a few months ago. His voice was changing as well. The frigid morning air bit at his exposed feet, causing him to pull back under the covers like a turtle into its shell.

Jian considered staying in his warm cocoon, but then he remembered that a heavy storm had swept through the city overnight. With a resigned groan, he swung his legs over the side and winced when his feet touched the cold, damp floor. He minced his way to the washbowl and splashed his face with icy water. He ran his hand through his now-short-cropped hair, tied his faded white robes tightly around his waist, and slipped on his fighting slippers.

A thick layer of morning dew hung low on the grass as Jian trudged out of his ramshackle hut and walked the length of the grounds of the Longxian Northern Fist School of War. The clouds above were still puffy and laden with rain, but were hastily moving westward. With a little luck, the next deluge would miss the school. He proceeded to the inner courtyard and hurdled the back of a stone chair set at the head of the training grounds. He landed softly between the armrests with his legs dangling off the side and surveyed the wreckage.

It was as expected for the morning after a storm early in the third cycle. Fallen branches, soggy leaves, and random debris littered just about every inch of the waterlogged courtyard. The weapons rack standing against the near wall had tipped over, spilling training spears, staves, and axes across the floor. Puddles filled the indentations formed from years of feet stomping on the stone tiles.

"You're up late," said a hard voice.

"I'm up early, Auntie Li."

"Not with this mess you aren't. You best get cleaning before first class." A short, plump woman with her sleeves rolled up and wearing a stained white apron appeared next to him, frowning disapprovingly. She wore a wrap over her hair like an imperial headdress and wielded a pair of long cooking chopsticks as if they were daggers. She shook them at Jian with each emphasized word. "How many times do I have to tell you not to sit on the master's chair?"

"As many as it takes before you realize I won't listen."

She tapped him lightly on the head with the chopsticks. "Ungrateful egg. Get to work before he wakes. You know how he feels about a clean training ground. You put him in a sour mood early, everyone will have a bad day."

That much was true. Every problem Guanshi noticed was always the biggest problem in the world. Jian rolled off the chair and accepted a straw broom from Auntie Li. Until dawn, he cleaned the courtyard, sweeping off the water and leaves and clutter, putting the weapons back on the racks, filtering the debris floating in the large drinking vases and refilling them.

Each of the vases was neck-high and four times his girth, and their smooth surfaces made them difficult to grip and carry. He had to squat down to lift them, then half carry, half roll them along the bottom rim to one side of the school to water the gardens. Then he would carry the empty vases to the back to fill them at the well, then return them to their places. Guanshi, the sadist, had forbade him from using a cart to transport the six vases dispersed across the training grounds. It used to take Jian the entire morning to navigate this chore when he had first arrived. Now it was almost a game to see how quickly it could be done.

Jian next went about scrubbing each stone tile in the training area. There were exactly 714 tiles; counting helped passed the time and kept him focused. Guanshi expected each to be cleaned, dried, and polished before the first students arrived, and the master was quick with the balance-a-pot-on-your-head-while-you-stand-on-one-foot punishment if any blemishes were found on his precious floor.

It was tedious work, but there was a reason this school was one of the most successful in Jiayi. While the family style had a respectable track record in tournaments and battles, the real secret to the school's success and popularity among Caobiu nobility was the master's excessive fussiness about immaculate cleanliness. War arts schools were notoriously rough and often dirty. Guanshi had discovered early in his career that there were few faster ways to earn the approval and business of a noblewoman about to send her child to a war arts school than to show her that her child would not live like a commoner.

Auntie Li reappeared from the kitchen as he was on his hands and knees scraping the grooves between the tiles with a sharp stick. "I'm off to the market. Clear out the sewer line in the back, then wash up. Wash up twice and change your clothes. I'll need help in the kitchen afterward. If any of the morning students are hungry, I've set aside a basket of fried dough and warm soy milk. *One* piece per student!"

He slumped his shoulders sullenly. "Yes, Auntie."

"No such thing as a free bowl of rice, Hiro." She waved as if to smack him again, and then broke into a sympathetic smile. "I'll look away when you pilfer a couple of bao later on."

"Thank you, Auntie Li." Jian watched as she left through the front gates. Auntie Li may only have been the school's cook, but she ruled everything inside the four walls as if she were the dowager, which was the nickname whispered behind her back. He appreciated that she looked out for Hiro, the pitiful orphan. She *did* smack him a lot, but he didn't mind. Auntie Li smacked everyone—including Guanshi—but it was rarely out of spite. Unless the offense was severe enough to require the long cooking chopsticks; then everyone—Guanshi included—became as still and quiet as the statues in the vegetable garden.

After he had finished with the courtyard, Jian went to work scraping the drainage lines that were routed from every part of the school into the sewer alley in the back. The storm had clogged several of the smaller channels with leaves and clumps of mud. That took up the rest of his morning. He was still trying to finish his chores when students began arriving for the first class.

The front and back courtyards soon became crowded. Many came early to stretch or practice, or just horse around. Jian avoided making eye contact as he hurried to finish up, feeling every smirk, snicker, and look. The humiliation didn't stop when Guanshi emerged from his residence in the east building. The master of the school passed Jian with a dismissive glance before taking his seat in the stone chair.

The senior of the class this morning, a girl named Gwaiya, clapped her hands as the students scrambled to their lines. She barked a command, and they bowed in unison to Guanshi; then she led the class through stretches and warm-ups. Morning classes were for novices, academic students and moonlighters, hobbyists exploring the arts for recreation. The majority here wouldn't make it to intermediate, but would walk away having learned just enough not to embarrass themselves in a scuffle or lop off a finger with a sword.

Auntie Li returned from the market a little later. Several of the students broke off from their exercises to help the Dowager carry groceries. She shooed Jian away when he offered to help, directing him to the nearest washbasin. After he dutifully complied, she carefully looked him over, checking under his nails and sniffing his robe before allowing him into her kitchen. The rest of his morning was spent working the stone oven and boiling water for the steamer.

Every once in a while, he would peek out the window to the training yard. The late-morning classes were for intermediate and advanced students. These were dedicated war artists—careerists and serious practitioners. Many of them had spent years studying at Longxian. Most, after obtaining a certain level, would enlist as officers in the state armies. Some would seek employment as magistrates, palace guards, or bodyguards. Others would specialize as duelists, bounty hunters, or assassins, or join mercenary companies.

There was a group of students who lived on the school grounds. Most did so because they had traveled to Jiayi from afar, but a few were truly dedicated to Longxian. These were the ones who were added to the school lineage and might eventually open their own schools. All of the students who could afford housing on-site certainly were well off enough not to have to work for room, board, and tuition. Except for Jian.

He was carrying a stack of baskets of small dragon bao over to the dining hall when Xinde, who was teaching a class, waved in passing. The school senior was running his students through a series of basic open-fist three-, four-, and five-stance forms that were shared among many war arts styles.

Jian had been drilling many of these same exercises since he had learned to walk and could easily outclass this pathetic bunch. As much as he wanted to show off, however, his life depended on keeping his identity a secret. Wen Jian may have been the Prophesied Hero of the Tiandi, the Champion of the Five Under Heaven, but Lu Hiro was still a novice, an orphan boy whom Guanshi had taken in out of charity.

"Paying forward my good fortune," the master told others when they inquired.

At least that was the story Taishi and Guanshi had concocted. Jian gnashed his teeth and slammed the basket of bao on the counter at the thought. Ling Taishi was a liar. She had promised to watch over him while he was here, but Jian had not seen her since she left him, barely risen from what could have been his deathbed. She had just dumped him here and gone on with her life. One would have thought he would have wised up and gotten used to disappointment by now, but the thought of abandonment still devastated him.

The last class before noon wrapped up, and the students broke for lunch, congregating at the dining hall. Lunch and dinner were easily the worst parts of Jian's day. One of his regular duties as an indentured servant was to work the dining hall during meals. This was one of the few times he had to interact with every student—his supposed peers—in order to serve and clean up after them. The daily humiliation never got old.

Jian spent lunch bringing out baskets of teriyaki buns, refilling cups of water, and busing dishes. When he wasn't running back and forth to the kitchen or wiping the tables, he tried to blend in with the wall, standing perfectly still while staring at his feet.

The chatter in the hall was always lively. The usually strict Guanshi relaxed discipline during meals, often saying that when bodies were nourished bonds between brothers and sisters were strengthened. The students took advantage. The little ones, some as young as six, sat at the near end, chattering animatedly and climbing over one another like a litter of puppies. Many of these children would train together for the next ten years until they graduated. Jian spent half of his time here cleaning up after them.

The older students sitting at the far end were louder and rowdier, with food and insults often being flung across tables. Bravado and gossip powered much of their conversations, inevitably leading to jokes, pranks, and the occasional food fight. This was all initially a shock to Jian, whose sheltered upbringing left him ill-equipped to deal with such social chaos. He considered this behavior childish and dull, but also couldn't help but feel as if everyone but him was clued in on some secret.

A girl sitting at the end of a table beckoned him over. "Hey, handsome boy." She wasn't flirting with him, and that wasn't a compliment. As he approached, she held up her plate. He opened the basket and placed a steaming bao onto it.

"I want one too," whined a boy next to her. He reached his hand into the basket.

Jian slapped it away. "You already had your second." There was a strict two-bao limit.

"Over here too, handsome boy." One particularly large youth raised his arm and shook his cup.

Jian pretended not to hear for a few seconds before meandering his way over with the glass pitcher of water. Cyyk was one of the louder and more confident students at Longxian. He had the haughty and confident air of a nobleman's son, and the perfectly manicured face and hair to match. To leave out any doubt, Cyyk's fine wardrobe reminded everyone that he was different. His higher-class upbringing and assertiveness made him popular. He was quick to tease and often the catalyst for taunts and bullying.

Jian kept his interaction with him as minimal as possible, quickly refilling the cup. As he turned to leave, Cyyk held up his plate expectantly. "Since you're going back to the kitchen, take this back with you."

Jian bit down on his lip, and his cheeks burned. He made as if to take the plate and then dropped his hand as soon as Cyyk let go. It clattered to the ground, scattering broken clay and rice all over the floor.

"I'm not your servant. Put away your own dishes," Jian growled, walking away. He didn't make it three steps before he was shoved in the back, sending him to his hands and knees, the pitcher breaking and spilling its contents.

Cyyk towered over him. "If you're not my servant, why are you serving me, handsome boy?"

"It's because he doesn't have parents," someone sitting nearby piped in.

"I hear it's because they don't want him," added another. Mocking laughter followed.

Cheeks burning, Jian lashed out, kicking Cyyk's knee at an awkward angle. The bigger boy howled as his leg gave way. Only his friends catching him saved him from falling onto his backside.

Cyyk snarled, hobbling on one leg. "How dare you, runt!"

Large meaty hands hauled Jian up by the collar. He was surrounded by the bully's friends, who slapped him on top of the head over and over. Jian had learned on his third day at the school that head-slapping was the way commoner children inflicted humiliation. By now, it had happened to Jian more than he cared to admit.

Xinde was there an instant later. The senior kept his hands at his sides, his face emotionless. The tussle ceased immediately.

"Sorry, senior," several of them called, bowing their heads.

He looked at Cyyk, who immediately let go of Jian. The bigger boy glared. "He kicked my knee. He could have crippled me."

"Are you injured?"

Cyyk shook his head. "I'm all right, senior."

"Good. That means you can carry your own plates to the kitchen. And while you're at it, why don't you help your brothers and sisters with theirs as well?" Xinde turned to Jian. "Hiro, you made this mess on the floor. Clean it up."

"Yes, senior," both said in unison.

The two exchanged daggered eyes one last time before going off to carry out their separate chores. Jian spent the rest of lunch mopping and cleaning, and then washing the dishes that Cyyk bused in. It had been worth it. It was probably one of the few times in his life the guy had to work a job. Cyyk's father was some high-ranking general under Sunri, and his mother's family ruled some commandery along the white devil border at Gyian. Many students passed the evenings trying to guess his father's identity, or whether Cyyk was even his real name. Children of high-ranking noble families were often sent to war arts schools anonymously for their training. Only Guanshi knew Cyyk's real identity, and by the latitude the master afforded the boy, his family's station had to be very high.

Everyone, again, except for Xinde. His influence over the other students had nothing to do with his family's status. He was just *that* admired. Even Jian felt nothing but respect for the senior, and he was usually an angry ball of resentment toward everyone. Xinde was standing by the door, exchanging pleasantries with the other students as they returned to the training yard for afternoon classes. He was good like that, always considerate and patient, and always doing the small things that mattered. He treated the highest students equally with the lowest ones.

After he finished in the kitchen, Jian fetched supplies and ran errands for Master Guanshi and Auntie Li before finally taking the late-afternoon beginners' class, which consisted of a group of children all five to seven years his junior. Because he had to hide his true skill, he was treated like a novice. That relegated him to learning and working on the most basic drills, most of which he had mastered as a toddler.

Jian trained diligently in those two hours, no matter how easy the class was for him. It was the only time he could exercise his muscles to maintain his reflexes. He hoped to feign natural talent in order to graduate to the advanced classes, but so far neither Guanshi nor any of the seniors were biting. Once he became an advanced student, he would have more autonomy in specializing his skill track. Maybe then he could start showing these commoners his true abilities.

It also offered him an outlet to vent his frustration: a virtual army of imaginary foes. From Cyyk and his cluster of goons to every single one of his former masters—except for Pai and Wang—to Riga and Horashi to those accursed dukes to even Taishi. Jian had a list, and he took his anger out on an imagined face every single training session.

Afterward, he returned to his role as everyone's servant for the evening meal. Dinner was fortunately uneventful. Other than a few glares, Cyyk and his lackeys left him alone to do his job. It probably helped that Xinde was checking up on him. Whether that would continue tomorrow was a different story. War artists tended to be a prideful and vengeful bunch.

Jian's last chore for the evening was to light the lanterns hanging along the interior of the outer walls, then he was free for the night. The Queen already ruled the sky with the Prince crossing from the south, but at least these precious hours were Jian's to do with as he pleased.

He spent the time well hidden in a small copse behind the vegetable garden, working through the forms Taishi and his previous masters had taught him. It frightened him how much he had forgotten in a few months. He struggled to remember the subtle differences between the Wang rolling punch and the Jang cutting punch, or when it was appropriate to throw the Sinsin chop punch. Or was that the Pai knife chop? It all jumbled in his head.

The techniques and exercises that he did work hard to keep embedded in his head were the ones Taishi had taught him. Even though he was angry with her—hated her even—he diligently ran through those forms every night.

Jian was an hour into his practice when he heard footsteps rustling through the garden. He froze, stopping halfway through the Luda eagle claw form thirteen. There shouldn't have been anyone out at this time of night. Some of the students who lived here sneaked out by climbing over the back wall to the sewer alley every now and then, but that was on the other side, near the outhouses.

For a moment, he feared he had been found out. There would be no talking his way out of being discovered running advanced forms. At the very least it would be a betrayal of the school's trust. They would expel him. At worst they would think he was a spy from a competing school. They would probably kill him then.

What if this was the Mute Men? Jian's blood ran cold.

He gave an audible sigh of relief when Cyyk and three of his goons appeared a moment later, although that too was short-lived. One look at their faces portended what would happen next.

"So, this is where the stray dog's been hiding," said a boy named Ulli.

"What are you doing here, runt?" asked Cyyk.

Jian stayed still while the four surrounded him. Short of crying for help, there was no way he could escape this, and he wasn't going to give them the pleasure of hearing him scream.

Another boy, Siang, shoved Jian. He did so again when Jian didn't stumble sufficiently for his liking. The second time, Jian stepped aside and stuck out a leg, sending Siang tripping to his knees. Both Ulli and Cyyk came at him next. Jian avoided their clumsy swings and was about to retaliate when he heard the voice clearly in his head.

"You must not under any circumstances show any skill. You are a complete novice. Your life depends on it."

Damn that Taishi. Jian stopped avoiding their attacks and ate a right cross to the mouth, then a kick to his stomach before covering up. The four bullies converged on him.

CHAPTER FIFTEEN

THE SOUL SEEKER

alminde stood at the prow of the lead pod as its wooden tracks crawled up the winding road severing the spine of the Shingyong Mountains. The last time she had ridden through this pass had been under very different circumstances: her first raid outside of the Grass Sea.

Sali had been wild-haired, raw, and ambitious, ready to prove her worth. For an entire glorious cycle, she had ravaged Zhuun lands with her Katuia brothers and sisters from Nezra and Fushand, making incursions deep into the fat farmlands inside Zhuun territories. She had even once come within eyeshot of the ugly and soulless city of Jiayi's outer walls.

It had been an exciting time, filled with adventure, promise, and many victories. Sali had been awarded her first kills, building her reputation as a talented warrior. She had returned to Nezra with many honors and rich bounties. But her highest reward was the invitation to the viper-strike sect and the right to shave her sides.

That was a lifetime ago.

A butterfly landed on Sali's shoulder. She admired it for a few moments before shaking it loose. Then she craned her head: Hundreds of thousands of pairs of shimmering blue, green, and purple wings threatened to blot out the sun.

The Zhuun called this pass Butterfly Valley. But her people had another name for it. The valley was flanked on both sides by curved jagged mountains shaped like an opened jaw, and when the red-and-yellow flags of the Zhuun army first appeared, it had looked like an endless, roiling flame devouring the land. The pass looked like a dragon's maw, and so it came to be called.

The tracks beneath Sali's pod begin to crunch on stone as the road transitioned from dirt to stone. They were nearing their destination. Their ascent leveled off a few minutes later, and they came around the last bend. The tops of the towers of the Zhuun commandery of Jiayi came into view.

Jiayi was an ugly place, even by Zhuun standards. The city was a brown blight on the lush green farmland around it, completely bereft of flavor or style. Its figure was squat and wide, stacked neatly together by raw sandstones all in barren straight lines and blocky square corners, with only the tips of a few buildings and towers rising above the plain outer wall surrounding it. According to Zhuun history, Jiayi had started out centuries ago as a simple military fort erected to defend against Katuia raiders, and over the years had grown and expanded into the architectural travesty it was today. How anyone could live in that prison empty of color or imagination was beyond Sali, but that wasn't why she hated the city. Jiayi, the military commandery of Caobiu duchy of the Enlightened States, held a sordid claim to a far worse sin.

Since the beginning of their never-ending war—that had just ended—every single Zhuun invasion of the Grass Sea had begun in Jiayi and gone through Dragon's Maw Pass. Every battle, every death, every lost generation, could be traced back to this accursed city. The fact that Sali and her people were arriving in Jiayi not as conquerors, but as indentured servants, forced to work the land-chained fields, left a bitter taste in her mouth. Her stomach churned, and she spat over the railing.

It wasn't just the sight of the city that made Sali queasy, it was also the Khan's Pull bubbling in her gut. She had assumed that it would weaken once Jiamin's body had been laid to rest, sunken into the Grass Sea. Instead, not only did it persist, the compulsion morphed, no longer a sharp, feverish pain but a dull scraping at the back of her mind. The need to return to the Black City and sacrifice her life to return her part of his soul was a constant ringing in her ears that never lapsed.

And it grew with each passing day. No matter how far she was or what service she was performing for the Khan and her people, all the compulsion wanted her to do was go back to the Sanctuary of the Eternal Moor in Chaqra to sacrifice her life. It was a struggle to suppress it, and Sali worried that it would eventually overwhelm her senses and thoughts.

"Keep it together a little longer," she muttered.

"What was that?"

Sali had been so lost inside her own head she had forgotten she wasn't alone. "Just speaking my thoughts, Batu."

"We will arrive soon, Soul Seeker," Sheetan's clan chief said. "The Zhuun have instructed us to set our city east of Jiayi, no closer than four hundred yards from the walls. If you wish to enter the city alone, I advise you to disembark now to avoid trouble with the guards."

"The transport is appreciated." Sali touched her chest with her fist lightly. "I hold in my memory the mighty city of fire and glass, the birthplace of our mastery of steam, and the might of my warrior brothers and sister in the Bullcrash sect. May you reach those peaks again in our lifetime."

The Sheetan chief bowed his weary head. He was not ignorant of the truth: The end of his lifetime was not far away. Batu would not live to see his beloved city free again. "It pleases this old soul to see you one last time, Will of the Khan, Viperstrike, and . . ." His voice trailed off.

Sali looked over the side of the railing for a place to land.

"A moment, Salminde, before you leave," said Batu, holding on to her. He leaned in. "I cannot let you leave without speaking my piece. Forgive me for talking out of turn."

She knew what would come next. It had been asked of her often over the past year.

The old chief took a long moment before speaking carefully. "No one doubts your loyalty and courage, Salminde, but you tread dangerously. Why have you forsaken your exalted place and lowered yourself to a Soul Seeker? You are a Will of the Khan. This is beneath you."

Sali looked on coldly. As either an exalted Will of the Khan or lowly Soul Seeker, she did not care to be lectured.

"I beg you to reconsider," he continued. "Think of the Whole and our people's future." In the khanate's warrior caste, one's courage and loyalty were taken for granted. To even mention them was considered a deep affront, and Batu had questioned not only her loyalty and courage, but also her wisdom, all in one breath.

Sali took it in stride, however. She was no longer a sprout, nor so prideful as to weigh his words without the intention behind them. Batu's motives were pure, and he was not wrong. One should never make decisions only on emotion, but that was exactly what Sali was doing. The chief was offering guidance born from his experience.

However, Batu was not a Will of the Khan nor a Soul Seeker, and he had not lived Sali's life. The chief had not grown up with Jiamin. He had not seen what becoming the Eternal Khan had wrought upon her friend. It was not Batu's city that had been destroyed, his clan scattered across the sea, and it was not his sister who was now indentured to their enemy. While all of these points should matter not to a Will of the Khan or a Soul Seeker, they meant everything to Sali.

In any case, these were political and theological discussions she did not intend to have as their final words. Sali turned away. "I forgive you for speaking out of turn, Batu. I have my reasons. Farewell, Clan Chief of Sheetan."

Sali jumped the railing and plunged down to the cobbled road three stories below as the pods continued rumbling past. She landed softly near a stable attendant, who handed her the reins of an old, faded overo horse. She yanked at the saddle, and then raked her fingers across the mare's coat.

Sali touched her forehead to the horse's body to whisper a prayer for their union, and, within seconds, had peeled away from Sheetan and was riding west down a series of dirt roads, cutting through fields and farmsteads. Several land-chained working the fields paused to watch her pass, a few reaching for their hoes and axes.

Sali paid them no attention, urging her overo west until she found another road south to finally merge with what appeared to be a double-wide main road heading back to the city. The stones for this main road were old and well worn, and the traffic going both ways was light but steady.

The other travelers—mostly merchants and small families—gave her one look and maneuvered their wagons and carriages to the far side of the road. Sali wasn't offended, nor did she blame them for keeping their distance. She tried her best to blend in, cloaked and hooded in appropriated Zhuun travel garb with her head bowed, but there was no hiding her heritage. Her nearly black eyes, wide nose, and bluish gray skin markings betrayed her as Katuia. Even if her distinct features didn't give her away, then certainly her overo's short gait and the long flat saddle she rode on did. To these ignorant land-chained, she was a savage from an alien land, worthy only of fear and hatred.

The Enlightened States and the Khanate Clans had shared open borders since the armistice—how else could her people work the Zhuun lands?—but she still felt as if she were riding into enemy territory. Fortunately, the land-chained left her in peace, as did the city guards, to her mild surprise. They eyed her with hands gripped tightly on their weapons, and more than a few unimaginative slurs were slung her way as she passed, but nothing more.

Sali barely heard them. Her eyes were wide and focused on the sprawling city that opened up as soon as she passed through the giant walls. She had never stepped foot in a Zhuun commandery before. It was at the same time magnificent and terrifying, evoking mixed feelings: awe and hatred, wonder and horror. The logistics behind its existence were incredible. How could so many people live on such a small amount of land? How could such a primitive civilization, who haven't learned to master spark stones or steam, build such a marvel?

Within moments of entering Jiayi, she received her answer: They couldn't, at least not without desecrating the land with waste and squalor. The pungent smell of the city was her first clue. Sali's eyes watered at the stench of the filthy, crowded streets. The streets were thick with the bodies of people, horses, and every pack animal she could imagine, all so close together she couldn't see the ground. The sheer number of souls packed in such tight spaces was abominable.

Sali's ears were inundated with the constant noise of humanity: Vendors shouting, people cursing, children laughing filled her ears with a cacophonic roar that made her head ache.

Since she wasn't able to read Zhingzi, Sali was forced to ask for directions, which of course proved a waste of time. No Zhuun would speak to her. Most pretended she didn't exist, although she could feel all of their sidelong stares. A few dared to spit in her path, but at least none dared to spit directly on her. They weren't that foolish. Sali may have been disguised as a commoner, but there was no denying the casual air of violence and danger surrounding her.

Over the next hour, she meandered through the city, repeatedly getting turned around. She had underestimated how truly massive the blight of these cities was on the land. You could walk across every pod in a Katuia capital city within an hour, perhaps two in Chaqra. Sali could wander through Jiayi for an entire day and still not reach the other end.

Moreover, she learned a valuable lesson as she crept through the heart of this military commandery: It was nigh impenetrable. In all her years attacking Zhuun lands, she had encountered only the settlements: farmlands, mining towns, ranches, fisheries, and trading posts. Her people were not trained or equipped for siege warfare. The khanate did not attack large settlements unless a capital city was involved, and even then it was a rare event, happening less than once a generation. Many of their leaders had entertained the idea of laying siege to this loathsome city, and now Sali was glad a campaign had never been attempted.

It would have been a bloodbath. Tall, thick walls not only encircled the perimeter, but spanned the interior as well, sectioning the city off into easily defensible districts. An invading army would shatter against these walls. And if by chance they did break through, half a dozen more awaited before they could reach the heart of the city. The invaders would be cornered in any of the subdivisions and find themselves besieged and surrounded in a cruel, expertly planned reversal of fortunes.

Sali finally noticed a small group of Katuia huddled near one of the district gates and stopped to ask for directions. She was heartened to see that her people were still kind to their own in this hostile place. They directed her toward what was known as the Kati District—Sali clicked her tongue at the slur. It wasn't far away. She located and followed the steady flow of her people passing through a large gate at the end of a busy marketplace.

Sali kept her head down, squeezed her knees, and guided the overo forward, passing through the raised iron gates. She was shocked to see that the filth and wretchedness here was even worse than in the rest of the city. The buildings on either side of the street were hardly more than dilapidated wooden sheds that looked ready to collapse. Many of these had so many holes and broken boards, she could see through to the other side. Some were more frames than houses. Lined along each wall were piles of garbage swarming with rats, flies, and stray animals fighting over scraps.

Many of the people here—her people—lay on the streets right alongside the refuse. Some were dressed in little more than rags, their eyes glazed over. Others wore the faded tatters of their past lives. Sali saw warrior tags on shoulders, tinker markings, even the robes of a spirit shaman. Seeing the survivors of her city in such a wretched state was overwhelming. She did her best to look on, not to stare, but it was a surprisingly difficult task. She bit down on her lip and forced her gaze forward, but could not avoid noticing her people's defeated, subdued faces.

The people on the streets had no such qualms ogling her as she passed, their gazes a mix ranging from curiosity to aloofness to outright hostility. Sali pulled her hood tighter over her head. She could almost hear their thoughts: *Where was she when Nezra fell?*

"Salminde?" a gaunt man with sunken cheeks and dark blemishes around his jowls called out to her. "Is that really you?"

Sali returned the scrutiny. There was something familiar about him, but she didn't recognize the face or raspy voice. That was when that gut-wrenching realization descended on her. "Quasa?"

"It *is* you, Sali." Tears burst from the man's eyes.

Sali slid off her horse and clutched his shoulders. Quasa was the viperstrike custodian, the caretaker of their sect's headquarters back on Nezra. A former viperstrike himself, Quasa not only maintained their home, weapons, and armor, but also shepherded the neophytes. This man was practically a father to three generations of viperstrikes.

After several long moments, she let go, clenching her teeth. The sight of him brought her so much joy, and so much anguish and rage. "What has happened to you?"

Quasa smiled ruefully. "I finally let go of that gut I've been meaning to lose. Who knew the secret to losing weight was starvation?"

The Quasa she remembered was a large man with a generous midsection. But now his shoulders and arms felt little more than bone and loose skin. "But you're alive. What about the other viperstrikes?"

Quasa's eyes darted over her shoulder. "Conversations like this best be had away from listening ears. Most of the residents of the Kati District are survivors from Nezra."

"That is welcome news, no? I was concerned our sect had fallen alongside Nezra. If people are still together, then the viperstrikes still live." Sidelong glances to either side revealed that their conversation wasn't private. She lowered her voice. "Why do they stare?"

"We should get off the streets." He lowered his voice and grabbed her elbow. "Clan sects have been banned. Someone may recognize you and turn you in."

Sali gasped. "They wouldn't."

"Desperate times make for desperate people, child." Quasa led her into an alley cutting between a pair of three-story buildings. He navigated around piles of garbage, stacks of discarded crates, and a sleeping vagrant. At least she hoped he was sleeping. They continued behind more buildings until they reached a weirdly shaped courtyard nestled awkwardly amid three buildings, as if the original architects hadn't bothered to check their measurements. They passed a small vegetable garden and a droopy citrus tree in the middle and went down a short staircase to an entrance below ground level.

Quasa opened the door and invited her in. The room was narrow and low. Sali had to stoop to avoid bumping her head against the ceiling. The place appeared to be an unfinished crawl space converted into living quarters. Quasa lit a lantern hanging from the ceiling and offered her a seat in the only place in the room to sit: a worn-down tree stump no one had ever bothered to root out.

"It's not much, but it's mine alone. Some live ten souls to a home." Before she could ask, he offered a weak smile. "My roommates all went out last month and never came back. I worried for a time, but there was nothing to be done. These days, no one asks if someone disappears."

Sali kept her hands in her pockets and sat on the stump as Quasa went to brew tea. She watched as he struggled to filter water from a washbasin through a strainer, then struggled some more starting a fire in the crumbling cooking stove. His hands shook so badly, he had trouble lighting a spark. But Quasa was a proud man, and to intervene would offend him.

Her soul ached to see the once strong custodian so frail. Quasa was an institution among viperstrikes, as strong and eternal as the sect's steel-wrought headquarters. The man had crafted her first training tongue and had been there for her as she struggled to master it. If it hadn't been for him, she might have given up and fled for home half a dozen times over.

Finally, after a chain of failed attempts to light the fire, Sali couldn't bear it any longer. She placed her hand on his, looking past Quasa's frantic, embarrassed expression, and waited until he let her take the spark stones. Then she led him to the stump as he stuttered, begging forgiveness.

"There is no shame, old warrior."

The custodian finally acquiesced and allowed her to finish the tasks. Within moments, a small fire was burning in the stove, heating the room and the kettle on the wok tray. It would take a while before the water boiled, so she turned her attention back to Quasa. "Have you heard from the others?"

He bowed his head. "Hyu and Vimma died defending the city. Olyi refused to guard his identity, or his tongue. The land-chained deemed all viperstrikes too great a threat to the peace, and executed him. Somi succumbed to pneumonia a few months ago. As for the rest of your brothers and sisters, and the neophytes . . ." He trailed off.

The news of her fallen sect was unsurprising, but it was still a knife thrust to the gut. Vimma had been Sali's dearest friend in their neophyte days. And while Sali was the most decorated and famous viperstrike of her generation, Hyu and Olyi were the most skilled. Olyi had always been far too prideful, that self-righteous fool. As for Somi, she despised the man, but he was also her brother, so she honored him just the same. For all Sali knew, she could be the very last viperstrike.

"What about you, dear child," he asked. "How did you end up here? The last we shared a hearth, you were leaving to campaign far to the north."

"The Khan brought me back," she replied. The words tasted sour in her mouth. "I remember the exact moment I felt his death. One moment I was with my raiding party ambushing a fat Zhuun trade caravan; the next a sharp stabbing pain in my chest knocked me down. At first I thought an arrow had pierced my scale mail. Imagine my embarrassment when I picked myself off the ground and realized there was no wound. I had just fallen off my horse."

"That's a relief," said the custodian.

Sali frowned. "What do you mean?"

"The Sali I trained would never have gotten stuck by an arrow while on horseback." The Quasa she remembered laughed loudly and easily at everything, and a little of his old self resurfaced as he threw his head back and roared, slapping his knee. But just as quickly as it came, the old viperstrike she fondly remembered was gone again as fits of wheezing and coughing overtook him. He waved her off when she reached out to comfort him. It took several deep, labored breaths before he regained control over himself. "What happened next?"

She raised the diluted tea—more flavored water than anything—to her lips. "So there I was, standing in the middle of a pitched battle, clutching my chest as if my heart had burst. That was when I knew: The

Eternal Khan of Katuia, the Lord of the Grass Sea, had moved on to his next incarnation."

"The pain must have been terrible," said Quasa. "Was that from the Pull of the Khan? Is that what guided you home?"

"It felt like a serrated blade burrowing through flesh, bone, and spirit." Sali's lips curled. "The Pull didn't guide me so much as drag me unwillingly. I lost complete control of my body after that. No sooner had the initial pain subsided than this strange compulsion emerged from the festering wound. It burned like a deep hunger and a mental compass, like an invisible leash, and it began to force-march me toward the Sanctuary of the Eternal Moor in the Black City. Any attempt to turn away or stop was met with fresh stabs of pain, like the sharp claws of a jungle cat tearing me up from within. Nothing else mattered; I just had to return my part of the Khan's soul back to the Whole where his body lay at rest."

"You just left the battle?"

"I had no choice. My feet simply started moving. I walked for several hours before I finally managed to wrest control away from the compulsion." The two fell into silence for several moments. When Sali spoke again, her words dripped with guilt and sadness. "Looking back, while I was shocked by Jiamin's death, my only real surprise was how long he managed to hold out before he succumbed."

"The mantle of the Lord of the Grass Sea is heavy," said the custodian. He was an old traditionalist.

Sali nodded. She had always known the Pull would come one day, had learned about it when she was first chosen to be a Will of the Khan, but she had never given it much thought. No one told her it would hurt so badly. But that wasn't why she was here. An even deeper pain had brought Sali to Jiayi. She gazed into the small fire crackling in the small hearth, surrounded by piles of ashes. "Have you seen Mali? Do you know if she is alive?"

Before he could answer, several dark shadows passed by the holes and cracks on the side of the wall facing the alley. Heavy knocks followed, shaking the entire structure. A cup filled with chopsticks resting on a hanging shelf rattled off the side, its contents scattering over the floor. Sali bolted to her feet, her hand resting on her tongue.

"Council guard, open up," a voice barked.

"The council is intact?" she hissed.

Quasa motioned for her to keep calm. "Not as you remember. Let me deal with them."

No sooner had he cracked the door open than a group of armed men spilled in, pushing Quasa aside. They were Katuia, young and self-important, armed with batons hanging from their waists. Their clothing was varied, but each sported a wavy green tag on his shoulder, ones she had never seen before. She noted with contempt that they all had their hands on the handles of their weapons. Sali folded her arms as they surrounded her and Quasa.

"What is the meaning of this?" Quasa exclaimed, trying to wedge his way between her and the group.

"You, stay put." One of the men shoved him to the ground.

Before the bully could take another breath, Sali's hand shot forward and dug a thumb into the base of his neck. He offered a strangled cry and fell to his knees, futilely pawing at her arm. The guard closest to them drew his baton, only to have Sali pluck it out of his hand and bonk him on the head. She didn't hit him hard, but he crumpled to the floor head-first, moaning and writhing.

The remaining guards jumped back when Sali swept the baton across the room. "Violence isn't the answer here. I suggest you answer my friend."

A guard who was looking at her in a slightly creepy, doe-eyed way raised his hand as if they were in a classroom. "The Council of Nezra received word of your arrival and have summoned you to an audience."

"Who are they to summon a viperstrike?" she said. "How do they even know I'm here?"

He looked apologetic. "We're just following orders."

"This particular council has the front gates of the district watched at all times," said Quasa.

"*This* council?" she muttered. "How many are there?"

Sali had thought she was being adequately cautious coming to the city. Apparently, she had been wrong. In any case, the council was as good a place to find answers as any. The baton slipped from her hand and clattered to the floor. "Lead the way."

The rest of the batons were sheathed. Sali let go of the bully. He collapsed on to all fours and, whimpering, scrambled back to the others.

Sali and the doe-eyed guard helped Quasa up. "I'll be back soon," she said.

The custodian clutched her sleeve and leaned in. "Be wary, Salminde. These are not the same people who once led our city. This Council of Nezra is a council in name only. They do not represent the clan."

"How dare you, old fool," one of the guards snarled. "You will respect—"

"Address Quasa with disrespect one more time and I will sever your arm from your body," she said matter-of-factly. "If word reaches me that anyone treats the custodian of the viperstrikes poorly, I will end your line."

Doe-Eyes stepped between them. "You have my word, Viperstrike. Please, this way."

CHAPTER SIXTEEN

LOCAL POLITICS

Jian winced and pulled away as Meehae dabbed the gash on his cheek with an alcohol-soaked cloth. Her fingers holding his face still were surprisingly strong. She slapped him lightly and blew on his face as she scolded him. "Hold still, you mewling baby. Next time, don't wait until morning."

Jian grunted. The last thing he had wanted to do after a beating was to run through the city to fetch the acupuncturist. After Cyyk and his friends had thrashed him, he had picked himself up and limped back to his shack. Caked with mud and dried blood, Jian hadn't wanted to dirty his bed, but was too worn to wash it off, so Auntie Li had found him shivering on the floor in the morning.

At least he had a reprieve from morning chores. Xinde and Auntie Li helped him to the infirmary and called for Meehae. The senior was leaning against the wall with his arms crossed, watching. He looked both concerned and annoyed as the apprentice acupuncturist cleaned Jian up.

Xinde tried to lighten the mood. "We need to work on your defense. Half of being a war artist is dishing out a drubbing, but the other half is avoiding taking one."

"Or being tough enough to soak up the punishment," grumbled Jian, pulling away as the acupuncturist dabbed the cut over his eye.

She held his head firmly. "You're going to be a great war artist then."

The senior's face turned serious. "How many times now has it been since you arrived? Three, four?"

"Five."

"All from Cyyk?"

"Only three times," admitted Jian. "I didn't say it was Cyyk."

"You didn't need to." The senior ticked his fingers. "Three from Cyyk and the other two from other students. All of those boys who beat you were in the wrong. There's no excuse for this."

"It was Songia one time." This rotten school was full of bullies. He hated it here, hated everyone.

"All right, all of those boys and the girl who beat you were in the wrong. I'm going to punish those responsible."

"Good. They should all get in trouble."

Xinde knelt down next to him. "What happens next time?"

"What do you mean?"

"What happens when you get beaten up again, Hiro?"

Jian was taken aback. "Then you should punish them more."

"Why do you think the other students pick on you? I want you to think about that."

"Because they're puss-sour nasty eggs."

Xinde chuckled. "Cyyk certainly carries an entitled stench, but that's not really the reason. As far as I know, he doesn't pick on anyone else. Why does this keep happening only to you?"

"It's the rich kids picking on the poorer ones."

Xinde shrugged. "Hua and Jindi's parents are peasants. Ulli's father is a homeless drunk."

"His ba died last winter," piped in Meehae.

"Oh, I didn't even know. He never mentioned anything. Poor kid." Xinde turned his attention back to Jian. "Ulli's an orphan. It's not about wealth. There are others who are poor who don't get picked on."

"They're just bullies who pick on the weaker students." Even saying that made Jian's face burn. If he could only show them . . .

Xinde shook his head. "You may be a beginner, Hiro, but you're talented. Everyone sees that."

Taishi's warning rang in his head. Had he blown his cover? He blamed Taishi. She had put him in this mess. "It doesn't matter why," he replied, lamely.

"I'm just trying to help you understand," said Xinde patiently.

"Understand what?"

"He's saying you're a mule-brained boob," snapped Meehae, her voice carrying all the way across the room. She plopped her medic satchel down on the floor. "Look, Hiro, you're my friend, but you're a whiny hissing cat, always spewing bitterness at everything."

Jian bristled. "Why are we friends?"

She smiled sweetly. "I like you in spite of you, but you do make it awfully hard."

Xinde nodded to Meehae, who left the room. "For someone who never throws the first punch, you pick a lot of fights."

"I do not!"

"I'm not blind." The senior's voice was calm and sympathetic. "If you are always looking for something to get angry about, you will find it. Your attitude influences every interaction you have with the people around you."

"I'm the victim here."

"And I'm going to punish Cyyk for that," said Xinde. "I won't begin to try to understand the difficult life you've had, but you can't treat everyone like they've wronged you. Because then eventually they will. You especially can't treat the other students this way. Longxian is not just a war arts school, it's a family. You and me, Cyyk too, we're brothers. Longxian war artists will never engage one another on the battlefield. Our bonds transcend blood and duty."

"Maybe for you," grumbled Jian. "You're Longxian's golden boy."

"For you too," said Xinde, "if you let it. But brotherhood under the lunar court is never freely given. It must be earned through dedication, comradeship, and *benevolence*. Sometimes, it's not about who is to blame or at fault. It's not even about right or wrong. Family and brotherhood run far deeper. Do you understand?"

"Yes." Jian didn't really.

"Excuse me, senior, you wanted to speak . . ." Cyyk appeared at the doorway and froze when he saw Jian.

Xinde winked at Jian, and then his face contorted into one of rage as he whirled on the larger boy. "Someone beat up Brother Hiro last night. I think you did it."

Cyyk was a terrible actor. His face paled and he swallowed as he froze in place. "I—"

"This behavior is beneath a Longxian brother's honor. I have a right mind to put you on yard duty for the rest of the cycle. Maybe that's what it'll take for you to learn some respect."

"But he—"

"Are you going to spout lies?" hissed Xinde. His glance shot to Jian for an instant. "I don't care what Brother Hiro says, I know you did it. I want you to march to the courtyard and kneel in the middle of the training field until tomorrow morning."

Cyyk's eyes bugged. "Until tomorrow morning?"

Jian had been fully embracing Cyyk's comeuppance right up to when Xinde mentioned his name. That was when the senior's intention became clear.

When Jian stayed silent, the senior continued to scold Cyyk. "You're lucky I don't expel you. Maybe then you'll finally learn what humility and brotherhood mean." He turned to Jian. "Well, what do you have to say?"

Jian stared at his big toe. The lesson Xinde was trying to teach was right there, but Jian's pride and anger stood in his way. He just couldn't let it go. He wanted to see Cyyk punished. That entitled bully always got away with everything just because he was rich and popular.

After a few awkward moments, Xinde gave up and sighed. "All right, since neither of you are willing to speak up, then you both share the punishment. On your knees in the courtyard until the dinner gong. Go."

Jian was startled. "But *I'm* the victim."

This was so unfair. He hadn't done anything. If he thought there was anyone who would be on his side, it was Xinde. Apparently not. Everyone was out to get him.

The first morning class was already in session when Xinde marched them into the courtyard. Guanshi, sitting on his throne, didn't bat an eye when he saw Jian. "Horse stance, block, turn, parry, bow stance, punch, kick-punch, step through. Horse stance, parry . . ." His voice trailed off when he caught sight of Cyyk.

Xinde marched the two to the front of class. "On your knees."

Both boys obeyed, facing their peers.

Guanshi's face grew dark and he exchanged a few sharp whispers with Xinde, who responded only slightly less sharply. The master looked unsatisfied as he snapped back to the class gawking at the pair. "Did I say stop? If you fools are waiting for my instructions, so be it. Everyone, horse stance and don't move until I say so." Guanshi got up and stormed off. Half of the poor novices had fallen over by the time the master returned near the end of class.

Another group soon took their place. Lunch rolled around and ended. Several practiced with staves and spears during the open workout period afterward. Jian and Cyyk stayed on their knees the entire time. A few of Cyyk's friends tried to speak to him, but were shooed away by a glower from Xinde.

At some point late in the afternoon, Jian's stamina began to fade. He struggled to stay upright. Cyyk was suffering too, his knees slowly folding in. Seeing his rival lag gave Jian a second wind. If he wasn't allowed to win in a fight, he was going to win this punishment. His rival apparently came to the same conclusion. Both boys became as stiff as staves.

Two more hours passed.

After having missed two meals, Jian's stomach growled at the aroma from the kitchen. He glanced over at Cyyk, who scowled. He scowled back. It became another contest.

Xinde was teaching the late-afternoon class when the front gates slammed open. Two students ran through, one bloodied, and the other looking as if he had taken a dive into a pig trough.

"Senior," a squat burly man named Hunra huffed, falling to a knee as he caught his breath. "There's an incident at the Pecking Crane near the west gate. Some of ours are getting into it with the Southern Cross."

"How many?" asked Xinde. "And how many of theirs?"

Hunra counted on his fingers. "Nine or so. There's many more of theirs."

"What were you doing there?" snapped Xinde.

Hunra looked abashed. "The army's temp quotas had already been filled this cycle, so some of us thought we'd try our luck with the merchants."

Now that the war had ended, this was becoming a more frequent problem. The Pecking Crane was a seedy bar popular with merchants of goods both legitimate and less so, and happened to be where many of them hired guards for their caravans. It was also generally considered a rival school's turf.

Xinde banged the nearest gong three times. Within seconds, every student on the school grounds had gathered around the senior. He picked out ten older students and instructed the rest to continue with their day.

"We're here to keep the peace and make sure no one—not our people, not theirs—comes to harm." He pointed at the assorted clubs, short swords, and staves several carried. "No weapons unless drawn upon first."

"Yes, senior!" the group chorused. The air was charged.

Xinde spotted Jian and Cyyk. "You two. Come along. Maybe you'll finally learn something about brotherhood."

Both boys leaped off their sore knees and joined the back of the group. A few of the students gathered around Jian and verbally questioned the wisdom of his attendance, much to his embarrassment. Cyyk was a known asset, having spent years training and fighting with the other students. Jian was just a novice with a poor reputation. However, Xinde was insistent they accompany the group as he led them out the front gates.

The crowds in the busy streets parted before the Longxian group moving down the street. They knew what to expect when they saw a cluster of armed war artists. If the duchy of Caobiu's primary industry was the military, then Jiayi's industry of specialization was war arts. Because all officers in the army were required to be skilled war artists, no other city in the Enlightened States had as many war arts schools as

Jiayi. Inevitably, this led to rivalries and competition. Longxian was one of the finest schools in the commandery, but they were one of more than a dozen premier academies.

Jian nearly tripped over a pair of legs jutting on the sidewalk. He grimaced at the body attached to them. It was a soldier, hugging his spear as he slept. An entire line of them was sprawled against the wall along their path. The military had been the primary employer of Caobiu duchy for centuries. Once the war with Katuia ended, the Enlightened States drastically cut back military spending, reducing staffing and head count. These cost reductions had affected the entire supply chain, which then cascaded down to everyone from blacksmiths and leather workers to farmers and traders, to even the bar and room salon workers. These cutbacks had been especially hard on Caobiu. There were now a growing number of unemployed soldiers and war artists looking for work with fewer and fewer positions available, which only exacerbated the already fierce competition between schools.

The brawl that had erupted at the Pecking Crane could be heard half a block away. It was the rumbling of a gathering mob punctuated by occasional screams and breaking glass. That wasn't what Xinde was interested in, however.

He raised a hand and motioned for the Longxian to stop just outside the bar so he could listen intently. "No metal or wood clashing. Keep your weapons sheathed. Open hand only unless absolutely necessary. Longxian will not draw first, do you all understand?"

Everyone nodded. Fights between rival schools had become so common, the local magistrates rarely bothered getting involved as long as the offending school paid for damages. They drew the line at death, serious injury, excessive property damage, or rioting. Everything else was fair game.

Many of the reputable schools, Longxian included, took great pains never to draw first in order to avoid liability. Guanshi's wrath after paying for damages or doctors' bills was terrible. For the most part, Longxian had managed to avoid squabbles with the other schools. The only exception was the Red Lion Academy of the Southern Cross based on the west side of Jiayi. Both schools were upper-echelon, respected, and popular. The source of their rivalry stemmed from the markets the schools fed into. Longxian dominated the military officer ranks, while Southern Cross was known for their security work, including palace guards, magistrates, and caravans. With jobs drying up, war artists were fighting fiercely for the dwindling scraps of opportunity.

Inside the Pecking Crane, it was standing room only, not only on the main floor but along the balconies overlooking the center area. The Longxian pushed through the crowd around the brawl. Jian's nerves tensed as the sounds of fighting grew louder. This was his first time seeing one of these things, and his nerves tingled with anticipation. He could tell the others felt the same way. Most looked eager and anxious.

There were only a few combatants, but there were several bodies scattered around the main floor. As far as Jian could tell, he counted four Longxian students fighting twice that number of Southern Cross. A larger group of Southern Cross had formed a perimeter around the fight to prevent it from spilling out of hand and damaging the bar's furniture. They too cared about avoiding the magistrates' and their master's anger.

Xinde was the first to reach the melee. The senior waded into the fray, pulling combatants apart as he came to the defense of his brothers and sisters. When one of the Southern Cross turned to attack him, Xinde disabled him efficiently, slipping a clumsy strike, trapping an arm, and pushing him out of the circle. The senior moved on, wrapping his arms around a woman from behind and spinning her down to the ground. When someone tried to charge at him from the side, he kicked the man's ankles from under him, sending him flying. Within seconds, the senior had smashed through all of the Southern Cross involved in the melee. The crowds clapped and cheered as Jian and the other Longxian dragged their wounded back to safety.

Xinde stood alone in the center of the open area. He folded his arms behind his back as he swept a thunderous gaze across the Southern Cross ranks. "Anyone else?" It was quite dramatic, half indignation and half theatrics. Brawls between schools, while real, followed unspoken rules and were often a school's best marketing tool.

Xinde knew how to leverage these incidents very skillfully, and was already a legend in this city. Jian had witnessed him practice his haughty mien for what amounted to hours in front of a mirror. The senior intoned in a clear voice, "War arts schools used to fight over skill and pride. We competed for bragging rights and the top honors at tournaments, not only for ourselves but for our schools, masters, and family styles. More recently, however, we've begun to quarrel over contracts and jobs . . ." He threw his hands wide and spun as if performing a dance turn. Jian had seen him practice that too. The man was awfully graceful. ". . . for the right to earn a couple of extra copper liang. And now—" He continued his dramatic pauses. "—now we are quarreling over the places where we apply for these jobs?" Xinde stopped abruptly. "Are we so petty and insecure that we can't even seek employment on our own merits?" Xinde took a step toward the Southern Cross. Several tripped in their haste to keep their distance.

A slow, deliberate clap began to echo across the Pecking Crane's tall ceiling. The sea of bodies parted as a tall, muscular man made his way into the circle. Jian's nerves ratcheted up another notch. Zhu Keiro was the Southern Cross's senior. He and Xinde had been rivals since they were children. Both were muscular and handsome, and Keiro was supposedly equally charming. If there was ever another person as perfect as Xinde, it was Keiro, but they were opposites. If Xinde stared into Mirror Lake down in the Eighth Hell, he would see Keiro.

The Southern Cross senior raked his fingers across his bald head and tugged at his braided goatee. "Great speech, Xinde. If that's true, then why is Longxian even here?"

Xinde crossed his arms. "Hello, Keiro. I'm keeping the peace, as should you."

The two men could not have looked more different. Xinde looked like a young noble: clean-shaven with long black hair, a perfectly symmetrical face, and a square jaw—these were all descriptions Meehae had given breathlessly to Jian—and Keiro played the part of a ruffian just as perfectly: bald with a long scar running from the crown of his head down between his eyes, an impressive goatee, and a nose so crooked it whistled every time he breathed. Meehae had also professed that Keiro looked roguishly dashing and would have been very swoon-worthy if it weren't for his bad breath. Meehae had firsthand knowledge, since her master sometimes provided care for the Southern Cross when their usual doctor was unavailable. Seeing Keiro up close for the first time made Jian question Meehae's taste in men.

Keiro stepped forward to confront his counterpart. "The Pecking Crane has always been Southern Cross turf. What is Longxian scum doing here?"

The students around Jian grumbled at the insult, but were held back by Xinde's raised hand. "No one owns public places, Keiro. The merchants are free to recruit whomever they please. Unless the Southern Cross are afraid of a little competition?"

"I'm sure you wouldn't mind, then, if some of ours went to the army recruitment center in Rose Ridge District. Would you?"

"May the better artist win." Xinde's hesitation was brief, but obvious. Master Guanshi would never allow competitors to seek employment near their school. The truth was Keiro and Southern Cross weren't in the wrong.

"Is that so?" Keiro raised his guard. "Maybe we should test that."

Xinde's hands stayed behind his back. "Are you sure you want to do this? We both know who wins the tournaments."

"Maybe it's time we see what happens without judges and points. The Southern Cross will not concede to Longxian. If you want to avoid a fight, go ahead and show your ass."

There was no way Xinde could walk away from that insult, especially under the lunar court. Although truthfully, it was the Longxian who had arrived with the challenge. The circle around the two men widened. While the two men were closely matched, Xinde had always had a decided edge in tournaments: more skilled, quicker, and better disciplined. In the realm of single-handed combat, those small advantages made all the difference and led to an undefeated record.

Several in the crowd began waving strings of liang and shouting names as bookies began collecting bets. Xinde emerged the overwhelming favorite, which only made Keiro's face darken even more. He raised his guard and tapped the ground twice with his lead foot. Xinde offered the war arts bow, his right fist touching his left open palm, and returned his hands behind his back. He tapped the ground twice with his lead foot as well.

Xinde's foot had barely touched the ground the second time when Keiro launched himself at him. His fists and legs snapped forward in a flurry of short punches and kicks. The Southern Cross style was aggressive, often forgoing defense in favor of overwhelming their opponents. Xinde, having sparred with Keiro many times, was ready for this. He slipped the initial barrage, parried several kicks with his own, and sidestepped to safety, all with his hands still behind his back.

The crowds oohed and ahhed. There was a disproportionate number of women cheering for Xinde, which was often the case. Jian and the other Longxian students cheered rowdily at their senior's confident display of skill, while the other side of the circle grumbled and jeered at the perceived disrespect. Their anger wasn't unjustified, but these fights were where war artists established reputations, so a degree of showmanship was generally encouraged.

The two men spun back and forth, their exchanges furious and quick. Keiro continued to press forward while Xinde was content to defend, his hands still behind his back. Panther Pouncing Along Low-Hanging Branch was countered by Lazy Flamingo Skipping Stones. It was followed by Fists of Stone meeting the Maiden Fanning the Air (but with Xinde's feet!). Some of their exchanges were so rapid and decisive that Jian couldn't follow exactly what was happening. When Keiro pushed Xinde backward, the crowd that surrounded them moved with them, everyone keeping one eye on the fight, and one on the rest of the students.

It wasn't until Keiro managed to grab hold of Xinde's shirt and land a glancing blow that the Longxian began to fully defend himself.

"A whole minute," murmured Cyyk in awe, standing next to Jian. It was showboating, but the crowd ate it up and clapped in appreciation while several strings of liang changed hands. Apparently, bets were made on how long Xinde could fight without using his hands.

Jian cheered along with the crowd, short of breath and flinching with each feint and punch as if he were the one fighting. Keiro landed a hard blow that knocked Xinde off balance. When Xinde tried to leap up to the second-story balcony, the Southern Cross senior latched on to his ankle and dragged him back down. Every time it looked as if Xinde was losing, he would pull off some miraculous maneuver, knock Keiro's face sideways, and step to safety.

Jian and the Longxian side went crazy, jumping up and down. He and Cyyk even whooped and slapped each other's backs until they simultaneously realized who they were celebrating with and quickly broke apart.

"That was a neat trick with those sticky hands," said Xinde, positioning himself back in the center of the circle. "You'll have to teach me that technique."

Keiro breathed heavily out of his open mouth. "Our enrollment is full, and the academy has a lengthy wait list, but I can put in a good word for you."

"I appreciate it." How did Xinde fight with a smile? "Seems expensive for what I get in return."

"How about I show you what else we offer?" Keiro's face contorted as he charged again.

The melee continued, except this time Xinde wasn't satisfied staying on the defensive. After weathering Keiro's opening, he attacked, throwing a dazzling combination of looping punches and flashy kicks. Lizard Leaping Between Trees was followed up by Monk with a Thousand Feet.

These moves were more for show than effect, but Xinde made it work, striking Keiro once in the chin and then once again in the chest, sending him tumbling to the ground. The Southern Cross senior recovered quickly, but Xinde kept the pressure on.

The longer the fight went on, the more punishment Keiro took, showing it on his body in the form of bruises and welts. To his credit, the Southern Cross senior refused to quit. However, after being on the losing end of several more exchanges, he began to try to break away. The Longxian senior allowed none of that, matching him step for step, until finally Xinde feinted high, swept low, and took Keiro's feet out from under him. The Southern Cross miraculously stayed upright, but then ate a kick to the midsection that sent him flying into the crowd. Jian and most of the crowd roared in approval. More money changed hands.

Xinde stood over his fallen opponent, triumphant. "Well fought, Keiro." He offered a hand. "Next time, let's settle our differences over some rice tea."

Keiro, sitting on his backside, looked up. "How about a cup of heady zuijo instead?"

He made as if to accept the outstretched hand. There was the metallic sound of a blade leaving its sheath as his hands blurred across Xinde's chest. The Longxian senior couldn't react quickly enough. The front of his robes split open. He stumbled backward, clutching his chest as it began to blossom crimson. Keiro rose to his feet, face dark, a saber in his hand. He charged at the stunned Longxian senior.

Jian stared in disbelief. Drawing blood with a blade after a fair fight was beyond the pale. He didn't think Keiro would actually follow through, but the rage on the Southern Cross senior's face was shocking. Why wasn't Xinde defending himself? The Longxian senior just stood there, frozen, mouth agape, his hands clutching his chest. He made no move to defend himself as Keiro charged him.

Intervening in a duel was highly inappropriate under the lunar court, but Jian didn't care. He moved on instinct and dove into the center of the circle. Keiro saw him approach from the side and would probably have killed him, saber or no saber, but then Cyyk appeared next to him. Together, they knocked the Southern Cross senior down and jumped on top of Xinde to pull him away to safety.

Around them, the other Longxian students began attacking Southern Cross. Jian did his best to shield Xinde with his body, but it wasn't stray blows that Jian had to worry about. He could feel the wetness on the senior's chest. The mayhem spread through the Pecking Crane and out, like a blaze across a dry field. Someone stepped on Jian's hand and another tripped over him. He was in very real danger of getting trampled when rough hands hauled him to his feet.

Cyyk, already sporting a bloody lip, shoved him toward the back. "Get the senior to safety."

Loud whistles began to shrill over the sound of fighting. "Magistrates!" someone yelled. The scuffle stopped abruptly, and the combatants scattered. Jian dragged Xinde as best he could, but they didn't make it very far down the street. He was about to hide Xinde in an alley when a loud and rowdy mob descended upon him.

Jian stepped in front of Xinde and raised his guard. Relief swept over him when he realized he was surrounded by friendly faces. Two older students took Xinde from him and began to carry him back toward the school.

Jian was about to help when Senior Gwaiya held him back. "Do you know where the clinic is located?"

He nodded dumbly.

"Fetch the doctor, as fast as you can." She shoved him along as a boost. "Hurry, run, fool!"

Jian ran like a fool.

CHAPTER SEVENTEEN

SANBA COMMANDERY

It took exactly sixteen days for Taishi to reach the southwestern tip of Xing duchy, where Sanba was located near the border of Lawkan. Covering the breadth of the Enlightened States was an impressive feat, considering she had departed the burial mountain in Shulan just as the second cycle's winter was blooming into the third cycle's wet spring.

When she had been a girl, a trip like this would have taken over a month, especially with unpredictable weather. Roads had been broken, were poorly planned, and were simply dangerous for travelers. It wasn't uncommon for two roads to miss each other by several hundred yards because some useless courtier specializing in bamboo flute had bribed his way onto the contract. The courtier would have ignored the actual work, underpaid the laborers, and siphoned project funds. By the time the mistake was discovered, no one cared enough to make it right. The underpaid laborers would shrug and go home. Travelers would have to leave the dead end and drag their horses and carts through fields or forests or swamps until they reached the next section of road to continue their journeys.

The prevailing corruption ended when Duke Yanso murdered his mentor. The newly promoted purselord of the late Emperor Xuanshing, may his greatness everlast, immediately saw an opportunity to expand commerce and reduce unemployment. He was also sapping the imperial treasury to keep funds out of the hands of his chief rivals, Sunri and Saan, the emperor's two greatest generals. Sunri, whose love for building armies was exceeded only by her love for marching them to war, quickly saw the benefits of well-maintained roads for her armies and followed suit on these ambitious projects. Soon, all the dukes got in on the game, and now there were orderly, connecting roads everywhere. Taishi, for one, was grateful.

She had spent the past few hours staring out the carriage window, admiring the white rapids of the dancing river spitting mist and fish into the air. The carriage shook as it skidded to a halt at the edge of a vast lake. Curious why they had stopped, Taishi opened the window and poked out, taking care to keep the scarf around her head tightly wrapped. She was immediately sprayed by the mist rising off the water and inundated by the sounds of crashing waves. Several of the other passengers barked at her to close the window. Taishi ignored them as she craned her neck to get a better look.

The fast-moving current swirled along the shore, moving in smaller and smaller circles as if circling a giant drain until it disappeared in a large black hole. A plume of mist rose from the lake's center and dispersed into the sky, offering glimpses of fragments of a rainbow that shimmered with the wind. Taishi was still wide-eyed as a peasant girl on her first trip to a commandery when she noticed a sparking of lights blinking beneath the water's surface.

What sort of mystical place was this?

Not quite trusting her eyes, Taishi nudged the passenger next to her. The slumbering man, an old miner with a frayed beard and weeks-old dirt on his face, barely opened his eyes before turning his back to her. Taishi was about to nudge the woman sitting on her other side when loud clicking sounds stopped her. The carriage shook as it began to sink into the earth. It was then that Taishi realized that the carriage had stopped over a wooden platform that was now being lowered underground. The sky and ground slowly disappeared from view, giving way to walls of dirt covered by dozens of large rattling chains, metal snakes crawling in both directions.

The platform descended for several hundred more feet before coming to a jarring stop on what could only be described as a public square in an expansive underground city. Crowds of people, many in fine garb, strolled around the platform, some with families, as if there were nothing out of the ordinary. Vendors lined the sides, hawking their wares and beckoning potential customers, all under the watchful eyes of yellow-clad magistrates.

The scene would not be out of place in any other city, except that the public square was in a massive cavern with a ceiling of dirt three stories high buttressed by wooden beams. Three walls of the square were composed of stone and earth. The fourth side off to Taishi's right was a curtain of rushing water falling past a wide opening. The rushing water shot plumes of mist out, giving the square a morning-fog-like quality.

The carriage rolled off the platform and carefully made its way through the throng toward the wall of water, turning left once it reached the outer edge. Taishi stared over the side and down into the vortex disappearing into an endless pit of darkness. It was as if the abyss were staring back. She looked up and saw just a glimpse of sky obscured by the rushing waters. It took her a moment to realize she was near the base of that plume of mist in the center of the lake. She noticed several large mirrors hanging from chains over the cap, reflecting sunlight to illuminate the underground city.

"First time to Sanba?" asked the woman sitting next to her.

Taishi only nodded dumbly as the carriage rolled along a road that curved around the vortex. "It's beautiful."

The old woman snorted. "Don't let it fool you. They don't call Sanba the asshole of the Enlightened States for no reason."

"Because it's an underground city?"

The woman pointed at the opening. "Because Sanba Falls is the anus of the Zhuun and all the eggheads down here are pieces of shit floating in the latrine. Watch yourself, woman. Sanba's reputation is well earned."

The carriage continued around the large vortex for three-quarters of a circle before breaking away into a side tunnel. The wooden wheels ground on stone tiles as it descended a road illuminated by sconces on both sides. The decline became so steep the passengers had to cling to railings to prevent from sliding forward. It continued a way before making a hard right, swaying so sharply the two inner wheels momentarily lifted off the ground. Taishi's knuckles were white from gripping her seat; dying in a carriage accident was definitely a poor way to go. Fortunately, the carriage managed to stay upright and continued down another decline.

Taishi lost track of how many levels they passed as they went deeper underground, each time passing an exit before making another turn. With every level, she noticed their surroundings turned a little bleaker, the lights a little dimmer, and the people walking about a little poorer.

The carriage finally rumbled to a stop at a coach station. The driver jumped down and began pulling luggage from the under racks and soliciting tips. Taishi pretended to ignore his outstretched hand as she accepted her small satchel and slung all her worldly possessions over her back. It was mostly undergarments and food. Her few remaining valuables were safely hidden under her tomb.

Taishi was about to ask the driver if he could lead her to this Wu Chown person when she changed her mind and asked a more pressing question instead. "Excuse me, boss, can you recommend a good, clean, cheap place to lodge and eat?"

He gave her a hard look and held out his hand again. This time, she obliged, flipping him two copper liang. The driver caught and pocketed the money with practiced ease. He considered her appearance and replied. "Which of the three do you want?"

In hindsight, Taishi probably should have given the driver another answer.

A heavyset cook with a perpetual scowl and dirty hands appeared carrying a large platter. She stopped at the end of the long wooden table and began to fling plates and bowls of food, sending them spinning and sliding across the tabletop as if she were tossing dice. Several bowls of rice, a plate of something green, two plates of chicken claws, and a platter of a roasted duck slid past Taishi, each coming to a stop directly in front of the ordering customer.

Taishi had to give it to her; the cook was exhibiting some serious skill. This was a good example of how jing could be wielded in every aspect of life, not just in the practice of war.

"Boss," signaled the man sitting next to Taishi. The plate of duck in front of him was starting to make her mouth water. "Hoisin sauce?"

The woman looked irritated but obliged, squirting a brown paste from a skin hanging off her shoulder into a small wooden bowl then sending it spinning across the table until it gently ricocheted off the man's platter.

A bowl of congee spun to rest in front of Taishi. Hopefully, the cook was just as great a master at preparing food as at serving it. One look down at the bowl of soupy rice told Taishi otherwise. She counted half a dozen dark specks of weevils flavoring her dish. Taishi sighed. So much for that. Somehow, within less than a year, she had gone from an emissary with a Ducal Mandate feasting at banquets to a fugitive eating bug-ridden porridge.

Well, she needed the extra protein anyway. Her stomach growled as she picked up her chopsticks and shoveled the congee into her mouth, weevils and all. With a little soy sauce, they actually didn't taste that bad, and added some much-needed crunch to the otherwise bland meal. Taishi wolfed down her congee, stopping short of licking the bowl clean. She managed to wheedle some duck skin from the man next to her, who for some inexplicable reason did not like the best part of the bird.

In the end, the meal was edible and her belly was full, which was as good as she could hope for. Taishi gestured to the cook as she paid the bill. "Excuse me, boss, could you direct me to a man named Wu Chown?"

The cook shot her the same irritated look she had given the hoisin sauce man and held out a hand. Taishi masked her grimace and passed over a copper liang. There really was no such thing as a free answer around here.

"Head out back to Ho Cliff on the other side. Two levels up, three bridges across. Follow the signs to a big orange sign." The cook turned away and stomped to the next table before Taishi could ask which direction was "across." Never mind. It would probably cost another liang.

Taishi picked up her satchel and left the inn through the rear entrance, stepping out into a narrow alleyway carved out of greenish limestone. She wound down the path until it opened up onto a windswept ledge of a giant gorge that cut long in both directions.

A constant swirl of wind shifted around Taishi's ankles, kicking up white sand and creating dozens of pretty but irritating funnels on the ground. So really, this was a terrible place to live. To visit. To breathe. To do anything. That beautiful view with the waterfall and the vortex in the lake, clearly where the titled and wealthy resided, was a distant memory. The real ugly, beating heart of Sanba was down here.

Most of the population of Sanba lived in the lower levels, deep within the tunnels in wooden buildings hanging off the sheer cliffs surrounding the abyss. The extensive mining operation here made this city one of the crown jewels of the Enlightened States. The commandery also served as the main trading hub for all the small mining clusters, desert settlements, and lawless camps to the south of Zhuun dominion.

Taishi looked over the side and found the bottom endless, fading into complete darkness. A wave of vertigo swayed the ground beneath her feet as wind blasted her face, cutting her cheek with specks of dust. She pulled the scarf tightly back over her mouth and nose, and continued down a wooden bridge spanning the frightening gap. Taishi clenched her teeth and gripped the thick rope railings tightly as she urged one foot in front of the other. Just because she could ride the currents didn't mean she was perfectly safe. Trying to ride these gusts would be suicide. A group of miners approaching from the other side smirked as they passed, their hands free and their pace relaxed and practiced on the swaying bridge. Taishi couldn't get off the rickety thing fast enough.

It took several wrong turns before she finally found the correct two-levels-up-three-bridges-across tunnel entrance that the cook had referred to. There were no signs that she could see and she doubled back several times before she finally found the dust-covered orange sign that was at best only medium-sized.

Taishi wiped dirt away with her palm, reading aloud: WU CHOWN'S HAPPY MAN'S GUIDE TO THE DESERT.

Underneath the sign in smaller letters: MASTER MAPMAKER.

"A mapmaker who is impossible to find," she muttered, yanking at the door. It was locked. She squinted at yet another smaller line below Chown's title. This business was supposed to be open. She took her frustration out on the door again.

"I'm closed," a voice yelled from the other side.

"Not for another two hours you aren't."

"Too bad. Come back tomorrow."

Taishi had spent months in a crypt and the past two weeks sleeping on a wooden bench in a rickety carriage. She wasn't going to wait a day longer just because someone felt like closing early, and she definitely wasn't going to pay for a night at an inn on his account. Taishi banged her fist more insistently. "I'm not leaving until you open up."

"Better make yourself comfortable. Best keep the lanterns burning. The temperature dips at night and the rats come out—"

Taishi hated rats. The front door blew open, breaking off one hinge and dangling limp on the remaining one. She strolled in and surveyed the room. It looked as one would expect a mapmaker's establishment to look. Dozens of maps of assorted sizes, shapes, and colors hung from the ceiling. To the right was a large drafting table. In the center a writing desk. To the left a half-dressed mousy man squatting over a bucket with his pants bunched around his ankles. He was frozen in place, quivering with his eyes wide, as if unsure if he should scream or pull his pants up.

"Wu Chown I presume. Finish up. I can wait." Taishi sat down at his desk. She wrinkled her nose. "Light a candle."

"Get out! How dare you?" It didn't take Chown long to finish and pull his pants up. He stormed up to her, his fear now replaced by fury, and pointed at his entrance. "You owe me a new door."

"I'm searching for the original Temple of the Tiandi. I'm told you can help. I can pay." She added, "A little."

The mapmaker crossed his arms defiantly. "Get out."

"I just kicked your door off its hinges. Imagine what I could do to your face. You're lucky I'm still offering to pay." A more tactful response was probably in order, but she was tired.

Chown stiffened. "You can't threaten me. I'm under the protection of the Silk Hands."

Apparently he was talking about either a face powder or some local criminal organization. Neither meant much to Taishi. There were already too many fops parading around court looking as if they had dunked their heads in goat's milk. There were also significant criminal organizations in just about every major city. What was one more set of people trying to kill her?

They were wasting time, and Taishi needed something from him. "Look, I can break some bones or I can pay you. Either way I'm not leaving until I get what I need." Diplomacy for her was still a work in progress.

It didn't take much to cow the mapmaker, who was now shaking so profusely his glasses slipped off. "I don't want any trouble."

"Then we're off to a great start." She channeled just a hint of a threat into her voice, using her sound to vividly paint how difficult it would be to draw maps with two broken arms.

Chown caved. "Fine, whatever gets you out of my shop. You said the original Temple of the Tiandi. The one in Fulkan Forest?"

"How many original temples are there?"

"You're still paying me, right?"

"I'm not robbing you if that's what you're asking."

Chown disappeared behind a shelf serving as a room divider and re-emerged carrying a long wooden box. He cleared the drafting table and slowly, lovingly even, opened the long box and pulled out a large colored map of the Enlightened States and the surrounding regions.

It became instantly clear to her how Chown and Mori knew each other. The calligraphy on the map was beautiful. The entire thing was a work of art, exquisitely detailed and gorgeously presented. The mountain ranges surrounding Sanba practically leaped off the paper, and the petrified forests to the southeast, twisted and intricately gnarled, evoked fear and darkness. Even the watery edge brought a sense of calm. This map wouldn't look out of place in the imperial palace.

There was also something strange—something magical—about the map. While she was admiring the details, the geography seemed to shift, albeit slightly, depending on the angle she viewed it from. That was when she realized that the map was actually several transparent sheets layered over one another, creating depth. Entranced, Taishi reached out to stroke a particularly beautiful waterfall falling over a cliff into the ocean.

That was an interesting moment for Chown to discover his spine. He smacked her hand away with surprising force. "Keep your filthy hands off the master map. You don't see me touching your—" He gestured at the Swallow Dances. "—thing."

Taishi let it slide. He had a point. "Is that Fulkan Forest there right next to Sanba with that fat squiggly line in between? That looks like only a few hours away."

"Distance does not correlate with travel time," he replied cryptically and rather smugly. "But yes, Fulkan Forest is within sighting distance of Sanba on a clear blue day."

Taishi's hopes rose. She had expected worse. "Perfect. If it's so close, I don't see why I even need a map."

Chown shrugged. "Suit yourself. I don't care what happens to you, but if you really want to reach your destination, you're going to need it."

"Fine. How much do you want for this thing?"

He sniffed his nose and scoffed. "Purchase the master copy? You're mad."

Taishi didn't mask her exasperation. "Then why even bring it out?"

Chown spoke as if to a child. "The way maps are created is, I focus on the area relevant to your journey, which is—" He used his finger to circle a portion of the map. "—here, and then I expand and copy it onto something a traveler can use."

Taishi pulled out her increasingly skinny purse. "How much for that then?"

Chown glanced over her shoulder at his door half hanging off its hinges. "Twenty silvers, and it'll take three days to draw."

Taishi guffawed. That price was outrageous. "Twenty? For a rotten piece of paper? Maybe I *should* rob you, because it seems like that's what you're trying to do to me."

"I'm a master mapmaker," Chown retorted, sounding indignant and righteously angry, "not some peasant off the streets with a piece of chalk. If you want quality, you pay for it."

That was fair. You couldn't hire a master war artist for the price of a street thug, so why not so for a master mapmaker? Still, twenty silvers would bankrupt her. Taishi wasn't going to sleep on the ground and eat only watery congee just because he was an artist. She waved her hand at some of the plain chalk drawings hanging on the wall. "It doesn't have to be pretty. Just give me something simple like one of those."

The two haggled for a good fifteen minutes before they settled on eight silvers, which was still an appalling cost, but at least he agreed to rush the work.

"Come back in three hours. It won't be up to standard and I won't put my name on it. I'll deny it's mine even." He pulled out a fresh stack of parchment and then framed the region he was going to copy with his fingers. Then he pulled back to a slightly larger region. "Make that four. In the meantime, you need to hire a guide."

"Why? I can read a stupid map."

Chown rolled his eyes. "You don't understand. You need to cross the Sand Snake to reach Fulkan Forest. That means you have to track true north, except when the entire Celestial Family is out, then you'll need to follow three degrees northwest. The map will require six layers in order to properly align the stars as well as taking into consideration wind, depth, and . . ." He took on a sly look. "How are you with three-dimensional geometry and multicausal navigation?"

"What's that?"

"My point exactly."

A young voice interrupted their argument. "I'm back. Are you done with your smelly squat—hey, what happened to the door?"

A young woman, lean and tall with straight black hair that rested on her shoulders, was standing at the doorway. She was plainly dressed and had a square face with bangs that covered her forehead. Pretty, but nothing particularly interesting, except for her eyes. They were sharp and intense, and moved about as if she was scanning the room, taking everything in. She was obviously the mapmaker's daughter, but while Chown wore an air of anxiousness, the young woman looked assertive and carried herself with a hardness that belied her age.

The daughter glared at Taishi and crossed her arms. "Is this your doing?"

"Yes." Taishi turned back to Chown. "Where can I hire a guide who can read your stupid map?"

"The Desert Trade Post on the lowest southern edge of the city at the cliff's base. I can sell you a map to it if you get lost." He held out his hand. "Now pay for the map to the Temple of the Tiandi. Eight silvers."

"When I return."

"What?" The young woman stormed up to the desk. "You're drawing a shifting map for this woman who kicked down our door for eight silvers? Are you an idiot? Your time is more valuable than that. You might as well just give away the shop."

Taishi couldn't help but like her.

"Watch your mouth, Zofi," Chown replied sharply. "Remember your place, daughter." He looked back at Taishi and took on a firmer tone, as if trying to compensate. "Pay first. Come back in four hours."

"And a rush job?" Zofi practically shrieked.

Taishi grudgingly slapped the eight silvers on the table. "I'll return shortly. I expect my map ready."

As she turned to leave, she found herself blocked by Chown's overly assertive daughter. "You may have scammed my weak, addled father, but you're not getting away with it while I'm here. You owe us fair payment and a new door."

Taishi didn't have time for this. She fingered the handle of her sword. "Move, girl."

Zofi was unfazed by the threat, her hands on her hips. "Wu Chown is one of the greatest mapmakers in the Enlightened States. He studied for ten years at Sunsheng University, and then spent twenty more ignoring Mam and me while he built up this miserable business. Now that Mam's dead and he's an old fool, this place is all we have. I'm inheriting it, I won't let you cheat me."

Taishi had a response, but something about this mouthy little thing proved too adorable. She broke into a grin and rubbed out three copper liang. "I'm not buying you a new door, but this should cover some hinges."

The coins disappeared in the girl's hand. She didn't budge. "Three more silvers for the map. We usually charge fifteen for a shifting map. You're still getting a bargain."

"Sorry, girl." Taishi shook her head. "Deal's a deal."

"Made under duress," Zofi countered. "You rattled your sharp, pointy thing, and he caved like the limp lilyweed that he is, I bet."

"Hey!" the limp lilyweed protested from behind the desk.

Both women ignored him as they sized each other up. "I want a fair deal," said Zofi. "Three more silvers or no map."

Zofi reminded Taishi of a certain brash little war artist when she had first set out to make her mark in the world: fearless and naïve. The world would beat all that naïveté out of her quickly enough, assuming she lived that long. As much as the girl was growing on Taishi, her little petulant act was also wearing thin. Taishi waved her hand aside, sending a small air current into her side. Zofi squawked and stumbled, nearly crashing into the shitting bucket.

"I'll be back in a few hours, mapmaker," called Taishi, not bothering to look back. "The map better be ready."

"Tell them you need to head to the area past the mining encampment in Manki, and then the guide will have to take you a day or two farther on foot."

Taishi offered Zofi a nod of encouragement as she left. There was a shortage of strong, assertive women in this harsh world. She considered tossing a silver liang as a sign of approval when her stomach growled, reminding her how much food a silver liang could buy.

Taishi left Wu Chown's Happy Man's Guide to the Desert without parting with another coin.

CHAPTER EIGHTEEN

THE COUNCIL OF NEZRA

S ali left with the council guards, returning to the alley and cutting across back streets. She noted that they took no main streets at all, except for one time when they crossed to the other side. Whoever had given the fetch order was taking pains to keep her presence quiet.

Their destination was on the opposite end of the district, which took about an hour to cross. Surprisingly, the Katuia District was even more crowded than the Zhuun ones. They passed dirtied streets littered with beggars. There were small fires on the ground everywhere, as if the people here had lost their story and simply given up. Sali gritted her teeth at the heresy and tried to keep her eyes forward, but she found it harder to maintain that wall as they tread deeper into the district. Anger resonated loudest within her, but also a deep, mournful grief.

They eventually turned in to a less congested street a little better maintained than the rest of the district and continued until they reached a run-down estate in a cul-de-sac. They entered the front gates of a nobleman's large row house that showed all signs of having been abandoned for decades.

"How did the council's eyes at the gates recognize me?" she asked as they entered the front gates.

Doe-Eyes looked at her with disbelief. "You're Salminde the Viperstrike. I grew up listening to tales of your campaigns. I used to pretend to be you when my friends and I played as raiders."

Sali rolled her eyes. "Oh, never mind."

They were met in the courtyard by a servant, who guided them to the back garden. They followed a winding path before stopping at the edge of a perfectly circular pond. In the center of the pond was an island with a bamboo pavilion. Two guards were standing at the end of a bridge connecting to it. Doe-Eyes approached them and exchanged a few words. Sali noted that these guards, a man and a woman, also wore green tags on their shoulders.

Doe-Eyes returned a moment later. "The guardlead is announcing you to the Council of Nezra. It shouldn't take long. I'm sure—"

"It's fine. I don't mind." The boy was nervous. Sali wasn't sure why, but his anxiousness put her on alert. Was this an ambush, an assassination attempt? Why would the Council of Nezra want her dead? Sali glanced to both sides: five guards within arm's reach. This council had better summon more help if they wanted to kill her.

Doe-Eyes suddenly jerked around to face her. He turned so quickly Sali nearly flinched. Nearly. If his hands had been anywhere near a weapon, he would have already been dead.

"A thousand pardons, Viperstrike Salminde," he blurted, his formality awkward. "I must ask. Now that you've returned to the clan, will you be restoring the viperstrike sect?"

"I . . ."

"If so, please allow me to be the first to call you master. My name is Hampa. I applied to be a sect neophyte the day before the fall of Nezra. It has been my dream—"

She spun the young man back the right way, silencing him. She murmured out of the side of her closed lips, "You're supposed to be guarding me, young Hampa." He recovered just in time to see the guardlead return from the pavilion.

The lead approached Sali and held out a hand. "The honorable

Council of Nezra accepts your request for an audience. Relinquish your weapons."

That was an interesting way to phrase it. "You're free to try to take them."

"You'll get them back after your meeting." Sali favored her with silence. The guardlead fidgeted, wilting under her gaze. "I cannot allow weapons in the presence of the council."

Sali turned to go. "If the council ever grows a backbone, they can come to me. They'll be allowed to keep *their* weapons."

"But—wait. You cannot refuse a council summons. Stop her!"

None of the other guards made a move; none dared. Sali was about to walk back into the row house when a gravelly voice barked out. "You twits, invite her back. If the viperstrike truly wished us dead, it wouldn't matter if she were armed. None of you wet lilies would be able to slow her down."

Sali recognized that voice. She turned, half wondering if the large man to whom it belonged had suffered a similar transformation to poor Quasa. To her mild disappointment, the man walking down the wooden bridge toward them was just as well fed and healthy as she remembered. "Ariun."

"Salminde," he offered a tilt of his head. "You look disappointed to see me."

"Just surprised," she countered. "I did not think Nezra's defensechief would have survived his responsibility."

"I can wonder the same about you, Will of the Khan." Ariun stepped aside and beckoned. "Join us, so we can both sate our curiosity."

Sali had no reason to refuse. She walked shoulder to shoulder with him across the pond. "You're part of the council now?"

"I *lead* the Council of Nezra now," he replied.

"How fortunate for you."

"Nothing fortunate at all," he replied. "There are no winners here, Salminde. No one wants this job. We serve suffering under the rule of the Zhuun while trying to lessen our people's plight."

"At least you're not starving."

Sali studied the man as they continued across the pathway. The lines along his face were deeper and harder than when their paths last crossed. His shaved sides now were speckled white. Nevertheless, he was still lean and muscular, and he cut an imposing and authoritative figure, looking every bit the Katuia warrior, except his warrior's mane had been shaved down to its burrs. There was one thing different about him, however. It was a missing piece of the man that she had never seen him without. "What happened to Sting?"

Ariun's jaw tightened. "After our surrender," he replied in a low voice, "the Zhuun general demanded a token of fealty from the surviving leaders of the city."

While the Katuia usually did not inject souls into their belongings— a horse was a horse, a sculpture was a sculpture, and a sword a sword— there were rare exceptions. Sali's tongue, which she cherished deeply, was just her tongue. It was a weapon, a tool. But just like she was *the* Viperstrike among viperstrikes, Ariun's Sting—a chain-whip weapon that stiffened into a straight narrow blade—was *the* Sting among stings. Passed down from his grandfather, who had been considered the finest weaponsmith of his generation, it had been Ariun's most prized possession for as long as she had known him.

"Sting is in the hands of the man who burned our city to the ground and sank it beneath the Grass Sea."

"It was a choice made and made freely, one I would make again for what it bought our people. I do not regret it." Sali didn't believe him. Ariun didn't sound like he believed it either.

The two reached the small island where a group of men and women were waiting expectantly, sitting along the wooden benches lining the perimeter of the bamboo pavilion. The Council of Nezra—thirteen in all—were all relatively well dressed and well nourished. Sali did not recognize any of their faces, although that wasn't surprising. She had spent more time in the past decade sleeping under the open sky of the Grass Sea than next to her home's hearth.

Ariun took his seat at the head of the pavilion. "Fellow advisers, Salminde the Viperstrike and Will of the Khan."

Sali bowed. "Council of Nezra." By the looks on their faces, they expected her arrival and were not particularly pleased with it.

"Welcome, Salminde," said a gray-haired woman. "The Council of Nezra welcomes back to her hearth one of our great warriors."

Sali studied each face closely. None, save for Ariun, looked like they ever had their sides shaved. "What happened to the old council?"

Ariun made a noise that sounded like choking. "The former council refused many of the Zhuun's demands after the capture, so they were made an example of."

"So this is a puppet council then," she spat.

"We maintain order. And we lead our people," the woman replied firmly. "A necessity we hope you see the wisdom of as well."

That was as far as the pleasantries went. The conversation immediately took a turn.

"Why are you here in Jiayi?" the young man next to the woman practically demanded. "You are a Will of the Khan, yet you still survive him. Why have you not returned to the Whole?"

"I will decide when my service to the khanate has concluded." The ice Sali put in her voice brooked no disagreement. "In these unseen times, I believe I can better serve our people alive than dead, so I pledged myself a Soul Seeker."

The council grumbled.

"This is unprecedented," said the woman.

"Outright dangerous," a wrinkled man wearing Zhuun garb snapped.

"Blasphemy," added another in shaman's robes.

Sali bristled, annoyed. She was really tired of hearing this from everyone.

Ariun held up a hand for silence and asked. "And your search for the reincarnation of the Khan has brought you here?"

Sali met his gaze and nodded. "It has."

"And is that your only objective here?" asked a councilman to her left.

Sali raised her chin and recited. "The Eternal Khan of Katuia is the salvation of our people. His return is all that matters. Your cooperation is required."

For months following her Return, Sali had journeyed throughout the Grass Sea searching for survivors of Nezra, combing refugee camps, following whispered rumors and faint leads. She once even allowed herself to get captured by a band that had turned to raiding. Bit by bit, through each survivor's spoken memories, she aggregated the individual stories to paint a picture of the battle's aftermath.

"These are indeed unseen times for the Children of Nezra," said the woman. "The only way we can exact our vengeance is by persevering. It took many months for this council to form and forge an agreement with the land-chained. The peace we've achieved required many meetings and conciliatory efforts. Only recently has this council returned a semblance of calm and stability to our people. We will not see that progress disrupted."

"Even in chains?" Sali growled.

"Even as servants," the young man cut in aggressively.

The events following Nezra's downfall were even more devastating than the battle. Sali had heard firsthand the stories of survivors who managed to escape the forced march to their internment at the commandery.

The old woman was the only one who sounded sympathetic. "All we can do at this time is see to the welfare of our people. Anything else," she said with resignation in her voice, "will take time until a political solution can be found."

Sali swallowed her fury. If this council was the voice of her people, then her people were truly defeated. It appeared most of the upper castes of the city were no more, likely by Zhuun design. Sali wondered why the survivors of Nezra had not resisted and risen up, but she also recognized that she had not experienced what the survivors had to endure. She had not had to spend every day of the past three cycles trying to survive in this alien land with dead earth beneath her feet.

The worst part of all this was how the spirit shamans had forsaken her city. The majority of Nezra had died protecting it. Most who survived the battle were captured and marched to Jiayi, and interned here as indentured servants. Sali's soul ached not to have fought alongside her people. As a term of the armistice, the spirit shamans had agreed to indenture the survivors to Jiayi and General Quan Sah, the general commanding the army that destroyed Nezra, now the governor of Jiayi for his victories. If Mali was still alive, she would be here.

"Now that we have come to an understanding," the woman continued. "What does the Soul Seeker require?"

"I need a list of every child under the age of eighteen." There were no limitations on whom the Khan would inhabit next, but it had always been a child. Once discovered, they would go to Chaqra to be trained by the spirit shamans, and then take part in the ritual to become the next Eternal Khan on their eighteenth birthday. Jiamin had been fourteen when he had been discovered.

"Done," the woman waved. "We will take a census and send word. Anything else?"

"That would be all, for now." Sali heart-saluted and turned to leave. She made it halfway across the bridge when heavy footsteps caught up to her. "Wait, Salminde."

She stopped and met him halfway. "Ariun."

"I just wanted you to know you have my support," he began.

"You did not come after me to tell me this."

He walked alongside her across the pond to the end of the bridge. "This council is the only voice our people have with the Zhuun. While we all wish to live free on the Grass Sea one day, fate has determined otherwise. It has taken almost a year for the council to carve a voice with the Zhuun. We've stopped beatings and executions. We had the afternoon curfews moved to the rise of the first moon, and have negotiated free passage between the districts. It is this council that ensures our people have food, clean water, medicine, and supplies."

"Our people owe you a debt of gratitude for keeping us together and safe." Sali meant it. "Speak frankly."

He stopped at the end of the bridge. "I need an assurance from you. The council has worked too long and too hard to establish the small peace that we now enjoy. The Children of Nezra are in no position to support an uprising. We are barely keeping things together as it is, and cannot lose our meager gains. Do I have your word that you will not cause trouble while you are here?"

Sali parceled her words out carefully. "You do what you think best, and I will do the same."

He grabbed her arm as she turned to leave. "That's not good enough."

She stared at his hand until he let go, and then continued walking. "It will have to be, for now."

CHAPTER NINETEEN

SCHOOL LIFE

Jian sped toward the acupuncturist's clinic as fast as he could. He waved his bloodstained hands wildly as he navigated the crowded streets. "Eyes up. Pay attention! Emergency! Out of the way!"

Most paid him no attention, nor bothered to move out of his way. The few who did look up just stared curiously. A few intentionally got *into* his way.

Jian had learned to expect this in his first weeks in Jiayi, when just about everyone kept knocking him down or bowling him over. At first, he thought people didn't notice him because of his plain brown robes—the only set he had. It was later that he realized it was because they didn't care. Some even did it for fun. That was when he had learned that this was a city of asses. All the vendors, war artists, soldiers, couriers, people walking about, all of them. All asses. Jian veered to the side to avoid an oncoming cart, moving as quickly as he could with his back pressed to a wall. He bounded over a couple of dogs who growled and nipped at him. Even the strays here were asses too.

He skidded to a stop at a busy intersection and was nearly trampled by a pair of mounted magistrates. To make matters worse, the officer, noticing him standing so close with his disheveled, stained robes, took him for a beggar or thief and kicked out. Jian fell into the mud and sputtered. He wiped the grime off his face and scowled at being submerged in ankle-deep goo. At least it covered up the bloodstains from Xinde's wound. Jian barely had time to sit up before having to dive aside to avoid another cart. That one didn't stop either.

"You rancid egg!"

Remembering the urgency of his errand, Jian picked himself up out of the hole and continued running, weaving among carts and rickshaws as he passed the Kati District. A whole city of Kati had arrived earlier in the day, and now the traffic around their district clogged everything. Jian shied away from an approaching group, suddenly wary of so many of his former enemies surrounding him.

"You're not the stupid Prophesied Hero anymore," he muttered under his breath as he hustled down the street.

It took almost two hours for Jian to make his way to the Saffron Tenet District on the other side of town, where most of the medical buildings were situated. Master Kui's clinic was located alongside a dozen other acupuncturists on a street known as Needle Row. Jian had questioned why all of these similar professionals were clumped together in such a way. It didn't make any sense for everyone in Jiayi to have to go to one place for their services. Xinde had explained that Duchess Sunri planned everything as if it were an army camp, so everything was grouped together in the interest of efficiency. For administrators, not people who needed services.

Jian barged into the clinic, swinging the door open with a loud bang. Meehae was standing in the center of the room staring at a red circle the size of a child's fist painted on the wall a few feet away. She paid him no notice.

"We need—" he huffed, slightly out of breath.

"Shh." Meehae threw up a hand. "I just need a second."

"But—"

"It's three seconds now, Hiro." The apprentice acupuncturist dipped her hand into a pouch hanging at her side and made a quick throwing motion.

Jian didn't notice anything at first, and then he saw four thin needles sticking out of the wall a good hand's length to the left of the red dot. Meehae scrunched up her face and tried again with her other hand, landing four more needles just above the dot. She fired two more times, landing clusters of needles to the right and to the bottom right.

Jian whistled. "That's pretty good—"

"Stupid miserable slick little dot," she swore loudly, stomping over to the wall and plucking each needle out.

"Wait, were you *trying* to hit the red mark?"

"You hush. I want to see how well you do flicking needles."

Jian wanted to tell her that Master Luda's eagle style utilized metal chopsticks as throwing weapons, and of course Jian was an expert, but he obviously couldn't. It probably was the wrong thing to say even if he could.

Then he remembered why he came. "Keinde's hurt, I mean, he hurt—"

Meehae looked nonplussed. "Keinde? Who's that? Do you mean Keiro? Why are you coming to me about him? His school has their own doctor."

"I mean Xinde. He's hurt badly. Keiro cut him with a saber across the chest."

Meehae had her bag in her hand and was halfway out the door before Jian had even finished the sentence. He followed after her.

"What happened to my Xinde?" she demanded.

"Xinde won the fight, and then Keiro cheated and pulled a saber and slashed Xinde across the chest." He struggled to keep pace alongside her as she raged down the street. The passersby gave Meehae one look and jumped out of her way.

"Blast that putrid hairless cantaloupe head and his stink breath. How deep is the wound? Is my Xinde conscious?" Meehae didn't slow when they reached the intersection. Shockingly, none of the traffic struck her.

"That's awfully possessive of you. I don't know how bad. There was a lot of blood." Jian became alarmed. "Are you sure you can handle this? What about your master?"

"Master Kui is with a client's dog."

"Dogs get acupuncture?"

Meehae shrugged. "She branches out when business is slow."

Fortunately, the Rose Ridge District was not far from the Saffron Tenet District. A large worried crowd had already gathered at the entrance to the infirmary. Jian escorted Meehae, pushing through. A wave of relief washed over the students when they noticed her.

"The doctor's here," someone said. "About time."

"Wait, that's Meehae, the apprentice. Where's the real doctor?"

She stopped at the doorway and slammed her bag on the floor. "My master's busy. I'm here to take care of it." The looks of relief quickly turned back to concern. She shooed the crowd clustered around her. "Everyone, get back. You're making me nervous."

Meehae slid the door open and went inside. Jian caught of glimpse of Auntie Li standing over a pale, prostrate Xinde, pressing down on his chest. The door slid closed with a loud thunk. The worried crowd, no longer held at bay, surged forward and surrounded the door. A few students went around the side to peek through the windows.

The door slid open a sliver a moment later. Meehae poked her head out, scowling. "I can hear all of you breathing. Don't you have anything better to do?" Apparently not, because no one moved. Meehae sighed. "Just keep it down."

Master Guanshi stormed into the courtyard a moment later. "His hairless rat drew a saber in the middle of an open-hand duel? What is shriveled scrotum Shiquan thinking? Does he want to go to war? With me? We used to be friends! I sent that man a grand opening flower arrangement! I'm going to run his little operation right out of Jiayi! Gwaiya, Cyyk, Kabi, break open the armory."

The rest of the riled-up students scattered with whoops and cheers. Some rushed to the back to do as the master had instructed. Others went to the training shed, returning with armfuls of padded leather jerkins. Cyyk and Kabi carried out two buckets of staves while Mooyan hugged a collection of sabers. They looked like they were preparing for war.

Jian stayed at the steps to the infirmary along with three other novices, unsure if he should participate. He watched as the others donned their tunics and helped one another tighten their straps, chattering excitedly among themselves, working themselves up into a frenzy. He frowned, disapproving of how excitable everyone was.

Jian used to spend hours in the arena anteroom with his personal guards before his training sessions. Every one of his guards was a skilled and decorated veteran. He always marveled at how they could be so calm and collected before their fights, not like this undisciplined bunch working themselves up into exhaustion.

His attention shifted to Wonna and her older sister and senior, Gwaiya, checking each other's armor. He could see this fight was important to them, to all the students at the school. They cared deeply about Xinde and about Longxian. This was why they were so agitated. Jian's personal guards had always been relaxed not because they were grizzled veterans, but because his training sessions were a joke. *He* was a joke to them, to the masters, the dukes, to everyone, just a spoiled brat they were earning liang babysitting.

No one at the Celestial Palace had cared about him. That was why it had been so easy to discard him after their worthless prophecy broke. No, that wasn't true. Uncle Faaru had cared about Jian, loved him even, and he had paid for that affection with his life.

"Hey, Hiro, what are you doing standing there?" Cyyk walked over and tossed him a padded leather vest. "You're a scrawny runt. This should fit you."

A sharp rebuke jumped to Jian's tongue, but he hesitated. Cyyk was insulting him, true, but the tone felt different. Not that it mattered. He didn't really belong at this school. This wasn't really his fight. He was just hiding from Mute Men and assassins. Getting involved would only risk his cover.

The bigger boy glanced over his shoulder. "Are you coming or not?"

All that reasoning was completely discarded the moment Cyyk asked. Jian threw on the tunic without hesitation. "Of course. I'll be right there."

Jian would not admit it, but all he had been waiting for was for someone to ask. As the Prophesied Hero, he had always stood alone. He was supposedly special, different, and everyone at the palace had treated him that way. Jian hadn't realize just how terribly lonely it had been until right now. For the first time, he felt a sense of camaraderie. He was excited to be part of something. He hungered for more.

"We depart!" barked Guanshi. He carried a tall ax with an elongated blade, an heirloom named the Steed Slayer. He signaled for Longxian to form behind him. The large group was about to file out the gates when a loud voice cut through the chatter.

"Where do you think you're going, Master Guanshi?" Auntie Li's voice carried all the way across the courtyard. She stepped out of the infirmary with her fists on her hips.

Guanshi froze and looked very much like a student caught stealing sesame dessert balls from her kitchen. "I'm taking care of business."

"I'll crack your head if you take another step." She stormed up to him shaking her finger. "You met with the magistrates just yesterday promising to minimize the violence between schools, and now you're going to personally feud with Shiquan? Are you missing a yolk?"

Every student remained perfectly still. Guanshi may have been the owner and master of the school, but everyone knew who was *actually* in charge.

All except for a yolkless egghead who opened his mouth. "But, Auntie Li, those Southern Cross bastards need to be taught a lesson."

The look she shot the mouthy boy nearly turned him to jade. "Am I talking to you, Phen?"

"Right now? Yes. Oh, I mean, no."

"Go clean the latrine."

"But Hiro already—" Phen bowed his head. "Yes, Auntie Li."

She turned her wrath back on Guanshi. "You start a war, and those magistrates will shut you down."

"They nearly killed my senior," he roared. "How would it look under the lunar court if we do not retaliate? I will lose face."

"You will lose face and still be open for business. If you get involved in two spats in one day, a fine will be the least of your worries." She walked over and prodded him hard with the end of a long chopstick. "Xinde will be fine, which will be more than I can say for any of you if you don't all turn around and go back to your lessons."

Everyone stood still, waiting for a sign. Then Master Guanshi spit out a string of curses, shoved Steed Slayer into Gwaiya's hands, and stormed back to the main house.

Just like that, it was over. Jian had just finished adjusting his padded tunic, and now he had to take it off. Everyone else grudgingly did as well.

Auntie Li stood at the double gates as if guarding them, her hands back on her hips. "Put all those pointy toys back into the armory. It better be organized. If I find one of those broom handles out of place, you're all cleaning the latrines too. Hiro's going to get the rest of the year off."

Jian grunted. "That's not a bad—"

"That wasn't an invitation to open your clap, Hiro." Her voice grew louder. "And while we're putting things away, we might as well tidy up the courtyard. Wipe down the statues and refresh the vases, trim the hedges. I want this place to look like a water painting. Now get to work."

The students goosed to their work, putting weapons back in their buckets and stacking the padded armor in neat piles. A small army of brooms came bustling out, and everyone was soon busy cleaning the stone tiles. Jian didn't mind this punishment at all. These were all chores he usually had to do. The students were still diligently tidying up the front of the school when the infirmary door opened and Meehae stepped out. She had been inside for less than an hour. Her expression was unhappy, and the front of her robes looked like she had just butchered a cow. Everyone gawked, horrified.

"It's not mine," she said hastily. Realizing that wasn't helpful, she added. "It's better than it looks. I have to get back to the clinic, but Xinde's going to be fine. He's resting with needles for the pain. Everyone, leave him alone. I'll come back to reapply needles and bandages."

A collective sigh of relief passed through the students. Some cheered and patted each other on the back as if they were the ones who had saved Xinde's life. It was a testament to how beloved their senior was. A few offered Meehae thanks, but most of the congratulations were to one another. Jian studied his friend as she picked up her medic satchel and weaved her way through the celebrating students. Her words did not match the look on her face. She looked puzzled, distracted.

Jian was about to ask when Auntie Li touched his arm. "It's almost time for dinner, Hiro. I need more wood. Fetch some from the back."

He nodded, his eyes still trailing after Meehae. What was wrong with Xinde?

CHAPTER TWENTY

NUISANCES

Taishi wandered lost through the tunnels of Sanba for more than an hour before she finally found the Desert Trade Post. It hadn't helped that the streets in the city were poorly lit and had sign-posts only at the larger intersections, not to mention everyplace she went looked exactly like the one she had come from. Maybe she *should* have taken up Chown's offer and bought a map.

The city, while not particularly wide or long as commanderies went, was shockingly tall, going quite a way up and down the cliffside. The trading post was not only at the far southern edge, but also fifteen levels below the mapmaker's shop. Taishi may have been a master war artist, but she hated stairs as much as the next person. By the time she reached the trading post, night had fallen. She hadn't realized how late it was. Time was nothing but numbers when you were underground.

The first thing Taishi noticed when she neared the trading post was the wind. It crept up on her, howling a sharp, high-pitched shriek that got gradually louder until she couldn't hear anything else. The entrance of the trading post led into a massive cavern with tall ceilings and walls far enough away she had to squint to see them. A thin layer of sand swirled around her feet, blowing in from outside. Taishi had hardly taken a few steps when she passed a large stone gateway carved directly into the rock leading out of the city. She stopped mid-step as a wave of agoraphobia washed over her.

Taishi had expected to see a forest outside the trading post at the cliff's base, Fulkan Forest being just on the other side of a squiggly line on Chown's map, but instead she was met with a desert that stretched as far as she could see. Not only that, it looked alive. Immense sand dunes rose and fell, like ocean waves crawling slowly across the landscape. She witnessed two rolling waves slamming and merging with each other, butting against each other and rising into a giant wall before toppling over. It was beautiful.

And terrifying.

And she had to cross it. Taishi wasn't a coward by any means, but there was a vast difference between fighting men and fighting nature. She would wade into a battle against a hundred enemies with barely any consideration for safety, but the thought of wandering in that vastness made her soul quiver.

"What happened to the trees?" she wondered aloud.

A caravan owner passing by shot her a puzzled look. "What do you mean?"

Taishi pointed outside. "This is Fulkan Forest? Where's the forest? Where are the trees and the bushes and the weeds?"

The man laughed. "Sorry, mistress. Fulkan Forest is on the other side of the Sand Snake, about three, maybe two days east if you have a good driver."

"I thought it was just a river."

"It is, in a way." His smile broadened when he saw her eyes go buggy. "First time surfing the Snake, eh? It'll be memorable. I hope you survive."

The very thought of having to pass through the hurricane made Taishi reconsider all her plans, first of which was crossing that hellscape. It took her a few moments to finally bully her spine stiff. A woman who had defeated some of the greatest war artists in the land should have no

problem crossing this—she looked out again—terrifying ocean of giant
sand tidal waves.

"You used to be afraid of heights too," she muttered.

Taishi turned her attention back to the trading post. It was surprisingly busy for this time of night. Dozens of guards, drivers, and team
bosses buzzed around their large caravans. Nine-wagon sleighs were
currently lined up in neat rows while a few more were pulling in and
departing through a large opening on the far side. She soon learned that
the majority of the caravans did most of their travel during these hours.
When she inquired with a caravan boss why that was the case, she was
given vague answers and amused smirks. It had something to do with the
heat during the daytime, but also how it was easier to navigate using the
stars, not just the Celestial Family.

She passed by the rows of giant sleighs laden with supplies, some as
tall and wide as a house, each in different stages of preparation. On one
side of the port, luxury goods were being off-loaded: Sacks of spices, several species of serpent and dragon skins, assorted colored vials, cut gems,
and beautiful, colored glassware were being pulled from incoming wagons by porters and carefully transported to holding areas. On the other,
rations and gourds of water and other supplies were being loaded onto
outbound caravans. Taishi approved of how orderly and efficient things
were. She passed the loading area and approached a counter where several caravan bosses were waiting to speak with the portmasters working
behind booths. Taishi joined the back of one line as it inched forward. It
took a good ten minutes for each boss to get processed, and there were
still many ahead of her.

Taishi could count on her good hand the number of times in the last
twenty years she had had to wait in a line. This was probably how things
usually went in these trading posts, since many of the bosses were prepared, having brought stools and drinks with them. Several were clustered in small groups sharing stories and bartering.

After twenty minutes, Taishi decided to cut to the front. She wasn't
trying to register her caravan, she just needed information. She ignored
the angry glares as she passed each boss, and offered a weak nod in apol-

ogy to a dusty sand-swept woman in a heavy turban whose turn was next. The woman's eyes flickered down to Taishi's sword resting at her waist, noting how easily it rested at her side and moved with ease with her, as if an extension of her body. She stood aside. Taishi's father had often said that a weapon and its wielder were like intimate dance partners. The way you moved with a weapon on your person was often a forecast of your skill with it.

"Excuse me, portmaster," Taishi said in her friendliest voice. "I need to book passage southeast. Could you please point me to the passenger carriages?"

The portmaster raised an eyebrow and looked her up and down. "You must be a ruck, or a really foolish and poor noblewoman."

Taishi had no idea what either meant. "That sounds very plausible."

"No carriages ferry passengers through the Sand Snake," replied the portmaster. "The only way to cross is to get your own sleigh or attach with a caravan."

"Simple enough," Taishi said, beaming. "Where can I book passage with a caravan? I'll need someone who can read shifting maps."

The portmaster pointed lazily behind her. "All these people who you just cut in front of can help. Now step aside. Next."

Taishi craned her head behind her and saw a row of angry faces. She stepped aside for the woman with the turban to pass, and then began working the line. She inquired about buying passage on the caravans with every single waiting boss and was duly turned down by each one. Most weren't heading in that direction. Some refused outright to even speak to her. The few who did quoted her outrageous prices for what should have been only a two-day trip.

One muscular dark-skinned man crossed his arms. "I doubled the price because you cut in line."

"Hah, that's what I did too," said a bald woman she had asked previously.

"Ask me next, woman." A bearded man waved farther back in line. "I'll triple it."

"I only had to ask a question," Taishi sputtered. "It just took a few seconds."

"It was two questions," the portmaster piped up.

"Well," the dark-skinned boss added, "I just spent the past four days locked down in a desert hurricane, and I still had to wait in line. What makes you so special?"

"The two worst sins in the sand are stealing a caravan's steeds and cutting in line at an outpost," someone shouted. "That's the trade life."

"Trade life," several echoed.

The price for passage grew more outrageous with every subsequent person she asked. No one wanted to sell passage to a line-cutter.

Taishi thought she had caught a lucky break when a new boss, unaware of her line-cutting ways, joined the back of the line. His face was clean and his robes weren't sanded, a good sign that he was on his way out. She approached him and spoke in a husky voice. "Hey, handsome boss, can you read a shifting map?"

The young boss, sunken eyes and high cheekbones, appeared a little delicate for this line of work. He looked confused. "Yes. Why do you ask?"

"I need to book passage southeast toward Manki. Are you headed that way?"

He nodded. "As a matter of fact I am, first thing in the morning."

"Can I book passage on your caravan?"

The young boss shrugged. "I don't see why not. I could use the extra coin."

"She's a line-cutter," the bald woman called.

A hefty older boss picked up a fistful of sand and hurled it at them. "Learn some manners, fresh fish."

The young boss looked confused at the angry faces. "I'm just—" He ate a mouthful of sand. More drivers joined in, showering them from every direction. It didn't take long for the young man to rescind his offer.

Taishi gave up for the night. This gaggle of stuck-up sand skimmers would make sure she wouldn't find a caravan willing to take her on. Her only hope was to try again tomorrow with a new group. Unless they put her picture up on some line-cutting board.

Taishi exited the trading post, dragging her feet in defeat. She passed by an inn just outside the entrance and considered taking a bed here. It was late. Her back desperately wanted to lie down while her feet begged for a tub to soak in. One peek inside, however, told her this was where all the caravans stayed in between their trips. She had received enough of their mockery for the time being, and decided to find other lodging.

Taishi began the slog back up the fifteen flights of stairs to the map-maker's shop. Maybe she could find a cheap hostel, or maybe even a clean alleyway. Better to save her dwindling money for food than use it on a smelly pallet, though she did wonder if Chown's claims about rats were actually true.

Taishi was about halfway back to Chowan's when she first sensed it, a presence. She casually looked back the way she had come, but saw nothing other than shadows flickering in the torchlight. She continued on to the next turn. As soon as she did, Taishi flattened against the wall and pulled the currents from that tunnel to her. At first she heard nothing. No footsteps or breathing. Her instincts rarely failed her. She waited a few moments longer, and sure enough there came a nearly imperceptible but unmistakable sound: a light pop. Air rushing to fill a vacuum. It was a sound Taishi had heard only a few times in her life.

Only one thing made that sound.

Taishi scanned the darkened corners of the stairwell. A lone sconce was the only thing keeping her from being shrouded in complete darkness. She scanned the stairs and noticed an exit three levels up. Taishi launched herself into the air, clearing the first flight in one leap, then the next two in two each. Muffled cries of alarm echoed from below. Footsteps soon followed, three sets by the sound of it.

Taishi burst out of the stairwell and entered a curved stone pathway. She wouldn't be able to outrun her pursuers, and these tunnels were a poor place to make a stand. Her best chance of survival would be to get aboveground, or at the very least out beneath the sky where she would have room to maneuver. Taishi broke into a sprint, reaching the end of the tunnel and entering what appeared to be one of the main passages. Fortunately, a faded sign above the entrance showed her which direction led to the gorge. Unfortunately, the way was a steep uphill climb. At least this area was better lit than the smaller tunnels.

Taishi pumped her arm and legs as hard as she could, feeling every bit her age. She had barely made it a few steps when she heard the popping sound again. This time it was a slightly lower pitch: air suddenly and violently being ejected outward. A shadow streaked toward her flank. She twisted aside, barely ducking beneath it as it passed. Another came at her from the other side. Off balance, Taishi managed to avoid this one as well, but her robe was not as fortunate, a gash appearing just below her armpit as it passed. Still another shadow came, this time charging her head-on.

Taishi sidestepped and spun, kicking into soft flesh. Her assailants were unarmored. She was awarded with a pained grunt as black wisps dissipated around a man's body. He rolled gracefully out of his fall and onto his feet, his face scrunched in pain. It was the handsome young caravan boss she had tried to book passage from earlier. He drew a curved saber as the last of the black wisps, like steam, evaporated off his body.

"Cockroaches," she snarled as the three shadowkills circled around her in the poorly illuminated hallway. Between the low air currents down here in the tunnels and the cramped space, this fight was a riskier and more tenuous situation than she would have preferred.

Shadowkills were expert assassins and infiltrators who employed a twisted sort of war art that poisoned the body, but gave them the ability to move through darkness. Not much was known about them, except they were relentless contract killers that operated under an umbrella group known as the Consortium, which may or may not have been a cult; no one really knew. Shadowkills were expensive to employ. Under the lunar court it was said that if a client hired a shadowkill to mark you, you probably deserved it.

Taishi had crossed paths with these expert killers on a few occasions, twice working alongside them. She honestly couldn't say which end of their blade she preferred. If it were up to her, she'd avoid them altogether. In her opinion, cults and capitalism made for an awful combination. Shadowkills had very annoying and strange rules of operation.

"You could have just sold me passage," Taishi muttered as the three circled her.

"Oh, trust me, I tried," he replied. "The caravan bosses saved you." That was likely true; she owed those jackasses her life.

The three came at her again, but Taishi was ready for them now. The key to surviving shadowkill battles was surviving the incredibly dangerous opening attack. Without the advantage of surprise, shadowkills were generally merely competent war artists.

By Taishi's standards, that meant they were dead. She easily dodged their attacks, flowing between their thrusts and kicks, striking out with the backs of her hands on the handsome one's face, slamming an elbow on an uglier man's face, then kicking a pretty woman's chest to send her flying.

"Give up and run back into the shadows, cockroaches," she mocked.

Taishi didn't mean for them to take her advice literally. Handsome caravan boy dove toward a shadowed area underneath one of the sconces. Before he could disappear into the darkness or whatever it was shadowkills did, Taishi surged forward and caught his face with her fist. His head snapped to the side and his eyes rolled to the back of his head as he toppled headfirst onto the floor.

The other two tried to come to his aid, but Taishi spun and stopped them in their tracks with just a look. Competent war artists knew when they were outmatched. "Maybe you should just surrender—"

There was a very light puff sound and Taishi caught a flash of a black streak out of the corner of her eye. She just barely blocked a knife thrust and spun to parry a second attack. The exchange continued for several seconds as this new shadowkill pushed Taishi out of position, forcing her to cede ground, backing her into a corner. This shadowkill was noticeably quicker and stronger than the others, the movement of their jing more powerful and refined.

After a protracted exchange, Taishi finally managed to break away and reset the battle. The wisps of darkness drifted off the shadowkill's body to reveal a young woman with pale, powdered skin, a sharp nose, and painted eyebrows. Her dark-red hair was ear-length except for two long wisps that curled along her youthful cheeks down to her chin, which made it look like she had fangs.

Taishi took stock of this new threat. There was something unsettling about the girl's yellow eyes, a wildness that glimmered in the lantern's light. That was when it hit her: This girl was relishing this fight, maybe even aroused. Taishi deeply understood love for battle, but her joy was in the practice of her war arts. This one enjoyed violence.

The young woman smirked. "I've been looking forward to meeting the legendary Ling Taishi for a long time. I grew up on stories of you. I even had a doll." She cocked her head to one side. "I wonder if your head will snap off as easily as hers did." She twirled black knives in her hands and then, humming, advanced on Taishi. The remaining two shadowkills followed close behind.

Taishi's war artist heart yearned to test her skill against this new shadowkill, but her war artist head urged prudence. In battle, it was always wisest to listen to the head over the heart. Instead of engaging, Taishi broke away and fled. The odds had now turned against her, and winning this skirmish earned her nothing.

One of the lesser shadowkills, the remaining man, tried to block her way, but succeeded only in getting bowled over. The path to her escape cleared. Taishi could just make out the night sky at the end of the street. She pumped her arm and legs, her already exhausted heart groaning with each step. Of course the route had to be uphill again.

A pop to her left gave her just enough of a warning to sidestep an attack. Taishi avoided the thrust, and then the tip of her big toe met one of the lesser shadowkill's eye sockets, snapping her head back and sending her careening to the ground.

Instead of finishing this pest off, Taishi kept on, jumping on a quick current and riding it toward the far wall. As it came hurtling toward her, there was a noticeably softer puff as the talented shadowkill stepped out of the shadows. Black knives flashed, nearly finding her throat.

The Swallow Dances leaped from her scabbard. One exchange had told Taishi all she needed to know about this new shadowkill. This little hornet was good. But like most who tested Taishi, not good enough.

Taishi feinted, sidestepped a thrust, and found a killing blow. The girl realized her mistake just as the tip of the Swallow Dances shot toward her chest. She was lucky they were fighting in the shadows, otherwise it would have been too late for her. As Taishi's blade touched her, her body puffed into a haze of black wisps, and she stepped out of a shadow on the opposite wall.

"I expected better from the great Ling Taishi," the girl called out. There was almost a singsong quality to her voice. "Has age caught up with you, or has the bar for legendary war artist fallen so far?"

"Who are you trying to fool, you pint-sized puppy?" Taishi clapped back. "You're awfully mouthy for an assassin."

The girl faked a yawn. "I just hate it when my childhood heroes end up so disappointing."

This encounter had been anything but dull. The chatty girl was just trying to save face. Both knew luck had saved her. That last maneuver, however—stepping into the shadows to prevent a blade—was still an impressive display of skill. As much as Taishi was tempted to continue chatting, she decided to take advantage of her upper hand. Praise and critique could come some other time. She turned away and sped to the opening of the gorge, the blue light of the Queen growing brighter with every step.

Three more times the shadowkill puffed in front of her, three more times Taishi avoided her black blades. Then Taishi was out of the tunnels and beneath the vast Celestial ceiling. Sensing her quarry escaping, the talented shadowkill puffed to the shadowed area closest to Taishi beneath the sconce of a lantern at the foot of the entrance. It was a desperate and ill-advised maneuver. It was too far from Taishi to get close quickly. The girl tried anyway, but Taishi was ready. She easily turned the tables, hooking her arm around the woman's armpit and using her momentum to fling her over the ledge. The girl had only a second to look surprised before disappearing over the side.

A long breath loosed from Taishi as she stepped to the edge to confirm her kill, tracking the shadowkill's descent. What a waste. She could have been a talented war artist. Taishi squinted. One moment the girl's body was falling, the next she had disappeared. Then a puff later, she flew out from a shaded nook in the wall. She poofed again and reappeared once more hanging off the ledge. The shadowkill pulled herself up and rolled onto her back, her body heaving as long black wisps evaporated off her body.

That last series of jumps was an amazing display of jing and skill. Taishi nodded in appreciation and approval. "You don't suck, girl. What's your name?"

The shadowkill responded with three knife throws one after the other. She may not have sucked, but she also did not know when to give up. Taishi knocked the first two out of the air with her blade. She quickly sheathed the Swallow Dances and caught the third with her hand. Taishi examined the expertly balanced blade and pocketed it. "Do you have any more for me?"

The girl screeched and produced two more knives. She charged, slashing only air as Taishi, anticipating this foolishness, grabbed on to a howling current. She was yanked into the air at a frightening speed. It was all she could do to hang on.

Taishi looked back. The talented shadowkill was shaking her fist and throwing a pinkie finger, screaming words Taishi couldn't hear over the sound of the wind as it whisked her away.

CHAPTER TWENTY-ONE

SHADOWKILL

Unlike most war artists, Maza Qisami was not above expressing her anger. "You got lucky, you limp one-armed hag. Next time I'm going to eat your face. And when I catch that holy boy, I'm going to use his skull for a piss pot and wear his skin for a coat!"

Her pinkie finger stayed waving in the air as her elusive prey fluttered away in graceful contrast with Qisami's vulgar outbursts. Qisami followed the woman's trajectory until the windwhisper disappeared into a cluster of buildings on the other side, marked by the faint screech of breaking glass. She admired Taishi's ability to fly through such powerful gusts and land against such a small target. What marvelous control.

Her mood seesawed between irritation at her cell's failure to capture Ling Taishi, and her delight to discover that the old woman was truly a mark worthy of her own considerable talents. This was going to make it even more satisfying when she finally caught the windwhisper and gutted her.

Qisami checked her knives—she was short three—and then used the sharpened fingernail of her pinkie finger to scrawl on her left forearm, cutting just deep enough to draw blood: *anyone dead?* The redness faded almost as soon as it appeared.

The responses came back one by one, each an itch on the same forearm that also vanished nearly the moment it came. Qisami didn't even need to look down to read the message. The character strokes alone were sufficient.

we okay. on way back.

Deciphering Burandin's bloodscrawl was always a puzzle. He had been a muck-wallowing farm boy when he had joined the Consortium. Though literacy and clear bloodscrawl were required skills among shadowkills, no amount of instruction could wash the peasant out of his grammar and penmanship.

His much smarter half had the opposite problem. Koteuni couldn't help but write a three-part saga every time she admired a pretty flower off the side of the road, much less whenever she described or explained anything important. Qisami hardly wanted a novel on her arm either. Koteuni had been a court brat. Her father had been a mnemonic official in Duke Yanso's court when a jealous rival had purchased a mark on Koteuni's father. To stave off his assassination, he had bargained for the brood atonement and offered up the least favorite of his nine children. Qisami's second-in-command had killed both her father and his rival as soon as she had learned to step into the twilight, as they called it.

Koteuni was always quick to remind their cell that she was far too overeducated for "this." Which was true. No shadowkill would ever need to recite Goramh's five hundred or so holy proverbs or recite Lady Leehua's erotic rhymes (that inflamed the passions of the emperor before setting his palace aflame). Or was it the other way around; Qisami could never remember.

The last reply came several minutes later: *I'm alive.*

That was everyone. Qisami had begun to wonder about Haaren. *On me* she directed.

She began to hum, trying to match her tone with the whistles of the shrill wind as she stepped to the edge of the chasm, leaning forward and tempting fate as the updraft blasted her body. She closed her eyes and spread her arms, imagining herself a hawk, gliding through the air, swooping down and preying upon rodents and stray cats.

Qisami bet she could have succeeded as a windwhisper given the opportunity. The rumor about Ling Taishi's particular lineage of windwhispering was that the student had to murder the master to achieve mastery, which was fine. Qisami was all about killing her teachers. She had tried to do just that several times while at the Consortium. No self-respecting shadowkill trainee didn't try at least once.

Qisami was still pretending to soar the sky searching for prey when the rest of her cell found their way to her. Burandin and Koteuni, walking hand in hand, found her first. Koteuni's lips were cut and bleeding, and one of her eyes had swelled shut in a purple knot. Her usually perfect hair, parted directly down the middle and pulled into two short ponytails, was a disheveled mess.

Burandin looked even worse. Koteuni's husband's bulbous head and queue hairstyle had always made his head appear too large for his rail-thin body, which made the two beautiful knots on the shelf he called a forehead all the more conspicuous. He also appeared to have trouble putting weight on his left leg as he limped toward her.

The couple beamed at Qisami and waved. She waved back. Every time she saw them like this, she wondered what Koteuni saw in ugly-stupid Burandin.

Haaren arrived shortly after, still wearing the caravan driver outfit, now blood-splattered. The youngest shadowkill in the group was one Qisami had lured away from a rival cell a year ago because she needed someone who could operate in disguise, and she had thought he was cute. Less so now that his face looked like pulverized meat.

He brought his hands to his cheeks gingerly. "This somehow hurts, but I can't feel a thing at the same time."

"You should have done a better job convincing the mark to join your caravan then."

"I tried, but those filthy sand skiers kept dusting me. Turning her down was the only honest response. I had to stay in character."

Qisami eyed him and grunted. Banana-brained thespian. "Did anyone cut her?"

All three shook their heads.

"No one managed to nick a drop of blood off this woman?" She ground her teeth. "I guess we'll have to track her the old-fashioned way."

Koteuni raised a hand. "Not to doubt our chances, but that mark laid us all out pretty good. Maybe we should bring in another cell?"

"No way," Qisami sneered. "We're not sharing. She just caught us by surprise, that's all."

"We were the ones who ambushed *her*," said Burandin.

She crossed her arms. "No other cells. We spent a year tracking her down. We are going to get famous gutting this old rag, and we are collecting the bounty."

"A shared bounty is still better than no bounty," said Koteuni.

"Or death," added Burandin.

"I don't want to hear it. This one is ours and ours alone," Qisami snapped, her eyes flaring, her decision final. "We already pay enough stupid dues to the Consortium. I'm not splitting it more ways, not to mention the penalty for pulling in additional cells."

"Never a good look," Haaren agreed, shaking his head. "It'll tarnish our reputation."

Qisami dug her sharpened nail into her forearm once more: *What about you, Tsang? Do we need to go back and kill the baby death shepherds?*

No, the information looks good. It's some sort of mapmaking shop. I'm sitting outside right now. Something happened here recently.

That was a relief. That particular burial mountain was far from here. It would have been a hassle to go back there to repay bad information, but threats were the one promise Qisami always kept. If people found out Maza Qisami's threats were empty, then everyone would lie to her. It would be chaos.

What happened? she scrawled.

The door is blown off its hinges and there's a skinny man inside with spectacles working at a table in the middle of the night.

Tsang was their grunt. He was usually assigned scouting, stakeouts, tailing, and any other boring job with which the rest of the cell couldn't be bothered. The boy also handled logistics: He managed finances, arranged lodging, and cooked meals, which probably made him the most important member of their cell. *Someone* had to wash the blood off their clothes.

She scrawled: *Keep eyes on him.*

Qisami turned to the others. "If no one is on their deathbed, let's go."

Burandin stared out across the space. "What about the mark? We're just letting her go?"

"Of course not," replied Qisami. "But our shot's gone for now. We can't catch her in the open like this unless you can sprout wings. The big cheater will just fly away, especially with this gorge providing cover whenever she chooses. We need to find the right moment, when escape isn't an option."

"Like trap her inside a building?" said Haaren.

"Or a cave," added Burandin unhelpfully.

"Maybe we can get a big net."

"We were just *in* a cave," said Koteuni. "It didn't matter. What our illustrious and glorious leader means is that we need to catch her in a situation where she has no choice but to stand and fight."

"Exactly." Qisami slapped Koteuni's butt as she walked past, earning her an appreciative glance, a promise for later. She peppered the rest of her cell with instructions. "Haaren, lock down the trading post. Make sure she doesn't buy her way out of Sanba on a caravan." She circled a finger around his face. "Use a different disguise. You look like a prostitute on a pleasure barge."

He nodded, his face melting a bit, adding weight, twenty years, and a few droopy chins. His walnut hair speckled white, and lines etched around his eyes. Haaren still kept himself relatively handsome in any disguise, however, because his frail ego couldn't help it. Pompous peacock.

She turned to the couple. "Burandin, put a word out to the underworld. Just information, nothing more. Keep the bribes modest. Anything too large attracts the wrong sort of attention. Koteuni, do the same with the lords and diplomats. Loose some local magistrate lips. Again, nothing alarming, just more eyes. The mark is ours and ours alone."

"What about you?" asked Koteuni.

"I'm going to pay Tsang's candle-huffing wrist-wagger a visit."

The cell broke to go their separate ways. Tsang scrawled instructions to his location, and Qisami stepped into the shroud beneath a lantern and stepped out three levels up, just at the edge of her line of sight. She did this two more times until she reached one of the public lifts. From there, it was a short jaunt through Sanba's tunnels until she reached the last member of her cell.

Tsang was sitting in a dark corner next to a trash heap, his legs splayed out. He was drawing in the dirt with a long, thin stick. The grunt perked up when she appeared from the darkness. Shadowkills did not startle easily. "Did you know there are some ferocious cats crawling through these tunnels? A couple tried to eat me."

Qisami smirked. "If you're still alive, they can't be that ferocious." Tsang couldn't keep a toddler from swiping sweets, let alone put up a fight against feral strays. She pointed at the shop with the broken door. "Is the wrist-wagger still inside?"

"Hasn't moved since I first poked my head in. He's still drawing at his table."

Haaren did say the old woman was asking for caravan bosses who could read shifting maps. "Is he alone?"

Tsang shook his head. "A girl was bringing in food and carrying out buckets of piss and shit."

"And?"

"And what?"

"Is she inside now?"

Tsang frowned. "I'm not sure. I had to retreat around the corner when the feral cats tried to steal my pack. It's hard staying inconspicuous when you're fighting off a clowder of vicious felines."

"One job, you worm-face. That's all you had." Qisami smacked him across the back of the head. She turned her attention back to the shop. "Worry about it later. Time to get some answers."

"Want me to come in with you?"

"No, you keep those kitties at bay."

Qisami strolled up to the shop and decided to fix the crooked door. A swift kick separated the heavy wooden slab from its remaining hinge, sending it tipping over flat into the shop. The wrist-wagger startled like a rabbit, smearing a black mark across his paper and sending a tray of ink over the side of the table. He cursed and, like a typical candle-sniffer, knelt down to clean up the mess. It was several moments before he realized he had company.

Qisami leaned against the doorframe. "I knocked, but I think there's something wrong with your door."

"What," the man stammered, the blood draining from his face. "We're ... I'm closed. Please come back tomorrow."

"Since I'm already here ..." Qisami hummed as she casually took in the details of the shop, her soles clicking on the fallen wooden door. No windows. Shelf obstructing a possible back room. No other exits in sight. Lack of a breeze made it unlikely, but they were deep in the mountain, so the airflow could just be poor. After a slow pivot, she fixed the startled rabbit with a bright smile. "Are you the famous Wu Chown?"

He stuttered, uncertain, "I am."

"It's such an honor to meet you. You're reputed to be the greatest mapmaker in the entire duchy. Everyone says so."

Chown's cheeks blossomed red. The man took praise just about as well as he took being startled. "I ... I ..."

Qisami went on. "I need a map. One that only you can draw."

The lines of fear around his eyes softened, as did the stiff arch in his back. He bowed. "Your kind words honor me, madam, but modesty prevents me from accepting such heavenly praise."

Qisami walked past him to his drawing table. Six black-and-white maps on translucent parchment, seemingly identical, were laid out in a neat row. She picked up two pieces, laid them over each other and held the combined map up to the candlelight. The mountains and rivers seemed to jump from their pages, causing her to throw her head back. She beamed. "So pretty."

Chown plucked it from her hand with an assertiveness Qisami didn't think the little man possessed. "It's not finished yet. This is for a rather poor client, so it's in no way indicative of my craft. For you, however, if you come tomorrow, I assure you I will draw a cartographic masterpiece."

"But I like this one," she drawled.

The mapmaker looked confused. "Was it a particular map you were interested in or did you want something beautiful as a display item?" He bowed. "Because if so, I have some truly unique pieces that would serve as a fine display for any noble house."

"I want the one you're drawing for Ling Taishi."

The fear returned to Chown's face. He began to shake. "Who?"

A contented sigh escaped her lips. There was something so satisfying about playing with a prey's emotions. It was a welcome appetizer. First frighten them, then lull them into a sense of security, then shatter their confidence once more. The process of toying with a mark's fragile psyche was a lovely experience.

Qisami's fingers drifted to one of her blades. "This is how things are going to work. I'm going to ask a few questions. If I—"

Chown fell to his knees. "Please don't hurt me. I'm drawing this map for the woman who broke the door. I think she's a windwhisper. She could be Ling Taishi. I don't know her. In fact, I dislike her greatly."

She snorted. "I haven't even touched you yet. I was saying, I have questions. If you don't answer, you're going to bleed. If I don't like your answers, you're going to bleed even more."

"She's headed for the Temple of the Tiandi," he babbled. "It's two days' journey from Manki. She's going to hire on to a caravan at the trading post. She'll be looking for someone who can read shifting maps. There are only a few—"

Qisami smacked him across the face. "Stop answering. I'm trying to ask a question."

A soft breeze could have blown the weak-kneed man to the ground. He collapsed into a whimpering heap. "But I told you what you wanted to know."

She gritted her teeth. "Stop cutting me off. Don't you know it's rude?"

He looked confused, then changed tactics. "The map. Take it. It's yours. Free of charge."

The fact that it had even crossed his mind that she'd pay for it was amusing, and a little offensive. This floppy fish had taken all of the fun out of her interrogation. Qisami drew her knife and stuck it into the man's thigh. Just as the pain registered on his face, she cupped his chin with her other hand and pinned him to the floor. "If any more words escape your lips that are not directly preceded by one of my questions, I'm going to split your spleen. And since I'm not a doctor and have no idea where it's located, I'll have to dig around with my knife. Do you understand?"

He nodded frantically. She released her palm and hovered her blade close as the mapmaker's cries were reduced to pathetic whimpers.

"It hurts," he moaned.

"The pain is sort of the point." Qisami added under her breath, "You big baby." She had barely stuck more than one knuckle's length of blade into his leg. In any case, the fun was ruined. A good torture required a little defiance, a little struggle. Otherwise, no one was having a good time. "Now you're probably going to die tonight, but depending on how useful you are, you can have a quick death or a slow, painful . . ."

Chown was no longer paying attention to her, which was altogether insulting. She was about to stab his other thigh when she sensed it as well.

They were no longer alone.

Qisami turned to see a group of men wearing randomly assorted armor and weapons spilling into the room. Most looked barely a step above common thugs. She wasn't worried. The shop was poorly lit, so there were plenty of shadows to operate from. But there were at least ten of them, so she didn't have the best odds. Not the worst either. If she took out the two wall lanterns and the chandelier, the shop would be curtained in complete darkness.

Qisami hauled Chown to his feet and slung her arm over his shoulder. She waved with her other hand. "Hello, boys. Was my friend here being too loud? I told him to be quiet. We were just working a few things out." Roughly half waved back, always a good sign.

Chown sniveled with relief. "Thank the Celestial Family you're here."

She cut him off loudly. "It would have been awfully nice if my lookout had, you know, kindly informed me about a group of armed men coming in."

"You mean this boy?" A thug hauled Tsang in by the scruff and shoved him to the ground at her feet. "You should thank us. A pack of rats had cornered him and were about to eat him when we came along."

Tsang's voice was shrill. "Those things were rats?"

"You should have let them have the meal." She glared at the grunt. "I'll deal with you later."

A man smaller than the thugs around him wedged his way to the front. "It looks like you're shaking this gentleman down. This establishment is insured by the Silk Hands. I'm Hanno, the floorboss, and you're messing up my bottom line."

"Fear not, friend," replied Qisami smoothly. "No need for trouble." She gave the signal, tapping two fingers to her thumb and turning her wrist.

The boss perked up. "Shadowkill business, eh? My nephew is one. Goes by Machi these days. Know him?"

As if all shadowkills were supposed to know one another. Qisami was tempted to ask the floorboss if he knew her imaginary thug cousin named Sop. In this particular case, however, the man wasn't wrong. She actually did. "I do, as a matter of fact."

"How's he doing?"

"He's dead."

The floorboss didn't flinch. "Serves the boy right. Always talked like he was better than the rest of the family because he was Consortium."

Qisami mentally patted herself on the back for not pointing out that they *were*, in fact, better.

Hanno walked up to Chown and looked the man over. The mapmaker's blood-soaked pants, pale face, and shaking hands made him look much worse off than he actually was. "Who would hire a shadowkill for this soft melon? Did a client get lost following one of his maps? As for you, shadowkill, the Silk Hands were not notified of a cell operating here."

The Consortium usually considered it just a courtesy, but the local underworld apparently did not agree. "Consider yourself notified, friend," she replied. "Now that we've established ourselves, I hate to keep your band of brothers up so late."

"Is this man your mark?"

Qisami forced her smile to stay on. She knew where this was going. For a moment, she was tempted to say yes, but she wasn't the lying type. If an assassin couldn't be honest to a gangster, what did that say about society? "No, but I need him."

Hanno made a tsking sound. "Now we have a problem. You know the rules. The Consortium's arrangement with underworld organizations such as ours allows them property rights over an individual *only* if they are the mark. If Master Wu here is not your target, then his policy with the Silk Hands is still active. Let him go."

"Oh, thank the Tiandi." Chown squirmed out of her grasp and limped toward the Silk Hands. He appeared to have found his confidence as well as he scolded the floorboss. "About time you got here. I don't know what I'm paying you an insurance policy for. First that woman war artist accosts my shop. Now this assassin."

What a beautiful fool.

Qisami violently yanked the mouthy idiot back by the collar, dragging him to the ground. She held up her other hand. "Actually, Hanno, my good man, are you open to an equitable middle ground?"

"A good businessman is always open to new business," the floorboss said.

"Let me have two days with our friend here. I'll give him back, on my word. Report back to your big boss that your guys erred, and you'll do better next time." She tossed two strings of silver liang at Hanno's feet. "This should cover it."

The floorboss didn't react to the coins at his feet. "My crew's silence needs to be paid for as well."

She tossed two more strings.

Hanno considered her offer. "Very well."

"What!" stammered Chown, panicked again. "But I'm insured. This is what I pay you for. You can't do this."

Hanno shrugged. "No offense, mapmaker. It's just business."

"Just business," Qisami agreed.

Chown's voice had risen several octaves. "Well, I'm not going to stay silent. I'm going to tell all the other businesses how their insurance policy means rot, and then I'm going straight to the Big Boss and tell him how you're cheating him. Then we'll see who pays!"

An awkward silence passed over the room.

Floorboss Hanno sighed. Qisami did as well. He shook his head. "You shouldn't have said that."

"Shouldn't have said that," she echoed.

Hanno turned to Qisami. "It's going to cost another three strings for lost business until a new one gets established and buys a policy."

Qisami grimaced. This was getting expensive. Any more and it might just be cheaper to kill this bunch of copper-plated thugs. She tossed the rest of her purse to the ground. "Not quite three left but enough of a friendly difference."

"We're friendly enough." Hanno looked around the room. "Too bad. Chown always paid on time. Never complained. It's hard to find customers like that."

"I'll wipe the room clean for you," she offered.

The mapmaker began to panic. "What does that mean?"

"Much obliged, shadowkill." The floorboss pulled out a neatly folded white handkerchief and tossed it to her. "Here's the paperwork. Let's go, boys."

That was when it dawned on Chown. "No, please. There's no need. I swear I won't say a word. On my life. On my family's honor. Just take what you need and let me go." He fell to his knees. "Please, I beg of you. There's no need for cruelty."

Qisami gave the dead man a sympathetic smile. "The cruelty is sort of the point."

"Sort of the point," agreed the floorboss. He winked at her and left the soon-to-be-formerly Wu Chown's Happy Man's Guide to the Desert with his crew in tow.

CHAPTER TWENTY-TWO

RIPPLES

Sanba. Had. Lifts.

Taishi gawked as the chains clanged up and down the walls, lowering the wooden platform to the next level. Her blood boiled. Where were the signposts directing her here? Why hadn't anyone bothered to tell her this before she had walked up and down all those stairs? She should have realized in hindsight that of course Sanba would have lifts. This was a mining colony with probably dozens of deep shafts converted for public use. Her carriage had arrived in one at the main entrance, for Tiandi's sake. She had just been so preoccupied with finding a meal that she had forgotten such things existed, bless her weary feet.

Taishi felt a sharp pain shoot up her spine as she shifted her weight. Her weary back and neck as well. That shadowkill cell attack had been too close for comfort. Their leader was certainly skilled, and Taishi considered herself fortunate to have escaped unharmed. The winds screaming through the gorge were so strong she couldn't tame the currents. It was sheer luck and desperate adjustments that had crashed her through a window instead of, say, a stone wall or the side of a cliff.

Taishi had limped away from where she had crashed as soon as she could stand and spent the night in a wicker basket inside a grain ware-house. She hadn't dared leave her hiding place until late into the morn-ing. Shadowkills mostly operated at night. The darkness was when their jing was strongest. While that mattered less in an underground city, shadowkills still needed sleep like everyone else, and usually did that during the day. This gave Taishi a window to finish her tasks and leave the city.

She moved past the public lift and into the tunnels toward the map-maker's shop. The shifting map should have been ready hours ago, and with luck Taishi would be crossing the Sand Snake toward Fulkan For-est before nightfall.

That was a big if. *If* Chown hadn't panicked when she hadn't come on time and changed his mind. *If* Taishi could actually hire a caravan. *If* those caravan bosses weren't at the trading post again. Most important, *if* the shadowkills weren't already lying in wait. Perhaps having engaged the local magistrates, or the criminal underworld, or both. For all she knew, the entire city was already hunting her.

Smoke wafted to her nostrils and scratched her eyes as Taishi ven-tured deeper into the tunnels. She didn't think much of it. The ventila-tion in some parts of the city was noticeably poor. Someone had probably gotten a little too enthusiastic brewing tea this morning. Taishi grimaced as she neared the entrance to Chown's shop. It was becoming more ob-vious with each step where that enthusiasm was concentrated. Hand on the Swallow Dances' hilt, she flattened herself against a wall and crept toward the entrance. The smells of burnt wood and tar were overwhelm-ing.

Taishi stopped at the entrance to Wu Chown's shop, feeling sud-denly deflated. "You careless old fool. You should have waited with the map."

A blaze had ravaged the shop in the middle of the night. Everything inside, the maps, furniture, shelves, even the walls, was charred black. A mixture of guilt and anger burned in her gut. War artists, by the nature of their chosen profession, were accustomed to violence and misery. Tai-shi herself had rained more destruction than most over her long career. However, it was one thing to ravage your enemies, it was another to afflict the innocent. There was no honor, no challenge, or satisfaction in sowing wrath on the helpless. Even if it had been unintentional. In many cases, especially if it had been unintentional. Carelessness toward the weak was a sin for the powerful.

Even if she had been able to sift through the ashes, she knew there would have been no point. Nothing useful could have survived. Anything she was looking for would have been paper. At least there was no charred body or smell of burnt flesh. Taishi held out a little hope that maybe Chown was still alive.

She walked around the blackened shelf to the back room. Columns of cabinets and drawers rose along the three walls. Most of the drawers were already opened. Everything inside had been reduced to ash. Not stolen, but burned. Someone had taken the effort of opening every drawer and cabinet before setting the fire. The blaze had been thorough, which only confirmed arson.

The mapmaker's shop was a dead end now. She needed to find another way to get to the Temple of the Tiandi. Taishi was about to leave when she felt a rhythmic current of air faintly swirling from behind a set of cabinet doors. She listened but heard nothing save for the occasional snap of cracking wood. Someone was close, pushing out short bursts of breath, shallow, labored, and tense.

Taishi drew the Swallow Dances and sliced, cutting clean through the cabinet door. She was rewarded with a panicked cry as Zofi tumbled out, clutching a long wooden case. The sword was sheathed as quickly as it was drawn. Taishi resisted embracing the girl, and instead patted her on the head. "What happened here? What are you doing in there?"

Zofi looked as relieved to see Taishi as Taishi was to see her. The girl's face was red and wet with tears. Strain around her eyes told Taishi all that she needed to know about Chown. Zofi pursed her lips, as if doing her best to hold everything in. "I stayed late to help Ba last night, and slept in this morning. By then, the fire brigade had already put out the fire. I asked the brigade chief and my neighbors what happened, but no one would even speak to me."

Taishi frowned. "Why not?"

"Someone pinned this over the sign outside with a knife." The girl handed her a crumpled white cloth dusted with heavy layers of ash. Taishi felt the silk fabric between her fingers, and then unrolled it to reveal a yellow outline of an outstretched pinkie-less hand.

For a guilty instant, a wave of relief washed over Taishi. If this was the work of the underworld, then perhaps she wasn't to blame for the shop getting burned down. Maybe this tragedy was just a coincidence. Deep down, though, Taishi knew this was a lie. There were no such things as bad coincidences, only bad players. Luck, good and bad, was nothing more than a product of planning, will, and work, or lack thereof. If Chown's shop had burned to the ground hours after she had visited, Taishi was willing to wager Sanso's soul that her presence there had had something to do with it.

"Once the brigade and my neighbors saw that, we were dead to them," explained Zofi. "No one wants to get in trouble."

"What could you have done to cross the criminal underworld?"

"The yellow means non-payment of policy," explained Zofi, bitterly. "I know for a fact that is not true. I handle all of my father's books, and we always paid on time. This is a mistake."

"Quite an egregious one to make," muttered Taishi. The black knife that the silk cloth was wrapped around was a shadowkill blade. "Not a mistake, though. Assassins were working with the Silk Hands. I'm sorry about your father, girl. Do you have a place to go?"

Zofi bowed her head. An awkward silence passed. Taishi wanted to offer comforting words, but couldn't come up with anything. The girl was bright and capable; she could take care of herself. That wasn't what she needed to hear. Instead, Taishi fished out three silver liang from her purse and dropped them into the girl's hand. "You were right. I should have paid a fair price for the map. Did it by chance survive the fire?" Taishi felt like a tax collector's perfumed ass for asking, but Chown had been her only lead.

Zofi shook her head. Fresh fat tears began to stream down the map-maker's daughter's face. "Nothing survived except this." She huddled a long wooden box close to her body.

"I hope it's something valuable you can sell. I wish you good fortune, girl." Taishi turned to leave. She wished she could do more for the girl, but orphans were as abundant as stray dogs in the Enlightened States.

She had just stepped out of the doorway when Zofi ran after her. "Wait, mistress, master . . ."

Taishi stopped at the doorway. "Master Nai Roha."

The girl laced her fingers and bowed. Trying to look submissive and deferential was not her strong suit. "Are you still trying to reach the Temple of the Tiandi?"

Taishi nodded. "I am."

Zofi opened the long wooden box she was clutching close to her chest, revealing the master map inside. "Father kept this in a stone safe. That was the only reason it escaped the fire."

Taishi's eyes glinted at the sliver of hope. "How much do you want for it?"

Zofi's response to that question would have made her father proud. She clutched it close to her. "I couldn't. This map is his legacy. It's all I have left of him."

Taishi felt shame for asking. Images of Sanso flashed through her mind. "It wouldn't be right for me to take something so precious from you. Good luck, child."

Zofi grabbed her sleeve as Taishi turned away. "Wait. If you're leaving Sanba, I can lead you across the Sand Snake."

The battle with the shadowkills was still fresh on Taishi's mind. She shook her head. "Where I am going will be dangerous, girl. You don't want to be near me."

"I have a sand sleigh and can read shifting maps. I can take you all the way to the temple, not just to Fulkan Forest."

Taishi grimaced. That almost swayed her. It would be difficult enough to latch on with a caravan heading toward the Manki settlement, let alone find someone who could guide her through Fulkan Forest. But her presence had already brought tragedy to the girl. Taishi didn't need another child's blood on her conscience, especially since it was likely she would have to abandon Zofi somewhere like she had Jian.

She turned away. "I'm sorry. You're safer here in Sanba."

Zofi clutched her sleeve. "No, you don't understand. It doesn't end with killing my father and burning down his shop. Once the Silk Hands place their mark on your family, they don't rest until it's finished. That's how they maintain control. I'm not safe anywhere in the city anymore. That's why I was hiding in the shop. I have no money and nowhere to go."

Taishi averted her eyes. She *did* owe a debt to Wu Chown, one she was honor-bound under the lunar court to uphold even if the girl didn't know it. Leaving Zofi to the mercy of the Silk Hands was not an option, although she was not doing the girl any favors by bringing her along. The less-bad choice won out. "Fine, you can come."

"Thank you, thank you." She didn't hesitate before saying, "I have to gather my things. Please come with me." Zofi rushed past Taishi and sprinted down the corridor. That last part almost made it seem like she was asking for protection, but Taishi knew better. This was all part of a plan, one Zofi had been able to concoct while hiding in a charred cupboard scared half out of her mind. Taishi was impressed.

They ventured deeper underground, where the walls crowded closer together and the ceilings threatened to bang into your head if you weren't careful. The air down here was thinner, with barely a current drifting through. Taishi grew wary. Between the cramped space and the listless air, she was at a disadvantage. Taishi pulled her scarf over her mouth and nose. It also stank.

Fortunately, their stay in the warrens was brief. The home Zofi had shared with her father was a hole barely large enough for two beds, a table, and a tiny cooking area. Zofi was able to pack all her belongings within the span of a few minutes while Taishi cleaned out the cupboards and the small stack of spark stones in the hearth. Then Taishi had to suffer the long painful uphill slog back to the surface.

"Where is your sleigh?" Taishi asked between long, labored breaths.

"The Peasant Docks, on the west end, on the other side of the gorge," answered Zofi, her breathing unchanged as she kept moving at a decent clip.

"We should hurry." Taishi, who was lagging behind the girl, picked up her pace. It had been a terribly long two days.

Zofi paused at a chart hanging on the wall of a square they were passing through. "It says here the winds are high. We should wait until they calm."

"When will that be?"

"Do I look like a weather diviner?"

The mouth on this one. "Then we'll leave now. I don't want to remain in the city a moment longer than necessary."

"But—"

"The Silk Hands, remember?" *And those blasted shadowkills.* "The longer we remain, the likelier that they'll find you."

Zofi must have decided that thugs were worse than poor weather. "The docks are this way."

It was late into the afternoon by the time they got up the hundreds of stairs back to the main floors and crossed to the other side of the gorge. Zofi insisted they pick up supplies at some of the local shops before heading to the Peasant Docks. Taishi had asked if they could use the lifts but Zofi refused, because Silk Hands thugs liked to hang out around the public lifts. Taishi couldn't argue, although her sore feet wished she would. Instead, the girl led her through more back tunnels, going up and down hundreds of more stairs that circled around large sections of the city. By the time they had reached their destination, her feet were congee and the pain had spread to her back.

The Peasant Docks were as luxurious as their name implied. Whereas the commercial and trading posts were docks where money flowed in and out of Sanba, the docks here were just a large cavern with an awkward mouth shaped like a jolly man's sneer at the bottom of a very long and not particularly well-lit tunnel leading, presumably, to the Sand Snake.

The sleighs, hundreds of them, were piled loosely on rickety wooden shelves stacked six high all the way to the ceiling, with long ramps leading down to ground level. The entire place looked like a death trap waiting to collapse. Zofi hurried past six shelves and up five levels before they reached what looked like a large oval-shaped wooden bucket with a pole sticking up in the center and a rudder on one end. The bottom half of the hull curved inward toward a shallow keel.

Taishi gawked. "This isn't a sleigh. It's a bathtub. How do we even fit in it?"

"This is the Slidewinder." Zofi beamed proudly. "I built it myself. It's not much, but it can fit two. One of us will have to hug the pole once we open the sails to catch the wind."

Taishi's worst fears were realized. She couldn't believe they were about to journey on that terrifying ocean of moving dunes in this over-sized soup bowl. Her stomach churned just looking at the thing, but she was clean out of options. "Fine. Let's take this stupid toy for a ride."

Zofi stepped between Taishi and the Slidewinder and held out her hand. "All we need to do is negotiate my rate and we can leave right away."

Taishi's voice turned shrill. "Rate what?"

Zofi smiled sweetly. "You didn't think you were going to hire a sleigh and a navigator for free, did you?"

CHAPTER TWENTY-THREE

FAMILIAL BONDS

Sali rented a room on the fifth floor of a narrow inn near the front gates of the Katuia District. She had found it strange that the penthouse units were the cheapest, but discovered that going up and down four flights of stairs grew tiresome very quickly. The rental was more a large box than a room, with a lone window offering a view of the stone wall that enclosed the district. She could almost touch all four walls if she lay on the floor and spread her arms and legs. If she jumped, her head would smash into the ceiling.

The first thing Sali did was map out her contingencies. Another disadvantage of the top floor was that there were only a few ways to escape. The window was just large enough to squeeze through, and although it was a long drop to the stone tiles below, the wall on the opposite side was close enough for her to jump, catch a foothold, and then leap back and forth until she reached the roof of the inn.

Sali perched on the corner eave and spent the rest of the day observing traffic flow in and out of the district to get the lay of the land. Almost every soul inside the district was Katuia, a mixture of Nezra and Sheetan emigrants by the style of their clan garb.

A row of carts lined one side of the street, hocking everything from potstickers to shovels. Weapons were banned, but entrenching equipment, step hammers, anchor drills, and other tools weren't. When one lived and labored in the Grass Sea, every tool was by needs a weapon.

Only a few Zhuun wandered through the thick crowds. None of the land-chained's businesses operated inside the district, and their guards stayed close to the checkpoint at the gates. Not even magistrates, with their tall cone-shaped hats, dared wander too deep into the district.

After a while, Sali caught herself staring more at her own people rather than the enemy. Many of the Katuia here looked without hope, lying on the streets, leaning against walls, sitting next to fires that burned on the ground. In small cruel ways, they were losing themselves in this alien land of stone walls and dead earth. The very fabric of her people had been torn by their defeat in a war that had been waging long before any of them had been born.

Even so, there were glimmers of hope: former comrades coming together solemnly clasping forearms, long-lost friends finding one another, and separated family members reuniting with rough embraces and streaming tears.

A wave of nostalgia passed over her as the day curtained into evening. Back when she had been a little girl, long before she had shaved her sides, Sali used to compete with Jiamin to see who could climb to the top of the lookout nests. Jiamin would always win. She couldn't be better than him at everything. The two of them spent hours hiding in the nests watching sunsets.

The last time the two had been together as children was in a tower. It was the night before Jiamin participated in the ritual that made him the next host of the Eternal Khan. Sali had held him close while he bawled like a baby, telling him over and over again that things were going to be wonderful, that he would make a great Khan, and that many great victories awaited him.

She ground her teeth. "I was such a fool."

Maybe she had been. After that ritual, Jiamin had never really been himself again.

Sali climbed back down to her room once the moon appeared, and was in bed and half asleep before she remembered she hadn't eaten since Sheetan. The price of having to go down and back up all those stairs was too steep for food, so she slept.

No sooner had she drifted off than a knock on the door roused her. She was on her feet immediately. Birds were chirping and morning light was shining through the window.

She pawed for her tongue with one hand and her shirt with the other. "Who is it?"

"Message from the Council of Nezra," piped a child's voice.

How had they even known where she was staying? Of course. She was right not to trust them about Mali. She held on to her tongue as she opened the door. A barefoot boy of about ten in ragged clothing looked at her nervously as he held up a piece of folded paper. "From the council, mistress," he repeated.

Sali unfolded the note. Scribbled on top were the Katuia pictographs for "flower," "sunrise," and "morning mist." Below each pictograph was a list of names with numbers next to them, totaling fifteen in all. Everyone on this list was between four and sixteen. At least the council was making good on their word.

"May you rise to greatness." Sali tossed the boy a coin. "Wait," she added, grabbing his sleeve before he could escape. Since he was already here, she might as well test him. She dragged the nervous boy to the bed and sat him down. "This will only take a moment. Close your eyes. Relax. Take a deep breath. Let your mind wander."

He shied away. "Will it hurt?"

"Not at all, but you may leave this room the next Khan of Katuia."

His eyes widened. "Really, me?"

"Better hope not," she muttered under her breath. She spoke slowly in a clear voice. "Now, think of the Grass Sea. Can you see it? Do you hear the chitter of skarn beetles eating rocks, the gasflies hissing above your head in the early evening? Can you smell the scent of burst orchids and black sunflowers?"

He fidgeted and shook his head.

"Hold your arms forward. Imagine you're holding a spear in your right hand and smoke in your left. The spear grows longer and thicker. The smoke drifts into the air. What do you sense?"

The boy stammered. "How do you hold smoke?"

"Never mind that. How does the rising smoke make you feel?" Sali bit her tongue, having erred. Her training as a Soul Seeker had been rushed, and her skill giving these tests suspect. Considering their plight, the spirit shamans had far greater concerns than providing her adequate instruction.

"Can I touch the smoke? Will it burn me?"

Sali struggled to mask her annoyance and keep the test on track. This was her first time performing it unsupervised. She felt a tinge of uncertainty as she dangled a light green crystal off a rope. "Let's move on. Open your eyes. Stare at this crystal. Watch it spin. Focus, focus, focus."

The boy tried his best. His face tensed and his breathing sped up as his pupils darted side to side, eyeing everything except what he was supposed to. And just like that the test was over. Sali had expected nothing from giving her first test, but still felt a pinch of disappointment that he did not pass. She glanced down at the paper in her hand. There would be many more failures to process.

"I'm sorry," the boy said, confused and downtrodden. "I must have done something wrong, mistress."

"On the contrary," she replied, "you did very well, lad."

He brightened. "Did I win?"

"In a way." If Jiamin's experience was any indication, he absolutely did.

The boy crossed his arms and stood his ground. "What do I win?"

Sali appreciated the hustle and handed him another coin, though if she had to pay every child she gave the test to, she would end up in the poorhouse by the end of the week.

Sali walked with the boy down the stairs and then sent him on his way. The stench of the street hit her the moment she stepped out of the inn. She had been here for two days now and still couldn't get used to the smell of manure, filth, and poverty permeating the air. Unlike the air back in the Grass Sea, which always blew, in Jiayi it felt stagnant, trapped within these walls like the people who lived here. She looked around and began walking deeper into the district. It wasn't long before she stumbled upon a yellow wooden beam jutting from the ground. Painted eloquently down all four sides were several Zhingzi words. Etched roughly with a blade at the top of the post was the Katuia pictograph for "scale."

Sali continued down the main street searching for more pictographs, finding the one for "flower" on a side street just before the main street ended. A small wedding party with three hearts—two young men, an adorable elderly man and woman in obviously their second or third marriages surrounded by their many grandchildren, and three women—danced down the street to the beat of half a dozen tuur drums. Sali stopped along with everyone else close by and slow-clapped a hand to her heart in the rhythm of the drums as the procession passed. The crowds were thinner and the mood more somber, but Sali appreciated that their traditions were still being kept alive. She was mildly surprised and thankful the land-chained allowed this, considering their sometimes more rigid beliefs. The only things missing were the wedding dresses and robes, and the processional of horses, which was understandable considering the circumstances.

Sali checked the note again and began her search, knocking from door to door. She tested her next child, a toddler, a few doors later in a second-floor unit that housed three families. The third was a girl working in the horse shop selling sinew, hair, and meat. The fourth was a teenager working in a brickyard. Sali took one look at the manure caked all over his hands, face, and body, and immediately rescheduled to return later that evening, preferably after he had washed up.

Sali had managed to test everyone else on the list and was just finishing up with the herbalist's daughter when her empty stomach grumbled, reminding her that she still hadn't eaten. How did she keep forgetting? This was one of the strange side effects of the Khan's Pull. It still had not lessened. In fact, it had grown so strong now, it blanketed her other senses, so much so she often couldn't sense the needs of the rest of her body. All she could feel was that gnawing, twisting desire to drop everything and sprint all the way to Chaqra.

Once Sali focused specifically on her empty stomach, the hunger came roaring back, sending sharp pains through her midsection. She grimaced as she finished speaking with the mother of the child.

The herbalist noticed her difficulty. "Is everything all right, Soul Seeker?"

"I am fine," she replied through gritted teeth.

The healer was not easily swayed. She cupped Sali's hand and squeezed, holding her still and gauging something. "Are you suffering from withdrawal of some sort?"

"No, it's nothing of the sort. It's . . ." Sali didn't know how to describe the compulsion. She tried to pull her hand away, but the herbalist's grip was firm.

"An addiction then?" The herbalist gave her a sympathetic look. "There is no shame in seeking help. I have treated several former clan warriors. Many have struggled lately."

Addiction was taboo among her people. Still, perhaps this herbalist could help. Sali leaned in and spoke in a low voice. "Do you have anything that can suppress urges?"

The woman nodded. "What sort? Zhuun alcohol? Giddy smoke? Opium? The treatment depends on the substance."

"It's nothing like that. It's more mental than anything else." The last thing Sali needed were rumors of the local Soul Seeker suffering from such a vice.

"Then something like a gambling addiction?" The woman's eyes widened. "Do you have an urge for violence or murder? Sexual—"

"No, no." This was getting her nowhere. "Apologizes, master herbalist. I am wasting your time. I'll be all right."

"One moment, please." The herbalist hurried to the hundreds of small wooden drawers behind her and returned a few moments later with a steaming cup in one hand and a small jar in the other. "Rat-tail leaves and hawkblood. Two pinches mixed into tea or hot water every morning. No more than one cup. This should soothe the mind and last through most of the day."

Sali didn't reach for it. "How much?"

The herbalist pushed both across the counter. "Consider it my contribution toward aiding in the search for the Eternal Khan."

Sali tried the concoction and found the taste as pleasant as anything involving rat-tails could be. Warmth spread through her body and she immediately felt a calm follow it. The gnawing pull in her head lessened, and she could feel some of her other senses again. She hadn't even realized her leg had been itching fiercely until just now.

Sali sucked in a long breath. "Thank you."

"Come back if you never need more, Soul Seeker."

She remained standing at the door for a few moments, replaying what had just happened in her head. She had never fully considered how important Soul Seekers were to her people. It was interesting to feel appreciated. It was not something she had ever experienced as a Will of the Khan or viperstrike, because her interaction with those from lower castes was kept to a minimum. Now that she walked among them, her relationship with them felt strange, but not unwelcome.

Sali left the shop and jogged—sprinted almost—to the nearest street vendor. Now that her mind was clearer, it let her know her body was ravenous. She bought one of everything and wolfed it down as quickly as the vendor cooked it, savoring nothing. The rice meal was bland; the spicy noodle stew was surprisingly devoid of noodles, or spice for that matter. The meat on a stick tasted nothing like the advertised horse, and she wasn't sure what the supposed taro cakes were made from. Not that any of this mattered.

Sali didn't put forth her critique of the food until she had finished the last bite. "That was terrible. What did I just eat?"

The vendor took her criticism in stride. "I can tell how much you hate it by the way you cleaned the plate. Would you like seconds?"

"Yes, friend." Sali pointed at the display. "This all looks like food from home, but tastes nothing like it. Why is that?"

The vendor sighed. "I used to be the chef for the clan heads on Fushand, but there is only so much I can do here without the proper ingredients. We do not have access to any of the spices from the Grass Sea, so we have to make do with what the land-chained provide."

She made a face. "Zhuun cuisine is terrible."

"No disagreement there." He held out his hand. "That'll be nine copper liang."

Sali paid the bill without complaint. This became her routine for the next several days. The same boy would appear at her door early in the morning with a new list. Sali would canvass another section of the district, then try her luck at a different food vendor. Disappointingly, the alleged clan-head chef from the first day was the best of the lot, and she found herself a regular at his stall.

Sali spent the rest of the week covering the entire district. Mali, now seventeen, should have appeared on one of the lists, possibly under a pseudonym. Sali had daydreamed of walking to a home to conduct a test and finding Mali at the door. The two would burst into tears and she would pick up her little Sprout and swing her around fiercely like she used to, and then they would steal away in the middle of the night under the glow of the three moons.

Sali had clung to hope even until the final morning, when the errand boy told her these twelve names were the last. That day, once she finished the last child, a three-year-old, reality finally punched her in the gut. Her knees buckled as a body-shuddering sob overtook her. Mali wasn't here. That meant she had likely fallen alongside Nezra, perished on the forced march, or succumbed to illness in this accursed city. It didn't matter how she died. Her precious and beautiful Sprout was gone, alongside the last of their blood. Sali was all alone in the world.

The poor toddler's mother, fearing something terrible had happened to her son, reacted poorly to Sali's sudden display of grief. "What's the matter?" she cried out. "What's wrong with my son? Is he cursed?" She paused, her hand fluttering to her chest. "Wait, is he the Eternal Khan?"

Thinking of Jiamin, Sali nearly broke into cynical laughter. "No, mistress, your son is not the Eternal Khan."

The disappointment was apparent on the mother's face. It disappeared when she saw Sali's red eyes. "Then what's the matter, Soul Seeker?"

Sali's grief was quickly masked. She shook her head. "It's nothing. I've been searching for someone, and she does not seem to be here."

The woman touched her shoulder lightly. "I understand your loss. I lost my husband during the battle and my oldest daughter from sickness after we arrived here. Are you sure you looked everywhere?"

"I've searched for and tested everyone under eighteen years of age here in the district."

The woman furrowed her brow. "Did you also check the ones living on the general's estate?"

Sali perked up. "What general's estate? How many live there?"

"I'm not sure," the woman replied. "About a quarter of the number in this district, I'd say. They're General Quan Sah's personal servants. My heart-sister is among them. She works as a gardener. Every once in a while, she comes here to recruit workers for large jobs. From what I hear, they live well, but aren't allowed to move about as freely, and have to adhere to an early curfew. If it were up to me . . ."

Sali stopped listening. Quan Sah, the general who had razed Nezra, was holding hundreds of Katuia at his estate. How had this escaped her knowledge? Was this an oversight on the part of the council or a deliberate attempt to hide it from her? There was only one way to find out.

Sali excused herself from the woman's rambling, patting the toddler on the way out, and marched down the main street. Her thoughts seethed as she stormed down the road. She couldn't remember walking to the estate where the Council of Nezra held court. A squad of guards staffing the front gates saw her all the way down the block. They noticed the fury on her face and hastily formed up.

The squadlead met her halfway down the street and leveled her spear at Sali. "Stop, not one step farther. State your business."

Sali's hand snaked out and clutched the end of the spear. She snapped her body like a whip, pushing and transferring her jing from the ground, through her body, over the shaft of the weapon, and into the guard's hands. The squadlead cried as the shock tore the weapon out of her grasp. Not taking her eyes off the front gates, Sali hurled the spear into a nearby wall with a loud thud, then continued on without missing a step. The rest of the squad realized who they were dealing with. Fearful cries of "viperstrike" passed through them as they melted away from her until only one guard bravely, or foolishly, remained.

To Sali's surprise, it was that doe-eyed man from a few days prior. He stood alone, quivering. "I'm sorry, Viperstrike Salminde. I can't let you pass."

Sali stopped as the tip of his spear touched her scale armor lightly. "Hampa, isn't it? Your courage and commitment are admirable, if not your sense of self-preservation."

Hampa looked pleased that she remembered his name, but still held his ground. "I will die in defense of Nezra."

The lad had a good head on his shoulders. It was going to get him killed, which was a pity. "What you're defending now is not Nezra, and I am not your enemy."

"It is not a warrior's place to choose when to follow their duty."

Another fair reply. However . . . "It is always a choice, young Hampa. Never fight blindly, and never throw your life away." That last comment hit Sali a little too close to home. Hampa wavered for a few seconds before slowly lowering his spear.

Sali offered him a curt nod as acknowledgment and continued walking. The rest of the squad gathered and followed close behind, but none dared impede her progress. She passed through the gates and continued around the estate toward the back garden. Word must have raced ahead to the council, because two squads of guards were waiting for her at the end of the bridge as she was crossing over to the pavilion. She was trying to figure out how to best dispatch all ten guards without hurting anyone when Ariun arrived and saved her the trouble.

"Salminde," he said. "To what do we owe this pleasure?"

"Your council was supposed to provide me the names of every Katuia under the age of eighteen," she said flatly.

He nodded. "And so we did. Why, did you not get the lists?"

"You forgot the ones living in Quan Sah's estate. I need those too."

"Unfortunately, those are out of the council's jurisdiction."

"They're our people." She was not containing her rage. "They need to be included! Their children need to be tested!"

"Out of the question." His forced calm did nothing to assuage her. By now, Sali was aware that another squad had formed up at the end of the bridge behind her. "The council provided what we could, but the general's personal servants are off-limits."

"Even for the ruling Council of Nezra?"

"And even for Soul Seekers and viperstrikes," he affirmed. "Interfering with the Zhuun general will cause many problems for our people."

Sali glared at the former defensechief with contempt. "How many children live there, Ariun? How many possible Khans are you asking me to overlook?"

"I do not know. It's none of my business at this time, and it is none of yours. The council forbids you from getting involved with the general's servants. It will cause trouble for the people."

"It is absolutely the business of a Soul Seeker." Sali reached for her tongue.

The guards at both ends of the bridge closed in. Ariun did not bother reaching for the weapon hanging off his waist. He crossed his arms and dared her to strike. "Is this what it comes down to, Viperstrike? Will you now spill the blood of your own people?"

"If I must," she growled.

The seconds ticked by. Deep inside, Sali knew that Ariun had successfully called her bluff. As much as she blustered, inflicting violence upon her own people was beneath her. That was not why she had come to Jiayi. This was not a measure she was willing to take. With a snarl, she turned and stormed back the way she had come.

"What will you do now, Salminde?" Ariun called after her.

"I will cause trouble," she replied, without looking back. The guards parted, giving her a wide berth. None were foolish enough to make a move.

Sali glanced at Hampa as she passed. "Still want to be a viperstrike? Come along." A moment later, her new neophyte, spearless and helmetless, fell in beside her. His face was bright and eager as a puppy's as he marched alongside her out of the estate.

"I won't let you down, Viperstrike," he exclaimed, trying to keep up with her pace. "By Nezra I will make you proud."

Sali gave him a sidelong glance and groused. "You could have at least kept your spear."

CHAPTER TWENTY-FOUR

SAND SNAKE

In hindsight, Taishi probably should have heeded Zofi's advice and set sail after the winds had died down.

Her first journey in a sand sleigh on the fine, granular surface of the Sand Snake was indeed a memorable one. That was good because she never wanted to do it again. No sooner had they pulled out of the tunnel exit of the Peasant Docks than the howling winds caught the sail and swept Zofi's little bathtub sleigh spinning out of control into the churn of the rolling dunes, like a true ocean storm tossing a fishing boat around.

Unlike many war artists who had put forth tremendous effort to maintain a stoic expression at all times, Taishi suffered no qualms about vocalizing her feelings, and she preferred those under her to do the same. It was better to show fear than false courage. A soldier who showed fear—in moderation—was an alert and sharp soldier, and more likely to follow orders. Someone who was busy acting brave was preoccupied with the wrong thing.

That was why, as their little sleigh dropped several stories in near free fall down the side of the first dune in the Sand Snake, Taishi felt com-

pletely free to scream herself hoarse. Zofi, who was also screaming, albeit from an altogether different emotion, pulled on the rudder, and the
sleigh caught an edge as it barreled down the bowl of the dune. As it
passed the bottom and began to climb up the other side, two rolling
waves, each as tall as buildings, crashed together, forming a giant wave
that blotted out the sky ahead of them. Taishi's screams intensified as
the new mountain of sand began to topple over, showering them. For
some inexplicable reason, Zofi continued to steer the sleigh toward it.

Taishi tugged at the girl's sleeve, her voice quiet with terror. "Are you
trying to get us killed, you suicidal idiot?"

Zofi replied with a whoop that sounded strangely like a mix between
a war cry and a giggle as sand and air spit in their faces. Just as the Slidewinder was about to go vertical, she banked sharply, causing the sleigh to
surf sideways along the wave as it curved and fell over them.

Taishi went back to screaming and screaming, and screaming some
more until her voice got hoarse and she got a little bored. After the
adrenaline had fled her body, she realized that everything—the sleigh,
the sands, the winds—were actually moving pretty slowly. It felt terrifying only while they were in the thick of it. Zofi howled triumphantly as a
strong gust caught the sails and shot the sleigh like a crossbow bolt out
from under the wave and onto the next swell.

The Slidewinder repeated this pattern several more times before
eventually escaping the turbulent, undulating dunes and hitting a stretch
of calm desert. The tall cliffs of Sanba soon disappeared, completely enveloped by the giant dust clouds that bubbled into the sky. Taishi allowed herself to breathe and moved to the rear of the tub. She studied
the wake pattern kicked up by the Slidewinder's hull. Soon all the mark-
ers shrank into tiny blemishes on the horizon, leaving her feeling small
and alone in this expansive ocean of sand.

Zofi never looked worried, and guided the sleigh through both the
rough churn out of Sanba and now across the calm expanse with complete confidence. The girl was a skilled sailor and steered with a soft
touch, knowing exactly how to coax the most wind out of the sails.
Under her control, the Slidewinder moved toward the southern horizon
with an easy grace.

Taishi was reasonably sure by now that their lives were safe in the mapmaker's daughter's hands. "How did you learn to sail so well?"

Zofi loosened the lines and retied them. "There's not much else to do for fun in Sanba besides surfing." Satisfied, she relaxed, sitting down and stretching her legs across the length of the boat, her feet sticking over the side. She leaned back and eyed the evening sky. "I used to dream of running my own caravan someday. Getting out of the caves and out under the Celestial ceiling."

Taishi grunted, settling down beside Zofi but still hugging the mast tightly. "You southerners have a strange sense of leisure."

"Try living in a cave your entire life."

Taishi glanced at the last desert clouds disappearing in the distance. "Will we encounter more storms?"

"Hopefully not, with luck. The waves are always roughest near solid land, and especially bad around Sanba because of the sand waves breaking against the cliffs."

"Just like the ocean," remarked Taishi, thoughtfully. "How does a place like this even exist?"

"No one knows for sure," said Zofi. "Most say it's always been here, but some historical records mention that the Sand Snake only appeared a few centuries ago. Everyone agrees, however, that it's growing, eating up solid land every year. Two hundred years ago, it was just a small stream that cut across the forest. Travelers just had to take proper precautions to cross it. Now it's everywhere."

"Will we sink in it?"

"Slowly, if we stop moving," replied the girl. "The people here call it slowsand. The sleigh has to keep moving to stay afloat."

That sounded familiar. Taishi glanced toward the northeast. The currents on the Sand Snake moved chaotically, but they generally swept westward. According to the map, just behind the Sand Snake region to the east was . . .

"The Grass Sea," muttered Taishi. Of course. A large body of water probably resided underneath this layer of sand. Just as the Grass Sea was layers of vegetation sitting on a bed of water, the Sand Snake was the same except with a desert as the surface.

She turned her attention closer to their boat and admired this strange and beautiful landscape. There was something hypnotically calming about the way the surface waves lapped and folded over one another, occasionally forming walls that rose up before collapsing under their own weight. She leaned over the side of the tub and touched the fine grains of sand—like silk—with her fingers.

Eventually, after a few hours, as with most things, wonder turned to familiarity and then eventually to tedium. The King changed from his imperial yellow garb for the evening, taking on his mandarin hue as he sank into the western horizon.

Zofi beckoned. "Hold the rudder. I need to check our navigation."

Taishi was grateful to stretch her sore legs. Her knees and hips groaned as she shifted, carefully trading places with Zofi on the small craft as the girl opened the long wooden box.

Zofi took out the map and pored over it intently, flipping through its many layers as she checked the stars, the last remaining sliver of the King, the Queen beginning her ascent, and even the direction of the wind. This continued for a while. Taishi was content to mind her own business and let the girl do whatever it was she had to do with the navigation, but she couldn't help but notice the lines on Zofi's forehead. The page flipping became more frantic.

"Is everything all right?"

Zofi responded with a guttural growl.

"Want me to just stay the course?"

Zofi nodded without bothering to look up.

Night had set, and Taishi was still on the rudder. Zofi had loosened the sails so now they were really moving at a crawl, but she was still struggling with the map, going back and forth between the many layers.

Taishi finally had to say it. "I thought you knew how to read one of these things."

"Ba taught me a few times, but I'm not that good at it yet," Zofi admitted.

Taishi scanned the horizon. It looked like desert and mountains in every direction. "Does that mean we're lost?"

"No, of course not. I'm just not exactly sure where we are at the moment, and I'm not positive we're heading in the right direction."

The pit of Taishi's stomach dropped. Every time she thought she had found a terrible and humiliating way to die, another worse way presented itself. She tried to stay optimistic. "Well, the Sand Snake isn't that wide. Two days' journey, right? I'm sure it'll be all right even if we're a little off course."

Two days passed and they were still sliding in the middle of the wide-open expanse of the Sand Snake with no land in sight. They ran out of food on the third day, and pretty much patience as well. Taishi didn't know what had gone wrong, but there was no use asking Zofi. The girl was still diligently studying the map, still trying to make it show them the way.

Everything resolved itself on the morning of the fourth day when the mining settlement of Manki appeared on the horizon. Taishi had thought it was a mirage at first, but then Zofi jumping excitedly confirmed that she saw it too. There was some awkward attempted hugging and pats on the back as the relief of knowing they weren't going to die in the desert set in.

Their joy was short-lived. Manki, like most rural settlements, was little more than a few rows of buildings along four or five intersecting streets. It had just large enough of a population to call it civilized, but was also lawless enough that it looked like a bandit camp. Makeshift tents and clay hovels flanked narrow, muddy streets. Rough-looking residents, showing more grime than skin, sharpened tools and heated pots over open flames. Most paid them little more attention than an unfriendly side glance before continuing with their day. Unlike in the interior of the Zhuun lands, transients were common here.

Taishi kept her face covered and her head bowed. "I see as many blades as I see shovels."

"It's the way of these parts. We're outside the borders of the States, so the people here have to fend for themselves. As long as Dongshi can collect taxes from Sanba, there's no need to annex places like this." Zofi scanned the horizon. "According to the map, Fulkan Forest begins just on the other side of that hill. It should only be a day's journey to the temple. We should probably rest during high heat and move out in the evening."

That's what the girl had said about the journey across the Sand Snake. Taishi relished moving about. Her legs were practically numb after so many days of inactivity. A long walk, even in this heat, was a welcome change. "Let's head out now. I've done nothing but sit on my butt for weeks."

Zofi looked dubious, but then shrugged. "Suit yourself. We should at least resupply first."

The two stopped at the only store in the settlement. Taishi walked in fully expecting things to cost more than at Sanba, but was left shocked by just about everything. A bag of rice cost as much as a pig's rear quarters. Smoked meats the price of the whole pig. Gourds of water cost their weight in gold.

"This is robbery," she spat.

The shopkeeper, a wiry crackled man who looked as windswept as the desert, shrugged. "You're free to take your business somewhere else."

Zofi began picking through the small piles of food and sparse supplies scattered on the shelves and floors. "The fortune to be made in these places isn't the mining, but in keeping the miners alive. Don't worry, I'll get the prices down."

Zofi spent the next several hours haggling with the shopkeeper on every single purchase. At first, Taishi didn't mind. It was *her* money they were spending, after all. She was even impressed that the girl had the thoughtfulness to go to such lengths to save her liang. Eventually, though, as the day dragged on, her impatience began to overwhelm her frugality. By the time the third hour rolled on, Taishi no longer cared.

She reached over Zofi's shoulder and yanked the burlap sack off the counter. "Who cares about the price of potatoes," she snapped.

Zofi crossed her arms. "I'm not paying a copper more than twelve."

Taishi slapped the two-copper difference they'd been haggling over for the past twenty minutes onto the table. "Let's go."

"Have a safe trip to the temple," the shopkeeper quipped. "Try not to die."

Taishi stormed out of the shop and scowled. They had wasted half the day at the shop. She rounded on the girl, shaking her finger. "You did this on purpose!"

Zofi shouldered their sack of supplies and grinned. "I just saved us at least four gourds of water and probably death by not traveling during the day. Next time, just do what I say."

"Why, you little . . ." Taishi shook her head. "Never mind. Let's go before we lose more light."

"Actually," added Zofi, pointing back the way they came. "We need to hide the Slidewinder, else it'll get stolen."

Taishi shot her a hard look that would have killed a lesser person, but she complied. The only way her current situation could get worse was if she were stranded here. They wasted another two hours dragging the Slidewinder to an isolated clearing and loosely burying it under a mound of sand. By the time they actually began moving into Fulkan Forest, evening was breaking. Just like Zofi had planned.

Taishi was impressed yet again. "Well done, girl."

Fulkan Forest . . . was not a forest. In fact, there was nothing remotely forest-like about it. It may have been one centuries ago, but now it was just vast clusters of petrified trees, a collection of twisted branches barren of leaves or wildlife sitting atop a desert landscape that stretched as far as the eye could see. Taishi rapped on one of the trunks. It was harder than stone. Any hope of walking underneath the shade of a forest canopy was crushed as they slogged through the slush of loose gravel on uneven terrain. The ground was hot to the touch from the heat of the day. Sweat soon glistened on her forehead, and she struggled to stay upright and maintain her pace. She didn't need to verbalize how grateful she was that they had begun this leg of the journey so late.

They continued deeper into the forest well after the Queen was in the sky, blanketing the yellow sands with her deep-blue hues. The Prince, just beginning his own journey, was layering his own colors, quickly turning the landscape cyan. The two moons being so close together was a reminder that the Princess would soon join the rest of the Celestial Family, and with her the harsh third cycle. Whatever traveling Taishi needed to do had better wrap up before then.

An hour after sunset, the temperature plummeted from scalding to near freezing, and by the sixth hour, her breath frosted the air and she could no longer feel her toes. By the time they stopped for the night, the ground had completely frozen over, the chill had permeated all of Taishi's layers, and she was regretting every decision she had ever made.

The two set up camp inside a small grove of petrified trees. It wasn't much, but it did provide some shelter from the winds that swirled and kicked up sand all around them. They huddled around a small fire drinking boiled potato soup.

"What will you do after we finish our business here?" asked Taishi.

Zofi shrugged. "I always wanted to escape Sanba, but Ba needed me close. He was the smartest person I know, a true master at his craft, but he couldn't run a business to save his own life."

Taishi grunted as she held her four pieces of potato on a stick. It was a fair assessment. If her own father had spent just a little more time teaching her to leverage her war art abilities for profit, then perhaps she could be living large in luxury like Guanshi right now instead of sunburned and frostbitten huddled next to a bossy orphan in a tree graveyard.

Zofi stared off into the darkness. "Now that Ba doesn't need me anymore, I guess I'm finally free to explore the world." She reached for her satchel and pulled out an intricately carved leather pen case and carefully unfurled it. A dozen fine pens were lined neatly inside, each expertly crafted and lovingly maintained. "It's my father's treasured painting set." Zofi touched each of the pens before closing up the case again. She stood. "Excuse me, I need to say goodbye properly." She walked away from the fire and disappeared into the darkness just outside their grove.

Taishi could just make out the girl's outline as she dug a hole in the soft ground and placed her father's belongings inside. Small sobs soon followed. The sounds faded, leaving Taishi to wait alone next to the dying fire.

When Zofi failed to return, she began to worry. Taishi picked up the Swallow Dances and went looking for the girl. She found Zofi sleeping, shivering huddled in a fetal position next to a mound of freshly disturbed sand.

Taishi touched her shoulder. "Come back next to the fire, girl. You'll catch a cold."

Zofi woke with a start, groggy but compliant as Taishi led her back to the fire. She accepted Taishi's offer of a cloak and wrapped it around her shoulders as she stared into the fire. "My mam died when I was a little. My ba was the last of my family. I'm all alone now." She shuddered as fresh tears ran down her cheeks.

Taishi understood well that extraordinary feeling of utter loneliness when you were the last of your family lineage. It was one thing to lose a close family member. It was another altogether to be the last. That meant you had no other connections, no more blood to bind you. She did her best, placing a hand on the girl's shoulder. "I know how you feel, girl. You'll get used to it. It's not so bad." If her words reached Zofi, she didn't show it. She tried again. "When I—"

"Please just shut up?"

That was probably for the best. She continued to pat Zofi's shoulder awkwardly. "I'm here if you need me."

"Go away."

She let her shoulder go. "I'll be over there if—"

A low, guttural howl that sounded eerily like laughter cut through the air. It was soon joined by several others.

"Rock jackals," said Zofi, bolting to her feet.

Taishi's veins went even colder as she scanned the blackness just outside their cluster of trees. She turned slowly, her eyes catching the dancing shadows from the fire. "That sounds close. We should be safe, though. Jackals are small and don't eat people. They're also afraid of fire."

"I don't think they're actually jackals."

"What does that mean?"

"It means rock jackals will probably eat us, and we'll have to fight them off near the fire. The stories about them are they're gray as night and nearly invisible."

Taishi scrambled to break camp, rolling up her blanket and scooping their meager supplies and rations into her satchel. "We can't fight them."

"Why not? Aren't you a war arts grandmaster? You can easily beat a bunch of wild dogs."

"I don't like to fight animals. I find it unnecessarily cruel."

"You don't like to what?" sputtered Zofi. "Well, get over it!"

Taishi slung her satchel over her shoulder, dipped the ends of two branches into the fire, and handed one to Zofi. "Why are you still standing still? Run!"

CHAPTER TWENTY-FIVE

FRIENDS & FALLACIES

Jian stood at his usual spot in the corner of the dining hall with three tiers of baskets in one hand and a damp cloth hanging off his free forearm. There were no seats left, and a small line had even formed just outside the doorway, but the chatter was unusually subdued. It was early the second morning after the fight. Xinde had not yet left the infirmary, and people were beginning to worry. Rumors were rampant. Some thought the senior was on his deathbed. Someone had suggested that he was already dead, but that Guanshi was hiding the fact to save face. The very imaginative believed that he was actually using his injury as cover to sneak out over to the Southern Cross to exact his revenge. Nobody knew how badly hurt he was except for Meehae and Auntie Li, and neither was talking.

One of the students finished his meal and left, leaving clusters of rice, a puddle of cucumber juice, and a torn banana leaf wrap on the table and bench. Jian grunted. "Sloppy savages, the lot of them."

As he went to wipe the table down, Siang stuck his leg out. Jian bobbled the baskets, nearly losing all three, but managed to save them by clutching them to his body as he fell to his knees. The room roared with juvenile howls. Jian snarled and turned to face Siang, but Cyyk beat him to it. Jian's former nemesis came out of nowhere and shoved Siang, sending him toppling over the bench and onto his back. A new chorus of laughter followed.

Cyyk's fists were to his sides as Siang picked himself up off the ground. "What do you think you're doing? You almost wasted good bao."

Siang, who moments earlier was eager to bully Jian, was instantly cowed by the bigger boy. "Sorry, big brother. I just thought—"

Cyyk pointed toward the kitchen. "Stop trying to think. You're not good at it. Go get me more juice." He grimaced and turned to Jian, offering just the slightest of nods. "Filthy animals, right, Hiro? Toss me that rag, would you?"

Jian lobbed one over.

Cyyk caught it, wiped down his area, and tossed it back to Jian. "Any more bao?"

The limit was still two per student, but Jian wasn't above bribery. He scooped a wooden spatula under two lotus paste buns and flicked them one at a time. Cyyk plucked both out of the air deftly and stuffed them into his mouth in one smooth motion, then gave Jian a thumbs-up before turning away.

Jian returned to the kitchen wondering what any of this meant. Cyyk certainly wasn't his friend, but it felt as if they shared a strange connection now. Jian peeked back through the doorway at the crowded dining hall. He had never realized how much he needed acknowledgment and recognition until he had a small taste of it. He still hated everyone, but things felt a little different. Jian was about to return to the hall with a refilled basket of buns when he heard a heavy knocking at the infirmary next door.

"Xinde," said Guanshi gruffly. He banged more insistently when no one answered.

Auntie Li appeared out of the milling shack a moment later with a basket of dough in her hands. "What are you doing, master?" Her question was more of a statement. "The young man needs rest."

"Nonsense. He's received worse injuries in training." Guanshi knocked more insistently this time. "Come on, Xinde, it's been two days."

"Give him time," she cajoled. "He needs to be in the right frame of mind."

"He can get his head straight doing his work." Guanshi was about to barge into the infirmary when the door slid open.

Xinde stepped out. "It's all right, Auntie. How may I serve, master?"

"About time you got up. I'm having breakfast with a group of masters. Teach the rest of the morning classes." Guanshi pointed his thumb at students working on head-to-toe stretching in the training yard. "You know what to do. The intermediates are practicing fixed-method sparring forms. No open-hand freestyling. Not with that clumsy group. The novices are starting basic spear. Work on holding the shafts correctly. Nothing more. With the children's class, have them play tag, I don't care. Just tire them out."

"Yes, master."

It was good to see the senior up and about. He looked tired, his face was pale, his eyes sunken, and his hair damp and plastered to his forehead. His shirt was hanging loosely off his shoulders and his chest was heavily wrapped, but the bandage was clean. Xinde disappeared into the infirmary and reappeared moments later wearing his robe.

Jian continued his work in the dining hall, occasionally peeking out to check on Xinde as the senior worked with the morning class. Any concerns he had about Xinde's health were quickly set aside. The self-assured Xinde had returned, his voice ringing clear across the grounds. He demonstrated techniques and ran drills, and even put in a few rounds of sparring. He did not seem hesitant or slowed from his injury, nor were his movements limited.

Jian finished his chores, wolfed down a couple of bao, then stretched for his afternoon class. He was soon squatting in a wide horse stance holding the shaft of a dull spear alongside the rest of the beginners working drills across from a retiree named Soome with too much time on his hands living out his war artist dreams.

Xinde followed Guanshi's normal routine exactly. The senior had them practice holding the spear with the proper technique. They weren't thrusting or parrying or swinging, just gripping and holding and staying in stance for the entire first hour of class. Luckily, they moved to basic sparring—only hands, half speed—for the second hour. And, of course, Jian was paired up with Soome.

"Hiro," barked Xinde as he walked up and down the line of novices. "What part of half speed do you not understand?"

"This *is* half speed," he growled under his breath. "Some half speeds are faster than other half speeds."

Jian had never had to hold back like this at the Celestial Palace. It was driving him crazy. He wanted nothing more than to unleash his full abilities. He became so frustrated and preoccupied that old Soome managed to land a punch, causing Jian to lose his balance and tumble onto his backside.

"By the heavens, are you all right, young orphan?" The white-haired grandfather patted him on the cheek. "Sometimes I just don't know my own power."

Jian touched his face and felt the blood trickle out of his nose. First blood by old man Soome.

Xinde kept his face neutral, but the mirth in his eyes was evident. "Novice Soome, what did I tell you about controlling your power? It's too much for some of these children."

The septuagenarian held up his bony fists. "I just don't know my own strength."

Xinde sent Soome off to practice on the wooden dummy and turned to Jian. "Is it broken?"

Jian, leaning his head forward and pinching his nose, shook his head. "I was just careless."

"That's the difference between life and death in battle," said the senior, checking his bloodied nose. "You have talent, Hiro. We need to hone your focus. You could be exceptional one day."

Every word of encouragement only made Jian feel worse. "Thank you, senior."

"So stop holding back."

Jian frowned. "You mean I can go faster?"

Xinde shook his head. "I want you to go even slower."

"What?"

The senior held up his guard. "Attack."

Jian obliged, launching a basic combination at his usual practice speed. Xinde, gliding in slow motion, slipped his punches and ended up with a spear hand touching Jian's armpit.

"A true war artist can read an attack before his opponent commits," recited Xinde, following through with a sharp tug to Jian's shoulder and tripping his ankles. If the senior had not been holding on to his robes, Jian would have fallen. Xinde kept him upright and patted him on the back. "It is more difficult to fight deliberately and at quarter speed than swiftly without control. Once you master fighting slow, fighting fast will be easy."

"I think I understand." He didn't, really.

Xinde patted him on the shoulder as he moved on to the next pairing. "Next time you spar with Soome, I want you to try to move as slow as possible. Without getting a bloody nose."

Jian was dubious, but took the lesson to heart, following the senior's instructions for the remaining hour of class. Soome came back and rewarded him with two more punches to the face—he seemed to have only one target—resulting in a cut lip and a black eye to go along with his bloodied nose. Soome really *didn't* know his own power. It took most of the rest of class before Jian got the hang of fighting slow. He was just beginning to anticipate his opponent's moves when Guanshi returned from his dim sum.

The master looked pleased as he walked through their ranks, offering instruction here and there, and occasionally adjusting his students' practices.

"The yard is yours, master," said Xinde as Guanshi approached. The class stopped what they were doing and saluted, putting fists to open palms and bowing.

Guanshi waved them off. "Xinde, I have a job for you."

"Continue practicing. Remember, control and technique," Xinde instructed, before turning his attention back to Guanshi. "How may I serve Longxian, master?"

"Fusan announced his retirement today." The master, his hearing already fading with his age, made only a halfhearted effort to speak quietly. Jian, in between eating punches from Soome, overheard everything.

"Master Fusan is a great teacher," said Xinde. "The lunar court will be poorer with his absence. His Gungar style has produced many excellent artists. Who is his successor?"

"No one," he replied. "He's shutting down all of his schools."

Xinde looked startled. "All three? Why? He has even more students than we do!"

The master grunted. "Call it a failure from an abundance of success. Fusan is so wealthy he doesn't need to work. His daughter is so spoiled she doesn't want to work. Rather than sully his family style's good name, he's just going to sell the schools and quit the business."

"Are you planning on buying them?"

"Not during this recession. What I want to do is to take a crack at Gungar's security contracts. I'll be setting up meetings to discuss taking them over. I need you to visit the owner of the Really Best Box warehouses. Every other school is scrambling for a bite of these contracts as well. Have Auntie Li assemble a gift basket for your meeting. Tell her to put in a bottle of rice wine, nothing top-shelf. This will be good practice for you to build these relationships."

"Of course, master."

"I'm glad to hear that. You didn't look ready to see anyone this morning. Training always does a body good. The meeting is tomorrow morning. Make sure the basket is ready by then. A good head for business is just as important as one's fist in war arts. It will be good practice for you."

He gave Xinde some more instructions and retreated to his office, leaving the senior to dismiss the class. Jian bowed to his sparring partner, still silently cursing his old-man strength.

CHAPTER TWENTY-SIX

THE "ORIGINAL" TEMPLE OF THE TIANDI

Taishi and Zofi fled from the rock jackals almost until daybreak, plodding uphill in ankle-deep sand, losing a step for every three forward.

The jackals remained just out of sight in the darkness, but made their presence heard with persistent howls from every direction. There was no outrunning or outwitting them. The pack waited patiently, herding the humans until they were too exhausted to fight back. The women's only chance would have been to find shelter, and this arid wasteland had little to offer. Taishi considered climbing the skeleton of a tree, but Zofi couldn't say if these animals knew how to climb.

At some point, their pace must have slowed so much even the rock jackals grew impatient. Their unnatural grousing crescendoed and harmonized. Their darting shadows closed in. Taishi swung her burning branch back and forth as eight or nine pairs of glittering orange eyes circled them, with more appearing by the second.

Zofi, standing a few paces away, suddenly cried out and fell to one knee. A rock jackal had pounced on her shoulder and was tearing at her satchel. There was really nothing jackal-like about these animals. Whoever had given them that name deserved a beating. The creature was a hairless animal the size of a large dog with a long ratty snout and mangled, droopy ears. Two long fangs curled downward from its twisted mouth, which crinkled its gray skin around it like a dried-out riverbed.

"Duck!" Zofi did just that as Taishi swung her burning branch over the top of the girl's head. The creature yelped as her blow sent it flying into the darkness.

More jackals took its place. One jackal bit down on the branch while another tried to take a bite out of Taishi's shoulder. She dropped the branch and dodged its jaws. Several came at her from all sides, a few sneaking up by crawling along the sands.

It was getting claustrophobic. They needed to get to higher ground. The silhouette of a ridge with four spikes rose up from the sands, blocking the Princess's full purple face as she was finishing her journey. Taishi grabbed a handful of Zofi's shirt and leaped, catching a current and riding it toward the ridge.

The girl was heavier than she looked. That or Taishi was exhausted. She teetered off balance and misstepped when she tried to move to the next current. The two crashed ungracefully, well short of her intended destination. Taishi came up sputtering bits of sand and dirt. She dragged Zofi along and reached the base of the ridge, but there was no way to climb up.

A boil of the creatures appeared over the nearest hill and converged on them. Taishi could theoretically have made it up there herself, but leaving Zofi to scavenging monsters was beneath saving her own life. Damn that Jian. If this was where she was going to die, Taishi was going to do it with her honor intact. She drew the Swallow Dances and waited as the rock jackals surrounded them.

"I'm glad you changed your mind about killing animals," said Zofi.

"I'm really not happy about that." Realizing that the girl was unarmed, Taishi yanked her knife out and lobbed it to the girl.

Zofi promptly bobbled the catch and nicked her hand. "Ow." Blood gushed from the cut, down her forearm and off her elbow onto the ground. That worked the rock jackals into a frenzy.

"That's just great. Just stay behind me."

Taishi brought the Swallow Dances down and decapitated the first rock jackal that dared come within range. The Swallow Dances blurred seven more times, killing seven more. Soon the main body of the animals arrived, and three rock jackals replaced every one she killed.

They were going to die. To a bunch of overgrown rats. This surpassed any other humiliating demise Taishi could have ever imagined.

"I'm sorry I got you into this, girl," she shouted over the chorus of mocking howls.

"I think I'd be better off if I had died in the fire," the girl replied.

Some jackals began to eat their slain while others jumped over the bodies to get to the two women. They leaped high and came at them from above. Taishi continued to cut them down by the dozen, but her arm was tiring, and they had run out of room to back up.

Just then, two long shadows fell over them. Taishi was too preoccupied with keeping the jackals at bay to notice until a pair of giants landed on the ground in front of her with a heavy thud, spraying sand in all directions.

One began swinging his fists in looping arcs, crushing the rock jackals in twos and threes. The other wielded a staff that was as tall as a tree with one end ablaze. The burning end of the staff left a trail of colored smoke in the air as if a spirit wisp danced under the light of the Twins.

One jackal leaped at the unarmed giant and bit down on his forearm. Metal jingled as the giant shook the creature loose. Taishi caught a glint in the moonlight on his arms: iron rings. Then she caught a glimpse of his bald head.

"Hansoo brothers," she said, her voice breathy at the welcome sight. They belonged to the militant arm of the Tiandi religion and were known to be devout and formidable warriors. The training at the Stone Blossom Monastery was reputed to be extraordinary, causing the monks' bodies to grow to unnatural proportions.

The two Hansoo brothers cleared the rock jackals in short order. Taishi wasn't sure why their actions managed to scare away the pack, since these creatures didn't seem to care about their own lives. Yet somehow, within a few moments of their arrival, the surviving jackals had backed off, forming a large circle around the four humans. Then, howling, growling, and laughing all the while, they peeled away in groups until the last disappeared.

Taishi still couldn't believe their good fortune. One of the monks turned to them. The gigantic man laced his hands together and spoke in an unusually soft voice. "Pardon the confusion, mistresses. Are you all right?"

She nodded. "Thank you for your assistance, both of you. We are in your debt. What are two war monks doing out here in the middle of nowhere?"

The giant Hansoo smiled. "What else but the watching over the most holy of lands."

The other Hansoo joined them shortly after. He had walked the perimeter with his smoking staff, waving it about. "That's the last of them. It's a good thing we arrived when we did."

The Hansoo who'd spoken first, gestured. "I am Liuman. This little one is Pahm."

The two Hansoo brothers could have passed for father and son. Both were bald and muscular, and they wore matching yellow-and-blue robes that hung loosely off their shoulders and were bound tightly around their waists. Liuman, the older and larger Hansoo, was easily half again as wide and tall as a normal man. His arms were unnaturally large and long, rivaling his legs. His forearms were completely hidden by a row of large iron rings.

Pahm, the "little" brother, was a head shorter than Liuman, but still a towering mass of a man. He was young, with a head as smooth and pale as a toddler's ass. The four rings on each of his forearms signified that he had not yet completed his monastic training and physical transformation.

Taishi inhaled deeply. "What is that? Is that caramel?"

Zofi, staring at the two giant men with her mouth agape, nodded. "I smell it too. Now I'm hungry."

The younger Hansoo brother grinned and glanced at his burning staff. "Burning sugar. Rock jackals can't stand the smell."

"How did you find us?" asked Taishi.

"It wasn't difficult," said Pahm. "Your screams carried."

"We've been keeping track of you since you set up camp," added Liuman. "We keep a lookout for pilgrims, so we've been tracking your torchlight since evening, and came to your assistance when we heard the jackal howls."

"You're from the Temple of the Tiandi?" said Taishi.

"What else would anyone be doing out here?" chuckled Liuman, the giant bundles of taut muscles around his shoulders shaking almost disconcertingly. The dozen iron circles around his wrists jingled in harmony. The entire display was a little unsettling. There were muscles on this man in places where muscles just didn't belong on a normal person.

"The *original* Temple of the Tiandi," Pahm emphasized, not without a hint of pride in his voice. Both Hansoo put their hands together in unison, and bowed. "Welcome, pilgrims."

"This is the original one that birthed the broken Prophecy of the Tiandi?" pressed Zofi.

Irritation flashed across the younger monk's face at her words. Taishi elbowed the girl in the ribs and quickly changed the subject. "Are we close then?" As soon as they were out of danger and the adrenaline had left them, the raw biting feelings of hunger, thirst, and extreme sunburn returned in a hurry.

The older monk pointed at the ledge behind them. "You're standing in the shadow of the Monkey's Paw now, friends. That means you're near the Temple of the Tiandi. Allow us to escort you the rest of the way."

"We would be honored." The relief in Taishi's voice was palpable, her appreciation deep as they fell in line with the two monks. Taishi looked forward to finally sleeping on a bed.

Unfortunately, it didn't take her long before she realized that the Hansoo brother was lying. The last leg of the journey to the Temple of the Tiandi took the rest of the night and well into the morning. Fortunately, it was uneventful and the rock jackals stayed away, although they remained close to the group. They must really have hated the smell of burnt sugar. The small group reached civilization just as the King was at his peak.

Taishi caught the shapes of the tops of two towers sticking out from the side of a hill. Surrounding them were what appeared to be several levels of terraces circling a small cluster of hills.

They couldn't have arrived any sooner. Pahm had to carry Zofi for the last hour. Liuman had offered to carry Taishi as well, and she responded by offering to stick her sword up his ass. No matter how tired she was, Taishi would rather get boiled alive than be carried by a man, especially if she could still walk. The Hansoo had taken her jibe in stride.

They reached the outskirts of the settlement at the foot of a hill and found its residents just starting to stir. A large group of children were herding the farm animals to graze, women were fetching water from the wells, and several monks were praying. Strangely, there were no men—excluding the monks—in sight. Zofi inquired and found out that it was just the way of this settlement. It was tradition for the women and children to start the day while the men slept in until evening. It had something to do with the heat, crops, and some other superstitious rubbish.

"This place sucks," groused Zofi.

Taishi wholeheartedly agreed.

The Hansoo led them up a worn stone path half covered by sand. It snaked through the heart of the settlement and then zigzagged all the way to the top of the hill. Taishi could just make out the face of a large building carved directly into the stone. Liuman narrated everything they were seeing, talking terribly slowly and taking very small steps for someone with such long legs.

The original Temple of the Tiandi was once a humble settlement that mined gold and copper from deep underground. The earth in this region was red clay, which was why the Tiandi religion's colors were red and gold. Every structure here was hundreds of years old. This building here up front used to be the tower that formed part of the defensive wall built to protect the settlement from early raiders. It was where the legendary Fongjue defended the temple with only his blood brother Xinwei against a horde of fifty raiders.

That building near the well with the oxen grazing next to the tree stump was where the fifth abbot of the temple offered his head in order to appease a group of terrible raiders who had planned to raze the temple. So moved were these evil men by his sacrifice that they immediately recanted their ill ways and instead dedicated their lives to defending the temple, which eventually led to the creation of the Hansoo order.

Taishi knew this game. Liuman was selling the pilgrimage experience, as all temples with visitors did. These stories were well known to any Zhuun child, recited regularly from even before their first Tenth Day Prayer.

The entrance to the original Temple of the Tiandi was far less impressive up close. Sure, it was tall and wide and garish, but the blemishes, cracks, and flaked paint were prominent once she stood beneath the arch of the double doors. She brushed her fingers along the ridged columns, feeling the thick layers of dust wipe away alongside small bits of stone.

Zofi, standing next to her, clicked her tongue. "It's a little musty and underwhelming, no?"

Taishi grunted, not taking her eyes off the doors with a burning cauldron and four large stone columns on either side.

"I would have thought there'd be more"—she gestured—"pomp and majesty for a holy place like this."

"It's a shit hole," Taishi muttered.

The two Hansoo, conversing quietly nearby, must have overheard, and appeared a moment later. Pahm looked deeply offended while Liuman was covering his mouth, his massive body shaking with laughter. He exclaimed loudly, "Welcome to the original Temple of the Tiandi, the birthplace of the Zhuun religion."

"It doesn't look like much."

"What did you expect?" the Hansoo replied, mildly. "Soaring towers and elaborately decorated temples with intricately carved statues and golden murals?"

"That's what all the other Tiandi temples have."

The large war monk grinned. "But there's a reason you made this long and dangerous pilgrimage, friend. If you could find what you were looking for in any other temple, you would have just made an afternoon trip there instead."

"Your words do not sound like those of a devout woman," Pahm noted, his eyes still smoldering. "If you're not here to experience the blessing of the birthplace of the Tiandi, then why are you here?"

Liuman cut him off gently. "That's enough, little brother. Inform the rest of our brothers that we have visitors. Off with you." Pahm's gaze lingered on them for a few more seconds before he split away and did as he was told.

Taishi watched the Hansoo disappear inside the temple. He was still young enough to take everything awfully seriously. A vice or two would have loosened him right up, a couple of drinks or a night of good sex. Her own years had introduced her to more than her share of fanatics. Chances were, if he did break his vow of celibacy, it would just make him all the more miserable and insufferable. Such was the way of the world.

"Shall we enter?" asked Liuman.

"I hope it's better maintained inside than out," she grumbled as he led them inside.

It wasn't.

The interior of the original Temple of the Tiandi looked much like the prayer hall of every other Tiandi temple, except it was smaller, messier, and with worse props. The Tiandi mosaic hanging at the front of the hall looked as if it were finger-painted by one of the child-monks running about. Taishi sniffed. It also smelled really badly of unwashed bodies.

What the temple lacked in aesthetics and modern amenities, however, it more than made up for in the monks' attentiveness. Two rows of monks were waiting right as they walked through the entrance. They all stared at Taishi and Zofi with wide-eyed eagerness, almost with hunger, as they bowed and shuffled the two women deeper into the temple.

"We are honored by your devotion, pilgrims," a monk said from off to the side.

"The Tiandi praises your struggle and will reward you in your next life," added another.

"Your good soul will soon bask in the light of the Celestial Family."

The platitudes continued as they walked the length of the hall, each monk trying to outdo the next in their praise. Taishi found the entire scene uncomfortable and inappropriate. When was the last time these people had had visitors? The only thing worse than a shopkeeper desperate for a sale was a priest desperate for a donation.

The retinue stopped at the incense vases just before the kneeling cushions. Zofi picked out three colored incense sticks. No fewer than four monks scrambled to light them for her. Everyone in the room—Zofi included—turned to Taishi expectantly.

Taishi stared back. She had not prayed to the Tiandi since Sanso's death, and she had no intention of doing so now. She spoke carefully. "Apologies, holy brothers and sisters, but I can't. I'm not here on a pilgrimage."

She was met with confusion. "You're not here to praise the Tiandi?" one asked.

"Or make a donation?" another piped from behind her.

"You didn't bring anything?" That one sounded indignant.

Taishi shook her head. "We have a big bag of potatoes."

The smiles on the monk's faces dropped one by one. A few, looking deeply disappointed, just turned and wandered off. One of the older monks spoke more directly. "Why are you here then?"

"This is awkward," she muttered. "My name is Nai Roha, and I'm a scholar seeking knowledge about the Prophecy of the Tiandi, or more specifically why—" She gesticulated trying to find the right words without offending. "—events did not unfold as expected."

Taishi explained herself as best she could, making sure to leave out the important bits about who she actually was. The mood in the prayer hall collectively fell as she went on. By the time she finished, only a handful of the monks remained.

"I traveled all this way for answers. I need to know what happened with the prophecy. Why did it seem to fail, and is it truly broken?"

An older monk stepped forward and bowed. "I am Templeabbot Sanu. Your journey to our temple is a virtue to the Tiandi, and your inquest over recent events conveys your deep understanding of our lore. Rest assured that the Tiandi weaves fate in mysterious ways. All will be brought to light at the will of the divine."

Taishi snorted, but tried some more diplomacy. She seemed to be off to a good start there. "Thank you, Templeabbot. I've come a very long way for more than mystery. The dukes have turned their backs on the prophecy and people all over the Enlightened States are abandoning the Tiandi in droves. This religion, the one that we have followed for three hundred years, is about to collapse. I believe you know more."

Sanu did not seem to be prepared for confrontation, and was saved only when one of the other monks whispered in his ear. He turned away as the rest huddled up, conferring quietly, occasionally glancing her way. Taishi considered carrying their voices to her, but thought better of it. Spying on a bunch of monks in their own temple felt like crossing an invisible line.

"Five hundred," said Pahm quietly.

"Excuse me?"

"The Tiandi religion has guided the Zhuun people for five hundred years."

"Whatever." Taishi flipped her hand. She had forgotten about the tight-ass Hansoo altogether.

Finally, the templeabbot spoke. "We cannot help you."

"I understand your time is valuable." Taishi nodded. "We are happy to wait for an appointment. If you can show us where—"

"You are mistaken," the direct and less friendly-sounding monk cut in. "You are *not* welcome here at the Temple of the Tiandi."

"Please, just . . ." Taishi scanned her audience. The eager monks who had been here when she arrived were now replaced by stern, even hostile ones. Something had just turned very ugly. There was a time to talk and a time to fight. She had somehow slipped into the latter without realizing. That was when she realized they knew her true identity. "Oh damn."

Zofi must have picked up on the tense vibe too. "What just happened?" She threw a thumb at Taishi. "Did she say something wrong?" Zofi turned to her and hissed. "What did you do?"

"You probably should have asked before you decided to come with me, girl," muttered Taishi.

"What is your true purpose here, Ling Taishi?" asked the abbot.

At the sound of her name, the two Hansoo rumbled alive, Liuman positioning himself between the monks and Taishi while Pahm moved behind her. Both wore shocked and furious glowers. The dark faces of the rest of the old monks weren't much better.

Taishi resisted the urge to drift her hand toward her sword. If spying on monks was a sacrilege, killing a few of them would basically fast-track her down to the Tenth Hell, which, at the rate her life has been going, might not have been that far a drop.

Zofi looked equally startled. "Master Nai, you're . . . You . . . She . . . killed the Champion of the Five Under Heaven?" The girl, Taishi's ride back to civilization, slowly backed away.

"Everyone keeps saying that," said Taishi. "I assure you. He's alive. Everything you've heard is a lie. In fact, I'm trying to figure out why the prophecy failed. Why else would I be here?"

"Probably to desecrate this holy temple," said Abbot Sanu.

"Perhaps to kill us all like you did the Prophesied Hero," suggested Pahm.

"Maybe she's here to repent her evil," someone added.

Taishi appreciated that sliver of positivity. "For the last time, I didn't kill him." Taishi held up Mori's wooden coin. "Look, I was sent here by the abbot of the Vauzan temple of the Tiandi. Here's proof."

Sanu made no move to take it. He squinted, his eyes darkening even further. "Lee Mori of the Shulan Duchy gave this to you?"

"He asked me to seek the truth." A harmless exaggeration.

"The arrogant templeabbot of the Vauzan Tiandi temple who speaks with overly flowery words?" he pressed.

"That sounds like him," she admitted. Maybe dropping Mori's name wasn't a good idea.

Sanu snapped his fingers. "Seize her."

The two Hansoo were almost upon her when Taishi regained her senses. The Swallow Dances sang from its scabbard. "Touch me and your blood will desecrate these sacred grounds. I assure you I deserve my legend."

Her blade hummed and wavered between the two war monks before settling on the younger Hansoo. While Liuman respected her with wariness, Pahm's fervor burned in his eyes. He looked as if he could hardly contain himself. The tension in the room was thick.

Sanu was speaking sharply. Zofi was shouting. The rest of the old monks were huddled in fear. Only the three warriors stayed silent, riding the calm before battle. The seconds ticked by and, as she predicted, Pahm was the first to tense. Taishi continued to give away nothing. The young Hansoo pounced, leaping forward and throwing a wide punch. She had an eternity to counter. He didn't just look like a lumbering ox, he moved like one as well.

Just as the two were about to clash, a rail-thin man in worn, stained blue robes burst through a beaded curtain adjacent to the mosaic. "What is this meaning of all this racket? Stop this at once!"

To Taishi's surprise, Pahm obeyed, pulling back his oversized fist. The tip of the Swallow Dances was already committed and much closer to its mark. Taishi managed at the last possible moment to turn her blade aside, barely avoiding the soft flesh under the Hansoo's chin.

Liuman was there a second later, wrapping his arms around Pahm and tossing him out of the way. He turned to Taishi, his hands held out in the universal gesture for de-escalation. "Thank you." The more senior Hansoo knew what would have happened otherwise.

"He's slow as a mule," she replied, "and telegraphs his moves for days."

"He'll learn."

"If he lives that long." Taishi turned her attention to the newcomer, who was admonishing Sanu and the other monks. Who could possibly have the authority to talk to an abbot so harshly?

"How dare you preach violence in this holiest of places!" the thin man was ranting, his voice hoarse and labored.

"This woman killed the Champion of the Five Under Heaven, Your Holiness," stammered Sanu.

"Nonsense. She did no such thing. First visitor in years to inquire about the prophecy. We finally receive a chance to fulfill our divine duty, and you fools try to kill her. Clean this place up and tell everyone to keep it down. It is indecent to make such a terrible commotion in the middle of the night."

Sanu bowed deeply. "Forgive us."

"I'm going back to bed. Wake me up in the morning."

The templeabbot bowed even lower the second time until his tiny thimble hat fell off the top of his head. "Holiness. It's already afternoon."

Taishi stared at this strange man. There was something deeply familiar about him: his blue-and-silver robes, the long horizontal creases running along his bald head, his near mono-brow and overly sharp crooked nose. Those strange blue eyes with the white irises and earlobes that hung halfway to his chin.

Apparently she wasn't the only one. Zofi approached him hesitantly. "I've seen this man before."

It hit them both at the same time. They *had* seen him before. Everyone in the Enlightened States had, in fact, ever since they were children. They were raised on stories about him. His image was prominent in religious paintings, sacred texts, on the damn mosaic itself. There were statues of this man in every city, in every home, above every hearth.

Taishi gaped, dumbfounded. "By the Queen's fertile blue ovaries, you're the Oracle of the Tiandi!"

CHAPTER TWENTY-SEVEN

DANGEROUS BUSINESS

The next morning, Xinde found Jian while he was still cleaning the training grounds and told him to tidy himself up and pick up the gift basket from Auntie Li. Jian would be going with him instead of breakfast duty. He couldn't believe his good luck. He quickly ran to his room to splash water on his face, and ran all the way back to the kitchen where Auntie Li was waiting for him with a large basket of food, wine, and negotiating favors, including a small golden statue of a luck cat. She hadn't forgotten to have some buns ready for him and Xinde too. He made his way only slightly less slowly to Xinde, who was already waiting just outside the front gates, chewing as he jogged with the basket under one arm.

The streets weren't too crowded as they began their walk east. "I asked you to come because I wanted to talk to you," said Xinde once they were a few blocks away. "Is Cyyk still giving you problems?"

Jian shook his head, thinking of the previous day's breakfast. "Things have improved between us."

"And the other students?"

"Somewhat," he admitted, "but not as much."

"Who is still giving you problems? Give me names and I'll take care of it."

"I can take care of it. We don't need management involved."

The ends of Xinde's lips curled up. "I'm glad you listened and learned. Tell me if things get bad. I don't want to see you hurt again."

"Yes, senior," said Jian.

Xinde grinned and clapped Jian on the shoulder. "This is what it means to be part of the Longxian family. Bonds are often forged by the blade, especially during interschool rivalries. I heard you were the one who helped me to safety when Keiro slashed me. Thank you. That makes us brothers now."

For Xinde to call him "brother" meant more than he cared to admit. Jian's lips quivered, and he tried his best to hold back the tears brimming in his eyes. Fortunately, something distracted them both before anyone could realize.

That something was a small object about the size of a pebble. The first flew past his nose. The second flew over, and then a third went over as well. Jian frowned and picked it off the ground, rubbing it between his fingers. "Hmm, a piece of dried plum candy."

Three more dried plum candies flew past him. He turned toward the source and took a dried plum candy on the bridge of his nose right between his eyes. He stumbled, nearly dropping the gift basket.

"Hey, cut it out," he barked, rubbing his eyes.

"Hey yourself," an angry voice yelled back, stomping toward them from the opposite direction, still lobbing candies. They continued to fly wide to either side of him. Jian caught one and popped it in his mouth.

Xinde waved. "Hi, Meehae."

The apprentice acupuncturist continued to lob candies at Jian. "You're supposed to be resting, Xinde."

"If he's the one disobeying doctor's orders," said Jian, "why are you throwing stuff at me?"

"Because he's my patient and I don't throw things at patients."

"I'm your patient too."

"Stop whining." She turned to Xinde. "You march straight back to the infirmary right now. I need to change your bandages."

"I have to run an errand for Master Guanshi," he explained. "We can stop by your clinic on the way back to take care of that."

Meehae did not look convinced. "How long will this errand take? I'm very busy."

Xinde shrugged. "I'll buy you both lunch afterward."

Her schedule miraculously cleared up. "Deal."

Meehae fell in on the other side of Xinde, fussing over the senior and making googly eyes. They continued through the Kati and Saffron Tenet districts and then past the entrance to the Onyx Flower District in the heart of the city. The crowds got denser through the center and then thinned back out the closer they got to the Painted Pots District, which housed the warehouses and grain silos.

Xinde took the gift basket and excused himself to meet the owner of Really Best Box while Jian and Meehae waited outside.

Once Xinde was out of earshot, she asked, "How has he been? Did he look sluggish or tired?"

Jian shook his head. "He looks fully recovered. He taught three classes yesterday and sparred with several students." He frowned. "Why do you look like I just gave you bad news?"

Meehae clicked her tongue. "I'm not sure. It's probably nothing, but there's something unusual about his injury."

"Is it infected? Does he need an herbalist?" Jian became worried. "Was he death-touched? I've never heard of a death touch with a weapon. Is that even possible? Sounds like overkill."

"Nothing like that. Quite the opposite. If he was death-touched, he'd be dead." Meehae paused. "His injury wasn't severe at all. That's why I wanted to check it again. Make sure it wasn't poisoned or infected, but that doesn't seem to be the case, since he's up and about and acting like himself."

Jian didn't understand. "What do you mean not severe? He was bleeding everywhere. He was so badly wounded we had to carry him back to the school."

Meehae did not look convinced. "I don't know why he was incapacitated. Xinde has always been a bleeder, but that cut was shallow. Like really shallow. I didn't even have to stitch him up. I've received worse cuts from my cat."

The two stood in awkward silence. Jian didn't know what to make of it. The senior was the most skilled war artist at Longxian, and possibly throughout all of Jiayi outside of the masters, and maybe even a few of those. How could a scratch incapacitate him for two days? He shook his head. Xinde was fine now; that was what mattered.

He nudged Meehae. "Do you have any more plum candies?"

She held out a small leather pouch, and then slapped his hand when he grabbed a handful. "Just one, greedy pig."

"Why so stingy? Here, I'll hands you for it." Jian held up both hands, fingers splayed out. It was a popular drinking game. The object was to try to guess how many open fingers were being held between the entire group every round. In their case, the choices were between zero and twenty, with the winner who guessed right every round earning a piece of candy. To Jian's dismay, Meehae had a good read on him and beat him the majority of the time. He didn't overly mind because they were gambling with her candy. They managed to keep themselves amused the entire time they were waiting outside the warehouse, which was fortunate, since it appeared Xinde's meeting was running long.

"What's taking him so long?" she complained after they had run out of candies.

Jian spit out the remnants of a plum pit. "Xinde's trying to earn the Really Best Box security contract. I assume that takes time, even with all his charms. Master Guanshi is trying to get Xinde more involved on the business side of the school."

"That means he doesn't think Sasha is coming back." Meehae was referring to Master Guanshi's elusive daughter. He'd heard her name, but had yet to discover why she wasn't at the school alongside her father.

Jian shrugged. "I don't see why not. Guanshi runs a very successful school."

"That's because you've never met Sasha," she replied. "She could not wait to finish her training and adventure the world. She and Xinde were best friends growing up. Guanshi betrothed them when they were children and it became apparent that Xinde was the school's heir."

Guanshi's oldest son had died in the war. If Sasha ever returned—which was quite in doubt—the school would be hers. The master had been grooming Xinde just in case. Jian knew the mysterious Sasha had left a year before he arrived and had not visited her family once.

Jian grinned and nudged Meehae. "I guess you're glad she's staying away."

"Hardly." Meehae blew a raspberry and stuck out her tongue. "What about you? Any novices catch your eye?"

Jian snickered, but his voice trailed off along with his thoughts. He realized then that no one had caught his eye. It was because he wasn't sure what it meant to actually like a person. He had been so preoccupied wallowing in his bitterness lately he viewed everything with a sour lens. Looking back on his past behavior now made him blush.

A plum candy bounced off his cheek. "That wasn't an invitation to daydream about her."

"No, that's not . . ." His voice trailed off when a group of four approached them. Jian immediately stood more upright. "Oh. We have company."

Keiro led the way toward them, stopping just outside arm's reach. He crossed his arms. "How are you, Meehae?" Jian was pretty used to being ignored.

She glowered. "I'm very cross with you, Keiro."

"Oh, did I scar your pretty doll? Is he dying?" He put his hand to his heart. "I am terribly sorry."

"What you did was unnecessary and mean."

"I disagree. It was very necessary and just business, and business can be deadly. Xinde lost. It happens."

Jian couldn't contain himself. "You're lying."

The Southern Cross senior fixed Jian with a dismissive look. "Who's this cracked egg? I've never seen him before. He must be fresh." His tone with Jian was decidedly different than with Meehae.

"I was there," Jian retorted. "You drew a weapon after you lost a fair fight."

"Fair fight," Keiro sneered. "This isn't a tournament, you whiny hen."

"You agreed on rules."

The senior shrugged and gave Jian a light shove. "Penalize a point then, scoring judge." He looked much larger and more intimidating up close. Jian's eyes came up only to Keiro's chin, offering him a close-up view of the man's goatee, which made him deeply envious. Unfortunately, Meehae was right: The guy also had noticeably bad breath.

"Keiro's right," said a familiar voice. Xinde came out from the warehouse and approached the group. "Rules are only as effective as those who follow them. It was up to me to protect myself."

"Oh please, golden boy," Keiro snarled at his rival. "Could you be more condescending?"

Jian exclaimed, exasperated. "What's the point of having rules if there's no punishment for breaking them?"

Xinde positioned himself between the Jian and Keiro. "The reason we make rules, Hiro," he said slowly, "is so war artists can follow agreed-upon parameters. You're right that there is no punishment if someone breaks the rules. However, if you do, then all under the lunar court will know that you are a rule-breaker who cannot be trusted. Everyone will know that you have ... no ... honor. Isn't that right, San Keiro of the Red Lion Southern Cross, first lineage senior of Master Ho Shiquan?"

"How dare you!"

The two men stood nearly nose-to-nose. Their eyes locked, daring each other to make the first move.

"Hey," snapped Meehae. "Can you dumb oxen not do this right now? I was promised lunch."

Keiro kept his eyes locked on Xinde. "Stay out of this, girl."

"Who are you calling 'girl,' stink mouth?"

Xinde didn't break his gaze either. "He's right. This is strictly under the lunar court."

Jian had been grateful for Xinde's arrival, hoping to see him beat

Keiro again. But then he noticed Xinde's hands; they were shaking. Something was very wrong.

He tried to squeeze in between the two. "There's been enough fighting. Why don't we all just go our separate ways?"

Keiro must have noticed Xinde's hands too. He chuckled derisively and shoved Jian, sending him tumbling to the ground. "What's the matter, Xinde, still stewing on your loss?"

"Bastard," snarled Xinde.

And just like that, it began again. This time, Xinde wasted no time using his jing, causing each strike of his hands and feet to echo, his movements blurring until Jian could barely see his shape. Keiro did the same, using his sticky hands to latch on to his foe to keep him close enough to throw short, hard punches. There was a difference between this fight and the last. The dynamic had changed. Jian had witnessed Xinde spar dozens of times; the man fighting now was not the same person. He was fighting without confidence, seeming almost timid.

Keiro, on the other hand, pressed on aggressively, forcing the Longxian senior to cede ground. Keiro's lackeys cheered while Jian and Meehae looked on anxiously.

"Everything's moving too fast. What's happening?" she asked.

Jian's apprehension grew. "He's losing."

"How? Xinde never loses. He wins all the tournaments."

Jian had no answer. Keiro's attacks appeared to overwhelm Xinde's defenses easily. Jian was tempted to intervene, but what could he do? Hiro was only a novice. He would blow his cover. He wasn't sure if he could make a difference even if he did get involved. These two were high-level.

One of Keiro's blows eventually broke through Xinde's guard, striking him in the gut, doubling him over. A knee to the face sent him flying backward. His eyes were unsteady; he looked dazed again. Keiro closed in to finish the job.

Jian couldn't bear to stand by any longer. He thought about Taishi's warnings, and then about Uncle Faaru sacrificing everything to save him. He couldn't live with himself if he let this happen. Jian charged forward and tackled Keiro just as his foot was coming down on Xinde's head.

The two tumbled onto the pavement, bashing Jian's head on the ground. Keiro rolled to his feet gracefully. Jian was slower to rise. No sooner had he picked himself up than he ate a foot to the chest that sent him skidding along the hard pavement.

"You dare interrupt a duel?" Keiro hissed.

"*Now* you want to follow the rules?" he shot back.

The two circled. Keiro showboated, flowing through several stances and forms. The world slowed as a fist flew toward Jian's face. Jian's head was crowded with chatter from every single one of his former masters.

"Linear Jang side guard!" Luda's voice was low and soft. "It's the best."

"Defense is for the weak. Just chop-punch harder," Sinsin would say.

"Hack the attack! Hack the attack!" Sun would flap his arms like a bird when he said that.

The most prevalent voice in his head, however, was Taishi's, warning him to not give away his identity. "Don't be a fool. Take the hit. Don't blow your cover."

That meant another beating, this time from someone who could really hurt him, and his friends, for that matter. Jian couldn't abide that. If Taishi were standing here in front of him right now, he would tell her to suck an egg.

Jian bobbed just as the punch arrived, leaving it to brush past his ear. He retaliated with two punches of his own. Keiro, and likely everyone else present, was so caught off guard by Jian's crisp display of skill that it actually found its mark right on Keiro's cheek. The element of surprise was fleeting. The Southern Cross senior quickly recovered and ducked the second punch. The exchange lasted a few more seconds before a blow to the stomach knocked the wind out of Jian, and he collapsed onto his knees, gasping for breath.

"Looks like we have a live fish here, brothers." Keiro circled him, amused, rubbing his ear. "Where did you find this chickling, Xinde?"

Xinde just stared, mouth agape. The senior couldn't have missed the fact that the stance and combinations Jian had just used were not taught at Longxian. Keiro tried to punt Jian in the ribs. At the very last second, Jian threw an uppercut into the Southern Cross senior's groin.

Keiro screamed and hunched over, hobbling away a few steps before falling to his knees. His lackeys cringed, and Meehae gasped loudly. Jian picked himself up and hesitated. What should he do? Finish off his opponent? Run? He looked over at Xinde, who hadn't moved from where he had fallen. Why was he still sitting there?

Those seconds of indecision proved costly. Keiro's face was now a violent storm. "I'm going to beat you within an inch of your life, and maybe a little past that."

"Or we can call it a draw—"

That was nearly the last thing he said. Keiro covered the distance between them in an instant. Jian barely had time to block a kick that almost broke both arms. He retreated, trying to shake off the pain. Keiro was really pissed.

Once again, every one of his former masters barked instructions in his head, Xinde and Guanshi's voices joining in on the fun. Through all of them, Taishi's coarse, sharp contralto came across most clearly. His reflexes responded: Gauge your distance, study your opponent's eyes, react proactively. He had noticed that every punch combination Keiro used ended with a right hook.

For a moment, with Taishi yelling in his head, Jian managed to keep up with the Southern Cross senior. But like all other moments, it passed. Keiro feinted a punch and folded out his elbow to hit Jian so hard on the shoulder his entire left side went numb. After that, Jian's defenses crumbled. The only reason he didn't fall was because he was practically sprinting backward trying to get away. Unfortunately, there was only so much ground for retreat. He nearly knocked himself unconscious slamming his head into the wall of the warehouse. His legs buckling saved him from Keiro's fist, which crumbled the brick behind where his head had been. Jian managed to scramble to the side, away from more heavy punches, which indented the brick wall in several places and shattered a windowpane.

The door to the warehouse slammed open a moment later and a wiry older man with a queue haircut, popular in the Gyian duchy, stormed out. "What are you doing? You're destroying private property!" He turned to Xinde, who hadn't moved. "Do something, Xinde! I just hired Longxian to protect my business. Why are you just watching?"

Jian really wanted to know why as well. However, it was all he could do to keep from getting his head smashed. It would be only a matter of time. The Southern Cross senior was faster and stronger. The only reason Jian wasn't already defeated was because of muscle memory from Taishi's training, and the fact Keiro had underestimated him.

"If you can't help, then you're fired, you useless hens." The wiry man ran off down the street, his long tail of hair whipping behind him.

Keiro had just knocked Jian down and was towering over him when a loud, shrill whistle pierced the air. Three uniformed men with pointy green hats appeared at the end of the street.

"Big brother," said one of the Southern Cross, "magistrates! The master is going to be furious if we get caught again."

Keiro gave the magistrates a dismissive snarl and hammer-fisted down on Jian anyway. Fortunately, the distraction had bought Jian enough time to roll away. He scampered back to his feet and realized that he was alone. Keiro and the rest of the Southern Cross were fleeing while the magistrates closed in on him, Xinde, and Meehae.

Jian rushed to help Meehae pull Xinde to his feet. The senior's legs were rubber, and his eyes wide and unfocused. His breath was shallow and quick, and the trembling in his hands had spread to his body.

"We have to go," he urged. "What's wrong with him?"

"I think he's in shock," she replied.

"Shock from what? He took one punch."

"I don't know," she yelled. "Slap him!"

Jian recoiled at the idea. Averting his gaze, he swung his arm out and slapped Xinde on the shoulder. Nothing happened.

"What was that? Did you just pat him on the arm? Get out of the way, you soft ox." She shoved Jian away and cupped Xinde's chin. "Sorry, beautiful man. This will hurt me more than it'll hurt you." She slapped him hard across the face.

That finally got Xinde out of his stupor. He blinked several times, and his eyes focused. "What? I'm fine."

Jian waved his hand in the direction of the magistrates.

Xinde nodded. "We have to get back to the school before they do."

"Why bother?" said Meehae. "The warehouse boss knows it's us. Even if he didn't, every magistrate and war artist in Jiayi knows who you are."

"If we get caught," Xinde explained, "there will be at least one night in jail before anyone can bail us out."

"Jail?" Meehae's voice went up an octave. "What are you standing around for?" She shoved them both out of the way.

The three took off in the only direction available to them, sprinting along the warehouses, jumping bales of hay, and avoiding moving wagons. Jian glanced up at the nearby roofs as they ran. He began to imagine himself jumping onto them like a windwhisper. If only Taishi had accepted him as her disciple, things would be so different now. He'd be learning to fly instead of mopping floors, sparring with legendary masters instead of getting into street fights. He was so distracted he nearly bowled Meehae over when she and Xinde stopped at a dead end.

Xinde, looking uncertain, spun frantically. "I can't find the way out of here."

Meehae threw her arms in the air. "How did you manage to lead us into a corner? The Painted Pots District is an oval with fourteen gates."

"I never come here," he shot back.

"Stupid boys. This way." Meehae pulled Xinde by the sleeve into one of the buildings. It was a factory with two rows of noodle looms. There was white powder everywhere and dozens of people in aprons. She paused to get her bearings and then led them to the far end.

"Where are we going?" Jian asked.

She ignored him as she approached a rough-looking man wearing a baker's apron standing against the wall and made a quick sign with her hand. The man lazily pointed to his left. Meehae continued in that direction, out of the warehouse. They crossed a short field to the nearest district wall and then went down a set of stairs leading to a large iron gate. Another rough-looking man, this time wearing a cutoff shirt and short fisherman pants, was guarding it. Meehae flashed the same sign, and the man opened the door.

The three continued down a short tunnel that appeared to pass under the district walls. Meehae hugged the left side of the tunnel, carefully avoiding the small stinking stream that flowed down the middle. "Try not to get your feet wet. You'll have to throw away your shoes."

"What is this place?" asked Jian. "How did you know to come down here?"

"I know everything about this city," she declared. "There's a whole system of catacombs, sewers, and tunnels. This is how the underworld moves contraband from Painted Pots and out of the city."

"And those hand gestures?"

"My ba taught me. He was a sub-boss, Iron Steel." She pumped her fist in the air with pride.

Jian was puzzled. "Aren't iron and steel just two different types of metals?"

"Shut your mouth, Hiro."

"I thought your ba died in a botched robbery," Xinde asked.

She fixed him a look. "Yes, botched."

"Oh?" He looked confused. "Oh!"

They emerged from the sewage tunnel into the Sunset Market District on the other side of the wall. Jian had managed to keep one shoe dry but he was pretty sure the other was not salvageable.

"See," Meehae said, beaming, "all we need to do now is make it two districts over to my clinic. We can wash up there. This way."

Xinde patted her on the shoulder. "Good work."

Unfortunately, and in no small part thanks to Jian's shoe, they smelled like they had brought the sewers with them. The people around them began to hold their noses and clear away. It was impossible to stay inconspicuous for long. Another group of pointy hats appeared at the end of the street.

"There's Xinde!" one of the magistrates yelled. More shrill whistling followed.

Meehae shoved and admonished the Longxian senior. "That's what you get for being a celebrity."

"I have an idea," he responded, spinning around. "I know a place the magistrates won't follow."

He didn't give them a chance to ask where—just ran toward a narrow path behind two rows of merchant tents. Meehae and Jian followed, half hurtling, half tripping over the ropes that tied the tents down. Wooden stakes began popping into the air, collapsing roughly a third of them. They came out from behind the destruction and joined the thick crowds entering the next district, weaving through the traffic when they could and pushing others out of the way when they had to.

They were well past the gate before the senior finally called for a halt. Jian and Meehae hunched over as soon as they stopped, panting.

Jian quickly realized why the magistrates wouldn't follow them here. This was the Kati District, and the stares from everyone around them told him how inviting the locals were to Zhuun.

"I don't think we're supposed to be here," said Jian quietly.

Meehae looked equally alarmed. "I think I'd rather spend a night in jail."

"Nonsense. They signed the armistice." Xinde pointed deeper into the district. "Let's get away from the front gates and wait out the magistrates."

"I'm pretty sure that armistice isn't going to do us a whole lot of good." Jian fretted, looking back as the gates leading back to his people disappeared around the corner. He glanced from side to side, seeing the faces of the Zhuun's mortal enemies, the hordes he had originally been destined to conquer. This was the first time he had seen Kati up close. They looked more alien than he had ever imagined, from their unusual hairstyles of bewildering colors to their clothing woven from grass and wood. By the looks on their faces, they were just as wary of him.

Jian was so preoccupied that he didn't notice his friends jogging ahead. His neck was craned to one side when he ran into a woman who was standing with her back to him. He lost his balance and fell over. This was happening to him an awful lot today. Jian looked up to see a striking Kati standing over him, muscular and intense, with a wild mane of black hair on top of her head, the sides shaved. This person did not seem like someone to trifle with, or to shove in the middle of the street. She held out a hand, which caused Jian to flinch.

"Are you injured, lad?" she asked.

"No," he mumbled, averting his eyes. Something about her gaze made him not want to meet it.

"You should be more careful of where you're going," the woman said firmly, but not unkindly. She lightly tapped his foot with hers, and gestured with her hand again. "Are you planning on sitting in the dirt all day?"

He stared at her outstretched hand as if it were the end of a blade. He wondered if he should accept. He clenched his teeth and berated himself. *Don't be a yolkless egg.* It was *he* who had run into her and it was *she* who was offering her hand. He certainly wouldn't have done so if their situation was reversed. Perhaps he had erred in thinking these alien Kati were all baby-eating village-pillaging devils. Perhaps the Kati were just misunderstood. Or perhaps this woman simply was nice.

"Forgive me, mistress. I was not looking." Jian reached out. Her hand was callused and strong as she effortlessly hauled him to his feet. He bowed hastily and turned to leave.

The woman didn't let go. Jian tugged again, but her grip was like steel. She pulled him closer until their faces were nearly touching. Her eyes glinted as she cupped his face, her sharp nails digging into his cheeks. "I sense—" She sniffed. "—something strange about you. What's your name, lad?"

So much for being nice.

CHAPTER TWENTY-EIGHT

STAR-CROSSED

Sali forced herself to hold on to the boy. It felt as if she were clutching a white-hot poker. Touching his skin sent waves of revulsion crawling up her arm, worse than a sleep sack full of bedbugs. Every fiber of her being screamed and begged her to let go. The Khan's Pull lashed at her other senses so violently she nearly blacked out. Yet as much as she wanted to let go, the need to know had seized control of her.

"What are you doing, you crazy woman?" he yelled. "You're hurting me, let go."

"What is your name?" Sali repeated.

He launched a kick that nearly hit her head. Sali had to tilt away just slightly as she raised her left shoulder to block it. The boy had war arts training, which only reinforced her suspicions. From that kick, she could tell he possessed good technique, though he moved frantically. That was understandable, considering his predicament.

"Help! This Kati is trying to kidnap me."

The slur was not helping his case. The boy attempted several more attacks, none coming close to their mark. She yanked his arm and spun him around like a dance partner until she had him cradled in a headlock. "I sense the taint of your Tiandi religion upon you. Who are you to them? It will go better for you if you cooperate."

Then all the pieces came together: his age, his face, that strange loathsome connection she felt. All children of the Grass Sea were familiar with the Zhuun prophecy that sought to kill the Eternal Khan and enslave their people. His discovery some fifteen years ago had set off a firestorm. A small army of khanate spies and assassins had been dispatched over the years to cut this threat, but the Enlightened States had fiercely protected the boy. The best they had were rough sketches based on secondhand descriptions, but those were distributed to every single warrior the day they shaved their sides. Sali had seen this child's face etched in her mind throughout her entire career.

All were given one standing order: Kill the Prophesied Hero of the Tiandi at all costs.

The news about his death at the hands of his own teachers had shaken the world. All Katuia had raised their arms and praised the skies. After their terrible defeats, this was one sliver of triumph they could cling to. If the Zhuun's supposed Champion of the Five Under Heaven was dead, then there would be nothing to stop the Eternal Khan once he Returned. The spirit shamans were spinning up news that the Eternal Khan's and this hero's death were part of some grand plan. Now, if what Sali suspected was true and this was actually the Champion of the Five Under Heaven, it was a truly devastating discovery for all Katuia.

Unless Sali did something about it right this instant.

She held the boy in the middle of the street while he flailed. Sali wasn't sure what to do next. This was the first time she had ever captured anyone. For her, enemies were either freed or dead. Katuia did not take prisoners. Her gut instinct was to drag him to a back alley and slit his throat, regardless of whether he was actually who she suspected. Sali wasn't a fan of kill-now-ask-questions-later thinking, but the stakes were too great. This would be the closest any of her people had ever gotten to the Zhuun's Prophesied Hero. Also, her people were currently enslaved by the land-chained. There were no innocents in this matter.

There was also the matter of killing an Enlightened States citizen inside the Katuia District. What would the ramifications be? No doubt the land-chained would rain vengeance on the district, flooding it with magistrates and guards who would beat, rob, and murder her people. It would bring a fresh wave of oppression and violence to the survivors of Nezra. Killing one Zhuun could lead to the death of dozens if not hundreds of Katuia. Was it worth killing this boy who may or may not even be who she suspected? Could she sacrifice all of her fellow Children of Nezra?

The answer was resoundingly clear. If this boy was their hero, then it was worth sacrificing her entire clan to ensure that the Eternal Khan rose again without the threat of the Prophecy of the Tiandi looming over him. Killing him could literally save all Katuia. Sali understood this, and she knew everyone in this district would as well. To lessen the blow to her people, Sali would give herself up to the Zhuun authorities after she committed the crime. It was the least she could do.

"Why are you doing this?" the boy croaked through his clamped mouth. "Let me go, Kati scum."

That settled it. Sali dragged him toward the nearest alley. There was no need to slit his throat in public. She would make it as quick and painless as possible. She passed several Katuia. No one so much as gave them a second look.

They had nearly reached the alley entrance when someone cried out, "Hey, hands off my friend!"

She turned to see a diminutive woman with a wild tangle of hair and thick-rimmed spectacles rushing her. Sali was so focused on the girl that she nearly missed the flash coming at her from the side. Almost. She turned at the last moment, parried the attack with one hand, and swung the possible Prophesied Hero around as a shield. This new land-chained coming at her was also a war artist, and from what she could tell a more skilled one than the hero. His jing was moderately strong but not yet fully developed. She easily dodged several more attacks before popping the young man in the chest. It was a glancing blow, but it stopped him cold. He stumbled, and his knees buckled.

Was he faking it? No, his eyes had glazed over. Sali had seen men's spirits break on the battlefield before. They wore the same distant look when fear and trauma took over. Still, she had rarely seen it in one so young.

Sali began to drag the Prophesied Hero toward the alley again when it became apparent that something was wrong. Her right arm lost its strength, and her entire side drooped. Her right leg soon dragged as well. Sali glanced down and saw a small needle at the back of her wrist. Two more pricks followed, one on the outside of her elbow followed by the back of her shoulder. Her other arm soon went completely limp, and the supposed Prophesied Hero slipped from her grasp. Snarling in frustration, she flopped around, pawing for her tongue. Unfortunately, Sali had lost all control and had opened herself up to another flurry of needles, about half of which pierced the skin of her neck and face. Her entire body stiffened, and the world moved beneath her as she fell flat on her face. Fortunately it didn't hurt because her entire body had gone numb.

She watched, one cheek pressed down upon the cold and wet cobblestone, drool leaking out of her parted lips, as the girl helped her two friends up and they sped off together. The numbness began to fade almost as soon as it set in. Sali, grunting heavily, pushed herself up and began limping after the three, feeling returning to her limbs with every step. A few seconds later, she was chasing after them at a full sprint. Sali closed in on her prey. It would have to be done in public, and the guards would likely kill her afterward. There was little chance of her surviving this, but it would be worth it. There was no worthier sacrifice she could make to Katuia than the death of the Prophesied Hero.

Sali drew her tongue and was nearly within striking distance when the only thing under the sun that could have drawn her away from her target, did.

"Sali?" a familiar voice called out.

Sali nearly crashed headlong into an oncoming donkey and rickshaw. She skidded to one knee and glanced over, fearful that the voice was just a figment of memory. At first, she saw nothing except the people walking by on the street. Her apprehension grew, until finally Sali caught sight of a lithe figure, a good half a head shorter than most, wearing a familiar pair of blue tinker suspenders.

Malinde, soul of their mother Mileene, heart of their father Faalsa, Sali's cherished little sprout and last of her blood, stood just on the other side of the street. She was taller than when they had last breathed the same air, longer in face and body, and thinner as well. Her face had blossomed full and womanly, but there were fresh lines around her eyes.

The sisters collided and embraced in the middle of the street, nearly leaping into each other's arms. "You're alive," Mali cried. Even her voice sounded older.

"As are you." Their foreheads touched. "I have searched everywhere since I arrived."

Mali squeezed her hand and put a finger to Sali's lips. "We have so much to say, but out here isn't safe. Come off the streets. I know a place."

The two sisters were soon hunched over a small table at a stall tucked under a canvas awning. They went through several rounds of hugging and laughing and crying, and more than a fair amount of hand clutching as two wooden cups of steaming zuijo sat untouched between them. After confirming each other's welfare and health for the fourth or fifth time, Sali and Mali finally caught up on missed time. Usually, it was Sali who, after returning from a campaign, would regale her wide-eyed little sister with accounts of her battles and campaigns in the Zhuun lands. Now, sitting across from each other, it looked like they both had stories to share.

Mali's eyes brimmed as she recalled the three days and nights of battle as Nezra desperately tried to hold the line against the bulk of the Zhuun army while recovery parties searched for the Khan's body. An all-out guerrilla battle and siege was waged all around the city until, pod by pod, the city crumbled under the onslaught. The other cities arrived just in time to recover his body from the Zhuun, but it was too late for Nezra. Crippled and sinking into the Grass Sea, the city had little choice but to surrender once the enemy had broken into the inner pods.

"I saw Mother fall," she sobbed, bitterness on her face. "She and Ratya—just the two of them—held back scores of Zhuun soldiers on the western artillery pod for over an hour. There must have been over fifty enemy dead at their feet." With that bitterness was also pride.

Sali bowed her head. She used to play in that very pod's tower with Jiamin as children. Though she had suspected, it also pained her to confirm that her mother's neophyte had died as well. "What about Father?"

"The last time I saw him was just before the pods accelerated to ramming speed." The two shared a few more tears over their beloved parents. Sali found it difficult to let go of Mali's hand, even to hold her drink, as if fearing she would lose her little sprout once more if she did.

She squeezed both Mali's hands. "And what about here? Are you well? Have the land-chained mistreated you? I returned as soon as I felt the Khan's passing. It took many months to track you here."

"I'm surviving, so far," Mali replied. "I'm a tinker for the general. He's fascinated by Katuia gear. A small group of us are responsible for fixing and maintaining his collection. And he has us teaching him how it works. I believe he plans to adopt it for the land-chained's own military."

Mali had always loved gear. Every time Sali told her stories about her campaigns, Mali wanted to know about wargear or trackgear or podgear or every other sort of gear. It wasn't surprising in the least when Mali announced that she intended to apply to become a tinker's apprentice instead of following her family's warrior tradition. While the family publicly grieved their littlest daughter's decision, Sali was secretly glad. The signs of a warrior had never developed in her Sprout. She had always been clumsy, and her reflexes were three days late.

"Quan Sah, the man who destroyed our home city?" Sali became incensed at the mention of his name. "That's who you work for?"

"A whole village of us are indentured to him. Sunri used whoever survived their death march after the Battle of Nezra as a 'reward' for the conqueror of the 'savage hordes.'"

Sali ground her teeth. "The hypocrisy of these land-chained. Has he mistreated our people?" She really only meant Mali, but was too anxious to hear that answer.

Mali shook her head. "We live not as terribly as we feared. The general is stern but not cruel. To him, we are tools, and why show cruelty to a shovel or an ax? We have a living area on the general's estates, about a quarter the size of the Kati District."

Sali leaned closer. "Listen, Sprout, pack your things. I'm taking you home."

"Our home rests at the bottom of the Grass Sea."

"Then I'm taking you back to the Grass Sea. It will be a difficult journey back, but I am confident I can lead us home."

Her sister fixed her with a look. "And then what, big sister?"

"What do you mean? Then you'll be free. We'll make a new life together, just you and me. We'll be away from this nightmare." That was a lie. Sali's barely-held-in-check chattering teeth were a reminder that she had no future. Any time she had was being stolen from that piece of the Khan's soul she carried, but this was the best use of what fleeting moments she had left.

To her surprise, Mali did not appear eager. "But our clan—our people, everyone we have left of Nezra—is here."

Sali buried the irritation growing inside her. "We don't have the time for this. I grieve with you, Sprout, but freeing the entire city would not require a plan, it would require a war. I can't help everyone, but I *can* set you free."

A sad smile crept across Mali's face. "Did you know, Salminde, that during the Battle of Nezra, behind our father's back, Mother tried to send me away? She ordered Vimma to steal me into the night. Could you imagine that, trying to assign me a guard, a viperstrike of all people?" She chuckled. "I was truly honored, touched, and a little insulted that Vimma did not flat-out refuse the order. Imagine my shock that she actually agreed."

Sali also couldn't believe Vimma had agreed to Mileene's request, knowing what she did about the stout and inflexible viperstrike. "Mother never took no for an answer," she replied. "She also only tolerated tradition when it suited her. What happened?"

Mali shrugged. "I refused. I may not be a warrior, but I am still a child of Nezra. I wasn't going to flee my home like a broken horse while everyone I ever knew and loved died defending her."

Sali held up her cup and signaled for another round of zuijo. When it arrived, she made a toast. "Fortune must cherish you, Sprout, because you have a second chance to make the right decision."

"You are not hearing me, big sister," Mali insisted, now with an edge to her voice. "I didn't abandon my people then, I'm not abandoning them now. Our people need help. They need *me*."

Sali was taken aback, and it showed on her face. The Sprout she knew was not a fighter or a leader. She was a scholar, which in the eyes of the khanate was a higher calling. Outside of the spirit shamans, few were talented and dedicated and patient enough to study the art of the gear.

Mali read her expression correctly. "I may still be just a tinker to you, Sali, but I am the last of our blood to have survived Nezra. Our blood still speaks to the people. They look to me for guidance and leadership, for the stability we once had. Scoff all you like. I may not be much, but I'm all they have. I will not abandon them!"

Sali felt shame for valuing her sister so little, even though Mali was worth more to her than all the tales of their people's history written in the constellations in the sky. This woman sitting across the table was no longer the little girl she remembered, but a leader of Nezra, of Katuia. She had grown up strong and surprisingly willful.

Mali was still her beloved Sprout, though, and by tradition, as the oldest, Sali expected—demanded—her younger sibling to adhere to her wishes. Her decision was final. "Malinde, by the familial line of Viper-strikes Faalsa and Mileene, by the souls of our ancestors, we will leave this accursed city tonight. I speak as the head of our blood."

It wasn't meant to come across as a threat, but it was absolutely a threat. Mali, however, did not look intimidated. She held her cup up lazily. "That flashing of your eyes. That lowering of your voice. Growling like Father. That doesn't work on me anymore, Weed." That was Mali's nickname for her, because she was tall and impossible to kill. "I'm staying to help my people, and you can't stop me."

She threw her head back and downed her drink, slamming down the wooden cup in emphasis. Zuijo, an extremely bitter and potent drink, should never have been drunk this way. However, Sali was a career soldier and had spent thousands of hours among the roughest and hardiest people. If this little stunt was supposed to impress her, it had failed miserably. She wasn't about to allow Sprout to throw her life away simply because her silly sister had a dull and desensitized palate. Her taste in food and drink—and men, for that matter—had always been highly questionable. Mali had made her point, however. This woman here definitely wasn't the young, hormonal, sweet Sprout she remembered.

Sali sighed. "You know, I could just truss you up, stuff you in a potato sack, and drag you out of the city in the middle of the night."

"You're only allowed to do that to me once in my life, Sali." Mali ticked her fingers. "Four times I mean."

"You always did love to visit the other cities without permission." While Mali was the gentlest soul, she was also the wildest, always believing that rules were optional. It drove her strict parents to such distraction they nearly sent her to the soul shamans. Fortunately, her discovery of gear technology tamed her thirst for exploration and focused her many interests into one.

"Promise me you won't take me back against my will, Sali." This was not a request. "As far as I'm concerned, this is where I belong. This is home."

"This isn't home," snapped Sali. Her skin itched fiercely. It itched from irritation. It itched from the Khan's Pull, and it itched from drinking this ghastly zuijo. "Fine. What would it take for you to come with me willingly?"

Mali lazily swept her finger across the street. "When everyone can come home with us."

Sali slammed her fist on the table. "Damn it, Sprout, that's impossible!"

Her sister leaned in and covered Sali's fist with her hands. "Then stay and help us make it possible. There's a small group of us back at the estate trying to organize a resistance. We could use you."

"You mean the Council of Nezra?"

Mali rolled her eyes. "That lot rolled over and exposed their bellies ages ago. There're actually three groups who all claim to lead the survivors of Nezra. I'll set up a meeting for you with mine."

"How large is your group?" The idea of joining a resistance had its attraction.

Mali ticked off her fingers. "Twelve. Wait, Juno and Mina got caught last week. Ten."

"Ten resistance fighters. Trying to free some two thousand Katuia. In a city of twenty thousand land-chained." Still, it wasn't like Sali had any better plans. "Fine, but if I don't like what I hear, then you aren't allowed to complain when I kidnap you in a potato sack again."

"I won't even scream." Mali tightened her hand over Sali's. Her smirk disappeared when she felt Sali's hands trembling. "What's wrong?"

Sali drew away. "There's a few things that you need to know. I'm—"

"Wait." Mali ordered two more cups of zuijo. Only after they arrived did she gesture for Sali to go on. "Go ahead."

"To begin," said Sali. "It may have surprised you that I'm still alive and did not perform my obligation as Will of the Khan during the Return."

"Never crossed my mind," said Mali. "That tradition stinks."

Her words were heresy, but by the Grass Sea, Sali loved her sister exactly for that. "I defied the Return to find you. I didn't anticipate this, but the Pull from the Khan's death is still in me. It will keep growing until . . ."

"Until what?"

". . . until it consumes me." Sali tapped her ear. "It already feels like a waterfall rushing in my head. It gets worse with each passing day."

Mali had a hand to her mouth. "Can anything be done? Is there a cure?"

"Death is a cure, I gather," she replied. "An herbalist nearby gave me medicine that muffles the Pull. Other than that, I do not know of a remedy. This is why time is short."

"We'll get through it together," said Mali, giving her hand a soft squeeze. "Is there anything else?"

"I'm a Soul Seeker now. That's how I squirmed out of killing myself."

"Oh, Soul Seeker, eh?" Mali frowned. "That's an unexpected career change for you. Slumming it a little, eh?"

"Also, all the viperstrikes are dead. But I have a neophyte now. His name is Hampa."

"I never thought you were the nurturing sort," Mali mused. Sali let that slide. "Where did you find him?"

Sali pointed down the street. "Right there actually. He and a group of guards tried to arrest me."

"Sounds about right." Mali ticked her fingers. "So, to recap. You're cursed with a dead man's soul, you're searching for the reincarnation of that same dead man, and you tricked a dunce into polishing your weapons and cooking your meals. Is there anything else?"

Sali snapped her fingers. "One last thing. I think I ran into the Zhuun's prophesied Champion of the Five Under Heaven."

Mali spewed zuijo all over. "What! He's alive?"

Sali wiped the alcohol off her face. Zuijo stung. "Yeah, I tried to kill him. It didn't quite work out as planned."

"I see." Sprout studied her for a few moments before pouring herself another drink. She leaned back, her eyes narrowing as she crossed her arms. "Now I know the *real* reason you came looking for me, Weed."

Sali was taken aback. "What? How can you say—"

"You landed thigh-deep in horse shit again, my dear sister." Mali broke into a grin. "It seems the real reason you're here is because you need me to bail you out again."

CHAPTER TWENTY-NINE

ORACLE

"You must have many questions."

That could have been the biggest understatement Taishi had ever heard. It had been almost a week since she had discovered that the Oracle of the Tiandi was still alive, and she still hadn't recovered from the revelation. "You bet your soft shell I have questions."

The two sat across from each other at a small table in the holding room she shared with Zofi, otherwise used for grain storage. When it wasn't being used as a jail cell. Taishi had surrendered to the Hansoo the moment she realized the damn Oracle of the Tiandi in the flesh was standing before her. The monks had moved the two women here while they deliberated their fate.

For a whole week, Taishi and Zofi rotted in here. Taishi didn't mind, really. She could have broken through the flimsy wooden door at any time, but the food was delicious, the room clean and dry, and the beds surprisingly soft. Other than an annoyingly wobbly chair and a table so covered in splinters she might as well have been petting a porcupine, this was a pretty nice jail. Taishi caught up on much-needed sleep.

The monks must have finally come to a decision on the morning of

the sixth or seventh day—Taishi had lost track. Sanu appeared at the
door carrying a tray of tea. "Let me begin with the oracle," he continued.
"To understand who he is, it's important to know what he is."

"And how he's five hundred years old," said Taishi. "Is that man I saw
the actual oracle? It's not possible."

"There is only one Voice of the Divine, and he is indeed five hundred
years old. As to whether he is the actual oracle, the answer to that is a bit
more nuanced. His Holiness is and is not the original oracle who birthed
the prophecy." The abbot hovered the pot over her cup. "More tea?"

"That's not helpful in the slightest, and no thank you." Taishi had
taken one sip of her tea and not touched it since.

Sanu refreshed his own cup. "The original oracle was a man by the
name of Sang Junfan."

"I don't need a children's lesson on the Tiandi, Templeabbot."

"Junfan was responsible for the Prophecy of the Tiandi," continued
Sanu, speaking as if giving a well-worn lecture. "A few months after he
passed, an infant in this village by the name of Huangxi was born possessing the gift. He became the next oracle. For eight generations, the
Voice of the Divine has reincarnated in this very settlement."

That explained why there were so many children here. Many of the
most devout probably lived here with the slim hope of raising the next
Oracle of the Tiandi. "So the oracle I saw isn't the original one, but the
eighth man in line in reincarnation?"

"Two of the oracles were women."

"If all eight were women, we wouldn't be in this mess," she muttered.

"Sorry? I don't understand."

"You wouldn't. If two of the oracles were women, why have all de-
pictions of the oracle shown the same man?" She pointed at the picture
embroidered on Sanu's chest. "In fact, the oracle I saw in the room the
other day looks exactly like him, except dirtier. How is that possible?"

"To properly answer your question, it is important you understand
how the gift is passed," said Sanu. "Once a child is gifted the Voice of
the Divine, they become the vessel of the oracle and experience a divine metamorphosis that alters body, mind, and soul. In every way and
essence, they incarnate into the original oracle, even possessing the

memories of the oracles' previous lives." Sanu gestured at her cup. "Your tea has cooled. Would you like it refreshed?"

"I'm fine, thank you." She was terribly thirsty, but she also had standards. "Do these oracles still have—" She waved her hand. "—oracle abilities? Do they still have visions and predict the future? Can they still form prophecies that have wide-reaching effects on an entire race of people and culture and dictate government policies for half a millennium only to fall apart right as the prophecy is about to get fulfilled?" Her lingering thoughts were almost as bitter as the tea.

"The gift of prophecy remains unchanged in all the oracles," Sanu replied cryptically. There was a pained hesitation in his voice. "However, the burden of having lived so many lives is tremendous."

Taishi wasn't sure what that meant; she didn't care either. This information, while interesting, was hardly relevant to the crisis at hand. "So the oracle is alive and his oracle-ing still works. That doesn't explain why the prophecy failed so spectacularly."

"Ah, the prophecy. That is a separate matter entirely. Let's continue this discussion in a more pleasant environment. Walk with me."

Sanu must have finally decided she was no threat to the temple. That or he had run out of awful tea. Taishi was more than happy to oblige. While her jail was comfortable, there wasn't much else to do other than sleep. She had been contemplating breaking out just to have something to do. Pahm fell in beside them as they left the storage room. The young war monk had not strayed more than a few feet away from her since she had arrived.

"Where's my traitorous companion?" Taishi asked.

"Some of the brothers are giving a pottery lesson."

Taishi grunted. For reasons unbeknownst to her, the Tiandi monks had decided right away that Zofi was no threat, and allowed her to walk around freely, returning her to the grain storage room only for the night. The girl had struck up a friendship with Pahm and had voluntarily spent hours on end with him while he guarded Taishi's jail.

The three walked through several hallways to the rear of the temple through the kitchen, living quarters, and prayer rooms, passing several monks going about their daily lives. Without fail, every monk stopped what they were doing and bowed as they passed. The abbot ran a tight ship here, a far cry from what she had witnessed in Vauzan.

"How many live here?" she asked as a girl no older than five bumped into her on her way to embrace Sanu.

The templeabbot patted her head and sent her on her way. "Thirty or so, and eighteen children currently. We always have a few come and go. Temple life is difficult for most; it is even harder here in this isolated place. Many of our brothers and sisters last only for a short while before moving on. This calling is not for everyone."

Taishi could see why. She had been dismayed at the primitive conditions. There was no running water, heating pipes, papyrus on the windows, or any other modern amenities. She had not even seen any water clocks, ice chests, or even mirrors. Only after watching the monks go about their lives had she learned to appreciate this world free from distraction. Unlike their brethren in the cities, these monks did not involve themselves with political, societal, or cultural issues. The need for donations, however, was universal in every temple. The older monks referred to it as secular taint.

Sanu led them several stories up a staircase carved directly from stone to a leveled garden area at the top of the hill. Taishi stood at the doorway and raised her chin, welcoming the King's rays. Pahm, ever the guard dog, crossed his arms and took his place next to the door while Sanu exchanged words with several monks tending the rows of vegetables and fruits along the graduated terraces at the top of the hill. He reached a wooden sitting area with a bench and table at the opposite end and beckoned for Taishi to join him.

She walked past him up to the edge of the wooden platform jutting out of the side of the hill and surveyed the vast sprawl of Fulkan Forest. There was the Monkey's Paw, surprisingly closer than she imagined it would be. Farther was the near edge of the Sand Snake. If she squinted hard enough, she thought she could make out the other shore, where Sanba lay.

An initiate appeared with a tray. Sanu accepted a cup of tea and offered her one. "Now, where did we leave off? Tea?"

"No thank you. We were about to talk about the prophecy and why it failed so spectacularly."

"Yes, although I would disagree with your conclusion that the prophecy failed in any way. Tell me, Master Ling, what do you know about how prophecies work?"

Taishi studied the five levels of graduated terraces that dropped off sharply. The tomatoes wanted picking. "What's there to know? They're supposed to come true."

A chuckle escaped the abbot's lips. "Your belief is common among the masses, and that's the problem. Nuance and context have become lost arts. The people desire simple, direct answers, easy to digest and process. All they want is for someone to point them in the direction to walk, without realizing that some places require turns and multiple stops before they reach their destination. The great misconception about the Prophecy of the Tiandi is that prophecy is destiny."

"Well, isn't it?" said Taishi. "What is the point of having a prophecy if it doesn't come true?"

"Prophecy cannot predict free will," explained Sanu. "The visions of the Voice of the Divine are true, but only so within the context that people make the choices that lead to those visions."

Taishi mulled his words over for several moments before she came up with a response. She exploded. "That's the stupidest thing I've ever heard. If people make choices that differ from what the oracle saw, then that destiny will not come true? If the Prophecy of the Tiandi requires everyone and everything to happen exactly as it needs for it to come true, then of course it's not going to work. The entire thing is . . . is worthless!"

"Free will can be such a hassle," smiled Sanu wryly. "Would you prefer that destiny robs you of choice?"

"I prefer that a prophecy actually works the way it's supposed to work, especially if our entire civilization has placed all our faith in it." Taishi had hoped to discover why the prophecy had broken, hopefully to find a way to repair it. She hadn't expected to learn that the damn thing was never supposed to be right at all. "What is the point of all this?

The oracle could have at least warned us about this free will crap. Then maybe the Zhuun wouldn't have taken this stink so seriously."

"Oh, but he did."

She perked up. "*That* is not mentioned in the sacred texts."

"The oracle did warn that the prophecy did not free the people from responsibility. The Zhuun still had to make the right choices to see our desired outcome. Because he knew free will could lead destiny astray, the oracle decreed directly to Empress Yihsanna to return every nineteen years to hear his refreshed vision of the prophecy. It was his hope that these insights would offer the wisdom to help forge a better future."

"So what happened?"

"No one came."

Taishi couldn't believe it. "What do you mean 'no one came'? Even if the emperors decided to skip the prophecy, how could the Tiandi monks allow it?"

Sanu raised his palms to the air in a shrug. "Because monks are people, fallible and susceptible to secular taint."

"That's an awfully roundabout way of saying they were bribed."

The abbot looked pained. "Bribery is such a harsh term. Change can be difficult to embrace. The next emperor, Yihsanna's son Yiyue, actually did visit the oracle nineteen years later. By that time, the Tiandi religion had swept across the Enlightened States and become the Zhuun's official religion. It was the agent that, for the first time in history, united our people as one. The masses embraced the belief that a Prophesied Hero would rise to unite them to defeat their mortal enemies, the Katuia Hordes and their dreaded Eternal Khan.

"Emperor Yiyue, however, had just ascended the throne when he made his pilgrimage. He did not like what he heard. He had not yet consolidated his power in court, and feared that unrest would follow if the people learned that their faith was as solid as slowsand. Yiyue made a deal with the Tiandi monks in power to suppress the truth about the prophecy's changes in order to maintain peace and stability, to keep the people united as one."

Taishi's blood had reached a boiling point. "Why would the Tiandi monks agree to such a thing? Religious doctrine and prophecy should not be up for debate. What could the emperor possibly have to offer them?"

"Why do you think there is a large, beautiful Temple of the Tiandi in every city in the Enlightened States?"

That stopped her dead, but only for a moment. "The prophecy isn't broken. People are such lazy, soft-brained idiots," Taishi spat out in disgust.

"Our fates are in the hands of heaven." Sanu put a reassuring hand on her shoulder. "Put your trust in the Tiandi. Let the divine work in its own ways. The River of Fate will guide us where we need to go."

"Don't touch me!" The abbot was just trying to help, but his attempts to soothe Taishi only enraged her. Everyone, from the abbots to the dukes to those pathetic masters to even that blasted emperor five hundred years ago, was just looking for the easiest, most convenient excuse to do nothing.

"Better to hand the problem off than make the hard choices. Let future generations deal with it instead of getting it right at the source," she lamented through clenched teeth. That was when the idea, like lightning, struck. Taishi's eyes flared open and she grabbed a fistful of the abbot's robes. "Take me to the source. Take me to the oracle. If he still has the vision, then he can determine what to do next. He was the one that got us into this mess. He can get us through it."

Sanu did not show fear as she shook him like a rag doll. "I'm afraid that's impossible. The oracle no longer offers his guidance."

"He'd better for me," she growled. "The prophecy owes us answers. I threw away my entire life to save the Prophesied Hero. Both our lives are now forfeit. At the very least, I need to hear from his mouth that Wen Jian, the Champion of the Five Under Heaven, is truly free from his destiny."

"How dare you lay a hand on the templeabbot!" Pahm roared as he barreled down toward them. She wondered if the big man was nimble enough to stop before plummeting off the edge. Part of her was curious to find out.

Sanu waved the war monk off. "No, Brother Pahm, it is all right. Master Ling and I are just having a spirited discussion."

The Hansoo hovered close by and shot Taishi an icy glare. "It will be best if you release him."

Taishi suddenly remembered where she was and who she was man-handling. There were more than enough failures to go around, but to take it out on him was misguided. She let go, ashamed. "Please forgive me, Templeabbot. I was not right in the moment."

Sanu looked resigned. "I see that you will not be satisfied until you have your audience with His Holiness. I warn you: You will not like what you see."

"I don't care what I see. It's what I hear that's important. If things have changed so much from the original prophecy, then maybe it's time someone actually listens to the oracle to correct our course, like it was originally intended."

The abbot stood and adjusted his robes. "Very well. I will take you to him now. He may not answer you, however."

"We'll see about that," she muttered.

A low, guttural growl emanated from the Hansoo.

Sanu led them back down the stairs and back to the heart of the temple. The kitchen was bustling as a small army of cooks prepared meals for the entire temple. The smell of roast duck and egg drop soup wafted to her nostrils. A group of monks were sitting in a row at a long table wrapping dumplings. Two of the younger monks were flicking flour at each other as their brothers nearby cheered them on. The situation nearly escalated to a full-blown battle of white powder before one of the cooks snatched their bowls away and admonished them. Even in her sour mood, Taishi couldn't help but smile. She had always considered Tiandi monks a serious, humorless lot.

They continued to the front of the temple, weaving their way through the main hallway when they ran into Zofi, who must have just finished her pottery class. The girl was now the proud owner of a misshapen thing that looked somewhat like an oversized chamber pot.

She beamed, struggling to wrap her arms around it and walk at the same time. "Look at what I made."

"That will come in handy if you ever need to piss ten times in a night," Taishi replied drily.

"It's a water pitcher."

"That will do the job too."

She frowned at the somber group. "Where are you going?"

"Master Ling has requested an audience with the oracle."

Zofi's eyes widened. "Can I come too?"

"Might as well. At least you can keep Pahm here company."

The normally sour-faced Hansoo had brightened at the sight of her. Zofi fell in line next to the war monk, who was more than happy to take the chamber pot off her hands. The two chatted animatedly, Taishi and Sanu already forgotten.

Taishi hoped all that had blossomed between them was a kindred friendship. She had intimate experience with loving someone married to their religion. The abbot led them to a guarded room just behind the prayer hall in the heart of the temple. It wasn't until after they had walked inside that she realized this was the temple heart sanctum. While this traditionally was the abbot's residence, it made sense that in this particular temple, the sanctum would be reserved for the oracle.

The first thing that hit Taishi when they entered the dimly lit room was the odor. What had smelled like stagnant water escalated to something that had her gagging. The room was windowless, and had only a daybed in the center of the room. An entranceway off to the side led to what appeared to be a bedroom of sorts. Scattered pipes, half-eaten plates of food, and dirty clothes littered the floor. Piles of gourds and bottles stood on a small table leaning against the near wall, all empty.

Zofi sniffed and waved her hands side to side, swirling the heavy smoke the hung in the air. "What's that stink?"

"Opium and head dust." Taishi scowled.

They found the oracle in the bedroom, splayed out on the bed on his side, a gourd of plum wine next to him overturned, its dark-red contents staining the sheets. At first, she thought him sleeping, then she noticed his blank eyes open and the long, thin pipe huddled close to his body as a wisp of smoke puffed from its opening.

Taishi gawked at the rail-thin man with the sunken cheeks and skin as blotched as his robes. His head lolled in an awkward angle against his pillow as if he were too weak to lift it. This was the oracle who had birthed the Tiandi religion that had spread across every corner of the Enlightened States? The man whose wisdom had not only united the Zhuun, but guided fifteen generations of emperors?

Furious, she rounded on Sanu. "The founder of the Tiandi religion is a drunk *and* an addict? How could you let this happen?"

"I warned you that you wouldn't like what you saw," the temple-abbot replied, resigned. "The burden of this gift is great, especially after the spirit of the oracle has lived so many lives. We've tried to help him, but this is the only way he can ward off his nightmares."

She knelt next to the bed. The oracle's eyes were lazy, unfocused, and staring off into nothing. If he had noticed her there, he offered no indication.

"Your Holiness," she said. "Can you hear me? I require your wisdom."

No response.

Taishi tried again, speaking louder and closer to his face. When was the last time this man had taken a bath?

Still nothing.

She snapped her fingers in front of him and patted his face. She turned to Sanu. "How long has he been like this? Is he coherent at all?"

"His Holiness has been declining for nearly two decades. We fear his time on this plane will soon come to an end."

"Some gift," she muttered. "How do I get through to him?"

"He has good and bad days," he replied. "More bad than good. We do what we can to make him comfortable, but the only thing we can do is to wait until he experiences a lucid moment."

"When does that come about?"

"Sometimes days, sometimes weeks."

"I can wait. I'm not leaving until I get my answers," Taishi declared.

Sanu nodded. "I honor your piety to the prophecy and the Tiandi."

Taishi dragged a chair next to the bed and sat down, crossing her arms. "Bring food and drink. I'll sit in this shit-stinking room for the next decade if I have to."

The next decade lasted for only four days. In her defense, it was because of the screams coming from outside the sanctum.

CHAPTER THIRTY

KILLING PROPHECY

They charged out from their hovels and down the path from the temple in bunches, unorganized, wielding bamboo staffs and rakes, wooden boards and other tools that belonged to the fields rather than the battlefield.

Qisami stifled a yawn as she engaged the first two, a portly man and an elderly woman. She parried the hoe the man was swinging and punctured his heart with a thrust of a black knife. The woman wielded a washboard with both hands and posed a more serious threat, moving quicker than Qisami would expect, and with some heft behind her efforts. Her swing nearly clubbed Qisami's head, and would have at the very least bruised her face had it connected.

"Now, madam," she remarked, avoiding another fierce grandmotherly blow. "You look like you've lived a long, very boring life. Is this really how you want to go?"

"The Tiandi protects me," the grandmother replied, putting her faith in the washboard. The black knife blurred across her neck, ending her long life in very little time.

"The Tiandi is bad at its job." Qisami continued up the winding path, taking out two more, a pair of brothers who may have been twins, then a crippled man with a dog at his heels. A few others were smart enough to just run. A young buffoon attacked her by himself. She dispatched him quickly and continued upward, killing everyone in her way. Except for the dog, of course; she took pains not to harm it.

Qisami reached the first hard turn up the path and caught up with an older monk herding a group of fleeing children. He hurried the children ahead and turned to face her, blocking her way. The monk wasn't even holding a weapon. To add further insult, he pressed his palms together and bowed. "Peace to you. Know that the pain you inflict upon this world will return tenfold in the Tiandi."

"Oh, get over yourself." Black knives twirled in Qisami's hands, sinking into his heart. She stood over the fallen body as his soul fled up to the Tiandi, or wherever it was supposed to go. An irritated hiss escaped her lips.

Koteuni, fighting a few steps behind, caught a fleeing man and impaled him with her spear. "You don't look like you're having fun. What's the matter?"

"This just feels so unnecessary."

Her second-in-command looked concerned as she yanked the spear out of her victim's back. "But you love to kill. You're not losing the urge, are you?"

Qisami barked a laugh. "If you think I've gone soft, my blades are waiting."

"I could never take your . . ." Koteuni grunted as a burly man leaped off the path higher up and tried to tackle her. The two struggled for several moments until Koteuni reversed her grip and tossed him to the ground. She finished him with a boot to the neck, and then joined Qisami, sucking in a few deep breaths. ". . . place. Besides, my husband would never follow my orders. I'd have to kill him, and then I would be sad."

"Good." A man with a rake came at Qisami. She caught his elbow and spun him around. She pawed for a knife at several of her sheaths and came up empty. Annoyed, she snaked her arm around his neck and snapped it. "Though not trying to take the top of the ticket shows a real lack of career aspirations."

"Why so glum then, Kiki?" asked Koteuni.

"What I meant was, all these senseless killings feel unnecessary, not to mention boring." Qisami began to backtrack to pick up errant knives. "You know me. I'm all about quality kills, interesting kills, not all this trivial death. I would have thought a cell of our reputation, a shadowkill of my stature, would be long past expending energy and talent on helpless peasants. Did you know that during training, I was the top of my litter?"

"You remind us at least once a cycle, maybe twice."

"Our cell should be big and prestigious enough that I should only have to get my hands dirty against worthy marks, not culling defenseless herds."

"Are you sure you want to create subordinate cells?" asked her second. "That's a lot of administrative work to deal with."

"It does sound like a lot of work for you, doesn't it?"

She waited at the top of the next turn for Koteuni to catch up. Her second handed her three black knives. Qisami sheathed them and patted her body. She had still left two somewhere down in the carnage.

"That's not really it, is it," Koteuni said. "You don't care about these mush-brained peasants. What's really bothering you?" Her second knew her far too well.

Qisami made a face. "It's near the end of the second cycle."

Koteuni looked sympathetic as they continued up the next bend together. "Ah, yes. Your ba's birthday. You should take care of that one of these days. I'm surprised you waited this long."

"I should. Just never got around to it." That really wasn't why. Qisami was just biding her time until she had made a name for herself under the lunar court.

The next time Maza Qisami crossed paths with her father, he was going to know her by reputation and be in awe of her accomplishments. He would realize what a terrible mistake he had made all those years ago choosing her for his brood atonement. He would tell her, *You really are my most worthy child.* Qisami's father was going to be *so* proud of her, right up to the moment she gutted him from navel to throat.

A black blur streaked past Qisami's head and plunked through the eye and out the back of the skull of a man sneaking up on them. Her second-in-command glanced at the corpse at her feet and beamed at a figure hidden in a ledge halfway up the adjacent hill. "Thanks, sweet meat." The figure waved back with his shoulder-mounted dragon crossbow.

Qisami grunted at the thought of Burandin. She was annoyed with him. He was to blame for this shoddily slapped-together assault in broad daylight. The original plan had been to ambush the mark when she left. A few anonymous bribes had verified that Ling Taishi was indeed inside, but in the three days they had waited for her, she had failed to appear.

It was only a matter of time before someone discovered them. You could stage an ambush in the middle of a settlement for only so long before your luck turned. A shepherd and his nine goats had come across Burandin's surveillance nest. Instead of doing his job correctly and gutting the boy, Koteuni's idiot husband had pushed the boy off the cliff. The shepherd had had a long way to scream and had alerted the village before the ground permanently silenced him. Once that little complication had occurred, the only options left were to abort the ambush or to attack the temple.

The two reached the top of the path leading to the ugliest Temple of the Tiandi she had ever laid eyes on. Most temples looked as if they had been designed with a wealthy nobleman's estate in mind. The façade of this one looked like it had been carved by blind monkeys. Qisami could only imagine what a dump the interior was.

A Hansoo brother waited at the temple entrance. He knelt on the ground, meditating with his eyes closed and palms pressed together. The war monk's body was so wide, he blocked nearly the entire doorway. He made no move as the two women approached. Out of curiosity, Qisami tossed a knife toward the war monk's big, bald head.

The war monk's eyes flew open, and he deflected the knife, his iron rings clanging loudly as he knocked it out of the air. Then he rose to his feet. Both women's eyes widened. Qisami had seen her share of war monks, but this one was a particularly spectacular specimen. He looked older than most of his kind, with a weathered face, deep creases along his forehead, and blemishes on his bald head. His bushy white eyebrows were out of control, and his forearms were completely covered by iron rings, marking him an elder of his kind, which was rare. War monks, like big dogs, tended not to live long lives.

The Hansoo bowed. "The Tiandi watches from above. This is a sacred place. Violence is forbidden, even for shadowkills. Have you no shame?" There was an intensity under that calm demeanor. He flexed his massive fists, stretched his neck from side to side, and stepped forward to meet them.

"Not really," replied Qisami.

"None here either," Koteuni agreed.

"Then the Tiandi forgive me for this stain on hallowed ground." The Hansoo flexed his fingers, muscles rippling up his arms to his shoulders. He advanced on them.

"Ever killed a war monk?" asked Qisami, softly.

"Never got the chance to check that off the achievement list. You?"

"Me neither. I'm excited." Qisami checked her blades again. "The two of us shouldn't have a problem with this one. Remember, they're reputed to be strong, impervious to pain, and tough-skinned. I bet someone this big must slow and tire easily."

Koteuni nodded. "Dance until they die?"

"Like taking down an elephant. Try to take the battle inside the temple, out from this accursed daylight."

The women spread apart. Qisami's nerves tingled in anticipation. What with the boring journey across the Sand Snake from Sanba, three days of boring surveillance, and now killing these boring peasants, she was ready for a challenge. Two shadowkills against a Hansoo would make things interesting. It beat slaughtering all those sheep on their way up here.

The war monk waited until Koteuni was just outside his range, then he pounced. He was far quicker than she had given him credit for, and his sudden move almost threw Qisami off guard. Almost. A fast turtle was still a turtle.

The war monk windmilled his arms, swinging them at the shadowkills' heads. Koteuni raised her spear to block him, and the shaft shattered when the iron rings smashed through the thick wood. She managed to duck to the side as his fists hammered the ground where she stood. His next windmill swing, however, caught her full in the chest and sent her crashing against a column. Koteuni bounced off the hard stone and crumpled to the ground.

Qisami was intrigued. "Silverback boxing. Fascinating."

She came at the Hansoo from his flank, slipping under one of his wide swings. Her black blades raked across the back of his knee to little effect. She followed up with four more hard thrusts before he could react. Each of her blows failed to break skin.

The Hansoo must have felt something, though. He roared and flailed harder: left, right, body turn, left, right again, each time his ringed forearms and fists smashing and chewing up the stone tiles. By his fifth sequence, Qisami had him timed. No sooner had his last strike hit the ground than she jumped on top of his arm and then onto his back in two steps, as if she were riding a wild stallion. A knife appeared in each hand, and she stabbed downward into the base of his neck. This time, she broke skin and drew blood, but barely, not a killing blow.

The war monk staggered, and a big hand grabbed her by the arm and tossed her like a rag doll. The earth and sky traded places as she tumbled and skidded onto her hands and knees. It wasn't her best landing. Qisami picked herself up, shaking off the fall. She singsonged, "Koteuni, you can help anytime."

Her second groaned, picking herself up off the ground and drawing her saber. "I'm still alive."

The shadowkills circled the war monk again, this time with more respect. When they came at him again, they attacked together from opposite sides, taking turns darting in and out of his long reach. Koteuni would come in, her saber sparking around his iron rings, and then once he was committed, Qisami would come from behind, her blades probing for weaknesses. There weren't many, but even the stabs that didn't break skin were showing their effects. The large war monk, after several exchanges, did seem to tire.

Qisami was so focused, she nearly missed the constant scratching on her forearm. When she finally did check, it displayed only the phrase *clear line of sight* over and over again. That was all she needed to know. She assessed her position and then juked hard to the right. "Now press!"

Her shadowkill cell was so in tune as a team, they needed no further prompting. The two women launched coordinated attacks, Koteuni's saber going high from one side while Qisami dashed low. The war monk caught the saber with his palm and tried to sweep Qisami aside. Instead of dodging, she timed his momentum and launched herself on his arm, one knife glancing off the iron rings while the other sank inside his elbow.

"Now!" shouted Qisami.

Both women did their best to force his guard open. There was a twang in the distance, followed by a long black streak blurring through the air. The Hansoo saw it coming, but it was too late. He shook the women loose and crossed his forearms just as Burandin's long bolt slammed into him.

Several of the iron rings exploded into fragments, and the Hansoo was thrown backward through the entrance of the temple. He landed roughly and slid a way before coming to a crashing halt beneath the mosaic at the far end of the prayer hall. The long bolt had punched through both arms and into his chest.

"Hansoo dead. Achievement crossed off." Qisami and her second bumped fists and hurried after their prey. As soon as they entered the temple, Koteuni began extinguishing all light sources while Qisami went to confirm the kill.

She was halfway across the room when another Hansoo appeared. This one was younger and smaller. He and a young woman were leading a gaggle of children to safety when they saw his brother. The Hansoo peeled away from the group and rushed to his side. "Liuman!"

Qisami grinned. "Looks like we orphaned a cub." This war monk was almost half the size of the other one, and looked probably half the age as well. His face was almost childlike.

Koteuni's voice joined in from somewhere in the shadows. "He's a cutie. Can we keep him?"

"No," replied Qisami. "Think about how much work it'll take for poor Tsang to feed and potty train him."

The puppy realized his mistake too late as he turned to face poor Liuman's killers. He balled his fists and assumed an aggressive stance. "Zofi, take the children and flee."

"Pahm, no, there're two of them. Forget about them. Just come with us," called the young woman, gesturing frantically to him. "We need you!"

"Just go. Now!" The young Hansoo, not taking his eyes off Qisami, continued advancing.

"You should listen to your friend," hummed Qisami. "She looks smart. We may even let you get away."

"She looks smart, unlike you," added Koteuni, "considering we killed your master."

The war monk assumed an aggressive fighting stance. "You'll pay for this."

While not as large as the other war monk, this Hansoo was still a big boy. It was too bad he wasn't going to live to get bigger. He wore only four rings on each forearm, but that wasn't the first giveaway that this cub was inexperienced. It was his rage, which betrayed his lack of control. The second giveaway was his overly aggressive stance. The third and most telling sign of this young Hansoo's lack of experience was—

Qisami cocked an eye. "Are you crying, puppy? Silly little thing, there's no crying in battle." The war monk's eyes were indeed red; long fat streaks were running down his cheeks.

"Maybe he was reading romantic poetry earlier," Koteuni quipped.

Qisami ratcheted up the taunting. "Maybe we killed his mama on the way up."

The Hansoo wiped his face with his sleeve. "The Tiandi will curse you for your sins, monster. If I don't send you to hell first."

The children, huddled together, stood at the doorway. "Brother Pahm, what's going on?"

"Run," he told them as he charged Qisami. The little dears stood frozen in place.

The young war monk was just about to reach Qisami when she took a casual step backward into the darkened alcove. She disappeared into the shroud and reemerged from a shaded corner near the ceiling. Qisami dropped down onto the cub's shoulders, kicking him in the back of the head and sending him crashing into the wall.

As soon as he picked himself up to face her again, Koteuni strafed him from the darkness, her saber taking his feet out from under him, sending him to the floor again as she disappeared back into the darkness. The young Hansoo roared as he swung wildly, fighting in the same silverback style as his master, but in a much less refined manner. Qisami danced around his clumsy swings, slashing him everywhere until his robes hung off his body in ribbons. Splotches of crimson began to expand on parts where her blade had pierced skin.

The two shadowkills played with the inexperienced war monk, slowly cutting him down to size. His swings were getting slower and further between. While his rage and reach kept him in the fight, his fate was inevitable.

Even the children realized this. Their cries grew louder the more the war monk bled, until soon their screams were drowning out the sounds of combat.

Qisami paused to shout at them. "Can you brats keep it down? I'd like to kill your monk in peace here." The children only grew more frantic.

The cub tried to take advantage of her distraction to lunge, which was exactly Qisami's plan. His face met the sole of her boot, snapping his head. A knife flew from her hand, plunging into his chest, followed by Koteuni striking him from behind, digging her saber into his shoulder.

The two women retreated as the Hansoo staggered and spun around, then fell to his knees. The fight was over, although the cub didn't know it yet. He pawed at the air futilely before falling onto all fours.

"May I?" asked Koteuni.

"Be my guest."

She walked up behind the boy and yanked his head back, exposing his neck. She slipped her saber under his chin and winked. "Check Hansoo off two times."

Koteuni had just begun dragging the blade across his neck when an invisible force sent her saber spinning from her grasp. Then it hit her again, and her body flew across the room. Qisami turned in time to take a blow to the face. Her vision went black for a moment, then the room was spinning, and she crashed to the floor with a bone-jarring thud. She blinked away stars. When her sight finally cleared, she saw a very enraged grandmaster windwhisper stalking toward her.

Finally, a worthy opponent. This was the fight Qisami had been looking forward to. When word spread that Maza Qisami had killed the legendary Ling Taishi and captured the boy hero, she would become so famous, the Consortium would certainly have to allow her to leave the organization. No one had a use for a celebrity assassin.

"I was wondering when you were making an appearance. Now that we're alone, let's see who deserves their reputation."

A snort emanated from the old woman. "You really are as stupid as you sound."

With a quick twist, a knife flew from Qisami's hand. It was followed by two more in rapid succession. The windwhisper batted them out of the air without missing a step.

Qisami, using her own modified version of the Consortium's "house style" known as Rolling Boxing, attacked with a flurry of overlapping short punches and quick kicks as she attempted to overwhelm her one-armed opponent.

Taishi didn't even look flustered as she dodged, blocked, or countered everything that came her way. The exchange continued with neither giving ground. Qisami realized an instant later that the only reason that was the case was because Taishi hadn't bothered to attack yet.

Nothing Qisami tried could penetrate the windwhisper's defense. The old woman moved with a mastery of space and distance, and her lone arm defended as if it were eight. Qisami redoubled her efforts, her arms and legs frenetic as she probed for weaknesses. None presented itself.

"You must have wonderful imagination for devising so many useless flashy moves," yawned Taishi.

"You're a bitch," she spat.

"And you're mediocre."

Qisami's anger simmered as her concern and impatience ratcheted up. She tried to chain together a series of unorthodox maneuvers, switching levels to punch low followed by a high kick before dashing to the side and sliding into a front sweep. She even tried flinging incense ash into the woman's face. Every attack missed by a hair, and by the calm look on Taishi's face, the near misses were completely intentional. The exchange ended with a kick to Qisami's midsection that pushed the air out of her lungs and sent her tumbling back to the floor. She spat blood and scrambled to a knee.

"Not so easy now that you don't have your goons fighting alongside you, is it?" Taishi flicked her hand toward Qisami.

Qisami dove to the side as the stone tile beneath her feet exploded into fragments. The detonating tiles followed her, forcing her to roll. She reached the darkened corner of the prayer hall and pounced in, coming out from the shadow of one of the columns behind the windwhisper.

Black knives flashed in her hands and she dove at the old woman's exposed back. Somehow, Taishi knew exactly where she was and parried with a long looping kick that smashed into Qisami's side, sending her crashing into the mosaic, collapsing the whole display on top of her.

Taishi looked amused. "Is this fight unfolding like you imagined it would?"

Qisami sat up and pushed the broken mosaic off her head. Her breathing was labored and painful; definitely a few broken ribs. "And you called *me* chatty. I'll let you know I'm just getting—"

"What is the meaning of all this noise? Who has made this dreadful mess?"

Both women turned to see a hunched man storm into the prayer hall. His gold-and-blue robes were flapping open and he was wearing nothing underneath. He gasped at the broken Celestial Mosaic of the Tiandi and jabbed at Qisami with his finger. "Are you responsible for this?"

"Your Holiness, get back!" yelled Taishi.

"Who . . ." Then Qisami realized. Her childhood had been filled with a leather switch and pages upon pages of this man's face. She had no idea if this was actually the oracle or not, but if that wretched Taishi valued his life, then Qisami knew what to do. She broke into a grin. "Don't you know it's not nice to point?"

A black blur passed between the two, and then the offending finger fell to the floor. The shock on the oracle's face registered before the pain. He stared at his severed finger, gushing red, and opened his mouth to scream, but no sounds escaped. Before he could utter that sound, she stabbed him. A long hiss left his lips as he clutched the handle embedded in his chest and collapsed. His body spasmed, and blood leaked from the corners of his mouth.

"No!" Taishi screamed in his stead while she rushed to the oracle's side. She was too late. The Hansoo, who was still lying on his side in the middle of the prayer hall, began to wail in anguish. He was soon joined by the squeaky cries of the children still huddled at the doorway. Then Qisami screamed as well, because everyone else was and why the hell not? Her scream, however, turned to mocking laughter.

Taishi cradled the oracle's head. She glared death at Qisami. "Do you realize what you just did? You will pay with more than your life. I will see to it that—"

The windwhisper gave a start when the oracle went rigid. His legs and arms stiffened. His eyelids, lazy moments earlier, flared open. He pointed at the ceiling.

The oracle intoned in a clear, strong voice:

> *The Celestial son carries the mandate of the divine*
> *On his shoulders. Heavy the burden weighs.*
> *Made fateless by freedom and driven to slumber,*
> *Seek him forth, oh curious wind, in the city at the edge of peace,*
> *For only when destiny aligns once more*
> *Will the children of heaven and earth and hell—*

The oracle's last words dribbled into a fit of coughs and gurgles, and then he toppled backward. His head bounced on the stone tiles and came to a rest looking to the side, eyes opened and blank. The room grew quiet. Everyone stared, stunned into silence. Had they just been in the presence of a divine prophecy, or were these just the last words of a madman? Moreover, had the Oracle of the Tiandi just died?

Qisami hadn't known he was even alive. What did it mean if word got out that a shadowkill—Qisami specifically—had killed the Herald of Prophecy? Maybe there *was* such a thing as bad publicity.

"You!" Both Taishi and the Hansoo lunged for her.

Qisami was ready for it. She had a good nose for when she wasn't supposed to be someplace, and that intuition had never felt stronger than it did now. She dove into the nearest shadow just as both of them reached her. She stepped out of a corner near the front, picked up the still-unconscious Koteuni, and hoofed it out of the temple, scrawling frantically on her forearm: *kill everything that comes out.*

She had nearly reached the path heading down the hill when the whoosh of an eagle bolt flew past her head. Several more followed. Someone behind her cursed as Burandin covered their escape to freedom.

The cell regrouped an hour later. Tsang nurtured a campfire while Burandin tended to his wife, who was only now regaining consciousness. Haaren, who had been operating at the far side of the settlement during the battle, was the last to return.

He glanced once at Koteuni and the fact there was no prisoner, and shook his head. "What do we do now? We've lost the element of surprise, and there's no way we can keep watch on everything. It'll be easy to slip past us."

Qisami gnawed on a drumstick. "We don't need her anymore. I know where the boy is hiding."

"I thought the plan was to acquire both bounties," said Haaren.

"No, the Prophesied Hero is the main prize. The old woman isn't worth the hassle. She's just extra fruit on top of the shaved ice." Truth was, after two failed, pathetic attempts, Qisami was no longer eager to fight Ling Taishi.

Tsang raised his hand. "Ling Taishi is still a big score, and she's right over that hill. We should just collect the bounty while we're here."

"Open your mouth one more time, Tsang, and I'll reach all the way in and squeeze your balls from the inside."

The grunt's mouth snapped shut.

"How did you acquire this information?" asked Koteuni.

"I got it directly from the original source." Qisami cleaned off the last piece of meat from her drumstick and tossed it into the fire. She wiped her greasy hands on her pants. "Pack up. We're off to the city at the edge of peace or, as I like to call it, the worst place in the Enlightened States."

CHAPTER THIRTY-ONE

KATI UNDERGROUND

S ali stood on top of the loading platform staring uncomfortably at the extremely worn armor piled inside a wagon bed that was as deep as a man was tall. She crossed her arms and shook her head emphatically. "I am not going in there."

"Why not?" said Mali. "It's just armor."

"Because I know what soldiers do in 'just armor,'" she shot back. "We sleep in it. We pee in it, and it's practically standard practice for cavalryman to shit in theirs as well. Worst of all, we die in it." Sali nudged her toe at a bloody helm with a little turtle ornament on top. "There're probably livers and other organs and brains splattered over everything in there. I've seen it up close. It's disgusting."

"It's a good thing you're used to it already, because this is the only way I can smuggle you in."

Sali scowled. She was not wholly loving this new assertive Sprout.

"Look," Mali continued, "half of our people are assigned to cleaning this garbage or melting it down. This is the only way I can be sure only Katuia will see you. So many loads of this come in, the guards barely bother checking it. Quan Sah is stripping everything from the fields and sending it back here for restoration, resale, or salvage. Caobiu has no other resources, and with the war over, no money either. One of the house servants heard the general complaining about how the other duchies have cut off supplies. Every military unit is scrambling to find alternative ways to generate revenue. This is the general's." Mali paused. "Why do you think he needs such a large workforce? They're ramping up for something big."

"Barely a year after ending their war with us?" Sali shook her head. "Who are they fighting now? Warmongering monsters."

"The military complex is getting restless. The guards gossip about it constantly. Straw Hats in the west, maybe. Or wild lands to the south. But the betting favorite is one of the other duchies."

That stopped Sali cold. "Is that true? A civil war? Which one?"

Mali shrugged. "No one knows for sure, but this army is devouring itself trying to find someone to fight. According to the soldiers, Xing is the weakest and most mineral-rich of the five. Gyian the wealthiest. "

"Good. I hope they all kill one another. I am amused by the delicious irony that our defeat will lead to the Zhuun's downfall," Sali concluded haughtily. She grimaced once more at the wagon bed, took off her good travel cloak, and handed it to Hampa. "I will need a drink after this meeting. Have a bottle ready in my room. Anything but zuijo. And clean this cloak."

"Yes, Sali." Hampa heart-saluted and ran off.

Sali and her sister watched him go. "Does he just follow you around like a puppy all day?" asked Mali. "It's adorable."

"He is terrible at house chores, but he tries." Sali refocused her attention on the wagon. "This really is the only way?"

"I'm afraid so."

"I don't really want to go," she replied. "You're the one who wants me to go."

Mali snapped, "Oh, just get in the stupid wagon, Weed."

When did her little Sprout become so bossy? "I miss the old you," she muttered.

In the end, Sali found herself exactly where she did not want to be:

hidden deep in the wagon buried under two layers of well-worn armor off the bodies of an unfortunate army, which by the angles of the puncture holes on both sides of the armor had gotten caught in a pincer move and then soaked by arrows. The entire bed smelled exactly as she had feared: a mix of rot, decay, and putrid, stale sweat. She closed her eyes and drew within, muttering through pursed lips her pre-battle meditation to calm her mind and, more important, slow her breathing.

The wagon jostled the loose armor and her like marbles in a half-filled jar. Something that felt like the tip of a steel boot kept jabbing the small of her back every time they hit a bump. She was pretty sure the bloody chain mail shirt with large gashes on both sides rubbing against her cheek belonged to someone who had come out on the losing end of a cavalry charge.

Fortunately, the journey was short and uneventful. The wagon stopped a few times along its way, each time punctuated by brief, muffled exchanges between the driver and guards. It was followed by the sounds of clanging metal that Sali soon realized were the guards stabbing their spears into the piles. Now she was thankful Mali had insisted she be buried so deep.

"All clear," someone said before the pieces of armor lying on top of her began to pull away.

Mali's grinning face appeared on one side. Sali let loose a long breath. "The land-chained stink like a cannibal's ass end."

"I'm sorry to hear that." Mali didn't sound sorry at all. "Because this is the same way you'll leave the estate too."

Sali sat up and scanned her surroundings. They were in a large warehouse with stone walls framed by long wooden beams. Her wagon had pulled up behind three others of the same size, and a small army of Katuia were wading thigh-deep in the cargo.

"Where are we?" she asked.

"This is where all the recycling happens," said Mali, offering a hand and pulling her out of the wagon bed. Sali had never felt the need to bathe more than at that moment, and she had spent Warchief Iraza's campaign in Xing not bathing for an entire cycle.

As soon as she stepped onto the wooden platform, three Katuia surrounded her. Someone draped a heavy wool blanket around her shoulders. Rough hands grabbed both arms and the small group began half herding, half dragging her down the stairs. Sali was about to object to being escorted, but let it slide. Mali knew what she was doing. Her sister led them down the length of the warehouse, past rows of tables of her people sorting armor, washing it in large tubs, and stripping the metal down.

She shook her head. "The population of an entire capital city reduced to this. It looks just as bad as toiling the fields."

The man to her right grunted. "I would give much to work under the sun with my face in the breeze. The land-chained live a filthy existence." Others muttered their agreement.

They left the warehouse, ducked behind a low wall outlining several horse pens, and followed it down to the far end. Mali peered around the corner and ticked down from four fingers. As soon as she made a fist, the group rushed across the dirt road, passing behind a patrolling guard who had just turned his back to them.

Sali marveled at the expansive estate in the heart of a cramped and claustrophobic city. With the heavy blanket mostly covering her line of sight, she lost track of where they were going. She noted that they sneaked past more than one horse barn, cut through a smithy, and zigzagged across a field, marked by dozens of bales of hay that they used as cover. The Katuia were laboring everywhere. Some were planting fast-growing crops resistant to the harsh third-cycle weather, ready to be harvested in three weeks. Others were herding sheep, feeding cattle, and laundering clothes. Most of the smiths she saw working the anvils were her people.

The small group entered what looked like an unused storeroom nestled at the rear of the estate. The man who spoke earlier opened a door in the floor, and they continued down a set of stairs to a long, narrow dirt tunnel with dozens of barrels stacked along one side. They entered a small room packed with people. The ceiling wasn't tall enough for anyone to stand. Most were content to squat or sit on the floor. There were no chairs.

Sali squeezed Mali's arm. "You said your group has only ten."

"It does. The rest are here to see you," she replied. "Word spread quickly. People are curious and hopeful."

Sali, rarely one to be self-conscious, felt a tinge of nerves as she made her way to the front of the room. Many bowed their heads and placed fists over their hearts as she passed. A few called out "Viperstrike" and "Nezra will rise again."

Sali would have returned the gesture if she weren't hunched over with her head bumping the ceiling. She was surprised to see familiar faces, people who had served under her, old neighbors from her pod, and several from her childhood. Interestingly, no city guards, former councilmen, or spirit shamans. The Zhuun were thorough when they sorted out potential troublemakers.

At the front of the room, Mali broke away to exchange a few quiet words with a shirtless young man wearing a heavy leather apron. It took a second glance for Sali to recognize Daewon, an apprentice tinker who had been friends with Mali from early childhood. The two had always been close—too close—much to Sali's family's dismay. The boy was obviously in love with Mali, and though less obviously, she had been equally fond of him. It was a childish infatuation, but dangerous considering the chasm between the families' standings within the clan.

Her family had been content to wait for the budding romance to wither on its own. When that failed, Mileene took matters into her own hands and challenged Daewon's entire family to a duel. It would have been six against one, an unfair fight in her mother's favor. Fortunately, Mali and Daewon relented, and agreed to stop entertaining the thought of a union. That had appeared to be the end of that, until now.

Sali winced when she saw Mali touch the boy's arm. Maybe it had been true love after all.

Daewon made his way to Sali and heart-saluted. He looked ill and anxious when he spoke, stuttering over his words. "Welcome, Salminde. Your presence inspires us all. I . . ." He swallowed.

She waved him off. "I have more important things to kill than you, for now."

He deflated, visibly relieved. "Of course. I didn't . . . welcome, I mean."

"You already said that." She leaned in. "We'll have a separate talk about Mali when this is all over."

He deflated again, becoming visibly unrelieved. Sali tapped him on the shoulder with a fist playfully as she passed and moved next to her sister. Mali glared and elbowed her in the ribs. It didn't hurt. "What did you say to him? He looks like he's about to faint. Be nice."

"That *was* being nice, Sprout." Sali elbowed her back, except her pointed elbow greaves were of hardened horsehide. Mali gave a muffled yelp and would have doubled over if Sali hadn't slipped an arm around her and kept her upright. It was a good reminder for Sprout.

Daewon began to address the crowd. "My heart-family of Nezra. Welcome to the meeting of the Kati Underground. Your sacrifices of your time and possibly your very life marks your dedication and bravery."

Sali rolled her eyes at the histrionics. She leaned in to Mali. "Why aren't you the one addressing them?"

"I hate talking to people," Mali answered. "Besides, Daewon's better at it."

The young man did indeed appear to have a knack for public speaking. He had launched into a punchy speech about the Children of Nezra's journey from the falling of their beloved city to this cellar. He weaved their struggles with personal examples, and displayed a level of emotional intelligence that held them to his every word even as he swept them back to bitter memories. Once all of this was over, the young man had a career announcing khanate war games between the capital cities, if they were ever to hold those again.

Daewon wrapped up his little oration with a swath of hope alongside her introduction. "And now," he concluded, gesturing her way. "We are blessed by the spirits to have returned to our family the famed and mighty, the conquering and unconquerable, the Lashing Tongue of Nezra"—*the what?*—"the mighty and, uh, famed huntress"—*he really needs to expand his vocabulary, though*—"the Viperstrike Salminde!"

There was much heart-saluting. Sali offered a curt nod, which was followed by an extended awkward pause. That was when she realized that Daewon expected her to speak. She kept her face even, but inside she was reconsidering her promise not to kill him. Like Mali and everyone else in her family, Sali wasn't much of an orator.

Her mouth suddenly dry, Sali stepped forward and promptly banged her head against the ceiling. She bit down on her lip and coughed, searching for the appropriate words. She decided to address the crowd as she would her warriors during their final meal before battle.

"Citizens of Nezra, I see that we are now living as we are, not at our greatest." A mutter passed through the crowd. The crowd seemed more taken aback than anything. At least she had gotten their attention? "The enemies of our fathers' fathers have razed our homes. Our people are scattered, and we have been brought to this soulless place. We have no home, no hearth, no people. The tale of Nezra has reached its conclusion . . . or has it? That choice is yours to make."

Sali paused for breath and surveyed the room. Her speech wasn't eliciting the response it would have from her troops. Usually, her warriors would be beating their chests and harrumphing in unison as she hammered each point home. These people looked scared and hurt.

She felt like a fool. These weren't warriors. They were farmers, tinkers, fathers, widowers, and mothers of mothers. Most of all, they were broken, beaten down, displaced refugees and servants who had lost everything. They wouldn't be sustained by the idea of vengeance or get riled up for war. They came here thirsty for hope and comfort. They wanted someone to tell them that they had a future.

Daewon appeared next to her to try to salvage this mess. "Everyone has felt tragic losses. We—"

Sali raised her hand. "Let me continue, please." She regathered her thoughts. What was she doing here? Why was she here? Why had Mali ask her to come? What did Sali want out of this meeting? The answer became clear. She took a deep breath and looked steadily at her audience. This time, she spoke from the heart.

"I will not lie to you. I originally came to Jiayi to find and free my sister from the Zhuun. I thought Nezra already dead, sunk deep beneath the

Grass Sea. I was overjoyed to finally find my Malinde. I was enraged when she refused to abandon all of you and escape with me back to the Grass Sea."

Sali nodded at her Sprout. "When I asked why, Malinde told me she was already home. I didn't understand what she meant until now. Nezra may rest at the bottom of the Grass Sea, the lucent lantern domes and pods carved from the spines of thousand-year trees may be splintered, but her people live on. Her spirit lives on. As long as we hold her memories in our souls, she lives within us."

Some in the audience were nodding. Most still offered blank stares.

Sali coughed. "I want to return Malinde not just to the Grass Sea, but to our home, our Nezra. A reborn Nezra. To do so, I must bring back the spirit of our beloved city, which means I need to bring all of you back with me." Sali offered her hand. "It won't be easy. Many of us won't make it, but will you join me in the fight to build Nezra anew? What say you, my heart-family? Are you with me?"

Sali expected a more rousing response this time around. Her second attempt was still met with silence and uncomfortable shuffling. No one cheered or clapped, or even smiled. But they weren't looking at her as if she had slapped their horse.

"How do you intend to do that?" an old man asked.

"That's a very good question." Sali should have been better prepared for this meeting. She hadn't even wanted to come in the first place. "The first thing we have to do is free everyone. It'll have to be done at the same time here and in the Kati District."

A woman raised her hand. "Most of us can come and go as we please. We can even walk out through the front gates if we wish."

"A large group of us are assigned to work in the fields every day," someone shouted.

"I visited my cousin in Sheetan just this morning," another added.

Mali had made her way next to her. She spoke softly. "Indentured servants aren't prisoners. We can come and go within most districts of the city, within limits."

Sali became confused. "So what's keeping you here? Why don't you just leave and return to the Grass Sea?"

"Because," said a new but familiar voice, stepping out from within the crowd. "Anyone who goes missing for more than a day will get hunted down by a Caobiu army. There's a healthy bounty for runaway indentured servants and a heavy punishment for the guilty. You would know that if you were one of us."

As if this meeting could get any worse. She acknowledged the new voice. "Ariun."

The former defensechief emerged from the crowd, pulling his hood back. Dirt and grime stained his robes, and the side of his head was stained with a dark-red smear. He must have arrived at this estate the same way as Sali. Other than that, Ariun looked just as well fed and prosperous as the last time they met. His eyes were piercing and sharp, and they were unwaveringly focused on her. "Word reached us that you were attending this meeting, Viperstrike. I thought it prudent I come as a representative of the Council of Nezra." His voice carried across the cellar. "All of us are here because the spirit shamans signed an armistice with the Zhuun. Our servitude is the price for peace. To break it is to incur the wrath of the Enlightened States."

"No one here signed it," spat Sali. "Why must Nezra pay the ultimate price while the other cities only work once a year? Chaqra pays nothing for the armistice."

"The scales of fortune are never balanced. The leader of our clan, Faalan, your uncle, my heart-brother, knew what he was doing when he chose to put the city in harm's way in order to recover the Khan's body. No one here was given a say in that decision either. To have someone who wasn't even at the battle disrespect our collective sacrifice is insulting."

"The spirit shamans should be doing everything in their power to bring us home," she shot back. "If they are not defending their people, then it's on us to do it alone." Ariun moved toward her until he was within arm's reach. Sali was aware of this because she had to restrain herself from reaching out and wrapping her hands around his neck.

Ariun turned around and addressed the crowd. "The Zhuun send out hunting parties to chase down anyone who flees their debt. They run you down and bring back your head as a lesson to other debtors.

Who among you would take the chance? Our people have finally settled here in Jiayi. It took over a year of hardship, but we've survived. We've made the best of this situation. We're not at our greatest, but it's who we are now, and it's home. Who here is willing to risk everything we've built to return to the Grass Sea, and for what? Even if we can avoid the Zhuun hunting parties and make the long journey, then what? We have no city, no place to call our own. We have already lost everything once. Do we throw away what little of this new life we have built for ourselves just to follow her?"

A fresh round of grumbling passed through the crowd. Sali was losing them. "The land-chained may call this indentured servitude. They may claim reparation and restitution and debt for the war. They may even be correct. However, here's what I do know. This is not free. This is not home with the rolling ground beneath our feet. We do not bask under the same stars as our ancestors. Our children do not climb to the tips of the tall grass. They do not glide along the canopies of the Grass Sea. And if you accept this indentured servitude, then your children never will, nor will their children. I now offer you a chance to reclaim our heritage as well as build a new city and forge a new destiny. Together, Nezra can rise again."

A silence fell over the room, punctuated only by an occasional cough. A woman sitting on the floor next to the man who first spoke raised her hand. "What if I don't want to go with you?" She picked herself up off the floor. "I lost six children and three grandchildren when Nezra died. There's nothing left for me back at the Grass Sea. I'm old and heartbroken, and I'm tired. Everyone I know left in this world is here in this cursed place, so here is where I'll die." Most in the crowd, it appeared, agreed with her.

"You can choose to stay," Sali replied. "There is no honor or loyalty lost if you do."

Daewon interrupted them before any more damaging words could be spoken. "Thank you, honored Viperstrike, honored Defensechief. You've given us much to discuss. Unfortunately, the evening gong will ring soon. We all have to return to our tasks before we're discovered."

People began rising to their feet and making their way out of the room one by one or in groups of two or three. Ariun stood stock-still with his arms crossed. He looked smug. Sali had failed to win her people over. They were two different visions of their people's future. Sali admitted she understood Ariun's intentions, traitorous and misguided as they were, but he could say the same about her. Most of their people would probably stay. She didn't blame them. They had lived through enough suffering and death. Sali only wanted to give them the choice; she would respect their decision.

As the room emptied, Ariun spoke softly to her. "Don't do this, Salminde. You'll bring death to us all."

Sali swallowed the urge to wrap her hands around the man's neck. Ariun wasn't wrong in this matter, however. There were just no good solutions. She remained where she stood while he joined the throng by the door as the crowd dispersed. This was not what she had hoped for, nor what she had expected. While a few approached to speak kind words, most did not appear keen to her invitation. She had assumed her people would be eager to fight for their freedom. It had never occurred to her that the survivors were done fighting, or running. They only wanted peace.

Soon, the only people left with the two sisters were Daewon and the two men by the door who had regulated the dispersal of the crowd. "I didn't know about Ariun," said Mali. "I'm sorry."

"It's all right." She met her sister's eyes.

"What happens now?"

Sali tried to put on a brave face. "We'll see how many decide to take me up on our offer. It'll probably be just a handful."

"Better than just you and me, big sister."

"So you'll come?"

"I just wanted our people to have a choice," said Mali.

Daewon stepped closer. "The Kati Underground is united behind you to a person, Salminde."

"All ten of you?"

"We're fourteen now, as of just now."

"That's just wonderful." She turned to leave. "At least with a small group, it will be easy to escape and avoid capture. Can you change the name of the group? I hate that slur."

Daewon shook his head. "I don't think that's a good idea."

"Why not?"

"Branding purposes. The people already know us by this name. We've built a reputation."

Sali was tempted to reach out and wrap her hands around *his* neck, which reminded her of one last loose end to tie, or kill. "By the way, I need your assistance before we leave. I need to find someone in this city. A boy, about sixteen or seventeen. Short hair, lean, athletic. Can your people help?"

Daewon frowned. "Of course, Salminde, but that description fits just about every boy that age in the city."

"Possibly, but I think he's the prophesied Zhuun hero."

His reaction was similar to Mali's. Before he could ask, her sister interrupted. "I'll fill him in later, but we really have to get Sali back out of the estate before the gates close. Unless you want to sleep in this cellar tonight."

"Get me out of here." Sali hesitated, and then offered her hand to Daewon. This was not a time for more enemies.

He looked surprised, slightly fearful even, and then clasped forearms.

Sali left the estate the way she had arrived, tucked between crates of armor and weapons. At least these were cleaned and renewed for use. She met with Mali at the same food stall over the next few days. By the end of the first day, thirteen people had approached Daewon about leaving Jiayi. By the second, forty-one more had joined the Kati Underground. By the third day, that number had swelled to more than three hundred.

Sali had somehow started a movement. Now she was really in trouble.

CHAPTER THIRTY-TWO

COVER-UP

No one at the Longxian Northern Fist School of War was having a good time. The magistrates had paid Guanshi a visit that very evening with a summons to the Tower of Fiery Vigilance, which Jian had always thought a peculiar name when the magistrates' uniforms were a dull lime green and their work hours extraordinarily reasonable. The master was gone for most of the next day and had returned late in the evening red-faced, drunk, and furious. The school had also obviously lost the warehouse security contract. At the very least Southern Cross hadn't gotten it either.

Xinde avoided everyone. He didn't teach classes, nor had he shown his face at the dining hall. He wouldn't even see Jian when Jian brought his meals. Worse yet, news of the altercation had spread like weevils on rice. By the time Guanshi left for the tower, everyone knew that Xinde, the golden boy of Longxian, had choked in battle, twice. Students were whispering that he was a porcelain prince, a lot of pretty smoke. His very presence became a black mark on the school and the style. Guanshi made no effort to break through his senior's self-isolation.

Rumors about Jian spread just as quickly, cobbled together from the

Southern Cross's mocking embellishments. In their account, Jian had had to step in to defend his hapless senior because Xinde couldn't get back up after Keiro's first attack. Jian had ambushed Keiro from behind like a coward, but had fought with the skill of a master. Keiro had managed, albeit barely, to prevail over this stranger who masqueraded as a novice.

Students brought the stories back thinly wrapped in disdain and disbelief, but that didn't stop them from telling and retelling what they had heard. No one gave him credit for saving Xinde or defending Longxian's honor. Everyone just glommed on to the idea that he was a master who had infiltrated their ranks. Never mind that no one in the history of the lunar court had ever become a master-level war artist before the age of twenty-five, let alone twenty. No one, not even the Longxian students, not even Auntie Li, even bothered to challenge the facts or ask Jian for his account. The outlandish tale was far more salacious.

They whispered to one another that Hiro, if that was even his name—that hit too close to home—was a spy sent from another school. Or he was here to steal war arts secrets? Or to rob Guanshi of Steed Slayer? Also, wasn't there a rumor about Hiro getting death-touched? Who death-touches a beggar boy? For that matter, why would Master Guanshi take him in, offer him free room and board, and train him for nothing? Certainly not out of the goodness of his heart. Could Hiro be Master Guanshi's bastard love child?

A week later, Jian was right back where he had started, an outsider. Or worse, since everyone assumed he was a traitor. The theft of war arts secrets was considered especially heinous. Even Auntie Li regarded him warily. Unfortunately, there was just enough truth in the rumors that neither Meehae nor Xinde could deny their veracity. In fact, their defense of him and explanation of the events made things worse. Xinde admitted to remembering very little, which made stories about how he had panicked and frozen even more plausible. And Meehae, sweet bighearted and terrible-liar Meehae, had tried to spin a story so bizarre it *sounded* like a cover-up.

Surprisingly, the one person everyone thought would go absolutely crazed, didn't. When word of the incident reached him, Guanshi only grumbled and jabbed Jian on his forehead with a finger. "Stay out of trouble." Then he turned and marched into his residence. The fact that Guanshi didn't immediately expel him only further fed the rumors.

Jian wasn't sure what to make of that. Did the master believe him, or did he not care? It was more likely Guanshi was more concerned about Xinde and what his rapid fall meant for the school. Regardless, Jian did his best to stay out of sight. He spent the days volunteering to polish and clean the school's weapons and reorganize the kitchen storerooms. He cleaned out the drainage pipes to the city's sewer system and swept debris off the roofs. He cleared out the chicken coop. Unfortunately, he still had to return to kitchen duties, which put him in range of everyone's silent, judging glares three times a day. He had felt just lonely before; now he felt hated.

It was a shock that the days went by without incident. No one tried to pick a fight with him—he's a secret master!—nor was he taunted or ridiculed to his face. No one hurled food or insults. The only things he had to deal with were glares and isolation. In retrospect, he would much rather have taken a beating.

By the sixth day, he had had it. Jian climbed the back wall and spent the early night on his back gazing up at the sky. It was the night of the Ash Revelry, when the twins intersected. The Princess ascended from the south and aligned with the Prince, who was disappearing into the northern horizon. The two moons together cast a hazy, eerie gray ghostly light across the land.

It was a stark reminder that the last season of the third cycle had arrived, with the burning steaming summer and soon the bitterest freezing winter. This could be a problem, because Jian had decided to leave, not just the school, but Jiayi and Caobiu entirely. It was the worst time of the year to travel, but he didn't have any other options. His cover may have been blown, Taishi had vanished, and it wasn't as if he would learn anything from Guanshi. He should have been promoted a cycle ago, but Guanshi kept making him do basic drill after basic drill.

Worst of all, and this bothered Jian the most, nobody liked him. Piled on top of their months of mockery now were those constant judging glares, and it was intolerable. Jian wanted a fresh start, a real one this time, not one haphazardly strung together by Taishi as a means of getting him off her hands. He had been a nuisance to her all along, as he probably had been to everyone.

Jian glanced on the other side of the wall down to the sewage alley running between the walled estates. He wasn't given a choice the last time; maybe now he could be. For the first time in his life, he could control his own destiny. Jian stood up and pointed to the end of the alley. "I'm going to go this way and not look back, ever." Then he realized that that direction led to the Grass Sea. He faced the other way. "I'm going to go this way, and not look back, ever."

He dropped back down into the garden and made his way to the ramshackle hut he called home. It wouldn't take long to gather his few meager items. He paused and held up the old robe that he had worn when he first arrived in Jiayi, the once fine silk now dirtied and torn. It was the robe that the tailor had made for him the night all five dukes came to the Celestial Palace. It felt like a lifetime ago. Now it was just a torn and tattered rag. Jian didn't know why he had kept it, just that it brought him back to his time at the Celestial Palace, the bitter and the good, mostly bitter. He packed it anyway.

When he was finished, all he had to show for it was one small satchel. He had few possessions and even less money. Really, no possessions save for the school uniform he wore now and padded robes, both of which he was pretty sure he didn't actually own. He took them anyway; he was owed that much. He and his small knapsack were back out the door within a few minutes.

Jian considered creeping to the main hall and kitchen to pilfer some food and valuables. The two strings of copper liang he had wouldn't get him very far. In the end, he decided against it. Longxian hadn't been the kindest, but it had provided him shelter and food. He didn't want to leave here a thief. Besides, a war artist's reputation followed him for the rest of his life. He shouldn't squander what little goodwill he had left on petty theft.

Jian was about to drop down the other side of the wall and be away from the Longxian Northern Fist School of War forever when a voice called out. "I would be careful there. The other side is a slippery slope of mud and sewage. From our drains, I might add. At worst you'll break your ankle. At best you'll slip and slide in shit. Instead, might I suggest this thing we have called a front gate?"

Jian looked back down into the garden and noticed Xinde lying on a bench near the pond. "Senior," he acknowledged. "What are you doing out here?"

"I was going to say, probably the same as you, but judging by your pack, you have more extreme measures in mind. Want to talk about it?" He didn't wait for an answer. He crossed the garden to the wall and climbed to the top on the tips of his toes and fingers. It was a Longxian technique, although Xinde had adjusted it for his individual talent and style. Jian personally thought this skill bland—truthfully that's what he thought of most Longxian uses of jing—but who was he to talk? He was the one who had had to climb up a tree to get to the top of the wall.

Xinde was next to him a moment later. The senior pulled out a gourd and offered it. Jian gratefully took a swig and turned a little green as he choked and forced it down. He was not ready for the harsh burn of cheap zuijo. He passed it back to Xinde, and the two sat together silently under the two moons.

Jian was very grateful when Xinde finally spoke first. "I feel like we have much to discuss."

They probably did, but Jian couldn't share his secret, and he was just as fine not prying into Xinde's personal business. It wasn't like they were ever going to see each other again after Jian skipped town. The senior was his only friend at the school, although to be honest he wasn't sure why. Everyone wanted to be Xinde's friend, but why did Xinde care about the lowest student in the school? Still, Jian was dying to know what the senior's deal was. Jian's concern for his welfare was genuine. Plus, he could tell the man needed someone to talk to. For once, it was the senior who needed a friend.

After a brief, uncomfortable silence, he probed. "Well, you first." He was still figuring this friendship thing out.

Xinde looked like he was expecting another answer, but shrugged. "That's fair. I *was* the one who invited myself up here." He looked up at the stars. "Do you know why I enrolled in Longxian?"

"Because you wanted to be a great war artist?"

Xinde chuckled derisively. "I actually wanted to be a dancer. I hated violence, it made me queasy." He raised one leg straight up in the air and pointed his foot. "I was good too. My teacher said I had a chance at the Songgua Academy in Allanto. A couple months before the test, my ba decided that no son of his was going to join the opera to be some painted dancer, so he dragged me to Longxian's front gates and dumped me here. Told me not to come home until I could best him in a fight."

"That's fortunate." Jian hesitated. "Or is that bad?" He actually wasn't sure.

Xinde shrugged. "It is neither good nor bad. It is simply what happened. Turns out the physical qualities that make a great dancer are not that different from the ones that make a great war artist. My talents translated well from leaps and twirls to punches and spin kicks, so here you have it"—he gestured at himself—"the dancing senior of Longxian."

"That explains why you're so graceful," said Jian. "Even if this wasn't your dream, you didn't do too badly for yourself. It could have been much worse."

"Or much better. I could have been the next great opera star at Songgua Academy. We'll never know. I honestly have no regrets." Xinde did not sound like he meant his words. "Life here has been good, mostly. Master Guanshi treats me like the son he never had. Auntie Li acts like the mother I never had."

"To have a mother and father, to have a family, is all most of us can wish for." Jian couldn't mask the wistfulness in his voice. At least Xinde *had* parents.

The senior gazed off into the night sky, lost in thought. "A family can be more than just a mother and father, husband and wife, parent and child. My father views me only as an instrument to carry on the family name. My stepmother stopped acknowledging my existence the day she moved into our home. Love and respect is what makes family, not blood. It can manifest in different ways and shapes, sometimes from people you least expect."

The senior must be referring to the Longxian school, or was he? Jian wasn't sure anymore. Thinking about his parents, whom he didn't remember, only grew the empty black hole in his heart and made him feel raw. He decided to change the subject. "What happened with Keiro? I've never seen you fold from a punch like that. I've seen you take harder blows in practice."

Xinde cracked a sad smile and tapped the side of his head. "That's the thing about sparring and tournaments. They're games; it's not real. They have judges, rules, and limits. The competitors—most of them—don't *want* to hurt the other person. Fights on the street are completely different. No judges, rules, or limits. No one wears pads, and the weapons are *sharp*. I've been lucky up until now. I've avoided most street fights on sheer reputation. I'd show up and talk everyone down. And I managed to avoid getting hurt the few times I've had to fight."

His voice cracked when he spoke again. "I don't like violence, Hiro. I'm afraid of fighting, I have been ever since I was a boy. My ba thought Longxian would drive that fear out. I thought so too. I had a trick. Whenever the fighting got real, a little voice in my head convinced me to treat it just like a tournament. But the first time Keiro cut me, the little voice went silent. I got so, so scared, and now that trick doesn't work anymore. I've broken."

Jian started intently at his own feet. What do you say to someone who just called himself a coward? He had always thought the opposite of Xinde. The senior was strong and brave. He was everyone's idol. Half the students at Longxian wanted to be him, and the other half couldn't decide if they wanted to be him or be with him. Maybe that was what Xinde needed to hear. Jian could tell his friend that he was completely wrong and absolutely not a coward. Or instead maybe Jian should try to help him overcome this problem? Wasn't that why the senior was telling him this, so he could help? Jian could perhaps offer personal examples of how he had overcome his own fears.

What Jian really wanted to do was just play dumb and gloss over this uncomfortable conversation, pretend it wasn't happening. He racked his brain, and ended up going with the first thing that came to mind. "Wow, that sucks. I'm sorry."

To his surprise, Xinde looked genuinely relieved. "Thank you, Hiro." Jian tilted his head at Xinde quizzically.

The senior continued. "For once, it's nice not to have someone think there is something wrong with me and want to fix me. And it feels good to finally tell someone."

Jian didn't understand. Something *was* wrong with Xinde, but he kept that thought to himself. "You're welcome."

Xinde breathed out a long sigh. "What about you, Hiro? What secret are you keeping? I remember enough from that fight to know you are not any sort of novice I've seen before."

It was Jian's turn to explain himself, except while he trusted Xinde to an extent, Jian knew he couldn't tell him the truth. They may have been exchanging secrets, but there was a slight difference between *I'm a coward* and *I'm the central figure of our religion.*

Taishi had told him several times that he was a terrible liar, so he decided to just tell the truth, but as little of it as possible. "You're right," he began. "I'm not who you think I am. There are people after me, so I'm in hiding."

"I don't think you're a spy," mused Xinde. "The techniques you used didn't come from any of the local schools. Now that I think about it, you exhibited northwestern, southern, and central flavors." He paused. "You must have been trained in multiple styles."

That hit uncomfortably close to home. Jian gulped. "Maybe."

Xinde fixed him with a look, as if perhaps if he stared hard enough he could decipher Jian's real identity. "Nobleman's son, I knew it. Your hands were always too soft for a street beggar."

"That's not true!" Jian held up both hands. "I have calluses."

Xinde snorted. "At the base of your fingers from holding weapons. You also have no accent." His grin grew sly. "So I'm right."

For the first time since Jian arrived in Jiayi, he felt important. "Maybe."

Xinde rubbed his hands. "Interesting. Are you blood with any of the dukes?"

Jian shook his head.

"So, your noes are noes, and your maybes are yeses. Are you from the Caobiu court?"

"No, I mean—no you're right, no." Damn that smart guy.

The senior went on excitedly. "Another duchy then. You don't have an eastern face, but you're skilled enough at a young age to give Keiro a good fight. Lawkan nobles frown upon their children practicing war arts." He snapped his fingers. "You pointed north a little bit ago. You must be from Shulan!"

"Maybe." This was too easy.

Xinde smirked. "You say people are looking for you. Are you a runaway? Is it your family searching for you, or enemies?" Xinde snapped again. "Enemies. You were death-touched, which means your family had powerful enemies. The assassins sent after you weren't common thugs, but why would you hide out at a war arts school instead of in one of your family estates?"

Jian could hardly believe how far the rumors had gone, but before he could answer, Xinde went on. "You're not at a family estate because the threat must be coming from within." He paused and leaned in. "You were betrayed, weren't you?"

"May . . . Maybe." Jian squirmed.

Xinde suddenly frowned and fixed him with a hard look. "You're not the missing Champion of the Five Under Heaven, are you?"

Jian could feel the blood drain from his face. He tried to speak but couldn't manage to push the sounds up his throat. The wall felt like it was suddenly spinning under him. Then Jian realized Xinde had broken into a laugh.

Jian chuckled along weakly. "Hah, good one." Was he really that easy to read?

Xinde held up a hand. "It's all right. You don't have to talk about it. Your secret will be safely guarded, Lord Hiro." He clapped Jian on the shoulder and dropped gracefully back into the garden.

"Hey, Xinde," he called after the senior. "You've gone out of your way to be friendly to me. Why? I appreciate it, but you don't need me, I'm nobody. Why did you go put in all this effort?"

Xinde shrugged. "Since we're both spitting out truths, Master Guanshi asked me to watch over you when you first arrived. I saw in you a kindred spirit. I could tell you didn't want to be here like I didn't when I first came to Longxian. So I wanted to be your friend and look after you."

"Are we really friends?"

Xinde shook his head. "No, we're not friends, Hiro. We're brothers. Regardless of what the others think, one does not choose their brothers, nor shed them easily. Think about that before you decide to leave." He turned. "By the way, if you still plan on running away through the back, I wasn't kidding about that slope of shit." Then Xinde turned and disappeared into the night.

ACT III

CHAPTER THIRTY-THREE

FAMILY DISCOUNT

Qisami slipped through the west entrance to Jiayi just before the gates closed for the night. She was grateful to have made it, sparing her another horrible humid night under looming thunderclouds. The journey from the Temple of the Tiandi to Sanba and then straight to Jiayi had been unpleasant even by Qisami's standards. It was now late summer in the third cycle, and the weather couldn't make up its mind, alternating from humid heat wave to freezing hailstorm every other day. Sometimes on the same day. Traveling during the third cycle was just the rotten worst. One time it had even rained leeches, likely scooped up from the Sea of Flowers to the west—more like Big Rotten Swamp, since the flowers that once bloomed there hadn't done so in hundreds of years.

After eight days of misery, Qisami was ready to murder someone, literally. She almost had when the carriage driver got deterred by the havoc on the roads caused by the inclement weather and severely delayed their journey. She had paid the man double to get to Jiayi as fast as possible, telling him he wasn't really trying unless at least one horse died along the way. She had gotten to stab him once after the carriage got stuck in mud for half a day, which lifted her mood a little, but then Koteuni and Burandin had stopped her, mainly because no one else wanted to take over driving. They arrived two days late, and worse, no one had died, not the driver nor any of his horses. Qisami's only comfort in this fiasco was the knowledge that Taishi had had to go through the same putrid weather to get here.

What was most important, of course, was that they had arrived ahead of the windwhisper. It wasn't by as much as Qisami had hoped, but they had enough of a lead to lop off the precious prophecy-boy's head. Once the damn windwhisper arrived, her cell's odds of pulling off this contract would dramatically decrease. It was a good thing she had a secret weapon . . .

Qisami took a deep whiff as soon as they came through the outer gates and smacked her lips. "I love this hellhole."

She really meant it. Jiayi was probably her favorite city in the world. It was the largest commandery in Caobiu, and like most large cities, it smelled like shit and anxiety. There was really no place like it. Allanto might have its debaucherous allure of decadent food, sex parties, and great opera; and Manjing, the capital of Lawkan, might have the largest and most exotic searfaring vessels and yachts, not to mention great noodle shops; but Jiayi was its own blend of urban misery and lawless bravado.

What made the city extra special, made it stand out above all other cities, was its heady air of violence and desperation. Most soldiers, mercenaries, and war artists stayed within these walls only when they were between contracts or looking for work, and idle war artists were often stupid war artists. Add the recent unrest and instability that had plagued the Enlightened States, and the city felt positively electric.

They continued deeper through the commandery, parting the crowds and not slowing for stragglers who didn't get out of their way quickly enough. The city was even more crowded than she remembered.

Haaren leaned over the side and studied the row of vendor stalls. "Everything is so cheap."

"That's because everyone's so broke," said Koteuni. "I've never seen so many unemployed soldiers and war artists waiting around in one place."

"That's what those dummies get for winning the war," replied Qisami.

Burandin pointed at a recruiter off to the side enlisting soldiers. The crowd surrounding him looked like piranhas during a feed. "The army's mustering again."

Koteuni snorted. "To fight whom? There's no one left."

He shrugged. "There's always someone to fight."

It took another hour of wading upstream before her cell reached the Onyx Flower District. No sooner had they passed through the check-point than Qisami peeled away from the group. "Book rooms at that inn I like with the patbingsu chef. Have dinner ready by the time I get back, preferably with lots of vegetables. I'm sick of eating potatoes and jerky. I want healthier options for this holy temple." She gestured to herself. "Tsang, scrounge up a pouch of opium too. The good stuff, none of that street funk."

"I want some too," added Haaren. Koteuni and Burandin raised their hands as well.

"Where are you off to, Kiki?" asked Koteuni.

"I'm meeting a contact. The rest of you take baths and get some rest. You smell like farts. Watch for my scrawl. Be ready to move."

"Which is it, get some rest or be on alert?" asked Burandin.

"Of course get some rest, but if you don't come the moment I blood-scrawl, I'll skin you alive."

Qisami soon found herself alone on a quiet street flanked by neatly pruned hedges and intricately shaped bonsai trees. It felt almost too quiet, with only the sounds of her horse's hooves clip-clopping against the smooth, paved roads. There were no street vendors, and everyone who passed looked dressed in their Tenth Day Prayer best. Even the air smelled like flowers.

She inhaled deeply. "I do love the smell of wealth."

The Onyx Flower District was mainly residential and housed nobil-ity and wealthy merchants. The streets were lined with palatial estates and gardens, and one intersection even boasted a two-story fountain.

She turned right and continued to the district's commerce block, where dozens of colored lanterns hung from two rows of alternating pink and white magnolia trees.

Qisami chuckled at the guard bowing as she passed through the entrance. The cell had taken the time before they reached the city gates to change from their travel attire into court finery. The guards and magistrates at the city and district gates had taken one look at her riding cloak and the dress underneath and assumed she belonged. Commoners did not ride in silks.

She reached her destination at a busy three-way intersection in the heart of the block. Qisami dismounted and passed the reins to a waiting attendant. She ruffled out the matted parts of her dress and accepted the hand of another attendant who escorted her up the three steps to a nondescript black building nestled between a dress shop and a cake shop. The building was plain, absent of Zhingzi or signage, and the only hint of what sort of establishment it was was a pair of obscenely bright doors polished daily to a distractingly white sheen.

The hostess of the room salon eyed Qisami warily, taking in the obviously rich and intricately embroidered red dress clinging tightly to her body dragging mud across the floor. Her eyes locked on the unbuttoned flap near Qisami's right shoulder that hung lazily forward before drifting down to the slit that ran all the way up to her thigh.

Qisami could see the uncertainty in the hostess's eyes. Was Qisami here for leisure or employment? She smirked and threw her hips side to side as she approached, daring the woman to draw the wrong conclusion. The hostess eventually decided that no one employed at a room salon would ever show up to work in such an obviously expensive dress.

She gestured with a limp arm. "Welcome to the Willow Swaying and the Maiden's Tail. Will you require a table and bottle service?"

"I'm here to see the Black Widow."

The hostess did not miss a beat and parted a curtain of beads. "This way, mistress."

Qisami's cloak slipped off her shoulders as still another attendant appeared to receive it. She followed the hostess through the beaded curtain and into a long corridor sectioned off by sheer floor-to-ceiling drapes.

Dozens of candles hung from chandeliers and sconces dotting the ceiling and walls, giving the space a luminous dreamlike quality. The smell of opium and perfumes hung heavily in the air. Tentacles of smoke curled around the furniture and decorations and tickled Qisami's nose. Waving her hand about did little for the itch.

Qisami counted heads as they walked, noting the bouncers with holstered clubs standing guard every few feet. Several waitresses and provocatively clad salon companions shuffled past, some hanging on to older well-dressed men like ants on rotten food.

The hallway opened up into a busy lounge area with several small circular tables and chairs neatly arrayed in a sunken center pit. The sides of the lounge were lined with large booths, and the far end held a long bar counter. The hostess navigated without looking back to see if her guest was keeping up, leading Qisami to the back corner.

She pulled back a sheer curtain surrounding a booth, revealing a large bearded man wearing a puffy red dress with sparkling sequins lining the cuffs. The body of a golden sequined dragon with its jaws opened around the throat of the dress curled around his shoulders, its body wrapping several times around the waist before its tail came to a rest at the crotch. It was gloriously tacky.

The man, who had his arms draped around a pretty young man and woman on either side of him, looked her up and down. His eyes narrowed. "Bitch."

"*You're* the bitch." Qisami added reluctantly, "I love your dress, Eifan."

The man known as the Black Widow preened, and then admitted even more reluctantly, "I like yours too."

She gazed back and forth at their strikingly similar outfits. "Well, this is embarrassing. We should have coordinated. We look like background dancers in a bad troupe . . ." Her eyes narrowed. "You did this on purpose."

Eifan broke into a grin. "Did you actually think you could enter the

Onyx Flower District without my knowledge? Jiayi is my playground, Kiki. I'm tired of you upstaging me every time we breathe the same air." He gestured to the young man to his right. "Serve my guest plum wine."

"You know I don't drink while I'm working."

"Who says you're working?" The Black Widow looked around suspiciously. "Are you?"

She accepted the drink. "Get out."

The two hastily obliged and she slid in next to the Black Widow.

"Hey," protested Eifan. "I wasn't done with them yet."

"Pour your own drink, you lazy crab."

He clicked his tongue. "I most certainly will not. What sort of commoner do you take me for?"

"I know the wine-soaked rat you call mam. You're as plain as white rice."

"Only because your rich father is a heartless bastard."

"No argument there, white rice."

"I'll have you know you're speaking to nobility. As Jiayi is my domain, I am the weblord of Jiayi."

Qisami sneered. "That sounds like a fake title. You made that up."

"How dare you!" Eifan sneered back. He pointed at the pitcher. "The job's yours now. Fill my drink. Don't spill any of it."

Qisami was tempted to spill something else of his. "You're still so high-maintenance."

"You're one to talk, trotting around the Onyx Flower District in a widow's dress."

"I killed her husband, and she was starving," she shrugged. "The least I could do was buy it off her. It wasn't like she was ever going to use it again."

Eifan drained his glass and rudely reached over Qisami to pick up the pitcher. "Since you won't serve me . . ." She waited patiently as he refilled and redrained his glass in one smooth motion. He placed it down and waggled his fingers. "So, what brings my favorite shadowkill to my corner of the web?"

The web the Black Widow belonged to happened to be the largest spy network and most powerful information brokerage in the world. It was supposed to have been disbanded by Emperor Xuzinan over a century ago for budgetary reasons. That was probably the gravest of all the errors Xuzinan had made in his short error-prone reign. By all accounts, the emperor fancied himself a better ruler and general than his abilities allowed, which was how he had led the empire through six years of continual defeats on the battlefield, two recessions, and one long famine before a Kati arrow through the eye had put the Zhuun out of their misery. Instead of allowing the web to wither and fray, the silkspinners had consolidated and turned mercenary, leveraging their expansive network for power and profit. By the time Xuzinan's successor had tried to correct the mistake and bring the spy network back under imperial control, it was too late.

"I'm looking for someone in Jiayi."

Eifan yawned. "First time since forever you come to me for information and it's a missing person? How boring. Let me guess. You're on the Zobu job."

"Already collected for that."

"The Hambao one?"

"That too."

"The Three-Legged Abbot?"

She stuck out her tongue. "Do I look like a common footpad to you?"

"The Tangerine Fox then?"

Qisami faked a gag. "I passed on that. I don't get involved with the dairy industry."

Eifan nodded emphatically. "Wise decision. Cow people are unhinged." He leaned back, brought his palms together, and waggled his fingers dramatically. The Black Widow did everything histrionically. "So if it's not the Fox or the Abbot, but you're here in Jiayi, what else could we possibly have to attract a shadowkill of your fee?" His eyes glittered. "A mark in the ducal court, or a cold case?" The Black Widow tapped his temple as he studied her. Finally, his eyes widened. "You're not still after that Prophesied Hero bounty, are you? It's already ancient history. Most have moved on by now."

"Warmer," she admitted.

Eifan's jing in deciphering information was strong, and it was a big reason he ran the information web in Jiayi. He had a keen ear and a knack for reading people, just as she had amazing reflexes and a knack for murdering them. Qisami kept her face straight, which was as much of a tell as if she had screamed the boy's name across the lounge.

"I knew it was something juicy," chortled Eifan. "Come, let's continue our business in private."

Qisami eyed a pretty woman who walked past. "What's wrong with right here?"

Eifan snorted. "You can't be serious. The Maiden's Tail is practically a country club for every spinner in Jiayi. Throw a dagger and you'll hit a spy." He surveyed the room. "In fact, I count . . . six, seven, nine who are actually here for the entertainment and the drinks. The rest are silkspinners who will sell the breath right out of your mouth. Come, I reserved a room in the back."

Her eyes narrowed. "If you reserved a room, why are we out here with the rest of the peasants?"

Eifan shrugged. "I like the background noise, and I like to listen. You would be *amazed* at how many silkspinners have diarrhea of the mouth."

"Is stolen information fair game to resell?" She swept a finger. "Aren't you all on the same team?"

"Absolutely, but only up to first rights." He led her to a back hallway that at first was invisible to the eye. "You see, if anyone was careless enough to get overheard, then it is entirely in the right of the silkspinner who obtained that information to sell it again. The brokerage takes a higher cut of secondary rights, but in the end everyone wins, in a way."

"What way is that?"

"It's twofold," the Black Widow explained. "First, information is both the most valuable commodity in the world and free to replicate. It's pure profit." The two walked down a corridor that again, by some trick of the eye, appeared to shrink as they got farther along. Eifan abruptly stopped and opened a hidden door Qisami had completely overlooked. "Second, it's a double-edged sword," he continued. "Because that means it must be guarded closely. A leaky spy can no longer be trusted with secrets, and without secrets to peddle, we're just a bunch of perverts hiding in closets."

Qisami followed him into a room with black padding on the walls. It was furnished with an ornate ebony square table flanked by matching chairs in the center, and a lounging daybed on the side. Her guess was that it was some sort of fetish chamber built with privacy in mind, which explained the deadweight of the air. Her voice felt muffled. The same two salon companions reappeared a moment later with a fresh pitcher of wine and a bowl of fruit. They placed them on the table and bowed before Eifan shooed them off.

Qisami nudged one of the spongy cushions attached to the walls and ceiling. "You must have a lot of fun parties in here."

"That's unfortunately not allowed anymore. Cleaning the fabric is a dreadful nightmare." The Black Widow took one of the chairs. "So, how can I help the beautiful and deadly Maza Qisami?"

"I'm looking for a boy, sixteen. He arrived in Jiayi within the last year, is skilled in the war arts, and by all accounts carries himself like he's a duke's uncle. Last seen with long hair, slender, and he may have a mark on his chest from a death touch."

Eifan raised an eyebrow. "You weren't joking about the Prophesied Hero. He's really here in Jiayi?"

Qisami ignored the question. "Can you find him?"

"Of course," he sniffed. "There is nothing I can't find in my city. It'll cost you, though."

"That's not a problem." She reached for her purse. "How much?"

"Five strings of gold liang," Eifan said all too casually.

Qisami was stunned. She earned well as a shadowkill. Some would even consider her wealthy, but she wasn't trample-a-child-over-with-a-horse-for-fun wealthy. "That's outrageous. Five strings is half of the reward for the boy."

The Black Widow smirked. "I guess that makes us partners."

A bubble of rage expanded inside her gut. "I'm all for getting rich together, but this is robbery."

"The price for information is always set to its value," he explained. "In this case, there is literally nothing more valuable than locating the Hero of the Tiandi."

"Be reasonable, Eifan. If I had that much coin I wouldn't be sniffing around this rotten hole hunting a runt with some holy prophecy wrapped around his tiny baby cock."

Eifan's face grew shrewd. He jutted his chin forward not unlike a badger stalking a henhouse. "I'm going to help you out, Qisami. Only because I love you. This could be the score of a lifetime. For both of us, really. Pay me one gold string now. The other four you pay after you collect the dukes' bounty. That way, we both come out ahead."

"I've been on this case since the beginning. You can't just swoop in here and expect half!" That bubble was growing, and multiplying. "I'm the one doing all the work and taking all the risks, you brainless, opium-puffing, badly dressed peacock."

"Now you're just being rude." He sipped his wine and held up one finger in the air. "There's one more thing."

Qisami's eyes narrowed. "What?"

"Don't take this the wrong way, Kiki," he continued cheerfully. "You know I think you're the best and you will absolutely crush this job, but—" He paused, dramatically. "—there's a tiny chance you won't. I have to take that into consideration; hedge my investment. So because I recognize your first rights, I'm going to give you three days to fulfill the contract. After that, I'll have no choice but to broker the information to someone else—"

Qisami's arm had a mind of its own. She wasn't even thinking when she plunged a black knife into his belly. They both looked surprised for a moment, then Eifan spasmed.

"What the living dog piss, Qisami? I'm your cousin! I used to babysit you. I should have drowned you in a shitting pot." He choked and wiped the blood leaking from the side of his mouth. "You know I hate the sight of blood."

This hadn't been part of her plan, but it was now. Qisami was committed to this path. She grasped the hilt of the knife. "You should have given me a family discount then. Now you're going to give me everything you know that will help me find this runt. After I collect the bounty, I'll give you one gold string, because I'm not a thief. And the only reason I don't gut you right now is because I really don't want to get annoyed with your mam talking bad about me at family reunions. Because I'd have to kill her too, and that would ruin everyone's evening. Are we clear?"

He groaned and writhed frantically. "Argh, I'm bleeding like a gutted pig. Didn't I just tell you that this room is hard to clean?"

"Stop moving. You're just making a bigger mess. Also, no selling this information to anyone else."

"I'm dying," the silkspinner croaked. He tried to yell. "Help."

Qisami settled in for the long haul. That soundproof room was really working out in her favor. Eventually, just as she expected, Eifan saw reason and a deal was struck. She left the Willow Swaying and the Maiden's Tail in a far better mood than the one she had arrived in, having had to pay less than she had expected, and not only with the information she needed, but also with the full support of the Black Widow's web for the duration of her stay. Eifan had always been her favorite relative. He could be so sweet sometimes.

Qisami hummed as she strolled out of the room salon, hissing at the hostess as she passed. Things were proceeding quite well, but she was still going to have to throw away this dress. She scrawled on her arm: *did you get the opium, grunt?*

Yes. I found a place with shark fin soup too.

Qisami clutched a fist in the air at the unexpected news about the soup. Things were looking up.

CHAPTER THIRTY-FOUR

PREPARATIONS

Sali sat alone in the corner of the balcony of the Drunken Monk, overlooking the alley and main street of the Rose Ridge District. The barkeep and bouncer had eyed her when she walked in but hadn't given her any trouble. She had pulled out her pouch of liang, and they were suddenly as content to serve her as they were anyone else.

The waitress, a plump woman with the look of a stern headmistress, was slow on the refills, but no slower than for any of her other customers. Sali thanked her politely, and continued watching the street below, specifically the gaudy yellow double doors of the building across the street.

Daewon and Mali eventually emerged. Her eyes narrowed when they, holding hands, looked both ways before flitting across to the tavern. The two were very public with their affection here, much more so than she ever remembered them being in Nezra. Sali was willing to offer the pair latitude, but they were trying her. What were they going to do next, get married without asking her permission?

"He really doesn't want to live to see the Grass Sea again, does he?" she muttered, taking more of a gulp of zuijo than she intended, searing her tongue.

They arrived at her balcony a minute later, hands unclasped. They sat down and leaned in. "We couldn't get very far," sniffed Mali. "They don't teach Kati."

"Of course not. I would rather die than teach land-chained viper-strike techniques." Sali leveled a look at the two. "Unlike the services our tinkers are providing the enemy."

Sprout remained unfazed. "You can keep your righteousness. You have the option to fight your way out. We tinkers have no intention of dying on account of gear."

"I wouldn't want you to either," she admitted. "So what did you see? Tell me about the layout."

Daewon pulled out his leather-bound drafting binder and sketched perpendicular lines with a charcoal pencil. "Front door leads to an open courtyard. Row of buildings on the left connects to a larger building in the center of the estate. A roof connects the two sets of buildings with a pathway in between leading to the back. On the right side are several clusters of bushes and trees with a pond halfway to the back. There are light sources here, here, and here."

Mali added, "The corner building here appears to be a kitchen. These buildings here have chimneys here, here, and here." She looked around. "Where's your puppy?"

"He scouted the back alley and then headed back." Sali drained her cup and studied the rough scrawl. "Has anyone actually seen the boy inside?"

Daewon ripped out the paper and offered it to her. "No, but Yoon-sa's working as a rickshaw driver and picked up several of their students who couldn't stop warbling about him."

Sali grudgingly conceded that Daewon was fairly competent. He was organized, detail-oriented, and fearless with ideas. As her mother would say, Daewon paid attention to the grain in the wood.

Sali left a small tip and led the three out of the Drunken Monk. They moved through the back streets and alleys, avoiding the crowds, keeping their profiles low. Rose Ridge was known for its war arts schools and housed several military buildings, so few Katuia wandered these streets. Any who did received unwanted attention.

"How many mouths?" she asked.

"The Kati Underground broke a thousand this morning." Mali beamed like the proud mother of triplets.

Sali held her tongue as her shoulders tightened. Their sudden success was becoming a disaster. How could they possibly smuggle this many people back to the Grass Sea safely?

Daewon added quickly, "A fifth are planning to stay. They just want to help out, spit in the Zhuun's eyes." He understood the logistical ramifications of trying to move such a large group. It wasn't just about avoiding and fighting off the Caobiu hunting parties, it was also about the challenge of feeding and caring for such a large group. Their meager supplies wouldn't even feed and shelter half for a week, let alone for the entire journey to the Grass Sea.

They stopped at the end of the alley and turned back in to the main street before cutting across and hurrying through the checkpoint into the Saffron Tenet District. Their conversation died in the bustling street. They kept their heads low and moved carefully until they had safely crossed into their own district.

Sali received nods from several people on the street, including Soa, the food vendor she favored, who had thought it necessary to move his stall next to the inn. She was becoming far too recognizable, and the number of Underground going in and out of the inn was becoming far too conspicuous. All it would take was one inquisitive magistrate to see the steady traffic and grow suspicious.

Fortunately, Esun the innkeeper was also a Katuia Underground volunteer—Sali refused to use the other term—and had opened the back door for the Underground and offered his top two floors. The first was used as storage for their impending exodus, and the top for their headquarters.

Hampa was guarding the stairwell when they arrived. The young man put his fist to his chest and bowed. "Mentor."

"Stop saluting every time you see me," she muttered. The first few days of it were cute. Now she just wanted to headbutt him. *Mentor* was a formal honorific rarely used outside of ceremony or death. Sali remembered using it during her first week at the sect before Alyna—*her* mentor—had ordered Sali to refer to her as sister and threatened to beat her with a cane. Sali loved her mentor all the more for it, but she was not yet ready to give this boy that honor, if ever. "How are things here, Hampa?"

"Your new clothes are folded and packed. Your boots are cleaned, and I organized your pack in preparation for travel. Your favorite vendor has your lunch ready."

That wasn't what she meant when she asked. Sali grunted. "Soa is being a little presumptuous there. And what new clothes?"

"The tailor on Flower Street thought the leader of the Kati Underground deserved clothing befitting her position."

Sali rolled her eyes. Just about every word in that sentence was an abomination.

"Congratulations on the promotion, Weed," quipped Mali.

"Wipe that smirk off your face before I stuff you in a sack."

"Always so quick to violence."

They proceeded into the room next to her sleeping quarters, which had been repurposed as a war room. She greeted the small group clustered around a bed turned into a makeshift table. Every organization, whether it was a capital city or a raiding party, needed administrators. These few in here kept the Underground working.

Sali stood at the end of the bed. "With the new numbers, we don't have enough backs to carry all the supplies. Where are we on transport?"

"We've procured sixteen rickshaws and nine wagons. Paolo works in Quan Sah's stables, says he can steal fifty horses, but that window will be open less than twenty minutes," said an ancient woman named Samaya with a reputation for having once been a fierce beauty and warrior. She was someone Sali's mother had looked up to as a little girl. Samaya was also one of those who did not intend to return with the Underground, but wanted to fight any way she could.

"Eight wheeled vehicles." Sali struggled to do the math. "It's hardly sufficient. No matter. It's the first few days out in the open that will be most pressing. We'll have to curve southeast. The ascent is more gradual. We'll chop the carts to pieces to set up obstructions once we reach the Shingyong Mountains."

"How many are in the exodus now?" asked a bearded man next to Samaya. He sounded shaken. "We only prepared for six hundred people."

"The numbers have changed since last night," said Mali. "It's nearly double."

The man visibly paled.

Daewon was studying the map. "We're not traveling down Dragon's Maw Pass?"

Sali traced her finger along the map down a narrow pass left of the Dragon's Maw. "With these numbers, we'll never stay ahead of the hunters. Our best chance will be to lose them through these passes that run alongside the Maw. There's a maze of paths we can take back east. We used them extensively when we raided Zhuun farmlands. It's heavily forested and easily defensible."

Samaya did not seem to like how things were unfolding. "It'll take three weeks, possibly four or five to reach the Grass Sea with these new numbers, if at all. A few more days to prepare would greatly benefit the exodus. Otherwise, our people may starve or freeze before we reach the Grass Sea. This is not a good cycle to travel."

There was also the matter of killing the Prophesied Hero. As much as Sali was loath to admit it, eliminating that threat was far more pressing than the exodus. Salminde, the Will of the Khan, or any loyal warrior of Katuia for that matter, would focus solely on killing the boy. Salminde, daughter of Nezra, needed to see her people safe with a chance for a new beginning. Sali the Viperstrike, however, refused to let either fail, though it was quickly becoming all too clear that there was only enough time and resources to complete one objective.

The problem they faced was that succeeding in one task would likely doom the other. If Sali led the Underground to safety, there was little chance she would ever again get close enough to kill the Prophesied Hero. But as soon as a Katuia murdered a Zhuun, the city would go on alert and close the gates, making the exodus impossible.

Unless . . . She drummed her finger on the bedpost. "How quickly can we leave?"

Samaya shrugged. "A day preferably, possibly eight hours, but again I encourage you to allow us a few more days to prepare."

Sali turned to Daewon. "You have people watching the boy?"

He nodded. "Yoonsa in front and two at both ends of the back alley."

"Good." Sali tapped the map. "Here's the plan. As soon as we receive confirmation that the boy is inside the school, we raid the school and end the threat to our Khan once and for all. At the same time, we set fires throughout the city. Then, in the chaos, the Underground rushes the south gate and escapes into the night toward the mountains before the army can assemble."

Her plan was met with silence. Daewon crossed his arms. "We tinkers have a phrase. The more gears there are to break, the more breaks there will be."

"One small break breaks everything," added Mali.

"I know," replied Sali. "But it's the only way to accomplish both objectives."

"What about you?" asked Mali. "If you're in the heart of the city while the rest of us are escaping, how will you get out?"

"The raid on the Longxian school will be right behind you. As soon as we kill the Prophesied Hero, we'll follow through the south gate and catch up to the main body. It shouldn't take the night to reach you." Sali pulled out the layout Daewon had provided earlier and studied it for a few moments. "I'll need twenty of our best warriors for the raid. How many does that leave for defenses?"

Daewon counted on his fingers. "Including me? Possibly eighty, maybe a hundred?"

"You don't count."

"I can lead the expedition and fight at the same time."

"You don't count because you can't fight your way out of a fishnet. I need real warriors."

"I am a—"

"Seventy," Mali interjected. "That's including some old enough to have given their weapons away. There's also a sizable group of young men with inflated senses of their prowess."

Sali didn't love these numbers. "Pick your best. Have them here and ready to move at a moment's notice."

Hampa, standing at the doorway, fist-saluted. "I'm part of that twenty, right?" There was definitely a tinge of desperation in his voice.

Speaking of young men with an inflated sense of their prowess . . . Sali was tempted to put him in his place, but also remembered her own time as a neophyte. She had only touched upon the boy's training in their brief stint together. He was strong and not untalented, but he was raw and far too excitable. Sali herself had been just as raw and even more excitable.

"Of course, Hampa." There were other ways to keep him out of danger. "I'll need you to guard the back alley."

Daewon got up. "I'll see to it. So nineteen?"

"Do it quietly." She pulled him by the sleeve down to her level and whispered into his ears. "Make that twenty still."

Sali sat through the group's meeting for another two hours, dozing on and off. She had never had the talent or the patience to deal with this side of warfare. If she had wanted to work with supply chains and logistics all day instead of raiding, she would never have left Nezra.

A stampede of footsteps roused her. Sali bolted to her feet, hand at the handle of her tongue, right as Mali and Daewon burst into the room.

"We have problems," they said in unison, panting.

"You're lucky I have a disciplined trigger." Sali relaxed. "What happened?"

"Ariun's on his way here with a bunch of his council goons to arrest you!" Sprout tensed with rage.

"He's accusing you of sedition," added Daewon, resting his hands on his knees. "He's telling everyone to turn you in if they see you."

Sali shrugged. "He's not wrong. That's exactly what we're doing."

"He's going to arrest you," Mali pleaded. "They will be here any moment."

Sali grunted. "That fool. Whose side is he on? It doesn't matter. He can't stop us."

Daewon's voice dropped low. "He could report you to the Zhuun."

"He wouldn't!"

The tinker's face looked unsure. "It's no secret the Council of Nezra is against our escape."

"Are you going to face him?" asked Mali.

Sali considered how the fallout from a confrontation between them would affect the rest of the district. She shook her head. "There's no need to divide our people. We won't be here much longer. I'll go out through the window."

"There's something else," said Mali. "The overseer at the estate stumbled across a group of Underground smuggling grain onto one of the armor shipments."

"Does he suspect anything?" asked Sali. "Can he be bribed to stay quiet?"

"They killed him."

Sali's stomach dropped. "They killed one of General Quan Sah's overseers?"

"The workers panicked," said Mali. "They didn't know what else to do."

Sali curled her hands into fists. "That shortens our timetable. We don't have much time before he'll be missed, and the Zhuun start asking questions."

Samaya cut in. "Apologies, Viperstrike, but we still need eight hours at least."

"What about the hero?"

"Still in and out of the school every few days, always back by evening, and never leaves after nightfall," said Daewon. "His last sighting was yesterday."

"That will have to be good enough." Sali weighed her options, which were few. She checked the sun still riding high in the sky and came to the only conclusion available to her. "We need to enact our plans tonight."

"What?" said Daewon and Mali simultaneously.

"We don't have a choice. We have to go tonight." Sali spoke firmly. "Get the word out. Make sure everyone is ready and at their places. The decoys, the ones leaving, the supplies, everything. Have those hand-picked for the raid meet me at the Drunken Monk."

Daewon nodded. "I'll see to it."

"We won't be able to gather all the supplies in time," warned Samaya.

"It'll have to do." Sali turned to Mali. "As soon as you see my flare, you break through the south gate and keep going. Don't rest until you hit the mountains. I'll catch up."

Her sister threw herself into Sali's arms. "You'd better be right behind me, Salminde."

Sali squeezed her tightly. "I didn't come all this way just to die now, Sprout." She broke away with renewed determination. "No time to waste. It's time to go home."

CHAPTER THIRTY-FIVE

SERENDIPITY

Qisami's business arrangement with Eifan paid off immediately. A courier arrived with a lead the very next day. The silkspinner had begun to pull his many strings, which gave her three possible leads to the Hero of the Tiandi.

The first was an orphan prince living in sewer tunnels. The boy had organized all the street rats in the city and turned them into a legitimate criminal organization. Now hundreds of orphans were strategically hitting vendors, soliciting protection money, and robbing commerce wagons.

It didn't take long for Qisami to grab the nearest urchin off the street and get him to squeal. She learned quickly that the orphan prince was actually just the rice production cartel trying to seize market share over the noodle cartel. The food industry, much like the dairy, was downright cutthroat.

The second lead was the adopted son of a lord in Sunri's court. Adoption into noble families wasn't uncommon, but this particular lord was young and had not taken a bride, and his son was only a few years younger, which made the stories of the adoption suspect. Many in the web speculated that he was hiding the Hero of the Tiandi. It took Ko-teuni and Burandin most of the afternoon to penetrate his estate's security, but in the end, it was simply a case of true love.

Qisami was now researching the last lead. There had been rumors floating around about a boy studying in a war arts school who had suddenly displayed extraordinary skill. He had arrived in the city only a year ago and had no other family. Eifan had assured her that the information was completely reliable. Then again, he had also been completely sure she wasn't going to stab him, so there was that.

She headed to the Rose Ridge District, which felt especially impoverished and filled with smelly people after her stay at the Onyx Flower District. It didn't take long for her to arrive at the so-called Longxian Northern Fist School of War. The school didn't look like much. Just some tall brick walls and hideous yellow half-moon doors. The outer wall was sturdy, and the tiles on the roof were purposely designed to dislodge from their holds and shatter upon impact as an alarm system. Some of the tiles were a different color from the others, likely meaning they had been replaced in the last year or so. This could have been because of burglaries, but was more likely due to school rivalries. There was easier prey for thieves than a war arts school. The lighting just above the walls offered indications that the interior was heavily lit with lanterns while a layer of soot on the left side of the gates signaled a hearth or kitchen. As with most war arts schools, the guards were likely useless students, but even a harmless pup could bark a warning before losing its intestines.

To gather more information would require looking inside. The school had already closed for the evening, but it was still too early to prowl. Qisami had a few hours to kill. She scanned her surroundings and brightened at the sight of a bar directly across the street. Whistling, she hurried into the establishment, found a table on the second floor next to a window, and ordered plum wine for dinner. In hindsight, she probably should have eaten something first. By the time the Queen rose two hours later, Qisami was resting her chin on her elbow, swinging a drinking urn in the air and singing along to some stupid song about some stupid something stupid. Her vision was blurry and everything was downright hilarious.

A small commotion at the balcony of the bar caught her attention. Qisami craned her head over and saw a gaggle of soldiers clustered around a corner table. She perked up. A bar fight would be the perfect way to end the evening. She reached for her purse to place a bet, then stopped when a few of the soldiers blocking her view parted, revealing a Kati woman sitting alone.

The woman wasn't a normal Kati, however. The sides of her head were shaved, and her hair rose up and was teased back, resembling ram's horns. Her ears had a dozen or so piercings each and her skin was rough with scars. Her expression was perfectly tranquil, and she sipped her drink even while several of those silly soldiers goaded and taunted her. What drew Qisami's attention was the woman's eyes. They were large, sharp, furious, and black as midnight.

"Tell me, Kati scum," a paunchy soldier taunted. "Is it true that you Kati and your horses take turns riding each other?"

The others soldiers around him roared. Qisami's brow furrowed. That joke was low-hanging fruit, worth at best a chuckle. Whatever was happening there really wasn't any of her business, but when had that ever stopped Qisami before? She was about to whip out a dagger when something about the woman's demeanor stayed her hand. This woman did not need saving. She was a lioness tolerating sheep. Those morons were alive only by the grace of her goodwill, and were simply too stupid to realize.

One soldier wearing an eye patch chortled like a braying donkey. "I hear your cities have to keep moving because of the stench your people leave behind."

An older, huskier guard added, "I guarded these savages on the march home after we broke their city. A whole bunch of them cried like babies the first night. I poked one with my spear and asked why, and he told me it was because we built our campfires on the ground!"

The soldiers roared. That last comment had struck a nerve and earned a reaction from the Kati. It was slight, easy to miss if one wasn't looking carefully. Qisami admired her grit no less than her cool, danger-ous beauty. She was especially jealous of the woman's fierce, manicured eyebrows.

After a few more moments of verbal abuse, the woman appeared to have had enough. She stood up abruptly, towering over most of the rab-ble. The chatter died, and the pack of yippy puppies melted back, carv-ing open a path for her. She patiently drained her drink, gently placed the cup on the table, then casually walked past her harassers. The sol-diers stood there, mute, like the used poop rags that they were, and then that was that. The show was over.

Or so Qisami thought.

The soldiers eventually found their spines again after the Kati left. They gathered together and began to gab loudly. She caught phrases like "kinky weapon," "souvenir," and "extra booze money." A moment later, the paunchy one signaled to his men to follow, and the group dis-appeared down the stairs.

She went to the balcony and leaned over the side just in time to see the soldiers turn down the alley. Qisami counted six bodies, which wouldn't be a problem for her, but she doubted this Kati was anywhere as skilled as she was, because no one was. Qisami absently reached for her urn and found it empty. She was about to order another drink when impulse struck her.

Qisami leaped over the balcony, dropping to the ground like a prowl-ing cat. She whistled softly, criminally off-key, as she listed drunkenly from side to side trailing after the soldiers. She caught sight of them right when the soldiers surrounded the Kati. Their coarse laughter echoed against the alley walls.

"It's against the law for Kati to possess weapons. We can have you flogged. If you hand that thing over, and whatever coin you have, we may be willing to overlook this."

"I also like her armor. I've always wanted to own a set of Kati scale mail."

"We don't have time for that, fool."

The paunchy one drew his saber and casually poked the woman in the chest. "Well, what will it be, Kati scum? Hand over your weapon or we'll pick it off your dead body."

Qisami reached for a knife. She had so many targets on that large, plump body. Where would cause him to squeal loudest? She was deciding between inside his right armpit into the lung or his lower back when, unfortunately, the choice was taken from her.

Just as she was about to throw, the woman lashed out, two spear thrusts that sent that many soldiers down within an instant. She grabbed the wrist of another who was drawing his blade and kneed him so hard in the gut his feet left the ground. She dodged a thrust against her back and spun away to safety even as a long whip-like weapon uncoiled from her waist. It twirled above her head and found Eye-Patch's good eye, flattening him on his back.

One drew a large warhammer, only to have the ends of the whip wrap around it. A tug yanked it out of his hands, and his fat mouth ate his own hammerhead when the Kati swung the whip back at him. His head whipped back and cracked against the stone wall. He was already dead by the time his body slid to the ground.

It took three more seconds for Qisami to reach the fight, which was exactly how much time the Kati woman needed to finish the three remaining soldiers. Two lay unconscious at her feet, while the last looked definitely dead, given the way his neck was bent. The Kati whirled on Qisami, her long weapon curled around her body, looking ready to pounce again.

Qisami held up her hand. "Hi! That was magnificent," she beamed. "I saw the commotion and thought I'd join in on the fun, but it seems you're awfully greedy."

The Kati hesitated. "Thank you," she said finally. "Aid is unnecessary—"

Qisami's black knife streaked just past her shoulder. The Kati woman immediately raised her guard, but glanced behind her in time to see the soldier's saber slip from his fingers as he pawed at his throat, spurting blood. He mouthed silently and keeled over.

The Kati lowered her guard but eyed Qisami warily as she walked over and yanked her knife out. She wiped the blade off on the man's tunic and sheathed it. Qisami stepped over two bodies and made her way toward the Kati. "You might want to make yourself scarce, cute stuff. The magistrates get real pissy when soldiers turn up dead."

The woman nodded. "You have my gratitude." She headed to the opposite end of the alley.

"Hey," Qisami called after her. "What's your name?"

The Kati woman turned back. "My name is none of your business." And then she was gone.

Spicy. Qisami appreciated that. "I'll see you around."

She was certain their paths would cross again. There weren't many women like that in Jiayi. Whistling, she walked out of the alley and checked the three moons in the sky. Night had finally fallen, and there was not a cloud in sight. It was near time to sneak into Longxian. She stopped at the entrance to the Drunken Monk and looked inside. Or she could go back in and continue drinking. It was probably best to wait a little while longer for everyone in the school to fall asleep. And she might need to sober up a bit. She'd decide which once she sat down.

Just then, a flare streaked upward and burst into a kaleidoscope of red and yellow bursts. So pretty. Who could be lighting that now? Out of the corner of her eye, she noticed several grappling hooks fly and catch on to the roof. They were soon followed by a line of silhouettes scaling the school's walls. And just as she had predicted, several of the tiles on the roof slid off and cracked loudly against the ground.

A few seconds later, a scream pierced the night.

CHAPTER THIRTY-SIX

RUDE AWAKENING

J ian's sleep was interrupted by a commotion. He opened one eye and blinked. Footsteps trampled past his door. A noise, like a shout, echoed in the distance. He yawned and turned to the other side. A door slammed somewhere. Late-night mischief among the students was not uncommon, although they were usually not so stupidly obvious. A couple of these hooligans were going to pay the price come morning. Jian was just glad he wouldn't be the one getting punished. With a little luck, he might have some chores taken off his hands. He closed his eyes.

A loud, piercing scream cut through the air.

Jian's eyes popped open. That one did not sound like a prank, not even gone wrong. Someone was injured, badly. He bolted upright and reached for his club leaning against the bed. He had pilfered it a while back to maintain and practice his swordplay in private. Swords were reserved for intermediates and above. Another loud crash followed by more screams informed him that something was indeed very wrong. He crept along the floor in the darkness, pawing for his trousers.

Heat blasted him as soon as he opened the door, followed by the smell of smoke and the crackling of burning wood. Something terrible was happening. The school was under attack. Jian froze. Were they after him? He eyed the wall at the opposite corner that led to the alley. Should he escape while he still could, or should he investigate and help out? A voice inside him clamored to leave. He was about to a few days ago anyway. Who cared what happened here?

It was tempting. Jian nearly took a step away, but then Xinde's words rang in his head. He thought about the right thing to do, and wondered if he could live with himself if he fled now. Not on his own terms, but because he was a coward and too callous when his brothers and sisters needed help. If he fled now, that would mean he had learned nothing.

Jian steeled himself and crept toward the sounds of violence. Gripping the club close to his body, both knuckles white, his arms trembling, he moved along the row of sheds and outhouses, then crouched low to the ground as he made his way through the garden. He was doing his best to hide behind a cage of tomato vines when a figure climbed out the back window of the kitchen and fell roughly to the ground.

Jian ran to Senior Gwaiya writhing on her back. Her face was contorted in pain and her breathing was shallow. "What happened?" He noticed the red stains on her hands and arms as she clutched her thigh. Her shirt was gashed open, as if by a blade. "By the Tiandi, are you hurt? Damn those Southern Cross bastards."

"Hiro, I don't think . . ." she huffed in short hard breaths. "You have to run. There are many attackers. Call for help. Summon the magistrates."

"Who did this?" he said as he helped her up.

Just then, a head, wrapped completely in gray save for the eyes, poked out of the window and looked straight down at them. Jian pulled Gwaiya away from the window, but the senior made it only a few steps before her legs gave out. She collapsed, clutching her thigh. The masked figure dropped down, crushing a bitter melon as he landed. He raised his saber.

Jian held out his club. "Get away if you can. Go!"

He didn't check if she moved as he stepped forward to confront the masked man. The first thing Jian noticed about his opponent was that the saber moved unnaturally in his hand, as if the two were not comfortable with each other. Behind the wrappings, his eyes were strangely dark.

The masked man charged, thrusting with his weapon. He was using it as if it were a short spear. Taishi's gravelly voice grated in Jian's head, but he wasn't listening or thinking; his body just remembered. Dancing Girl Spins in Spring parried the blade to the side as Jian brought his club down on the attacker's shoulder, staggering him. He couldn't quite make out his muffled curses and didn't have time to dwell on it as his opponent surged forward. Jian deflected the second thrust and this time brought the full weight of the club onto the man's forehead. The attacker stiffened, then toppled over into a flower of lettuce.

Jian wanted to pull the man's mask off, but decided he needed to check on Gwaiya more. She was still grasping her thigh but now eyeing him as if he had grown a second head. She recoiled when he got close. "The rumors are true. You really are some sort of infiltrating master."

"Thank you for saving my life, Hiro," he shot back. "Don't mention it."

She still didn't thank him as he hauled her to her feet. "Who are you spying for?" she demanded.

Jian rolled his eyes as he boosted her up to the top of the back wall. "We don't have time for this. I'm going to try to find more people. Go get help. Watch the drop on the other side. I hear it's slippery and full of—"

Gwaiya disappeared from the top of the wall and then landed with a splat and a squawk on the other side. "Ack, this is disgusting!"

Another scream snapped his attention back to the school. Jian hurried to the kitchen and crept along the main corridor to the front. He could just make out the sounds of fighting: steel clanging, flesh striking flesh, and cries mixed with grunts and growls. He reached the training ground and was momentarily dumbstruck by the carnage and destruction. There were five bodies—three of them students—strewn across the field. A fierce fight must have been waged here. The water pots were overturned and shattered, the stables were on fire, and escaped animals were dashing wildly to and fro across the courtyard.

Jian caught a glimpse of two more masked figures. One disappeared into the main hall while another had pinned a student to the ground and was holding their head down in the koi pond. Jian was about to jump the drowner from behind when another masked person stepped out from the kitchen. Jian ducked into a split water pot and huddled in ankle-deep water. This one carried a chain whip, leaving behind a trail of dripping blood across the courtyard. The two were dressed similarly in a patchwork assortment of clothing, roughly sewn, loose fitting, and haphazardly assembled. They looked more like field hands than assassins.

The two nodded to each other, then one disappeared into the main residence while the drowner continued the job. The student's flailing arms and kicking legs were weakening. Once the coast seemed clear, Jian jumped out from the vase and charged the assailant. Unfortunately, he slipped with his first step, accidentally kicking a piece of crockery and sending it skidding loudly across the ground. This gave the drowner all the warning in the world to look up and watch Jian's sloppy, off-balance charge. The assailant let go of the student and rose to meet Jian, drawing from his back a pair of tigerhook swords.

Jian recoiled at the sight but did not slow. Tigerhook swords were designed to counter other swords, but were just as effective against staves and clubs. A practitioner would use the hook ends to trap and lock an opponent's blade and then use the bladed pommels to punch an enemy. In a skilled war artist's hands, tigerhooks were extremely deadly. Jian hated them with a passion because in the hands of the unskilled, tigerhook swords were more likely to injure the wielder than their opponent. He had the scars to show for it.

Jian's hope that his opponent was not very skilled faded the first time he brought down his club. No sooner had the weapons touched than his masked opponent slipped the club to the hook and turned his blade. The club twisted violently in Jian's hands, and he nearly dropped it. Jian had to contort his body to hang on, which left him exposed for the other sword. Only by losing his balance and falling flat on his face did he avoid getting his arm cleaved from the rest of his body.

He groaned, catching his breath. Those things were a lot more effective than he could have ever guessed. He rolled onto his back and watched helplessly as his opponent kicked the club out of reach and advanced on him, flaring his tigerhooks in a figure eight.

Jian pawed for a weapon, a rock, anything, but managed to grab only a few small twigs. Hurling them did little to slow his opponent down. Just as he thought this was the end, two large arms wrapped around the man's neck from behind and squeezed. The masked figure struggled, swinging his blades over his shoulder, but then his head twisted sharply to the side and he went limp, falling to the ground.

Standing behind him, chest heaving, was a very wet and very angry Cyyk. The large boy scowled and gave the body of his would-be drowner a swift kick to the ribs for good measure. He walked over and offered Jian a hand. "You saved my life, runt."

Jian accepted it and returned to his feet. "You saved mine. Who are these guys?"

"Only one way to find out." Cyyk tore the hood off the dead person at their feet. He swore. "Kati scum."

The veins in Jian's entire body froze. He had been sure it was just Southern Cross looking for revenge. The dukes would have sent Mute Men, while professional bounty hunters wouldn't have been so poorly equipped. It had never even occurred to him that the Kati would be after him.

The memory of the Kati woman who had tried to kidnap him flashed through his mind. They *knew* about him. *He* was their target. The Kati had likely come to exact revenge for their fallen Khan. He suddenly saw tonight's attack in an entirely new light.

He tugged at Cyyk's sleeve. "We have to get out of here. There could be an army of them here. I know a way out." He began to lead the other boy toward the back.

Cyyk, who was looking over at the main residence, had other ideas. "We need to find the master."

Jian immediately fell in beside him as they crept to the servants' entrance near the back. The sounds of fighting continued around them. They could make out the noises of furniture breaking and several voices yelling over one another.

"That's Guanshi," said Cyyk. "I recognize his grunts anywhere."

"That's Xinde too."

The sounds of battle grew as they crept along the deserted hallway.

They were just outside their master's sitting room when a body exploded through the wood-and-paper walls. Jian took a running start and kicked the masked Kati in the face as they struggled to rise.

The two looked into the sitting room to find a bloodied Guanshi battling three black-clad attackers while Xinde struggled with one more who had pinned him to the wall. That frozen look on his face was becoming too familiar.

Master Guanshi was wielding his long ax, Steed Slayer, with a fury worthy of his title and reputation. The giant golden ax was a blinding arc of light as it twirled around his body and over his head. Something so large and unwieldy shouldn't have moved so gracefully or quickly, but it swung in the master's hands as if an expert dance partner.

They watched Steed Slayer run one attacker through. The master put the heel of his boot to the woman's chest and freed the blade. He brought it around just in time to parry a straight thrust from a Kati coming in from the side. The quicker blade darted left and right before the attacker shot low. The large ax somehow kept pace with the sword as their blades clashed rhythmically, almost like ringing bells.

Guanshi seized an opening when the woman swung too high. He slipped the attack and brought the blade of Steed Slayer down across her wrist. Blood sprayed the ceiling and floor as the sword and the hand attached to it flew across the room. The woman's scream was cut short when he mercilessly ended her pain. The last of his attackers was taken down by Cyyk while Jian hurried to help Xinde.

The four paused in the middle of the room to catch their breath. "Can everyone still fight?" asked Guanshi, eyeing Xinde specifically.

"Yes, master," Jian and Cyyk said crisply.

"Yes, master," added Xinde several seconds later, his words a low mumble.

"You three need to go now and summon help," said Guanshi. "Head out the back way."

"But what about the others? What about the school?" asked Jian.

"I need to search for survivors."

"But—" protested Jian.

"Do not argue with me, son," snapped Guanshi, herding them out of the room. "A good war artist knows when to share his thoughts, and when to follow orders."

They followed their master to the back of the building, moving in and out of rooms and hurrying down darkened hallways. Signs of battle were everywhere. Tables and shelves were overturned, chairs and walls broken. They passed four bodies: two more students, the gardener, and a masked Kati. Xinde's eyes watered when he found Kaosan, a promising student who had joined the school only a few weeks ago. Cyyk cursed when he discovered that the other body was his friend Siang. As much as Jian had despised Siang, he too couldn't but feel deep sadness and rage at his fellow Longxian's fate. Apparently, he was not the only one.

"This is my fault," swore Cyyk. "I'm the reason they're here. The damn Kati are seeking revenge against my father. I'll make them pay."

They had almost escaped out the back, and had just turned down the corridor leading into the garden when a lone masked Kati appeared at the door. She seemed relaxed and undeterred by the odds against her. She held a spear with one hand by its butt end and extended it, slowly lowering it until the tip touched the floor. A formal challenge.

"We don't have time for this." Guanshi hefted Steed Slayer and moved to dispatch the woman. The spear tip sprung from the floor and flexed as soon as Guanshi came within range, almost curling around the ax head to gash his legs. Guanshi flew over it and brought Steed Slayer downward. That should have ended the fight right there, but the Kati eluded the initial attack and parried the second by dancing around the shaft. Her movements were artful, almost relaxed, but quick and effective.

Guanshi's powerful swings and the reflecting light of Steed Slayer were met by the woman's longer supple spear. Back and forth, each sought an advantage. They appeared evenly matched at first.

The spear moved in the Kati's hands in a way unlike any Jian had ever witnessed. It wasn't just an extension of her body, it was its own living creature, a slithering snake that constantly flexed, swayed, and writhed, striking and slashing at his master's defenses.

Sensing the urgency, Guanshi blurred his movements to mask his ax's attacks. Jian had always found Xinde's skill with echo strikes impressive, but it paled in comparison with Guanshi's mastery of Longxian techniques. Whereas Xinde blurred his actions with the memories of his movements, Guanshi's echoes moved chaotically and in all directions, as if they had minds of their own. It was impossible to keep track of what was real and what was an illusion. His two arms became eight just as his two legs became four. Steed Slayer shone so brightly and moved so quickly it looked like a glowing wisp darting around the combatants.

To Jian's—and likely Xinde's and Cyyk's—dismay, the Kati not only held her own against Guanshi's barrage, she absorbed his initial flurry without backing down.

The three boys gaped. "It's another master," Xinde said in a hushed voice.

Duels between two masters were rare and impressive events. These two weren't just masters, however, but powerful ones. As the battle continued, both began to show signs of injury. Guanshi needed just one blow, and nearly landed it several times, but Steed Slayer never found its mark. The Kati, on the other hand, was content to stay far back and use the superior length of her weapon to whittle Guanshi down. Slowly, cut by cut, the Kati master began to mark him. Guanshi's robes grew shredded as the battle continued. Crimson blossoms soon followed.

Their long exchange ended when Guanshi slammed Steed Slayer down on the woman to cleave her in two. The ax bit into the stone tile and stuck momentarily. The Kati master seized the advantage and darted forward with her spear. Guanshi had to drop Steed Slayer to catch the spearhead with his hands, and they struggled even as blood seeped through his hands. Finally, after an intense few seconds, the two traded places and broke apart, with Master Guanshi coming away with the Kati's spear.

The woman walked up to Guanshi's fallen ax, slipped a toe under it, and effortlessly bounced it up and caught it. She admired the weapon, turning it in her hands. "Fine weapon, master." She tossed it back to him, sliding it along the floor to his feet. She offered a more formal bow. "There is no need for more meaningless violence. Give me the boy and there can be no more deaths tonight."

Guanshi returned her respect and tossed her the spear. "Longxian would rather perish to dust and be forgotten in the winds of history than sacrifice one of our own."

"Then honor is the way."

"It is the only way," he agreed.

"Your weapon will be untouched and returned to your family," she said.

Guanshi nodded appreciatively. "And who would claim yours should you fall?" The woman hesitated. He added, "I swear there will be no further retribution from Longxian in its return."

She considered and accepted his offer. "There is a man named Quasa in the Katuia District. He will know what to do."

"Please see that my body is not desecrated," Guanshi said. "It has been years since I have last seen my daughter."

"Burn my body before the magistrates arrive," she replied simply. "My family perished with Nezra."

The two masters continued to relay their wishes for last rites. Guanshi refused to hide the fact that it was a Katuia attack, but offered to safeguard her body from the authorities and return it to her people. In return, the woman promised that the only death after his would be her mark. Lastly, both parties agreed that no word of tonight's events would be spoken to the magistrates. Jian wasn't sure why Guanshi was insistent upon this, but the Katuia master was more than happy to agree.

"It will be done," Guanshi said finally, completing their negotiations with a bow, his fist touching his open palm.

"It is done," she replied, placing her fist to her heart.

The two masters prepared for another round. Guanshi rolled up his sleeves and hefted Steed Slayer over his shoulder. He spoke in a low voice. "Listen, boys, this is where you leave. Right now. I'll buy you as much time as I can."

All three were shocked. Xinde's and Cyyk's eyes brimmed with tears. For Guanshi to order them away before the duel reflected poorly on the master's confidence.

"Master." Xinde's voice broke. "You may need us afterward if you're injured."

"That will be unlikely, son," said Guanshi. He turned to face them. "Listen closely, all of you. Get as far away from here as you can. There is more at stake than you realize."

"This is all my fault, master," choked Cyyk. "These Kati scum are after me. They seek revenge for my father. Allow me to sacrifice myself."

"Don't be an egg white and throw your life away." Guanshi did not take his eyes off the woman. "You have a more important task now. Xinde and Cyyk, I charge you, as disciples of the Longxian lineage, Guanshi family style, to protect Hiro and see him to safety."

"What?" Both boys were near speechless.

Jian was stunned as well. "You . . ."

The master turned and met his gaze, and nothing else had to be said.

Cyyk was staring openmouthed. "Hiro? What does this have to do with him?"

"No time to explain." Guanshi spun his massive ax in his hand as if it were a child's stick. The shaft came to a stop atop his shoulder, and then he settled into the classic Longxian stance, perhaps for the last time. "If you see Sasha again, tell her . . ." His hard warrior face cracked slightly. ". . . tell her I wish I were a better father than a master. Now go!"

Guanshi charged the woman.

Cyyk and Jian had to drag Xinde away as the three fled the masters' duel. They entered one of the dry goods storerooms, shattered the window, and climbed out one by one. They dropped to the corridor next to the kitchen and retreated down the narrow path to the garden at the rear of the estate. Jian and Xinde helped Cyyk up, then Jian went next. As soon as the senior joined them atop the wall, Cyyk hung off the wall on the outside and dropped down to the slippery slope. He loosed a string of curses.

Jian was about to follow when Xinde looked back to the main building. "The fighting stopped," he said softly. "Maybe we should go back."

"Master Guanshi charged us with an oath," said Cyyk, looking up. "What makes Hiro so special anyway?"

"Nothing. I'll gut just as easily as you if we get caught." Jian dropped down next to him and lost his footing. He slipped roughly on his backside and would have taken a ride down the sewer drain on a stream of brown sludge if Cyyk hadn't grabbed the back of his collar and yanked him up.

Xinde landed softly and surely on the ground a moment later. "I warned you about that drop."

They continued down the rest of the slope to the sewer alley. Jian fell two more times, and Cyyk once. The two nearly dragged each other down into the running stream at one point. Xinde, on the other hand, was perfectly poised and made it look effortless.

They sneaked to the end of the back alley and looked up and down the street. The air was heavy with smoke and soot, forming one of many black columns drifting into the sky. A small crowd had gathered to spectate the flames leaping high into the night sky. The three fled to the end of the street, stopping at the end of the block to look back at their school burning to the ground.

"What do we do now?" asked Jian.

"What Master Guanshi ordered. Get you to safety." Xinde scanned the sky. Scattered bright-yellow and orange glows illuminated the night. "What is happening? The entire city is on fire!"

"We should go to my father," said Cyyk. "He'll have this city quarantined by dawn."

"How about the clinic?" Jian suggested instead. Getting involved with the nobility would be the surest way to blow his cover.

"What good is that?" said Cyyk. "One word from my ba and—"

Xinde put a hand over Cyyk's mouth and yanked both to the shadow of the wall. He pointed at the silhouette that had leaped atop the roof adjacent to the school with a long black cloak fluttering in the wind. He couldn't make out her features from this distance in the poor light, but there was no mistaking the Kati. That meant Master Guanshi had fallen.

Cyyk must have come to the same conclusion. His voice cracked. "No, that's not possible."

As much as Jian hated to admit it, he knew that was the likely outcome. Both were masters, but that woman was a level above Guanshi, quicker and more fluid. That and their master was twice her age. "Do you think she can see us?" he asked.

Just as the words left his mouth, the woman turned directly toward them, and he caught a glimpse of what could only be described as two greenish glows from her eyes, like gems reflecting light. The Kati ran along the spine of the roof and leaped completely over the street to the other side, then closed in on them.

Panicked, the three fled with no destination in mind, just anywhere away from this Kati. The possibility of being found out by the dukes and the Mute Men was still better than certain death by the woman who had just killed their master. Jian looked back and caught her running near parallel to them, jumping from rooftop to rooftop while running down their spines. By how quickly she was closing in on them, it appeared he was not going to have an actual say in the matter.

"We're only three blocks from the nearest guard post," huffed Cyyk. The large boy was slowing down.

"We won't make it," said Jian. The Kati was practically on top of them.

Xinde slowed. "You both go ahead. I'll try to slow her down." Before he could break away, Jian grabbed his sleeve and wouldn't let go. When the senior tried to pull free, he pulled back even harder.

The realization that Guanshi knew about him all this time had shaken Jian deeply. For most of his life, people had placed him on a pedestal. He had been the Prophesied Hero, the center of the Tiandi religion, the savior of their people. Jian had never realized the responsibility and consequences of that exaltation, and had just taken it for granted until people started dying around him. Now people who were important to him were throwing themselves in harm's way in order to save his pathetic life. The school was burned down and Master Guanshi was dead. All that weighed heavily on his soul. Jian just couldn't imagine bearing any more of that burden.

The three turned at the next intersection and could see the signpost for the local garrison at the district checkpoint. They summoned the last of their energy and ran, waving their arms and yelling as loudly as they could. For a second, it looked as if they were going to make it. They were less than half a block away from the garrison and had attracted the attention of the guard on duty.

"Help!" Jian screamed. "Someone's trying to kill us."

"Rouse your captain! I demand to speak with him immediately." Cyyk must have found his second wind, because he began to pull away from them the moment he saw the garrisoned soldiers. He huffed loudly. "My father . . . my father . . ."

That was the last thing Jian heard. One moment his feet were pounding the stone tiles and his heart was hammering in his chest, the next, a shadow passed overhead and something caught around both of his feet. Jian found himself tumbling with the world rolling around him. Something had latched on to his ankles and yanked his feet from under him. He had just enough time to cry out before he slammed his head on the cobbled street. His vision dimmed. His ears roared, and everything hurt so badly that nothing hurt.

He blinked once, staring up into nothing. A large plume of black smoke was roiling into the air, stinging his eyes. His left side wasn't responding, and he was having trouble feeling his toes. Jian blinked once more, and then Xinde was there, hauling him to his feet, his mouth opening and closing but making no sound. Jian leaned against the senior, his legs dragging uselessly across the ground.

After what felt like an eternity, Jian regained his senses, as if a bubble had burst and his senses—sight, hearing, and touch—came rushing back. His eyes focused just in time to see the Kati standing close. Her cloak was fluttering in the wind, and this time she wielded a whip of some sort.

Xinde appeared a moment later, looking like he had taken a bad fall as well. He tried to help Jian to his feet as the Kati stalked closer.

"Xinde, Hiro," yelled Cyyk farther down the street.

"Keep going! Don't stop. Get help," Xinde yelled back. He pulled Jian behind him and raised his guard. "Stay back." His hands were shaking so badly, he looked as if he might pass out.

"There need only be one more death tonight," she replied. "Let me keep my promise to your master. Step aside."

Xinde charged her. The Kati flicked her hand, and the whip snapped him once on the shoulder, staggering him. The second time it wrapped around his waist, and she pulled to the side, yanking him with ferocious strength and sending him flying into the wall with a heavy thud.

She then turned her attention to Jian. "We meet again, lad."

"I'm not who you think," he stammered. "You don't need me. The prophecy is broken."

"Your two statements contradict each other," she said mildly. "And I won't make the same mistake I made the last time we met." She snapped her arm out and the whip stiffened into a spear. If Jian hadn't been so terrified, he would have been awfully impressed. The Kati aimed her spear at him. "For my Khan and my people. For Nezra and all Katuia!"

Jian saw the tip plunging toward his heart. This time there was nothing he could do, and nothing else to be done. This was his disappointing, pitiful end, at the hands of a deadly Kati master. He had expected so much more from his life.

The last thought that passed through Jian's mind was one that strangely enough had never worried him before. How would the people react once they learned he was dead? Would they grieve for their fallen hero, or would he become a joke in the annals of history? His mind flashed to the Celestial Palace, the place where he had spent most of his life. What was it like now that he was no longer there? Had it fallen to ruin, or was it a more prosperous, happy place? How would his parents react once they learned that their son, the Prophesied Hero of the Tiandi, the supposed Champion of the Five Under Heaven, had not only failed to fulfill his destiny but also died like a beggar rat in the streets?

Would his parents cry? Would they miss him? Would they be disappointed in him?

He stared dumbly as the point pierced through his shirt. He felt a sharp pain, and then the world exploded. Something hard struck him across the face, sending him flat on his back.

He cried out loudly. That was the second time in so many seconds that someone had sucker-punched him. He sat up, his legs splayed out. He patted his chest to feel the wound. Finding nothing, Jian looked up and stared, dumbfounded. It couldn't be. "Is . . . is it really you?"

Ling Taishi stepped in front of him, her sword drawn and eyes focused on the Kati master. Her lips curled into a snarl. "What did I say about keeping a low profile, you stupid boy?"

CHAPTER THIRTY-SEVEN

REUNION

A single fat tear rolled down Jian's cheek. The emotion was visible on his face, and he reached out as if to touch her to see if she was actually real. It was a pitiful and pathetic display.

Taishi pulled away from his outstretched hand. "What are you doing? Stop it. Get your head straight. We're not out of this yet." She turned toward the viperstrike. "You had your shot. You blew it. It's time to leave while you still can."

"This isn't over," growled the viperstrike, launching herself forward.

Taishi wielded the Swallow Dances in a reverse grip and deflected the woman's furious barrage of angled strikes trying to reach Jian. Taishi kept her position between the two as the spear desperately tried to snake past her defenses. This woman was very skilled, even among viperstrikes, who were widely considered to be the deadliest war artists in the Grass Sea. Given her age and looks, the tongue being her chosen weapon, and the style with which she fought, Taishi knew her name. This master wasn't just any viperstrike, but their standard-bearer.

Taishi came out of the flurry untouched, then she refocused a powerful air current at the viperstrike, blasting her in the chest and knocking her back. It was to her credit that the woman managed to stay on her feet. Taishi sheathed her blade in one smooth motion as the two circled each other.

"Your reputation precedes you, Salminde the Viperstrike," she exclaimed, keeping the Swallow Dances relaxed by her side.

The Katuia's eyes narrowed. "I don't know who you are."

"Now, *that* stings," Taishi said, smirking. "It is never too late to learn. Here are your options. You can attack me and lose, and then I'll hand you over to those two hundred soldiers or so forming up and charging this way. Or you can leave now and fail again the next time our paths cross."

Salminde, glowering suspiciously, checked to confirm. There *was* a group of soldiers spilling out of the garrison. Two hundred was an exaggeration. It was more like fifty, but did it really matter after you counted past ten?

The viperstrike cursed, probably realizing there was no winning this fight. For a Katuia warrior to get so close to killing the Hero of the Tiandi only to come short had to be devastating. Taishi remained calm, but she too was starting to get antsy. That woman wasn't the only one who preferred not to have to deal with Zhuun soldiers.

"Can you hurry this up?" she asked as the mob of soldiers crashed toward them.

The viperstrike, stuck between a horde of soldiers and one of the greatest war artists of this generation, waffled. Finally, she turned away and leaped onto a nearby roof.

"Good call. I'm sure we'll meet again." Taishi spun and hauled the boy to his feet.

He was still staring at her like a creepy ex-lover. "How . . ."

"Later. We have a bunch of eggs rolling our way." She hooked her arm around his waist and was about to jump on a current when he tugged on her sleeve.

"Wait, my friend is over there."

Taishi saw the slightly older boy rising to his knees. She distinctly remembered him trying to fight the viperstrike as she was landing, and taking a beating for his troubles. It was the effort that counted. She walked over to the boy and hauled him up by the collar. "Anyone else?"

Jian pointed at the garrison. Taishi caught sight of a third boy who was being escorted away by a protective circle of soldiers. He had to be a nobleman's son.

"Your friend will be fine. You, me, not so much if we don't go now."

Taishi took off and just managed to catch on to an air current as she teetered with two young men weighing her down. Fortunately, they did not have far to go. As soon as they rode to the top of the nearest roof, she dropped the pair and landed lightly beside them. Both boys were still openly gaping at her, which only irritated her more.

"You came back, Taishi," Jian reiterated in hushed voice.

"You gained weight," she scolded.

"Master Nai, you're the legendary Ling Taishi?" The older boy was equally breathless. "I have so many questions."

She waggled her finger between them. "Cut it out, both of you. What happened to Guanshi? Never mind." It took her a few moments to orient herself. "This way."

The three ran to the end of the building. Taishi, laden with their additional weight, couldn't make it across to the next building with one leap, so she had to drop down to ground level then head back up to the other side. She was glad to see the other boy was able to scale the side of the building using a method Guanshi had developed back when they were sleeping together. The Longxian boy stepped up to the side of the building with his arms and legs moving quickly, almost like a Katuia horse galloping up the wall.

Taishi thought the technique looked ridiculous in what she otherwise considered a relatively bland style, but it was effective. Guanshi's style had always been merely utilitarian. But then he was also fabulously wealthy and owned a large prosperous school in the heart of a commandery, so who was she to judge?

They eventually ran out of roofs to run along and had to stay on the ground. Taishi led them between several buildings before reaching a small plaza at the edge of the district.

"Why did we come here?" asked the older boy. "This is taking us deeper into the city. We should consider . . ." His voice trailed off when a large figure stepped out of a darkened alley. "What in the Tiandi is that?" he whispered.

"Tiandi indeed," Taishi scoffed as her two companions stepped forward to meet them. "Pahm, Zofi, this is Jian and . . ."

"Xinde," Xinde mumbled. He couldn't stop gawking at the hulking Hansoo.

Pahm was directing his own wide-eyed gaze at Jian. The Hansoo's face was stupefied by awe, which looked ridiculous. She couldn't fault him. To meet the central figure of his religion had to be an extraordinarily spiritual experience for the young monk. She glanced over at Jian, who was openly glaring at Zofi for some strange reason. Maybe spiritual, but likely disappointing.

Taishi gestured between the two. "Do you two know each other?"

"No." Zofi waved. "Hello."

Jian's jaw tightened and he looked away. "Hi."

What was wrong with these kids?

"Hero of the Tiandi," said Pahm. "It is the honor of my life to bask in your glory." He lowered to one knee and still had to look down at his object of worship. The Hansoo's obvious spirituality made everyone feel only even more awkward, Jian especially. Taishi had seen this sullen look almost every day she had trained him. She had hoped Guanshi would have stomped it off his face. That apparently was too much to ask.

"The entire city guard will be out like stinkbugs to a flame," she exclaimed. "Is there a place we can hole up tonight?"

"Our school burned down, master," said Xinde. "Where are you staying?"

"We got into the city only a few hours ago," said Zofi. "Taishi wouldn't have reached you in time if she hadn't rushed ahead and left us here."

The two boys exchanged glances. "One of the students' homes, perhaps. Maybe Cyyk's or Auntie Li's?" suggested Xinde.

Jian shook his head. "Cyyk is probably surrounded by Mute Men at his estate in the Onyx Flower District. As for Auntie Li, I don't want to bring danger to her doorstep. She has young nieces. What about the clinic?"

"Meehae probably won't like us bringing trouble to her doorstep in the middle of the night," Xinde mused. "Actually she probably wouldn't mind. But we should ask first—"

"We are long past asking for permission." Taishi herded everyone back into the shadows as a patrol of Zhuun soldiers ran by the alley entrance. "I hope your clinic friend is a good friend. Can we get there by side streets?" She gestured at Pahm. "We have an elephant."

"What's an elephant?" asked Pahm.

"You are, big guy."

Fortunately, the city was in complete chaos, and the magistrates and soldiers were stretched thin. From what they could glean from the people standing about, dozens of buildings throughout the city had been set ablaze. The rumor was that several Kati arsonists had been caught. Also that one of the main gates has been seized by an unknown enemy. Half the people on the street seemed to believe Jiayi was under attack, while the other half had gotten bored and gone back to bed.

The soldiers, magistrates, and fire brigades were too preoccupied to pay attention to a small group scampering in the shadows. They managed to sneak past the gates to the Saffron Tenet District, and from there, it was only a short jaunt to the clinic. The greatest danger to them was the ten minutes of banging on the front door before the glow of a lantern illuminated the darkened window.

It appeared Meehae, their friend who probably wouldn't mind, actually did mind a little that the two boys had appeared at her front door in the middle of the night with a gaggle of strangers.

"Hi Meehae," Xinde began. "We're really sorry—"

"You jerks woke me up." The diminutive woman yawned and turned away, dragging her long, ratty sleeping robe along the floor like a poorly arranged wedding train. "Don't track mud in here."

Jian shut the door as they spilled into the clinic. "Where's Doctor Kui?"

"She's at home in her big house in the countryside," said Meehae, already retreating to her room. "Only her poor apprentice lives here.

Grandma can sleep on the acupuncture table. The rest of you, I don't care."

Taishi bristled. "Who are you calling a grandmother?"

Xinde gestured. "Meehae, this is Ling—"

Not bothering to look back, Meehae waved over her head. "Tomorrow." She disappeared into her room.

Taishi appreciated the girl's single-minded focus on sleep. She turned to survey her little band of misfits. The Hansoo brother had found his way to the clinic's tiny garden courtyard, which was the only place in the clinic where he didn't have to duck his head. Taishi worried about the Hansoo. She wouldn't have brought him along if not for Liuman, who had used his last few breaths anointing Pahm the Guardian of the Tiandi. He confided to Taishi a few seconds later that no such title actually existed, but the young Hansoo needed to hold on to something to keep his faith. Liuman had begged Taishi to see Pahm safely returned to the Stone Blossom Monastery.

"He's a fine stripling," the giant Hansoo had choked in between rough gasps. "Please, watch over him, Master Windwhisper. Help keep his faith and deliver him home."

"I'd rather not" had been her reply, but Liuman had died, and now she was stuck looking after an overly sensitive monk suffering an existential crisis. Pahm had been morose and insufferable since they had laid Liuman to rest, and barely uttered ten words in the entire trip to Jiayi. Not even Zofi could cheer him up. He also cost as much to feed as three men.

Speaking of dour, she eyed the Hero of the Tiandi, who was sulking off to the side as if she had just confiscated his favorite toy sword. What was *he* so glum about? "How are you, boy?" she asked.

His eyes squinted together and he pursed his lips as if he were about to challenge her to a fight, and then Taishi realized he was fighting back tears. "What's wrong with me?" His voice was hoarse.

A little context would have been nice. *Say something nice. Comfort him.* "That's a little broad of a question, isn't it? There could be lots wrong with you."

"Admit it!" He jabbed a finger at Zofi. The dam had broken. Tears streamed down his face. "It's not that you didn't want a disciple. You didn't want *me* as your disciple. That's why you left me here to rot while you found yourself someone else to teach."

Taishi guffawed. "What? You think that gangly, mouthy skin-and-bones is my disciple? The heir to the Zhang windwhisper lineage?" She picked up a small wooden bowl and held it up. "Hey, Zofi."

The mapmaker's daughter looked up from the shelves of herbs she was perusing. "What?"

Taishi lobbed the bowl along a nice lazy trajectory across the room. It slipped between the woman's outstretched alligator arms and bounced off her forehead. Zofi bent over, clutching her head. "Ow, you cheap witch! What was that for?"

Taishi turned back to Jian. "Satisfied?"

He looked abashed. "She's not . . . then what is she doing here?"

Taishi sighed. "I'm not sure myself, but I don't train lost causes."

The truth was, Taishi was glad Zofi had decided to tag along. She had thought the woman was going to set off on her own after they had reached Xusan, and again after they stayed overnight in Loyia, but every time it looked as if she was going to take her leave, Zofi declared that she would accompany them to the next stop.

Taishi wasn't sure if Zofi had nowhere to go or was too scared to leave, but her dry-humored company was welcome, considering the only other person Taishi could talk to was the pouty Hansoo. In any case, the young woman was still here and had proved her worth with her sharp mind. She was better at counting and reading than both Taishi and Pahm combined.

At least Jian looked abashed now. "I didn't know. I just didn't think you were coming back for me."

"Why would you ever think that? I promised, didn't I? The thought of abandoning you never crossed my mind." Never mind those dozens of times it had. At least he wasn't sulking around like a bathed kitten anymore. Taishi looked him up and down. "You've grown, gotten fat with muscle."

"What took you so long?" He was still hiccuping from his fit. "When you said you would come back for me soon, I thought you meant a few weeks. It's been over a year!"

"A few weeks..." Taishi tensed. "Jian, since I left you here, I've been hunted by literally every ambitious pissant with a pointy stick and a suicide wish. I've slept in ditches, trees, mausoleums, and jails. I've had to deal with Mute Men, bounty hunters, shadowkills, the entire Zhuun army, and I nearly got eaten by a pack of ugly dogs with dry skin. I'm deeply sorry you had a difficult time adjusting at this war arts school."

His lips quivered. "It was hard."

Taishi let it slide. Self-awareness had apparently not been in Guanshi's curriculum. She sat down on the acupuncture table and invited him to join her. "Tell me about your time here. Catch me up."

He pulled a stool next to her and followed her request literally, starting with the day after she had left. Taishi was impressed by his clear memory, especially when it came to every small thing that had bothered him. Jian painted a vivid image of the dirty storage shack that he lived in, went into painstaking detail about his chores, and dwelled for a while on his abject poverty. Mostly, though, he ranted about his treatment at the hands of Guanshi and the other students.

Taishi failed to not roll her eyes several times. Everything he described sounded typical for most people who didn't have noble titles and live in sprawling palaces. Even his time at the war arts school didn't sound unusual. "The lunar court can be savage and unforgiving," she said. "It's wolves fighting for fame, dominance, and sometimes just scraps. A war artist often has no one to rely on except those from their school. The school is their pack. That's why it's so important for students to forge strong bonds."

He nodded. "I was just starting to understand that when everything fell apart."

This is what she was really interested in. "What happened next?"

Jian told her about the scuffles Longxian got into with their rival school, and how things escalated when the senior of that rival school cheated and drew a blade on Xinde. Strangely, though he went into excruciating detail about everything else in his narrative, Jian intentionally glossed over his friend's injury.

"Then things got worse from there. The second time Xinde and Keiro fought—"

"Keiro's the other senior?"

He nodded. "Keiro was going to hurt him badly so I just had to help. I didn't want to give away my cover, really. I had no choice." He stopped. "Xinde's my . . . my brother."

"I thought you hated everyone at the school."

"They weren't nice," he added quickly, then reconsidered, looking slightly crestfallen. "But I wasn't nice either."

Taishi leaned forward. Her eyes twinkled as a twist of nervousness jittered inside her. "Explain."

"I was angry for so long. Mad at you, at Guanshi, at the other students. I was mad at the world. Once you get used to being the Champion of the Five Under Heaven, being an impoverished, peasant nobody stinks." Jian became contemplative, almost mournful. "I thought things had turned around a few weeks ago. After that brawl with the Southern Cross, the other students began to accept me."

"That's an important lesson. Brotherhood is an important practice, Jian."

His face turned troubled again. "It didn't last long. After I blew my cover protecting Xinde, rumors spread that I was some sort of master war artist who was spying on Longxian to steal their secrets."

"A master, hah! They really are handing that title around like plum candies," Taishi chortled. "Although war art style theft is also a common practice under the lunar court."

Jian looked a little hurt, but quickly recovered. He had matured somewhat in their time apart. The boy she knew would have stewed for hours if not days over every perceived hurt. He continued. "Now the school's burned down and Guanshi is gone. Everyone will probably blame me. I'll never regain my honor."

The fact that honor meant anything to Jian meant he had learned another important lesson. "Tell me about your training with Guanshi."

Jian became animated once again dredging up the perceived insult that the school had purposely held him back and stunted his development as a war artist. "Six months on the basic three-, four-, and five-stance forms. Half a year, wasted! A week on the basic punch, three on a hammer fist!" He waved his hands emphatically, growing visibly agitated. "These are all skills I mastered as soon as I learned to walk. I did them perfectly in front of Guanshi a thousand times, and he still refused to promote me. He just made me practice the same stupid drills over and over and over again. I swear I've forgotten ten times more from my time at the Celestial Palace than I learned at the Longxian school."

Taishi didn't bother hiding her smirk. "Of course. That was the whole point."

"What?" Jian was taken aback. His eyes narrowed. "You knew about this?"

"It was my idea," she said, shrugging. "Technically Guanshi was following my instructions to break you back down to basics and forget all that drivel your useless old masters had put in your head. I wanted you to start over with a clean slate and a rock-solid foundation."

"But an entire year was lost!"

"Not at all. You were a feral, unruly dog before, and now you've reverted to a freshly housebroken puppy that has finally stopped pissing all over the furniture. You are now finally ready to learn."

"Learn?" His eyes bulged. "What am I ready to learn?"

Best not to get ahead of themselves. She glanced over at the mapmaker's daughter, who had taken it upon herself to reorganize the floor-to-ceiling shelves full of medicine bottles. "Why don't you reintroduce yourself to Zofi. You made faces at her all night."

Jian slid off the stool. "I *was* being a jerk again."

All right then, credit him with a little self-awareness. Another improvement. Taishi watched as he picked his away around the growing collection of jars all over the floor. He stopped halfway across the room and looked back. "I'm glad you're here, Taishi. I really missed you."

I missed you too. Instead, she shrugged. "Good."

CHAPTER THIRTY-EIGHT

AFTERMATH

I t took Sali most of the night to make her way back to the Katuia District. The city had erupted into anarchy. Buildings burned, a haze of smoke enveloped the skies, and fire brigades were confused about which fire to put out first.

The arson decoy teams had overachieved. They had managed to simultaneously set flame to a building or checkpoint in every district, even the Onyx Flower District. It was as if the earth had cracked open and unleashed the Ten Terrors of Hell onto Jiayi. Katuia warriors easily overpowered the guards at the south gate and held it long enough for the entire exodus to escape into the night. By the time the stunned Zhuun authorities could wrap their head around what was happening, runaway servants were the least of the army's worries.

The entire night went off surprisingly well, save for Sali's part of the plan. She had not only failed to kill the Prophesied Hero, she was also now trapped in this accursed city. Magistrates staffed every intersection, gate, and watchtower, while soldiers swarmed to lock down the streets.

It was lively, to say the least. All three moons painted their colors across the earth. Stealth wasn't one of Sali's strengths, but there were many other distractions competing for attention. She managed to avoid most of the commotion by staying on the rooftops, hurdling narrow gaps or sneaking across balconies. Several times she had sighted small black-clad groups moving above the city as well. Were they Zhuun operatives, or opportunistic thieves? Sali couldn't be sure. She didn't get close enough to see.

A dozen or so thick columns of smoke, blacker than night, drifted into the air, forming their own cloud ceiling over the city. The fiery blooms pushing back the night provided the perfect distraction. Like moths to lanterns, they lured eyes and bodies, leaving Sali a clear path back to the Katuia District.

She really should have been heading in the opposite direction and finding a way out of the city. If things had gone according to plan, she would have linked up with the exodus and been halfway to the Shingyong Mountains by now. But of course things were rarely easy. It physically pained her to have come so close only to fail.

Dawn was threatening by the time she breached the perimeter walls of her district, finding a small gap between parapet patrols. It was a race against the rising sun as she jumped onto and over the wall. Her fingers contorted into claws as she skimmed down to the ground, then retreated to a darkened corner. She quickly oriented herself and proceeded toward the inn on the opposite end of the district. The early morning still provided some shadows, but they were quickly receding.

Sali was just about to turn onto the main street when she was forced to backpedal behind cover. There were pointed hats everywhere, kicking down doors and dragging people out of their homes. A large group of people had already been rounded up and were huddling on their knees in the middle of the street. Sali bit down on her lips. There was nothing she could do to help them, and a death wish helped no one.

Sali retreated deeper into the alley, staying low as she crossed through a small tent city, past a landfill, and into a narrow pathway wedged between two buildings covered from the sky by several layers of cloth canopies dangling overhead. She turned abruptly at an intersection when she spotted a group of pointed hats heading in the opposite direction. A shout from them notified her that they had spotted her as well.

Sali turned, weaving around obstacles while hurdling over debris and garbage. She crossed a short bridge and continued down a walkway running parallel to a sewage stream curling around a bend.

"Stop her!" That voice coming from close behind her was all the warning she needed.

Sali turned again and ran smack-dab into another squad of pointed hats. Both sides were momentarily startled. It was up to the one who recovered first to seize the advantage. In this case, Sali punched the consciousness out of the nearest magistrate, and then threw the second down into the sewage channel. A club glanced off her chest, and then she spearhanded the third in the throat, sending him gasping like a fish on land.

The last soldier, a large, brawny man, wrapped his arms around her and threw her into the wall. Fortunately, her armor saved her ribs from cracking. They struggled loudly and brutally as they bounced from wall to wall, smashing a wooden fence. His death was quick and violent. Sali ended it by impaling him on a sharpened fence post.

She continued on as more cries of alarm drew closer, which were soon joined by others from every direction. Sali stopped at a small, awkwardly arranged courtyard nestled in among four buildings and scanned the area furiously. There had to be a way to get back on the roofs, but the walls were sheer with no handholds in sight. It would take too long to scale on her own.

This place also looked vaguely familiar. Then Sali noticed the citrus tree wilting in the center of a sad garden area. Her eyes followed to a nearby staircase leading belowground. Of course!

She jumped the railing and rapped on the door quietly, but insistently. When no one answered, she drew a dagger to wedge it into the doorframe. Kicking it down would make too much noise.

Sali was about to force the flimsy door when it swung open, revealing Quasa with an arm drawn back and a short spear in hand, ready to strike. He lowered it and beckoned her in. "Salminde, what are you doing here? You're supposed to be far away with the exodus."

"Something happened." Or more like something didn't happen. "I'm on the contingency plan now." She actually had none. "Can you shelter me?"

The custodian of the viperstrikes beckoned her in. "Of course."

He closed the door behind her as she stumbled inside. Sali drew her dagger and crouched facing the door. Quasa took the position to the side of it. The two waited. The quiet was interrupted first by shouts and footsteps, then the knocking of fists on wood, before, slowly, returning to the morning calm.

Finally, Quasa moved to a crack in his walls and peered outside. "The enemy have moved on." He leaned his spear against the wall and looked up and down. "I see you're still up to your old habits, sneaking out and staying up all night again. I always tell you, nothing good happens after nightfall." He pointed at the stove. "Would you like some tea?"

The strain of the previous night finally broke. She cackled softly as the tension drained from her. "That would be wonderful, heart-uncle."

Sali, exhausted, melted on the wooden stump and watched as Quasa puttered around his home wearing a torn burlap apron. For a moment, Sali was a sprout again sitting at the sect's hearth, listening to Quasa weave his outlandish tales of his viperstrike days as he cooked over the communal griddle or roasted duck over the fire. Quasa had once been known for his paired spears, and likely could still match spears with many of Katuia's finest.

She was ashamed not to have spent more time with him since her arrival. Time had passed so quickly. There was so much that had had to be done, and with the burden of the exodus and killing the hero boy, she had completely forgotten about her old friend. "Quasa, I'm so sorry not to have visited you earlier."

"Nonsense, Salminde." The custodian smiled. "You've been busy since you arrived, as I would expect from the daughter of my heart-sister Mileene."

She frowned. "How did you know about the exodus? Did you join the Katuia Underground?"

"Didn't everyone?" He broke into a wide toothless grin. "I was one of the first when I learned who was leading us."

"I'm not the leader," she replied. "I don't know where that rumor started."

"Oh, it was never spoken that you were, officially. I hear it's some tinker boy." Quasa brought over a cracked clay pot and two drinking urns. "But Nezra knows her shining stars. We all assumed—all knew—that once you joined the Underground, you would become the voice of our people."

Sali's cheeks flushed. She glanced to both sides. "I need to admit something."

"You are always free to speak your mind, Salminde."

"It's all a lie. They all speak of me as if I came to lead our people to salvation. I just wanted to find my sister. I had not considered for a moment—" She gestured at their surroundings. "—this suffering afflicting our people. In fact, Mali had to convince me to help. This shames me."

"I knew that, child. Everyone does. Your family had always been ambitious, far too haughty and elitist, but always acted with honor. No one holds your motives against you. What matters is what you chose. You could have walked out the front gates with Mali and been back in the Grass Sea by now. None would have held it against you. Instead, you stayed to risk everything."

"I was out of potato sacks," she muttered. Deep inside she knew she would have been just as happy to abandon those here if she could have just stolen Mali out of the city. Fortunately, her kind and caring sister would have never allowed it.

The two settled down over their tea to wait out the turmoil outside. The morning turned into a fine distraction after the previous night's debacle. Quasa, always the storyteller, regaled her with tales of her early years. Sali had heard them many times before. Quasa tended to recite the same stories over and over again, but hearing his familiar, comforting voice warmed her.

"I just don't understand how you can ice-cold stare down a herd of charging raptors without blinking yet scream like a seedling at a harmless garden spider." Quasa wheezed between fits of coughing and laughter, "I have a confession. Remember when that sack of spiderlings exploded in your saddle during mounted exercises?"

"Don't remind me." She shuddered.

"That was me. I was the one who planted it in your bags. Alyna ordered it as a mental exercise. If I recall, you failed spectacularly."

"What!" Sali's face turned crimson. "I ran my horse straight over the falls and nearly drowned us both."

Quasa's chuckle was raspy and labored. "I know. I was the one who fished you out."

It had happened a long time ago, but the burning humiliation still felt hot and fresh. The mentors did eventually stamp out her fear of spiders, but only after leaving her hanging in a pit of them for three days. Even then, to this day, those demonic bugs made her uneasy.

Sali passed the time with one hand on the urn and the other on her tongue. The truth was, she was only half listening as her mind replayed the events of the previous night. She had come *so* close. The boy had been within her grasp. It had been her chance, possibly the only one she or any of her people would ever have, and she had failed. She had failed twice now. This was a shame for which she could never atone. There was only one way to wash it clean. A curse escaped her lips.

"Is something the matter?" asked Quasa, noticing her clenched fist. Her emotions had always been unshaded to him.

"I'm sorry. I'm distracted." She glanced at the morning rays piercing into the room between the cracks. "I do not know if the exodus made it out of the city. I sent the rest of the survivors of the raid to join them. I don't know if Mali or my neophyte made it out."

Quasa arced an eyebrow. "You, Salminde, have a neophyte?"

She grunted. "Long story. It was an impulsive decision made out of anger."

"Would you like me to see? I can ask around. An old worn-out man will not attract attention."

"No, you have done enough already, my friend." Sali drained her tea and stood. "It's late morning now. I should go. Thank you for the shelter and comfort." The realization that this likely was the last time she would ever see him temporarily overwhelmed her. "Thank you for everything."

Quasa's smile and steady calm were as comforting now as the first day a terrified and nervous girl had walked into the sect's headquarters. "You've gifted an old man a fond last memory, child."

Sali embraced him and turned to leave. "Why didn't you join the exodus? You don't surely prefer it here. You belong in the Grass Sea."

Quasa shrugged. "There are dozens of us old ones who joined the Underground, but chose not to go. It's not because we don't want to return home, but we are old and frail, and would only slow the exodus down. Our lives have been lived. We hope by staying behind, we help ensure that future generations will live to see what we will not."

Sali's eyes brimmed and her voice broke. "You will always have a place at my hearth, heart-uncle, and live as long as my heart beats." Their embrace was long and gentle. Her arms trembled. Even if Sali succeeded in escaping Jiayi, she was leaving a piece of herself here.

"I will return for you one day," she said finally.

"This old man is at peace." There was a finality to his words as he ushered her out. "Now lead our people home."

Sali was awash in a torrent of emotions as she left Quasa's home. It had never occurred to her why many of their people who'd joined the Underground still chose to stay. If the exodus managed to succeed, it would be those left behind who would be the forgotten heroes. Except Sali was intent on making their sacrifices known.

The chaos from the previous night had died with the sun, but the air was still tense as pointed hats staffed the intersections and patrolled the streets. Sali had to creep around the back streets for the better part of the morning until she neared the entrance to the district. She hid in an alley across the street and watched as a crowd gathered around the inn.

Her breath caught when the magistrates marched Esun, the innkeeper, out of the inn and dropped him to his knees. The charge, a magistrate with two feathers sticking up like rabbit ears proclaimed loudly in Katuia for all to hear, was housing and abetting a terrorist. Then, to cries and gasps of the crowd, another pointed hat looped a noose around his neck and pressed down on his back with his foot.

Sali had to once again fight back the temptation to charge into the fray and kill as many Zhuun as she could. She had to remind herself that useless sacrifices were not sacrifices all. It was merely an empty meal for her wounded pride. Still, Sali's heart and outrage nearly overrode her head.

"Pst, hey, mentor, Salminde," a voice hissed from somewhere up above.

She looked up and saw Hampa on a nearby roof failing to look inconspicuous as he waved to get her attention.

She cursed. "Hampa. What are you still doing here?"

He pointed toward the back of the alley and disappeared.

"That fool." The one time he decided to disobey her. Sali had no choice but to go where he directed.

At least the young man had survived the raid unscathed, although that was mainly because she had made him guard the front doors. She had lost over half of her warriors last night, good and loyal people—at least loyal—who had offered themselves for the greater good of Katuia.

The two met just inside the broken door of an abandoned building. If anything, he looked even more drained than she.

Sali grabbed a fistful of his shirt. "You were ordered to leave with the rest of the raid to join the exodus."

"And I *said* my place is by your side," he shot back. "And nothing *you* say will change that."

Finally, a little spine. Sali had been waiting for it. The Rite of Defiance was an old tradition among viperstrikes. How long could a mentor push their neophyte until they finally pushed back? Hampa had taken much longer than average. But then Sali had taken just as long, if not longer. At least Hampa wasn't scraping to her like she was the blasted Khan. Not even Jiamin required so much groveling.

She was about to congratulate him on finally growing a backbone when she sniffed the air. "What is that stink?"

"I jumped into that green river that cut through the city." He shuddered. "That's how I escaped. The Zhuun are terrible to their waterways. It was full of garbage and refuse."

Sali didn't have the heart to tell him that there was no river that ran through Jiayi.

"What were you doing up there?" she demanded.

"One of Samaya's men found me. I've been keeping watch for you ever since. Come, follow."

Hampa led her a short distance to a small abandoned Tiandi temple half submerged in a pond of sewage. The rear of the temple housed a storeroom that was still dry. It had a small bed of hay in the corner and a recently used hearth in the center of the room.

"We can rest here for now," said Hampa. "Samaya will meet with us soon. You can use the bed."

Sali didn't have the energy to object. Last night's battle had taken more out of her than she thought. It was the fights with those two masters. Sali had already been worn down after Longxian. The man had been skilled, and may have posed a real threat in his younger days. Both knew the outcome as soon as their blades crossed. She would have let him live had he surrendered, but the master was intent on buying time for the boys. Sali respected that.

That old woman, however; she was something else. From their very first blow, Sali had felt her strength. Who was she? What was she doing here? The jing Sali had had to expend even to withstand her blows was frightening. The last time Sali had felt such power was when she and Jiamin had taken their sparring too far. She had always hated the fact that she had usually bested her friend before he became the Eternal Khan, and had never bested him since. This woman was on his level. If she was the Prophesied Hero's protector, then Sali's mission was over. There was little chance Sali could defeat a grandmaster on her own.

Her worries about this new dilemma receded as exhaustion took over. The bed smelled like rot and vomit, and the hay scratched her skin, but sleep overtook Sali nearly the moment she closed her eyes.

CHAPTER THIRTY-NINE

IN HIDING

Meehae barged inside the clinic, banging the doors open violently and shaking the walls.

Jian, who was quarreling with Zofi on how best to reorganize the medicine drawers, looked over. "Hey, Meehae, how did that meeting with your—" He coughed. "—friends go?"

"No time! Everyone hide, hurry. She's coming."

To Jian, there was only one woman who could elicit such a response. He bolted to his feet and pawed for the nearest weapon, which happened to be a broom. "What? She found us, how?"

Both Pahm and Xinde, who were squatting over a small kettle set over a firepit, rose to their feet. "Who found us?" asked the senior.

"Who else, my master! She has an emergency client on her way here now." The apprentice acupuncturist began sweeping the counters clear and kicking the clutter into the corner. "Why is this place such a mess?"

Taishi, who was napping on the acupuncture table in the middle of the room, lifted the towel off her face. "What are you blabbing about, girl?"

"Doctor Kui is coming here! She'll arrive within the hour. We have to clean up. Get moving!"

"Oh. Wake me up a few minutes before the hour's up." Taishi lowered the towel back down and rolled over.

"I thought your master was in the country," said Jian.

"An emergency, Hiro!" Meehae sniffed the air. "What's that stink?"

Pahm pointed at the steaming pot. "We're making congee. Would you like some lunch?"

She cocked an eye. "Yes, I'm famished, but why does it smell funny?" She cocked an eye at some plants on the cutting board set next to Pahm. She pointed. "Is that what I think it is?"

Pahm picked it up and sniffed. "You mean ginger?"

Meehae stomped over and snatched the gnarled plant from his large hand, then shook it in his face. "No, this is rabbit root. It's used to cure infertility and costs its weight in silver. Who told you to pull this from the shelf?"

Pahm looked confounded. Even though he was squatting, his head towered above the others. "I didn't know."

"My master's going to kill me, you dumb ox. This root matures only once every six cycles!"

The Hansoo bowed his head. "I'm sorry," he mumbled and walked away.

Meehae looked equally confused as the large Hansoo retreated, shoulders slumped, feet dragging, back into the garden. "What's wrong with him? Never mind. Everyone clean your mess up. If Kui finds out I've turned the clinic into a fugitive camp, she'll have all of us out on the streets."

"Hey," said Xinde softly. "It was an accident. Go easy on the brother. Pahm was just trying to help out. All we had was rice, and he wanted to cook something nice for everyone."

"I *was* going easy."

"Pahm tends to take things a little personally. Please be kind."

Meehae shrugged. "Whatever. It's already forgotten. I just have to source more of the root, and it's not easy." She turned toward Jian. "Hey,

Hiro, I mean Jian, or whoever you are, light that row of candles. I need them melted into oils before my master arrives."

"I'll take care of it," said Zofi, moving away from the stacks of jars. When he reached out to grab the next one, she reappeared next to him in a blink to slap his hand away. "Not until I return. I don't want you messing up my system."

He clutched his hand and watched the woman go to help Meehae. Who was she to tell him what to do? He reconsidered. What Jian had learned about her in the three days they'd been cooped up in the clinic was that Zofi was detailed and sharp. Almost too sharp. Nothing seemed to get past her. Not only could she do math well, she had an incredibly frustrating ability to predict several steps ahead and guess what he was thinking. She demonstrated this by crushing him at Siege, a popular game using a wooden board with grids and a pouch of colored pebbles. The woman not only beat him mercilessly nine out of ten games, she did so in the most unsporting way. She took great glee in chewing up the board bit by bit until he was one lone little piece.

Everyone set about helping clean, including Pahm after Xinde convinced Meehae to apologize. It was filthy with the consequences of so many people in such a cramped space. The least they could have done was tidy up after themselves, something they had neglected up to that point. The only one who didn't lift a finger was Taishi, who was snoring softly in the middle of the room. At one point, Meehae was going to kick her off the table, but both Jian and Xinde rushed to stop her.

"Who does the mean old lady think she is, anyway?" she snarled, reluctantly backing off.

"Just let her sleep," said Xinde.

"You probably shouldn't call her an old lady either," added Jian.

The place was made presentable enough to satisfy Meehae just in time for her master's arrival. She stuffed four of them into her bedroom and managed to hide Pahm behind the back shed.

A little while later, several new voices entered the clinic. They were followed by a small stampede of clip-clopping footsteps. Kui's distinctive high-pitched voice crackled for more lights. Meehae went out to greet their new patient, and then a cow mooed.

"This is my apprentice, Meehae." Kui's voice could be heard through the walls. "Why is this place so filthy, child?"

"My deepest apologies, master," she responded. "I haven't had enough time."

"Make the time," the master snapped. "This is a medical establishment."

"Yes, master."

"Now, move that table aside for our guest." Kui took on a noticeably softer tone. "There, there, my sweet thing. Come closer. Give the girl some room."

Another low, rumbling moo followed.

Taishi, who was still half asleep, blinked. "Is her patient a cow?"

"Only when business is slow," Jian explained. He wasn't sure why he thought this was something she needed to know.

They spent most of the day hiding. There was much mooing and panting. At one point the cow kicked the wall and Meehae was told to scoop up all the droppings. Eventually, the voices on the other side cleared up. The cow was the first to go, followed by the voices of three men who trailed away one by one. Kui gave Meehae final instructions before the sound of a door shutting shook the walls.

The door to their room swung open, and a worn-out Meehae looked inside. Her apron was stained and covered with guts. "You can come out now," she said, waving tiredly.

They shuffled out of the room into what looked like a slaughterhouse. All of the furniture had been pushed to one side, and there were bloody rags everywhere.

Xinde's mouth dropped. His eyes were full moons. "What happened in—?"

She held up a hand. "Just. Don't."

"Sure. Oh," he said, trailing after her. "What happened with your meeting?"

Meehae snapped her finger. "Yes, I forgot. I got an answer. My people have agreed to help smuggle you out of the city. You can all thank my ba."

Jian experienced a surge of relief and anxiety. "Really?"

Zofi raised an eyebrow. "Who exactly are *your* people?"

"It's a long story," said Jian. "You don't want—"

"Iron Steel." Meehae did her little double fist pump.

Zofi blinked. "Is that the underworld?"

"Did you say you have a way out of the city?" Taishi demanded, pushing her way to Meehae. "How, when?"

"With the next shipment of weapons. They wouldn't tell me when, just to be ready. It could be tonight, or a week from now," she replied. "When it happens, a waste wagon will drive by around midnight. It'll drop us off at the entrance to the sewer hub. Someone will meet us to guide us out."

"Are you coming with us?" asked Jian.

"Just to the city walls. You'll need me to talk to the Iron Steel."

"What about you?" Jian asked Xinde. "Are you coming with us?"

The senior hesitated. "I haven't thought that far ahead."

Jian was reminded at that moment that he wasn't the only one who had lost everything. The senior's entire life up until now had been Longxian. Not only had Xinde lost his war arts lineage, he was now homeless. If Jian hadn't been so self-absorbed, he would have considered how his presence had affected those around him.

He didn't have long to dwell on it, because Meehae made them pay for their housing by putting them to work not only cleaning up the cow guts, but also scrubbing down every last thing she could think of so her master never chastised her again *for someone else's filth*, she made sure to add before stomping off to bathe.

Xinde wiped the floors while Pahm rearranged the furniture. Zofi helped sterilize the needles, and Jian disposed of the bloody rags. They cleaned into the night and the next morning, pausing for subdued meals. Each time, Pahm lifted the heavy acupuncture table with one arm and carried it across the room as if it were a sack of flour to clear the way for them to picnic on the floor, then carried it back when they were done. Jian marveled at the war monk's strength. They had exchanged hardly four words since they had met, which was a feat considering the limited space they occupied.

"Hey, Pahm." He smiled. "We haven't really gotten to know each other. I'd love to learn more about you, since we're related in a way."

Pahm's eyes widened and he mumbled something low and incomprehensible.

"What was that?"

"The Hansoo serve the Tiandi, Holiness." It was surprising to hear such a soft voice from such a huge body.

Jian gave a start. "Me? Oh, you don't need to call me that. I'm just Wen Jian. Taishi tells me you're a Hansoo brother. I've never seen one up close. You're very impressive. Xinde tells me you recently lost your mentor. I'm sorry."

"Brother Liuman served the Tiandi."

"I see." An awkward silence passed. "I've heard great stories about the Hansoo's prowess in battle."

"We dedicate our body and soul to—" Jian couldn't make out the rest. "Excuse me, I have to move ... things," said Pahm abruptly. He put the acupuncture table down and retreated to the far corner of the room.

This guy didn't just look like he was made out of stone, he was acting like it too. Jian's patience ran thin. "Hey, did I offend you?"

Pahm stiffened. "Of course not, Holiness. Please excuse me." The war monk fled back to his spot in the garden.

Jian was dumbfounded. "Was it something I said?"

Taishi chuckled nearby. "You really don't get it, do you?"

"What do you mean?"

"You don't understand your significance to these people. The Hero of the Tiandi is the central figure of the Zhuun religion. You are their mythological savior, practically a god even." She glanced at Pahm. "Of all the clergy in the Tiandi, the Hansoo are the most dedicated. Their dedication allowed them to survive the torturous transformation they go through to become that." She looked back at Jian. "All this for *you*. And you don't even know it."

"Of course I do," he sputtered.

"Do you, really? Think about it. *Really* think about it, boy."

Now that she challenged him to look inward, Jian realized he wasn't sure if he really did. He had always taken the enormousness of his position for granted. But after meeting the Hansoo and seeing the many sacrifices that so many had made protecting him, Jian felt it more deeply. He had taken their devotion for granted in the past, but after the recent events, he was beginning to receive their faith with a sense of humbleness instead of pride, and, for the first time, a feeling of responsibility. His stomach sank.

He peeked over at the Hansoo slipping the iron rings onto his wrist one by one. "If I'm the center of his religion, then why is he acting so weird around me?"

Taishi didn't mince words. "He's probably disappointed."

Those words bit deep. "In the broken prophecy or in me?"

"Think about it, boy. The prophecy is about a mighty warrior who vanquishes the invincible Eternal Khan. His destiny is to lead the Zhuun to victory and usher in an era of peace and so on and so on. There are songs and poems and children's tales about how the Champion of the Five Under Heaven ushers in paradise. Think about how a devotee must imagine their savior looks." Taishi plopped herself into the chair where he worked, forcing him to clean around her. She grabbed him by the shoulders and spun him toward a mirror. "Now look at that."

"That's not fair!"

Taishi shrugged. "Don't take it personally, boy. Put yourself in Pahm's very large slippers. Not only has the central premise of his religion failed—or so he thinks—" Something about the way she said that rubbed Jian the wrong way. "—but when finally given the holy blessing of meeting the legendary savior of his people, instead of a mighty warrior god, he is delivered someone so utterly and completely ordinary."

"I'm still young. I just need more training," he protested. "I will be ready by the time I—"

"It doesn't matter. The young Hansoo is looking at the wrong things anyway."

Jian frowned. "Are we still talking about me?"

Taishi rolled her eyes. "Pahm, like most, is too busy looking for the obvious. What do you see when you look at me, Jian?"

"Well," he stammered. "You're . . ."

"Old, feeble, crippled? A weak old woman." She pressed her finger into his forehead. "Until we cross fists and I crush your head like a sun-baked melon. Even war artists too often believe that strength and power are derived from the body, when in fact the body is simply a conduit for the mind and the jing." Still staring intently at Jian, Taishi flicked a finger at the mirror; instantly cracks crawled across the glass.

"Hey," shouted Meehae.

"I'll pay for it," said Taishi, still eyeing him. "Pahm is disappointed because you don't look like the Hero of the Tiandi should look." She cracked a smile. "Not that it matters. All our heroes will eventually disappoint us and let us down, one way or another. Best remember that, Wen Jian."

"You won't let me down, right, Taishi?" he asked.

"I already have, boy."

After the cleaning was done, the group spent the rest of the day preparing for their escape. Jian was a blend of anxiousness and excitement as he packed his clothes drying on the line in the garden. It had been a little over a year since he had arrived from the Celestial Palace hidden inside a vegetable wagon. It felt like a lifetime, yet it also felt like everything was still the same. He was still the Prophesied Hero and still being hunted. His skills had still not developed. He was no wiser or more experienced, and no closer to fulfilling his destiny.

At least Jian had *had* a destiny a year ago. He had had a purpose. He had lived in a palace that had once been the home of ten generations of emperors. An army of soldiers and servants had served him, and he had had the best teachers from all over the Enlightened States. The fate of the world had rested on his shoulders. He had been an important person.

Now he was just a commoner like everyone else, and fleeing Jiayi the same way he had arrived: sneaking through the dead of night in a wagon, hunted and impoverished. The only difference was he had been on his deathbed a year ago.

Jian grunted. He wasn't out of the city yet. There was still time to end up on a deathbed. He pulled down the still-damp robe he had worn when he fled the Celestial Palace. He still didn't know why he kept it. It was torn in several places, faded in others, and several spots were so stained he couldn't tell what color had been underneath the grime. He rolled the robe up and threw it into his satchel.

Jian looked back and saw everyone working. Xinde and Meehae packed food for the trip while Taishi and Pahm polished and cleaned their armor and weapons. Zofi was on the other side of the garden packing the rest of their wash. These were all the friends he had in the world, two of whom he had just met. He loved Meehae like a sister, looked up to Xinde, and worshipped Taishi, and all three of them were commoners.

For the first time in his life, he was all right with that. It didn't bother him anymore. The mantle of the Hero of the Tiandi was heavy, and Jian had carried it his entire life, even after the prophecy had broken. Even now its corpse weighed heavily upon him with every bitter step. He shook his shoulders, feeling the muscles across his back move and shift. Everything still felt the same, but it also didn't. He couldn't quite put his finger on it, but it made him smile as he finished getting ready to leave everything he knew for a second time.

CHAPTER FORTY

WILL OF THE PEOPLE

I t felt like no sooner had she closed her eyes than someone was shaking her awake. Sali groaned. "I would kill someone right now to get eight good hours."

"It's well into night, Viperstrike," Samaya said. "I'll give you a moment to wake."

Sali nearly rolled over and asked the elder to come back tomorrow when every worry that had been weighing heavily upon on her pricked her mind. She sat up, blinking away the sleep. Her body protested the movement, and she grimaced as she rolled her shoulders. That was when she realized that her armor had been stripped off.

Sali glanced at the doorway and noticed Hampa standing guard at the door. Splayed out on the floor next to him was her scale armor. It had been somewhat cleaned and repaired. He had even managed to pull out some of the damaged scales and work them back in place. Her neophyte had made a few mistakes in its repair and reassembly, but had otherwise done passably at maintaining it. In his defense, it had taken quite a beating during the fight. Stripping her armor while she slept was a little presumptuous, but Sali gave him a pass.

She walked over to a relatively clean water basin and washed her face. "What's the news outside?"

The elder sat on a broken stool. "By last count, one thousand four hundred thirty-four freed souls made it out of the gates, Viperstrike."

"How many didn't make it?"

Samaya turned mournful but nodded appreciatively at Sali. Those in the warrior caste rarely inquired or even cared about civilian casualties. "We lost over fifty at the south gate, and then another hundred forty-six were caught with a wagon and two oxen laden with ground meal within sight of the city walls. Another eighty-four are unaccounted for—either they didn't make it or they changed their minds. Everyone else made it free, including your surviving warriors from the raid."

That was one small sliver of good news. "And Mali?"

"Both your sister and the leader of the Kati Underground are at the head of the main group. They are safe for now, with each step taking them closer to the Grass Sea. That is more than I can say for you, Viperstrike."

That much was true. Sali loosed a resigned sigh. In hindsight, the decision to stay behind could prove to be a fatal one. "How bad is it out there?"

"Like you kicked a hive of acid wasps. I haven't seen this many soldiers on the street since the day we arrived. Quan Sah has declared martial law over the entire commandery. Every district gate checkpoint is now crewed by an entire squad, and the Kati District has been completely locked down. Pointed hats are going door-to-door harassing and beating people. Half of the army has encircled Sheetan, and the other half is mustering to pursue the exodus. It'll likely take them no more than three or four days before they depart."

This was all expected, but Sali had not anticipated the land-chained moving so quickly. Every day she remained in Jiayi was another day the exodus was pulling away without her to protect it. The penalty of breaking indenture was steep. If the Zhuun army caught the exodus, they might not return with survivors.

"I'm going to need our spies to locate the Prophesied Hero again."

"That would be a problem." Samaya's tone sounded more like a negative. "Almost all of them are gone with the rest of the exodus. Those few who remain have limited reach."

"How am I going to find this boy?"

Samaya considered for a moment. "There are groups of Zhuun that may sell this information. It is their business to know things. I do not know if they will work with Katuia, but I can inquire, if you wish."

"Do so, if possible. The reemergence of the Hero of the Tiandi takes precedence over everything." *Almost* everything.

The elder nodded. "I will do what I can. For now, I believe it would be best if you stayed here out of sight. The pointed hats are taking everyone in. Most who remain are old, are sick, or have willingly shackled themselves. You stand out like a lion in a herd of antelope."

"Please do so quickly. The longer I stay in Jiayi, the farther away the exodus gets."

"I will return soon when I have news." Samaya heart-saluted and ambled to the door.

"Soon" stretched from one night to two. Samaya sent word by the end of the third day that the Zhuun data brokers had rebuffed her inquiry for their services. The silkspinners would not sell information to any Katuia. She would keep trying, however.

By the fourth day, Sali could no longer keep her anxiety at bay. She had little to show for her decision to stay in Jiayi, and was beginning to question her mission altogether. That night, feeling the need to do something, anything, she left the hideout to return to the school to search for clues. However, the pointed hats' hold on the Katuia District was still tight, with constant checkpoints and patrols on every street, and soldiers on the parapets at every twenty paces. It was far above Sali's abilities to sneak past the perimeter walls without discovery. The entire district had turned into a prison.

Sali's already limited choices took an even darker turn when an armed group arrived at her hiding spot the next day to arrest her. What was surprising was *who* came to take her.

Sali crossed her arms as they flooded the room and surrounded her, their leader entering last. "So this is how it ends, with the mighty defensechief of Nezra carrying water for the land-chained. How did you find me?"

"The Council of Nezra still leads the people here, Sali. Who's left of them." In truth, Ariun looked haggard, like he hadn't slept in days. There was still steel in his eyes though. The man was ready to kill. "Do you know what you've unleashed on our people?"

She nodded. "I do."

"They're rounding up those who remain: the old, the sick, those innocent to your plot. They're all being beaten, interrogated, killed even, because of you."

"My heart aches," she replied, "but doesn't that prove my point that our people need to be out from under the boots of the land-chained?"

"We had peace," he roared. "Stability, order, even prosperity for some."

"There's no peace or stability or any of those aspirations for those bound to indentured servitude!"

"Three-quarters." He paced the floor. "Your so-called exodus led three-quarters of our people to their deaths."

"Not if they make it back to the Grass Sea."

Ariun drew a large club from his waist and leveled it at her. "The weight of their deaths will rest on your soul." The defensechief was a formidable man, especially in cramped quarters and flanked by a dozen guards. Each had made their point. He stepped closer. "Listen, Salminde, the Zhuun are demanding your arrest. Just like offering Sting was the price I had to pay to have a voice for our people, your life will be the price for peace."

She met his gaze. "Our people in the exodus will need me to survive. Like you said, they are my responsibility."

"Will you come willingly?" he hissed.

Sali stood firm. "There are greater things at stake, Ariun. Think of it. The Hero of the Tiandi is out there, here, in this city. The next Khan must be found. The exodus needs protection and leadership. Nezra can be reborn. Now is the time to rise, not cower."

"Turning yourself in is how you can repay those who remain. Come willingly." The defensechief reached for her tongue.

Sali caught his wrist with one hand and drew her knife with the other. "I will not do the land-chained's deeds for them, but I will also not come willingly. If you are to hand me over to the Zhuun, then you will hand them only my body. My soul will be free."

Ariun looked down at the knife in Sali's hand with the blade aimed back at her.

"You have to be the one to do it, Ariun," she said, hovering close to his ear. "I hold you blameless."

Ariun studied the blade for so long she wasn't sure what to expect. Then he wrapped his large, callused hand around it, gripping it tightly until his fingers turned white. His arms shook. Sali stared intently at his face, waiting for the killing blow.

An eternity passed.

Then Ariun's body spasmed. He uttered a muffled, pained cry and tossed the knife down on the floor. He swore, pacing the room, occasionally jabbing the air. Sali and the guards stayed still as the leader of the Council of Nezra kicked over a wooden barrel. Finally, after he had expunged his rage, Ariun refocused on the object of his anger. "Promise me you'll see the exodus to the Grass Sea. Promise me you'll see them safe. Promise me that Nezra will ride again. All of this!"

"Upon the stars that map the sky, the legacy of my blood: my father Faalsa and my mother Mileene, the continuing strength of the Eternal Khan, and the spirit of our people," she responded solemnly, "the exodus will see the dawn rise over the Grass Sea again. Nezra's curved towers will sail once more. Our people will have a home again."

It took several moments for her words to sink in. She could see the many lines around the defensechief's eyes quiver and recede, slowly fading to smoothness. He finally nodded. "A person cannot offer more than everything. You better make good on this, Salminde." He looked around the room. "You should move to our headquarters. We can protect you there. This swamp is a dump. You'll catch malaria."

Sali watched, puzzled, as the council guards left one by one. "What happens now, Ariun?"

"What else is there to do? The Zhuun demand a price for the welfare of those who remain, and it still must be paid."

"No, that isn't necessary—" she protested.

He cut her off as he turned to leave. "Save your breath. It is done. If your paths ever cross, get Sting from that mangy-faced bastard Quan Sah, and return it to my family."

CHAPTER FORTY-ONE

STRANGE ALLIANCES

The old Kati woman asking questions looked nothing like Eifan's mnemonic artist had sketched, but his description of her had been perfect. That man needed a new line of work.

Qisami stepped from shade to shade staying on the woman's tail, moving with the practiced invisibility required of her profession. The old woman stopped frequently, talking to shop owners and passersby alike. It was obvious she was a person of stature within this community, although she looked as ragged as anyone. She had offered to pay the silkspinners a princely retainer too. Qisami wondered how an indentured servant could scrounge up so much liang. She had to represent someone powerful.

It was unusual for the silkspinners to be unwilling to sell to the Kati. The brokers were many scummy things, but normally they were equal-opportunity capitalists, never biased against any particular group, even the Zhuun's enemies. To them, information was information, gold was gold, power was power.

Qisami made her move once the woman entered a run-down building. Just as she opened the door, revealing plenty of darkness inside, Qisami stepped into a shadow across the street and reemerged in the room. The Kati gave a start when she walked in upon Qisami teetering on a wobbly stool.

Qisami waved. "Hello."

The woman stopped. "I apologize, mistress. I must have entered the wrong building."

Before the woman could retreat, Qisami spun off the stool gracefully, stepped around into the darkened hallway, and reappeared behind the door. She pushed the woman back and closed the door behind her.

The old woman gasped. "What sort of demon are you?"

"I'm the helpful kind," she quipped. "Word on the street is that a Kati hag was inquiring about the whereabouts of a young man attending the Longxian war arts school."

The woman's eyes narrowed. "Are you a silkspinner?"

"Not exactly," she replied, "But I think we can help each other. I have a proposal for your client, because we both know this information isn't for you. Take me to her, and I promise you this will end well for all parties involved."

The woman considered her offer, then rejected it. "I'm sorry. You have mistaken me for someone else." She tried to walk past Qisami, but the shadowkill continued to lean against the door. The woman asked. "Am I a prisoner here?"

Qisami pulled her hand back. "Just a friendly proposal. If you change your mind—" She looked around. "—mark a circle on that wall."

"I do not understand. I am just a simple commoner, mistress."

"Sure you are."

Qisami allowed the old woman to leave, then followed her again. The woman was now moving at a quicker pace despite her age, no longer bothering to stop every few steps to chat with everyone. Qisami stalked her deeper into the district until she eventually came to a stop at a run-down estate with guards at the front gate. The woman exchanged a few words with them and entered.

It took Qisami all of three seconds to slip past these buffoons, and soon she was following the woman through a decrepit manor house swarming with busy Kati. If she hadn't known better, she would have thought this was some sort of government house. It made keeping up with the old woman even more fun. It became a game, avoiding the Kati walking about, creeping through the hallways, slipping in and out of shadows. The old woman eventually made it to the back of the manor and continued into the rear garden. She reached a bridge and proceeded across it to a gazebo set on a small island in the middle of a pond.

This was as far as Qisami could go undetected. There were two armed guards at the foot of the bridge, and the pond was just large enough, and the area around it just out in the open enough, that no amount of shadow-stepping was going to get her across undetected. That left her favorite option. All she needed to do was wait for confirmation, which she received a few seconds later when a tall figure with that fierce mane of hair stood up to greet the old woman.

Qisami scurried from the bed of flowers in which she had camouflaged herself and closed the distance to the two guards at the bridge. She could tell from the way they leaned on their sharpened broomsticks that neither was alert. They were the sort of fodder you used to soak up enemy arrows before you sent in the real soldiers.

Qisami was upon them before they could react. She waved. "Hello, you two tadpoles." Because she was here on a diplomatic mission, she decided to be gentle. She had learned from experience that murder was a terrible way to start a relationship.

Both guards were slow to wield their spears. She punished their failure to return her greeting with hard shoves. Both had time to cry out an alarm before they plunged into the green waters. Qisami plucked a reed from the pond and placed it in her mouth. Whistling, she strolled across the bridge.

Another guard emerged from the gazebo and charged. "Hello to you too," she called, waving, before she sidestepped his rusty sword. His blade sliced down into the rotting wood. Qisami swept his legs, flipping him onto his head and bouncing him into the pond. The next guard was a little more skilled than the previous three, and was properly armored with a heavy metal chest plate. She was also strong, competently wielding a large poleax.

Qisami played with her for a bit, allowing the guard to practice thrusting at air. Then she grabbed the shaft and, with a quick twitch, knocked the woman into the murky water. She watched curiously as the guard flailed and struggled to stay afloat before the waters finally overtook her. This one might actually drown in all that heavy armor. Well, the Kati couldn't hold Qisami accountable for a drowning, could they?

Qisami turned to give the next Kati a bath when the fierce woman from the bar leaped from the gazebo and landed with a thud that shook the rickety bridge.

Qisami brightened. "Hi, remember me?"

It took a breath before the woman actually did. Her eyes narrowed while her hand curled around the handle of the tongue holstered at her side. "You just attacked my people. My adviser says you accosted her earlier."

Qisami held up a finger in protest. "'Accost' is such a strong word. I was merely asking for a meeting."

"What business do you have that you would attack our hearth?"

Qisami glanced over at the pretend-soldiers fishing themselves out of the water. The one in the heavy armor was still nowhere to be seen. Qisami would probably have started worrying about her right about now if she had actually cared.

"Hardly an attack," she scoffed. "More like a . . ." She struggled for a less aggressive term. Failing that, "So how are you?"

The woman pressed. "Speak quickly, land-chained."

"Straight to business. I like that." Qisami nodded at the old woman in the gazebo glaring at her. "That old bag over there was making quite a bit of noise trying to buy information. She returned empty-handed, but because I am such a phenomenal person and I think you are too, maybe we can work something out." She waggled her eyebrows and leered.

"You have the information we seek?"

"Not yet. I will, but that's not your real concern."

The fierce woman drew her weapon. But instead of pointing it at Qisami, she snapped the tongue and straightened it, lowering it into the water. A moment later, the armored guard emerged, clinging on for dear life. After she was done with the rescue, the fierce woman spoke again. "Tell me, what is my concern?"

Qisami put her hand over her heart. "First of all, I'm Maza Qisami. And you are . . . ?"

"Still none of your business. Speak, or leave."

Qisami rolled with it. "All right, None-of-Your-Business. I'm going to call you Business for short, also because you're all business. We both have a problem, which I think I can solve for both of us."

Business's expression didn't change.

"Fine, if I have to spell it out," said Qisami. "I watched you dazzle from afar that night. Very impressive, I might add. You had the hero in your grasp, but that old windwhisper whipped you from the Ngyn Ocean all the way to the Grass Sea. You're pretty 'pretty' and pretty good, you hot spicy soup, but you can't beat her."

"And you can?" said the Kati, coolly.

"No, I've tried. That bitch is *good*. I'm after the brat too." Qisami flashed her brightest smile. "So let's do it together. Let's team up, kill the windwhisper, and then gut the brat. What do you think?"

"What do you want with the boy? What's in it for you?"

"Just his death," she replied nonchalantly, "same as you."

"We don't know where he is hiding. He may have already fled Jiayi."

"Aha! That's where you're wrong," exclaimed Qisami triumphantly. "The silkspinners won't talk to your servant over there."

"She's not my servant."

"Whatever. They won't deal with her, but they'll deal with me. Don't you worry that luxurious mane of yours. I'll take care of it. I know for a fact both he and the windwhisper are still in the city, probably desperately trying to find a way out, especially now that the entire commandery is under martial law."

"And you need my help to kill this windwhisper, and then you'll hand over the Prophesied Hero?"

Qisami held up a hand. "I'll even let you make the killing blow, but I'm afraid I will need his body, or his head at least. Something to confirm the kill."

The Kati's eyes narrowed. "You're a bounty hunter, then."

That was an insult in shadowkill circles, but Qisami let it slide. She was a little soft for this woman. "A girl has to eat. So what do you say, Business?"

The woman considered her offer, and then nodded. "You may call me Salminde."

Salminde had several more demands before accepting the arrangement, most of which Qisami was happy to either acquiesce to or lie about. The viperstrike would need to know the plan ahead of time. She wanted a map of the area in which they would be operating. She needed a way out of the city immediately after the kill. The list went on.

So high-maintenance, but so worth it.

In the end, Qisami satisfied the woman's concerns. "Very well. This arrangement is acceptable, but if I sniff betrayal in any way, one of us will not survive our next meeting."

"That sounds fabulous, Salminde." Qisami enjoyed how that name rolled off her tongue. What a pretty name. "I'll send word once we're ready."

"You will come personally, alone."

"Even better."

Just like that, their conversation was over. As Salminde turned to leave, Qisami decided to go for it. "One last thing."

"What is it?"

"Do you like zuijo? Or plum wine? I have a fine stash of quality opium. We could get some . . . at a nice establishment . . . together . . . sometime?"

"No." Salminde walked away without looking back.

"Take that as a maybe," Qisami called after her cheerfully.

Every guard she passed shot her darts of death with their eyes. She met each of their looks with her own plus a smirk. No doubt they were all wondering how she had sneaked all the way into their inner sanctum. As she passed the outer walls of the estate, Qisami lightly touched the Kati in charge of security and wrinkled her nose smugly in passing.

"It was easy."

Koteuni was waiting for Qisami when she finally emerged from the sewer system on the other side of the wall a while later. Security around the Kati District was so heavy, she almost hadn't made it out. It required a lot of patience to creep from shadow to shadow across the guard stations before she finally got to the lower levels.

Qisami waved at her second as she stomped up the street. Koteuni was leaning against a wall with her face buried in an opened banana leaf wrapped around sticky rice she held in her palms. Qisami scratched her forearm to get her attention, and Koteuni fell in line beside her. Qisami held out a hand.

"What?" asked Koteuni.

"Where's my dinner? I'm starving."

The woman's mouth stopped chewing. "I ate it."

"That was mine!"

"Sorry, Kiki, but you were gone all day. What was I supposed to do? I don't even know why you even wanted backup for this errand."

"To hold my sticky rice," Qisami snapped. Koteuni offered Qisami hers. "No I don't want yours."

"What took you so long anyway?"

She sighed. "Everyone looked alike down there. Everywhere I looked it was old people."

"But you found the viperstrike." Koteuni gestured for more information. "How did it go?"

Qisami's face lit up. "I think we have a connection. She's a cold one, but I'm hot pepper enough for us both."

Her second rolled her eyes. "I mean about helping us take down the windwhisper."

"She'll do it, for me." Qisami chortled as they continued through the Saffron Tenet District. This was a good opportunity to dazzle and get acquainted with this mysterious Kati while they both went after the same score. There were few activities more intimate than fighting alongside someone. Killing that hateful windwhisper witch was just a nice, fat bonus.

The pair entered the Onyx Flower District and stopped by a nicely decorated restaurant with elegant calligraphy on the signage and bright yellow Zhingzi: THE DRAGON'S POINTED TEETH: HOMESPUN NOODLES AND FRESH RED BEAN BUNS. "Come on, I'm starving."

They were soon sitting at a booth, using their wooden chopsticks to drum on the table and generally making a ruckus. Qisami flicked her chopsticks around her finger as she glared back at any stares. They ordered one of everything and settled in for their meal.

She slurped loudly from the teacup. "Hey, so I'm thinking about closing the atonement for my father."

Koteuni clicked her tongue disapprovingly. "About time, Kiki. You know how much the Consortium hates keeping cold contracts. It's bad for business, an annoyance to keep on the books, and that coin just dwindles in escrow until the job's completed, which by the rules only the brood can atone."

"You don't have to lecture me." Qisami felt sheepish. This was a loose end she *should* have burned off years ago. Something was holding her back, which was annoying. She didn't like emotional tethers of any sort.

"When are you thinking about going for it?" Her second pulled out a neatly folded paper. "Honestly, our schedule is pretty busy until next spring of the next third cycle. We have jobs lined up, and a long list of people to kill." She licked her thumb and turned several pages. "Maybe I can move a few things around, maybe skip that whole trip to Lawkan. That place is boring anyway, though I was hoping to spend some time on the beaches."

Qisami dreamed about the look on her father's face when he learned of her accomplishment, but this was not the time. "Don't do anything yet. We'll talk more after we bag this mark."

"I'll come with you if you like. The progenitor kill always feels a little weird." Koteuni reached out and squeezed her hand. "You might want someone to cry on afterward or something."

Both women shuddered, and then broke into laughter.

"I could use someone reliable to carry my dinner," said Qisami. "Maybe Haaren."

"But hey, a little cell business," Koteuni continued. "I have a suggestion. Promise me you won't boil until you hear me out." Her second leaned in. "I think we should let Tsang go."

Qisami was aghast. "How can you say that?"

"Come on, Kiki. He's a terrible grunt. He can't cook, he can barely count, and he launders like a pea-brained chickpea."

"That's all true, but he's *our* pea-brained chickpea," replied Qisami. "I really don't feel like housebreaking a new grunt, and Consortium rules say we need one." She scowled. "Stupid rules." There were always so many rules. Her eyes narrowed. "Tsang's a cracked egg but he's not *the* worst. Why do you really want to get rid of him?"

Koteuni looked a little wistful. "I really want a girl."

Qisami brightened. "Me too!"

"Think of how much more fun it would be if we had a girl," chimed Koteuni. "We can mold her in our own image."

"She would definitely be smarter than Tsang, and probably launder clothes better too. Imagine, neat, folded, and carefully put away."

"Backrubs during baths," added Koteuni.

"We could go to room salons and stab men for fun." Qisami slapped the table loudly. "You know what, let's do it. Let's get a girl."

"Really? That's great. You're the best cell leader a girl could wish for!" Koteuni reached out and planted a kiss on her lips. "Can I pick her out?"

"Sure, but no blondes. I'm not loading up on dye vials again."

Their embrace was interrupted when a waitress brought over a pot of tea and a bowl of fruit. Koteuni poured two cups, and they were about to toast to getting a girl when a stuffy-looking bald man in fine robes invited himself to their table and ruined their moment.

Qisami glanced irritably and flashed a blade. "Whether you're buying or selling, we're not interested."

"Your interest is irrelevant, Maza Qisami. My name is Sabana Yoshi, and I am with the Central Orb."

There went her appetite. A quick glance of the man's appearance, the quality of his spectacles, and the refined embroidery lacing his collar, added to that ugly scholar's bag hanging off his shoulder and the intentional creep of a tattoo climbing up the side of his neck, and Qisami knew exactly whom she was dealing with.

"Look," she began. "To be fair, Eifan's my cousin, so it's just a little family . . . drama. He's still breathing. It's no big deal."

The rat-faced man acknowledged that with a blink of his beady eyes. "The fact that you are related makes it worse. However, the weblord of Jiayi's health is not our concern."

"What do you know. He didn't make that stupid name up," Qisami muttered under her breath.

"Pardon?"

"Never mind." She crossed her arms and leaned back. "What do you want then?"

"I am here regarding your recent inquiry into the Hero of the Tiandi. A conflict check submitted to us the other day by silkspinner Eifan raised concerns about some rather delicate information. Given your reputation, Maza Qisami, we have a small situation that requires addressment. How certain are you of the Prophesied Hero hiding here in Jiayi?"

"As certain as if the Prophet of the Tiandi himself had told me. I just need your web . . ." Her eyes narrowed. "But you already knew he was here, didn't you?"

Yoshi made no attempt to deny it. "The silkspinners know the world better than the world knows itself." This was their official motto, on their pamphlets and everything. "Our organization was made aware of the boy-hero of the Tiandi's presence in Jiayi within days of his arrival, even before the bounty was placed on his head."

"Why have you held on to this information? Everyone in the world was looking for him. You could have sold it to the dukes for a fortune."

His eyes scanned the table and stopped on the fruit bowl. "The key to a perfect banana is to pick and eat it at the right moment." He chose one out of the bunch, slowly peeled it, and took a bite. "Picked too early, the banana tastes bitter and waxy. Too late, it's too sweet and soft."

Oh, but he was irritating. Qisami eyed the fruit as she gnawed on her lip and suppressed the urge to stick her butter knife into the wrist-wagger's neck tattoo. She hated being talked down to, but even *she* knew not to mess with the Central Orb. "The payoff for this banana metaphor better be good, or you're going to walk out of this room less than perfect."

Yoshi smiled. "The Champion of the Five Under Heaven is an unripe banana. He's just a harmless, confused boy. The dukes simply want to rid themselves of this nuisance to tie up loose ends. Boys, however, if given the opportunity, eventually grow up to become men. Men with ambition and drive, and likely a thirst for vengeance. The boy-hero's unique status lends itself well to this path. In three or four years, the boy will man up and inevitably try to fulfill his destiny."

"You want him to become a threat before you sell him," nodded Qisami. "Then the silkspinners will sell him back to the dukes for two to three times the current offering price."

"More like ten." He bared a set of yellow-stained teeth.

Qisami and Koteuni stared wide-eyed. A hundred strings of gold liang could probably purchase their own duchy.

"What happens if someone finds the boy before he ripens?" asked Qisami.

The silkspinner shrugged. "It is a calculated risk. No investment is without uncertainty, but to the Central Orb, the Prophesied Hero is a long-term asset worth nurturing."

"And no one has found him in the middle of one of the largest cities in the Enlightened States except me?"

"If only you were so clever," said Yoshi. "You're not the first one to have discovered his location. A bounty hunter six months ago dug too close. We put a stop to her inquiries."

Qisami yawned and stretched her arms out, curling her hands into fists. "Is that what you plan to do with me?"

"Unfortunately for us," explained Yoshi, "you're not a lowly bounty hunter we can simply erase, so we'll have to come to another arrangement."

"Is that so? And here I thought I had to pay you for the information. What are you offering? If you're going to ask me to hold back from killing him for another five or so years, save your breath. The boy is mine."

"The Central Orb was certain that would have been your position.

Excuse me." Yoshi signaled to the waitress. "Oolong tea, please, right off the boil." He turned his attention back to them. "Here is our offer. The situation in Jiayi has become untenable for the boy, especially with the Kati uprising. The silkspinners will pay you to capture him alive and bring him to us unharmed. The Central Orb will relocate him to a safer environment for the time we believe he needs to fully ripen. In exchange for your cooperation, we will release the information you seek and provide you all of the logistical support and connections with the local underworld. This must be accomplished in complete secrecy and you must never speak of it again."

Qisami shook her head. "That won't work for me. No deal." Half the reason she wanted to capture the boy hero was the notoriety. What was the point of going after the most wanted fugitive in all of the Enlightened States if no one heard about it?

"We'll pay you triple the current bounty, provided the boy is delivered safe and on our terms."

It was a testament to her acting skills and control of her face that her jaw didn't drop, which was more than she could say for Koteuni, who erupted into a fit of coughs. Triple the highest bounty ever offered for any contract was more than her cell could earn in two lifetimes. Still, greed could scratch only some of her itches. The game wasn't only about coins. The notoriety they would earn from collecting this bounty was so much more delicious.

"Sorry, still not good enough."

Koteuni, who was staring pointedly at the fruit bowl, nudged Qisami with her foot under the table.

Sabana Yoshi stared intently at Qisami for a while, long enough to make the exchange awkward. Finally, he nodded. "The Central Orb will also offer to buy out your contract with the Consortium."

This time Qisami's mouth did drop. She recovered quickly enough, but the damage was done. "For my entire cell?"

"Everyone except for your grunt. Unfortunately, the Consortium, per policy, do not relinquish trainees."

"That's not a problem," said Koteuni quickly before she realized she had spoken out of turn.

"Not a problem at all," echoed Qisami. She racked her brain. The offer was already too good to be true, but she would rather drown puppies than take a deal without getting the last word. "Three times the bounty is not enough. My cell will need five, which makes my cell and the silkspinners equal partners." Her second could barely hold in her consternation. This time, the nudge was a sharp kick.

Yoshi's face betrayed nothing, but the silence that followed reflected his opinion on her outrageous request. "Four times the original bounty. Half upon delivery and half when the boy's bounty is sold."

The two went back and forth a few more times, but the contract amount and the offer to buy her servitude from the Consortium was all that really mattered. Everything else was just toppings on the patbingsu.

"Then we are agreed," said Yoshi after their negotiations were concluded. He brought out a knife and a small wooden block. He sliced open his forehead, dabbed a drop of blood from it onto the flat part of the wood, then slid it across the table to Qisami. After she did the same, he took out a matching block and pressed the two together. A few seconds later, after the porous wood had absorbed the angry red liquid, he handed one of the blocks to Qisami. "Consider our negotiations complete. Return to the Willow Swaying and the Maiden's Tail and present this to Silkspinner Eifan. He will know we've come to an adequate arrangement, and that he is allowed to release the restricted information. Which by the way is quite time-sensitive, so I suggest you pay him a visit right away." He stood up. "Good day."

Yoshi had barely stepped out of the room when the two women held each other's hands and squeezed. Koteuni basked ecstatically. "We're rich, Kiki."

"And we'll be free." That meant a lot more to Qisami than any amount of liang. The lack of acknowledgment for fulfilling the greatest bounty in history still bothered her, but everything had a price, and their freedom was a steep enough bounty to cover that.

"Wait," said Koteuni after the two touched glasses in a celebratory toast. "What about the Kati? You promised her the kill."

"Meh." Qisami waved dismissively. "We'll worry about that later."

CHAPTER FORTY-TWO

THE ESCAPE

The waste wagon pulled in front of the clinic shortly before midnight on their fifth night there. It could not have happened soon enough. Everyone was growing impatient waiting for the Iron Steel.

As described, the waste wagon was laden with junk: twisted metal, rotting vegetables, splintered beams of wood. The driver, a small weasel of a man, climbed down to reveal a secret compartment under the wagon bed. He held the lid open and chittered with his lips. The five hurried from the clinic and slid into the cramped hold, all but Pahm. The Hansoo was forced to hide in the back of the wagon underneath a tarp.

The driver and Meehae exchanged hand signals, and the latch closed. The wagon creaked all around them as the wheels ground against the stone pavement. Narrow slits between the wooden boards offered glimmers of the outside. Jian caught flashes of buildings and walls, lanterns hanging off poles, and a staffed guard tower with torches. If he listened closely, he could hear Pahm directly above him muttering a Tiandi mantra over and over again. Strangely, it was something about him, so it made Jian rather self-conscious.

A soldier barked a muffled order to stop, the driver offered a gourd of wine, and then they were off again. The rest of the way was mercifully short, and the wagon finally rolled down a ramp before coming to a stop at a wrought-iron half-moon gate. The compartment door swung open, letting in a blast of cool air. The driver looked around furtively and beckoned them out. He pulled out a large black key and went to work on the lock.

"Someone is coming," Zofi hissed. Jian tensed as a patrol turned the corner and came into view.

The driver craned his head back and waved. "Oh hi, Faodi."

One of the four guards waved back. "Working again?"

"Feels like every night, doesn't it? What I would do for some overtime pay." The two men traded playful barbs and the patrol kept going.

Once the gate opened, the driver ushered them inside, then closed it behind them.

Zofi grasped the bars. "Hey, what if we need to turn back?"

"One-way trip, little egg. You should have thought about it before you bought the ticket," the driver replied, locking the gate and backing away. The sound of grinding began again as the wagon rumbled off.

She returned to the group, scowling. "I don't like this."

But as the driver had said, there was no turning back now. The group stepped deeper into the passageway with the darkness closing in at every step. The tunnel was wide, but low, which gave Pahm some trouble. The Celestial Family's shine through the iron gate faded. The air smelled like moss and dankness. A steady stream of running water gurgled and splashed with constant plinks and plunks of water dripping on stone.

Zofi continued to disapprove. "Something feels wrong."

That riled Meehae. "Relax. Iron Steel uses this route all the time. What did you expect, a garden pathway and a parade of roses?"

Zofi did not seem convinced. "And this Iron Steel is abetting out of charity? Why would they do that?"

"Iron Steel is family," sniffed Meehae, dismissively.

Zofi harrumphed. Apparently, the mapmaker's daughter had had a far different experience with family than the acupuncturist's apprentice. The two lagged behind the rest of them and whispered heatedly.

"The underworld does nothing for free," hissed Zofi.

"They're not doing this for *free*," snapped Meehae. "My father was Iron Steel for most of his life. His service is what's paying for *your* escape."

Xinde found a lantern hanging off the wall and lit it, illuminating a long tunnel that curved around. They followed it for a way as Zofi and Meehae continued their argument. Jian found the strong and very differing opinions puzzling. He hadn't known any of these underworld groups existed until only a few days ago.

The tunnel opened into a large oval connected to several smaller tunnels. A stream of sewage flowed through a channel down the length of the chamber. A narrow bridge arched over the gap. A large grated opening in the ceiling allowed the three hues of moonlight to illuminate the area near the center of the room, but left the walls in darkness.

"Where to next?" asked Pahm, taking the lantern from Xinde and panning across the room. "Every way looks the same as the next."

"You're late," a voice echoed across the room. A light on the other side of the chamber blinked on, growing larger until they could make out a muscular tattooed man with a sharply trimmed goatee and a smooth handsome face. "I almost left. Come along now. This way." He pointed at one of the tunnels.

They followed, crossing the narrow bridge and moving single file to the other side of the room. Meehae hurried ahead to strike up a conversation with their guide. "Those are nice body markings. Who tatted them? I haven't seen you before."

He flexed, making the dragons curling around his arms undulate. "Freshly beaten in."

She giggled, her voice bouncing all over the chamber. "I know that. My father was a sub-boss, but he started out on the pig farm."

"Ah yes, the pig farm. Swine is big for us these days."

"Oh no, not an actual pig farm. I meant disposal." She eyed the young man curiously. "You really are new, aren't you?"

"Very," the man admitted. "Why do you think I got this lousy assignment?"

Zofi, the last to cross the bridge, stopped in the middle directly under the grate and looked straight up. "Hey," she called, waving. "Which way are we going?"

"Quickest way out of the city. Where else?" said the Iron Steel, pointing at one of the tunnels.

Zofi scrunched her face and studied the sky through the grating, then stared at a tunnel in the opposite direction. "We're on the north side of the city. That tunnel you're leading us into takes us southwest, back deeper into Jiayi."

"Some of the paths collapsed. We have to go around," he explained.

Zofi cocked an eyebrow. "Are you sure you know where you're taking us?"

He bristled. "I don't have all night. You can follow me or I can leave you here to rot until a sewer patrol finds you."

"I'm sure the good man knows where we're going," said Jian. "Everything will be fine. I just want to get out of here."

Zofi did not budge. She stood in the middle of the bridge and crossed her arms. "He's taking us the wrong way."

Meehae was glaring at Zofi at first, but then directed her attention back to the young man. She flashed him a hand signal. When he failed to respond, she gestured again. Still nothing. Her eyes narrowed. "Who are you, really?"

The tattooed man brushed her off. "I said I was new."

She began to back away. "Nobody calls themselves Iron Steel without the signals."

"Whatever." He rolled his eyes, and his short sword hissed from its scabbard.

Meehae had no time to react to the blade swinging toward her neck. The killing blow never landed, however, as Taishi was there to block its path, her own sword shimmering blue in the moonlight. She knocked his weapon out of his hand, sending it bouncing away into the darkness, then plunged her blade into his gut. The man blinked, and his jaw dropped. Blood poured from his mouth, and he shuddered as he fell to the ground.

Taishi stood over him, wiping her blood-soaked blade on his pants. "The wound went clean through. You'll live, if I allow it. Who sent you?"

The man spat and fumbled for something in his pocket. He produced a twig of some sort and stuck it into his mouth. Before he could bite down, however, Taishi stuck the tip of her sword between his teeth. She then twisted the blade ninety degrees, forcing his mouth open. "I won't ask again. Who sent—"

A black blur darted out of the darkness. Somehow, Taishi heard it coming and knocked it out of the air with a flick of her wrist. Something came at her from the opposite side. This time, Pahm placed himself between Taishi and this new threat. He swung his giant fist and knocked the attacker down. The blur landed roughly and rolled several feet. Tentacles of black smoke drifted off the body, clearing until a black-clad man was revealed.

"Shadowkills," Taishi spat.

Another blur dropped down from directly above. Taishi fended off the flurry of attacks but was forced to give ground. This new danger stepped in front of her fallen associate, revealing a woman with shoulder-length red hair holding two black knives.

"Hello again, Ling Taishi," the shadowkill singsonged, twirling her blades. "We never formally met. The name's Maza Qisami, and I'm a huge fan. I'm going to be so-o-o-o-o-o famous after I kill you."

Two others, a man and a woman, appeared behind them on the opposite side of the room. Taishi scowled. "Still haven't learned your lesson, I see. You cracked eggs couldn't beat me back at the Temple of the Tiandi. What makes you think you can beat me now?"

"Oh, I learned my lesson all right." Qisami whistled. "Come out, beautiful."

A new figure stepped from the darkness, this one dressed in dark scale armor. A long cloak hugged her body down to her ankles. "Don't ever call me beautiful again." Jian, standing close by, drew his breath sharply. He didn't know who this strange short woman was, but he recognized the Kati master. The woman snapped her arm out, and the looped rope in her hand went taut into a long spear. "We have unfinished business, Master Windwhisper."

CHAPTER FORTY-THREE

THE WINDWHISPER

Taishi drew in a calming breath and assessed the situation as the viperstrike and shadowkill, and their second-rate lackeys, surrounded her. The circumstances had become much more interesting. Having dueled both women previously, she knew exactly how well each matched up to her. Fighting together, they posed a serious threat.

Women like the three of them were rarities, sharks who had thrived in an ocean dominated by mediocre men. Qisami was talented and cunning, and Salminde deadly and skilled. The two together might be more than she could handle, but Taishi was eager to test her strength against these women in their prime. This would be a fitting way to conclude her biography if it came to that.

Taishi took a second breath and pulled the Swallow Dances out of the mouth of the shadowkill lying at her feet. Killing him was probably the smart call, but killing a helpless opponent was frowned upon under the lunar court. The unwritten rules had to be respected, even if nobody actually knew them. It had always been more of a feeling.

She said drily, "When did viperstrikes start working with hired shadow puppets?"

"Hey, watch it," Qisami shot back, still trying to show off her knife skills. Shadowkills took being called shadow puppets as a grave insult. "The two of us have been friends since forever."

"No we haven't." Salminde, on the other hand, was focused and serious. Her eyes telegraphed her readiness for battle. Her stance was aggressive, her entire body coiled, ready to pounce.

Taishi considered her options. Fighting was too risky, but running would be worse. The shadowkill cell would easily pick them off in these dark tunnels. That left one option.

Taishi's third breath was the longest. "Everyone listen carefully," she sent on the barely moving air currents of the sewer tunnels. "Zofi, find a way out of this city. Pahm, protect Jian with your life. I'll buy everyone as much time as I can. When you run, don't look back. Just keep going. I'll catch up if—"

A loud roar shook the chamber. Pahm rushed Qisami. He barreled down on the shadowkill and launched a large meaty fist with such fury it would have likely pulverized the small woman had it connected.

Qisami looked almost amused as she skirted the attack. "Puppy! You made it!"

The blow instead slammed the ground with such force it cracked several stones. The shadowkill sliced the Hansoo twice across the arm and then skipped out of the way, smirking. Unfortunately, she was so busy toying with him she underestimated how badly Pahm wanted to get his hands on her. The Hansoo's arm immediately shot out and grabbed her ankle before she could flit away. Qisami squawked as he pulled her to the ground. She spun around, sending two knives flying. Pahm blocked one knife with the rings on his left forearm, but the second sliced him in the chin before bouncing off his hardened skin. He roared and threw her across the room, sending her flying over the ledge into the sewer channel, followed by a loud splash.

Qisami screeched. "Ew, gross!"

"That was for Brother Liuman, you devils!" The Hansoo turned his attention to Salminde, who gracefully hurdled his running charge, raking him across the back with her spear.

Taishi threw up her hands. "Oh fine, we'll fight." It was what she had wanted anyway.

She surveyed the erupting chaos. Pahm had moved on to another target, hounding after a shadowkill, while Jian and Meehae had become entangled with another. Zofi had disappeared—hopefully to do as she had been told, and the Longxian senior—

"For Master Guanshi!" Xinde yelled, rushing past her toward the viperstrike.

That was a phenomenally terrible idea. Taishi decided to save the young man from himself by sticking her leg out and tripping him, sending him skidding out of death's way face-first.

Taishi leaped over him to meet Salminde before the viperstrike could skewer the young Longxian. The Swallow Dances clashed with the tongue as she closed the distance. All things being equal, a sword was usually at a disadvantage against a spear. It was a good thing Taishi had few equals, but she had to admit the spear in Salminde the Viperstrike's hands was sublime. She wielded it like a true extension of her jing, and its ability to soften at will only made it more dangerous.

The tongue flicked and writhed in the air, biting and snapping from every angle, keeping Taishi at a distance and unable to close in. Anytime she did manage to find an opening, Salminde would retreat and retract the tongue, wrapping the rope around her waist or looping it over her shoulder or neck, until she was able to launch the spearhead back at Taishi like an arrow. One strike sliced her cheek while another nearly tangled her up.

These tricks were cute, but Taishi wasn't having any games. The Swallow Dances knocked the body of the tongue aside as she leaped to the air and pushed and pulled the weak air currents blowing in from the grated opening in the ceiling and tunnels. It was a good thing Taishi was very skilled at working with so little. She twisted several small currents and refocused them into one blast spiraling toward the viperstrike.

Salminde lost her footing as the tiles beneath her feet erupted. Another bolt of air temporarily blinded her, and Taishi scattered the sound around her ears, rendering her without senses for an instant. Taishi launched herself back at the viperstrike, her sword aimed for the death blow.

The Swallow Dances blazed blue through the air. Just as it was about to strike its mark, the air puffed nearby, and Taishi caught a flash coming her way. She pulled out of the dive and parried a knife thrust that gashed her robes. She blocked another slash and kicked away.

Both Taishi and Qisami landed lightly on the ground, one with sword held high, the other with blades crossed. Taishi sniffed the air. "What's that stink?"

"Your stupid Hansoo mutt threw me in a stream of shit!"

Taishi began the dance again with her new partner. The angry shadowkill tried to eviscerate her. Gone was the playfulness. There were no cute tricks or flashy moves, just solid, quick Consortium bladework, of which Taishi had made a thorough study on each of the occasions she had encountered it.

The Consortium utilized a boutique hybrid war art, originally created in a far-off land and improved upon once it immigrated to the Enlightened States. The style relied on short, hard, straight strikes, whether kicks, punches, or blade slashes. Never fancy, and each thrust always meant to kill, followed up, if missed, by relentless offense until the target was indeed dead. Quick and effective, it needed only a brief training period. However, it was easy to counter once a war artist became familiar with its limitations and pacing. The whole point of shadowkills, of course, was that their marks would only ever see this style once in their lives. Unfortunately for Qisami, Taishi had proved a much tougher egg than a carton of shadowkills.

Lunging Snake in the Weeds was countered by Crane Waves at Starlight, just as Cutting the Giant's Knees was countered by Sweep the Floors. The two weapons, one reflecting the light from the Celestial Family, the other absorbing the darkness, fluttered around each other and then past each other as the artists broke their exchange.

Salminde soon recovered her senses and joined the dance, her attacking tongue now a second threat with which Taishi had to contend, pushing her back on her heels. Every time Salminde shot with the long tongue, Qisami would follow, stepping in from just about anywhere. Inarguably masters in their own right, the viperstrike and shadowkill melded their offense seamlessly, covering each other's weaknesses and bolstering each other's strengths. What had been near misses and deflections began to find their marks. Taishi's robes were tattered, and her skin began to bloom bloody from paper-thin cuts.

She took a low current flowing just off the ground, trying to get some space between their suffocating attacks. She rode it out of the tongue's range directly to a waiting Qisami, who nearly sank a knife into her skull. Taishi parried and struck back, her thrust just missing. They tangled in the air briefly, then split apart as the tongue's spearhead shot between them. The three landed simultaneously on opposite ends of the channel.

This could have been Taishi's chance to escape, but the longer she held the attention of these two threats, the longer they were not going after Jian and his friends. Hopefully, the rest had wised up enough to follow directions and had escaped by now.

Just then Pahm blundered across her field of vision, chasing his shadowkill across the room. The woman was chatting up a storm to mock the lumbering Hansoo, who appeared to be slowing down and weakening the longer she evaded him. Then Taishi spied Jian, Xinde, and Meehae still loitering on the other side of the room.

She snarled, exasperated. "Those yolkless imbeciles! What is everyone still doing here?"

The boys were trying to take on the remaining shadowkill. The two idiots were keeping him in check more with frantic tenacity than any semblance of a plan, or skill, for that matter. Learning to fight as a pair required a level of coordination or experience that neither boy had, and the results would have enticed a chuckle out of Taishi if she hadn't been preoccupied. The senior was actually quite skilled with Longxian echo strikes, but that did not make up for Jian's shortcomings.

Shadowkills were not to be trifled with. Eventually, their target would capitalize on the many mistakes Jian and Xinde were making. He fell into a shadow and came up behind Xinde. He would have gutted the senior had Jian not jumped in. The shadowkill shucked him off easily and nearly ended the Prophecy of the Tiandi right there and then, but Meehae managed to flick a needle into his hand, causing his knife to slip out. He smacked her away, sending her flying.

Taishi's people were losing ground. A soft puff snapped her attention back to herself, but she was a moment too late and suffered a laceration for her lapse. She gave back by slicing open Qisami's shoulder. The shadowkill staggered, and Taishi followed through with a slash that would have severed the shadowkill's head had Jian not emitted a panic-induced shriek.

She looked over to see his shadowkill on top of him. The boy had both hands on the assassin's wrist, but the blade was slowly driving down into his chest.

When she refocused on Qisami, the shadowkill was gone, having fallen through the floor and disappeared. Taishi didn't have time for this. Cursing, she hopped onto a current and rode it across the chamber to Jian. She landed next to the shadowkill and kicked him in the ribs—breaking several—sending him tumbling across the room. The assassin was lucky he was too tangled up with Jian for a clean sword thrust.

Taishi hauled the boy to his feet and rapped him on the head. "What did I tell you about countering an inside knife guard? Have you forgotten everything?"

"I tried. I had it under—"

Taishi frowned when she noticed Xinde standing on his knees off to the side, eyes glazed over staring blankly into nothing. "What's wrong with Longxian?"

"Uh, nothing," said Jian. "He took a hard hit—"

Her attention was already elsewhere. Someone else badly needed her attention. This was why she hated operating in a team. "Never mind. Find Zofi. Get out of here."

Taishi dashed off toward Pahm. The Hansoo was a tree that was slowly being chopped down. The other female shadowkill had brought him to his hands and knees with a hundred scratches. His robes had been shredded off, and his trousers were hanging on by threads. Pahm leaked blood from every inch of him, and he looked spent. His head hung low, his shoulders were slumped, and his knees had given out.

"You remember me?" the woman taunted. "I killed your baba bear back at the desert temple."

"That was my kill, Koteuni!" Qisami's voice echoed in the chamber.

"We can share it," quipped the one named Koteuni. She examined one of her knives, then tossed it aside. "You've dulled all my blades, my handsome golem." She took a three-step running start and kicked Pahm in the chin, flattening him to the ground. She winced and hopped on one foot. "Lucky for you," she gloated, "I always carry spares."

Koteuni pulled a knife from her boot and tapped the tip on Pahm's head as if she were about to split a coconut. She pulled her other palm back to slam it down on the butt of the hilt when Taishi swooped in, lopping off the woman's hand at the wrist. It was a clean cut, smooth and efficient. The shadowkill didn't even realize her injury until the blood sprayed back into her face. She stared at the stump, more surprised than pained. Before she could verbalize how she felt, Taishi dropped her with a spin kick across the side of the face that threw her into the center channel.

"Get up, war monk," she growled, emphasizing each word as the Hansoo looked up at her. "You have a sacred duty—"

Taishi was interrupted by Salminde returning for another hard-earned lesson. The viperstrike had bounded up to the curved ceiling and run along it before diving downward. Taishi would have missed it if it were not for the sudden shift in the currents above her head. The tongue thrust at her in rapid lunges, like a striking snake. Taishi parried and dodged the initial barrage, but failed to protect Pahm, who took a spear gash across his chest the moment he rose to his feet.

Taishi didn't have time to check on him. She and the viperstrike were already dancing again, with eyes only for each other. The results were similar to the first time, although it was clear both were tiring. Taishi suffered more injuries to the shoulder and thigh, and inflicted a dozen small wounds. The only reason Salminde was still standing was her armor, which was all that was keeping her organs from spilling out.

Taishi was very nearly about to disarm her overwhelmed opponent when of course Qisami decided to rejoin them. Oh, but Taishi's body was indeed starting to tire. There was little chance she could keep up with strong women in their prime. Superior skill and experience could compensate only so much for a worn body.

Her opponents must have sensed this. Both were fighting more cautiously than before, neither playing too aggressive a hand. They were going to let Taishi tire out and start making mistakes. First, she was late to sidestep a low attack, which resulted in a kick to the shin that nearly broke it. Her guard crumbled against an overhead spear swing, causing one of her knees to give, and she didn't even notice a knife strike coming from her blind side, which nearly resulted in her getting her eye cut out. Then Taishi blocked only four of a five-flurry combination and took a crack to the ribs that sucked all the breath out of her.

They kept her just busy enough to prevent her from catching her breath. Out of the corner of her eye, Taishi caught Zofi emerging from one of the tunnels. She ran to the fallen Pahm and signaled to Meehae, who was with Jian tending to Xinde.

"Get out of here, you stupid hatchlings." Taishi sent her whispers to them between quick breaths. "While you still can."

Of course, instead of doing as instructed, Jian sped toward her wielding a black short sword.

"Why does no one ever listen?" Taishi shouted, her frustration boiling over. If she could tear her hair out, she would, but her good hand was on her sword.

Qisami looked amused as well. "I love it when the mark comes to me."

Salminde agreed. "He might as well just slit his own throat."

"Well, actually . . ." said the shadowkill.

"Stay back, Jian," she yelled. "In fact, just go away."

"I won't leave you."

Well, that was going to get him killed. Qisami peeled away to meet him as soon as he crossed the bridge, and within a breath had sent his weapon flying into the channel. She swept his feet from under him and smashed his face into the ground.

Taishi threw the shadowkill onto her rump with a blast of air, and desperately tried to intervene before it was too late. No sooner had her feet left the ground than a scorching pain blinded her. A spear tip exploded out through her stomach. Taishi teetered and lost her balance, pitching over to the side headfirst. Her chest spasmed as her stomach twisted and screamed in agony.

Still, Taishi tried to paw and claw her way toward Jian. It was a good thing she was in shock, because she was pretty sure she was in a lot of pain. She had nearly pushed herself back to her knees when another shock hit her as the tongue violently whipped out of her body.

Gasping and coughing blood, Taishi used what little strength she had remaining to sit up, and then she was spent. She clutched her belly, feeling the life drain from her body. Her fallen sword was nowhere close. The room swayed as she unsuccessfully struggled to one knee before falling over again.

Salminde appeared, holding her bloodied tongue coiled in one hand and the Swallow Dances in the other. She bowed respectfully. "You fought well, Master Windwhisper."

"You're lucky I have one useless arm and the other one tied behind my back trying to protect these dumb droplings."

"I recognize the circumstances, and swear to never embellish these events." The viperstrike held the blade up respectfully, almost reverently. "Your sword is a work of art. Do you have an heir to whom you wish to pass this?"

"Go milk a rooster." Then Taishi changed her mind. She looked over at Jian. "I assume you're going to kill the boy, aren't you?"

"The sword would not belong to him for long," Salminde confirmed.

Taishi grimaced and considered her options. It was a little embarrassing she couldn't come up with anyone. It finally came down to two names, and Saan had more toys than he could use in three lifetimes. "There's a templeabbot in Vauzan named Mori. He can use it for a butter knife or something."

Salminde nodded. "It will be done."

"No!" Jian struggled futilely while Qisami pinned him down.

The shadowkill smacked him on the back of the head. "Stop squirming." She glanced over at Salminde. "Get on with it and kill the old bag. I really need a hot bath."

"Give the boy a clean death," Taishi said quietly. It was as close to a plea as she could muster. "Don't have him paraded through the streets or leveraged as a trophy. He's as much a victim in this as any of us. He deserves his dignity."

The viperstrike placed a fist on her chest. "As you will bear witness." The tongue in her hand uncurled and straightened into a spear. The viperstrike strode toward Jian. "Wen Jian, Prophesied Hero of the Tiandi, ordained Champion of the Five Under Heaven, I, Viperstrike Salminde of the Glass City of Nezra, am here to free you from your chains of fate."

Qisami held up a finger as the Katuia master approached. "Hang on a minute. You know, before we get ahead of ourselves, I have an idea. What do you think about—"

"Know this, your death comes from a place of justice and honor," Salminde continued. "I bear you no malice, receive no personal joy for these actions. What must be done will be done in the name of duty and loyalty to the Eternal Khan and the Katuia people. I hope that one day, perhaps, we can share a hearth in the next life."

"No, really"—Qisami's voice became shrill—"I mean it. Hear me out. I think it may be much more beneficial—"

Salminde launched the tongue at Jian's heart. At this distance, there was no missing its target. Taishi watched the execution unfold as if it were a cursed dream. Her gaze was glued to the tip of the spearhead, slicing through hundreds of tiny air currents, splaying them in all directions in its wake. Jian's eyes were wide, panicked. At that moment, he probably had no idea of the enormity of his own death. He couldn't grasp how much the fate of the Zhuun rested upon his beating heart. He probably didn't care. Jian was a frightened young man, staring down the end of his life with little to no reflection.

He shuddered. Two heartbeats passed. Taishi, even with blood filling her lungs, held her breath. Jian, eyes squeezed shut, slowly pried them open. The death blow never came. Grabbing the tongue's shaft with both hands was Qisami.

The shadowkill's eyes gleamed with exasperation. "I *said* hang on a minute!"

CHAPTER FORTY-FOUR

THE VIPERSTRIKE

S ali couldn't believe this was happening. Actually, she could. A double cross was the first thing she had expected when she had agreed to ally with the shadowkill. Sali had had reservations about working with the infamous Consortium, but Qisami had come across as awkwardly earnest and believable. Besides, it wasn't like Sali had had any other leads.

The arrangement had been simple and straightforward: The silk-spinners had paid to have Iron Steel lure the Prophesied Hero down to them. All Sali and the shadowkill cell had to do was kill the Hero of the Tiandi and anyone else who got in the way.

For most of the night, the gamble appeared to have paid off. Iron Steel brought the boy and his friends. The cell took care of most of the others while Sali and Qisami focused on Taishi. The fight had ebbed and flowed, but they emerged victorious. Now all Sali had to do was to kill the eventual murderer of the Eternal Khan. Just as she was on the cusp of saving her people, the double cross came.

And still Sali found herself somewhat shocked and dismayed. "Release my tongue."

Qisami obliged and threw up her hands. "Sure, fine, but before you get all stabby, hear me out. I know you were very much looking forward to stopping the kid's heart forever. I get it. Murder is the best part of an assassination, but . . ." She held up a finger. ". . . I have another idea. How about we *not* kill him? At least not yet. What do you think of that? This little kitten here would grow up to be so much more valuable alive and fresh on the open market as a big lion with sharp fangs. We just have to hold off a few years. In fact, I already have a buyer. Let me hand him over and we'll split sixty–forty. You don't even have to thank me. We can just snuggle."

Sali blinked. "You think I'm doing this for money? Do you actually think I can be bought?"

Qisami winced. "'Bought' sounds harsh." The shadowkill tried to reassure her. "Don't worry. He'll die, just not right away. Trust me, nobody wants him alive."

"Hey!" exclaimed Jian.

Qisami ignored him. "The buyer isn't interested in the boy fulfilling some stupid prophecy. He just wants him killed at a more appropriate and dramatic time. You know, more fanfare and spectacle. Like a ripe banana."

"Like a what?" Sali's eyes narrowed. "No matter. I'll save your buyer the hassle."

Qisami reached for the spear again. "I know I just sprang this on you, but trust me when I say I'm thinking about us. So how about this: We'll club the kitty over the head, stuff him in a sack, and you let *me* take *you* out for a nice dinner. Afterward, if we can't square up, then you can lop his head off or carve out his spleen to your heart's content—"

Sali didn't wait for her to finish. The shadowkill's blades flashed in the air. One deflected the tongue just enough to miss the boy. The other she brought up to Sali's throat as she lunged forward.

"This is your last chance. Don't push me. I'm having a really rough day." The playfulness was gone.

Sali relaxed the tongue to swing it at Qisami, then immediately hardened it again. The shaft was like a drawn bowstring, launching the shadowkill into the air. Qisami squawked as she flew across the room. Sali turned her attention back to Jian when something slammed into her back, knocking the tongue out of her hand completely and sending her sprawling face-first to the floor.

The edge of a sharp blade once again kissed the back of her neck. Qisami hissed in her ear. "I *said* don't push me! That was not nice."

Sali exploded upward and bucked the small woman off easily. She rolled to her feet and faced the shadowkill. Oddly, even though she had been betrayed, Sali wasn't eager to fight Qisami. A warrior was trained to fight without emotion, but now facing Qisami with their blades drawn, Sali couldn't help but hesitate when facing the assassin. She was a curious creature, this shadowkill. There was something *untethered* about her that irritated Sali like a slime beetle that found its way into your sleep sack. Yet it was her oddities that made her so intriguing.

In their next life, the two might have become friends. Sali raised her guard. Which, for one of them, could be happening sooner than expected. Only one of them would survive this night. The two women stepped back and circled each other.

Jian, who stood nearby, frozen, raised a hand. "Should I just get out of your way?"

"You stay put!" both Sali and Qisami snapped, their eyes still on each other.

Sali settled into the classic Serpent Fang stance, which was a Nezra home-brewed style that had achieved widespread popularity among her people centuries ago. Mastery of it was now a prerequisite for any who aspired to join the sect. Sali stayed in her coil with her palms flattened and arms waving in slow circles, and waited as Qisami came at her with a barrage of blade thrusts and kicks.

The light shining through the grating in the ceiling offered all too many opportunities for Qisami to retreat and emerge. She would leave Sali bleeding from several gashes in her arms, back, and legs, and then reappear elsewhere.

Sali soon wised up. The next time Qisami disappeared, Sali turned and leaned to the side. Her coil guard snapped forward and slapped the knife out of Qisami's hand as she reemerged. She clutched Qisami's wrist with one hand, and the other slithered up the shadowkill's arm to bite into the soft flesh of her armpit, transitioning into an arm lock. Qisami managed to twist away, but not without suffering several more hard shots on the way out.

Qisami rubbed her jaw as she retreated, her face contorted with rage. "We could have made such beautiful murders together."

The shadowkill's aggressive style matched Sali's suffocating Serpent Fang defense well. Qisami would charge forward like a rampaging ox, and Sali continuously slipped away to create distance, using her long reach for counters. They danced, their exchanges carrying them from one side of the room to the other.

Sali wasn't sure how long the shadowkill could keep this impressive pace up, but after several furious exchanges, Qisami did not appear to be breathing heavily, let alone tiring.

Whenever Sali had a moment to catch her breath, she would survey the room. Jian hadn't moved from where they had left him. He sat there on his knees with his mouth agape, watching. The windwhisper was still lying in a pool of expanding blood on the other side of the chamber. At various points during the fight, Sali would notice the others, but she wasn't too worried about any of them.

Sali managed to trap Qisami's arm on her second attempt and flipped her over, tossing her headfirst to the ground. Qisami fluttered her legs, striking Sali in the face several times before she crashed. Both women collapsed in a heap. Sali recovered first and pounced on top of Qisami. She grabbed the shadowkill's tunic, lifted her off her feet, then slammed her back down. To her dismay, Qisami fell through the ground with Sali's fists pounding nothing but hard stone. This trick was starting to get annoying.

No sooner had she looked up than Qisami sprinted up to her and kicked Sali in the face, snapping her head back and knocking her to her backside. The shadowkill climbed on top of her and drew yet another knife. She plunged it down at Sali's heart.

The only thing Sali could do was use her forearm as a shield. The blade sank into her flesh from one side and came through the other, its tip managing to keep going and wedge into the gap between three pieces of scale armor.

Sali muffled a cry and sucked in several short hard breaths, calming her agonized nerves, willing her body to relax. The knife in Qisami's hands continued to press downward, slowly digging deeper. The overwhelming pain threatened to rob her consciousness.

Sali steeled herself, then launched her head forward. The first blow fractured Qisami's orbital bone, the second shattered her nose. The shadowkill reared back just enough for Sali to follow with a hard kick to her knee that cracked and bent it to an unnatural angle. Qisami cried out and fell to the ground.

Sali rolled onto all fours, gasping, her chest heaving and blood gushing from the wound in her chest and half a dozen other cuts, but not from her arm, where the blade was still lodged. She found herself short of breath as she tore at her scale armor until she popped out the three scale pieces that were digging into the gash. Sali fumbled for a small sack hanging at her belt. She ripped it open with her teeth, and with two fingers clawed out a dark-green spotted paste, then muffled an agonized cry as she applied it liberally on her chest. The paste from the hong fruit tree oxidized with her blood and burned like fire as it cauterized her wound. Thankfully, slowly, the pain wore away.

A few long, deep breaths helped Sali regain control of her functions. The wound had closed, but the seal could just as easily break open again. She had to repeat the agonizing process with the fruit paste on both wounds through her arm. She bit down on a leather strap of her armor as she yanked the blade out and cauterized as quickly as possible. Sali was drenched in sweat and blood by the time the pain finally faded.

She could barely stand, let alone fight, and she had no idea where her tongue had gone. Her armor had chipped and lost its shape. Hampa was going to have his hands full with repairs when they get out of here, assuming she ever made it out of this mess.

Qisami, still on the floor a little ways away, appeared to be in equally bad shape. The shadowkill's face was a wreck. The left side had puffed up, nearly completely closing one eye. Blood poured freely from her broken nose down her chin and neck. Qisami moved her jaw back and forth until she plucked out a tooth, spat out a glob of blood, and smeared her face and arms. She caught sight of Sali staring, and then broke into a wide unsettling grin, exposing red-stained teeth and a black gap up front.

What a puzzling creature.

Sali glanced over to where the Prophesied Hero was sitting on the ground and found him missing. "Oh damn it." She should have expected this. The fool wouldn't have stayed there like worm bait forever. She craned her head back to where Taishi had fallen, and found that the windwhisper had disappeared as well. She listened for sounds of footsteps or voices or anything and found none. Sali grunted and slammed her fist onto the stone floor, but then remembered which tunnel the other woman had disappeared into and reemerged from. That had to be the way out.

She shot to her feet and instantly regretted not taking it a bit more slowly. The room swayed. The balm she had applied to her wound had stemmed the bleeding, but she had already lost a lot of blood. Sali bent over and sucked in a few deep breaths, and then returned to the chase after the Hero of the Tiandi, running with a lopsided gait that threatened to rip the wound open with each step.

"Hey, where are you going? This is just getting fun." Qisami called out, trying to stand. "Ow, you broke my leg."

Sali glared back and lobbed the balm at Qisami. She wasn't sure why she did it. A moment later, just as Sali entered the tunnel, she heard a bloodcurdling scream, and her lips curled into a smirk. She refocused her attention on the Hero of the Tiandi. His fate was now all that mattered. The cramped passage closed in on her as it faded into darkness. Sali concentrated her jing, focusing it into her vision until the uniform blackness broke apart into different shades of darkness.

The sewer system under the city stretched everywhere between the outer walls. It was a maze of passageways, catacombs, collapsed structures, and natural caverns. The old city had been razed centuries ago by a long-dead clan. The Zhuun had rebuilt over bones. Several of the buildings that still stood now formed much of this current iteration's sewer system.

If she had led the now-extinct Qadan, this cursed place would have been salted.

Sali was grateful that she had demanded to see a map of Jiayi's sewer system before agreeing to tonight's plan. She had no idea how Taishi's group had found which tunnel to take. Sali knew this tunnel led to the rendezvous point where Hampa was waiting with their horses, as agreed with the shadowkill and the Iron Steel. With the betrayal, however, who even knew if the rest of the plan was still intact.

The tunnel curved around a wide bend, and all remaining light shining from the chamber disappeared, pitching her into total darkness. Sali didn't fear moving in darkness. The tall foliage in the Grass Sea often blotted out the sun. The viperstrike's night gaze was especially useful then. She soon caught the sounds of footsteps splashing in water, which were accompanied by heavy breathing and loud whispers. Sali stayed against the left wall, moving as quietly as still air. She caught sight of a single spark of light in the distance. Someone up there was holding up a spark stone, which, while it illuminated their way, blinded them to the darkness. The Hansoo was carrying something, or someone, in his arms, likely the windwhisper. The woman with the short hair was leading them with the hero at her side, while the Longxian boy and the little acupuncturist brought up the rear.

Sali reached for her tongue and cursed. What a foolish thing to have forgotten back in the chamber. She drew her long dagger instead and continued to creep closer. If found out, she wasn't sure how effective she would be in her current state. However, the element of surprise made the kill simple. After that, what happened to her was unimportant. She still preferred to survive this encounter in order to get back to Mali and the exodus, but that was just a bonus.

Sali was nearly on top of the group at the end of the tunnel when they all fell flat on their stomachs in unison. She became as still as a statue as she listened intently, just making out several garbled and echoey voices coming up from the next room. The hero's group moved away from the tunnel's mouth and disappeared from view. Sali followed until she reached where they had lain down overlooking another chamber directly below. A set of stairs curved from her hiding place. This chamber was different from the previous, showing only a half oval with a large curved wall save for a set of iron gates set in the middle, flanked on one side by a guardhouse.

A small group of soldiers with their bowl-shaped helms huddled around a small fire beneath a kettle passing around gourds of wine. They were chatting with an equal number of rough-looking individuals, likely Iron Steel henchmen. This had to be the sewer garrison stationed at one of the three underground passages leading out of the city. It was also the route the Iron Steel used to smuggle contraband out of the city. In this case, Sali and Hampa were the contraband. This was their way out.

She scanned the area below. Her neophyte was nowhere within sight. A moment later, three figures emerged from the guardhouse. Hampa appeared in the light first, with two uniformed men holding his arms. Her neophyte had his wrists and ankles trussed up like a snared rabbit, and they marched him toward the fire.

The one who looked like he was in charge, wearing a pitchfork on his helm, shoved Hampa roughly to the ground next to the kettle. "The mangy gutter toad won't speak." The guard nodded appreciatively at the Iron Steel. "Thanks for lending him to us anyway. He's a little worse for wear, but who cares."

A bald Iron Steel with a long mustache that flared out like a catfish's whiskers waved it off. "Don't mind it one bit. Always willing to do favors for friends."

The guard captain, missing half a nose, crossed his arms. "I don't like owing favors to the underground."

"Oh no," the bald catfish said with a wave, offering one of the gourds. "I only meant it was a courtesy, a gesture of goodwill based on our long-standing business arrangement."

Half-Nose grunted. He drank deeply from the gourd and tossed it back to the Iron Steel. Then he unlatched a clasp at his waist and hoisted a small ax. "You want us to take him off your hands? Free of charge."

Catfish waved it off. "Hold off. The shadowkill might want him."

Hampa had risen to his knees next to the fire. The bright flames licking from under the cauldron reflected off his face and brought to light the beating they had given him. Blood ran down his cheek, and a piece of his ear had gashed open. The boy's eyes were purple, and his lips were cut so badly the wound would need to be sewn shut. He stared intensely out into space. A muffled cry escaped his lips when one of the Iron Steel walking by smacked him. He struggled back to his knees with a grunt and continued to keep his head up.

Fury coursed through Sali's veins. These land-chained had beaten Hampa badly, but they could not break him. He was too hard for them. Sali had no intention of escaping this city without her neophyte. She stayed close to the ground and considered her options. Navigating the situation below would be tricky. The hero's group was creeping down the stairs and making their way toward the gate. Could they escape without detection? Likely not. The gates would be locked, and not even the Hansoo could break through them. That meant a confrontation was inevitable. With their injuries, Sali wasn't sure who would win the fight against soldiers and Iron Steel. They would certainly lose if she intervened, but those guards and Iron Steel would just as likely turn on her the moment she revealed herself. In the end, she decided to heed the wisdom of her warchief mother: If two of your enemies choose to fight each other, let them.

The group around the fire had no idea what was coming. One of the Iron Steel was half dancing, half acting as he told a joke, each hand gripping a gourd. The man took a swig of his gourd and was about to down the other when he stared off into the darkness and stopped. One gourd slipped from his hand as he pointed, his fingers shaking.

Sali followed his gaze just in time to see the large silhouette of the Hansoo emerge from the shadows like some monstrous creature out of a nightmare. His roar echoed as he charged into the light, his rings jingling around his wrist. The torn shreds of his robe streamed behind him, making for a terrifying scene. His giant arms swung wildly, pounding the ground and knocking over chairs and barrels, as if he were some sort of devil from the lower levels of the ten hells.

The war monk crashed into the group, running over one Iron Steel and sweeping two off their seats with his long arms, inadvertently knocking over the black kettle of stew. He was followed close behind by the hero and the Longxian boy. Her focus was initially on the hero, but the Longxian boy stole her attention. He flew at a guard with a flying kick, then knocked down an Iron Steel with a spectacular assault of his blurred movements. He had talent.

Jian, on the other hand, was several steps beneath his peer. He fought competently, but his lack of experience was blatant. He was just good enough to knock down one of the Iron Steel thugs, if barely. Jiamin would have squashed him like a brittle bug had their paths crossed. Sali had to remind herself that the hero was still just a boy.

A melee erupted around the fire, throwing giant shadows up on the walls. It quickly became apparent that these guards and Iron Steel were more incompetent than she had given them credit for, and they were drunk. That was probably why they were all relegated to assignments in the sewers. Interestingly, the windwhisper was nowhere in sight. Just how badly was she hurt?

The door to the guardhouse slammed open as the remaining guard, with only one boot and a chest plate dangling off one shoulder, ran out. He made it two steps before he clutched his neck and toppled over. The two women appeared from behind the building. One ran inside while the one with the wild hair checked her handiwork, sticking the downed guard with more needles and locking his joints before running off to help the hero, who was losing decisively to Half-Nose.

The Longxian and Hansoo were doing the bulk of the work, keeping at bay five times their number. The Longxian especially was doing an admirable job fighting off two soldiers, as well as a spearman, when Catfish struck him across the face with his club. Longxian's eyes immediately glazed over, and he dropped to his knees. Before Catfish could finish him off, the Hansoo came to his rescue. He picked up Catfish by the neck and threw him screaming all the way across the room.

Sali refocused her attention on the Hansoo, who now stood alone, looking spent, breathing and bleeding heavily. What was wrong with the Longxian? She had witnessed people freeze during battle like that, but rarely war artists. And where were the rest of his friends?

The short-haired woman reappeared a moment later, swinging a large black ring of keys in her hand. The Hansoo picked up the Longxian and threw him over his shoulder like a bag of rice, and they retreated toward the gates.

The head guard barked orders to the few remaining people around him. "You, pull the bell rope to alert topside. You, put that pathetic Kati dog out of his misery. The rest of you, come with me. They can't escape."

This was her cue. Sali waited until the main group went off to pursue the Prophesied Hero, then rose, feeling her body groan. The injury in her chest flared, and her left arm felt like a lead weight. Even in her weakened state, she could still clear that rabble below. She leaped off the ledge, diving headfirst toward the fire. She rolled roughly onto her feet—it was not one of her more graceful moments—and glared at the spooked soldier who was making his way to Hampa. She kicked high, sending him sideways into the dying fire.

She offered her wide-eyed neophyte a curt nod. "I'll be back. Stay put."

"But—"

Sali sprinted to the guardhouse. She kicked the door down just as the other soldier was about to ring the bell that would send alerts throughout all of the guardhouses and summon patrols down to investigate.

Sali threw a dagger, slicing first through the rope and then into the soldier's throat. The unfortunate young man flew into the wall as the blade thudded into the hard wood. The thick rope at neck height, now dangling by a thread, fell to the floor a second later.

Unfortunately, she had been a few seconds too late. The soldier had managed one pull. Somewhere above her, Sali could just make out the faint tinkling of a bell. It was soon followed by others.

She cursed, plucked her last dagger from the wall, and burst out of the building and toward the gates. That meant she had only minutes to catch and finish the boy. Who knew if they had already made it into the tunnel or how far they had gone. If she didn't get to the hero before reinforcements arrived, it would be over.

To her surprise, the hero and his friends still hadn't made it past the gates. The woman with the keys was trying to find the right one, the needle-thrower was squatting next to an unconscious Taishi and the

Longxian boy, while the hero and the Hansoo were finishing off the last of the soldiers.

The Hansoo was holding Half-Nose by the arms and slamming him to the ground. Then the war monk's strength finally gave and he fell onto his knees and hands. He barely had the strength to raise his head as she approached. With a resigned look and sigh, he summoned whatever he had left inside and came at her, half running, half crawling into a dive.

Sali skipped over the attack and planted a boot to his face. She landed behind him and sliced him twice across the back in a crisscross. To his credit, he only flinched. Two more exhausted swings missed by miles, and then she was on top of him, wrapping her arms around his neck. She avoided his futile grabs at her as she yanked him drunkenly side to side. He eventually lost his balance and crashed to the ground. His breathing became tortured and slowly faded. Sali stood over him and placed a heel to the side of his face.

"Stop!"

Sali looked up to see Jian standing right there gifting himself to her. "Are you sacrificing yourself for your holy warrior? There's irony in that, Hero of the Tiandi."

"No, this is a formal challenge. Leave the others out of it. I'm the one you want."

Sali let the war monk go. She stood and faced Jian, the hero, the boy. "Very well. I accept your challenge."

"What are your terms?" he asked.

"That's not how it works."

"What?" His bravado momentarily broke.

"When you challenge another war artist"—she couldn't believe she was explaining this to the supposed Champion of the Five Under Heaven—"you're the one offering the challenge. The one you challenge is the one who requests formal terms."

"Oh." Realization sparkled in Jian's eyes. He frowned once more. "So, uh, are you going to ask me?"

She shook her head. "I feel no need to parlay."

"But . . ." He swallowed hard and looked down at his fallen Hansoo friend. "Can you at least let them go?"

"Are you surrendering to me?"

"No, I'm going to fight you."

Sali was about to slap him down again when she realized she was wasting time. "Your friends can go."

The Hero of the Tiandi turned his head without taking his eyes off her. "Meehae, Zofi, help Pahm up and get out of here."

"What about you?" one of the women said.

"Just go. I'll catch up." He refocused on her and began to stomp the ground like an eager colt being freed from a pen.

Sali stared blankly. "What are you doing?"

"I was . . . never mind," he growled. "You killed Master Guanshi. You almost killed Taishi. You'll pay."

Sali didn't waste any time. She attacked as soon as he finished speaking, aiming for a quick death. She was sapped from the night's long encounters, but was confident she had enough strength left to kill the Hero of the Tiandi quickly and unceremoniously. The boy had eluded her too many times already. To her mild surprise, Jian blocked her first few strikes, sidestepped a low kick, and escaped when she grabbed a fistful of his shirt. He even landed a solid punch to her wound that momentarily wobbled her knees.

Those would be his only highlights.

The boy put up a respectable fight and made a fair account for himself in the same manner toddlers surpassed expectations for not pissing their pants. Sali ignored his meager attacks, cracked a few ribs with her knee, and followed up with two good clean punches. Then she caught his arm dangling out and put him in a joint lock, disabling his elbow. She yanked his head one way and his body the other. One more crank and the Hero of the Tiandi would be no more.

"Your prophecy will plague the Katuia no longer." The time for ceremony was long past. Jian fought against her but was helpless in her grasp. His breathing became labored. A high-pitched squeal echoed through the chamber walls.

Something sharp and hard punched Sali in the back, piercing her scale armor and lodging in her collarbone. She stumbled, losing control of the boy. Grimacing, she reached over and broke the shaft of the arrow.

She turned around to face this new threat just in time to take an ax into her shoulder. Sali stared, and then her legs gave. She fell to the ground as several soldiers surrounded her.

"What happened here?" shouted one.

"It's a Kati! She killed the entire garrison!" One soldier pinned Sali with a spear to her chest.

"Are you all right, son?" Another helped Jian to his feet. "What happened here, boy? What are you doing here?"

Another, who was checking the bodies, reported back. "By the Tiandi, sir, everyone in the garrison is dead."

"There's one more Kati back there. He's tied up."

"The gates are unlocked, Captain. Someone escaped."

Sali looked to the side and saw Jian slowly retreat to the gate while all the soldiers focused on her. She pointed at him weakly. "You don't understand. He's . . . he's the Hero . . ."

The soldier pressed the edge of the spear to her neck. "Not another word, Kati scum. What should we do with her, Captain?"

The Zhuun soldier with the two bright-red plumes on his helmet nudged her lightly with his toe. "This one looks half dead already. Kill her. We can interrogate the other one."

"Yes, Captain." The soldier who had a spear pointed at Sali's neck raised it. He was about to send her to her next life when his head violently snapped back, a small black throwing dagger in one eye. The remaining soldiers barely had time to look around before they too went down.

Sali struggled into a sitting position as three shadowkills stepped out on all sides. They all looked in pretty poor shape, but Qisami most of all. She limped badly and was using Sali's tongue as a walking stick.

"You had all this fun without me." The shadowkill surveyed the carnage, and then glanced into the tunnel past the opened gates. "Did the mark get away?"

Sali nodded.

"That's going to be a problem," Qisami muttered. "Those wrist-wagging silkspinners are going to shit a fit when they find out I lost their golden egg." She glanced down at Sali. "You're going to live, right?"

Sali was too weak and weary to go another round with her. "Depends. Are you going to kill me?"

"There's no point anymore. Besides, now you owe me a favor."

Sali struggled to stand. She was in so much pain she didn't actually know where she was injured anymore, other than the obvious arrow in her back and the ax head still buried in her shoulder. She couldn't even feel the Khan's Pull. In a way, she actually preferred it this way. "I owe you nothing. You betrayed me and then tried to kill me."

"I know you're good for it." Qisami smiled sweetly. Her teeth were still bloody and the gap still very conspicuous. "Now get your grunt and get out of here before more of these tin-cans arrive."

Sali didn't need to be told again, especially with her current luck. She wasted no time untying Hampa and helping him onto a piebald horse tied to the guard stand. Sali mounted a nearby dun and led both straight for the gate, passing the three shadowkills without saying a word.

They were just about to pass through the gates leading into the gates leading out of the city when Qisami called out. "Hey, Salminde."

Sali turned the horse around. Qisami picked up the hardened tongue, aimed, and threw it at Sali, with force. Sali caught it with one hand and relaxed it, letting it coil back around her saddle horn. She tipped her head. "Why are you letting me go?"

"No reason. Maybe I want to see you again." Qisami shrugged in an exaggerated fashion as she twirled a knife in her hand before accidentally losing control and dropping it. "Our paths will cross again someday, yeah?"

Sali turned her back to her. "We're still not even." But this time the harshness in her voice was gone. She glanced over at Hampa. "Come, little brother," she said, ignoring the startled look on his face, "let's go home."

CHAPTER FORTY-FIVE

CLOUD PILLARS

Jian sat on the rickety balcony hanging at the cliff's edge, overlooking a vast forest surrounded by impossibly tall mountains. The entire structure creaked and rattled, not exactly inspiring any confidence. After everything that he had gone through, falling off a mountain would feel like a bit of a letdown.

That had been the first thought to cross Jian's mind the first day he arrived at Taishi's home nearly two weeks ago, having traveled by donkey, cart, and river barge most of the way. They had ridden within eyeshot of Vauzan but chosen to avoid the capital of Shulan entirely. After that, it had been three days until the tips of the Cloud Pillars appeared on the horizon, two more days until they reached the base of the mountains, and another four up incredibly difficult terrain on foot. Fortunately, Taishi had recovered enough by then for Pahm to carry her on his back.

The Cloud Pillars were known for their treacherous peaks and beautiful, dense forests. Jian's mouth had dropped the first time he saw the rock formations layered on top of one another rising to the heavens, yellow and purple stone layers stacked into near-vertical buttes covered with brightly colored vegetation. Along the way, they had had to walk carefully along narrow paths that hugged the sides of cliffs, navigate swampy land where one misstep would have plummeted them into quicksand-like pools filled with leeches, and cross worn-down rope bridges hundreds of feet up in the air.

In any case, Jian wasn't supposed to be dwelling on dying right now. He wasn't supposed to be thinking at all. Jian was *supposed* to be meditating. His legs were crossed, and the backs of his palms were resting on his knees while his thumb touched the middle finger on his right hand and the ring finger on his left. His concentration broke as he momentarily became confused about which finger was the ring finger. Pahm, who had been instructing him in meditation arts, wore rings on all his fingers.

Jian shifted as a gust of cold breeze blew up his robes. He drew in a deep breath and let it seep out slowly through his pursed lips. This was supposed to allow him to tap into his jing, to clear his mind and focus his thoughts, or was he supposed to focus his mind and clear his thoughts? Not like it made a difference. No matter which variation he tried, Jian couldn't get into that stupid meditative state. He was completely aware and present in his surroundings and felt every painful, boring second of this feeble attempt to find peace of mind and enlightenment.

He was still struggling with this when a small voice called to him over the shrill wind. "Hey, Hiro, I mean, Jian."

He kept his eyes closed. "Yes, Meehae?"

"You have a few moments?"

"I have all the moments in the world." He patted the bench next to him. "Have a seat."

"I'm not stepping foot on that death trap."

That was fair. He kept his eyes closed as he turned around. He hadn't realize he was terrified of heights until the first time Taishi had dragged him here. To be able to sit out here now was progress. Jian slid off the bench and joined Meehae back on solid ground. "What is it?"

Meehae stared toward the horizon. If they squinted hard enough, they could just make out the tops of Vauzan in the distance. "It's time."

Jian's stomach twisted into knots. "So soon?"

She pointed at the clear skies. "The last of the storms have passed. The Twins are tucked in bed for the next month. If we leave now, we'll make it before winter. Traveling in snow isn't any fun, even during the first cycle."

Jian pursed his lips. He couldn't meet her gaze. "You could always wait until spring."

Meehae laughed. "I'm lucky if Master Kui hasn't already found another apprentice. If I wait any longer, she'll assume I'm dead and give my room away."

"What about Taishi?"

She put a hand on his elbow and dragged him away from the ledge. "Master Ling will recover soon enough, assuming she doesn't start war-arts-ing all over the place. I left the recipe for her brew on the shelf. Remember, twice a day, and keep a piss pot close."

"I might mess it up," he muttered, staring at the ground. "Maybe you should stay until she's fully recovered."

"I need to go back and finish my training." She squeezed his arm. That was when she noticed the wetness in his eyes. Meehae wrapped him in a big hug. "Hey Jian, you're going to be okay."

"It's just," he said grudgingly, "I'm going to miss you both. I don't have anyone else."

"I'm going home, Jian, not leaving to colonize Merea across the Blue Sea. We'll see each other again soon. I promise."

The two walked down to the crumbling three-walled hut they used for a stable. Only the donkey was there now. "And Xinde? Is he going with you?"

"I don't know. There's nothing left for him in Jiayi. Wherever it is, though, I hope it's not too far from me."

The two came around the side of the wooden fence that lined the perimeter of Taishi's home. According to the windwhisper, this place had once been a temple for an old sect of cannibal priests known as the Diyu Red Lanterns who worshipped a twisted form of the Tiandi. Their ultimate goal was to have their templeabbot eat the Prophesied Hero in order to assume his place within the prophecy. Taishi had come to clear the temple after a war artist friend's nephew had gone missing. They weren't able to save the boy, but Taishi had exacted justice by wiping the entire sect off the face of the earth. Then she had become so enamored with the view that she had moved in.

Jian wasn't sure what to make of staying in a place with such a violent and wretched history, but at least the temple was spacious and the rooms comfortable. He guessed he should be thankful that Taishi had rid the world of crackbrained cannibals who wanted to eat him. But if those religious fanatics had wanted his job, they could have just asked. Jian would have been happy to give up the mantle of the Champion of the Five Under Heaven.

They continued around to the front gate, where Xinde and Pahm had saddled the horses and were loading supplies for their journey. The Hansoo had a hand on the senior's shoulder, looking almost as if he was leaning into the senior to hold him up. Xinde was looking up at Pahm, conversing in a low voice as their heads huddled close together. The two had become quite inseparable in the brief time here, with one rarely seen without the other. Jian was happy Xinde had found a kindred spirit, but couldn't help feeling just a sliver of jealousy over their close relationship.

The Longxian senior and the Hansoo monk stepped apart as he and Meehae approached. Xinde waved as he hastily adjusted the saddle. He carried no noticeable limp as he walked around to the other side of the horse. "Ready to go?"

"What's the hurry?" Maybe Jian could convince them to stay awhile longer. Meehae wouldn't go anywhere without Xinde. "You can stay and train with Taishi for a bit. Maybe we can all be windwhispers together."

Xinde gave him a good-natured grin. "Only one of us can. Let it be you. Besides, there're a couple of things I really need to work through." He extended his forearm to Jian, and Jian clasped it. He looked at Pahm. "Brother Pahm has offered to help me work through them. He needs to report back to his templeabbot and lay Brother Liuman's rings to rest. It's on the way, so we all decided to travel together."

Jiayi and the Stone Blossom Monastery were in completely different directions. Jian chose not to bring that up, but turned to Pahm, who immediately dropped to one knee.

"Stop that," Jian grumbled. He didn't know why it bothered him so. Back at the Celestial Palace, everyone bowed every time they saw him. Now it just made him uncomfortable.

"You are the Champion of the Five Under Heaven, the Prophesied Hero of the Tiandi. There is no act more sacred than kneeling in your presence. When I tell my brothers and sisters about your return, it will bring so much healing to the faithful."

"You will do no such thing," a sharp voice barked from behind them.

Everyone turned to see a hunched-over Taishi, leaning heavily on a staff as she made her way toward them. Trailing by her side was Zofi, fussing to make sure she didn't fall over.

"Hey," snapped Meehae. "What did I say about keeping her in bed?"

"How am I going to stop her? What do you expect me to do, tie her down?" Zofi snapped back.

"Hush, Doctor," Taishi replied. She turned to Zofi. "You too, girl." The individual titles she addressed them with were not lost on anyone. Taishi waved her staff like a club as she marched up to Pahm and bonked him on the head. "You will not whisper a word of the Prophesied Hero to anyone. Do you understand, Hansoo? I need you to swear."

Pahm shook his head. "That I cannot. Wen Jian is the treasured breathing fount of the Tiandi religion, and he is not only found, but alive as well. How can I keep this from the faithful?"

"Because if you don't, someone stupid in your faithful is going to spread the word to the wrong people and I'll soon have Mute Men paying us a visit, and then your breathing fount will not be breathing. Do you understand?"

Pahm did not appear to take her chastisement well. The large man slumped his shoulders and averted his eyes. Xinde patted him on the shoulder. "Don't worry, Master Ling. I'll speak with him. He won't give you or Jian away."

She grunted. "You better. If I find Mute Men at my front steps and live to survive it, I'm going to hunt young Pahm down and carve his hard skin into a suit of armor." Jian and Meehae exchanged wide-eyed looks. Taishi did not make idle threats.

There were a few more goodbyes and promises to stay in touch before Xinde, Meehae, and Pahm began their winding descent. Taishi retreated to the house when the breeze grew frigid, leaving Jian and Zofi to watch their friends depart until they were just a tiny dot at the base of the mountain.

Even though they had been gone for less than an hour, Jian already felt loneliness closing in on him. He had grown accustomed to it most of his life, but now that he had finally found friends—true friends—he could only watch helplessly as they disappeared from his life. Maybe as Meehae said it would only be for a little while, but it could just as likely be forever.

Jian must have worn his worries on his face. "Are you all right?" asked Zofi, gently touching his shoulder.

"I'm going to miss having friends." He was *supposed* to say he was going to miss *them*, but with so many jumbled thoughts, his words came out more honest and pathetic than he intended.

"Well, I'm not really your friend yet, but I'll hang out with you." She looked around the quiet plateau. "Seems like neither of us has much of a choice."

"You're staying?" he asked, surprised.

One end of Zofi's lips curled up crookedly. "I'm here for a little while. I have much to learn from Taishi, for now."

"Learn what exactly?" he asked. "You're not a war artist. You don't train or fight. What could you learn from her? All I've seen her do since we've met is boss you around."

Zofi chuckled derisively. "Oh, you are of such a simple mind. Taishi is one of the greatest war artists alive, which means she excels at being the best. There is much to learn from someone like that."

"I don't understand." That was often the case when Jian spoke to Zofi. Still, he was glad for her company. He wasn't sure if he could have survived being up here with just Taishi.

Zofi crinkled her brow in amusement. "Besides, Taishi hired me on to instruct you in grammar, math, and history. And your lousy etiquette."

"Wait, what?" stammered Jian. "You're my teacher, Zofi?"

"You may address me as Master Wu." Her laughter trilled up and down as they headed back to the cave. The woman was having far too much fun at his expense.

Taishi was waiting for them when they returned. The King was setting in the west and his orange rays illuminated her from behind like some sort of heavenly spirit.

"It's about time you came back," she barked, the sound of her sharp voice dispelling any semblance of holiness. "I'm getting hungry. Get the fire started and the water boiling."

"Yes, master," the two replied together.

Taishi stuck an arm out, blocking their way as they tried to pass. "Jian, one moment."

"Yes, Taishi?"

She leaned heavily on her staff. "Show me a punch."

He frowned. "Now?"

Taishi just looked on.

Jian did as he was told. He chambered his fist and threw a simple front punch. It was short, clean, and sharp.

"Your other arm."

He repeated the technique with his left. No sooner had he rechambered his fists than Taishi whipped the staff at his head. So much for needing a crutch. Jian managed to block it with his guard. Taishi followed through with a series of staff strikes from several angles. She obviously wasn't trying too hard.

Jian let his movements speak for themselves, keeping his guard close to his body as he blocked each blow. He eventually made an error. His guard went high when he should have still kept it close. Taishi poked him in the ribs just hard enough to double him over. She followed up with a rap on the chin, then brought the butt of the staff straight down on his big toe. Jian howled as he hopped on one foot, so Taishi swept his other foot, sending him flat on his back.

"To the gut and then the foot. That looked painful," Zofi narrated a little too cheerfully.

"What was all that for?" he asked as Taishi helped him up.

Taishi noted approvingly. "Basic, clean, reflexive. You've unlearned all your poor habits. Your slate is clean."

"What?" He scratched his head.

"You are finally ready to learn again." The windwhisper sounded strangely formal. "I, Ling Taishi, offer you, Wen Jian, a place as my heir in the Windwhispering School of the Zhang lineage of the Ling family style."

Jian could only gape. "Huh?" Her words at first didn't register with him. Then bit by bit, they slowly sank in. He blinked several times, tears welling in his eyes. "Are you sure?"

"I am sure I'll regret this many, many times over the next few years, but yes . . ." She offered several small nods. ". . . I am sure."

Jian's legs wobbled and he dropped to his knees.

"Stop that," she snapped immediately. "Do I look that insecure to you?"

He scrambled back to his feet. "Now what? Is there some sort of ceremony?"

An amused chuckle climbed up her throat as she gave him a side-eye. "Ceremony? What sort of retail bright-sash marketing war arts school do you think you've joined? There's no ceremony, boy. You're a windwhisper now. It's all about the work, not the formality."

"I see, yes, master," This time, the title rolled easily off his tongue. He even relished it. "What happens next?"

"We train you to be the best damn windwhisper the world has ever seen," she continued. "One day, the Tiandi will have need of you, as will your people. When that time comes, when the prophecy needs the Prophesied Hero of the Tiandi, the Champion of the Five Under Heaven to fulfill his destiny, when the Zhuun need their savior to bring peace to the land, you, Wen Jian, will be ready for whatever challenges the prophecy throws your way, chief among them the Eternal Khan of Katuia."

"I'll make you proud, master." He again felt the urge to drop to a knee, but caught himself in time. "I am ready to train."

Taishi leaned on her staff and made her way back to the main building with Jian and Zofi following close behind. "No you're not. Stop standing around and fetch water from the stream. After that, get a fire going and help Zofi with dinner. I expect a warm basin and breakfast ready by sunup. Then you can start on the roof tomorrow. This place has fallen into disrepair."

"And then we can start with the training?" he asked eagerly.

"Nonsense. It'll take weeks for you to fix this place up."

Ling Taishi reached the stoop of the building and stubbed her toe on a loose board. She hissed and banged it with her staff, then disappeared into her house.

CHAPTER FORTY-SIX

THE GRASS SEA

For Sali, each step of the journey home felt more perilous than the last. With gritted teeth she had dealt with a constant low-grade anxiety as she fled with Hampa while riding a pair of stolen draft horses across the Zhuun farmlands. That worry only grew once they reached the Shingyong Mountains and tried to track down the exodus without falling into the hands of a Zhuun patrol.

But reach the exodus they did, which meant Sali barely slept for the next several weeks as she, Daewon, and Mali shepherded nearly thirteen hundred hungry and desperate Children of Nezra toward the Grass Sea with the Zhuun army nipping at their heels.

Reaching the Grass Sea brought its own set of woes. While the rest of the exodus cheered and hugged and burst into song at the first sight of the tall, leaning blades of vegetation, Sali was grappling with how so many of her people, nearly all on foot, were going to survive their hazardous homeland. The sea was unforgiving to the ill prepared.

Shockingly, they survived the journey deep into the Grass Sea mostly intact. The journey sent two in ten to their next life, but at that price, they finally escaped to freedom.

And Sali's trepidation grew.

She glanced around the stretch of flattened vegetation that lay in the wake of the constantly moving city that was finally in sight. The foliage would spring back within a day or two. By week's end, there would barely be any sign that a mechanized city housing thousands had come through. For now, however, the field served as an area for the Black City's camp followers—the poor and migrant who could not afford to live in pods—to camp during the nights. It dawned on Sali as she rode through the crowds that even after nearly two years, Chaqra's wake still looked like a refugee camp.

Meanwhile, the constant gnawing itch from the Khan's Pull lessened as they approached, and then finally ceased. Its absence made Sali feel almost hollow inside.

A squad of black-armored warriors awaited her at the bottom of the ramp. None stepped forward to meet her. They seemed wary of her. Sali bristled; Chaqra should be meeting her people with food and blankets, not distrust.

The squadlead raised an arm and surveyed the long line of Katuia following her. "Viperstrike, Soul Seeker, you are being summoned to the Sanctuary of the Eternal Moor."

"I bet I am," she muttered, dismounting. She handed the reins of the sorrel over to Mali. "He's a good horse, young, strong with spirit. Keep him close. Our people will have need of him."

Mali placed her hands over Sali's and kissed her fingertips. "You're coming back. If the shamans order you to Return, you *will* refuse, sister. You're needed. Here, with me!"

Again, more often than not these days, a command, not a request. Sali smiled but remained noncommittal. "I will do what I must for our people."

Sali harbored no illusions of what the spirit shamans would demand of her as a condition of safeguarding her people. No clan would simply embrace the survivors of another clan. That was just not their way. As little as a few centuries back, the clans had waged constant ferocious wars on one another just as enthusiastically as they had on the Zhuun. It was only after the Eternal Khan had risen to power, backed by the power of Chaqra and the spirit shamans, that their people had united.

The orphans of Nezra would need special protection, which only the spirit shamans could provide. To secure that, however, there would be a price. It was a price Sali would gladly pay to guarantee her people's survival. Everyone knew of this eventuality, as illustrated by nearly every Child of Nezra at some point over the past two days paying her their respects. Everyone except for Mali, who adamantly refused to see the truth.

Her sister did not let go of Sali. "You are *not* leaving us, not after all that you've done for us. It's not fair."

"I will see you, Sprout, sooner or later, but all the same. Be happy, my beloved Malinde." She pulled away, offering a small nod to Daewon. He placed his fist to his heart.

The last to see her was Hampa. He was ugly-crying and failing to hide it. To make matters worse, he couldn't decide between heart-saluting and bowing and ended up muffing both.

Sali embraced her neophyte and whispered in his ear. "Stay strong, little brother. I order you to search the Grass Sea for another surviving viperstrike, and they *will* complete your training. It is the way."

"Yes, mentor."

"Sister." It was the ultimate honorific.

Hampa fell to his knees, crying openly.

Sali loosed a long breath and pulled away from her loved ones before her emotions betrayed her. She proceeded to the waiting squad, no longer caring in the slightest if this was being perceived as an escort.

Mali yelled after Sali, her voice rising above the sounds of the living jungle. "I'll be waiting right here until you return. I'm not leaving here without you. Do you hear me, Sali? I'll burn this place down if you don't come back."

The end-pod had lowered its ramp and was waiting for her as she walked up to the city. Sali was halfway up and near the tops of Grass Sea's canopy when she looked back one last time. The Children of Nezra had clustered around the base of the ramp, standing silently, their ranks stretching across the long, narrow field as far as the eye could see. Every soul to a man, woman, and child had their fists over their hearts. The usual loud chatter of the Grass Sea seemed to have subsided as well, the living land beneath their feet paying its last respects.

Sali returned the gesture, although this time, she broke tradition and met their eyes. They were *her* people, and she drank in each of their gazes until finally resting on her sister. Many heartbeats passed before she finally turned away.

Sali was mildly surprised to find a group of fully armed black-armored towerspears waiting for her at the top of the ramp. The squadlead heart-saluted. "We are here to take you to the council, Viperstrike."

Viperstrike, not Will of the Khan or Soul Seeker. Interesting. In official matters, her bond with the Khan should have taken precedence. In holy matters, her religious calling as a seeker. To refer to her by her sect raised fresh alarms.

Sali shifted in her armor, feeling the dull ache in the shoulder still healing from the ax wound. Her forearm had mostly recovered, thanks in part to the healers in her camp, but her grip was still infantile and would need another cycle to be anything near what it had been. Not that any of her injuries would matter for much longer. Sali had no intention of fighting the judgment of the spirit shamans. The remainder of her life was now numbered in hours, not days.

The towerspears were respectful. They made no attempt to confiscate her tongue or make her escort appear too much like one as they made their way across the pod. Sali noted a small crowd of onlookers waiting on the other end of the first bridge, no doubt curious to catch a glimpse of the errant Will of the Khan returning to the Whole. Her impending arrival had not been a secret, considering the small army she had brought with her.

She was surprised when the towerspears turned just before they reached the bridge and proceeded down a set of stairs into the underbelly of the pod. Known as the gear level, this underground layer was an entire alien world of steel and steam that housed each pod's machineries and powered its section of the city. They passed by an army of tinkers maintaining the gears and laborers stoking steam furnaces. Several of the workers, faces black with grease and soot, offered cursory glances, but nothing more.

Why would the spirit shamans go through the effort of shielding her from Chaqra's residents when she had come to fulfill her final service to the Khan? They should be singing her glories and shoring up the people's faith in the Eternal Khan and their guiding wisdom. Things weren't adding up. Sali's mind raced as they crossed the bridge that ran directly beneath the one on the surface. She looked over the side as the large tracks ground the earth below, propelling the pod at its current crawling pace, continuously moving just enough to prevent sinking beneath the soft earth.

Every once in a while, a muffled voice would carry over the sound of the pipes to blare commands: synchronizing and maintaining speed, trajectory adjustments, spark stone supply runs in order to keep all the pods—nearly a hundred in Chaqra's case—working in unison.

Mali had spent much of her youth in the gear layer, having fallen in love with the many moving parts and the shrill songs of the steam whistles. Sali hated it and rarely ventured down here, finding it loudly abrasive and claustrophobic.

She lost track of her progress, making many turns at intersections and crossing a dozen bridges. The towerspears eventually led them up another flight of stairs and back into daylight. Sali blinked and shielded her eyes from the strong sun, then turned to realize that they were standing at the base of the Sanctuary of the Eternal Moor in the heart of Chaqra.

A young black-robed shaman at the large double doors pulled it open. Sali acknowledged her with a nod and entered the Sanctuary of the Eternal Moor. She was met with a wall of heat and humidity as well as the heavy scent of patchouli and musk oil. A light honey-colored smoke hung in the air, wavering between shades of sunlight yellow and dark blood-gold. The room was symmetrically domed, with dark-green curved beams that rose up from the floor and met in the center at an opening that revealed several more levels of the increasingly narrow tower. On the floor was a similarly sized opening framed by a low railing. Leaning over the side revealed the earth three stories down, scrolling slowly along as Chaqra moved along the Grass Sea.

Sitting in a large circle around that opening were twelve of the holiest and most powerful religious leaders of the Katuia. These elder spirit shamans were the guiding wisdom behind the light of the Eternal Khan, and the caretakers of the Grass Sea. Sitting at their head, facing Sali directly on the opposite end of the room, was Jhamsa.

Her heart-father looked unchanged from the last time she had seen him, save for his firm grimace and his tightly pursed lips. He gestured for her to enter. "Viperstrike. You are expected."

"And I have come," she intoned.

"And you brought those from Jiayi here with you."

She nodded. "I brought as many Children of Nezra as I could back to the hearth of the Grass Sea."

"I see." He looked on intently. "Are your people well?"

And there it was. "They will be, after much-needed food and shelter."

"Good." Jhamsa paused and listened as one of the shamans picked up a pipe and blew green smoke that trailed into Jhamsa's ears. His eyes focused back on her and hesitated before finally speaking once more. "You have waded into a pool with which you are not familiar, Salminde."

She frowned. "In what way? Is this in regard to my delayed final duties as a Will of the Khan? If so, I beg for forgiveness. I am *now* ready to perform my holy duty to the Eternal Khan and thank this council for allowing me leniency. It has allowed me to still do some good with this body before my next life."

"It has nothing to do with that!" A shaman to her right slapped the table. "We signed an armistice with the Zhuun, and you broke the pact!"

Sali was dumbstruck. "I . . . what does that sham of a treaty have to do with this?"

The bald, rail-thin shaman burst to his feet, leveling a finger at her. "You've endangered everyone with your selfish, illegitimate, unlawful act."

"Selfish?" Her indignation grew. "I freed and brought my people home!" She inadvertently took two steps toward the shaman before she remembered she was standing in her people's holiest place.

Jhamsa interceded quickly. "What Brother Vanus is saying, is that your *courageous* act in bringing the Children of Nezra back has created a political crisis. The Zhuun have already sent word, demanding we denounce the theft of the services of their indentured servants, and return them immediately."

Her heart stopped. "You wouldn't."

"And they insist that the saboteur be returned for justice," Vanus added, dripping with malice.

Sali's mouth was dry. Her voice wavered, almost desperate. "I am the Will of the Khan. If you betray me to the land-chained, his soul will not be whole. How can you allow that?"

Another spirit shaman, this time sitting to her left, shrugged. "We're far past that now. What matters now is preserving the armistice."

"Preserving the . . ." She couldn't believe these sacrilegious words were being spoken by one of their holiest.

"You will turn around and march these people straight back to Jiayi."

Sali couldn't make sense of what she was hearing.

"We will, of course, make arrangements to preserve and return the fragment of the Khan's Will back to our people," said Jhamsa hastily. Several more shamans began to speak at once, some rising to their feet, talking at her or to one another. The cross talk began a buzz of anger and threats.

"Return the fragment . . . Far past . . . what could be . . . ?" Sali couldn't hear anything other than a roar in her ears that was as loud as silence. She had come here ready to die. Death was not the problem. Her life had been marked forfeit a long time ago. But dying for her people and her religion was one thing. Dying as a prisoner to the Zhuun was something entirely different. Even worse, if the spirit shamans, the holiest men in Katuia, viewed the treaty with their enemy as more important than their faith, that made their religion . . .

". . . a sham," Sali said, her voice hoarse. "A lie."

Watching these old, pompous men, layered with comfort and fat from decadence, their mouths twisted in curses and self-righteousness,

Sali blinked and saw clearly for the first time. These spirit shamans were not wise and not benevolent. They were charlatans, self-interested leeches doing whatever it took to keep the body alive for feeding.

Something deep inside Sali burst. It was a taut silvery string of pure light that snapped, growing dim and cold. She stared dumbly at the crowd of fat old men.

"I do not accept this." She spoke quietly at first, and then her voice found its legs. "I do not accept your judgment today."

"How dare you!" The closest shaman shot to his feet.

"I do not accept an unjust order. I do not accept the righteousness of holy men who choose to send their own people in chains to the enemy. I do not accept the authority of a council that betrays its own people." Sali was practically shouting.

"Silence." Jhamsa slammed his fist on the table. Every spirit shaman was now standing. "You have gone too far. Know your place, Salminde. Your sacrilege will not be tolerated, and our word is not up for debate. The Sanctuary of the Eternal Moor has spoken, and you will obey, Viperstrike, or risk being stricken from the stories of our people along with everyone you brought with you."

"Strike us then," Sali snarled. "Strike us with your petty threat. You all are nothing but empty husks of flesh decaying in the murky waters. I will not listen to your diatribes and obey spineless commands expressed out of cowardice and fear. I will not give credence or audience to your charade."

"Seize her!" someone yelled.

More joined in the chorus. "Take away this blasphemer."

Sali had not forgotten that there were four armed towerspears positioned directly behind her. She twisted away from several jabs of their mancatchers and then ran, stumbling, toward the spirit shamans. The two closest to her threw their arms up, but Sali sped past them. She reached the opening and gripped the railing with one hand. She swung her legs over and dropped into the darkness.

Sali wished she could have landed gracefully on her feet, but she was lucky she didn't break her neck in the fall. A large bent grass blade or tree branch cushioned her descent somewhat before she crashed into a copse of bramble.

She looked upward as the illuminated opening slowly continued moving past. She rolled to her feet and found her bearings, noting the tracks to every side. It took just a blink for her to orient herself to where she needed to go, and then she was off, half sprinting, half limping in the opposite direction of where the city traveled.

Sali had to weave around large tracks and stabilizing beams that intermittently hung from the main bodies of the pod. It was pitch-black beneath the city, and the ground was uneven. Luckily, Chaqra was moving at a toddler's crawl, and it wasn't long before she had escaped from beneath it. She sighted the Children of Nezra huddled on one side of the indented field where they had set up camp for the night.

Several of her people saw her approach and shouted an alert. Mali, Daewon, and a few others rushed forward to meet her.

"You're back!" shouted Mali in disbelief. "What happened?"

"Are they going to help?" said Daewon. "Will the spirit shamans stand with us?"

Sali grimly walked past them as they fell in behind her. "Forget the shamans. Rouse the people. We're on our own."

EPILOGUE

Cyyk sat in the courtyard of his father's estate and watched a large school of koi swim over one another. He wondered why they all moved in the same direction. Every once in a while, one of the fish would change directions sharply, and then the rest would follow. It was a hypnotizing display that used to keep him preoccupied for hours on end. He always wondered if the lead fish knew that it was leading.

A group of statues carved mostly out of one large piece of rock stood in the middle of the pond. Tallest in the cluster was his father, most of his face covered by his ceremonial winged helmet with purple plumes jutting skyward. Only his eyes and mouth were visible, but there was no mistaking who he was. The sculptor had painstakingly created his father's bushy eyebrows, humped nose, and long, sharp goatee. Cyyk could almost feel his father's disapproving scowl.

To the right of his father was his mother, carved when she looked just about his age now. She stood demurely by her husband's side in a tulip-shaped headdress and a formal dress still popular in the Gyian court.

Cyyk missed seeing his mother badly. She had died from lead poisoning during one of his father's campaigns. Cyyk had been too young at the time and had been left at home, which had likely saved his life.

Flanking his parents were his four siblings. Two were now commanders in Sunri's famed Avalanche Legion. His brother Lisiu had disappeared, presumed kidnapped and killed, before Cyyk was born. The oldest of his father's children, Cyyan, had married into one of the oldest and most powerful families in Xing. The lord was old and sickly, with a face like a diseased potato, which meant Cyyan would soon ascend in court as well. On the far end of the statues, carved out of a separate, newer stone, was Cyyk, the baby. That right there perfectly explained how expected his birth was to the family.

An attendant approached. "Younglord, your father will see you now."

Cyyk's stomach twisted and bugs crawled up his throat. It wasn't that he was frightened of his father per se, just that there had never been an instance when his father summoned him that had ended favorably.

He followed the attendant past the courtyard and through a zen garden, then a greenhouse. His father liked to claim that he was only a simple farmer who had accidentally become a general.

Two other attendants slid a set of annoyingly tall doors open as they entered the main house. They continued into a large room that looked more like a museum than someone's personal chamber. An array of pedestals littered one side of the room. On each pedestal was a strange alien item, all Kati gear. On the other side was a mostly intact bixi, minus the tracks. Next to it were the bones of one of their flying glider contraptions, including a tattered cloth. At the far end of the room was a partial hull of one of their supposed under-the-sea boats, although at some point Cyyk wasn't sure what was truth and what had come from the overactive imaginations of frightened soldiers. He felt another quiver once they reached his father's audience room. He closed his eyes and took in a deep breath.

The first thing Cyyk did upon walking into the room was shield his eyes. It was abnormally bright, with every sconce lit, and a large fire roaring off to the side. Several floor candelabras had been brought in as well, excessively illuminating the entire room. His father was sitting at a table up a short flight of stairs on the other end of the room. Curiously, he had donned his combat armor. Hanging on one wall was Caobiu's yellow ducal flag. Underneath it was the Quan family flag, and then beneath that were the many torn and shredded flags of his father's many defeated enemies.

There were two Mute Men flanking his father at his desk. Father usually shunned them, preferring to rely on his own skills, but there were times when having the Quiet Death's protection was necessary. Cyyk furrowed his brow; it appeared this was such a time. He had thought this was a private meeting between father and son, but there were a few others in the room: a woman with two strangely garbed people who obviously had arrived with her.

"Younglord Quan Cyknan, my lord."

General Quan Sah, marshal of Duchess Sunri's armies, didn't look up from his papers. "You may leave." The attendant bowed low and retreated backward out of the room.

Cyyk knelt. "Father, how may I serve?"

"Stand." Quan Sah looked him up and down. "You've grown tall and broad."

"I train all the time, and eat even more."

"Your training at Longxian went well? Pity about what happened."

"Yes, Father. I look forward to continuing my education in the war arts at another school of your wise choosing."

"I see." General Quan Sah glanced over at the woman standing off to the side. "I trust then our business is concluded."

The woman had red hair in an unusual, foreign cut. She was small, but Cyyk could feel the danger of her. She made a face at him, and sighed. "He'll do, I guess."

"Watch your tongue," Quan Sah snapped. "The blood of the Quan flows through him."

"The fifth Quan," the woman said, shrugging.

Cyyk froze. He had never see anyone speak to his father so, not even the duchess.

"If nothing else, it satisfies the brood atonement," said Quan Sah coldly.

"Your mark shield has been renewed, General. The Consortium sends their regards." There was a hint of mockery in her voice.

"Now get out of my city." General Quan Sah returned his attention to his papers. "Never return unless you are on contract."

Before Cyyk could protest or demand to know what was going on, the woman weaved an arm through his elbow and began dragging him back out of the room.

"You said we were getting a girl!" the other woman hissed.

"After the heat the Central Orb put on the Consortium, be happy they didn't knock us all back to grunts," their leader retorted.

"What are you doing? Release me! Do you know who I am?" Cyyk tried to break free of her, but she flipped him into a neck lock and flicked the tip of a knife to his chin.

"First lesson of being a shadowkill. Always fight in darkness." She leaned in and whispered. "The second, the cell shares everything: food, spoils, lovers, and information. Now tell me about your time at the Longxian school, my stupid little baby grunt."

ACKNOWLEDGMENTS

The idea of The War Arts Saga was born from a steady diet of wuxia movies that spanned nearly half a century. Having immigrated to the United States from Taiwan at the age of five, wuxia was my connection to my history, culture, and people, and was the inspiration that led me into a kung fu school one day to begin my own journey to the lunar court. I never did learn to fly or break walls or death-touch someone (probably a good thing!), but I came away from that martial education with so much more.

It is only fitting that the first people I would like to acknowledge are those who brought those wuxia stories to life, both in front of or behind the camera, in the books and scripts they wrote, and the many incredible stunt coordinators and martial artists who made magic on the screen. I'd like to give a call out to some of the truly great ones in this field: Yuen Woo-Ping, Wong Kar-Wai, Jet Li, Jackie Chan, Tony Leung, Bridgette Lin, Maggie Cheung, Zhang Yimou, Michelle Yeoh, Stephen Chow, Tsui Hark, Donnie Yen, Bruce Lee, and many, many more. A special thank you also to my master, Wei-Chung Lin (RIP, Sifu), my brothers and sisters in the Extreme Kung Fu family, and the Mortal Kombat crew.

To my wife, Paula, who has provided unimaginable encouragement and support over the years, especially when writing *The Art of Prophecy* while we raised two young boys during the great quarantine of 2020.

To my beautiful boys, Hunter and River, you two are my exuberant forces of nature. Your father cannot be more proud.

To my family, Mike, Stephen, Yukie, and Amy, for always making sure I knew I was never alone.

To my agent, Russell Galen, who didn't even blink when I told him my next project was "a kung fu book." His faith and support mean everything. To my manager, Angela Cheng Caplan, for taking my words and finding the right partners to adapt this idea. I couldn't have asked for a better team.

To the amazing crew at Del Rey Books: Bree Gary, David Moench, Julie Leung, Ashleigh Heaton, Scott Shannon, Keith Clayton, Cassie Gonzales, Jo Anne Metsch, and Nancy Delia. Thank you for your dedication and making this gorgeous book. This has been a dream project, and I am so grateful for having the opportunity to work with everyone. Bonus points to Benjamin Dreyer, who looked out for me and is just a really cool dude.

A very special thank you to my editor, Tricia Narwani. You know that feeling when the moons and stars just seem to align perfectly? Well, that's you.

To Alexandra Kinigopoulos, whose critical eye and savage honesty makes every book I write the best book I can write.

To Tran Nguyen and Sunga Park, whose incredible artwork graces the jacket and endpapers.

Lastly, to my awesome readers and fans, I wouldn't have made it this far without your support. Thank you for walking this journey with me. I hope *The Art of Prophecy* brings you as much joy to read as it did for me to write.

ABOUT THE AUTHOR

Wesley Chu is a #1 *New York Times* bestselling author of twelve published novels, including the Tao, Io, and Time Salvager series. He was the 2015 winner of the Astounding Award for Best New Writer. His debut, *The Lives of Tao,* won the American Library Association's Alex Award and was a finalist for the Goodreads Choice Awards for Best Science Fiction. He is the coauthor of the Eldest Curses series with Cassandra Clare. Robert Kirkman tapped Chu to write *The Walking Dead: Typhoon,* the first Walking Dead novel set in Asia.

Chu is an accomplished martial artist and a former member of the Screen Actors Guild. He has acted in film and television, and has worked as a model and stuntman, and recently returned from summiting Kilimanjaro. He currently resides in Los Angeles with his wife, Paula, and two boys, Hunter and River.

wesleychu.com
Facebook.com/wesleychuauthor
Twitter: @wes_chu

ABOUT THE TYPE

This book was set in Electra, a typeface designed for Linotype by W. A. Dwiggins, the renowned type designer (1880-1956). Electra is a fluid typeface, avoiding the contrasts of thick and thin strokes that are prevalent in most modern typefaces.

White Ghost Lands

Diyu
Mountains

Cloud
Pillars

Vauzan

Manjing

Ngyn Ocean